"I'm afraid there have been some changes in your orders," said Company-Captain Vargan. "The Powers That Be have decided they need you home as quickly as possible, and not as just one more platoon-captain. Which means, I'm sorry to say, that this is the last thing you're going to do as an Imperial Marine . . . Your Highness."

Janaki had been prepared to protest. But he didn't—because even as Vargan spoke, a lightning bolt seemed to stab through his brain. It hit so hard, so suddenly, his breath actually caught.

The Glimpse made no sense. Not yet. The images of fire and explosions, the sound of screams and the thunder of weapons, were ripping through him now.

"Are you all right, Your Highness?"

"I'm sorry, Company-Captain," Janaki said, shaking himself vigorously.

Whatever he'd just Glimpsed, it was going to happen here—*right* here, so he needed to be at Fort Salby. But the one thing he knew with absolute certainty was that if he explained what he'd Seen to chan Skrithik, the Fort Salby CO would literally throw him onto the next train to get him as far away as possible—if Janaki told him the one crystal-clear image he'd brought back from his Glimpse in the instant his eyes refocused.

The image of Company-Captain Orkam Vargan's decapitated body sprawled across torn, corpse-strewn ground while his blood soaked into Fort Salby's parade ground.

BAEN BOOKS by DAVID WEBER

Honor Harrington: *On Basilisk Station* • *The Honor of the Queen* • *The Short Victorious War* • *Field of Dishonor* • *Flag in Exile* • *Honor Among Enemies* • *In Enemy Hands* • *Echoes of Honor* • *Ashes of Victory* • *War of Honor* • *At All Costs*

Honorverse: *Crown of Slaves* (with Eric Flint) • *The Shadow of Saganami*

edited by David Weber: *More than Honor* • *Worlds of Honor* • *Changer of Worlds* • *The Service of the Sword*

Mutineers' Moon • *The Armageddon Inheritance* • *Heirs of Empire* • *Empire from the Ashes*

In Fury Born

The Apocalypse Troll

The Excalibur Alternative

Bolos! • *Old Soldiers*

Oath of Swords • *The War God's Own* • *Wind Rider's Oath*

with Steve White: *Crusade* • *In Death Ground* • *The Stars At War* • *The Shiva Option* • *Insurrection* • *The Stars At War II*

with Eric Flint: *1633* • *1634: The Baltic War*

with John Ringo: *March Upcountry* • *March to the Sea* • *March to the Stars* • *We Few*

BAEN BOOKS by DAVID WEBER & LINDA EVANS

Hell's Gate • *Hell Hath No Fury*

BAEN BOOKS by LINDA EVANS

with John Ringo: *The Road to Damascus*

with Robert Asprin: *Time Scout* • *Wagers of Sin* • *Ripping Time* • *The House That Jack Built* • *For King and Country*

HELL HATH NO FURY

DAVID WEBER
& LINDA EVANS

HELL HATH NO FURY

This is a work of fiction. All the characters and events portrayed in this book are fictional, and any resemblance to real people or incidents is purely coincidental.

A Baen Book

Baen Publishing Enterprises
P.O. Box 1403
Riverdale, NY 10471
www.baen.com

ISBN 10: 1-4165-5551-X
ISBN 13: 978-1-4165-5551-3

Cover art by Kurt Miller
Map by Randy Asplund

First Baen paperback printing, July 2008

Library of Congress Control Number: 2006100465

Distributed by Simon & Schuster
1230 Avenue of the Americas
New York, NY 10020

Pages by Joy Freeman (www.pagesbyjoy.com)
Printed in the United States of America

For Megan, Morgan, and Mikey Paul,
who put up with their Dad.
See? I really *was* working on something!
—David Weber

For David and Aubrey, Bob and Susan,
and all the people who keep me going
when the going is rough.
—Linda Evans

CONTENTS

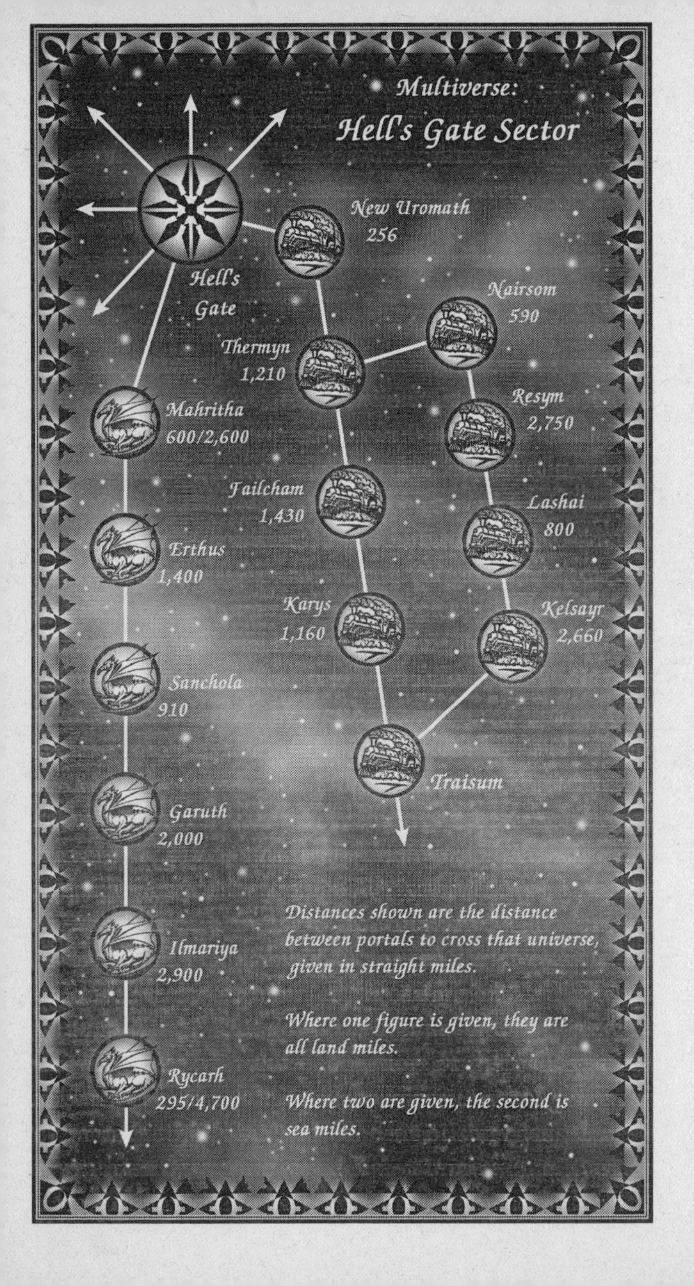
Multiverse:
Hell's Gate Sector
New Uromath
256
Hell's
Gate
Nairsom
590
Thermyn
1,210
Resym
2,750
Mahritha
600/2,600
Failcham
1,430
Lashai
800
Erthus
1,400
Karys
1,160
Kelsayr
2,660
Sanchola
910
Traisum
Garuth
2,000
Ilmariya
2,900
Rycarh
295/4,700
Distances shown are the distance between portals to cross that universe, given in straight miles.
Where one figure is given, they are all land miles.
Where two are given, the second is sea miles.

PROLOGUE

THE VERTICAL CUT in the cliff face only looked razor-thin. Even the broadest railway cut looked like a narrow crack when it was cut into the face of a sheer precipice over three thousand feet tall.

Darcel Kinlafia knew that. He'd already passed through what the guidebooks had taken to calling the Traisum Cut once before, outbound, but it was the sort of sight not even the most jaded trans-universal traveler could ever tire of.

That was why he'd climbed out of his seat in the rattling, banging so-called "passenger car" and stepped out onto the front platform so that he could see it better as the train started up the four-mile approach ramp to the cut. Now he stood there, hands on the guard rail, staring out and up at one of the most spectacular pieces of scenery imaginable.

The portal between the universes of Traisum and Karys was one of the smaller ones Sharona had explored. Or, rather, it was *effectively* one of the smaller ones. The theorists believed it was actually much larger, but that most of it was buried underground in both universes. Only the uppermost arc of the circular portal was exposed, and the terrain in the two universes it connected was . . . dissimilar, to say the least. The Karys side of the portal was located near what would have been the Arpathian city of Zaithag in Darcel Kinlafia's birth universe; the Traisum side was located in the Ithal Mountains west of the city of Narshalla in Shurkhal.

That was what created the spectacular scenery. Zaithag was barely seven hundred feet above sea level; the mountains west of Narshalla reached heights of over forty-six hundred feet . . . and the portal's Traisum nexus was located smack in the middle of one of those mountains.

Most people who saw it from the Karys side for the first time felt a peculiar sense of disorientation. It was something the human eye and the human mind weren't trained to expect: an absolutely vertical, glassy-smooth cliff over a half-mile high at its shortest point and four and a half miles wide.

The good news was that Karys was outbound from Sharona. That had allowed the Trans-Temporal Express's construction crews to come at it from the slopes of Mount Karek rather than straight out of the mountain's heart. The portal was actually located east of the mountain's crest, which made the impossible cliff several hundred feet shorter from the Karys side and the approach slope perhaps three or four miles shorter from the Traisum side. Even so, and even though TTE's engineers were accustomed to stupendous construction projects fit to dwarf the Grand Ternathian Canal or New Farnal Canal, this one had been a stretch even for them. It had taken them years (and more tons of dynamite than Kinlafia cared to contemplate) to complete, and all meaningful exploration down-chain from Traisum had been bottlenecked until they'd finally finished it. The cut was five miles long, eighteen hundred feet deep where its Karys terminus met the top of the approach ramp, and wide enough for a four-track right-of-way *and* a double-wide road for wheeled traffic. The grade, needless to say, was steep.

Now the locomotive chuffed more noisily than ever, laboring as it started into that deep, shadowed gulf of stone with its tender and single pair of passenger cars. Its smoke plume fumed up, adding its own fresh coat of grime and soot to the stains already marking the cut's rocky sides, and he heard the haunting beauty of the whistle singing its warning.

He stayed on the platform a little longer, looking up past the edge of the passenger car's roof overhang at the narrow strip of scorching blue sky so far overhead. Then he drew a deep breath, went back inside, and settled himself into his seat once more.

Not much longer now, he told himself. *Not much longer . . . for* this *stage, at least.*

* * *

Less than two hours later, Kinlafia gazed out the passenger car window as the train clattered and banged to a halt in a vibrating screech of brakes and a long, drawn-out hiss of steam.

It was hot, and despite the welcome interlude of relative coolness in the Traisum Cut, the car's open windows had done little more than help turn its interior into an even more efficient oven by letting the hot, dry wind evaporate any moisture it might have contained. Still, it had been a substantial improvement over the wearisome horseback journey through Failcham, across the desert between what should have been the cities of Yarahk and Judaih.

As a Portal Authority Voice—and a certified Portal Hound—Kinlafia had seen far more of the multiverse than the vast majority of Sharonians could begin to imagine. Yet even for someone like him, it took a journey like this one to truly drive home the immensity involved in expanding through so many duplicates of humanity's home world. Under normal circumstances, it tended to put the silliness of most human squabbling into stark perspective. With such incredible vastness, such an inexhaustible supply of space and resources available, surely anyone ought to be able to find the space and prosperity to live his life in the way he chose without infringing upon the interests or liberties—or prejudices—of anyone else!

Except that it doesn't seem to work that way, he thought, as he collected his valise from the overhead rack. *Part of that's simply ingrained human cussedness, I suppose. Most people figure somebody* else *ought to move away, rather than that* they *ought to go off looking for the life they choose. And then there's the godsdamned Arcanans.*

His jaw tightened for a moment, and his brown eyes turned bleak and hard. Then he shook himself, forcing his shoulders to relax, and drew a deep breath. His weeks of grueling travel had given him enough separation from Shaylar's murder for him to at least concede that Crown Prince Janaki had had a point. There was no way Darcel Kinlafia was ever going to forgive the butchers of Arcana for the massacre of his civilian survey crew and—especially—Shaylar Nargra-Kolmayr. For that matter, he still saw no reason why he should.

But there was a difference between refusing to forgive and building an entire life on a platform of hatred, for hatred was a corrosive drug. Nourished too deeply, cherished too closely, it would destroy a man as surely as any rifle or pistol bullet.

And it can do exactly the same thing to an entire civilization, he thought grimly. *"Call-me-Janaki" was right about that, too. Besides I've known plenty of Sharonians I wouldn't exactly want marrying into the family. No, be honest, Darcel. You've known plenty of Sharonians who ought to've been put on someone's "needs killing" list. So, logically, there have to be at least some Arcanans who are going to be just as horrified as any Sharonian by the prospect of an inter-universal war. Of course,* finding *them may be just a little difficult.*

He snorted in wry humor, which he was half-surprised to discover was only slightly tinged with bitterness. Well, maybe a little more than "slightly." Still, the tearing, savage spasms of fury which had wracked him whenever he thought about the massacre at Fallen Timbers truly had lost much of their virulence.

Petty-Captain Yar told me they would. I suppose I should have listened to him.

Kinlafia made a mental note to drop Delokahn Yar a Voice message. It was the least he could do for Company-Captain chan Tesh's senior Healer, he thought just a bit ashamedly, given how hard Yar had worked to force him to admit to himself that life truly did go on. Wounds like Shaylar's death might never go away, but at least they could scar over, turn into something a grownup learned to cope with rather than retreating into an endless morass of depression and petulantly refusing to have anything more to do with the world about him. And in his own case—

"Welcome to Fort Salby."

Kinlafia turned as the sound of the train master's voice interrupted his thoughts. Despite his Arpathian surname, Irnay Tarka was a Uromathian, from the independent Kingdom of Eniath. He was also an employee of the Trans-Temporal Express, one of the hundreds of workers pushing the railhead steadily down-chain towards Hell's Gate now that they could finally get their heavy equipment forward through the Traisum Cut. They'd driven the line to within less than four hundred miles of Fort Mosanik in Karys, which had been an enormous relief. No one was going to be sending any of the TTE's luxury passenger coaches out here to the edge of the frontier anytime soon, but even this spartanly furnished, bare-bones, pack-'em-in-cheek-by-jowl people-hauler was an enormous improvement over a saddle.

Tarka grinned, almost as if he could read Kinlafia's mind.

"Saddle sores feeling any better?" he asked, and Kinlafia snorted.

"It's going to take more than one miserable day for that," the Voice said. "Mind you, I'm not complaining. Just having the opportunity to sit down on something reasonably flat is a gift from the gods!"

"We aim to please," Tarka said. Then his grin faded slightly. "On a more serious note, Voice Kinlafia, it's been an honor."

Kinlafia half-waved one hand in a dismissing gesture that was more than a little uncomfortable. That was another thing Janaki had been right about. As the sole survivor of the massacred Chalgyn Consortium survey crew—and the Voice who had relayed Shaylar's final, courageous message—he'd acquired a degree of fame (or notoriety, perhaps) which he'd never wanted. It wasn't as if *he'd* done anything that wonderful. In fact, he would never forgive himself, however illogical he knew it was, for not having somehow managed to save his friends' lives.

Tarka seemed about to say something more, then stopped himself and simply gave a small headshake. Kinlafia smiled crookedly at him and held out his right hand, and Tarka clasped forearms with him.

"Good luck, Voice Kinlafia," the train master said. "And a safe journey home. A lot of people are going to want to hear from you directly."

"I know." Kinlafia managed not to sigh.

He nodded to the Eniathian, walked down the aisle, and then climbed down the carriage's steep steps onto the sunbaked, weathered-looking planks of the station under a sky of scorching, cloudless blue. It was only late morning, but the platform's heat struck up through the soles of his boots as if he were walking across a stovetop, and he was acutely grateful when he reached the cover of the shedlike roof built to throw a band of shade across the rearmost third of the boardwalk.

The locomotive lay panting quietly as the station's water tower topped off its tender and its fireman and his grease gun worked their way down its side. It wasn't one of the behemoths which pulled TTE's massive freight and passenger trains closer to the home universe, nor was it as beautifully painted and maintained. In fact, it was a shabby, scruffy work engine, with an old-fashioned half-diamond smokestack, grimy, banged-up, dust-covered paint, and no pretension to the grandeur of its more aristocratic brethren. No doubt it was out here in the first place because newer and more powerful engines had replaced it closer to home. The TTE could spare it from passenger and normal freight service, and the construction planners and operations people had probably figured they might as well get the last of their money's worth out of it before it finally went to the boneyard. Yet even though it couldn't come remotely close to matching the speed and effortless power of something like one of the new Paladins, Kinlafia had never been happier to see one of those more splendiferous lords of the rails.

His mind ran back over the wearisome journey since he'd separated from Janaki's platoon and its little column of Arcanan POWs. The ride to Fort Ghartoun had been hard enough, but the journey across Failcham had been worse. Much worse.

Normal Portal Authority policy called for the forts which housed the Authority's garrisons and administrative centers to be located, like Fort Salby, on the Sharonian side of the portal they covered. The planners had made an exception in Fort Ghartoun's case, however, for a couple of reasons. One was that the Failcham side of the Failcham-Thermyn portal was located very close to the spot occupied by the city of Yarahk in Sharona. Unfortunately, "very close," especially in multiversal terms, wasn't the same thing as "in exactly the same spot." Yarahk had grown on the banks of the mighty, north-flowing Sarlayn River, just below the Sarlayn's first cataract and almost six hundred miles south of the Mbisi. The Sarlayn Valley was fertile enough, and Yarahk was fairly popular as a winter resort, but the portal was thirty miles outside the valley, in the barren desert to the west. It sat on a thoroughly unpleasant piece of dry, sun-blasted dirt and rock, with very little to recommend it aside from the portal itself. Just providing a garrison with water would have been hard enough.

Admittedly, Fort Ghartoun (only, of course, it had been Fort Raylthar when it was built) was also located in a remarkably arid spot, but at least water was closer to hand. And so were Snow Sapphire Lake and the Sky Blood Lode. It had made sense to put the local Authority administrative center on the Sky Blood Mountains' side of the portal, given the availability of water and the fact that keeping a watchful eye on the development of that massive silver lode was eventually going to become the local authorities' primary concern.

But locating Fort Ghartoun on the Thermyn side of the portal hadn't made the journey across Failcham any more pleasant. The Karys-Failcham portal was located in the North Ricathian Desert, close to what would have been the city of Judaih, better than fourteen hundred miles west of Yarahk. Fourteen hundred miles of desert, in point of fact, in which the water a traveler could carry was altogether too often the margin between survival and something else.

The letter of priority Crown Prince Janaki had gotten Regiment-Captain Velvelig to endorse for Kinlafia had helped enormously. Among other things, it had allowed him to requisition Portal Authority horses—and, for the desert-crossing aspects of his journey, experienced local guides. His homeward journey had been far more rapid (and strenuous) than his survey crew's outward journey, and his letter had provided him with dune-treaders, as well as horses, for the trip to Fort Mosanik, on the Karys side of the Karys-Failcham portal.

From Fort Mosanik, located in the general area of the Sharonian city of Queriz, the terrain had been at least a little friendlier than that between Mousanik and Ghartoun. Of course, only the North Ricathian Desert could have made the Queriz Depression seem particularly hospitable. At its deepest point, Kinlafia knew, the Depression was almost a hundred feet below sea level, dotted with salt lakes and covered with feather grass, tamarisk, and wormwood, where it wasn't outright desert in its own right. Still, oases were more frequent, and the much flatter terrain, once one got south of the highlands around Fort Mosanik itself, was much easier going. Not to mention the fact that he'd only had to cover around three hundred and fifty miles of it before he met up with the advancing railhead.

Which meant, he thought, hoisting his valise and starting along the platform towards the rudimentary station building, that he only had another three or four weeks to go to get home.

"Voice Kinlafia?"

Kinlafia stopped and turned around as someone called his name in accented Ternathian. The man who'd called to him wore PAAF uniform with the single gold rifle of a company-captain. He was also a sturdy-looking fellow, perhaps a couple of inches taller than Kinlafia himself, with the swarthy complexion and dark brown eyes of a Shurkhali. His nose was strongly hooked, and the eyes under his bushy eyebrows were very direct and intense.

"Yes, Company-Captain?"

"Orkam Vargan," the Shurkhali said, reaching out to clasp Kinlafia's forearm. "I'm Regiment-Captain Skrithik's XO here at Fort Salby. They sent word up the line that you'd be arriving today, and the regiment-captain asked me to keep an eye out for the train."

"Oh?"

"We understand your hurry to get back home again," Vargan said almost apologetically. "But you're the first person to come back *up* the line since it happened, and you're also . . . well—"

He shrugged slightly, and Kinlafia suppressed a sigh. It was hardly the first time someone had said that to him.

"I don't suppose there's another train headed up-chain this afternoon, anyway, is there?" he said instead.

"Not really." Vargan's slightly crooked grin suggested to Kinlafia that the company-captain had heard the sigh he hadn't uttered. "That's why the regiment-captain wanted me to ask you if you'd have supper with him tonight. Obviously, we'll all understand if you're too tired. Gods know *I'd* be! But we'd really appreciate the opportunity to offer you the closest Fort Salby has to hospitality. And, of course, to pick your brain ourselves."

"Actually, if I can extort a long, hot shower out of you, and maybe a couple of hours worth of nap, I think I'd enjoy a sitdown supper."

"No problem." Vargan smiled. "We've put you up in the BOQ. If you'll come with me, we'll get your bag dropped off, and then I'll personally escort you to the longest, hottest shower in at least two universes."

Kinlafia chuckled. "It's a deal."

* * *

Somewhat to Kinlafia's surprise, supper at Fort Salby turned out to be not only extremely tasty, but actually enjoyable.

Salby, unlike the other portal forts Kinlafia had passed through on his way back from Hell's Gate, had been established for quite some time. At one point, Salbyton, the settlement outside the fort, had been a construction boomtown as the Trans-Temporal Express labored on the Traisum Cut. Its peak population had been as high as seven or eight thousand, although it had declined from that quickly once the cut was completed. By the time the Chalgyn Consortium had set out on its productive but ill-fated survey expedition, Salbyton had been down to perhaps two thousand, and TTE, as was its wont, had collected and hauled off the temporary, portable housing in which most of its labor force had lived. Despite that, the remaining buildings of Salbyton had a look of permanency and solidity which was rare this far from Sharona, and the local railroad station had quite literally miles of heavy-duty sidings left from its days as the end of the TTE's line.

Neither the fort nor the town had changed a great deal—yet—despite all that had happened since, but that was about to change. All of that temporary housing TTE had pulled out was undoubtedly on its way back, although it might not be stopping at Salbyton this time. The new construction priorities closer to Hell's Gate were going to dwarf the importance of making the Traisum Cut.

There was a two-hour time difference between the two sides of the portal, which, fortunately was also one of the older portals which had so far been discovered. It must have been . . . lively around Fort Salby's present location for the first century or so after the portal formed, Kinlafia reflected. The altitude differential was less than that of some other portals, but it had still been sufficient to channel a standing, unending, twenty-four-hour-a-day, three-mile-wide hurricane through from Karys until the pressures finally equalized. There was ample evidence of the sort of sandblasting erosion portals at disparate heights tended to produce, although none of it was very recent. And there was still a permanent, moderately stiff breeze blowing through the portal, even now, which made it unfortunate that Zaithag was about as dry (and hot) as Narshalla. Fort Salby could have used a little rain, if Karys had had any to spare.

Now, as the Voice sat with his hosts on the covered veranda built across the back of the Skrithiks' house just outside Fort Salby's gate, the portal had already darkened to star-shot night. It was a striking vista, even for an experienced inter-universal traveler, as the midnight-blue half-disk of night loomed up against the coals and ashes of the local sunset. The veranda had been carefully placed to take advantage of the permanent breeze, and the air moving across it was distinctly cooler than the local air temperature.

"That was delicious, Madame Skrithik," Kinlafia said, sitting back with a pleasant sense of repletion. "I've been eating off of campfires for months now."

"I suppose that makes your approval just a bit two-edged," Chalendra Skrithik said. "I've eaten campfire cooking myself a time or two, you know."

"I didn't mean—" Kinlafia began quickly, then stopped as he recognized his hostess' slight smile. She saw his expression, and the smile turned into a chuckle.

"My wife, you may have observed, Voice Kinlafia," chan Skrithik said wryly, "has what she fondly imagines is a sense of humor."

"Actually, I have a very *good* sense of humor," the wife in question said, elevating her nose with an audible sniff. "All women do. It's simply unfortunate that so many males of the species fail to appreciate its innate superiority."

"Personally, I've always recognized its superiority," Kinlafia told her gravely. "Or, at least, I've always been smart enough to pretend I did."

"A wise man, I see," Company-Captain Vargan observed, then shook his head with a sigh. "I fear my own cultural baggage betrayed me when Madame Skrithik and I first crossed swords. Er, *met*, I mean. Met."

"But I had to draw so little blood before you recognized the error of your ways, Orkam," Chalendra said sweetly, and this time Kinlafia laughed.

He really hadn't looked forward to dinner when the invitation was extended, but now he was more than glad he'd accepted it. Chan Skrithik reminded him in many ways of an older Janaki chan Calirath. He wasn't as tall—few people were, after all—and he was considerably older than the crown prince, with much fairer hair, but he had the same steady, gray eyes, and there was something of Janaki's sense of . . . solidity about him. He and his wife had worked hard, with the smoothness of a well-established team, to make their guest feel welcome, and they'd succeeded in ample measure. They'd treated him as if they'd known him for years, and he found himself wondering if perhaps Chalendra had one of those traces of rogue Talent that turned up so often. She'd seemed to know exactly what to say and do to make him feel at ease, and he was guiltily aware that his personality had been . . . thorny, to say the very least, since Shaylar's murder.

Like her husband, Chalendra Skrithik was at least ten years older than Kinlafia himself, and she had that tough, capable air he'd seen among so many of the women who'd followed their husbands—or made their own independent ways—out to the frontier. Her dark hair was just beginning to show threads of silver, and there were crow's-feet at the corners of her brown eyes, but she remained a remarkably handsome woman.

"At any rate, Madame Skrithik," the Voice said now, "I intended my comment as the most sincere possible approval. This was delicious, and the opportunity to sit in a proper chair and use honest-to-gods silverware only made me appreciate it even more."

"I'm glad," she said, this time with simple sincerity of her own. "I've spent enough time following Rof around to realize just how hard you must have been pushing yourself to reach Fort Salby this soon. And I know why you're doing it, too. If we can make you feel welcome, then I think that's the very least we can do after all *you've* already done."

"Don't make me out to be some sort of hero," Kinlafia said quietly. "I happened to be the one to Hear Shaylar and relay the message. The real heroes were the ones at Fallen Timbers, or the people like Company-Captain chan Tesh."

"I have enough Talent to have Seen the SUNN rebroadcast of Voice Nargra-Kolmayr's last message," Vargan put in. "I won't embarrass you by running on about it, but I wouldn't be surprised if those of us who've Seen it don't have a better appreciation than you do for just how much you do qualify as a 'hero.'"

Kinlafia made an uncomfortable little gesture, and the company-captain left whatever more he'd been about to add unsaid.

"At any rate," chan Skrithik said, stepping into the brief hiatus in the conversation, "we appreciate what you've been able to tell us about what's happened since. I've been getting the intelligence synopses and copies of most of the official reports, but it's not the same thing as talking to someone who's actually seen it. You've really helped me put a lot of it into context."

"I'm glad I could help," Kinlafia said, and he was. *And I'm also just a little surprised by how little it hurt*, he thought. *Either the scab's getting even thicker, or else I really am learning to deal with it. Or both, maybe.*

"I could wish you hadn't left before the negotiations began," Vargan said.

"Oh?" Kinlafia looked at him, and the company-captain shrugged.

"You were there at the beginning," the Shurkhali pointed out. "You might say—" Vargan's smile was grim "—that you Saw the way *our* first effort to negotiate worked out. I'd like to have gotten your firsthand impression of whether or not they're serious . . . and whether or not anything's likely to come of it."

"I wouldn't be the right person to ask." It came out a bit more flatly than Kinlafia had intended, and he gave himself a small mental shake. "I'm afraid I'm a bit too emotionally involved in what happened to Shaylar and the rest of our crew to stand back and think about anything those people might come up with."

"I can understand why that might be," Chalendra said quietly. She reached out and touched the back of Kinlafia's hand. "I don't think anyone who Saw the

SUNN broadcast of Shaylar's final message could expect you to feel any other way, Darcel."

"Maybe." He managed not to sigh and gave her a small, grateful smile. "Having said that, though, I really do hope that something comes of the talks. But for that to happen, they're going to have to agree to punish whoever was responsible for that massacre. I don't see how Sharona could settle for anything less than full accountability for that."

"From what I've been seeing in the Voicenet transmissions, that's probably the absolute minimum any Sharonian government is going to be able to settle for," chan Skrithik agreed. "On the other hand—"

The regiment-captain paused as his batman stepped back onto the veranda with a bottle of slightly chilled wine, which he proceeded to pour.

"I'm afraid that finding *good* wine out here at the bleeding edge is all but impossible," chan Skrithik said, "but this vintage is at least decent."

"Wine snob!" his wife snorted.

"I take my pleasures where I can find them," the regiment-captain replied with an air of dignity as the orderly withdrew with an admirably impassive expression.

Chalendra's lively eyes gleamed, but she declined to take up that particular challenge, Kinlafia noted. For now, at least.

"I noticed what looked like a Uromathian cavalry regiment's standard," the Voice said, changing the subject before she changed her mind. "Does that mean Emperor Chava is sending forward reinforcements?"

"Not as many as he might like," Vargan muttered, and chan Skrithik gave his executive officer a slight frown, more imagined than seen.

"Actually, Uromathia was the first to get any of its national units moved up to support us," the fort's CO replied to Kinlafia's question. "And I'll admit I had my own doubts when I heard they were coming. For that matter, and just between the four of us, I still don't trust Chava's motives one little bit. But Sunlord Markan, their senior officer, has done nothing but dig in and do everything he possibly can to integrate his troopers into our force structure here. In fact, he's out on maneuvers this evening, or I'd have invited him to supper, too. I don't think anyone could fault his efforts or how energetically he goes about them. And to be brutally honest, he's come very close to doubling our available troop strength."

"But you're not sending any of them farther forward?"

"No, I'm not. Or, rather, the PAAF isn't. For several reasons, I feel certain. Logistics would be a problem, for one thing. The Uromathians don't use standard PAAF equipment, so just keeping them supplied with ammunition would be a pain. And until the railhead reaches Fort Ghartoun, Salby is the natural 'stopper' for the Karys Chain. In fact, we've turned into a collecting point for a really odd collection of odds and ends that've been emptied out of various arsenals and armories up-chain from us. Some genius in Reyshar actually sent us an even dozen Yerthak pedestal guns." Chan Skrithik snorted. "They were intended for the Authority revenue cutters in Reyshar—they've been having some smuggling problems—and apparently the panic immediately after word of Fallen Timbers hit got them rushed ahead to us here. And until they get the rail lines laid at least to Ghartoun, I'm *keeping* them here, too. The damned things weight a good half-ton each, and at the rate they eat up ammo, just keeping them supplied with shells would be a genuine pain in the posterior. Exactly what chan Tesh needs in his field fortifications, aren't they?"

The regiment-captain's expression was so disgusted Kinlafia had to chuckle. For a moment, he was afraid his laughter had given offense, but then chan Skirithik grinned wryly and shook his head.

"Better to have people sending us stuff we'll never use than not get sent the stuff we *will* need, I suppose. But that's just one more example of the logistics headaches we'd be looking at if we deployed the Uromathians forward."

Kinlafia nodded gravely, but he also heard all of the things chan Skrithik wasn't saying. The Voice didn't doubt for a moment that Balkar chan Tesh would have done almost anything to get another couple of thousand men forward to help hold Hell's Gate. But the "almost anything" undoubtedly didn't include effectively putting Uromathia in command of future contact with Arcana. No matter how conscientiously this Sunlord Markan was working to cooperate with chan Skrithik, letting him supersede chan Tesh—which, given his combined military rank and aristocratic precedence, he would most certainly have done—wasn't going to be something any non-Uromathian in Sharona wanted to see happen.

Politics, he thought almost despairingly. *Always politics. And Janaki thinks* I *can do something about it?*

A vision of his parents' faces floated before him. His father was a professor of languages at Resiam University in New Farnalia, while his mother was a Talented Healer, and both of them had . . . pronounced views on politics. Which, though he hadn't explained it to Janaki, was one reason he'd hesitated before jumping at the Prince's offer. Both of them were staunch opponents of the "outmoded, class-based" system of "paternalistically justified aristocratic denial of the basic right of decision-making." Given that the two of them lived in one of the more militant of Sharona's republics, they had little personal experience with that "aristocratic denial" of the right to make political decisions, but he very much doubted that they were going to be performing any Arpathian drum dances of joy when they found out about their baby boy's career-move decision.

"Has there been any word on the Act of Unification?" he asked after a moment. "There seemed to be a few . . . difficulties that still needed ironing out according to the last Voice message I Heard."

"My, you *are* tactful, aren't you?" chan Skrithik murmured with a crooked smile.

"Well, I'm neither Ternathian nor Uromathian," Kinlafia pointed out. "I hope you won't take this wrongly, but most of us New Farnalians have always been at least a little amused watching the two of you. Don't get me wrong. Of the two, I've always been a lot more comfortable with Ternathia. After all, that's where most of the New Farnal colonists came from in the first place. Still, I have to admit that with the entire multiverse out there, all of this 'great power rivalry' has always struck me as just a little silly."

"If it weren't for the constant potential for it to turn into something very unfunny indeed, I'd probably agree with you," chan Skrithik said. "Orkam, on the other hand, lives a little closer to Uromathia than you do, and I don't think he finds it quite as amusing. In fact,

I've noticed that the humor quotient seems to decline in direct proportion to one's proximity to Chava Busar's frontiers."

"I know." Kinlafia felt just a little abashed. "If it sounded like I don't think there's any difference between Emperor Zindel and Emperor Chava, I apologize. For that matter, I spent quite a while with Crown Prince Janaki, and I discovered that he's a . . . very impressive fellow, in a lot of ways. I guess it's just that I grew up far enough away that I never really felt threatened by either side, and I've seen just how big the multiverse is. I've wondered, sometimes, if it wouldn't have made sense to just hand an entire universe over to Uromathia, and another one to Ternathia, and tell them to behave themselves."

"I doubt very much you could've gotten anyone else to go along with the notion of giving Chava Busar an entire world to play around with," Company-Captain Vargan said dryly. "The problem is what he'd do with all those resources. I'm afraid Chava is one of those people who can never be satisfied, never feel he has quite enough power. The only thing he could see that sort of resource base as would be a springboard from which to conquer the *rest* of the multiverse."

"I'm afraid Orkam's probably right, about Chava, at least," chan Skrithik said with a sigh.

"And he's not exactly alone in that, either, Sir," Vargan pointed out. His voice was diffidently stubborn. Obviously, this was a topic he and his superior had discussed before, Kinlafia thought. "Markan's been a lot more . . . proddy ever since he found out about the Act of Unification and who'd been proposed as *everyone's* emperor, and you know it."

"Yes, he has," chan Skrithik agreed. "But you'd be 'proddy' if Chava had been elected as *your* emperor, too, Orkam. And Markan's a sunlord. Whether he wants to be or not, he's got to be deeply involved in Uromathia's internal politics. Bearing all of that in mind, how could you expect him to feel any other way?"

"I don't imagine anyone could," Darcel said, stepping diplomatically into the fray. "But has Sunlord Markan's attitude become a problem?"

"No, not really," chan Skrithik said. "Markan is as dedicated and professional an officer as I've ever met, and he hasn't let his unhappiness—his *natural* unhappiness—get in the way of cooperating with us here. In a way, though, that only emphasizes the nature of our problem. Most Uromathians are going to be at least . . . strongly influenced, let's say, by the attitude of their ruler. And if *most* Uromathians are no more power-crazed or power-hungry than anyone else, Chava, unfortunately, *is*."

"And he's Emperor of Uromathia," Chalendra pointed out, shaking her head. "For that matter, those sons of his are no great prizes, either."

"So thank the gods the Conclave had the good sense to pick Emperor Zindel over Chava," Vargan said with the sort of fervor Kinlafia seldom heard outside temple.

"I can't disagree with that," Kinlafia acknowledged. "But should I understand from what you've just said that the Act has actually been approved?"

"Not yet," chan Skrithik said, then snorted. "Well, what I actually meant, I suppose, is that it hadn't been as of a week and a half ago."

Kinlafia nodded in understanding of the qualification.

It was hard to remember sometimes just how far places like Fort Salby were from Sharona. The thought that it could take over a week for a Voice message to reach Traisum was sobering proof of just how great the distances involved truly were.

Of course, it wouldn't take that long if it weren't for the water barriers, he reminded himself. It was the need to transport Voices physically across the water gaps too wide for them to span—most of which were up-chain from Traisum—that accounted for the vast majority of the delay, after all.

"So we still don't know if Uromathia is going to sign on," he said, after moment.

"Oh, I think Chava will sign on the dotted line eventually," chan Skrithik replied. "It's not like he has a lot of choice, after all. Even he has to recognize how the appearance of these 'Arcanans' has changed everything."

"You think so?" Vargan said sourly. Chan Skrithik looked at him, and the company-captain shrugged. "Logically, I can't argue with you," he said. "But I'm telling you, Rof—that man is never going to sign off on the creation of a world empire, especially under the Caliraths, unless he figures there's some way for him to park his fundament on the throne eventually."

"You may be right," chan Skrithik conceded with the air of a man who'd had this discussion more than once already. "In fact, from what I've seen of Chava, you probably are. But even if you are, what he *thinks* he's going to get away with, and what he *is* going to get away with are two different things. I don't care how tough, how sneaky, Chava Busar may think he is, he does *not* want to piss off Zindel chan Calirath. Believe me."

"If he's anything like his son, I'm inclined to agree with you," Kinlafia said.

"Which doesn't mean Chava isn't going to try something, anyway," Vargan pointed out. "And if he does, it could get spectacularly messy."

"Yes, it could." Chan Skrithik nodded. "But what Voice Kinlafia was asking was whether or not Chava's going to accept unification at all. And my feeling, from the regular Voicenet messages and the dispatches I've received, is that he's going to. I'm sure he is going to have some . . . mental reservations, let's say, if he does, but if Emperor Zindel is willing to accept the demand that Janaki marry a Uromathian, I don't think Chava will have any choice but to agree to the unification."

"Janaki marry a Uromathian?" Kinlafia couldn't quite keep his repugnance out of his voice and expression, and Chalendra Skrithik snorted. It wasn't, Kinlafia noted, a particularly happy snort.

"That's what Chava's been holding out for," she said. "And, like Rof says, he may already have gotten it. According to the last report *I* heard, the Conclave was supposed to vote on the marriage amendment to the Act of Unification three days ago. So, we ought to be hearing about the outcome in another week or so."

"I see."

Kinlafia sat back and took a sip of chan Skrithik's "decent vintage" while he pondered what Chalendra had just said. It was odd to sit here and realize the outcome of the vote was probably speeding its way down the chain of universes to Fort Salby at this very moment. And it was even odder to realize just how ambivalent Kinlafia himself was about that possible outcome. Despite the optimism everyone else had felt when the

Arcanan diplomats turned up, Darcel Kinlafia's belief that Sharona had to reorganize itself into something capable of meeting the Arcanans toe-to-toe had never wavered. Sharona *had* to unify its competing, squabbling nations. And yet, the thought of the towering young Crown Prince of Ternathia being forced to marry one of Chava Busar's daughters or nieces revolted him. Perhaps it was the sort of dynastic, political calculation kings and emperors routinely had to face, but he *liked* Janaki. Liked him a lot.

And I don't much like what Vargan was saying, either, the Voice reflected. *Because if Chava really does think there's a way to put* his *arse on the throne, then there has to be at least a line or two in his plans for getting rid of Janaki, first.*

Darcel Kinlafia wouldn't like that. He wouldn't like it at all.

So it looks like there's another good reason to go into politics, where I might actually be able to do something about it, he thought, drinking his wine and gazing up at the twinkling stars of Karys.

CHAPTER ONE

COMMANDER OF ONE Thousand Klayrman Toralk sat upright in the personnel carrier strapped to his circling command dragon's back, despite the buffeting wind of the beast's passage, so that he could see clearly over the edge of the windshield. The sight was impressive, he admitted, watching critically while the final few transport dragons, scales glittering with gem-like intensity in the last light of day, settled like huge, multihued insects onto the handful of islets clustered in the middle of so many endless miles of swamp. Unfortunately, "impressive" wasn't exactly the same thing as "well organized." In fact, the words which came most forcibly to mind were "awkward as hell."

And the reason the maneuver looked awkward was because it *was* awkward, he thought sourly. Despite his deep respect for his immediate superior, this entire operational concept could only have been put together by a ground-pounder. Any Air Force officer would have taken one look at the topographical maps and informed his superior roundly that he was out of his mind. Crowding this many transport and—especially—touchy, often ill-natured battle dragons into such a constricted space violated every precept of peacetime training regulations and exercise guidelines.

Too bad Ekros never heard about all those regs and guidelines, Toralk thought. *Or maybe he did. After all, how could even a demon make sure that whatever could go wrong did go wrong if he didn't know* exactly *what he was screwing up?*

The thousand chuckled with a certain bare minimum of genuine humor. Yet even as he did, he knew that if Commander of Two Thousand Harshu hadn't pushed him—hard—on this, he would have told the two thousand it was impossible. Fortunately for Arcana (if not, perhaps, for the tender sensibilities of one Thousand Toralk), Harshu wasn't particularly interested in the artificial safety constraints of peacetime. He wasn't overly hampered by excess tactfulness, either. But he *was* completely willing to absorb a few casualties, among his dragons as well as his troops, to get Toralk's attack force into position with its beasts sufficiently well rested to maximize their combat radius.

And it looks like that poisonous little prick Neshok was right—barely—about whether or not I could fit them all in, Toralk conceded.

The last of the transports landed a bit short of its intended island, and a towering, mud-streaked fountain erupted as the huge dragon hit the water. Fortunately, it was shallow enough that the beast wasn't in any danger of drowning or miring itself in the muck, and the levitation spell kept its towed cargo pod out of the water while it floundered ashore. Of course, Toralk had no doubt that if he'd been a little closer, he would have heard an interesting chorus of yells and curses coming from the infantry inside that pod. It might have stayed out of the water, but that hadn't kept it from bouncing around on the end of its tether like some sort of insane ball. And all of that water and mud the dragon's impact had thrown up had had to go somewhere.

Toralk grinned behind his helment's visor, despite his tension, then shook his head and leaned forward to tap his pilot on the top of his flight helmet.

"Yes, Sir?" The pilot had to raise his voice to be heard, but not by very much at this ridiculously low speed.

"Let's set it down, Fifty Larshal," Toralk said, and pointed at the larger island at the center of the half-dozen congested, swampy hummocks which had been chosen for his forward staging points.

"Yes, Sir!" Larshal said, and the command dragon lifted onto its left wing tip, banking more steeply as it circled down towards the indicated perch.

Toralk gazed into the west, where the embers of sunset still glowed on the horizon. This particular bivouac wasn't going to be much fun for anyone, he reflected. Maybe that would be for the good, though. Men who were thoroughly pissed off after spending a wet, muddy, bug-infested night not sleeping were likely to show a little more . . . enthusiasm when it came to shooting at the people responsible for them being out here in the first place.

* * *

Hulmok Arthag was an unhappy man.

Someone who didn't know the platoon-captain well might have been excused for not realizing that. Or, rather, someone who didn't know Arpathian septmen well might have been excused for not realizing Arthag was any unhappier than usual, given how little an Arpathian's expression normally gave away.

He stood under the forest canopy—thinner than it had been when the Chalgyn Consortium survey crew had been slaughtered, just over two months ago—and gazed into the predawn darkness, longing for the empty plains of home. Life had been harder there, but it had also been much less . . . complicated.

"Copper for your thoughts, Hulmok."

The platoon-captain turned at the sound of Platoon-Captain Dorzon chan Baskay's voice. The Ternathian cavalry officer looked improbably neat and clean—not to mention well-dressed and freshly shaved—for someone who spent his nights sleeping in a tent in the middle of the woods with winter coming on. Arthag had sometimes wondered if there were a special Talent for that, one that was linked by blood to the families which routinely produced the Ternathian Empire's diplomats. Not that chan Baskay had ever wanted to be a diplomat, whatever the rest of his family might have had in mind for him.

Which just goes to show the shamans were right. No man can *outrun his fate*, Arthag reflected with the faintest lip twitch of amusement.

"I don't know if they're worth that much," he told the Ternathian after a moment.

"I'm pretty sure they are," chan Baskay responded. Hulmok raised one eyebrow a fraction of an inch, and chan Baskay shrugged. "I've heard all about your 'instinct' when it comes to picking people for your command. And while I'll admit you've got a remarkably good gambler's face to go with it, it's pretty clear to me that something's jabbing that 'instinct' of yours as hard as it's jabbing every single one of mine."

"Really?"

"Hulmok, they've been talking to us for over a month now," chan Baskay said. "In all that time, they haven't said one damned thing except that they want to talk, instead of shoot. And they've been throwing grit into the machinery with both hands for the last week and a half. Which, you may have noticed, exactly corresponds to the point at which I finally got formal instructions from the Emperor. You think, maybe, it's pure coincidence that they got even more obstructionist as soon as *I* stopped sparring for time?"

"No." Arthag shook his head. "No, I don't think that—not any more than you do."

The two men looked at one another. Chan Baskay's expression showed all the frustration and anger he couldn't allow himself to display across the floating conference table from the Arcanan diplomats, and Arthag's very lack of expression showed the same emotions as both of them contemplated the Arcanans' last week or so of posturing. Rithmar Skirvon, the senior of the two Arcanans, had hardened his negotiating posture noticeably. His initial, conciliatory attitude had all but completely evaporated, and he seemed determined to fix responsibility for the initial violence of the clash between his people's troops and the civilian survey crew on the dead civilians.

That was a pretty significant shift from his original attitude, all by itself, but it was obvious to chan Baskay that Skirvon's instructions were exactly similar to his own in at least one regard. Neither side was prepared to give up possession of the Hell's Gate portal cluster to the other under any circumstances. Chan Baskay hadn't found it necessary to be quite as . . . confrontational as Skirvon, since Sharona currently *had* possession of the cluster, but he could at least sympathize with the Arcanan on that point.

What he couldn't understand was why Skirvon seemed actively intent on forcing a breakdown in the talks. He wasn't simply stonewalling, simply withdrawing into an inflexible position which he could always have blamed on instructions from his superiors. Instead, there'd been a whole series of insults, "misunderstandings," and "lost tempers" coming from the Arcanan side. And by now, chan Baskay no longer needed Trekar chan Rothag's Sifting Talent to tell when Skirvon was lying. All he had to do was check to see whether or not the Arcanan's mouth was moving.

"Hulmok," he said after a moment, his eyes unwontedly somber, "I've got a really bad feeling about what's going on. But that's all I've got. I don't have a single concrete thing to hang my worry on. So, if you've got something specific, I damned well need to hear it before I sit back down across from those bastards in a couple of hours."

Arthag considered the Ternathian for several moments, then shrugged very slightly.

"I do have a Talent," he acknowledged. He wasn't entirely pleased about making that admission to anyone, for several reasons, but chan Baskay was right. "It's not one of the mainstream Talents," he continued, "but it's run in my bloodline for generations. We've produced a lot of shamans because of it."

"And?" chan Baskay prompted when he paused.

"I can't read minds, and I can't always tell when

someone's telling the truth, the way Rothag can. But I can read what's . . . inside a man. Tell whether he's trustworthy, honest. Recognize the ones who'll cave in when the going gets tough, and which ones will die on their feet, trying. And—" he looked directly into chan Baskay's eyes "—the ones who think they're about to slip a knife into someone's back without getting caught."

"Which pretty much describes these people's school of diplomacy right down to the ground, assuming Skirvon and Dastiri are representative samples," chan Baskay snorted.

"I'm not talking about double-dealing or cheating at cards, Dorzon," Arthag said somberly. "I'm talking about *real* knives."

"What?" Chan Baskay stiffened. "What do you mean?"

"I mean that little bit of 'lost temper' yesterday afternoon was carefully orchestrated. I mean that when Skirvon demanded that *our* people apologize for provoking it, he'd rehearsed his lines well ahead of time. I mean that the lot of them are pushing towards some specific moment. They're not only working to a plan, Dorzon—they're working to a *schedule*. And the thing that's driving me mad, is that I don't have any idea *why* they're doing it!"

Chan Baskay frowned. Commander of Fifty Tharian Narshu, the senior officer of Skirvon and Dastiri's "honor guard," had exploded in a furious tirade over a trivial incident between one of his soldiers and one of Arthag's PAAF cavalry troopers the day before. The Arcanan officer had actually "allowed himself" to place one hand on the hilt of his short sword, which chan Baskay was positive had to be deliberate posturing on his part, rather than a serious threat. After all, Narshu had to know what would happen if his outnumbered men wound up matching short swords against H&W revolvers.

But by the same token, an officer in Narshu's position had to be equally well aware of his responsibilities as part of the diplomatic mission . . . and if *he* wasn't, then certainly the diplomats he was there to "guard" were. Yet Skirvon had reprimanded Narshu in only the most perfunctory manner, even though both Arcanan negotiators must have been conscious of the example their escort's CO was setting for the rest of his men.

"How confident are you of that, Hulmok?" he asked after a moment. "The schedule part, I mean?"

"I'm not as totally confident of it as I'd like to be," Arthag admitted. "If these were Sharonians, I'd be a hundred percent certain. But they aren't." He shrugged ever so slightly. "I keep reminding myself that it's remotely possible I'm misinterpreting something. After all, it's only been two months since we even knew they existed. But still . . ."

Chan Baskay nodded again, wishing his stomach muscles weren't tightening the way they were.

"One thing *I'm* certain of," he said slowly, "is that they don't have any intention of actually negotiating any sort of real resolution. For one thing, they're still lying their asses off about a lot of things."

"For example?" Arthag raised his eyebrows again.

"Exactly how Shaylar died, among other things," chan Baskay said grimly. "And these repeated assurances about their eagerness to reach some sort of 'mutually acceptable' disposition of the portal junction, for another."

"And about who shot first?" Arthag asked.

"No." Chan Baskay grimaced. "On that point, they're actually telling the truth, according to Rothag. They don't have any better idea of who shot first than we do. And oddly enough, they also seem to be telling the truth when they insist that the officer in command at the time tried to avoid massacring our survey crew."

"I think maybe Rothag better have his Talent checked," Arthag said bitingly.

"I know, I know!" Chan Baskay had the air of a man who wanted to rip out handfuls of hair in frustration. "I've Seen Shaylar's message myself. I *know* chan Hagrahyl stood up with his hands empty and got shot down like a dog for his pains. But they insist that wasn't what their officer wanted, and Rothag's Talent insists they're telling the truth when they say it."

"They may *believe* they are," Arthag snorted. "But if they do, it's because the bastard lied to them about what happened out here."

"Maybe." Chan Baskay shook his head, his expression half-exasperated and half-hopeful. "I keep wishing Shaylar had managed to contact Kinlafia sooner." He grimaced. "That sounds stupid, I know. The fact that she managed to reach him at all under those circumstances, much less sustain the link through what happened to her and all of her friends . . . Gods, it was nothing short of miraculous! I can't even imagine the kind of guts it took to hold that link. But we didn't actually See or Hear anything until after chan Hagrahyl went down."

"But we know what happened, anyway," Arthag pointed out. "Darcel—Voice Kinlafia—was linked deeply enough to know that from the side traces. Besides, she *told* him so."

"Granted. But she Told him, and she Showed him her *memory* of chan Hagrahyl going down with his hands empty and the crossbow bolt in his throat. That's not the same as Seeing it happen for ourselves. We have what she told Kinlafia, but we don't have anything before the actual event, don't know if there was something Shaylar didn't see herself, or saw but didn't recognize, or didn't realize it had happened at all, in those few seconds we didn't actually See."

"I'm sorry, Dorzon," Arthag said after a moment, "but I can't think of anything which could possibly change what happened or why. And even if I could think of anything now, it's too late for it to have any effect."

"I know. I know." Chan Baskay gazed off into the depths of the forest. "But they're still insistent that they didn't want any of this, that what happened was against their standing orders to establish *peaceful* contact with any new human civilization they encountered, and Rothag's Talent insists they're telling the truth about that. Which presumably means it accurately represents their government's long-term policy, no matter how badly things have gone wrong on the ground. To be honest, that's the only hopeful thing I've heard out of their mouths yet! Unfortunately, it's outweighed by everything else . . . especially what *your* Talent is telling you."

"Well," the Arpathian said slowly, "what do you plan to do about it?"

"Gee, thanks," chan Baskay said. "Drop it on *my* plate, why don't you?"

"Well, you *are* senior to me," Arthag pointed out reasonably. "My promotion was only confirmed last week. And you're the official diplomat around here, too."

"I know." Chan Baskay drummed the fingers of

his right hand on his thigh for several seconds, then shrugged.

"The first thing is to have Chief chan Treskin Flick a dispatch to Company-Captain chan Tesh. I'll tell him what we're worried about, and ask him for instructions. And the next thing is probably to have Rokam pass the same message back to Company-Captain Halifu for relay up the line to Regiment-Captain Velvelig."

Arthag nodded. Chief-Armsman Virak chan Treskin was the Flicker who'd been assigned to relay messages to chan Tesh's senior Flicker, Junior-Armsman Tairsal chan Synarch. Petty-Captain Rokam Traygan was chan Tesh's Voice, but despite everything, they were still desperately understaffed with the long-range telepathic communicating Talents out here. Traygan had originally been slated to hold the Voice's position at Halifu's portal fort in New Uromath. In light of the situation here at the Hell's Gate portal, he'd come forward to replace Darcel Kinlafia when the civilian Voice headed back to Sharona with Crown Prince Janaki. Fortunately, the Portal Authority had managed to scare up a third Voice—Petty-Captain Shansair Baulwan, a fellow Arpathian—to hold down Halifu's fort, and they were working hard to get still more Voices forward. But for right now, at least, there was absolutely no one else to spare in Hell's Gate or New Uromath, and it was critical that chan Baskay have the shortest possible message turnaround time . . . and the greatest accuracy and flexibility when it came to relaying diplomatic correspondence. So they'd ended up assigning Traygan to him and Baulwan to Halifu, at the critical inter-universal relay point, while chan Tesh (who was in the potentially stickiest position of all) made do with written messages relayed through the Flickers.

It was clumsy, but until they could get more Voices deployed forward, it was the best they could do.

"And in the meantime?" the cavalry officer said after a moment.

"And in the meantime," chan Baskay replied with a grim smile, "we do the best we can. I'm inclined to trust your Talent, even if these aren't Sharonians. So, pass the word to your people. I don't want them going off half-cocked, but I don't want them taken by surprise if these people are working to a schedule and they decide to push further than they have."

"Swords and crossbows against pistols and rifles?"

"If that's all they have, that's one thing." Chan Baskay shook his head. "On the other hand, it's been a month now, and we need to be careful about letting familiarity breed contempt. So far, they haven't produced anything man-portable that looks like some sort of personal super weapon, but for all we know, they've just been waiting for us to get accustomed enough to them to let our guard down."

"Point taken," Arthag agreed. "I'll talk to my people."

"Good. And when they get here this morning, I want you handy. Close to Skirvon, as well as Narshu."

* * *

As he climbed down from the back of the completely unaugmented horse the Sharonians had "loaned" him for the trip from the swamp portal, Rithmar Skirvon found himself wishing he'd been in the habit of spending more time in the saddle. Whatever the rest of him thought of his current assignment, his backside didn't like it at all. And the miserable nag his "hosts" had provided didn't make it any better. He suspected they'd deliberately chosen one with a particularly unpleasant gait just for him.

He pushed that thought aside as he handed his reins to one of Fifty Narshu's troopers and started across the now-familiar clearing towards the Sharonian negotiating party. Deeply drifted leaves rustled about his boots like bone-dry dragon scales, and the air was cool and bracing, particularly compared to the hot humidity from which Skirvon had come.

Despite that, his "hosts" didn't look particularly happy to see him as they waited under the towering forest giants' multicolored canopy, and, as he contemplated what was about to happen, Skirvon had never been more grateful for all his years of experience across the bargaining table. For that matter, his taste for high-stakes card games had served him in particularly good stead over the last two or three weeks, as well. His face was in the habit of telling other people exactly what he wanted it to tell them, and while he'd developed a certain wary respect for Viscount Simrath, he was confident the Sharonian diplomat didn't have a clue what was coming.

Of course, he reminded himself as he reached the floating conference table and his waiting chair, *there's always the possibility that I'm wrong about that.*

But, no, that was only opening-day nerves talking. If the Sharonians had suspected the truth, they would certainly have reinforced their "honor guard" here at the conference site. For that matter, they wouldn't have passed Skirvon and his diplomatic party through the swamp portal at the crack of dawn this morning, either.

Face it, Rithmar, he told himself as he settled down

in the chair across the table from Simrath yet again, *your real problem is that you're scared shitless*.

His lips quirked ever so slightly at the thought as he waited for Uthik Dastiri, his assistant, to sit beside him. That, however, didn't make it untrue, and he reminded himself once again that this entire ploy had been as much his idea as acting Five Hundred Neshok's. In fact, Skirvon had probably done even more than Neshok to sell the concept to Two Thousand Harshu. Somehow, though, he hadn't quite envisioned his own direct participation in sufficient detail when it had sounded like a *good* idea.

Mul Gurthak is so *going to owe me for this one*, he thought. *He may be in the Army*, *but* I'm *damned well not drawing combat pay!*

He watched Viscount Simrath and Lord Trekar Rothag sitting down opposite him and suppressed a sudden urge to pull out his chronometer and check the time.

"Good morning, Master Skirvon," Viscount Simrath said, as courteously as if he didn't realize Skirvon had been deliberately stalling for at least the last two weeks.

"Good morning, Viscount," Skirvon replied, as courteously as if he really thought Simrath didn't realize it.

"I trust we may be able to move forward, at least a little bit, today," the Sharonian diplomat continued. Under the formal rules and schedule they'd agreed to, it was his turn to control the agenda for the day.

"Progress is always welcome, My Lord," Skirvon conceded graciously.

"I'm pleased to hear that. However, the fact remains that I'm still awaiting your response to the points I made to you following the receipt of my last message from Emperor Zindel," Simrath said pleasantly. "In particular, I note that you continue to insist that the Union of Arcana must receive title to at least half the portals contained in this cluster. A cluster, I remind you, which is in Sharona's possession and which was first surveyed by the civilian survey crew which your troops massacred."

"I'm afraid I must disagree with you, Viscount," Skirvon said in his most respectful tones. "You appear to be implying that Arcana has taken no cognizance of Sharona's insistence on retaining total possession of this cluster—despite the fact that it's still to be established who actually fired the first shot, and the fact that our total casualties have been much higher than your own. In fact, we have taken cognizance of that insistence. Our position may not have changed," he smiled the empty, pleasant smile of a professional diplomat, "but rejection *of* your emperor's . . . proposals is scarcely the same thing as not responding *to* them."

The Ternathian noble leaned back in his chair—the floating chair, provided by Skirvon—and folded his arms across his chest. The leaves whispering wind-songs overhead were growing thinner by the day, Skirvon noticed as a shaft of sunlight fell through them and illuminated the tabletop's rich, polished grain and glittered brilliantly on the translating personal crystal lying between him and Simrath. Those leaves remained unfortunately thick, however, and a part of him wished Two Thousand Harshu had decided he could wait just a little longer.

Which is pretty stupid of you, Rithmar, when you've *been pushing him just as hard as you dared from the beginning.*

"Master Skirvon," Simrath said, "I'm at something of a loss to understand Arcana's motives in sending you to this conference table."

"I beg your pardon, My Lord?"

"Officially, you're here because 'talking is better than shooting,' I believe you said," Simrath observed. "While I can't disagree with that particular statement, ultimately, the shooting is going to resume unless we manage to resolve the issues between us here, at this table. So it strikes me as rather foolish for the two of us to sit here, day after day, exchanging empty pleasantries, when it's quite obvious you're under instructions not to agree to anything."

Despite himself, Skirvon blinked. He was ill-accustomed to that degree of . . . frankness from an opponent in any negotiation. After all, two-thirds of the art of diplomacy consisted of wearing down the other side by saying as little as possible in the maximum possible number of words. The last thing any professional diplomat truly wanted was some sort of "major breakthrough" whose potential outcome lay outside the objectives covered by his instructions.

More to the point, however, Simrath had observed the rules of the game up to this stage and taken no official notice of Skirvon's delaying tactics. So why had he chosen today, of all days, to stop playing along?

"In addition," the viscount continued calmly, "I must tell you that the distressing number of . . . unpleasant scenes between members of your party and my own do not strike me as being completely, um, *spontaneous*, let's say. So I have to ask myself why, if you're so eager to negotiate with us, you're simultaneously offering absolutely nothing new, while either encouraging—or, at the very least, tolerating—extraordinarily disruptive behavior on the part of your uniformed subordinates. Would you, perhaps, care to enlighten my ignorance on these matters?"

Skirvon felt a most unpleasant sinking sensation in the vicinity of his midsection.

Stop that! he told himself sternly. *Even if they've finally started waking up, it's too late to do them much good.*

At least, he damned well *hoped* it was.

"Viscount Simrath," he said in his firmest voice, "I must protest your apparent charge that the 'unpleasant scenes' to which you refer were somehow deliberately contrived by myself or any other member of my negotiating party. What motive could we possibly have for such behavior?"

"That *is* an interesting question, isn't it?" Simrath smiled thinly. It was a smile which never touched his gray eyes—eyes, Skirvon realized, that were remarkably cold and clear. He'd never realized just how icy they could be, and it suddenly struck the Arcanan that Simrath was not only extraordinarily tall, like most of the Ternathians he'd already seen, but oddly fit for a diplomat. In fact, he looked in that moment like a very tough customer, indeed, and remarkably little like someone who spent his days carrying around nothing heavier—or more deadly—than a briefcase.

"What, precisely, do you wish to imply, My Lord?" Skirvon asked with the air of a man grasping a dilemma firmly by the horns.

"I wish to imply, Sir," Simrath said coolly, "that it's never actually been your intention to negotiate any sort of permanent settlement or mutually acceptable terms. For reasons of your own, you've seen fit to initiate these negotiations and to keep Sharona talking. To this point, I've been willing to play your game, to see precisely what it was you truly had in mind. However, neither my patience, nor Emperor Zindel's tolerance, is inexhaustible. So, either the two of us will make significant progress over the next twenty-four hours, or else Sharona will withdraw from the talks. We'll see," if his smile had been thin before, it was a razor this time, "how you prefer shooting once again, rather than talking."

Skirvon felt Dastiri stiffen at his side. Despite the Manisthuan's espousal of *garsulthan*, or "real politics," Dastiri's skin had always been thinner than Skirvon's. Fortunately, the younger man appeared to have himself under control, at least for the moment. Which was actually about as much as Skirvon could say about himself, if he wanted to be honest. He managed to keep himself from looking over his shoulder at Commander of Fifty Narshu, but it wasn't the easiest thing he'd ever done.

"That sounds remarkably like an ultimatum, My Lord," he said.

"Does it?" Simrath cocked his head to one side, as if carefully considering what Skirvon had said, then shrugged. "Good," he said in an even cooler tone. "After all, that's what it is."

"The Union of Arcana is not accustomed to bending to ultimatums, My Lord!" Skirvon's response came out harder and more clipped than he'd intended.

"Then perhaps you should seek to profit from the novel experience, Master Skirvon," Simrath suggested. "Or, of course, if my plain speaking has sufficiently affronted you, you can always withdraw yet again to . . . how *was* it you put it the other day? Ah, yes! Withdraw to 'allow tempers to cool,' I believe you said."

Skirvon was astounded by the sharpness of the anger Simrath's words—and scornful attitude—sent jabbing through him. He felt his expression congeal, his nostrils pinched in ever so slightly, and the slight flicker in Simrath's eyes as the Sharonian obviously observed the physical signs of his anger only made that anger even sharper.

At that moment, Skirvon would have like nothing better than to stand up and storm away from that table. Or to snatch an infantry-dragon out of some outsized pocket and blast the smiling aristocratic bastard across from him into a smoldering corpse. Unfortunately, he could do neither of those things . . . yet.

"My Lord," he said through gritted teeth, instead, "I must protest the entire tone of your comments and your apparent attitude. As I say, the Union of Arcana is unaccustomed to bending to ultimatums. However," he made himself inhale deeply and sat back in his own chair, "whatever your own attitude, or that of your government, may be, *my* instructions remain unchanged." *Which*, he reflected, *is actually the truth*. "As such, I have no option but to continue my efforts to achieve at least some progress in resolving the matters which bring us here before anyone else is killed. I will continue to pursue my duty, but not without telling you that I most strongly protest the insulting nature of this exchange."

"If the insult is too great," Simrath said, almost indifferently, "please feel free to withdraw. Otherwise, I trust, you'll at least stop insulting my intelligence by simply repeating the same, worn out, and completely pointless positions again and again and again."

* * *

Dorzon chan Baskay watched the Arcanan diplomats' faces darken with anger. The younger of them, Dastiri, had never been particularly hard to read, and his anger at chan Baskay's confrontational language sparkled in his dark eyes. Skirvon was obviously older and more experienced than his assistant, but despite that, he was nowhere near as good at concealing his emotions as he clearly thought he was. And the fact that even though Skirvon was as furious as he obviously was, he'd swallowed not just the content of chan Baskay's words, but the deliberately insulting tone in which they'd been delivered, as well, told the cavalry officer quite a lot.

Unfortunately, chan Baskay wasn't certain exactly what that "lot" was. The fact that Skirvon hadn't stormed away from the table in yet another of his patented temper tantrums was interesting, though. Whatever these bastards were up to, Skirvon clearly *needed* to be here this morning.

Which, coupled with Hulmok's observations, doesn't precisely fill me with joy.

He didn't so much as glance in the Arpathian officer's direction, but he did withdraw his gold fountain pen from his breast pocket and toy with it. He turned it end for end, watching it gleam richly in the morning sunlight. He had no doubt that the Arcanans would interpret it as another insolently dismissive gesture on his part. That didn't bother him particularly, but it wasn't the real reason for it, and the corner of his eye saw Arthag's tiny nod as the Arpathian acknowledged his warning signal.

"I deeply regret that you've apparently so completely misconstrued and misunderstood my efforts, My Lord," Skirvon told chan Baskay through stiff lips. "Since, however, you seem to have done so, by all means explain to me precisely what sort of response to your emperor's terms you would deem a sign of 'progress.'"

* * *

"For a start," chan Baskay told Skirvon in an only slightly less indifferent tone, "you might begin by at least acknowledging the fact that our current possession of this junction—paid for, I might add, with the blood of our slaughtered *civilians*—means we are not, in fact, negotiating from positions of equal strength. We need not even discuss sharing sovereignty over this junction with you. We already have it. As Sharona sees it, Master Skirvon, it's your job to convince us first, that there's any logical or equitable reason for us even to consider giving up any aspect of the sovereignty we've secured by force of arms, and, second, that there's any reason we should trust your government to abide by any agreement you manage to negotiate."

Skirvon ordered himself not to glower at the arrogant Sharonian. That sort of blunt, hard-edged attitude was far more confrontational than anything he'd seen out of Simrath to this point, and he wondered what had prompted the change.

But it's too little, too late, you prick, he told Simrath from behind the mask of his eyes. *All I have to do is keep you talking for another hour or so, and then . . .*

"Very well, My Lord," he said after a moment. "If you insist upon rejecting my government's efforts to reach some arrangement based on something other than brute force, I suppose I have no choice but to meet your proposal on your own terms.

"As you say, Sharona is currently in possession of this junction. I would submit to you, however, that it would be a grave error to assume that that happy state of affairs—from your perspective, at least—will continue indefinitely without some indication of reasonableness from your side. My government has stated repeatedly, through me, that talking is better than shooting. That doesn't mean shooting couldn't resume if our legitimate claims are rejected on the basis of your current military advantage."

Skirvon sat forward in his chair once more, hands folded on the rock-steady table floating between him and Simrath, and looked the Sharonian straight in the eye.

"In all honesty, My Lord," he said with total candor, "given the fashion in which you've just spoken to me, and spoken about my government, a resort to military force isn't totally unattractive to me. I suspect, however, that your masters would be no more pleased than my own if that should happen. So—"

Rithmar Skirvon went on talking, making himself pay no attention to the steadily ticking seconds and minutes flowing away into eternity.

CHAPTER TWO

COMPANY-CAPTAIN Balkar chan Tesh pushed back his canvas chair and stood. The morning officers' conference had run later than usual, thanks to the message chan Baskay and Arthag had Flicked to him, and that, in turn, had both delayed his breakfast and reduced his appetite. Now he left his mess kit on the folding field table for his orderly to deal with and stepped back out of his tent into the morning light.

It was an hour earlier in the day on this side of the portal, and he squinted his eyes as he gazed through it at the mist hanging above the hot, humid swamp on the other side. The autumn weather was growing steadily cooler on this side, especially under the towering trees, but the far side of the portal was much nearer to the equator. At the moment, chan Tesh was grateful to be spared the swamp's miserable climate, but if his people were still living under canvas once winter got here, that was going to change, he thought wryly.

Of course, by then we should have someone senior to me in here to take over, he told himself. *And we may have enough manpower to let me divert enough working parties to actually* finish *those winter quarters Frai's working on.*

He snorted at the thought, although his amusement was less than total. Master-Armsman Frai chan Kormai had been making pretty good progress on throwing together split-log barracks which would at least be weathertight, if not precisely luxurious. Until, of course, the Arcanan "diplomats" had arrived on the scene. Up to that point, it had appeared the mysterious enemy was intent on avoiding any further contact, which had suited chan Tesh just fine. The longer Sharona had to get its own reinforcements forward before they were needed, the better.

But the Arcanans' reappearance, and the transportation capabilities their magic-powered boats had revealed, had forcibly reminded chan Tesh of just how vulnerable his position out here really was. He had been dividing his efforts between improving his troops' fighting positions and trying to provide them with at least rudimentary housing . . . until the arrival of Rithmar Skirvon and Uthik Dastiri refocused his priorities. Following their appearance, he'd pulled his work parties off the barracks-building details to concentrate on strengthening his troop emplacements . . . and reduced his work parties' size to make certain those emplacements were adequately manned at all times.

Of course, "adequately" was an often slippery word, and chan Tesh wished he could be more confident that it applied in this instance. Unfortunately, while it was decidedly on the small side as the inter-universal gates went, the swamp portal was still four miles wide, and there'd never been much point in pretending the forces under his command could hold its entire frontage against a determined attack—especially not given that the actual frontage to be covered amounted to *eight* miles, not just four. Although the rest of chan Tesh's command had finally caught up with the three platoons he'd taken ahead in response to the Arcanans' original attack on the Chalgyn Consortium survey party, that still left him with fewer than eight hundred men. Instead of spreading them out and dissipating his combat power, he'd chosen to divide the command in two. Platoon-Captain chan Dersal, the senior of his two Marine platoon COs, was in command of the positions covering the southern face of the portal, while chan Tesh commanded the ones to the north.

In the face of such a broad frontage, he'd had to settle for attempting to dominate it by fire. Luckily, the rest of his mortars and half a dozen three-point-four-inch field guns had come up with the remainder of the relief column. He'd dug the mortars in in central positions on both Hell's Gate sides of the portal, with the field guns positioned on their flanks, prepared to sweep the approaches to the mortar pits with shrapnel. Also luckily, the ground sloped generally upward on this side of the portal, in both directions. That gave him pretty fair lines of fire into, across, and along the portal's Hell's Gate aspects. He'd taken advantage of that and located the rest of his firepower to protect and support the mortars, because only they had the reach to cover the full width of the portal's faces from their gun pits. He'd positioned his machine guns with the best supporting fields of fire he could arrange, and his men had spent a great deal of time clearing fire zones of scrub saplings, which had further improved upon his basic elevation advantage.

The fact that the water table was farther from the surface on this side of the portal—although the ground immediately *surrounding* the portal was heavily saturated with swamp water—was another factor in his decision to defend it from Hell's Gate. He'd been able to go down more than two feet on this side without striking water, and he'd taken advantage of that to dig his men and weapons in as deeply as he could. And after he'd gotten them dug in, he'd gone right on digging. The mortar pits had to be open if he was going to fire the weapons at all, and the field guns were equally open in order to give the quick-firing guns the best command possible. Despite their lack of overhead cover, the artillery should be relatively safe, given the Arcanans' apparent lack of any sort of indirect-fire artillery.

His other positions, however, were as heavily bunkered as he could contrive. They were the protective barrier between the portal and his gunners, and he'd ordered them dug in below ground level. The aboveground bunker walls were over four feet thick, with log retaining walls filled with tamped-down earth, while the roofs consisted of at least four layers of crisscrossed logs covered by multiple layers of sandbags, as well. He was confident that they would have stood up well even against Sharonian-style field or medium artillery, and judging from the Arcanan fireball spells' apparent lack of penetration, they ought to resist even direct hits almost indefinitely.

He'd also arranged a few other things he hoped would come as nasty surprises to any potential attackers, but he'd always been aware that he'd be hard-pressed to stop any attack in force.

Many of his men (and at least some of his junior

officers), on the other hand, thought he was being alarmist. He knew that. Despite his best efforts, they remained supremely confident—even *overconfident*—of their ability to deal with anything the other side might produce. Yet as chan Tesh had pointed out at this morning's conference, people always learned more from failure than from success, and what Sharona actually knew about Arcana's military capabilities remained pitifully inadequate. At least some of the Arcanan troops his command had defeated two months ago had managed to escape, however—that had been obvious from the moment Skirvon mentioned the confirmed death of that Arcanan civilian, Halathyn, in the attack—which meant the other side had probably learned more than he would have liked about Sharonian capabilities. But even if that weren't true, the natural response would be for Arcana to be bringing up the equivalent of *its* big guns (whatever the hells *that* might be) just as quickly as it could, and that could turn very ugly very quickly. Especially if those damned boats of theirs were any indication of their general mobility.

Chan Tesh himself was painfully well aware that much of his earlier victory owed its success to the Arcanans' complete lack of familiarity with modern firearms and mortars. The peerless stupidity of their commanding officer hadn't hurt, either, and that advantage, in particular, was something he couldn't count on the second time around. Just as—as he'd reminded his subordinates this morning—they couldn't afford to assume for a single instant that what they'd seen so far out of Arcana was, in fact, the best Arcana had.

There's a hell of a lot of difference between a four-and-a-half-inch mortar and an eleven-inch howitzer, he thought, *and the other side hasn't seen* that *yet, either, has it?*

At least chan Baskay's dispatch had helped him ginger up his platoon commanders. Which was remarkably little comfort compared to the way it had underscored chan Tesh's existing concerns.

He snorted again, this time without any humor at all. Chan Baskay's message had at least seen to it that chan Tesh's entire command was at a higher state of readiness. He hoped to all the gods that those among his subordinates who thought he was jumping at shadows turned out to be right. He was confident he and his men were as ready as they could be, but he was also more aware than ever of just how exposed, vulnerable, and—above all—unsupported they actually were.

* * *

Commander of Fifty Tharian Narshu had been carefully chosen for his present duty.

Despite his junior rank, Narshu had seen more than his fair share of combat against everything from brigands to cattle rustlers to claim-jumpers to landowners using "guest workers" as virtual slave labor. More to the point, perhaps, he wasn't the Regular Army officer he appeared to be. He'd been trained in the far harder, tougher school of the Union of Arcana's Special Operations Force, as had half of the men under his command. Two Thousand mul Gurthak had grabbed Narshu and the single squad of his platoon he'd had with him, snatched them (and the transport dragon which had been moving them to join the rest of his platoon in Jylaros) out of the regular transport queue, and hurried them forward to Two Thousand Harshu. Harshu had been delighted to see them . . . and he'd used them to provide the core of Master Skirvon's "honor guard."

The honor guard's other twelve men were primarily window dressing, along solely to make up the numbers, who had no idea their commanding officer and fellow troopers weren't, in fact, Regular Army at all. Narshu wished fervently that all of them could have been Special Operations, but there were never enough SpecOps available. Two Thousand mul Gurthak had been unreasonably fortunate enough to have found even one of Narshu's squads this far out into the boondocks when it had all hit the fan. Besides, a dozen SpecOps troopers ought to be more than sufficient, especially with Sword Seltym Laresk to run the squad. Narshu and Laresk had served together for almost two years now, and the fifty had total confidence in the noncom.

He was glad he did, too, because Tharian Narshu, unlike the late, unlamented Hadrign Thalmayr, wasn't about to underestimate his opposition. This Platoon-Captain Arthag, for example, was as tough and competent as anyone Narshu had ever seen. But competence didn't matter, he reminded himself, when it was offset by complete ignorance and total surprise, and these people knew *nothing* about even the simplest magic.

If there'd been any doubt about that, it had been dispelled several days ago when Narshu and his men first started bringing their daggerstones with them.

Narshu had been in two minds about the wisdom of issuing the daggerstones that soon. He'd been afraid that, despite Five Hundred Neshok's and Master Skirvon's assurances to the contrary, the other side might have some way of detecting them. It wasn't as if they were particularly hard to spot, after all—that was why they were so seldom used by the Spec Ops teams, despite their firepower—and their maximum effective range was barely ten yards. The possibility of getting the ridiculously short-ranged weapons close enough to do any good was minimal in the face of even the most rudimentary security spells.

Two Thousand Harshu had insisted, however, and Narshu couldn't really fault the two thousand for it. Unlike these Sharonians and their "Voices," there was no way for Narshu to report the success or failure of his current mission in time for the two thousand to modify his own plans. That was the entire reason Narshu was out here—to level the communications playing field, as it were—and if his mission had been likely to fail simply because the Sharonians could, indeed, recognize a daggerstone for what it was, finding out at the very last moment would be disastrous.

No one on the other side had noticed a thing, though. Nor did any of them seem aware of the real reason for all of the last few weeks' "incidents."

And, he thought, glancing idly at his chronometer, *it's about time the game began*.

* * *

Rithmar Skirvon kept his attention focused on Viscount Simrath, and *not* on Fifty Narshu, just as he'd been very careful to avoid any casual glance at his own chronometer. Despite that, he was almost agonizingly aware of Narshu's presence behind him, and despite the coolness of the dry northern air, he felt sweat gathering along his scalp as the tension coiled tighter and tighter inside him.

It was becoming increasingly difficult to maintain his air of concentration, to respond to Simrath's statements with the proper degree of normality. He'd expected some of that, but he hadn't anticipated just *how* difficult it might prove, and he found himself unexpectedly grateful for Simrath's earlier abrasiveness. The Sharonian diplomat had introduced a confrontational atmosphere which, in turn, offered an acceptable pretext for any sharpness on Skirvon's part, especially in the wake of all of the unfortunate outbursts of temper over the past couple of weeks. As a matter of fact, those "outbursts" had been carefully designed for the specific purpose of covering any last-minute tension on the Arcanans' part if the Sharonians happened to notice it.

None of which made the diplomat feel one bit calmer as the last few moments trickled past.

* * *

Tharian Narshu's right thumb hooked into his broad, stiff sword belt.

It was a completely natural-looking mannerism, if not precisely the most militarily correct posture in the world. In fact, he'd taken considerable pains to display that particular "sloppy habit" to the Sharonians for the last couple of weeks. It was about as unthreatening as it could be—his hand was on the opposite side from his sword's hilt, after all—but he'd wanted that sharp-eyed bastard Arthag to be accustomed to it. The last thing Narshu needed was for the Sharonian officer to notice anything out of the ordinary on the day when it finally mattered.

The fifty's own eyes never strayed from their slightly bored, incurious focus on Viscount Simrath, but his carefully trained peripheral vision made one last sweep to confirm that the rest of his men were in position. Only his SpecOps squad had a clue about what was going to happen. The rest of his "honor guard" detachment were all tough, capable vets, but they weren't SpecOps. They lacked the specialized training and experience of Narshu's own squad, and he'd decided against briefing them in ahead of time on the theory that what they didn't know was coming they couldn't inadvertently give away.

I'm going to have to apologize to them when this is all over, he thought. *They're good troops, and they're going to have a right to be pissed off when they find out what's really been going on.*

But he'd take care of that later; at the moment, he had other things to think about.

He completed his methodical check of his troopers' positions. Everyone was exactly where he was supposed to be. That was good. In fact, the only flaw in Narshu's satisfaction was that Arthag was outside his field of view.

It was just like the bastard to be uncooperative, the fifty thought sourly. He knew where Arthag was, of course, but he wasn't about to turn his head and look for the man—not at a moment like this. Besides, Arthag wasn't Narshu's target. Seltym Laresk was responsible for dealing with him, and the sword was perfectly positioned to Narshu's left rear.

Yes, he is, the fifty told himself. *So why don't you stop worrying about Seltym, and get on with it?*

It was, he decided, an excellent question, and his right hand flexed.

* * *

Hulmok Arthag's expression never even twitched—he was an Arpathian septman, after all—but he'd felt the tension coiling tighter inside his Arcanan counterpart for the last twenty minutes. The man was good; Arthag had to give him that. Looking at Narshu from the outside, there was absolutely nothing to indicate his spring-steel tension. But Hulmok Arthag was watching the Arcanan from the *inside*.

He wished, not for the first time, that his Talent had been more amenable to direction. He knew, beyond any doubt, that Narshu was totally focused on some action, some mission, but he had no way of knowing precisely what that mission was until the Arcanan actually acted. Which meant *Arthag* couldn't act until then, either. Whatever the Arpathian might "know," there was absolutely no supporting evidence. The other man's hands weren't even close to his sword, and his body language was relaxed, almost casual. Whatever Arthag *wanted* to do, he had to wait. Wait until Narshu gave him something more concrete than the warning of his Talent. Despite his and chan Baskay's suspicions, Narshu—like Skirvon and Dastiri—was part of a diplomatic mission. As such, their persons were inviolable, protected by their diplomat status until and unless their actions, not their *intentions*, changed that status.

Which hadn't prevented Arthag from briefing his own people about his suspicions. Or from leaving the retaining strap of his holster unbuttoned this morning.

* * *

The daggerstone slid cleanly out of the concealing compartment in Narshu's belt.

It didn't look particularly threatening to the naked eye. Aside from the peculiar, glassy sheen of sarkolis, it could have been a quarter-inch thick oval of natural quartz just under two inches across at its widest point. Only someone with at least a trace of a Gift could have used it, and anyone *else* with a trace of a Gift would have seen something quite different from a hunk of stone. Those were, of course, two of the reasons at least some Gift was required for anyone to qualify for SpecOps duty in the first place. Any Gifted observer would have seen exactly what Narshu saw—the nimbus of energy glowing around it, reaching out to envelop his hand and forearm—and, if his Gift had been properly trained (like Narshu's), he would have been able to sense the lethality of that energy, as well.

But no Sharonian had that Gift, or that training.

Narshu's hand rose smoothly, without haste, as his thumb nestled into the slight hollow in the daggerstone's upper surface. It rose just high enough to bear on Petty-Captain Rokam Traygan, and Narshu released the first spell charge.

Brilliant, stunning light flashed across the conference table in a solid bar of lightning. The lightning spell was almost silent, compared to the thunderclap a fireball spell would have produced, but it hammered into Traygan with brutal force, and the Voice flew backward, outlined in a dazzling corona of energy, until he slammed into the trunk of a tree ten feet behind him. He hit with bone-shattering force, but it scarcely mattered; he was dead before he smashed into it.

Two more of Arthag's troopers were caught in the fringes of the spell, and both of them were just as dead as Traygan before they hit the ground. Chan Baskay was just far enough away to be unharmed, but the near-silent concussion of arcane energy sweeping out from the spell's impact point was like being hit with a club.

* * *

Rithmar Skirvon was almost as stunned as chan Baskay. Unlike the Ternathian, he'd known what was coming, but the actual moment had managed to surprise *him*, as well. He jerked back from the conference table as the spell's violence hit him in the face like a fist. Although the plan had been at least partly his own, it was the first time he'd ever even seen a combat spell used, far less been this close to its point of impact. He'd tried to prepare himself ahead of time for what it would be like, but he'd failed.

Had his brain been up to the task, he would have been astounded by how *quiet* it was. Surely nothing that violent, that powerful, could make so little noise! "Quiet" wasn't the same thing as "gentle," however—not by a long shot—and his ears rang, his eyes watered, and he felt as if the breath had been knocked out of him. Yet even so, he knew the most critical part of the mission had succeeded perfectly. They'd managed to identify Simrath's "Voice," and Neshok's eavesdropping recon crystals had overheard enough conversations at the swamp portal to know that the dark-skinned Traygan was the only Voice Simrath and chan Tesh had between them. Which meant there was no way now for chan Tesh—or Simrath—to warn anyone else of what was about to happen.

* * *

Tharian Narshu felt an intense satisfaction as his target went down. Later, he knew, it might be different. The only difference between this and an act of murder, after all, was that he'd been ordered to do it by his superiors. But any regrets were going to have to wait unti—

* * *

Hulmok Arthag's right hand had started to move one thin fraction of a second after Narshu's. The H&W single-action revolver came out of its holster while the daggerstone was rising into position. The hammer came back as the muzzle rose, and the pistol's bellow was the thunderclap of the daggerstone's lightning.

Tharian Narshu's head exploded under the sledgehammer impact of the hollow-nosed .46 caliber bullet, and pulverized bone, blood, and tissue sprayed over Rithmar Skirvon as a stunning cascade of violence swept the clearing.

Narshu's Special Operations troopers had been fully briefed. They were primed, waiting only for their commander's attack on the Sharonians' Voice as the signal for their own attacks. Like Narshu himself, they had recognized the tough professionalism of their Sharonian counterparts. But, also like Narshu, they'd known the Sharonians had no way of detecting a daggerstone, no way of guessing what was coming.

Unfortunately, *they'd* had no way of recognizing Hulmok Arthag's Talent.

Sword Laresk and his men had been focused on Narshu, watching him, waiting for his attack, but Hulmok Arthag's men had been watching *him*. The instant his gunhand began to move, theirs did the same.

* * *

Skirvon was just beginning to realize Narshu had succeeded in his primary mission when the entire world went mad about him. The sibilant hiss of daggerstone bolts was abruptly punctuated by the thunder of Sharonian revolvers. Men shouted in terrified surprise, others screamed in sudden agony, and Skirvon's head snapped around just in time to see the undischarged daggerstone fly from Sword Seltym Laresk's hand as Chief-Armsman Rayl chan Hathas' revolver bullet struck him just below the left armpit from a range of fifty-two inches. The heavy lead projectile, as big around as chan

Hathas' little finger even before expansion, disintegrated a two-inch section of rib, drove straight through the Arcanan sword's heart and lungs, and blew a fist-sized hole out of his right side.

Three of Narshu's twelve Special Operations troopers managed to activate their daggerstones, but none of them got off more than a single spell. They'd ordered themselves to take their time, to avoid rushing those first, critical shots in order to make sure of their initial targets, because *they'd* expected to be the ones with the advantage of surprise, only to discover that their intended victims had been waiting for them all along. Thanks to Arthag's warning, *his* men were actually quicker off the mark, and the sudden, stunning reversal of advantage knocked even the highly trained and motivated SpecOps troopers back on their heels. Thirteen more Sharonians died in the short, cataclysmic exchange, but then every man of Laresk's squad was down and dead . . . along with nine of the other twelve Arcanan troopers who'd never had a hint of what was coming.

Skirvon started to lurch up from the conference table as he realized just how terribly wrong the plan had gone. He didn't know where he thought he was going to go, and it didn't matter. Even as he gripped the edge of the table to lever himself out of his chair, a pistol materialized in "Viscount Simrath's" hand from the shoulder holster Skirvon had never suspected was hidden under his civilian jacket. It was a much smaller weapon than the ones every single one of Hulmok Arthag's men had drawn, but the hollow eye of its muzzle gaped like a cavern as Skirvon abruptly found himself staring straight down it.

The Arcanan froze, mouth gaping open, and the

gray eyes watching him over the revolver's sights were colder than sea ice.

* * *

"Sit back down."

Dorzon chan Baskay's voice was even icier than his eyes, and the .35 caliber Polshana in his hand was rock-steady. Skirvon stared at him for just an instant, then half-fell back into his seat.

The senior Arcanan diplomat's face was the color of cold, congealed gravy. His eyes were sick, stunned—not from the carnage, but from who the victims had turned out to be. At that, he looked better than Uthik Dastiri. The younger diplomat simply sat there, jaw hanging, as if his brain flatly refused to accept what his eyes were reporting to him.

"If you move so much as an eyelash without my permission," chan Baskay continued in that same icicle of a voice, "I will shoot you squarely in the head. Is that understood?"

Skirvon only stared at him, and chan Baskay's thumb cocked the revolver's hammer. It wasn't necessary—the Polshana was a double-action weapon—but it had the desired punctuating effect.

"I asked if that was understood," he said in a very soft voice that sounded bizarrely quiet and calm even to him in the wake of the unexpected thunder. He had no idea where that self-control—if that was what it was—was coming from, but whatever his voice sounded like, something in his expression had Skirvon nodding with sudden, spastic speed.

Chan Baskay gave him one more glance, then looked up as Chief-Armsman chan Hathas stepped up beside him.

"I've got these bastards, Platoon-Captain," the chief-armsman grated, covering the Arcanans with his heavier, longer-barreled H&W.

"Thank you, Chief."

Chan Baskay slid his pistol back into its holster and stood. He turned his back on the two Arcanan diplomats . . . and on the almost overwhelming temptation to simply shoot them out of hand. Everything around him was absolutely crystal-clear, yet all of it also seemed to be much further away than he knew it actually was. He glanced down at his hands and discovered that they were completely steady, despite the quivering tingles running through them. Then he drew a deep, cleansing breath before he looked at Arthag.

"How bad?" he asked.

"About as bad as it could have been," Arthag replied, sounding preposterously matter-of-fact to chan Baskay. Then the Arpathian gave his head a little twitch. "Actually, that's not really true. We could all be dead. Short of that, however, I don't see how it could be much worse."

Chan Baskay looked past him to Rokam Traygan's contorted, broken body. The dead Voice's face was twisted in a final grimace of agony, and chan Baskay swallowed the foulest curse he could think of as he saw Chief-Armsman chan Treskin's body ten yards from Traygan's.

"How did they know?" the Ternathian officer demanded in a crushed-gravel voice. "How *could* they know to kill both of them?"

"I don't know. As a matter of fact, I'm not sure they did know," Arthag said.

"They must have. They went for Rokam first. That means he was their primary target all along. And that means they must have realized not only that he was a Voice, but what a Voice could do, in the first place."

"Maybe. No," Arthag shook his head, "not 'maybe.' You're right about him, at least. But chan Treskin wasn't even the intended target of the . . . whatever the hells it was they used. He just caught the very fringe of one of those blasts, and the bastard who killed him was already going down when he fired. I think it was simply a wild shot that just happened to take him out."

Chan Baskay gazed at the Arpathian for a moment, then shook his own head. Not in disagreement, but to clear it. They still didn't know how long Shaylar had lived after she was wounded, but obviously it had been long enough for the Arcanans to have learned at least a little about Talents and how they worked. It was the only way they could have realized just how vital the Voices were, and they obviously had. On the other hand, if Arthag was right about what had happened to chan Treskin, then the Arcanans *hadn't* realized how important the Flicker was. It was only sheer, incredibly bad luck that they'd gotten him, too.

Not that it mattered.

"We can't tell Company-Captain chan Tesh or Company-Captain Halifu about this." Chan Baskay knew he was stating the obvious. "So, the question is, what *do* we do?"

"They didn't just do this on the spur of the moment," Arthag replied. "And you're right, they obviously hit us first because we were the communications link between Company-Captain chan Tesh and New Uromath. I'm guessing they were pretty confident they could get us all, but I doubt they would have bet everything they had on that, however confident they felt."

"Which means they're going to be hitting chan Tesh anytime now, assuming they haven't already," chan Baskay agreed harshly. He closed his eyes, rubbing his forehead as if to clear away the last lingering cobwebs of shock while he thought furiously. Then he looked at Arthag once more.

"If they've planned this as carefully as I think they have, they probably allowed for the possibility that at least some of us might get away. From where I stand, that means they probably figure they can get here before any of us could reach Halifu."

"How?" Arthag's question was genuine, not a challenge, and chan Baskay shrugged.

"I don't have the least damned idea," he admitted. "Given what we've seen of their boats, and what they just did here, though," he waved one arm at the carnage sprawled about them, "I'm not going to assume they can't do it. Gods, man! If they can make *conference tables* float, maybe they can conjure up flying *carpets* for their people, too! Until I know different, *I'm* certainly not going to say they can't, at any rate."

"Me neither." Arthag tapped two fingers on his chin for a moment. Then it was his turn to shrug.

"I'll get the troops saddled up," he said.

"Good. And while you're doing that," chan Baskay's smile was razor-thin and cruel, "I'll just have a little chat with our guests."

* * *

Skirvon wrenched his eyes away from the revolver in Chief-Armsman chan Hathas' hand as Viscount Simrath waded back across the clearing through the deep leaves. The Ternathian's expression was no more comforting than the gaping bore of Hathas' revolver.

"So, Master Skirvon," he said in a voice fit to freeze the very air about him, "this is Arcana's idea of talking instead of shooting."

Skirvon kept his mouth shut. His belly was a frozen knot, and he swallowed convulsively, again and again. Somehow, despite everything, he'd never imagined anything like this. He'd been far too focused on what was going to happen to the Sharonians to consider what would happen if the carefully orchestrated plan failed.

"Not so talkative now, I see," Viscount Simrath observed. "I think, however, that you might want to reconsider that, Master Skirvon. In fact, I think what you really want to do is tell me exactly what's happening."

"I don't know what you're talking about," Skirvon managed to get out. "I had no idea Narshu was going to do anything like this!"

"Trekar?" Simrath glanced at the other apparent civilian standing beside him, and Trekar chan Rothag shook his head.

"That was a lie," the viscount said flatly, turning back to Skirvon. "Not that I really needed Trekar to confirm that. However, perhaps I should warn you that Trekar is what we call a 'Sifter.' You obviously know more than you wanted us to realize you do about our Talents. Well, Trekar's Talent is that he can always tell when someone is lying. I would strongly advise you not to lie again."

"Or what?" Uthik Dastiri asked. The Manisthuan had apparently recovered the ability to speak, although Skirvon wasn't at all certain that that was a good thing. He might be speaking again, but his eyes were still only half-focused and his expression was belligerent, and Skirvon recognized his associate's anger with a sudden, sinking sensation. Dastiri's temper had always been too close to the surface for a professional diplomat. Now his sense of shocked disbelief had transformed itself into unreasoning rage, and his hands twitched at his sides as he glared at Simrath.

The viscount seemed singularly impervious to his anger.

"You've systematically lied to us," the Ternathian said, and his eyes were far colder—and far more lethal—than Dastiri's. "You've violated the truce between us and killed our soldiers. No doubt, you intended to kill or capture Trekar and myself, as well. In short, you're guilty of premeditated murder, and the penalty for that is death."

"You wouldn't dare!" Dastiri shot back.

"I wouldn't?" Simrath repeated in a deadly calm voice.

"We're diplomats," Dastiri said. "Even barbarians like you ought to understand what *that* means! Besides, it's only a matter of time until our soldiers get here."

"Barbarians, are we?" Simrath's voice was very soft. "The sort of barbarians who massacre civilians, perhaps? Or who systematically lie when they claim to want a negotiated end to the violence? Or who commit murder under cover of their diplomatic status?"

"Uthik, shut up!" Skirvon said harshly.

"I won't!" Dastiri shot back. "This bastard thinks he can *threaten* us? Well, he's wrong!" He turned his glare on the Ternathian. "Go ahead," he sneered. "Tell us what you're going to do to us! Just remember, *our* soldiers are coming!"

"Really?" Something about the Ternathian's smile tightened Skirvon's belly muscles even further.

"I'm afraid you've been operating under a bit of a misapprehension, Master Dastiri," Simrath continued, reaching back into his jacket and withdrawing his revolver once more. "I really am Viscount Simrath, and I really am Emperor Zindel's accredited representative to these negotiations. But I'm also Platoon-Captain chan Baskay, Imperial Ternathian Army, on assignment to the Portal Authority Armed Forces. And I'm afraid that at the moment, I'm feeling much more like Platoon-Captain chan Baskay and very little like a *diplomat*."

Skirvon swallowed again, harder, and chan Baskay smiled icily.

"Under Ternathian military law, Master Dastiri, I have full authority to conduct summary courts-martial in the field and to carry out their verdicts."

"You can't bluff *me*," Dastiri sneered. "Not even you could be stupid enough to think you could get away with murdering an Arcanan diplomat!"

"Perhaps not," chan Baskay conceded. "On the other hand, I *am* 'stupid enough' to execute a murdering piece of scum."

He raised his pistol hand, and despite himself, Dastiri's eyes widened as the Polshana's muzzle aligned itself with the bridge of his nose. Chan Baskay's free hand waved two troopers standing behind Dastiri out of the line of fire, and the Manisthuan's nerve seemed to waver for a moment as the cavalrymen stepped aside. But then his mouth tightened once again, and he glared back at chan Baskay, as if his momentary weakness had only made him even angrier.

"I would most earnestly advise you to give me a reason not to kill you," chan Baskay said.

"Fuck you!" Dastiri spat.

"Wrong answer," chan Baskay said, and squeezed the trigger.

The black hole which appeared in Dastiri's forehead wasn't all that big, actually, a corner of Skirvon's brain reflected. But the entire back of the younger man's skull disintegrated in an explosion of red, gray, and splintered white bone. The body was flung backward. It thudded to the ground, quivering slightly, and chan Baskay brought that deadly muzzle to bear on *Skirvon's* forehead.

"You have five minutes to convince me not to kill you," chan Baskay told him. "I'm sure you know the sorts of things I'd be interested in hearing. And, just as a reminder, don't forget that Trekar will know the first time you lie to me. And if you ever lie to me again, Master Skirvon, I'll be very, very *unhappy* with you. Is that clear?"

CHAPTER THREE

COMMANDER OF FIVE HUNDRED Cerlohs Myr, CO of the First Provisional Talon, Arcanan Expeditionary Force, settled himself even more deeply into the cockpit hollowed out of Razorwing's neck scales. He felt the deep, subterranean rumble vibrating through the accelerating battle dragon, felt the prodigious power of Razorwing's sweeping pinions, and a matching flood of eagerness poured through him, for there was nothing—nothing in all the universes mankind had ever explored—which could equal the sheer thrill of piloting a battle dragon into combat.

Not that anyone's had all that much combat experience over the last couple of centuries.

The thought flickered through the back corners of his brain as the air stream began to scream just above his head. Battle dragon pilots didn't use the saddles transport pilots favored. They rode their mounts in a prone position, strapped into their cockpits—the depressions which centuries of careful breeding had formed in the backs of their dragons' huge, scaly necks. Carefully sculpted scutes in front of that depression acted as baffles, protecting it and fairing the airflow. At a battle dragon's maximum speed, that airflow could severely injure any limb which strayed into it, but the curved scales bent it up and around, leaving the pilot in a pocket of absolutely calm air, like the eye of a hurricane.

Of course, Myr could count on his fingers the number of times he'd taken Razorwing to the dragon's true maximum speed. That kind of flying was frowned upon during peacetime, even in the combat strikes, because of the potential for injuries. And not just injuries to pilots. In fact, replacing a dead or crippled pilot was the *easy* part; a fully seasoned and trained battle dragon like Razorwing took literally decades to hatch, raise, and train.

That was part of the reason the Air Force never had enough of them. They were expensive, they were irritable, they were dangerous, and—in peacetime—they were far less useful than the bigger, slower, more placid transports. There were those who'd argued for years that the combat strikes should be reduced even further. Aside from providing occasional support against unusually large and well-organized groups of brigands, they didn't really have a peacetime function which couldn't be filled just as well by the transports. After all, a properly trained transport dragon could fly aerial reconnaissance missions just as well as a battle dragon, and battle dragons were poorly suited to transport and SAR operations. Their function wasn't to carry or rescue things . . . it was to *kill* things.

The Air Force had fought off the pressure to completely dispense with battle dragons, but it hadn't been easy, especially after so many years in which no external threat to the Union of Arcana had ever been encountered. The decisive argument, in many ways, had been the time and incredible expense which would be required to reconstitute an aerial combat capability from scratch if the breeding and training programs were allowed to lapse. The fact that certain members of the Union Parliament had been determined to protect their constituencies' lucrative Air Force contracts hadn't hurt, either, of course.

But if the Air Force had managed to keep the breeding programs going, it had still been forced to accept severe reductions in total numbers. The slow, steady build-down of the combat forces had been going on for better than ninety years now, and the Air Force's ability to project fighting power and provide ground support was at an all-time low.

Which, of course, explains why Ekros dropped a godsdamned war into our laps now, Myr thought sourly. Or, at least, as sourly as it was possible for a man to feel as the incredible power of the dragon under him carried him through the endless heavens at better than two hundred miles per hour.

The lumbering transports were already out of sight, left far behind as the battle dragons sped ahead at two-thirds again their maximum speed. Not even a battle dragon could sustain that sort of sprint speed for long, but Two Thousand Harshu had stressed the vital necessity of hitting the enemy as quickly as possible.

Myr would have preferred to spearhead the attack in person, and his Razorwing could have flown the mission. Razorwing was a "black," after all—a lightning-breather. But a commander of five hundred had no business getting entangled in the opening stages of an attack like this one. Myr's job was to coordinate everyone else, and no one had commanded an attack on this scale since the Unification War.

He'd selected Commander of Fifty Delthyr Fahrlo for the most ticklish aspect of the operation. Fahrlo's Deathclaw was a "black" like Razorwing, and he was also well over eighty years old. Still in his prime, for a battle dragon, but with decades of experience behind him. It might be experience acquired in training missions, rather than on actual combat operations, but Deathclaw was still the most qualified beast for the mission, and Fahrlo had amassed an enviable record in his strike's exercises over the three years he'd piloted Deathclaw.

Now it remained to be seen just how good Myr's choice would turn out to be. As he gazed ahead, the five hundred saw the swamp portal looming up, growing rapidly closer and bigger, and wished his mouth didn't suddenly feel quite so dry.

* * *

Petty-Armsman Harth Loumas checked his watch.

It was just about time for another sweep, and he yawned and stretched deliberately, locking his fingers above his head and twisting his back to encourage the kinks to depart. Then he settled back on his haunches, closed his eyes, and once more reached out across the miles of water and mud with his Talent.

Loumas had always taken his duties and responsibilities seriously. Given the . . . energy with which Company-Captain chan Tesh had stressed Platoon-Captain chan Baskay's concerns over the Arcanan diplomats' attitude, he was more attentive even than usual today. And he also regretted the fact that they didn't have a decent Distance Viewer even more than usual.

But they didn't, and they couldn't get one, which

meant Loumas' Plotting Talent was the best they could come up with, and he frowned in concentration as he "felt" for the presence of living creatures. As always, he was bombarded with thousands upon thousands of flickers of life essence—birds, mammals, lizards, crocodiles, jaguars. . . . The list went on and on, but all of those essences, all of those glittering points of light in his Talent's field of view, were scattered randomly. They lacked the organization, the formation, which would have indicated a *human* presence.

Still no sign of the bastards, I guess, he reflected. *Good. I know some of the other guys are awfully full of themselves. Well,* they *can be as eager for another round with these people as they want to be. I'd just as soon not see a sign of them until our reinforcements get here.*

He opened his eyes and straightened, and Junior-Armsman Tairsal chan Synarch cocked an eyebrow at him.

"Nothing, huh?" the Flicker asked.

"Don't sound so disappointed," Loumas said dryly.

"Oh, I'm not, believe me!" Chan Synarch shook his head, hard.

"Good, because in that case, I don't have to throttle you for being an idiot."

Chan Synarch chuckled. He and Loumas had been teamed for lookout duty ever since Company-Captain chan Tesh had taken the swamp portal away from the Arcanans, and they got along quite well, despite very different backgrounds. Loumas was a New Farnalian who'd joined the PAAF almost fifteen years before, whereas chan Synarch was a Ternathian who'd been born less than fifteen miles outside Estafel, the imperial capital. He was an Imperial Marine on temporary assignment to the PAAF, and there was a lively tradition of rivalry between the Marines, who considered themselves a *corps d'elite*, and the Portal Authority Armed Forces' long-service regulars.

Upon occasion, that rivalry had spilled over into even more lively brawls, but not this time. Chan Tesh had pinched Loumas from Hulmok Arthag because he desperately needed a Plotter. Well, actually he'd *needed* a Distance Viewer, but he'd had to settle for the best he could get. Although chan Synarch was senior to Loumas, he'd confessed at the outset that he'd never worked with a Plotter before. He'd been refreshingly ready to ask questions in order to figure out how their Talents could mesh most effectively, and the two of them had quickly established a lively mutual respect.

"I wish we were on the other side of the portal," chan Synarch said now, swatting vainly at the insects whining about his head and ears.

"Well, if you can figure out a way to make a Talent work *through* a portal, I'm sure we can get the Company-Captain to sign off on it. For that matter, you'll end up filthy rich, I imagine."

"Instead of just filthy, you mean?" chan Synarch said, grimacing at one muddy boot, and it was Loumas' turn to chuckle.

* * *

Commander of Fifty Fahrlo felt himself trying to curl even more tightly against Deathclaw's comforting solidity. He'd never before dared to take the dragon to his maximum speed, given the bloodcurdling penalties awaiting any Air Force officer foolish enough to lame or cripple one of the expensive, almost impossible to replace battle dragons in a mere training exercise.

I hope to all the gods that Neshok knows what he's talking about this time, Fahrlo thought. *If he* doesn't, *if these people are maintaining any sort of a decent sky watch instead of concentrating solely on ground threats, things could be about to get pretty damned messy.*

Fahrlo would have been more confident of the Intelligence officer's assessment if he hadn't decided that Neshok was one of the half-dozen biggest pricks he'd ever had the misfortune to meet.

You don't have to like him, as long as he manages to do his job, the Air Force officer reminded himself. *Of course, if he were half as bright as* he *thinks he is, he'd probably be a two thousand himself by now, wouldn't he?*

Fahrlo gave his head a mental shake. He had other things to be concentrating on at this particular moment, he reminded himself, and pressed the fingertips of his gloved left hand into the control groove along the side of Deathclaw's mighty neck.

Transport pilots used reins and dragon prods to control their beasts, but the men who piloted battle dragons flew by the tips of their fingers—literally. Just as the dragon breeders had created the cockpit in which Fahrlo rode, they had formed two grooves, each just a shade over two feet long and conveniently placed for the pilot's hands. Those grooves were deep enough that Fahrlo's fingers touched Deathclaw's actual hide, not just the thick, protective scales which armored the mighty beast. That hide was acutely sensitive, and Deathclaw had been trained to respond to even the lightest touch. Fahrlo, like most battle dragon pilots, had long since developed the manual dexterity of a concert pianist, and after so long together, he and Deathclaw literally thought as one. The dragon knew exactly what each touch through one of the control grooves meant, and now he lowered his left wingtip, arcing into a steeply inclined bank, and lowered his head.

Fahrlo removed his right hand from the starboard control groove just long enough to press the sarkolis crystal embedded in his flight helmet, and a circular windowlike image appeared on the helmet's faceplate. It didn't look quite like anything Fahrlo had ever seen with his own eyes, because dragon vision was different from human vision. The color balance was subtly skewed, and no human being had ever been able to pick out such minute details from so far away.

Delthyr Fahrlo's father had been a battle dragon pilot. So had two of his uncles, and his grandfather. And his great-grandfather, for that matter. It was a calling which tended to run in families, because it absolutely required a particular Gift. The image projected across Fahrlo's helmet faceplate wasn't quite like something a scrying spell might have produced, although there were similarities. But the crystal embedded in the helmet contained no scrying spellware. Instead, it reached out to another sarkolis chip, surgically embedded in his dragon some three months after its hatching, which linked the two of them directly when activated. A pilot literally saw what his dragon saw, and the linkage worked both ways. A crosshair floated in the window, moving as Fahrlo moved his eyes. By turning his own head, directing his own vision on a specific object or creature, and marking it with the crosshair, the pilot was able to designate targets for his dragon's attack.

Nor was that all the crystal did. No one in his right

mind wanted a battle dragon's breath weapon to come online without direct human supervision. The weapon itself was an integral part of the dragon's structure, but the dragon couldn't use it without his pilot's consent. It was the pilot's job to *select* the target; it was the dragon's job to *hit* the target . . . but only when the pilot triggered the release code through the helmet crystal and allowed the dragon to attack.

Now Deathclaw's impossibly powerful vision focused on the pair of enemy soldiers so far below. The two men who had to be the first to die under Thousand Toralk's operations plan.

* * *

Something made Tairsal chan Synarch glance upward.

He didn't know what it was. Certainly, it wasn't because of any Talent, or because he'd heard anything. Perhaps it was some primitive instinct which cut deeper than any Talent, any Gift.

Whatever it was, it came too late.

The Marine's eyes went wide as he saw the incredible beast arrowing down out of the heavens above him. The thing's sheer size—and the fact that he'd never seen anything remotely like it—made it impossible to judge the range accurately. At first, for a few brief moments, he'd thought it was only some distant hawk, or possibly an eagle. But then he realized that it was far, far larger than that. And, as the sun caught it, it glittered with a peculiar, metallic sheen no feather had ever produced.

"What the—"

He never finished the question.

* * *

In many ways, the selection of Deathclaw for this particular mission cut against The Book on Air Force operations. Blacks were aerial-superiority dragons, not ground-attack beasts. That sort of attack was supposed to be the province of the fire-spitting reds and gas-spitting yellows. But Five Hundred Neshok and Thousand Toralk had made it clear that the lookout post they'd identified had to be taken out in the very first moments of the attack. One of those lookouts clearly had one of the Sharonian "talents" which allowed him to send messages back and forth almost instantly over at least short distances. According to Neshok, he didn't *seem* to be what the Sharonians called a "Voice," which meant he shouldn't be able to send messages over longer distances. But they couldn't be certain of that, and Arcana couldn't afford to let him relay a warning up the chain of universes behind him if it turned out Neshok was wrong.

That was why Five Hundred Myr had assigned a black. Reds and yellows were both shorter ranged than the blacks, and their weapons were appreciably slower in reaching their targets even across their lower effective ranges. That was especially true for the yellows, yet even the reds' fireballs traveled no more quickly than an arbalest bolt, which, combined with their short effective ranges, made both weapons relatively ineffectual in air-to-air combat.

But that was precisely the mission for which the blacks had been created. Their lightning weapon inflicted less damage than the reds' fireballs, but their attacks reached their targets at literally lightning speed. There was no time for evasive action, no time to dodge. If the bolt was accurately aimed, it *would* strike its target.

Fahrlo had fired Deathclaw's lightning more than once in training operations, at wood and canvas targets on carefully delineated training ranges. He'd never unleashed that weapon against a living, breathing target.

Until today.

* * *

Harth Loumas had just begun to turn his head to see what had so startled chan Synarch when a lightning bolt as thick as a man's arm came hissing down out of the cloudless sky. It struck directly between the two Sharonians, and its dreadful power dwarfed anything any Sharonian had seen out of the Arcanans' infantry weapons.

Their mouths opened in silent, agonized screams as the lightning enveloped them in a blinding corona of destruction. For an instant they writhed, their bodies convulsing in helpless reaction to the massive blast of electricity searing through them. The "CRACK!" as the lightning bolt struck was like a cannon shot, and heads turned towards the sound just in time to see Loumas and chan Synarch collapse like broken puppets of seared, smoking flesh, singed hair, and tattered clothing.

* * *

Five Hundred Myr saw the blinding streak of Deathclaw's bolt rip across the heavens. From Razorwing's present position, it looked perfect, and the five hundred triggered the spellware that released the brilliant red signal flare behind his dragon. It exploded in a spectacular burst of crimson light, and the 3012th Combat Strike obediently peeled off and dove into the attack at maximum speed.

* * *

Balkar chan Tesh was on his way back to his command bunker opposite the center of the portal's northern aspect when he heard the sharp, explosive sound. He spun toward it, and his eyes widened in sudden speculation. The sound wasn't quite like any explosion he'd ever heard, but it was too violent to call anything else.

He was too far from Loumas' and chan Synarch's position to see what had actually happened, but he knew. Somehow, he *knew*.

He stood for one more moment, and then some instinct made him look up.

* * *

Commander of One Hundred Horban Geyrsof watched the lead elements of his 3012th Strike separate and dive steeply.

The entire First Provisional Talon had approached the objective from the east. That had kept the portal itself between them and the enemy's lookouts, who'd been located at its western end. No one knew whether or not a portal would have the same effect on these "Sharonians" so-called "talents" that it had on spells, but according to Five Hundred Neshok, it appeared to. Geyrsof wasn't particularly fond of phrases like "appeared to" when it came to planning operations, but given the description of the enemy's horrific weapons, he was more than willing to play for any possible potential advantage.

Now, as Five Hundred Myr's flare announced initial success, all eight of the 3012th's reds split into two separate four-dragon flights which broke left and right, then came slashing back in diving turns. They stooped upon both faces of the portal simultaneously, wings swept, approaching speeds of two hundred and fifty miles an hour as they used the advantage of their altitude ruthlessly.

Geyrsof would have preferred to lead the initial attack himself, and not just because he possessed an abundance of the aggressiveness and self-confidence which were the fundamental qualities of a successful battle dragon pilot. This was the first Air Force attack on a regular, organized military opponent in two hundred years, and Geyrsof's Graycloud was a yellow. His poisonous breath weapon had been expressly designed for missions just like this one, but he was one of only three yellows—all in Geyrsof's strike—which Thousand Toralk had been able to scare up.

That was the problem. This wasn't just the first attack in two hundred years; it was also the first Air Force attack *ever* on an enemy from an entirely different universe, and they had too few yellows to risk losing them in the very first attack. Especially when no one had the least idea how well Air Force doctrine was going to work against such an opponent, or how effective the other side's weapons were going to be against Geyrsof's dragons.

Those were two of several things they were about to find out.

* * *

The instant he saw the impossible beasts screaming down out of the very heavens, Balkar chan Tesh knew the blow about to sledgehammer his positions would be far worse than any attack even he had imagined in his worst nightmares. The . . . the *dragons*, for want of any better word, would be horrendous opponents even if they simply landed among his men with talons and fangs. He'd never imagined anything outside a whale which could possibly have matched their size, and the mere fact that anything *that* big was actually capable of flight was enough to flood his mind with atavistic terror. But it wasn't just their size, for something gibbered in the back of his brain that if they *looked* like dragons, and if they *flew* like dragons, then they probably *breathed fire* like dragons.

Yet even as the primitive part of his mind recoiled from those horrifying images, the *thinking* part of his mind had already grasped a far more terrifying implication. If these people could fly, then every calculation and estimate of the relative mobility of the two sides had suddenly become meaningless.

And if that explosionlike sound had come from where he thought it had, then he had no way to get a message out to chan Baskay for Rothag to relay to Halifu's Voice. Which meant no one else could possibly know what he'd just discovered.

Those thoughts blazed through him like thunderbolts while he watched the trio of dragons coming straight at him.

And then they began to belch fire.

CHAPTER FOUR

COMMANDER OF TWENTY-FIVE Tahlos Berhala led the attack.

"Commander of Twenty-Five" was a purely Air Force rank, one which Berhala was perfectly well aware the other branches of the Union of Arcana's military deeply resented. He didn't really blame them for their anger over the Air Force's "rank inflation," although he had no intention of giving up the privileges (and additional pay) which went with his commission. But the Air Force had decided long ago that anyone responsible for flying a battle dragon had to be an officer. Once upon a time, Berhala knew, there'd been quite a few noncommissioned combat pilots, but they'd been eliminated in the course of the Air Force's build-down of its combat strength. If there were only going to be a limited number of battle dragons to go around, then by all the gods, they were going to have *officers* in their cockpits!

Which explained how one Tahlos Berhala and his red dragon Skyfire found themselves flying point for the first inter-universal air strike in history.

He concentrated on the targeting display projected

across the inside of his helmet's visor, trying to shut out all the other distractions, all the fear, all the excitement. He watched the incredibly clear image Skyfire's draconic vision produced, and the spellware built into his helmet's sarkolis crystal put a strobing amber crosshair directly in the center of his vision. He moved his eyes until the crosshair settled on one of the open-topped weapon pits and watched it flashing more and more quickly as the range dropped.

His fingers stroked gently, gently in the control grooves, and Skyfire swung slightly to port. Airspeed was still building when suddenly the crosshair stopped blinking. It settled into the steady, blood-red glare that indicated he was in range, instead, and he inhaled deeply.

"*Sherkaya!*" he snapped, and Skyfire's entire body seemed to buck indescribably beneath him as the one-word command—the ancient Mythalan word for "fire"—triggered the helmet spellware's release code.

* * *

Balkar chan Tesh watched in belly-knotted sickness as the first fireball impacted directly on top of the pit occupied by Morek chan Talmarha, his senior artillery officer. There was no overhead cover, nothing to impede the attack in any way. The fireball seemed to move impossibly slowly, yet at the same time, it flashed directly to its target, and it was obviously many times more powerful than anything the Arcanan infantry support weapons could produce. The mortar pit was almost a hundred yards from chan Tesh, but the searing flash of the fireball's ear-stunning detonation seemed to singe every hair on the company-captain's head.

For one bare fraction of a second, all he heard was

that sharp, concussive almost-explosion. But then came the shrieks, the screams of men far enough from its center to have been spared instant death in favor of a far more terrible fate. He saw flaming torches, rolling on the ground, trying to beat out the flames consuming them, and then the ready ammunition stored in the pit began to cook off, as well.

* * *

Berhala saw his target go up in flames, although he had too little time for any sort of detailed evaluation. The maximum attack range for any red was under two thousand yards. At better than two hundred miles per hour, it took barely fourteen seconds to cross that distance, which gave him time for two shots, maximum. Under the circumstances, he decided to assume that the leaping pillar of fire meant he'd knocked out his primary target and turned his head. His eyes moved as well, tracking the crosshair onto one of the sandbag-covered emplacements to the west of his primary target, and then it settled into position.

"*Sherkaya!*" he barked again.

* * *

More fireballs came streaking down to explode on their targets. All of the mortar and gun pits covering the northern aspect of the portal were hit, reduced to flaming crematoria filled with wrecked weapons and exploding ammunition, and the galloping pattern of overlapping concussions threw chan Tesh from his feet. He landed hard on his belly and, even as he hit, the onrushing monsters turned their attention to his bunkers.

Still more fireballs erupted, but this time the results were different as the thickness of the fortifications upon which he had insisted proved their worth. For all their terrifying noise, all the incredible heat radiating from them, the fireballs simply lacked the penetration to punch through that much solid earth and logs.

* * *

Berhala swore in furious disgust even as he pulled Skyfire up and around into a steep climb. The open weapons pits had been devastated, but those other fortifications—

He shook his head, unable to believe that anything could have stood up to Skyfire's devastating attack. But those heaps of dirt and logs were still there, smoking furiously, yet still intact. He glanced across at Lairys Urkora, flying off Skyfire's starboard wingtip on his own Cloudtiger, and the other twenty-five looked up, as if he'd felt Berhala's eyes. It was impossible for either of them to see the other's expression through the reflective, spell-hardened glass of their helmet visors, but they'd flown together for almost a year. Berhala could see Urkora's own astonishment at the survival of their secondary targets in the way the other man cocked his head.

They broke eight thousand feet, converting the speed they'd gained in their original attack dive back into altitude, and Cloudtiger followed Skyfire around. The other two dragons of the flight—Daggerclaw and Deathstar—followed slightly below and to port as they leveled out at just over nine thousand feet, because, despite his junior rank and relative youth, Berhala was the flight's senior pilot.

Five Hundred Myr and Hundred Geyrsof had warned him that the effectiveness of their dragons' breath weapons was unproven. Berhala doubted that either of his superiors had truly imagined that they would prove totally *ineffective* against the other side's fortifications, though.

He glared down at the position a mile and a half below and twice that far behind him. The smoke and flame vomiting upward from his flight's initial targets made it hard to pick out details, even with the assistance of Skyfire's incredible vision, and the looming portal made it impossible for him to see what had happened with the strike on the fortifications guarding its southern aspect. But he could see enough to know the dug in positions on *this* side were still there, still waiting, undoubtedly protecting the devastating rapidfire weapons which had massacred Hundred Thalmayr's company.

Those weapons might not pose a significant threat to Berhala and Skyfire, but the cavalry and infantry coming in behind them would be another story entirely.

He glowered downward for another few heartbeats, then looked back across at Urkora once more and raised his right hand. He was careful to keep it out of the slip-stream as he patted the top of his helmet, then pointed back downward. Urkora responded with a dragon pilot's exaggerated nod of understanding, and Berhala returned his hand to the control groove.

"All right, big boy," he said, although there was no way Skyfire could possibly hear him. "Let's try that again."

* * *

Company-Captain chan Tesh dragged himself back up off the ground. He felt physically stunned, as if someone had beaten him with clubs, but his many years of experience and training roused quickly, fighting his mental shock.

The destruction of his mortars and supporting field guns meant, ultimately, that his defense was doomed.

To be fair, however, that had probably been true from the outset. If the Arcanans' transport capability was as great as the existence of these "dragons" implied, then they'd probably moved in enough troop strength to have overcome his men eventually, no matter what. He simply didn't have enough ammunition to stop the manpower these people could have lifted in by air.

But that doesn't mean we can't bleed *the bastards first*, he thought harshly. *I don't care how fucking good their logistics are, they can't possibly have an unlimited number of men available . . . and however many they have now, they're going to have a hell of a lot* less *by the time they take this position away from* my *boys!*

He turned his head, craning his neck as he looked for the four dragons which had flown directly over him at an altitude of barely a hundred feet after belching their fire into chan Talmarha's gun pits. There! They were circling around, and his jaw clenched as he realized they were preparing for another pass.

Motion caught at the corner of his eye from closer at hand, and his head snapped back around in time to see six of his Ternathian Marines struggling to drag one of the Faraika II machine guns out of a bunker. He started to shout at them to get back under cover, then stopped as he realized what they were doing, and why. They couldn't get enough elevation to reach aerial targets—even targets flying as low as these were—through the firing slits of their bunker.

Obviously, they intended to do something about that.

As he watched, they dragged the two hundred and fifty-pound weapon across to one of the piles of dirt from which the fatigue parties had been filling sandbags.

They heaved the heavy tripod to the top of the pile and slammed its feet as deep into the soft earth as they could. The dirt pile tilted the entire weapon at an awkward, unnatural—and unstable—angle, but four of them threw their own weight onto the tripod, bracing it in place while the gunner and his assistant scrambled around to find some sort of firing position behind the gun.

They didn't have much time. The dragons were already sweeping back, sharpening their angle of approach as they dove back into the attack once more. Other Marines and PAAF troopers were pouring out of their bunkers, finding firing positions with their Model 10 rifles, and as he scrambled towards them, he saw at least a handful of troopers with grenade launchers clamped to their rifle muzzles. The rifle grenades were heavy, awkward, and short-ranged, but they were also specifically designed to take out bunkers and strongpoints, and he doubted *anything* that actually got hit with one of them would—

"Here they come!" someone shouted.

"Make it count, boys!" chan Tesh heard someone else shouting with his own voice, and then the dragons were upon them once more.

* * *

The amber crosshair in Berhala's visor began to steady down as Skyfire swept back into range once more. The commander of twenty-five watched with satisfaction as its rapid blinking slowed, but then he frowned.

Graholis! What were those frigging idiots doing *down there?*

He couldn't believe it. They were actually coming out of their fortifications! He hadn't noticed them quickly enough, either. By the time he could have retargeted and Skyfire's head could have followed the crosshair around to the exposed Sharonians, they would already be past them. But why—?

Then he realized. They couldn't have fired their own weapons against the attacking dragons from inside their prepared positions. So they'd come *outside* in order to be able to shoot back.

He felt himself tightening internally, some of the exuberance and wild adrenaline rush giving way to the sudden awareness that the same impossible weapons which had ravaged the Andaran Scouts were about to be fired at *him*.

Ground fire was a part of any red dragon's life. The reds' breath weapon was short ranged enough that they almost had to come into even arbalest range in a firing pass, and infantry- and artillery-dragons—the support weapons, not the living creatures—had more than sufficient range to engage any strafer. But the good news was that dragons, as a whole, were relatively resistant to the lighter versions of their own breath attacks which the artillery and infantry support weapons could throw. And while arbalest bolts could penetrate and lacerate the relatively thin, translucent hide of their wings, the heavy scales protecting a dragon's undersides and throat were another matter entirely.

And anything they've got will have to get all the way through Skyfire before it does anything to me, he reminded himself.

* * *

They shouldn't have come straight in on us this way, chan Tesh thought. *They should have come in at an angle—made us lead them with our fire.*

The company-captain had been on enough quail and duck hunts to know just how difficult a deflection shot against a passing bird could be. Of course, he'd never fired at a "bird" the size of one of these things in his life! But it didn't really matter very much, either, with the monsters coming straight down his men's throats.

Model 10 rifles began to crack viciously, spitting .40 caliber cupro-nickel jacketed hate back at their attackers. It was impossible for chan Tesh to see what—if any—effect the rifle fire was having, but then the Marine machine gunner he'd noticed earlier began to turn the crank on his weapon.

The Faraika II was a much heavier weapon than the Faraika I he'd had available for his own attack on the Arcanans' original infantry position. The Faraika I fired the same round as the Model 10 rifle; the *Faraika II* had been designed, among other things, as an anti-small boat weapon. It fired a .54 caliber round, which weighed better than three times as much as the lighter round, at an even higher muzzle velocity and with better than five times the muzzle energy. The Spitzer-pointed rounds had a range of close to four thousand yards, and the thunderous bellow as the weapon began to fire was stunning.

Even with four burly Marines heaving their full weight on the tripod, it was almost—almost—impossible to hold the machine gun steady against the hammering recoil, but they managed. And every fifth round was a tracer. They weren't as visible in the bright morning sunlight as they might have been in poorer lighting, but chan Tesh's eye followed them as they streaked towards the dragon flying just off the leader's right wing.

* * *

Twenty-Five Berhala heard—and felt—Skyfire's harsh scream of mingled fury and pain. The dragon shuddered under him, muscles bucking and jerking again and again, but Skyfire never hesitated, never even tried to swerve. He held his course, and the crosshair blinked suddenly crimson once again.

"*Sherkaya!*" Berhala shouted, and another fireball ripped away. Like its immediate predecessor, it impacted directly on one of the squat, thick fortifications . . . and achieved absolutely nothing.

Berhala's lips drew back in anger and frustration, but then he heard a sudden, ear-tearing shriek from his right. His head whipped up and around, rising dangerously close to the slipstream howling just above his cockpit, and his face went white as Cloudtiger's mighty wings seemed to crumple and the huge dragon slammed into the earth at almost three hundred miles per hour.

* * *

"*Yes!*"

Chan Tesh's fierce exclamation of satisfaction was lost in his men's baying shout of triumph. The stupendous creature hit headfirst, tumbling, rolling, broken wings flailing, and the man who'd been strapped to its back went flying like a discarded doll. He hit with an impact which must literally have broken every bone in his body, and Balkar chan Tesh bared his teeth in ugly satisfaction.

It might be small enough recompense for what that dragon and its companions had already done to his command, but at least the treacherous bastards knew now that their victims still had a sting.

* * *

Berhala's mind refused to wrap itself around what had just happened. None of the training texts had ever suggested anything like what had claimed Urkora and Cloudtiger. *Damage* from ground fire, yes. Even the occasional loss of a battle dragon. But not this sudden, almost casual blotting away.

It wasn't possible—shouldn't have happened, his mind insisted. It was—

All thought of his wingman chopped off abruptly as Skyfire made a sound Berhala had never heard out of the dragon before. It was a plaintive, mournful, moaning sound, and the rhythm of the beast's wings seemed to falter suddenly as another blinking icon appeared on Berhala's visor. The image of a blood-red sword flashed before him, and his hands moved instantly, instinctively, in the control grooves.

Skyfire moaned again, but he answered to the familiar touch, banking with a suddenly frightening clumsiness he'd never before displayed. Berhala closed his eyes for a moment, lips moving in a silent prayer for his mount. Then he opened his eyes once more, looking ahead, and brought the wounded dragon in as quickly as he could.

* * *

Commander of One Hundred Horban Geyrsof watched Skyfire hit the swamp like a skipping stone in a long, ragged line of foam and mud. He stared downward, literally holding his breath, then exhaled in ragged relief as Skyfire struggled doggedly towards the nearest islet. At least the beast was still mobile. That was a good sign; dragons tended to recover—eventually—from anything that didn't kill them outright.

Which didn't change the fact that he'd just lost a quarter of his reds, the 3012th's commanding officer reflected grimly. He'd been one dragon understrength to begin with, with only three yellows—his own Graycloud, Commander of Twenty-Five Sherlahk Mankahr's Skykill, and Commander of Fifty Nairdag Yorhan's Windslasher—to make up what should have been his third four-dragon flight. Now he was down to a total strength of only nine, and the effectiveness of the enemy's fire was dismaying, to say the very least. Especially given the battle dragons' low numbers and the time required to replace one. It would never do to say so where any of the Union's ground troops could hear him, but each of his precious battle dragons was probably as valuable as at least a couple of battalions of infantry, and now they'd lost one on only their second pass at the enemy.

He glared at the looming portal. There was plenty of smoke, and not a little fire, visible through it, yet it was painfully obvious that the reds' fireballs had proved singularly ineffective against the half-buried fortifications the Sharonians had erected.

He used Graycloud's vision to sweep the enemy's positions as well as he could through all of the smoke, and his mouth tightened. Some, at least, of the Sharonians had abandoned their bunkers, obviously in order to bring their weapons to bear on Twenty-Five Berhala's flight. He didn't know how many of them were still waiting under cover, and that didn't matter at the moment. What mattered was that the enemy who could hurt his dragons had to come out into the open to do it.

He thought about sending the two surviving reds of Berhala's flight back in. They'd have easier targets this time around, and the ground fire wouldn't take them by surprise a second time. But the Sharonians were more dispersed than he'd expected. He didn't know if they'd spread out on purpose, and it didn't matter.

The way they'd opened their formation would make the reds' fireballs less effective. The remaining reds could still get the job done, especially if he concentrated all of them into one attack force—Geyrsof never doubted that—but it would take more passes, give the other side more opportunities to cost him dragons.

His eyes narrowed as he considered his options, and then he nodded in decision.

A yellow's breath weapon was the shortest ranged of all, but it also had the widest area of effectiveness. It would take at least four passes by all of his remaining reds to clear the exposed Sharonian personnel he could see from here, and that didn't even consider any of the enemy who remained under cover inside their infernally tough fortifications. But his three yellows could cover the entire Sharonian position in only *two* passes, and the very fact that their weapon was so short ranged meant that they had been provided with the thickest, toughest ventral scales of any of the dragon breeds. It left them heavier, slower—more ponderous and less nimble—then any of the others, but it also made them much, much tougher targets. Geyrsof doubted that even a yellow could survive whatever it was which had literally blown Cloudtiger out of the sky, but the chances were good that Graycloud's natural armor could defeat whatever had wounded Skyfire.

He used his helmet spellware to fire the white flare which called off the surviving members of Twenty-Five Berhala's flight. Then he fired the yellow flare which announced the attack by his own flight.

* * *

For a few minutes, chan Tesh allowed himself to hope that the shock of having one of their dragons shot right out of the air would cause the Arcanans to reconsider their aerial attacks.

He spent those minutes dashing across to join the men who'd left their bunkers. He wanted to order them back into the fortifications' protection, but he dared not. Unless they could keep the dragons off their backs somehow, even the relatively ineffectual fireball attacks would be enough to keep his bunkers pinned down while the rest of the Arcanan forces maneuvered around them.

So instead of sending them back into a position of temporary safety, he spent his time rearranging them. Spreading them out even further to deny the enemy massed targets and allocating defensive sectors.

He wished fervently that he had more of the Faraikas. Unfortunately, he'd never had more than a single squad of the heavy-caliber IIs. That was only five weapons when it was at full strength, and he'd been one short to begin with. So he'd deployed two of them to cover each aspect of the portal.

One of the ones covering the northern aspect had been too close to the artillery pits. Its crew had died along with chan Talmarha and his gun crews, and he didn't know whether either of the other section's weapons remained intact. In fact, he didn't know anything about how the defense of the portal's other aspect was going, but he was afraid he could guess.

Whatever was happening over there, however, *he* had to worry about his own position, and his jaw tightened as someone shouted a warning. He turned back towards the portal, and his eyes were cold and bleak as he saw three more black dots plunging down out of the heavens.

* * *

Hundred Geyrsof led the attack personally.

By The Book, he should have let one of his two wingmen take the lead, but he was more experienced than either Mankahr or Yorhan, and the responsibility was his, anyway.

He pressed himself even closer to Graycloud's neck, hands gentle in the control grooves, fingertips moving with a slow, reassuring rhythm. He sensed Graycloud's determination, felt the dragon's own anger at what had happened to Cloudtiger and Skyfire. Dragons were far smarter than most non-pilots gave them credit for, and Geyrsof never doubted that Graycloud understood, at least in general terms, what had happened . . . and who was responsible for it.

And, like his pilot, the yellow wanted vengeance.

Geyrsof laid his strobing crosshair directly atop the tight little cluster of men whose weapon had downed Cloudtiger.

They're going to be shooting at me anyhow, he reflected. *I might as well take my best shot at* them, *too.*

Graycloud was still building speed. Geyrsof had never taken the big yellow to such a velocity, and he wondered if even Graycloud's mighty pinions were equal to the strain he was imposing upon them. But the dragon never complained, never resisted. He only put his head down and flew straight at the enemies who had killed his strike mate.

* * *

Chan Tesh was at the far end of his improvised line from the machine-gun crew as the fresh attack came streaking down upon them.

"Steady, boys!" he called almost gently. "*Steady!*"

The three huge beasts spread out slightly, coming in on a somewhat broader frontage than the original attackers, and he watched the Faraika tracking the leader. The shot wasn't going to be quite as easy this time. *These* dragons were coming in more obliquely, not attacking directly head-on, which was going to make deflection trickier.

Rifles began to crackle once more, but the dragons held their course. Then the gunner began to turn the Faraika's crank. The twin barrels spewed flame and tracers, and the gunner traversed, swinging his fire to intersect the oncoming dragon. The stream of heavy, deadly bullets streaked upward . . . and then one of the Marines helping to steady the tripod slipped.

It was a small enough thing . . . or would have been, under other conditions. And it was scarcely the Marine's fault. Standing up to the brutal recoil of that heavy caliber weapon was no picnic, and his boots slid in the soft soil of the dirt pile. His companions tried to compensate, but they couldn't stop the cascade effect, and the machine gun toppled over on its side.

The gunner was forced to cease fire while his assistants flung themselves on the weapon, wrestling it back into position, but they weren't quite fast enough.

* * *

Hundred Geyrsof's belly muscles had tightened convulsively as the fiery stream of . . . whatever it was coming up from the ground reached for Graycloud. He saw it moving to intersect their course, knew that the heavily armored yellow would never be able to dodge it.

And then, suddenly, it simply disappeared.

His dragon's vision showed him the Sharonians struggling to hoist their heavy, awkward weapon back into firing position, and his lips skinned back from his teeth.

Not this *time, you bastards*, he thought harshly.

The range spun steadily downward. He felt Graycloud quivering as other projectiles hammered into his belly armor from below, but there was no indication that any of them were getting through his thick scales. Skykill and Windslasher held formation on Graycloud's flanks as if they'd been tied together by a single rope, and he felt a burning pride in their steadiness.

And then the crosshair stopped strobing.

"*Larkima!*" he barked, and the ancient Mythalan word for "strangle" released Graycloud's breath weapon.

* * *

Something came streaking downward from the dragons.

Chan Tesh's eyes narrowed as they tracked it. It was even slower than the first dragons' fireballs had been, but it was also bigger. And . . . different. The fireballs had been like tiny, incandescent seeds when they were first launched, growing steadily until they were perhaps twice the size of a man's head. That was as big as they'd gotten until they hit the ground and detonated.

But these "seeds" were bigger from the outset, without the fiery glare of the fireballs. They were darker, dingier, and they grew rapidly. They were three times the size of the fireballs, at least, by the time they reached the ground, and they didn't *explode* the way the fireballs had. Instead, they *splashed*. There was no concussion, no savage flare of heat. It was almost like watching a bucket of water hitting, spreading out, washing over everyone in its vicinity as it spread wider and wider like some green-yellow fog.

For a heartbeat or two, that was all that happened. Then the first of chan Tesh's men staggered. He went to his knees, clutching at his throat with both hands. One of his companions turned towards him, as if to offer assistance, then went down beside him, writhing, choking.

Balkar chan Tesh's eyes widened with a horror even the fireballs hadn't awakened. Perhaps that was because for all their unnatural origin, the fireballs weren't all that different from the artillery with which he was familiar. This, though—he'd never seen, or imagined, anything like *this*.

More and more of his men went down. *Everyone* trapped in the area covered by those obscene breath weapons collapsed, strangling, vomiting, coughing up blood from rupturing lungs while they writhed convulsively, twisting in agony.

The dragons which had spawned that horror streaked overhead, climbing once again, and despair closed upon Balkar chan Tesh's heart like a vise of frozen iron.

That single pass had covered over two-thirds of his exposed personnel, and at least a quarter of the bunkers. Even as he watched, strangling, dying men clawed their way out of two of the bunkers, only to collapse in their own vomit as they reached the "open air" outside their position.

No one—not even Imperial Ternathian Marines—could be expected to face something like that. Not when it came at them cold, with absolutely no warning. He looked at the handful of men—there were only five of them—clustered around him, upwind from the killing clouds of vapor. There was still time, he thought. Still time to run, to put distance between himself and the dying, spasming men behind him before the dragons came back. He saw the same thought, the same recognition, in the eyes around him.

And, like Balkar chan Tesh, not one of them ran.

"All right, boys," he said quietly, looking past them, tracking the dragons with his eyes as they swept back up into the heavens. "They'll be back in a few minutes. It doesn't look like rifle bullets bothered the bastards very much, either."

He turned his head, taking his eyes off the dragons, and looked at the men around him.

"Whatever those people are doing, and however they're doing it, they had to come in close before they fired or whatever," he said.

"Yes, Sir," one of the others agreed. "And they opened their mouths, too," he added.

"Good point." Chan Tesh patted him on the shoulder, then gestured at their Model 10s.

"You've all got grenade launchers," he said.

* * *

Hundred Geyrsof studied the ground below through Graycloud's eyes as Skykill and Windslasher formed up on them once more.

The initial strike had succeeded even more completely than he'd hoped. The vast majority of the enemy was already down, dead or dying, and aside from minor damage to Graycloud's and Windslasher's wing membranes, all three of his yellows were unwounded.

He should have felt nothing but satisfaction. He knew that—and he *did* feel satisfied. But that wasn't all he felt. Graycloud's vision brought it all too close, made it all too clear. He saw the men he'd just killed, even though they weren't all dead yet. He saw them twisting, convulsing in agony, jerking like landed fish drowning in poisonous oxygen, and for the first time, he truly understood why some people had fought for so long to have the yellows banned. It was ugly . . . unclean.

Oh, fuck "ugly!" he told himself fiercely. *Dead is dead, Horban. There aren't any* good *ways to die, and better it should be them than us!*

He knew that was all true . . . and it didn't make him feel any better.

Anything he might feel couldn't change his responsibilities, though, and he watched the other two yellows settling into formation once again behind and to either side of Graycloud. He waited until they were both in place. Then his hands moved in the control grooves, and Graycloud slanted downward once more.

* * *

"Here they come," chan Tesh said quietly.

One of the Marines had found the company-captain a Model 10 whose owner would never need it again. Like the others, he'd mounted the grenade launcher and loaded the special blank ammunition that fired it. Now the six of them stood waiting, watching their executioners sweep towards them.

There were other Sharonians still standing, somewhere beyond the swirling haze of green-yellow vapor. Chan Tesh heard their rifles beginning to crack, and his heart swelled as he realized his men were still there, still fighting back, despite everything.

He took his own eyes from the oncoming dragons for just a moment, let them sweep across the Marines around him.

"Gentlemen," he said, "it's been an honor. Thank you."

No one replied. There was no need.

Chan Tesh looked back at the oncoming dragons. Only one of them—the one on the extreme left of the Arcanan formation—was going to come into the grenade launchers' range, he realized. Well, at least that guaranteed concentration of fire.

Onward, closer and closer. They weren't coming in as quickly this time, a detached corner of his brain observed. Was that overconfidence? Or were they just slowing down to improve their accuracy? Or was it simply that they'd started from a lower altitude, hadn't had the opportunity to build the same velocity?

It didn't matter.

Closer, and closer still.

Properly speaking, rifle grenades weren't launched from a normal firing position. Given their recoil, The Book called for them to be fired only with the rifle's butt firmly grounded. Chan Tesh knew that, but he didn't really care. Not this time.

He nestled the brass buttplate into his shoulder, tracking the incoming dragon steadily, waiting.

One of the Marines fired. The grenade missed, and the dragons swept closer. Another Marine fired and missed.

Chan Tesh and the other three waited. Waited.

* * *

"*Larkima!*" Hundred Geyrsof barked.

* * *

The dragon belched its dingy death seed.

All three of chan Tesh's remaining Marines launched their grenades. One of them missed completely. Of the other two, one struck a wing membrane and punched clear through without ever exploding. The third slammed into the dragon's left foreleg and exploded, blowing a huge, gaping wound into the limb.

But Balkar chan Tesh waited just a moment longer. Waited even as he watched the growing breath weapon streaking towards him. Waited for the dragon to come just that little bit closer. And then, as it opened its mouth in a bellow of pain, he launched his own grenade.

CHAPTER FIVE

RITHMAR SKIRVON SAT slumped in his chair while Fifty Narshu's splattered brains and blood dried into a caked residue on the back of his neck and the back and shoulders of his elegantly tailored civilian coat. There were probably at least a few specks of Uthik Dastiri's brains mixed in among the rest of it, and his face seemed to have crumpled in on itself. There was no sign of the confident, masterful diplomat now, Dorzon chan Baskay thought grimly, and felt a fresh ripple of anger roiling about in his belly like slow magma as he glared at the Arcanan.

Skirvon had, indeed, worked hard to convince chan Baskay to let him live. In fact, he'd spilled his guts, more than half-babbling in his urgency to tell chan Baskay anything—anything at all—which might placate the Ternathian's frozen rage.

Which meant chan Baskay knew just how utterly and totally screwed he and all of Hulmok Arthag's surviving troopers actually were.

"We're ready," a voice said behind chan Baskay, and the platoon-captain turned to find Arthag standing behind him. The Arpathian stood beside his magnificent Shikowr-Daykassian-cross Palomino stallion with his Model 10 slung over his shoulder, and the rest of their surviving men stood saddled and ready to ride behind him. Every bit of movable, useful equipment had been loaded onto pack horses at truly Arpathian nomad speed. Two of them had packed up chan Baskay's and chan Rothag's gear and saddled their horses, as well . . . and the bodies of every dead Sharonian were lashed across their saddles.

"Is that really necessary?" chan Baskay asked very quietly, nodding at the dead men.

"As a matter of fact, I think it is," Arthag replied. Chan Baskay couldn't quite hide his surprise. Arpathians, as a rule, weren't particularly sentimental about the bodies of the dead. As far as they were concerned, once the soul had fled, the body in which that soul had once resided had no intrinsic importance, which made Arthag's apparent concern for these bodies unusual, to say the least.

"We don't have time to bury them," Arthag explained, responding to chan Baskay's perplexed expression, "and one thing all of us canny Arpathian nomadic warriors get taught at a very early age is that it's important to keep an enemy guessing about your losses. Let the bastards find their men's bodies lying around here without a single one of ours. You don't think that's going to make them more than a little anxious about just what happened here?" He shrugged. "The way I see it, anything that can convince them to be even a little hesitant about chasing after us is well worth the effort."

Chan Baskay gazed at him for a moment, then nodded.

"Good enough for me," he said. "Of course, there's still the little problem of exactly *where* we're going to go while they hesitate about chasing us, isn't there?"

"I take it there's no point trying to make it back to Company-Captain Halifu?"

"You take it correctly," chan Baskay said grimly. "I'm sure Master Skirvon still has quite a bit to tell us, but I think I've got the essentials for our immediate problem. Which includes the fact that these bastards have *dragons*, Hulmok."

"Dragons?" One of Arthag's eyebrows rose perhaps a sixteenth of an inch, and chan Baskay snorted.

"Yes. According to Skirvon, they come in two varieties—one that's basically for transporting cargo, and the other that breathes fire and lightning. And the buggers can fly at up to a couple of hundred miles an hour."

"Marvelous."

"Wait, it gets better. The transport version?" Chan Baskay paused, and Arthag nodded. "They can transport entire companies of cavalry by air, and they've been shipping in men, weapons, horses, and still more dragons the entire time they've been talking to us here. They've got what sounds like at least the equivalent of a light division or heavy brigade, and they're probably rolling right over Company-Captain chan Tesh while we're talking."

"I see."

Arthag cocked his head, his expression thoughtful, and chan Baskay felt an incredible temptation to punch him right on the nose. At this particular moment, the Arpathian's total imperturbability was almost as maddening as it was reassuring.

But only almost.

"They've got something Skirvon calls 'gryphons,' too," chan Baskay said, instead. "He says they're about the size of a good-sized pony but with wings, beaks, and great big claws, and they're even faster—and more maneuverable—than these dragons of theirs. They aren't as smart, though."

"Can they get at us through the tree cover?"

"That seems to be about the only good news I've gotten out of the bastard," chan Baskay said, shaking his head. He waved one hand at the overhead canopy of leaves and towering branches. "They can't get down through that, and Skirvon swears the dragons can't see through it very well, either."

"And he's telling the truth?"

"That's what Trekar's Talent says. Of course, the son-of-a-bitch is scared to death. Trekar says that sometimes someone who's piss-himself terrified convinces himself that whatever the other guy wants to hear is the truth, and his Talent can't tell the difference in a case like that."

"Um." Arthag scratched the tip of his nose thoughtfully. "I'm inclined to believe him on this one," he said after a moment. "At least as far as their being able to get at us directly." He smiled crookedly. "You know, this is the first time I've ever been grateful for the way these godsdamned trees get in the way!"

"Maybe. On the other hand, it's not going to be enough to get us back to New Uromath. According to Skirvon, their horses are a hell of a lot better than ours, too."

For the first time, Arthag bridled. He straightened, one hand reaching up to Bright Wind's ears, and his eyes narrowed.

"He says they've used more of this damned magic

of theirs to 'augment' their horses," chan Baskay said. "They're faster than ours, according to him, and they've got a lot more endurance, and if they can breed *dragons*, I don't see any reason why they couldn't do that, as well."

Arthag nodded unwillingly, and chan Baskay shrugged.

"Assuming he's right about that, they'd almost certainly run us to ground long before we could get back to New Uromath. Besides, it turns out they've scouted the New Uromath portal, too. Apparently one of their people made it all the way to Halifu's fort and back again before we took out their base camp. They've known exactly where it is all along, and they're planning to attack it as soon as they've secured control of the swamp portal."

"I figured they must have something like that in mind," Arthag said. "I hadn't considered the possibility of these 'dragons' of theirs, of course. But none of this—" he waved one hand at the body-littered clearing "—would have made any sense at all if they hadn't planned on going all the way. I *had* expected to be able to outrun them back to Fort Shaylar, though."

"Agreed."

Chan Baskay turned to survey the area himself. The tangle of fallen trees where the Chalgyn Consortium survey crew had been massacred had seen far more than its fair share of bloodshed in the last couple of months, he reflected grimly.

Arthag's people had been busy doing more than just packing while he and Trekar chan Rothag interrogated Skirvon. The three surviving Arcanan cavalrymen sat on a fallen tree trunk, hands bound behind them and shoulders slumped. From their expressions, as well as their body language, chan Baskay was strongly tempted to believe Skirvon was right—those men hadn't had a clue what was going to happen here today. Nothing was likely to make chan Baskay feel particularly kindly towards Arcanans at the moment, but despite himself, he felt an unwilling sense of sympathy for those prisoners.

He felt none whatsoever for Rithmar Skirvon, however.

His mouth tightened at the thought as his eyes traversed the line of Sharonian bodies tied across their horses. There were sixteen of them, in all, and the twenty-three Arcanan bodies scattered about under the trees were no comfort at all as he considered their losses.

"We'll have to jackrabbit," he said after a moment, and Arthag nodded, then cocked his head slightly.

"Which portal?" he asked.

"That's the question, isn't it?" Chan Baskay's eyes slitted as he thought hard, considering their meager menu of options.

"I think we'd better go for the New Farnal connection," he said finally. Arthag grimaced slightly—the equivalent of a shouted protest, coming from an Arpathian—and chan Baskay shrugged.

"I don't like it a lot better than you do," he said, "and I know the horses are going to hate it. But if they've got these dragons, and these 'gryphon' things, we're going to need all the terrain advantage we can get. And if they don't like flying through tree cover like *this*—" he waved at the leaves overhead again "—then they're going to *hate* triple-canopy jungle."

"There is that," Arthag agreed. "It's a little farther to go, though. If they've really got better horses, they could probably overtake us."

"They'll probably figure we broke back for New Uromath," chan Baskay countered. "They know that's the only way home to Sharona, and, according to Skirvon, that's the only other portal they've actually located and scouted. Besides, they've been working extra hard to keep us from finding out about their dragons. If they think they've succeeded—and they did, after all—then they'll expect us to try to outrun them back to Company-Captain Halifu."

"But if they sweep through here on horseback, they're going to be able to tell which way we actually went."

It could have been a protest, but Arthag's tone was thoughtful, not argumentative.

"I know. But I still think it's our best option."

"So do I." Arthag nodded. "And I think I have an idea about how to . . . delay the pursuit just a bit, too."

* * *

"On your feet, you fucking son-of-a-bitch!" Sword Keraik Nourm barked.

The wounded Sharonian soldier just looked up at him. The Sharonian's expression was a mix of hatred, shock, disbelief, and pain as he crouched on his knees, cradling a savagely burned left arm against his chest.

"On your *feet*, godsdamn you!" Nourm snarled, and buried the reinforced toe of his combat boot in the Sharonian's ribs with a brutal kick.

The Sharonian went down, crying out in pain as his burned arm hit the ground, and Nourm raised his heavy arbalest to butt-stroke the wounded man's head.

"*Belay that, Sword Nourm!*"

The four-word command cracked like a whip, and Nourm's arbalest froze in midair. His head whipped around, and his face tightened as he saw the officer with the two silver collar pips of a commander of fifty striding angrily towards him.

"What the hells d'you think you're *doing*, Nourm?" the fifty demanded harshly.

"Securing the prisoners, Sir," Nourm replied half-sullenly.

"The hells you say!" the fifty snapped. "That man is severely wounded, Sword! Godsdamn it, you're the platoon sword—what kind of message do you think this is sending to the rest of the men?!"

Nourm opened his mouth, then shut it with an almost audible click. His face flushed darkly, more with anger than with shame, and he set his jaw stiffly.

Commander of Fifty Jaralt Sarma put his hands on his hips and glared at his platoon's senior noncom. What made Sarma's seething fury even worse was that Nourm was normally one of the best platoon swords Sarma had ever seen.

The fifty leaned closer, lowering his voice, and let his tone soften just a bit.

"I know you're pissed off with these people, Keraik, but that's no justification for violating the Accords. You know that's a court-martial offense."

"The Accords, Sir?" Nourm looked at him as if he couldn't quite believe what he'd heard.

"Yes, the Accords," Sarma said. "Do I need to remind you that they apply to *everyone*?"

The Kerellian Accords, drafted centuries ago by Commander of Armies Housip Kerellia, had set forth the Andaran military's official rules of war, including the standards for proper treatment of POWs. The Accords had been adopted by the Union Army following the Union's formation two hundred years ago, and officially incorporated into the Articles of War.

"Sir, these bastards aren't even from our *universe*!" Nourm protested.

"I don't recall anywhere in the Accords that specifies where the prisoners have to *come* from, Sword."

"But, Sir—"

"Don't make me tell you again, Sword Nourm," Sarma said very quietly, and the burly noncom closed his mouth again.

It was obvious he still couldn't quite believe what his fifty had just said, and Sarma shook his head.

"I understand you're mad as hells, Sword," he said in a more normal voice. "But that's no excuse for turning ourselves into something we'll be ashamed of later."

"Sir, I understand what you're saying, I guess," Nourm said after a moment. "I just don't see why we should waste the Accords on miserable fuckers like these."

"The Accords aren't as much for them as they are for us, Keraik. It doesn't matter what *they* do. What matters is how *we* go about being who we are."

"Sir, I just don't see it. These miserable bastards deserve anything they get. They should feel grateful we don't just shoot *them* in the back of the head!"

Sarma's lips thinned angrily, but that anger wasn't aimed at Nourm this time. Or, at least, most of it wasn't.

Neshok, you bastard, the fifty thought venomously. *You and your fucking "briefings!"*

"I'll remind you—once—Sword," the platoon commander said after a moment, "that the briefers specifically said those reports couldn't be confirmed."

Nourm's jaw set again, harder even than before. His shoulders hunched like a man preparing to dig in against a monsoon, and Sarma inhaled sharply. He started to launch into the sword again, then made himself stop. This wasn't the time or the place for him to turn his command relationships into a debating society.

"Listen to me," he said instead, his voice flat. "At this moment, Sword Nourm, I don't really care what you feel or think about these people. You *will* observe the letter of the Accords in your treatment of them, and you *will* see to it that every member of this platoon does the same. And don't think for one moment that I won't know whether or not you do. The recon crystals are activated and recording, and they'll stay that way. So you think about that, Sword. You think *real* hard before you abuse another prisoner, wherever the fuck he came from, while you're under *my* command. Do you read me on this, Sword Nourm?"

"Yes, Sir," Nourm grated.

"I don't believe I heard you, Sword."

"Yes, Sir!"

"That's better. Now, I believe this man needs medical attention."

"Yes, Sir."

Nourm's anger was obvious, but it was equally clear to Sarma that the sword was at least trying to control it, so he let it pass. Which didn't prevent him from keeping an eagle eye on the noncom as Nourm helped the wounded Sharonian back to his feet. He wasn't especially gentle about it, but he wasn't brutal, either, and for the moment, Sarma was willing to settle for what he could get.

He watched the sword half-dragging the prisoner towards the healers and sighed.

Sarma knew his own attitude towards the Sharonians was atypical. Which was . . . unfortunate, since it was *supposed* to be the entire expeditionary force's attitude.

Two Thousand Harshu's general orders had made it abundantly clear that the observation of the Accords was the official policy of the Union of Arcana in the present conflict. Unfortunately, unless Sarma was very much mistaken, it wasn't going to matter a great deal what general orders said.

It was Acting Commander of Five Hundred Neshok's fault, he thought bitterly. Sarma's platoon had been in the first wave of reinforcements to reach Fort Rycharn. That meant he'd had the opportunity to talk directly to Five Hundred Klian's men before the rest of Harshu's troopers and dragons had assembled. Perhaps more to the point, one of his uncles had served with Five Hundred Klian when they were both mere squires, and the five hundred had invited his old friend's nephew to join his own officers for dinner one night.

Which meant he'd heard Five Hundred Klian's version of what had happened when the Sharonians punched out the Andaran Scouts at this very portal.

Somehow, the five hundred's version was quite different from the official briefings Five Hundred Neshok and his staff had delivered. According to Five Hundred Klian, who'd spoken directly to the only Arcanan eyewitnesses, Magister Halathyn vos Dulainah had been killed accidentally by an *Arcanan* infantry-dragon after he'd been pulled out of his tent by a Sharonian cavalryman. But according to Neshok's briefers, although they'd been scrupulously careful to warn everyone they were still seeking confirmation, Magister Halathyn had been dragged out of the tent and shot dead by the *Sharonians*. And, those same briefers had said gravely, there were additional unconfirmed reports that the Sharonians had systematically executed all of the Scouts' wounded, as well, rather than providing medical care.

Nothing could have been better calculated to fill Arcanan soldiers with fury. Magister Halathyn had been quite possibly the most beloved single man in all the Arcanan-explored multiverse—outside his own native Mythal, at least—and the idea that he'd been murdered out of hand by the Sharonians had fanned the rage of men like Sword Nourm to an incandescent pitch. Adding the possibility that the Sharonians had murdered their own prisoners only made it worse . . . assuming that anything could have.

Sarma shook his head. He'd never seen troops in such an ugly mood. They were out for blood vengeance on the "Sharonian butchers," and the fifty felt a cold, icy shudder of fear when he considered where that might lead everyone.

But it's not too late, he told himself. Surely, *it's not too late. Two Thousand Harshu can still turn this around, if he'll just make Neshok stick to the facts.*

Only . . . the two thousand hadn't done that yet. Whether he agreed with what Neshok was doing or not was almost beside the point. Even the officers who might have questioned Neshok's briefings, or pointed out to their men that even the Intelligence briefers had stressed that the reports were unconfirmed, were going to take their lead from Harshu's *apparent* attitude. And until Harshu specifically addressed the issue, they were going to ignore his general orders' *official* position.

And when they do, what happens to the Union Army? Sarma asked himself almost despairingly. *What happens when we wake up and realize what we've done? And what happens if the way we treat* our *prisoners leads them to* really *start shooting our people out of hand when they're captured?*

Jaralt Sarma didn't know the answers to those questions . . . but he was afraid that was going to change.

*   *   *

Commander of One Thousand Klayrman Toralk was not a happy man.

In one sense, the operation had gone exactly as planned. They'd obviously taken the portal defenders completely by surprise, which meant Narshu must have succeeded in neutralizing the Voice at Fallen Timbers. And the force here at the portal had been almost totally eliminated. At the moment, they had exactly twelve prisoners, half of them wounded, and it didn't look as if there were going to be very many more.

But the attack had cost him. *Graholis*, but it had cost him! Bad enough to have had two of his reds killed outright, but he had three more which had suffered significant injuries. The odds were probably about even that they'd still lose Berhala's Skyfire, even with the healers, and one of the other wounded reds was hurt almost as badly. That was a much higher loss rate than he'd anticipated, and it suggested that these Sharonians' "rifles" were going to be dangerously effective against his ground attack dragons.

Yet as bad as that was, there was worse. He had no idea what the Sharonians called the things they'd screwed onto the ends of their rifles, but one of them had gone straight into Nairdag Yorhan's Windslasher's open mouth. The explosion had killed the yellow, and Yorhan's neck had snapped like a twig when his dragon went in at two hundred miles an hour.

It was obvious to Toralk that the yellows had been his

most effective weapon, and at least they'd demonstrated a relative immunity to rifle fire. Graycloud and Skykill both had wing damage, but punctured membranes were something the Dragon-Healers could repair quickly. Both of them had dozens of scarred and gouged belly scales, as well, but none of the fire they'd taken there had managed to penetrate, and he expected the healers to have both yellows back in the air within another half-hour, maximum.

Which made the fact that he'd lost a third of them even more painful. If taking a single portal had cost this much, then—

The sound of a sudden explosion snapped his head up, and his mouth tightened as he heard the fresh screams.

That bastard *Neshok*, the thousand thought viciously. *Why the hells didn't he warn us about* this *crap, if he's so frigging good?*

Even as the thought flashed through his brain, he knew it wasn't really fair. The truth was that most of the information Neshok had provided had proven amazingly accurate, but Toralk wasn't really in a mood to be fair to the arrogant Intelligence officer. Not when he'd already lost so many battle dragons. And not when one of the things Neshok *hadn't* warned him about had already cost Arcana at least twenty men.

He didn't know what the Sharonians called the devilish devices they'd buried around their defensive positions. He didn't even know—yet—how they worked, for that matter. But their effectiveness had already been made amply clear, and he expected them to have a significantly dampening effect on the ground troops' confidence.

Maybe not, he thought. *I may be being overly pessimistic. It's not that much different from a combat trap spell, after all.*

He watched the corpsmen making their quick yet cautious way towards the newest casualties and knew that there was, indeed, at least one very significant difference. The devices killing his men as they exploded were completely undetectable by any of the Army's trap-sweeping spells. They simply didn't register, since they didn't rely on any arcane technology at all, and that was the reason for the hesitancy he could already see in the gas-masked troops advancing cautiously through the Sharonian positions.

"Sir," one of his staffers said quietly. Toralk glanced at him, and the young man twitched one hand unobtrusively back over the swamp. Toralk followed the gesture with his eyes, and his lips tightened slightly as he saw Two Thousand Harshu's command dragon slicing down towards a landing.

He nodded his thanks to the young fifty and turned to walk back towards the safe zone on the swamp side of the portal where they were sure there were none of the whatever-the-hells-were-blowing-people-up to greet his superior officer.

The dragon landed in a spray of water and muck, and Harshu vaulted down from its back. He landed with a substantial splash, but he seemed completely unaware of it as he started for the shore, grinning fiercely around the stem of the pipe clenched between his teeth.

Somehow, Toralk wasn't surprised. The two thousand had always struck him as someone who was enamored of flamboyance for flamboyance's own sake. Someone who was constantly aware that he was "on stage" and played shamelessly to his audience. Over the past few weeks, though, Toralk had come to the conclusion that he'd been wronging Harshu, at least a little. The two thousand *was* constantly on stage, and constantly aware of it, but it was a sort of military theater which was part and parcel of his command style. And, somewhat to Toralk's surprise, it actually worked. Even with relatively senior officers—like one Thousand Klayrman Toralk, who damned well ought to know better.

Commander of One Thousand Tayrgal Carthos followed the two thousand down into the mud. The heavily built, red-haired Carthos was Harshu's senior infantry commander, Toralk's counterpart amongst the expeditionary force's ground pounders. He was also older than either Harshu or Toralk, with streaks of startling white painting themselves into his thick, spade-shaped beard to bracket the corners of his mouth, and his expression seemed to hover on the precipice of a perpetual frown. Now he and Harshu waded through the thigh-deep swamp to the solid hillock upon which the portal stood, then stepped through onto the firmer ground on the other side.

"Sir!" Toralk saluted briskly, and Harshu touched his own fist to his left shoulder in response.

"Before you say anything, Klayrman," the two thousand said around his pipe, "you and your people did well—very well. I know we've lost more dragons than we'd anticipated. Well," he grimaced, "that's not totally unexpected, is it? We knew going in that the first battle would be a learning experience."

"Yes, Sir. But I still—"

"Don't kick yourself over it." Harshu's voice was just a bit harsher, and he shook his head. "I said you did well, and you did. I was watching over the scrying spell. I know exactly what happened, and I know Hundred Geyrsof made the right call. I don't know just what they used to knock that one yellow down, but whatever it was, it was short ranged. And whatever else happened, we've got the portal."

"Yes, Sir," Toralk acknowledged, then showed his own teeth in what very few people would have mistaken for a smile. "On the other hand, these people seem to have left us a few rather nasty little surprises." He shook his head. "I know I'm just an Air Force puke, but it looks to me like these trap-spell equivalents, or whatever they are, are going to be a major pain in the arse."

"At least until we get a handle on finding them, at any rate," Harshu agreed, gazing past Toralk to where his infantry pointmen continued to pick their way gingerly and cautiously forward.

"I don't suppose we can blame the men for being a little hesitant," Carthos put in,"even if it is putting us behind schedule."

Toralk nodded. The cavalry was supposed to have been moving ahead, sweeping towards Fallen Timbers to relieve Narshu. The infernal devices the Sharonians had left behind, however, had put a significant kink into their timetable.

"I agree," he said. Under the Union of Arcana's joint forces doctrine, he and Carthos were currently in a sort of gray zone. Air-mobile operations technically came under Air Force control, but only until the ground forces were landed. At that point, control reverted to the senior Army officer present. Technically, that was Two Thousand Harshu as the expeditionary force's commanding officer, but Carthos was the designated tactical officer in command for the ground component. Which meant that Toralk was in a rather delicate position if he said anything that sounded like Air Force criticism of Army personnel.

"Part of it may be that we've . . . over impressed our junior officers with the need to conserve manpower," he observed.

"Maybe," Harshu said. "But it's a hells of a lot more likely that the fact that they can't detect the bloody things is giving them the willies!"

The two thousand stood for a moment, clearly thinking hard, then shrugged.

"Narshu obviously pulled off his primary mission," he said. "If he hadn't, these people would have been a lot readier for us. So, he most likely has control at Fallen Timbers. We still need to get someone up there to link up with him and confirm that he and Master Skirvon have the situation in hand, but it's more critical that we take the Class Eight and take out their portal fort. And any 'Voices' they have stationed there."

"Yes, Sir."

"All right, then." The two thousand turned to Carthos. "We'll leave one of your light cav companies and your engineer battalion here. As soon as the engineers manage to clear enough of these booby traps of theirs, we'll put the cavalry through and send it up the trail to Fallen Timbers. In the meantime," he glanced back at Toralk, "we'll push ahead to the Class Eight with the dragons and the rest of the air-mobile forces. We can't be positive they didn't have patrols or fatigue parties out somewhere, but if we close the Class Eight behind them, they aren't going anywhere, anyway."

"Yes, Sir," Toralk said, and Carthos nodded.

"Understood, Two Thousand," he said.

There wasn't much else he could have said, under the circumstances, but Toralk listened carefully to *how* he said it. If this entire operation was going to succeed, it would be solely because of the mobility and reach his dragons afforded. Which meant it wouldn't happen if interservice rivalry got in the way. He wouldn't say that Carthos sounded happy about the reminder that the Air Force had to be the senior service for this particular mission, but he didn't detect any overt resentment in the other thousand's tone or expression.

"Then let's get your dragons back in the air as soon as you can, Thousand," Harshu said, and slapped Toralk on the shoulder. "And remember this, Klayrman. The lessons you've learned here this morning may have been painful, but they still give *you* the advantage, because whoever's in command of that portal fort hasn't had any lessons at all yet. Now go change that."

CHAPTER SIX

"EXCUSE ME, SIR."

Company-Captain Grafin Halifu, commanding officer of the portal fort which had been named in memory of the murdered Voice Shaylar Nargra-Kolmayr, looked up from the paperwork on his desk with an undeniable expression of relief as Junior-Armsman Farzak Partha rapped on the frame of his office door. Halifu had never been one of those officers who was particularly good with paperwork. He was conscientious about it, but he managed to get through it only by sheer, dogged persistence. In fact, it was the one part of his chosen profession that he genuinely hated. And the situation had gotten significantly worse after those Arcanan lunatics massacred Ghartoun chan Hagrahyl's survey party. There was more of it, for one thing, and Halifu was prepared to swear it was getting increasingly trivial, as well. This morning's chore, for example, included trying to track down three cavalry mounts which appeared to have evaporated into thin air.

Not that the air's particularly thin around here, Halifu thought grumpily as he glanced out his office window. At least nothing was actively falling out of the sky at the moment. In fact, they'd had the better part of thirty-six hours without any rain at all, but from the look of the low, dark clouds, their record wasn't going to get a lot longer.

"What is it, Farzak?" he asked, resolutely turning his back on the charcoal sky.

"Petty-Captain Baulwan would like to see you for a moment if, of course—" Partha had been Halifu's senior clerk for almost a year now, and his eyes gleamed as he allowed them to drop for a moment to the sheafs of paper spread across the company-captain's desk "—you can spare the time away from your paperwork, Sir."

"Away from my paperwork, is it?" Halifu tipped back his chair and grinned at Partha. "I'll 'paperwork' you in a minute, Farzak! In fact," his eyes narrowed and his grin grew broader, "I've got a little chore for you. It seems that three of our horses have mysteriously disappeared. Why don't you go ahead and show Petty-Captain Baulwan in, and then take this report—" he picked up the offending sheets of paper and handed them over "—and trot right over to the stables and find out where these three miserable nags are."

"Of course, Sir," Partha replied, and somehow he managed to simultaneously maintain proper military decorum, radiate an air of martyrdom, and make it perfectly obvious that such a routine task was well within the limits of *his* capabilities, whatever might have been the case for his superior.

Halifu snorted in amusement and handed over the report, then watched Partha depart. The door opened again, a moment later, and Shansair Baulwan stepped through it.

"Good morning, Sir." The petty-captain came to attention and saluted.

"Good morning, Shansair," Halifu replied, returning the salute just a bit less crisply.

Baulwan had been on-post for only a bit over three weeks, and it was clear to Halifu that the Voice still didn't feel totally comfortable with him. In fact, he suspected Baulwan was taking refuge in military formalities precisely *because* he wasn't comfortable with Halifu. It was, unfortunately, an attitude to which Halifu had become unhappily accustomed when dealing with officers from Eastern Arpathia. Halifu himself was a Uromathian, and Uromathia—especially, Halifu was forced to admit, under its current emperor—hadn't proved a particularly friendly neighbor for Arpathia in general. Halifu didn't like it when he ran into an Arpathian who was prepared to dislike him simply because of where he'd been born. He couldn't really blame them, though, and he had to admit that when he finally got through to one of them and convinced them to separate him from the Uromathian stereotype, he felt an undeniable glow of pleasure.

It's too bad Hulmok is forward-deployed, the company-captain thought. *He'd probably be a big help getting Baulwan over the hump.*

"What can I do for you this morning, Shansair?" he asked aloud.

"I'm just a little concerned, Sir," the Arpathian Voice said. "I haven't heard anything from Petty-Captain Traygan this morning."

"Well, it's fairly early yet," Halifu pointed out. In fact, it wasn't quite ten a.m.

"Yes, Sir, it is. But it's not that early at Fallen

Timbers," Baulwan pointed out in return, and Halifu nodded. In fact, Fallen Timbers was three hours east of Fort Shaylar (and, of course, in a totally different universe), which meant it was almost one in the afternoon there. "They should have broken for lunch by now, Sir," the Voice continued, "and that's when Rokam—I mean, Petty-Captain Traygan—usually sends me a synopsis of the morning's negotiations."

"Maybe they're just running a little later than usual," Halifu suggested.

"That certainly possible, Sir. But when that's happened before, he's at least dropped me a short Voice transmission to let me know about the delay. After all, he knows I'm camped out on the Hell's Gate side of the portal, waiting, whenever I expect to hear from him and he's usually careful about not leaving me hanging around when there's not going to be any Voice traffic to receive after all."

Halifu frowned. Put that way, Traygan's failure to check in with Baulwan did sound a bit peculiar. In fact, his frown deepened, when he put that failure together with the message chan Baskay had transmitted up-chain about Arthag's suspicions, it became more than just peculiar.

He looked back up at Baulwan and saw the same thought in the youthful Voice's eyes. Of course, Baulwan was the one who'd relayed that very message to Halifu. Not only that, but Arthag was also an Arpathian, and one with a steadily growing reputation among his fellow countrymen. Clearly, Baulwan, at least, had taken his and chan Baskay's warning to heart.

"I understand your concern, Shansair," the company-captain said after a moment. "In fact, now that I've had a chance to think about it, you're starting to make me a bit nervous, too." He smiled tightly at the Voice. "On the other hand, we're probably both a little extra jumpy just now."

"I thought about that, Sir." Baulwan seemed to relax a little at Halifu's reaction. "That's why I tried to contact *him* when he didn't come through on schedule. I didn't get any response, Sir."

"I see."

Halifu grimaced and climbed out of his chair.

"Come with me," he said, and led the way out of his office and across Fort Shaylar's muddy parade ground. He always thought better in the open, and he needed to carefully consider what Baulwan had told him.

"Have you ever had trouble getting through to him before when you initiated the contact?" he asked the Voice as Baulwan walked a respectful half-pace behind him and to his right.

"Honestly, Sir?" The Arpathian shrugged. "I did have trouble making contact a couple of times. Once, he was asleep, and it took me at least half a dozen contact attempts to wake him up. The other time, he was concentrating on something else and it took him a while to Hear me. But both of those were unscheduled contacts. This time around, he should have been expecting to Hear something from me, I'd think, since I hadn't Heard anything from *him*."

"I see," Halifu repeated.

They reached the foot of the tall, steep, ladderlike stair that zigzagged up to the top of the fort's observation tower, and the company-captain started up it, with Baulwan following. It was a stiff climb, which Halifu made it a point to make at least three times a day on the premise that whatever didn't kill him would help maintain his current belt size, and he was slightly amused, despite his growing concern, as the considerably younger Voice began to puff before they were two-thirds of the way up.

They topped out, and Halifu crossed to the sturdy, split-log railing around the observation platform and leaned forward, resting his elbows and forearms on it as he gazed out through the stupendous portal in front of him.

It'd take a dozen damned forts this size to really cover this portal, he thought, for far from the first time. No one had ever seen a portal this size before, and their wasn't any real point in pretending Fort Shaylar was anything more than an administrative center. Technically, he was supposed to have enough manpower to let him send out patrols to cover the entire face of the portal for which he was responsible. Actually, he wouldn't have had enough men for that even if none of his assigned strength had been sent forward to chan Tesh.

Hell's Gate was thirty-seven miles across, which meant the actual frontage to be patrolled would have been seventy-four miles. Seventy-four miles of rainsoaked, incredibly luxuriant, virgin woodland.

Under the circumstances, all he could realistically hope to do was keep an eye on things, relay messages back and forth between chan Tesh and chan Baskay and the home universe, and keep at least a few of his dragoons available for field service in some sort of emergency.

And I've stripped my own support weapons to the bone sending them forward to help chan Tesh, he reminded himself sourly. Not that he—or chan Tesh—had had a lot of choice about that.

"When are you scheduled for your next transmission up-chain?" he asked Baulwan.

"I'm not, really, Sir," the Voice replied. Halifu arched an eyebrow, and the young Arpathian shrugged slightly. "I'm sorry, Sir. I thought you knew that."

"Son," Halifu said with a crooked smile, "there's been so much crap going on out here ever since we met these people that I'm willing to bet there're at least a dozen things people think I know about that I don't."

"I should have seen to it that this wasn't one of them, Sir," Baulwan said a touch stiffly. "I apologize for failing to do that."

"Why don't you save the apologies for something that deserves them?" Halifu said.

"Thank you, Sir." Baulwan seemed to relax just a bit. In fact, he actually allowed himself a slight smile of his own. "To be honest, Sir, we haven't tried to keep a set schedule because Rokam and I are all alone out here. The rest of the Voices are spread almost as thin as we are, and most of us are trying to get as much rest as we can whenever we don't *have* to be actively transmitting."

Halifu nodded. Fatigue could become a real problem for anyone who pushed his or her particular Talent too hard. In extreme cases, it could lead to Talent burnout, or even death. And Talent fatigue could be insidious, creeping in without being noticed. Voices were particularly susceptible to it, especially if they worked in one of the major Voicenet transmission junctions.

Or, he thought dryly, *if the poor luckless bastards happen to be the only two Voices available out here at the arse-end of nowhere and they're spending all their time transmitting diplomatic notes up and down the chain.*

"Erthek Vardan's the next Voice in the chain at the moment," Baulwan went on. "Petty-Captain chan Lyrosk is supposed to be relieving him as senior Voice at Fort Brithik, although I don't think he's arrived yet. Vargan's got pretty good transmission range, but his reception range is a lot shorter, and he's young—younger than *I* am, I mean, Sir," the youthful Voice said, flushing slightly despite his Arpathian rearing, as Halifu smothered a chuckle.

"I know, I know," the company-captain said after a moment. He patted the Voice on the shoulder apologetically. "I didn't mean to laugh at you, Shansair. It's just that I'm afraid that from where I stand, *neither* of you is what I'd call particularly ancient."

"I suppose not, Sir." Baulwan grinned a bit sheepishly. That was a good sign, Halifu thought. Maybe he was making some progress with the boy, after all.

"But what I was going to say, Sir," the Voice continued, "is that Erthek's sensitivity is a bit on the low side, and he tires quickly. Traygan and I are only about fifteen miles apart, and he's sensitive enough that he can usually Hear me if I 'shout' loud enough, even if he isn't actively Listening for me. Erthek's almost three hundred miles from here, and he has to settle into at least an upper-stage trance to receive from me, so I can only contact him at times when he's already expecting me to. And, like I said, he tires quickly, too. Early last week, when we had that long transmission from Platoon-Captain chan Baskay, he had to break it into two separate transmissions. So we usually try to conserve his strength. He mounts a Listening watch for me for ten minutes either side of the hour every two hours, and unless an incoming message for us is urgent, he holds it until the next time *I* contact *him* instead of his trying to initiate contact with me. Of course, the fact that I spend so much time on the other side of the portal maintaining contact with Traygan is another reason for him to wait for me to make contact. And since this entire leg of the Voicenet's been reserved solely for military traffic—well, military and diplomatic, I suppose—there isn't really all that much traffic, even if the amount we do have tends to cluster in fairly intensive bursts."

"But he's not going to be Listening for you right this minute?"

"No, Sir. Not for another—" Baulwan checked his watch "—ninety minutes or so."

"I see."

Halifu rubbed his chin, gazing thoughtfully through Hell's Gate at the autumn-struck trees on the other side. It was just like the gods, he thought sourly, to dump endless buckets of rain here in New Uromath while the universe on the other side of the portal hadn't seen a drop of rain in almost three weeks.

He really would have preferred for Vardan to be expecting a message from Baulwan at any moment. Unless a Voice's Talent was particularly strong, it was very difficult to attract his attention with an incoming Voice message he wasn't anticipating. It sounded as if it would have been even harder than usual in Vardan's case, and under the circumstances, Grafin Halifu really, really wished he could report Rokam Traygan's missed transmission to Baulwan to his superiors up the chain. There was almost certainly a completely innocent explanation for the Voice's silence, but Halifu would have felt much more comfortable if someone else knew about it.

We don't have enough redundancy in the Voicenet, he told himself sourly. *On the other hand, we never designed it for a crisis like this one. And, of course, it doesn't help any that the gods were inconsiderate enough to let this happen clear out at the end of the multiverse, where* all *Talents are in such short supply.*

He'd never truly realized just how fragile the Voicenet was until all hell had broken loose. Now, after Shaylar Nargra-Kolmayr's murder and Darcel Kinlafia's departure for Sharona, he was acutely conscious of just how overstretched their communications capability truly was.

"All right, Shansair," he said finally. "We may both be worrying ourselves over nothing, but I'd rather do that than *not* worry about something I *should've* worried about. So, as soon as your friend Vardan is likely to be listening for you, I want you to send the word up-chain that we're having trouble contacting Traygan. Unless, of course, we hear from him in the meantime, that is."

"Yes, Sir. I'll see to it."

"Good, Shansair." Halifu patted the youngster on the shoulder again, then turned and started down the steep stairway to the parade ground—and his waiting paperwork—once again.

* * *

Thousand Toralk had discovered something else to worry about.

It was barely thirty air miles from the swamp portal to the huge portal which had been christened Hell's Gate and lent its name to this entire universe. Of course, that was thirty miles of solid, impenetrable treetops, and like most dragon pilots, Toralk was always at least a little uncomfortable about flying over terrain where he and his beast couldn't put down in a hurry, if they had to.

That wasn't what was bothering him at the moment, however. No, what was *bothering* him was the fact that he'd just spent the better part of fifteen minutes with his entire force circling directly above Fallen Timbers without getting a single response from Narshu or Skirvon.

And I've got better things to do than hang around up here all day admiring the scenery . . . however damned spectacular it may be, he thought sourly, looking north towards Hell's Gate.

That portal was so huge that it was clearly visible at his present altitude, even from here. In fact, it dominated the entire northern horizon. Nor was it alone. Klayrman Toralk and his pilots had a ringside seat for something no human being had ever seen before, for Hell's Gate was a cluster.

The portal detector Magister Halythan had invented had already told them precisely where each of the associated portals was, but at this moment, Toralk scarcely needed it. He could actually see no less than four of them simultaneously—four semi-circular windows, of widely differing sizes, but all of them at least several miles across and high, opening into four totally separate universes. He saw a midnight-black night sky through one, a dark-green, fecund jungle through another, and an icy snowscape through yet a third. The incredible vistas dominated the horizons, making the incalculable value of this universe starkly plain, yet their very visibility only made the heavy tree cover even more frustrating. He could *see* all of them, even get dragons through any of them he chose, but he couldn't get the beasts on the *ground* anywhere in this massively forested wilderness . . . just as he couldn't even see the ground directly below him here!

Still, the visibility looking *up* ought to be considerably better, and despite the tree cover, Skirvon and Narshu had to know there were dragons overhead. Or they should have, anyway. Even if the canopy was getting in their way, the tangled scar of wind-downed trees where the original clash with the Sharonians had occurred was right next to them. It would never do to land a dragon, and even if Toralk had been able to get one down, he'd never have gotten it back into the air again. But Narshu should have been bright enough to post a lookout out in the middle of it, where the hole torn through the canopy would have allowed him to make visual contact.

We should have brought the gryphons, Toralk told himself irritably. He knew why they hadn't, of course. In fact, it had been his own idea. After all, the total distance to be covered on this leg was only thirty damned miles. How the hells' much reconnaissance capability were they likely to need? And gryphons were . . . problematical, at best, as a strike weapon without very exact pre-attack planning and programming from their handlers. They certainly weren't something anyone wanted to interject into the middle of a possibly confused infantry action!

But if he'd thought about it, he would've realized that he could at least have put a recon gryphon down through the Fallen Timbers opening to confirm what was happening there.

Oh, stop, Klayrman! he told himself. *You figured from the get-go that if anything went seriously wrong out here, the entire operation would turn into an utter fiasco. So, either you were going to find Narshu sitting here in control of the position, or else the shit was going to be so deep it really wasn't going to matter. So there actually wasn't much point worrying about sending gryphons in on recon missions, was there?*

He glowered down at the treetops for a few more seconds, then shook his head. He couldn't afford to hang around here any longer. Besides, Carthos' unicorns would be here within another hour or so, max, and he had his own mission to complete.

"Take us on!" he ordered his pilot.

"Yes, Sir!"

The command dragon broke out of its holding pattern and headed due north, and hundreds of steadily beating dragon wings followed in its wake.

CHAPTER SEVEN

"ANY TIME NOW," chan Baskay murmured.

The platoon-captain drew rein and turned in the saddle, gazing back the way they'd come. Not that he'd really expected to see anything.

One of the things Company-Captain chan Tesh had insisted upon was the necessity of finding at least the nearer of the secondary portals in the Hell's Gate cluster. Thanks to Darcel Kinlafia's ability to sense the compass bearings of other portals, he'd at least been able to tell them roughly where to look before he left, and they'd been astonished to discover that there were no less than three more portals within less than sixty miles of Fallen Timbers. Two of them, in fact, were less than fifteen miles from the site of the massacre which had started this entire confrontation. Of those, one connected to what was obviously New Farnal, while the other connected to an open, rolling expanse of grassland—currently covered in the first snow of winter—which could have been the heart of New Ternath or any of a score of other places.

At the moment, the thirty-odd men of what had

become Dorzon chan Baskay's command were still about five miles from the New Farnal portal. They'd concentrated on speed, pushing their horses as hard as the terrain permitted, and their trail through the drifts of the forest's bone-dry leaves was painfully obvious.

For now.

Hulmok Arthag's suggestion about how to "conceal" that trail had horrified chan Baskay when he first heard it. Of course, chan Baskay had spent much of his youth on his family's estates in Reyshar. They were located in central Chairifon, in an area of endless forests where the primary local industries all relied on forestry products, and he'd spent most of his boyhood hunting, fishing, and hiking in woods very much like these. That youthful experience had left him with a deep reverence for trees . . . and a matching horror of forest fires.

Arthag, on the other hand, was a son of the steppes. Forests held no special attraction to him, which had undoubtedly made it much easier for him to hit upon the idea in the first place. Once he had, despite chan Baskay's own emotional response to it, the Ternathian had been unable to come up with a logical argument against it.

Except, of course, for insisting that we had to have enough of a head start before he started playing with matches, chan Baskay thought now.

But Arthag had had an answer for that, as well. He and Chief-Armsman chan Hathas had quickly rigged a crude timer using several gallons of kerosene and a candle, and if his estimate of the candle's burning rate was accurate, it should be reaching the kerosene any minute now.

So stop looking over your shoulder and get your attention back where it belongs, chan Baskay scolded himself.

The last thing you need to do is hang around back here long enough for the fire to catch up with you!

He snorted, shook his head, and put his mount into a canter to catch up with the rest of the column.

* * *

Toralk's command dragon skimmed just above the treetops as it swept through into the next universe.

With such a huge portal to play with, there was no need for them to make the crossing where anyone in the Sharonian fort could possibly see them. And thanks to the successful scouting mission the Andaran Scouts' chief sword had carried out, they knew precisely where that fort was, and its exact coordinates had been entered into their navigation units.

That was the good news; the low cloudbase was the even better news.

While the cloud cover would make the coordination of his strikes—especially with the air-mobile infantry and cavalry—difficult, it also offered the possibility of additional concealment. He'd covered this possibility in his original mission planning, although the casualties they'd taken in the initial attack had led him to make some fairly substantial adjustments in light of the demonstrated efficacy of the Sharonians' weapons. He wished that he'd had more time to work on those adjustments, but the Air Force had always emphasized an officer's need to think on his feet, and he'd discussed his new attack variants with his strike COs in their hasty conference before leaving the swamp portal behind.

He'd been able to see how heavy the cloud cover was going to be well before he actually crossed the portal's threshold. In fact, the overcast was crowding through the portal into the Hell's Gate universe with the promise of at least some badly needed rain. He'd already fired the sequence of flares to indicate his chosen variant, and now he watched Hundred Geyrsof's strike disappear into the thick overcast ahead of his ponderous transports.

* * *

Shansair Baulwan was still on top of the Fort Shaylar observation tower.

It wasn't as if he had any other pressing duties he had to attend to, and one place was as good as another while he waited until Erthek would be Listening for him. In fact, this was a much better spot than most. He'd heard that Company-Captain Halifu liked to come up here to think about things, and leaning on the rail, looking out across the marvelous view, he could understand why. Like Hulmok Arthag, Baulwan was a child of the steppes, and all of the woods stretching out on either hand would have been bad enough even without the apparently inexhaustible and unending rain. Up here, he could get his head above the treetops, let his mind clear.

He was beginning to think he'd done Halifu a disservice by lumping him with other Uromathians he'd had the misfortune to meet. It was hard to remind himself that Uromathians could be just as different from one another as anyone else, but a Voice ought to be more aware of that than other people. He'd have to make a point of keeping his mind open where Halifu was concerned, he decided.

He straightened up, stretched, and checked his watch again. Fifteen more minutes before Erthek would start Listening.

* * *

Horban Geyrsof had never been more grateful for clouds in his entire life.

No dragon pilot really liked flying through soup this thick, especially in formation. Midair collisions between dragons were almost invariably ugly, particularly if battle dragons were involved. They were always touchy, and they seldom extended the benefit of the doubt to someone who ran into them in flight.

But, after his experiences at the swamp portal, Geyrsof was *delighted* to take the 3012th and its sister strike, the 4016th, into the clouds. The Dragon-Healers had patched up Graycloud's and Skykill's wing membranes, but both of the remaining yellows were still proddy. They'd not only lost wingmates, but they'd found out that Sharonian weapons *hurt*. They were going to be much happier if they didn't get shot at again . . . which summed up Geyrsof's own attitude quite nicely, actually.

As for the reduced visibility, all of the 3012th's and 4016th's pilots were experienced formation flyers, and all of them understood the necessity of tightening their intervals and holding their positions relative to one another when visibility fell into the crapper this way. And they were all experienced instrument flyers, too, putting their trust in their navigation units' position and altitude figures rather than trying to rely upon their fallible human senses.

And, best of all, the bastards in that fort aren't going to have enough warning to get their damned heavy weapons into action, he told himself grimly.

He kept one eye on his own nav unit and the other on his single remaining wingman as both strikes crossed over the boundary between the universes well to the east of its objective. Then they turned west, following the preplotted waypoints programmed into their navigation units, until they were sweeping steadily towards the back side of the Sharonian fort.

* * *

Petty-Captain Baulwan took one more look at his watch, then nodded in satisfaction. Erthek would be starting to Listen for him sometime in the next couple of minutes, and Baulwan began preparing himself to contact the other Voice. He closed his eyes, concentrating on his Talent, letting it flow up from the depths of his mind like a crystal-clear water welling up from the throat of a mountain spring. At moments like this, he *knew* the shamans were right about the wondrous touch of the gods.

He felt himself relaxing, and breathed slowly and deeply, preparing, getting ready to reach out—

* * *

No one in Fort Shaylar saw them coming.

Hundred Geyrsof's pilots, guided by their navigation units, had arrived at precisely the right spot at precisely the correct moment and tipped over into their attack dives when all they could see was the wet, soaking interior of the clouds through which they were flying. It was risky—they didn't know exactly how low the cloudbase actually was, or what obstacles might be hiding in it if their navigation was even slightly off—but it also meant they had perfect cover all the way down. Even if anyone in the fort had suspected the existence of Arcana's dragons for a moment, it would have done them no good under those conditions.

In fact, the lumpy gray ceiling was at barely twelve hundred feet. At that low an altitude, the attack dragons were already starting to pull out when they broke clear of the clouds. They were going to have time for only a single attack each, and they had mere seconds to find their targets for it, but seconds were enough.

Sixteen fireballs exploded in the interior of Fort Shaylar almost as one.

* * *

Grafin Halifu had just signed the report about the triumphant relocation of those incredibly irritating cavalry mounts when the first explosions began.

He lunged up out of his chair, snatched up his pistol belt, and charged out his office door.

By the time he reached Farzak Partha's desk, the entire parade ground was a roaring holocaust.

There couldn't be that much to burn, a shocked, horrified corner of his mind insisted while the shrieks and screams ripped through his very soul. The shrieks and screams of his men—*his* men—burning like living torches in that impossible inferno. There'd been no warning, no preparation. One instant, everything was orderly, normal; the next instant, devastation was upon them all.

Partha leapt up from his own desk just in time to tackle Halifu. The outer surfaces of the fort's log structures were already smoking and charring under the incredible heat radiating from the red dragons' fireballs, but they still offered at least some protection to the people inside them, and Partha's quick thinking saved Halifu's life at least briefly.

The company-captain hit the rough floor hard. Hard enough to shake him back into a semblance of rationality. He squirmed free of Partha's grasp and climbed back to his feet as the initial wave of fireballs exhausted their power and dissipated.

He moved forward again, then, this time with Partha

at his heels. The admin block's door was jammed, warped in its frame by the brutal heat, and he had to kick it open. Then he stepped out into a scene of nightmare.

The lucky ones were already dead.

Everywhere he looked, it seemed, there were bodies. Twisted, contorted, charred dead men, smoldering with an intolerable stench of burning flesh. Here and there among the corpses were the screaming, writhing bodies of hideously maimed troopers who were still alive. He knew those men, knew most of them by their first names, and he couldn't even recognize them.

He advanced onto the parade ground, and half the fort's buildings were on fire around him. The observation tower blazed like a huge torch, soaked in oil, and a seared scarecrow of a human figure hung over the platform rail like a shriveled, blazing mummy. His mind refused to absorb the reality, couldn't find a way to process the information. He needed time for that, and there wasn't any time.

Something made him look up at the sky just in time to see a final pair of huge, impossible creatures hurtling suddenly out of the clouds. They streaked down towards the flame-wracked abattoir which had once been Fort Shaylar, and Grafin Halifu found his H&W in his hand.

The heavy, long-barreled revolver rose, his thumb cocked the hammer, and he began to fire.

He was still firing when the gas cloud enveloped what was left of his command.

* * *

Commander of One Hundred Sylair Worka looked at his chronometer and grimaced in disgust.

It wasn't his fault, but that didn't make him any happier to be running well over two hours behind schedule. Those damned Sharonian booby traps had imposed a delay out of all proportion to their actual effectiveness, and he wished Fifty Narshu had at least been assigned a hummer handler.

But, no, Worka thought sourly. *We couldn't risk the Sharonians finding out about the hummers, could we? Of course not! So what if it makes it impossible to communicate when it all hits the fan?*

His expression grew briefly even more disgusted, then he shook his head. Part of the problem was that neither side knew what it ought to be concealing from the other, he reflected. So Arcana had wound up hiding just about everything . . . even when it was an operational pain in the arse.

He supposed it all made sense, but it would have been far more convenient—and, undoubtedly, more reassuring to Narshu—if Worka had been able to send him a message to explain the delay.

Well, we're only thirty minutes or so out now. In fact, the point ought to be—

"Sir!"

Worka looked up from his chronometer as one of his troopers came towards him at a stiff canter. A light cavalry unicorn could manage speeds of up to forty miles an hour and maintain a gallop for ninety minutes at a time in decent terrain . . . which, of course, this mass of trees most definitely was not. Still, Lance Ranlak was moving at a good clip.

The trooper drew up beside his company commander and saluted.

"What is it, Yurain?" Worka asked.

"Sir, Sword Kalcyr's respects, and he thinks we've got a problem."

"Problem?" Worka stiffened in the saddle. Senior Sword Barcan Kalcyr was the company's senior noncom. He'd been everywhere and done everything, and he didn't use the word "problem" lightly.

"Yes, Sir. He said to tell you he smells smoke. *Lots* of smoke."

Worka gazed at the trooper for a few moments, then pressed with his heels, and sent his mount galloping forward.

The constant coming and going of the diplomats who'd been negotiating with the Sharonians—not to mention all of the Sharonian traffic between the swamp portal and the Class Eight—had produced a well-worn, surprisingly broad trail, and Worka's troopers crowded aside to let him pass. He made good time, and well before he reached Kalcyr's position, he'd come to the conclusion that the senior sword had, if anything, understated the situation. The hundred's unicorn snorted uneasily, tossing its horned head, as the first sharp-smelling banners of smoke came flowing through the woods.

"What do we have, Barcan?" Worka asked as he drew up beside the noncom.

"According to my nav unit, we're only about five miles out, Sir," Kalcyr replied. "I don't think we're getting through *that*, though."

He pointed, and Worka's jaw tightened as he looked in the indicated direction. The stiff breeze was blowing across the trail at the next best thing to right angles. Now, as he gazed ahead, he realized that the smoke he'd smelled on his way forward had been only outriders, only the stray tendrils of the massive wall of smoke rolling steadily westward ahead of them.

"Where there's smoke, there's fire, Sir," Kalcyr observed in a tone which sounded as disgusted as Worka felt.

"Yes, there is, Senior Sword," Worka agreed. "In fact—"

He broke off, gesturing, and Kalcyr grunted as they both saw the first, abrupt crackle of flames coming towards them through the smoke. One of the towering forest giants went up like a torch in a glare of crown-fire, little more than two hundred yards farther along the trail.

Worka's unicorn flattened its lynxlike ears, and he felt the sudden tension quivering in its augmented muscles.

"Time to go, Senior Sword," the hundred said.

"You've got that right, Sir," Kalcyr agreed feelingly as a second tree flared up, and he blew his whistle.

The point men responded instantly—after all, they were even closer to that oncoming inferno than Kalcyr or Worka. The hundred and the senior sword waited until they were sure everyone had heard the signal, then turned their own unicorns and headed back the way they'd come—rapidly.

Worka knew he'd made the right decision, but he didn't like the implications one bit. He supposed it was remotely possible a random lightning strike out of the cloudless sky might have just happened to start a forest fire in this particular place at this particular time. It wasn't very likely, though. Unfortunately, he couldn't think of any good reason for *Fifty Narshu* to have been starting any fires. Which meant that if it wasn't the result of some sort of accident—which Worka strongly doubted was the case—someone *else* must be responsible.

Which probably meant things hadn't gone quite as well as everyone had been assuming, after all.

CHAPTER EIGHT

ACTING COMMANDER OF FIVE HUNDRED Alivar Neshok looked up from the notes transcribed into his personal crystal as two of the troopers assigned to his Intelligence section hustled the latest prisoners into the large room Neshok had taken over for interrogation purposes. The room in question had originally been meant to serve as a secondary armory, as nearly as Neshok could tell. It was part of the same building as their main armory, at least, although it appeared that the fort's garrison must have been awaiting substantially more weapons and ammunition, since it had been empty when the Arcanans occupied it.

The five Sharonians' hands were manacled behind them, and most of them were white-faced, obviously shocked and not a little terrified.

Good, the Intelligence officer thought. *Apparently even these barbarians are capable of absorbing object lessons . . . if the lesson's* pointed *enough, at any rate.*

He returned his attention to his crystal, ignoring the prisoners as obviously as possible while the handpicked, carefully instructed guards kicked and cuffed them into position.

Very few of the Sharonian garrison had survived. In fact, only eleven of the Sharonians actually in the fort at the moment of the attack had lived long enough for the healers to reach them. Two of those had died anyway, which was unfortunate. Prisoners represented intelligence, and intelligence was the most deadly weapon of all, especially in a war like this.

And it was Alivar Neshok's task to wring every single drop of information out of these Sharonian scum. Interrogation wasn't always a pretty job, but someone had to do it, and Neshok knew he did it well.

Too many of his colleagues seemed to forget the psychological aspect of interrogation techniques. Probably, Neshok often thought, because they'd basically been nothing but glorified policemen for the better part of two hundred years. There'd been no wars, no true "enemy" personnel to interrogate, since the founding of the Union, after all. For the most part, specialists in Neshok's particular area of expertise had been interrogating brigands, bandits, claim jumpers—the sort of scum who routinely preyed upon society out here in the frontier universes. In the process, they'd gotten lazy. That sort of criminal was hardly trained or motivated to resist questioning the way *soldiers* were, and the interrogator generally had a pretty detailed idea going in of what he expected to learn. A few basic verifier spells, and the prisoner's knowledge that those spells were in place (and of the consequences of adding perjury to the charge list), were usually enough to get them talking.

It was going to take a little more in a case like this,

though, which was why Neshok had designed his prisoners' "preparation" so carefully.

The healers wouldn't let him talk to their patients yet. That was also unfortunate. If he'd had his druthers, Neshok would have interrogated those "patients" before they were ever allowed to see the healers in the first place. Pain and terror were great psychological motivators, after all. But Commander of Five Hundred Dayr Vaynair, Two Thousand Harshu's senior medical officer, had other ideas. He'd gotten up on his high Andaran horse and taken the position that the Kerellian Accords applied even to these people, which made him irritatingly representative of healers in general, in Neshok's experience. Well, Neshok was Andaran, too, but he wasn't about to let the antiquated Andaran "honor code" get in the way of *his* responsibilities. All very well for Vaynair to stand upon his Healer's Oath without even bothering to hide his contempt for the people charged with securing the information the operational commanders simply had to have. This entire operation had gone so well so far solely because of the activities of people like Alivar Neshok, but did Vaynair recognize that? Did he realize he'd had so few *Arcanan* patients expressly because Neshok and his Intelligence team had done their jobs so well?

Of course he didn't! He was too occupied with his contempt for the despised Intelligence people's efforts to continue to do their jobs.

Well, we're just going to have to do something about Five Hundred Vaynair, aren't we? Neshok reflected. *But not yet. Not until I've had time to build my case, at any rate.*

But if Vaynair wasn't going to let him interrogate his

precious patients just yet, then Neshok would have to make do with prisoners like these.

So far, the cavalry patrols Thousand Carthos had sent spreading out from the captured fort had swept up over thirty Sharonians who'd been outside the fort at the time of the attack. Most of them had been engaged on the sort of work details any military post had to provide. The tree cover on this side of Hell's Gate was just as bad, from the prospect of aerial operations, as on the other side, which explained why Carthos had been forced to rely on his unicorns to get out under the branches to secure the prisoners. Neshok suspected there were still at least one or two work parties who'd managed to evade the cavalry this far, although the odds of their continuing to do so much longer were slim.

All of the prisoners they'd so far taken had been close enough to see the attack on the fort itself, which meant they'd finally realized that Arcana had combat capabilities which tremendously outclassed their own. They'd seen the dragons, seen the explosions of searing heat as the reds belched their fireballs. They hadn't seen the yellows' gas clouds, but Neshok had made certain they'd seen the *consequences* of both dragon types' breath weapons. That was why he'd had them marched straight here, across the fort's still-smoldering parade ground into this log building. The Sharonians hadn't peeled the bark off the conifer logs from which all of the fort's buildings had been constructed, and the radiant heat from the fireballs had turned that bark into flaking ash on every wall which had faced the parade ground.

The bodies hadn't been policed up yet, either. They lay where they had fallen, twisted and contorted. Those who'd died of gas inhalation after the second pass of the attack wore expressions of horror and agony. Most of those who'd been killed by the fireballs in the first pass, on the other hand, showed no recognizable expression at all. There wasn't enough left of the shrunken, twisted chunks of charcoal which had once been humans for that.

Now Neshok entered a few notes into his PC. They didn't actually say anything particularly important, but it was one more bit of window dressing, and he gave himself a curt nod of approval, then looked up.

The prisoners knelt in front of him. One of them—a short, wiry fellow kneeling at the left end of the line—reminded Neshok of Hulmok Arthag. That would have been more than enough to inspire the Intelligence officer with a lively sense of dislike, since there wasn't much doubt that whatever had gone wrong at Fallen Timbers, Arthag had almost certainly been at the bottom of it. Worse, though, this fellow wore the four red collar pips of a senior-armsman. That made him roughly the equivalent of a javelin, or possibly even a sword, according to the tentative table of organization Neshok had managed to work out for the Sharonians.

It also meant that he was the senior prisoner, which made his hard eyes and masklike expression unpromising.

The other four were about as physically diverse as a similar sampling of Arcanan military personnel might have been. One of them—a towering, broad-shouldered, red-haired bear of a man with the two red pips of a petty-armsman, which made him the next senior prisoner—was bigger even than the Sharonian diplomat, Simrath. The other three ranged in height between the big petty-armsman and the Arthag-like senior-armsman.

"Well," Neshok said finally, relying upon a translating crystal to render his words in fluent, idiomatic Ternathian, "I do hope you . . . gentlemen are prepared to be reasonable."

None of the prisoners said anything, and Neshok allowed himself a slight frown as their faces hardened defiantly.

"Now, I suppose you may be feeling heroic," he continued. "Of course, that would be a particularly stupid thing for you to do, under the circumstances. I'm sure that what you saw on your way across what used to be your fort has already suggested as much." He smiled thinly. "It isn't going to be very long before we move on to your next fort—in Thermyn, I believe you call it? And after that, we'll be continuing on up-chain. We won't be getting all the way to Sharona this time, of course. But by the time your reinforcements can get here, we'll be in position to run right over them before they even know what's happening."

He smiled again, even more coldly.

"You've seen what we did to your precious fort," he said. "I assure you, your portal fortifications were even less effective. So just what do you people think is going to happen when our dragons catch your reinforcement columns in the open, without any protection at all?"

Two of the prisoners' faces had crumbled as Neshok spoke. They had no way of knowing how vastly the Intelligence officer had overstated the ease with which chan Tesh's positions had been taken. Nor could they possibly know he'd just expended almost his entire store of knowledge about what Two Thousand Harshu's expeditionary force was likely to run into on its way up-chain. All they knew was that he seemed to be well informed, already. The big redhead, and the wiry little senior-armsman, on the other hand, appeared less impressed. The smaller man's expression showed no reaction at all—which, of course, was a reaction in its own right. But his taller companion seemed to be less adept at concealing his reactions. His eyes narrowed, his mouth tightened, and his shoulders squared.

Good, Neshok thought coldly. *Always best to start with the biggest one, especially when he's one of the noncoms the others will be looking to for leadership. It makes the point so much more effectively for the others.*

The acting five hundred looked at one of the two guards, and nodded very slightly.

Javelin Lisaro Porath stepped forward without a word in response to the silent command and raised his heavy infantry arbalest to chest level, then brought its butt down in a flashing, vertical stroke. It struck the top of the petty-armsman's left shoulder like a hammer. It also took the big man completely by surprise, and he grunted in hoarse agony, despite himself, as the vicious stroke landed. Privately, Neshok was impressed that the man had managed not to cry out, although he wasn't about to let any of that show in his own expression.

Pain and the physical impact drove the prisoner forward and down. With his hands behind him, he couldn't even try to catch himself, and he smashed face-first into the rough, split-log floor. Blood erupted from his flattened nose and pulped lips, and Porath reached down, caught him by his hair, yanked him back upright, and then drove a kneecap brutally into his spine. The impact hammered him forward again, his hair "slipping" from Porath's fingers, and he thudded back onto the floor, where the guard proceeded to kick him repeatedly in the ribs.

The second guard watched the other prisoners alertly, his arbalest ready, but they seemed too shocked, too stunned, to pose any kind of threat, and Neshok watched them closely as he let the brutal, systematic beating go on and on. He wanted them to *stay* shocked, wanted them to reflect upon what could happen to anyone who failed to provide the answers he sought.

By the time the acting five hundred finally waved one index finger gently and Porath stepped back, panting with exertion, the big petty-armsman was unconscious. The arbalest butt had almost certainly broken his shoulder badly, and Neshok rather doubted that he had a single intact rib. His face was a mass of blood, bubbling on his lips as he breathed through his mouth rather than his flattened, broken nose, and his right cheek and lower jaw were a caved-in ruin of shattered bone. Neshok never doubted for a moment that the prisoner also had internal injuries, and a dark, vicious light of purring cruelty glowed in his eyes.

"Drag that garbage out and get rid of it, Javelin Porath," he told the guard. The translating crystal obediently rendered the order in Ternathian for the other prisoners' benefit, and the trooper gave a harsh half-grunting laugh, grabbed the unconscious petty-armsman by an ankle, and dragged him out of the interrogation room. The sliding, scraping body left a trail of blood as the brutalized face scrubbed across the splintery floor, undoubtedly taking still more damage in the process, and Porath paused long enough to administer a final, savage kick to his victim's side before he dragged him the rest of the way out the door.

That door closed behind him, and Neshok allowed his attention to return to the other four prisoners. Or, rather, he allowed them to *see* his attention return to them, as if he'd forgotten the crystal would translate his instructions to the guard into Ternathian. He smiled coldly at them, then looked up again as the door opened once more.

Javelin Porath stepped back through it. His arbalest was slung across his back, and he was just settling his short sword back into its sheath. He rebuttoned the retaining strap across the quillons as he walked back to stand behind the remaining prisoners without a word.

Very nice, Neshok thought approvingly.

Porath had taken the Intelligence officer's instructions to heart, and he clearly had a thespian bent. Neshok had been half-afraid the trooper would do something like ostentatiously wiping his blade, or something equally obvious. Instead, he'd opted for something understated enough to clearly imply the desired effect without overdoing it, and his satisfied expression was more effective than any theatrically homicidal leer.

As if I had any intention of wasting an intelligence asset that quickly, Neshok thought contemptuously as he watched the prisoners draw the desired conclusion. The wiry senior-armsman's face showed absolutely no change of expression. If anything, his eyes simply hardened even further, but his companions were quite another matter. There was still anger in them, Neshok decided. In fact, their anger burned hotter and fiercer than ever, yet its heat was at least matched by fresh, choking terror. Obviously, they believed exactly what he'd wanted them to believe.

Hard to blame them for that, really, even without that neat little bit of acting, he admitted. *Just the beating probably would've killed the bastard in the end, and these fucking barbarians have never heard of proper healers. Even if they had, it might not have occurred to them—yet—just what that implies when it comes to the application of . . . forceful arguments in favor of cooperation. Well, they're going to find out* exactly *what that means, aren't they? Eventually, of course.*

He was going to have to deal with Vaynair first, no doubt. One of the things the Kerellian Accords specifically prohibited was the use of healers in the interrogation of prisoners. Alivar Neshok had no intention of allowing his hands to be tied that way, however. Which was really the main reason Five Hundred Vaynair had to go. Vaynair would almost certainly go ahead and heal the battered petty-armsman this time, but he'd never sign off on the use of torture or allow any of the healers under his command to cooperate by healing the physical consequences of a . . . rigorous interrogation session only to let the questioners begin all over again without accidentally expending their intelligence assets.

In the meantime . . .

"Perhaps the rest of you are feeling inclined to be a little more cooperative now?" he suggested, and one of the prisoners—a young under-armsman who couldn't have been much over twenty—swallowed visibly. Neshok noted the reaction with satisfaction.

"I'm sure, for example," he continued, "that one of you would like to help me out by telling me exactly which of the other portals Viscount Simrath and Platoon-Captain Arthag might have chosen to make for."

No one answered, and Neshok showed his teeth in something no one would ever have mistaken for a smile.

It had become abundantly and painfully evident that whatever else had happened at Fallen Timbers, Narshu's mission couldn't possibly have been a complete success. It was going to be a while before they could prove that conclusively, however. The forest fire which Neshok was personally certain Arthag had deliberately started to cover his tracks was rapidly turning into a demonic holocaust. The tinder-dry autumn forest, with its deep drifts of leaves, had proved the ideal target for the Sharonian's arson. A booming, crackling wavefront of flame was spreading out—it was actually moving *upwind*, as well as downwind—and there was no possibility of containing or controlling that raging fury. It had already completely blocked the overland route between the swamp portal and Hell's Gate, and unless some divine agency chose to intervene soon, it was going to burn all the way back to both of those portals. Not to mention burning the gods only knew how far in every *other* direction, as well.

From the Sharonians' perspective, simply blocking the trail would have been completely worthwhile in its own right, especially if they'd set the fire before they discovered the Air Force's existence. It was going to be a pain in the arse for Arcana even with the advantage of dragons and levitation spells; without that advantage, it would have delayed Two Thousand Harshu's offensive for days, probably even longer. The fact that it was going to completely destroy any possibility of tracking the Sharonian fugitives from Fallen Timbers was simply gravy from their viewpoint. But Neshok wasn't about to let them get away with that. If Rithmar Skirvon and Uthik Dastiri were still alive, Neshok wanted them back, and not just because they were accredited diplomats of the Union of Arcana. He wasn't supposed to know just how . . . friendly the diplomats were with Two Thousand mul Gurthak, but he was an Intelligence officer. As such, he had a pretty shrewd notion of how grateful mul Gurthak would be if Neshok could manage to retrieve them.

"Come now," he said almost gently as the silence stretched out. "I'm sure none of you want to be so . . . uncooperative that you make me angry. Believe me, you won't *like* me when I'm angry."

"We don't *know* where they'd go!" the young under-armsman blurted suddenly.

"That's enough, Sirda," the senior-armsman said quietly, almost gently.

The youngster darted a look at the older man, then clamped his jaws with a visible effort and stared at the floor directly in front of him, avoiding any possible eye contact with Neshok.

"No, Sirda," the Arcanan said, his voice almost as quiet as the senior-armsman's, but far, far colder. "It isn't enough. It isn't *nearly* enough."

The under-armsman—Sirda—clenched his chained hands into fists behind him. His face was pale, and he bit his lip, hard, but he didn't speak.

Neshok nodded to the second of the two guards, and the Arcanan trooper bent over Sirda from behind, twisted his fingers in the young man's hair, and yanked his head back so hard the youngster couldn't quite smother his cry of pain. The pressure on his scalp forced him to look up, meet Neshok's eyes, and the Intelligence officer's smile was cruel and thin.

"*Someone* is going to tell me what I want to know," Neshok said softly. "Whoever it is, will probably get to live. As for whoever it *isn't* . . ."

He let his eyes drift to the trail of blood the big petty-armsman's face had left across the floor, then looked back at Sirda. The young man's throat worked, and sweat coated his face.

"In that case," the senior-armsman said levelly, "why don't you ask *me*?"

Neshok allowed his eyebrows to arch and gazed at the Sharonian noncom thoughtfully.

"I hadn't realized you were so eager to be reasonable, Senior-Armsman," he said. "Very well, which portal did Simrath and Arthag make for?"

The senior-armsman looked back up at him for a moment, then said something in a language the translating crystal didn't understand. The long sentence—or sentences—sounded guttural, yet flowing and edged with a sort of harsh music, but the language certainly wasn't Ternathian, and Neshok frowned.

"Speak Ternathian."

The Intelligence officer managed to bring the words out calmly, suppressing—barely in time—the urge to snap them out. Using anger to generate fear in someone else was a useful interrogation tool, but allowing a prisoner to successfully bait him would be a sign of weakness.

"Oh," the senior-armsman said. "Your rock doesn't speak Arpathian?"

"Speak Ternathian," Neshok repeated almost tonelessly, and the kneeling prisoner shrugged.

"If you want," he said. "I said, he already told you. We don't know the answer to your question."

"And what else did you say?" Neshok asked softly.

"Actually, what I said was, 'He already told you. We don't know the answer to your question, you syphilitic, camel-fucking son of a diseased sow and a hundred pig-fucking fathers,'" the senior-armsman replied . . . and smiled.

"It was, was it?"

Neshok tried to keep his voice calm, level, despite the sudden, savage bolt of white-hot fury which burst suddenly through him, but he knew he'd failed. He heard the anger crackling in his own words, heard the way they quivered about the edges, and saw the satisfaction in the senior-armsman's eyes.

Eyes, Neshok suddenly realized, which, like the cold smile below them, held not a single trace of fear. Which dared the acting five hundred to do his worst. And as he realized that, Neshok realized something else, as well. The senior-armsman had deliberately redirected Neshok's own attention—and anger—to himself, and away from the terrified young under-armsman.

The five hundred glared at the Sharonian in front of him. It would have been inaccurate to say that Neshok reached a decision. That would have implied a deliberate, at least semi-rational process. He told himself, later, that it had been exactly that. That the coldly calculated need to undermine any defiance the senior-armsman might have managed to inject into his subordinates was what inspired him. Certainly a trained, determined interrogator would never allow a prisoner's words—the only weapon the prisoner possessed—to fill him with such sudden, volcanic fury that he acted without truly thinking at all.

Alivar Neshok looked at the guard standing behind the Arpathian prisoner, clenched his fist at shoulder level, and jerked it downward.

The Arpathian must have understood what that

gesture meant, but his eyes never flinched and his smile never faltered as the short sword hissed out of its sheath behind him and the guard's free hand gripped his hair and yanked his head back.

"Now . . . Sirda," Neshok heard his own voice say across the coppery stink of the huge fan of blood which had erupted from the senior-armsman's slashed throat to fill his nostrils, "I believe you had something you wanted to *tell* me."

CHAPTER NINE

"WELL, ISN'T *this* charming," Hulmok Arthag remarked.

It was quite astounding, Dorzon chan Baskay reflected, just how much disgust his fellow platoon-captain could put into a simple four-word sentence.

Not that he could really fault the Arpathian at this particular moment.

The Ternathian officer turned and gazed back the way they'd come. The portal through which they'd passed was far smaller than Hell's Gate. In fact, it measured barely three miles from side to side, which made it even smaller than the swamp portal. And at the moment, it was like a picture window into the very heart of one of the Uromathians' fiery hells.

The fire Arthag had created had rolled right up to the portal's very brink. The furious, heat-driven storm-front of wind had whirled bits and pieces of flaming debris through the portal as the bone-dry northern forest they'd left behind consumed itself in a vortex of searing devastation.

But there'd never been much chance of that fire

pouring itself through *this* portal, chan Baskay reflected. He could feel the fire's heat on his face even here, hundreds of yards away as he and Arthag stood side-by-side in the fork of a towering tree. Their chosen tree reared its impressive height—well over a hundred feet into the air, most of it far above their present perch—atop the same, sharp ridgeline over which Chief-Armsman chan Hathas was leading the other members of their tiny command. Other trees, *thousands* of trees, stretched away from this aspect of their arrival portal as far as they could see, and *those* trees were anything but "bone-dry."

As nearly as chan Baskay could estimate, they had to be deep inside the rainforest basin of the mighty Dalazan River, which drained the vast interior of the continent of New Farnal. That meant rain. *Lots* of rain, in daily, drenching doses. Rain measured not in inches, but in *feet* per year. In fact, it was raining right this moment, soaking the upper canopy of lush green foliage so completely that even entire flaming branches, borne through the portal in the grip of fire-born whirlwinds, simply hissed into extinction when they landed. When Arthag's holocaust had completed its work, this portal was going to thrust up out of a wasteland of ashes and soot like some surreal slice of verdant greenery.

A very *visible* surreal slice of verdant greenery.

"It may not be exactly 'charming,'" chan Baskay said now, in reply to Arthag's comment, "but in my own humble opinion, it beats the hells out of the alternative."

"There is that," Arthag acknowledged. "That doesn't mean I have to like it, though. And I don't—like it, I mean."

Chan Baskay snorted, but he had no trouble understanding Arthag's viewpoint. If the Arpathian hadn't liked the northern forest of hardwoods and conifers they'd left behind, their present triple canopy rainforest had to be even worse. On the other hand, the advantages for a small band of fugitives were enormous.

Although equatorial rainforests were undoubtedly home to the most diverse collection of plant and animal life on any world in the multiverse, they were quite different from the image which the word "jungle" evoked in most people's minds. They were composed primarily of trees, not vast, thick-growing thickets of fernlike vegetation. Instead, the surface of the ground tended to be marked by a layer of rapidly decomposing dead leaves, dominated by abundant tree seedlings and saplings. Most of those seedlings and saplings would never reach maturity, since only a minute fraction of the potential sunlight ever penetrated the upper tree canopies. The topmost layer of leaves reached heights of over a hundred and thirty feet, and additional, lower canopies intercepted any light that got past it. Visibility was still limited in a forest like that, of course, but not nearly so badly as the average Sharonian might have assumed.

But this particular portal sat in the middle of what the botanists would have called a "regeneration zone." Something—possibly even the formation of the portal itself—had killed back enough trees to open an enormous hole in the overhead canopies. The light streaming suddenly into the dim, dark recesses which those canopies had hidden had unleashed an explosion of growth of more light-demanding species. Herbaceous varieties had sprung up everywhere, creating something which truly was very much like the stereotypical idea of a "jungle." By now, the process was far enough along that the fastest-growing shrubs and trees were beginning to shade those varieties back out once more, but the transition was still far from complete. For the moment, the incredibly luxuriant masses of plant life made any line of sight much over ten or fifteen yards all but impossible to come by. The torrential equatorial rains were also able to get through, thanks to the thinner canopies overhead, and the combination of well over seventy inches a year of rain, plus the incredible rates of local plant growth, would quickly conceal any trail they might leave. Perhaps even more importantly, under the circumstances, the limitless possibilities for ambushes would force any pursuer to move with the utmost caution. And if anyone *did* manage to catch up with them, he would soon discover that not all of the Faraika I machine guns had been sent forward to Company-Captain chan Tesh. Chan Baskay had only three of the weapons, but once they were dug in in properly concealed positions, they would wreak havoc on any opponent.

This sodden, mucky, overgrown, dimly lit jungle was going to be hard on their horses, which undoubtedly helped explain Arthag's aversion towards it. It was also going to literally rot the clothes off their backs and the boots off their feet, and what it would do to improperly maintained firearms scarcely bore thinking upon. But they'd managed to bring along quite a bit more ammunition than chan Baskay had realized Arthag had managed to squirrel away at Fallen Timbers, and they had almost twice as many rifles as they had troopers to fire them . . . not to mention half a squad's worth of slide-action shotguns.

"Do you think they're really likely to follow us in here?" Arthag asked after a moment.

"Hard to say." Chan Baskay shrugged. "If it were me, I'd probably forget about us, at least for a while. They know there can't be very many of us, and from what Skirvon's told us, their emphasis has to be on getting as far forward as they can before they run into Division-Captain chan Geraith. Of course, they'll probably figure out we have Skirvon with us, and they may decide to mount some sort of rescue attempt." Chan Baskay snorted harshly. "From what I've seen of him, I wouldn't *want* him back in their place! They may have different standards, but even so, Division-Captain chan Geraith has to be their number one worry right now."

"Do they really know the division-captain is coming?" Arthag asked. Chan Baskay looked at him, and it was the Arpathian's turn to shrug. "I was just a little busy while you were talking to him," he pointed out mildly.

"Fair enough," chan Baskay conceded. "And the answer is that they do, and they don't, assuming Skirvon really knows what he's talking about. Apparently, they'd managed to plant 'reconnaissance crystals' on us. I suppose if they can record sounds and images in the 'personal crystals' they let us see, there's no reason they couldn't use other crystals and their godsdamned magic to record tactical information, too.

"At any rate, Skirvon obviously knows we've been expecting a substantial reinforcement. I don't think he knows exactly *how* substantial, or exactly when it's about to arrive, though. And from some of the other things he's said, it's even more obvious to me that they've significantly underestimated the firepower chan Geraith is going to be bringing with him."

"Nice to know we're not the only ones who've fucked up completely," Arthag observed in a conversational tone, and chan Baskay grimaced.

"I take your point," the Ternathian said. "And I wish there were some way we could get what we know—or get Skirvon, at least—to the division-captain before he runs straight into these bastards."

"Maybe somebody else will manage to get the word out," Arthag suggested.

"I hope so, but they've thought about that, too." Chan Baskay's voice was heavier, and Arthag quirked an eyebrow at him.

"They know about the Voices, Hulmok," chan Baskay said. "And they've come up with a plan for dealing with them. It's the same one they used to deal with Rokam and chan Treskin. According to Skirvon, they intend to shoot every Voice they encounter out of hand."

Arthag's nostrils flared, and his eyes went so bleak and cold that for just an instant, chan Baskay was frightened of him. Then the Arpathian drew a deep breath.

"I suppose that's one way to deal with the problem." His voice was matter-of-fact, almost thoughtful, but the eyes which went with it were carved from the heart of an obsidian glacier. "Still, eventually they're going to miss one somewhere."

"No doubt they are. But remember, the one big weakness of the Voicenet—aside, of course, from the fact that we don't have nearly enough Voices out here in the first place—is the fact that no Voice can reach another one *through* a portal, and Skirvon says they know it. That's the weak spot in the chain, and these people plan to exploit it and get as far up-chain as they can before anyone manages to pass the word that they're coming."

"And at the same time, they're going to be looking for someplace they can dig in against counterattack," Arthag said. "Someplace with a small enough portal to make defending it practical."

"That's the idea," chan Baskay acknowledged, impressed not so much by Arthag's ability to figure that out as by the Arpathian's ability to figure it out so quickly. "If they can't find one, though, they're planning to use their godsdamned dragons to devastate our supply lines in a running campaign."

This time, Arthag only nodded, and chan Baskay chuckled grimly. If there was anyone in the multiverse who'd understand the niceties of cutting an over-extended opponent off from his logistics base, it would have to be an Arpathian.

"You know," Arthag said after a moment, "this really and truly sucks, doesn't it?"

* * *

Five Hundred Neshok watched in profound satisfaction as the remaining prisoners were dragged out of his presence. They had to be dragged; at least two of them wouldn't be doing any unassisted walking until he'd finally gotten the healers to attend to them. Not that there was any particular rush about that.

He'd had a special holding area of jury-rigged but sturdy cells erected just off his chosen interrogation room. It allowed him to keep prisoners he'd already interrogated segregated from the general population of captured Sharonians. And it also just happened to keep them handy, close enough to hear the results of his troopers' efforts to . . . persuade the recalcitrant to tell him what he wanted to know.

And, he admitted to himself, *hanging on to them*

here ought to keep any nosy idiots like Five Hundred Vaynair out of my hair.

Sooner or later, he knew, there were going to be questions about his methods. That prick Vaynair would see to that, if no one else did. But by the time that happened, Alivar Neshok would have amassed enough solid, reliable, *useful* information to make it obvious just how ridiculous Vaynair's potential protests were. They *had* to have that information, and Neshok knew superior officers remembered subordinates who'd had the balls to do what had to be done, even if the strict letter of the Articles of War had to be bent just a bit in the process.

Two Thousand mul Gurthak already owed him. And the two thousand recognized Neshok's capabilities, as well, as his present assignment clearly demonstrated. But valuable as mul Gurthak's patronage would undoubtedly prove, the fact remained that the Union Army was overwhelmingly dominated by the *Andaran* officer corps. Adding someone like Two Thousand Harshu to his list of . . . sponsors would be even more valuable, and Harshu wasn't likely to forget the Intelligence officer whose efforts were about to make him the victor in the opening campaign of the first inter-universal war in history.

His lips quirked in a slight, satisfied smile at the thought, and he nodded to the trooper who was sluicing buckets of water across the floor to get rid of the worst of the mess, then stepped outside to catch a breath of some fresh air which wasn't tainted by the stink of blood and vomit. He had at least five or ten minutes before the next batch of intelligence sources arrived, and he crossed the covered veranda built across the width of the armory and leaned on its railing, watching the activity swirling around him.

The armory buildings formed an island of calm in the midst of all that action for several reasons. One was the result of his own insistence on the need for privacy to let him isolate his interrogation subjects in order to instill the proper psychological attitude. And another, no doubt, was that Thousand Carthos didn't want any of his troopers fooling around with the unknown, alien weapons which had been gathered up from where the slaughtered garrison had dropped them. They'd been hauled back to the Sharonians' own armory and stacked there, where they could be kept under guard, if only to prevent potentially lethal accidents.

He heard a monstrous flapping sound and looked up to see a quartet of tactical transport dragons, towing a pair of cargo pods and escorted by a single, slightly understrength three-dragon flight of reds, heading almost directly north, away from Fort Shaylar and deeper into the universe the Sharonians had called New Uromath. The terrain wasn't especially promising for aerial operations out there, Neshok reflected. Thanks to their navigation units, Two Thousand Harshu's forces knew exactly where they were, on the upper west coast of Andara, and Magister Halathyn's portal detector told them where to find the next portal headed up-chain. With that information, it wasn't hard to predict that the nearly three hundred miles between Fort Shaylar and the universe the Sharonians had christened Thermyn consisted of exactly the same rainsoaked, heavily wooded terrain. There was no place dragons could set down in that sort of terrain, and the improvements (such as they were) the Sharonians had made to the hacked-out overland trail between Fort Shaylar and the portal were minimal.

None of that worried Neshok particularly, however. There might not be any handy landing zones between here and the New Uromath-Thermyn portal, but there was also no reason for the expeditionary force to need any. The next portal was smaller than Hell's Gate—Magister Halathyn's detector had already told them that much, not that they'd really needed the detectors for that; no one had ever seen a portal Hell's Gate's size, far less one bigger. But his prisoner interrogations had confirmed that it was still the next best thing to ten miles across . . . and that the so-called "fort" built to cover it was little more sophisticated—or manned—than Fort Shaylar had been. The advance forces Two Thousand Harshu and Thousand Toralk were sending ahead should find it child's play to slip through a portal that size under cover of night without being spotted.

And the terrain on the *far* side of the portal was very different from that on this side. Fort Brithik lay in the midst of the vast, level plains of central Andara, which—unlike these miserable, dripping woods or the smoldering desert left by the forest fire still raging in the Hell's Gate universe—was ideal terrain for air-mobile operations. Those same prisoner interrogations had also told them which way to go in search of the next portal *beyond* Brithik . . . and where to find the next half-dozen Voice relay stations.

Magister Halathyn's detectors would undoubtedly have pointed them in the direction of the next portal, even without the information Neshok had wrung out of his prisoners. For that matter, the fact that the Sharonians had no dragons meant there were bound to be roads—or at least tracks—to point the way to their next destination. But it was thanks to Neshok's efforts that they knew how *far* they had to go (and where to look when they got there) to find those never-to-be-sufficiently-damned Voices.

The Voice relay between New Uromath and Thermyn, for example, was on *this* side of the portal connecting them. The distance was short enough to require only a single relay, but whereas Fort Brithik was built in Thermyn, where there was at least less rain and better lines of sight, the Voice outpost was in New Uromath. As far as the Sharonians knew, there was no real security need to put it under the cover of Fort Brithik's palisades, and by putting the Voice on this side of the portal, he was more handily available for contact from Fort Shaylar or the Voice at Fallen Timbers. Clearly, the Sharonians had decided messages moving up-chain were more likely to be time-critical than messages moving down-chain, which explained the Voice's location. He was close enough to the portal that he could easily cross it to transmit messages up-chain or check for messages coming down-chain at regularly scheduled intervals, yet always available at any other time for any potentially critical message from the Sharonian negotiators.

Without the information Neshok had gotten out of his prisoners, it was likely the relay station would have been overlooked by people who expected the Voice they wanted to be inside Fort Brithik's protection. And if that had happened, the odds were entirely too good that the Voice might have evaded the Arcanans long enough to break back across the portal himself and pass a warning back to Sharona.

That wasn't going to happen now. Those same interrogations had informed Neshok that the relay station had been built on ground which, unlike most of the rest of the terrain between here and Thermyn, was *not* covered in dense woodland. It was hard to conceive of a forest fire in these environs, and Neshok suspected that the one which had made the clearing in which the relay station had been built had actually been set by a prairie grass fire coming through the portal from Thermyn long before the Sharonians discovered either universe. Where the fire had come from didn't matter, however. What mattered was that it had been big enough to offer landing space for dragons relatively close to the relay station, yet far enough back to land unseen and invisible on a moonless, drizzling night.

And that the relay station itself was far enough away from the portal for the discharge of weapons less . . . showy than the Sharonians' to pass unnoticed by the fort's garrison.

And, he thought coldly, still watching the quartet of transports and their escorts fade into the early evening sky, *even if something should happen to go wrong* there, *there's always the next Voice relay* beyond *Fort Brithik.*

Their Voices might offer the Sharonians all sorts of strategic advantages . . . but only as long as the long, vulnerable chain of relay posts remained unbroken. And it would remain unbroken only as long as Arcana didn't know where to find it.

Alivar Neshok smiled again, baring his teeth in a snarl of triumph, then straightened. It was time to get his professional interrogation face back in place to greet the next batch of prisoners, he thought, and turned around to walk back inside.

* * *

"You wanted to see me, Fifty?"

Commander of One Thousand Carthos sounded brusque, as well he might, given the thousand and one details he had to deal with at the moment. The captured fort was a bubbling cauldron of movement, orders, questions, answers, and curses as the thousand's infantry and cavalry got themselves sorted out for the next day and the leap forward to position themselves for the attack upon the universe the Sharonians called Thermyn.

"Yes, Sir. Thank you for finding time."

Fifty Jaralt Sarma made his own voice crisp and firm—the sort of voice a senior officer might expect out of a subordinate who was determined not to waste his time.

"Well?" Carthos said impatiently.

"Sir," Sarma drew a deep breath and braced himself, "I'm afraid we've had a serious violation of the Kerellian Accords."

"Really."

The single word came out flat, devoid of any emotional overtone at all, and Tayrgal Carthos sat back in the chair behind the desk which had once belonged to the fort's Sharonian commander. He interlaced his fingers across his flat midsection and cocked his head to one side.

"What sort of 'violation,' Fifty?" he asked after a moment.

"Sir," Sarma said, "it's Five Hundred Neshok. My platoon has the guard duty on the fort's armory. We saw one of the five hundred's troopers drag a Sharonian prisoner out of the side of the main building where the five hundred's set up for interrogation. He—the prisoner, I mean, Sir—had been beaten. *Badly* beaten."

"And?" Carthos prompted with a slight frown as Sarma paused.

"And a little later we heard screams, Sir," the commander of fifty said. "A *lot* of screams. None of the other prisoners came back out. Not until two of Five Hundred Neshok's men dragged out another prisoner. Sir," Sarma met the thousand's eyes levelly, "the man's throat had been cut. He'd been murdered."

The fifty used the verb deliberately, and watched Carthos' eyes harden. Silence hovered for a moment, then the thousand allowed his chair to come back upright.

"As it happens, Fifty Sarma," he said, "I've already received a report on the events you've described. According to *Five Hundred* Neshok—and the corroborating testimony of five of his men who were physically present at the time—the dead prisoner attacked the five hundred. Exactly what the lunatic thought he was going to accomplish eludes me, of course, but five reliable witnesses—six of them, counting the Five Hundred himself—all agree that the prisoner managed to get his hands on one of the guard's weapons and that Five Hundred Neshok killed him in self-defense."

Sarma's jaw dropped. He couldn't help it . . . but he managed, somehow, to stop himself before he actually said anything.

Carthos' expression hardened ever so slightly, but the thousand kept his own voice level.

"I commend you for your obvious desire to see to it

that Two Thousand Harshu's standing orders extending the protection of the Kerellian Accords to any prisoners we take are adhered to, Fifty. And I assure you that any possible violations of the Accords will be investigated most carefully. In this case, however, given the existence of half a dozen witnesses, all of whose testimony corroborates one another's, I suspect that you've overreacted to a situation in which you weren't privy to all the facts."

Sarma got his mouth closed again, locking his teeth against the protests which hammered upon them from behind. Gotten his hands on another guard's weapon, had he? Then perhaps Thousand Carthos could explain just how that had happened when the dead man's hands were still chained behind him as he was dragged out of the interrogation room like so much slaughtered meat. Or explain where those screams had come from, or the reason for the savage beating the first prisoner had obviously sustained.

But those, Jaralt Sarma knew now, were questions he dared not ask. Not now, not here. Perhaps never, but definitely not today.

"I see, Sir," he heard his own voice say levelly. "You're right, of course. Obviously, I wasn't aware of all the details. Nor was I aware that you were already so well informed about the incident. I . . . apologize for wasting your time at a moment like this."

"Nonsense, Fifty," Carthos replied. "No officer is ever guilty of 'wasting' his superiors' time when he believes that something as serious as you obviously thought had happened has occurred. A deliberate violation of the Kerellian Accords?" The thousand shook his head. "The Articles of War themselves are quite specific about the responsibility of any Union officer to report something like that, after all."

"Yes, Sir, they are. I still appreciate your being so understanding, though."

Sarma was distantly surprised that he could get the words out without gagging, but he managed.

"Don't worry about it, Fifty." Carthos' smile somehow failed to reach his eyes, Sarma noticed. The thousand paused for a moment, then arched one eyebrow.

"Was there anything else, Fifty Sarma?"

"No, Sir," Jaralt Sarma said. "Nothing else, Sir."

CHAPTER TEN

"VOICE KINLAFIA?"

Darcel Kinlafia's head snapped up, like a startled rabbit exploding out of cover, as he turned to face the assistant chamberlain. His movement wasn't quite sudden enough to count as "whipping around," he realized an instant later, but it was too sudden for any other description.

"Yes?" His response came out half-strangled, and he cleared his throat, blushing furiously.

"If you'll come this way, please," the assistant chamberlain said with a small smile. Kinlafia didn't have to touch the man to feel the sympathy—and understanding—behind that smile, and a trickle of comfort flowed through him. Obviously, he was far from the first visitor to the Great Palace to wonder if his blood pressure was going to survive the visit. He supposed that the fact that most of them appeared to have made it through the ordeal intact should have been comforting, but somehow it didn't actually make him feel all that much better as the chamberlain led the way down the broad, marble-floored passageways with the walls adorned with paintings and tapestries, any one of which was probably worth a prince's ransom.

Don't be silly! Kinlafia scolded himself. *Most of them are only worth a* duke's *ransom, you twit, whatever the cliche says! And it isn't "the Great Palace," any more, either.*

He'd been more than a little surprised by the name change. For the better part of three centuries, this enormous, glittering fairyland had been known as the Great Palace, or the Grand Palace, depending upon how one chose to translate the Shurkhali. Now, though, it had reverted to the name it had borne for over two thousand years: Calirath Palace, the ancient and future home of the Calirath Dynasty.

The change in names had not met with universal approval. The palace had been renamed by one of the early seneschals who had been restored to rule after the Ternathian withdrawal from Othmaliz. It had been widely proclaimed as a gesture of Othmalizi pride in its restored independence, and Kinlafia had no doubt that at least some Othmalizis had seen it as a poke in the eye for the dynasty which had ruled over them for so long.

Of course, what none of them realized at the time was that the seneschal in question only got away with it because the Caliraths themselves agreed to it. It's amazing how few people knew the family never actually surrendered ownership. I suppose that's because it's been imperial policy for almost three hundred years to allow the Othmalizi government to use it as if it owned it. But given the most recent seneschal's track record, it's probably also the only reason it didn't get sold—or turned into a resort hotel!

None of the seneschals had gone out of their way to make known the minor fact of who actually owned the place (or the fact that it sat on what was technically still Ternathian territory, under the terms of the Empire's withdrawal from the rest of Othmaliz and Tajvana), and Kinlafia suspected that had the Great Palace belonged to anyone else, some seneschal would have seized title by force long ago. No one was quite stupid enough to do that to the *Caliraths*, however, and Kinlafia wondered how badly it must have irked generations of Othmalizi rulers to realize that they were living in someone else's house on sufferance . . . and that they couldn't even collect property taxes on it.

Judging from the current Seneschal's reaction to "his" parliament's decision to revert to the ancient and original name for the most historic single edifice in Tajvana, it must have irked them badly, indeed. The Seneschal had put the best face he could on the decision, but his mouthpieces had inveighed furiously against the entire notion in his usually tame parliament. Their failure to vote down the proposal had constituted a major political defeat for the Seneschal, and his irritation had been obvious despite his flowery speech of approval when the change became official.

Now Kinlafia remembered some of Shaylar's pithy comments about the Seneschal and surprised himself with a quiet chuckle of genuine amusement as he reflected upon how inordinately pleased she would have been by his current discomfiture.

The chamberlain glanced back at him, and this time Kinlafia's smile felt far more natural and unforced. The chamberlain gave him a slight nod, as if approving the change. Then they reached a huge, ornately carved door with the ancient motto of the Caliraths—*I Stand Between*—etched into the stone lintel above it. An armed guard in the green-and-gold of the Calirath Dynasty's personal retainers stood outside it, and the Voice felt something as the guard looked him up and down.

Kinlafia wasn't certain what he'd felt—or, rather, Felt. He'd never experienced anything quite like it before, and he found himself abruptly wondering if the occasional whispered rumors about the Ternathian imperial family's bodyguards and their Talents might not hold at least a kernel of truth, after all. Certainly there was *something* going on as the guard's eyes swept over him. Kinlafia could Feel a peculiar sort of . . . probing. Or *testing*, perhaps. Whatever it was, he couldn't put his mental hands on exactly the right label, but he knew it was there . . . whatever it was.

It lasted for no more than one or two heartbeats. Then the guard came to attention and nodded respectfully.

"Voice Kinlafia," he said quietly. "You're expected."

Kinlafia wondered if he was supposed to say anything in response, but before he could, the guard reached back—with his offhand, not his gun hand, Kinlafia noticed—and opened the door behind him. The Voice hesitated. He knew who was waiting for him on the other side of that threshold, and he abruptly discovered that even "call-me-Janaki's" letter of introduction wasn't nearly enough to prevent the butterflies in his midsection from launching into a complicated Arpathian drum dance.

In that moment, Darcel Kinlafia, who had accompanied Company-Captain chan Tesh's troopers through the swamp portal with rifle in hand, who had faced down brigands and outlaws, fought off claim jumpers and raiders, and stood his ground against charging bison, Ricathian cape buffalo, and even an infuriated grizzly bear, decided that the only thing to do was run. He was a fleet-footed man. If he started now, he could be all the way back to the train station in no more than twenty or thirty minutes. And from there—

The chamberlain's cleared throat interrupted the Voice's brief fantasy of escape. Kinlafia looked at him, and the chamberlain twitched his head at the open doorway. For an instant, Kinlafia actually considered backing away, but he discovered that he lacked sufficient nerve to chicken out at the last minute. And so he nodded back to the chamberlain and followed the palace staffer through the doorway with a surprisingly steady tread.

The room on the other side was on the small side—indeed it was positively tiny—by the scale of Calirath Palace, which meant it was no more than twenty-five or thirty feet on a side. It was furnished with surprisingly worn, overstuffed armchairs and a long, comfortable looking couch. A coffee table which appeared to have been made from driftwood stood in front of the couch, and an old leather-topped desk sat before the wide bay window which looked out over the sun-soaked palace gardens. Bookshelves lined the wall opposite the window, and the priceless artwork so much in evidence elsewhere in the palace had been replaced by what were very good but obviously amateur watercolors and oils of a land whose soft, misty greenery was far removed from the sunbaked heat of Tajvana.

All of that registered instantly, but almost peripherally. It couldn't have been any other way, when the man who'd been seated behind that desk stood and held out his right hand.

Kinlafia froze. No one had ever instructed him in formal court protocol and etiquette, but he had a shrewd notion that one didn't simply walk up to the Emperor of Ternathia, say "How the hell are you?" and shake hands with him. On the other hand, he had an equally shrewd notion that one didn't *refuse* to shake hands with him, either.

"Voice Kinlafia."

Zindel chan Calirath's voice was a shade deeper than his son's, but it sounded remarkably similar, and the physical resemblance between him and Janaki was positively uncanny. The crown prince stood eight inches over six feet, and he and his father were very much of a size. If anything, Zindel might have been a fraction of an inch the taller, and his shoulders were definitely broader. Aside from that and the strands of gray beginning to thread themselves through the dark, gold-shot hair of the Caliraths, the Emperor looked far more like Janaki's older brother than his father, the Voice thought. Then he gave himself a mental shake as he realized he was keeping the Emperor of Ternathia—no, the designated Emperor of *Sharona*—standing there with his hand held out.

"Your Majesty," Kinlafia got out. It sounded a little strangled to his own ears, and he drew a deep breath, then reached out and gripped the hand of the most powerful man in Sharonian history.

Darcel Kinlafia had come into this room determined not to intrude upon the Emperor's privacy in any way, only to discover that the stress of the moment was too great for him to shut down his Talent completely. He was far too well trained, and too experienced, to let things get fully out of hand, of course. He didn't even come close to tapping into Zindel's thoughts, but the Emperor's *emotions* were something else, entirely. Kinlafia couldn't *help* sensing those, and he felt a moment of something very like panic as he realized that was the case.

Yet that flare of almost-panic was brief. It vanished in a moment, blown away on the genuine welcome flowing out of Zindel like some warm, comforting tide, and something else swept over him in its wake. He remembered how Janaki's sheer presence had radiated that mysterious magnetism, that awareness that he was in the presence of the direct descendent of Erthain the Great. Yet whatever it was that Janaki had, it was far stronger, almost physically overpowering, as Kinlafia gripped Zindel's hand. It was like an electric charge, flowing through him, and he wondered if the Emperor was aware of it.

"My son has written me quite an epistle about you, Voice Kinlafia," Zindel said. "He appears to have been impressed by you."

"Ah, Prince Janaki is too kind, Your Majesty," Kinlafia got out.

"His mother will be glad to hear that." The Emperor released the Voice's hand with a smile. "I, on the other hand, know Janaki a bit better than that. He wouldn't have written me a letter like this one—" the Emperor gestured at the creased sheets of paper lying on his desk "—unless he truly felt it was justified. And I suppose I should add, Voice Kinlafia, that I have a very lively respect for his judgment."

"Your Majesty, I don't—"

Kinlafia broke off. The truth was, that he didn't have a clue what to say, and Zindel chuckled.

"I apologize, Voice Kinlafia. I'm sure this is all rather overwhelming after months out on the frontier. Tajvana traffic all by itself is probably enough to leave you longing to run for cover. And as if that weren't enough, here you are, dragged into the Palace for a face-to-face interview with that bogeyman, the *Emperor*."

There was so much genuine warmth and amusement in Zindel's expression that Kinlafia found himself chuckling as he nodded.

"I would never call you a *bogeyman*, Your Majesty," he said ruefully. "A little scary, now . . . that I might go for."

"I don't suppose I can blame you for that. On the other hand, at the moment what I most am is a father who hasn't seen his son in months. And you, Voice Kinlafia, are the man he picked to send his letters home with. That would be enough to make you welcome without any other recommendation from him. But you're also the Voice who relayed Voice Nargra-Kolmayr's last message to us, and from what Janaki's had to say in his letter about you, you're the sort of representative we're going to need in our new parliament, too. That's quite a combination of recommendations."

"Your Majesty, that was Prince Janaki's idea. Running for Parliament, I mean. It hadn't even crossed *my* mind until he raised the possibility."

"Which isn't a bad recommendation for office all by itself." Zindel's smile turned far less humorous. "Most people who start out wanting power for its own sake shouldn't be trusted with it in the first place. Which, I suppose, must sound a bit strange—if not hypocritical—coming from someone in my position."

Kinlafia made no response to that last statement, and the amusement returned to the Emperor's smile.

"I see Janaki was correct about your natural . . . diplomacy, Voice Kinlafia," he observed. "Don't worry. I won't put your native tact to any more tests. For now, at least."

* * *

Zindel chan Calirath watched the tanned, brown-haired Voice with careful attentiveness . . . and with more than just his eyes. He knew the fanciful rumors—legends, really—about the mysterious Talents which were somehow reserved as the exclusive property of the House of Calirath. Of course he did; everyone knew about those ridiculous tall tales. But what Zindel knew that most people didn't was that there was a solid core of truth behind them.

The Calirath bloodline extended far beyond the immediate imperial family. It could be no other way, after so many millennia, and the longstanding policy of the emperors of Ternathia to not simply permit but actively encourage periodic marriage outside the ranks of the aristocracy had only pushed that extension harder and farther. And yet there were the Talents which had been persistently associated with the imperial house for literally thousands of years but which scarcely ever manifested *outside* the immediate imperial family. And in addition to the Talents which everyone knew about, there were others, most of which were spoken of only in whispers, about which very few, indeed, knew a thing.

Zindel chan Calirath had always cherished his own doubts about the mythic, almost demigod stature of Erthain the Great as the sun source of all Talents. Yet he knew of no other explanation for the knowledge conserved within the Calirath archives. Ternathia had given the Talents to the entire human race . . . but the imperial dynasty had not shared all it knew. Only the Caliraths, their most trusted Healers, and the high priests of the Triad knew how to activate the potential to Glimpse the future, for example. And only the Caliraths and those same trusted Healers and priests knew how to awaken the other Talents bound up with the Winged Crown.

There'd been times Zindel felt more than a little uncomfortable with the notion that such knowledge had been kept secret for so long. The fact that no one was ever informed of it without first voluntarily agreeing to have that information placed forever under seal by a Mind Healer had also bothered him upon occasion. Yet, in the end, he'd always come back to the inescapable fact that the knowledge which reserved those Talents as the Crown's monoploy constituted one of the Empire's most important state secrets—one which had literally saved the Empire on at least two occasions. That was the sort of advantage no ruler could justify casting away.

The imperial family and its spokesmen had always been careful to smile at the "absurd notion" that such "secret Talents" existed. But they'd always been careful never to expressly *deny* their existence, either, which meant most people had come to the conclusion that there was *some* substance to the rumors, but not a lot. Still, the ability of the Ternathian Emperor to judge the fidelity of ambassadors and councilors, to recognize those driven by personal ambition, to pick out those who might betray his trust, was legendary, and as Zindel gazed at Darcel Kinlafia, he knew Janaki's judgment had not been in error.

Of course, Janaki didn't tell him everything, the

Emperor thought. *And I'm not going to tell him, either. Not yet, at least. I don't have any clearer Glimpse of why it's so important to Andrin to have this man in Tajvana than Janaki does. But Janaki's right about that, too.*

"I'm afraid my schedule for the day is on the full side, Voice Kinlafia. It always is, actually. However, I've read Janaki's letter, and my initial impression of you strongly suggests that he's right about both your character and your electability. And the importance of the service you could render not simply to this new world government we're seeking to establish but to Sharona as a whole. I also realize that having the Crown Prince of Ternathia—and the Emperor, as well—suggest that to you has to be overwhelming."

"'Overwhelming' is a grossly inadequate choice of words, Your Majesty," Kinlafia said with a grimace, and Zindel chuckled appreciatively. The fact that Kinlafia was able to make even that mild a joke in his very first private audience said truly amazing things about the Voice's resilience. Things, Zindel suspected, which Kinlafia himself had never even suspected.

"I hope we can get past that," the Emperor said now. "I'll be honest with you. For all of the power and indisputable prestige which clings to the Winged Crown and the Calirath Dynasty, we can never have too many allies in the political process. I hope you'll become one of those allies. Not out of any sort of blind loyalty to my House—the fact that you aren't Ternathian yourself will probably help there—but because we both have the best interests of Sharona at heart and recognize the need for those who share that commitment to work together."

"Your Majesty," Kinlafia said slowly, "I appreciate

what you've just said. And I appreciate everything the Prince said when he urged me to seek office. More than that, I hope we *will* find ourselves in agreement if I should manage to win election to Parliament. But if I do win election, my decisions as a member of Parliament will have to be *my* decisions. I hope you realize I mean absolutely no disrespect when I say this, but if I should find myself in disagreement with you, I would have no choice but to say so openly."

"An ally who isn't willing to tell you when he thinks you're wrong isn't an ally worth having, Voice Kinlafia," Zindel said, and it was hard to conceal his satisfaction. It took a huge amount of intestinal fortitude—not to mention a spring-steel spine—to stand up to the Emperor of Ternathia in a face-to-face audience. People who could do that were far too valuable to let slip away.

"I'm glad you think so, Your Majesty." Kinlafia's tone and expression were still somewhat guarded, and Zindel shrugged.

"I'm sure if you do disagree with me, and if I think you're wrong to disagree, we'll have the occasional . . . energetic debate, let's say. I've been told by my physicians and Healers that occasional bouts of elevated pulse rate and respiration are good for my circulatory system, though, so I don't think it will be a problem. Not," Zindel smiled charmingly, "from *my* perspective, at any rate."

"I hope you won't take this wrongly, Your Majesty," the Voice said wryly, "but you're really quite a bit like your son. Or possibly the other way around, I suppose."

"I've been told—especially by his mother—that it runs in the family." Zindel chuckled, and Kinlafia smiled. Then the Emperor allowed his expression to turn more sober.

"Seriously, Voice Kinlafia, I believe Janaki was correct about the political asset you represent. And I also share his judgment that it would be in the best interests of Sharona and of the House of Calirath for me to assist you in launching your political career. Mind you, it could be fatal for me to give you *too much* assistance. I have no intention of offering you any sort of *quid pro quo*, any sort of 'understanding' or obligation to become 'my man' in Parliament. First, because I don't believe you would accept my aid if I attached that sort of string to it. Second, because people who allow themselves to be bought by promises of power from one man are generally susceptible to being bought by bigger promises from someone else later on. And third, because people who share your beliefs and support your policies because *they* think they're the correct policies are far more effective as allies than people whose uncritical allegiance, as everyone knows, has been effectively bought and paid for.

"If, however, I campaign too energetically for your election, there would be those who simply refused to believe I wasn't buying your eventual support. I trust you understand that?"

"Of course I do, Your Majesty."

"Good. Having said all of that, though, I think we can contrive to get you off to a rousing start. And in the process, you can probably give the public's morale a fairly substantial poke."

"Your Majesty?"

"As I'm sure you're aware, the next week is going to be exhaustingly full of festivities to celebrate the formal ratification of the Act of Unification, culminating with the Coronation Ball and Coronation the week after that. In fact, you've gotten home in the nick of time. The actual signing ceremony is scheduled for this evening, in the Great Throne Room. It's going to be one of those unbearably formal affairs, with full regalia and the kind of shoes that have you limping inside five minutes. Fortunately, given how recently you've arrived and the fact that no one could possibly expect you to have proper formal attire, you can probably dodge that particular bullet."

Kinlafia's expression reminded Zindel forcibly of a cornered rabbit, and the Emperor smiled crookedly.

"What you *won't* be able to dodge," he told the Voice, "is the parade scheduled for tomorrow afternoon. I understand they're pulling out all the stops. It's going to be incredibly gaudy, with floats, marching bands, mimes, tumblers, military units from at least two dozen countries, and everything else you can imagine. And you, Voice Kinlafia, are going to be one of the prime exhibits."

"I beg your pardon?" Kinlafia's voice was curiously stifled sounding, Zindel observed.

"Of course you are, and for a lot of reasons. Probably the most important, and I'm deadly serious about this, is that you represent a living link with Shaylar." Zindel's eyes and tone alike were both level as he gazed into Kinlafia's eyes. "You may find that uncomfortable, but it's true, and the people of Tajvana—and of all of Sharona, for that matter—*need* to see you. The SUNN Voicecasts have made you a symbol, one inextricably linked with what happened to your survey crew out there. And at this moment, when everything is in such a state of flux and there's so much uncertainty, symbols are hugely important."

Kinlafia obviously wanted to reject Zindel's analysis. For a moment, the Emperor thought that was exactly what he was going to do. But then, manifestly against his will, the Voice nodded slowly, instead.

"At the same time, however," Zindel continued after a moment, "politics is perhaps the most pragmatic of all human endeavors. To put it bluntly, one always tries to kill as many birds as possible with a single stone in the political arena. And make no mistake about it, Voice Kinlafia—even the most high-minded of statesmen must be an effective practitioner of politics if he hopes to accomplish anything.

"In this case, the visibility of the Unification Parade will provide you with an invaluable platform from which to launch your political career. And, if you have no objection, I intend to see to it that the platform it offers is used as effectively as possible."

"I beg your pardon, Your Majesty?"

"In just a few moments, the chamberlain will escort you to Alazon Yanamar's office." Kinlafia looked blank, and Zindel shrugged. "Alazon is my Privy Voice. She's not simply one of my most valuable councilors, either; she's also my political chief of staff and probably my most trusted political adviser after First Councilor Taje himself. She'll see to it that you're slotted neatly into the parade in an appropriately visible niche. She'll also see to it that you're properly accoutered for the ordeal."

The Calirath smile flashed again, and Kinlafia returned it, although the Voice's smile seemed rather more nervous.

"Trust me, Voice Kinlafia. Alazon will make sure it doesn't hurt a bit. Besides, I think you'll like her."

"I'm sure I will, Your Majesty," Kinlafia said politely.

"At any rate, in addition to getting you launched

properly in the parade, Alazon will also be the most suitable member of my staff to serve as a neophyte politician's adviser. And she'll understand how the Crown can most effectively support your candidacy without being too obvious about it."

"I see, Your Majesty."

Kinlafia, Zindel observed, continued to nurse a few reservations about accepting too much of the imperial favor, which spoke well of the man's fundamental integrity. It would be up to Alazon to show him that Zindel truly intended to attach no strings to his support.

Well, not any political *strings, at any rate*, the Emperor told himself. *Personal loyalty, now. That's something else, entirely.*

Not that Zindel intended to tie that personal loyalty to himself.

"After you've had an opportunity to meet with Alazon and get your immediate schedule squared away," he continued, "I trust you'll be able to join us for supper. I'm afraid it will be a little late this evening, what with the signing."

"Supper?"

The panicky look was back in Kinlafia's eyes, Zindel noticed.

"Don't worry," the Emperor said soothingly. "It's not going to be a formal state occasion. In fact, you'll be the only guest. And, before you object, let me remind you of what I said at the very beginning of this interview. None of us have seen Janaki in months. You have. His mother is going to be just as anxious as I to hear anything you can tell us about him. She'll want to meet you, and the opportunity for you to begin experiencing this sort of affair will be extremely useful and valuable.

If you'll pardon my saying so, the chance to dip your toes into these waters in an intimate, friendly sort of way is nothing to sneeze at."

"Of course not, Your Majesty!" Kinlafia said quickly. "I understand. And thank you."

"Don't mention it. As I said, the Empress is looking forward to the opportunity to talk to you. And, of course, you'll also have the opportunity to meet my daughters."

CHAPTER ELEVEN

THE DOOR TO Alazon Yanamar's office was less ornately carved than the private audience chamber's. It was *more* ornately carved, on the other hand, than any other door Kinlafia had ever seen outside a Temple, he observed sourly, remembering his activist parents' views on "imperial trappings." And, for that matter, on "professional political operatives," which, from what the Emperor had said, undoubtedly included the woman behind that door, Voice or no Voice.

Great, he thought. *Just great. My political keeper's going to be another Voice, with all the opportunities for "subtle coaching" that provides! Won't* that *be fun?*

His guiding chamberlain rapped discreetly on the gleaming portal. The sound he produced was so soft Kinlafia doubted anyone could possibly have heard it, but he was clearly wrong, since the door was quickly opened by a young, golden-haired woman with bright blue eyes.

"Yes?" she said.

"Voice Kinlafia to meet with Privy Voice Yanamar," the chamberlain said, and the young woman's bright blue eyes moved to Kinlafia.

"Voice Kinlafia!" The welcome in the young woman's voice was genuine, Kinlafia realized. "It's an honor to meet you, sir! Privy Voice Yanamar is expecting you. Please, come in!"

"Thank you," Kinlafia replied, just a bit taken aback by her enthusiasm. Then he glanced at the chamberlain who had been his lifeline—so far, at least. "And thank you," he said, with utmost sincerity.

"You're welcome, sir," the chamberlain said. "It's been my honor." He bowed to Kinlafia, then bestowed a somewhat less profound yet still deeply respectful bow upon the young woman in the doorway, and headed off down the endless hallway.

Of course, Kinlafia thought, *they're* all *endless in this place, aren't they?*

The young woman opened the door wider and stood back, and he accepted her silent invitation to step across the threshold into a pleasantly furnished office.

"I'm Ulantha Jastyr, Privy Voice Yanamar's assistant," the young woman said. As he concentrated on her, Kinlafia realized she was a very strongly Talented Voice herself. "As I say, the Privy Voice has been expecting you. If you'll follow me, please."

He followed Jastyr across the outer office to an inner doorway. Unlike the chamberlain, she didn't knock; she simply alerted Yanamar via Voice, then smiled over her shoulder at Kinlafia, opened the door, and stood aside.

"Thank you," he said once more, and stepped past her into yet another of Calirath Palace's obviously infinite number of rooms and chambers.

This one was smaller than the Emperor's private audience chamber, although it was still spacious and high-ceilinged. It also had windows overlooking the same garden, and it was decorated with horses. Lots and lots of horses. There were paintings, two tapestries, and half a dozen large, framed photographic prints on the walls, and a long display shelf across the entire width of the office's bookshelves held literally dozens of ceramic, crystal, and bronze horses. Kinlafia was no art connoisseur, but he didn't have to be one to recognize that many of them were exquisite (and undoubtedly expensive) art pieces in their own right.

The plethora of equines distracted his immediate attention from the new office's occupant. Only for a moment, though. Then he turned towards her—and froze.

Alazon Yanamar, he realized, was about his own age. She was slender, high-bosomed, delicately boned and of little more than moderate height for a Ternathian woman, which meant she was perhaps an inch and a half shorter than he was. And she was obviously a very powerful Voice; he could feel the strength of her Talent from ten feet away.

All of that was true, he realized, yet it wasn't what registered upon him so immediately and powerfully. No, what registered upon him were the huge, incredibly deep, clear gray eyes and the mass of midnight-black hair framing an oval face which the gods had clearly designed for laughter, humor, and intelligence.

They trapped him, those eyes. He remembered the ancient saying, the description of eyes as the "window of the soul." Between Voices, that could be literally true, and as Darcel Kinlafia looked into *these* eyes' crystalline depths, he Saw the glowing power deep in the heart of her.

It wasn't until much, much later that he finally realized Alazon Yanamar, despite an exquisite figure, was not a beautiful woman in any classical sense of the word. Her cheekbones were too high, her nose was too pert, her chin too determined. And none of it mattered at all. Not then, and not ever.

"Voice Kinlafia." Her speaking voice was deep, for a woman. It was also rich and musical, shimmering with subtle undertones that rippled like clear water over beds of golden sand. It went through him like harp notes of sunlight, and he drew a deep, lung-filling breath.

"Voice Yanamar," he replied, and saw those gray eyes widen slightly even as he heard the edge of hoarseness in his own voice.

She started to say something more, then paused. He could Feel her looking into his own eyes, and then her nostrils flared.

"Oh, dear," she said softly, and Kinlafia reached out to touch her cheek with birdwing fingers.

He'd never done such a thing in his life. Certainly not with a woman he'd never even met before! This time, it was the most natural possible gesture in the multiverse.

I never really believed anyone when they told me about things like this, he thought. *Which just proves the gods* do *have a sense of humor, I suppose.*

"This is an unexpected complication," she said after a moment, and Kinlafia smiled as that magnificent voice sang through him.

"I suppose it is," he agreed. "*I* never expected it, anyway."

She laughed. It was a delightful sound, and Kinlafia found himself smiling hugely at her.

Under any other circumstances, a corner of his mind

recognized, he would have felt like an utter idiot standing here, touching a strange woman's face, grinning like a fool, and floating with his feet ten inches off her office floor. Under *these* circumstances, it was inconceivable that he could have done anything else.

Occasionally—*very* occasionally—Voice met Voice and, in that first instant of awareness, recognized one another. Felt the interlocking of Talent and heart. Other people might speak about "love at first sight," but for Voices, it could be literally true . . . and the bright glory of that moment of recognition could be the greatest tragedy in their lives. There was no guarantee that two Voices "meant for one another" would find each other at all, much less before one of them had met and loved someone else. When that happened, when one or both of them weren't free, this soul-deep fusion could cause incredible pain for everyone involved.

I just thought *I loved Shaylar*, Kinlafia thought. Then he gave himself a mental shake. *No, that's not true. I* did *love Shaylar, and I always will. But this—*

"What do we do now?" she said, as the laughter left her voice but not her eyes.

"You're asking me?" Kinlafia shook his head. "I didn't even know your name until ten minutes ago!"

"Does that matter?" she asked simply.

"Not at all," he told her softly, fingertips caressing her cheek.

"Good." She closed her eyes for a moment, leaning her cheek against his touch, then inhaled deeply, opened her eyes, and straightened her spine.

"Good," she repeated. "I'll remind you of that quite often in the future, I'm sure. But I'm very much afraid we don't have time to explore *us* at this moment."

"No, we don't," he agreed, yet even as he did, his Voice continued. <*But we* will *find time for it, My Lady. Soon.*>

<*Oh, that we will, love,*> she promised him in a Voice every bit as deep and musical as her speaking voice.

Most people, Kinlafia knew, would never have understood. Even another Voice would find it difficult—as Kinlafia himself always had, when he'd seen it between other Voices—to truly realize, or to *believe*, perhaps, that two total strangers could meet and know instantly that the gods themselves had crafted them to be the two halves of a single whole. That they could share such a serene, unshakable confidence that they were meant to be together. That, in fact, they already *were* together.

I *never understood it, at any rate, even when Mayla and Hilas tried to explain it to me.* He shook his head mentally at the memory of his friends trying to tell him how it worked. *But maybe it's different for everyone. Maybe it hits all of us in a different way. Or maybe it's just something no one* can *explain, even to another Voice, unless it's happened to them*?

He didn't know the answer to his own question, but he knew that *he* would never be able to explain it. Not how it had happened, or how potent it was, or how magical. Or how something so deep, so powerful, could be simultaneously so calm, so patient and ready to wait upon the future. It was like standing in the eye of a hurricane. All the incredible power and passion, the wonder of having met one another, the promise that so much more was still to come, roared about them with strength to shake the multiverse by the scruff of its neck until its teeth rattled, and yet they stood in a place of crystal clarity that was poised and peaceful, like gold fish drifting effortless as dreams over golden gravel in a deep, clear pool.

"Please," she said, stepping back and waving one graceful hand at the comfortable chairs placed to flank the coffee table and form an intimate little conversation nook. "Sit down. We've got a lot to discuss. Officially, I mean."

"Of course," he agreed, and obeyed the invitation.

She let him settle into his chair before she picked up the folder on her blotter, walked around the desk, and seated herself in her own chair, facing him. She looked into his eyes for a moment longer, then took a fountain pen from her pocket, uncapped it, and opened the folder in her lap. It was, he recognized, her way of announcing that it was time for business.

"Now," she said briskly, "about this parade . . ."

* * *

Zindel chan Calirath's eyebrows arched as Yanamar Alazon and Darcel Kinlafia were ushered into the private dining room.

That dining room lay in the Emperor's Wing, the most recently modernized portion of the palace (for Calirath Palace, "modernization" was an unending process which had begun literally thousands of years ago), and the gas-jets and oil lamps of the less modern areas had been augmented with the relatively new incandescent lights. Personally, Zindel didn't much care for them, esthetically speaking. Their light was much harder edged, in his opinion. But it was also undeniably brighter and a huge boon for people (like certain emperors he could have named) who found themselves forced to deal with ream after ream of paperwork and reports. And unlike him, Varena much preferred the new lighting—probably because of her interest in needlepoint—while even he had to admit that it made it easier to see people's faces and read their expressions.

Like now, for instance. For two people who had never met before that very afternoon, the two Voices were indisputably together, and the Emperor forcibly suppressed an all but irresistible temptation to grin like a triumphant urchin. The human being in him was simultaneously touched by and envious of the all but visible glow radiating from them. Like most Caliraths with the Calirath Talent, Zindel had often resented the fact that Glimpses were so often things of tragic portent and never of things like this. But he needed no Glimpse to realize what had happened, and that was the reason for his sense of triumph. He'd never expected, never dreamed, that anything like this might occur, but the Emperor in him recognized instantly how valuable it could prove.

Stop that, Zindel! he scolded himself. *Just this once stand here and be glad for someone without thinking about how what's happened to them can help you do your damned* job! *Besides, you've never seen Alazon look happier in her life.*

"Voice Kinlafia," he said, walking towards the Voice with his hand once more extended. The footman who had ushered Kinlafia into the chamber looked moderately shocked, but it was important to Zindel that this evening be placed firmly on a non-state-occasion basis as quickly as possible.

"Your Majesty," Kinlafia responded, and gripped the extended hand with rather more aplomb than he'd shown the first time Zindel had held it out to him. "I'm honored by the invitation," the Voice continued. "And

I'd be even more honored if you could see your way to using my first name."

"Oh, I think I can see my way clear to doing that," Zindel assured him, then turned and extended his free hand to the tallish, early-middle-aged woman standing beside him. She was an extraordinarily handsome woman, with the very first frosting of silver just beginning to touch her hair, and despite her height, she looked petite and delicate as she stood beside the Emperor in a simple little gown which even Kinlafia recognized had probably cost thousands of marks.

"Darcel Kinlafia," the Emperor said, "my wife, Varena. Varena, my love, this is Voice Kinlafia."

The footman who'd looked moderately shocked at Zindel's informal greeting to Kinlafia looked as if he'd dislocated his plunging jaw this time, the Emperor noted with a fair degree of pleasure. The Hawkwing Palace staff were accustomed to his often deplorably casual private manners. Many of them even recognized that his deliberate informality on private occasions was one of the ways he maintained his sanity during the endless *nonprivate* occasions to which he and his family were subjected. The expanded staff here in Calirath Palace were still figuring that out, and some of them were clearly scandalized by it all.

Well, it's just as well if they start getting used to it early, he thought. *I'm too old and set in my ways to change now. Besides, maintaining my sanity probably just got a lot harder.*

* * *

"Voice Kinlafia."

Janaki had obviously gotten his physique from his father's side of the family, Kinlafia decided, yet as he looked into the prince's mother's eyes, he saw an echo of Janaki's enduring patience. He could readily envision Janaki matching Zindel's famous Conclave outburst about the "godsdamned fish," but the patience which had taken the Crown Prince through Kinlafia's debriefing again and again . . . that had come from his mother. Darcel Kinlafia never doubted for a moment that Zindel chan Calirath would have been just as thorough, have taken just as much time, just as many pains, had that task fallen to him instead of his son. But Janaki's gently supportive sympathy, even as he forced Kinlafia to relive every horrible moment of Shaylar's last Voice message, had owed as much to his mother's compassion as to his father's iron sense of duty.

"Your Majesty," he replied now, and bent over the hand she extended. New Farnalians didn't spend as much time kissing ladies' hands as some, but Kinlafia's training—both as a Voice, and from the Portal Authority—had included the rudiments of courtesy from virtually all of Sharona's major civilizations. His instructors might never have anticipated that he would someday find himself kissing a hand quite as exalted as this one, and they might not have included the proper modalities for being privately introduced to the Emperor of Sharona, but they *had* covered this, at least, he reflected with profound gratitude.

<*She's really a very nice person who wouldn't dream of having your head cut off just because you didn't kiss her hand properly,*> Alazon's deep, rich Voice murmured in the back of his brain.

<*Really? What a relief!*> he replied as he straightened and met the empress' eyes.

"I'm very pleased to meet you . . . Darcel," Varena

said. "I wish that the events which have turned all of our lives on end over the last few months had never happened, of course. But everything I've read and heard tells me how very fortunate we were to have you out there at Hell's Gate. I only regret," her voice and eyes alike softened, "that you were forced to endure so much sorrow and pain for the rest of us."

"Your Majesty," he told her, "what happened to my friends—and to me, I suppose—had nothing to do with anyone except the people who killed them."

"Perhaps not," she acknowledged. "Yet the fact remains that you were the one who got Voice Nargra-Kolmayr's message to all of us. And so, however it was that that duty fell to you, the fact remains that all of us are deeply, deeply in your debt."

"And about to become more deeply so," Zindel put in briskly. Kinlafia and the empress both turned their heads to look at him, and he chuckled. "Darcel *is* a Voice, my dear. I think you're about to find that he's brought you more than just letters from Janaki."

"But I—" Varena began, only to pause as Kinlafia gently squeezed the hand he was still holding.

"Your Majesty, I realize you aren't a telepath yourself. That's one reason I asked if Privy Voice Yanamar might join us this evening, as well, when I discovered that she was a Projective, as well as a Voice."

<"One *reason?*"> a musical Voice rippled through his thoughts. <*I like that!*>

<*Hush woman!*> he replied. <*It's not only diplomatic, it's even true.*>

"I hadn't realized you were aware of that," Zindel told him dryly. "It isn't exactly something we've announced to the world in general."

"Oh, I've become aware of quite a few things about the Privy Voice, Your Majesty," Kinlafia assured him.

"Good. And, if I may be permitted to touch upon just a bit of official business after all, have you and Alazon gotten your schedule squared away for that never-to-be-sufficiently-damned parade we're all going to have to endure tomorrow afternoon?"

"We have, Your Majesty," Alazon replied for Kinlafia. "Mind you, I think the tailors left Darcel in a state of shock."

"Really?" Zindel's eyes twinkled, and Kinlafia shrugged.

"Your Majesty, I hope you won't mind my saying that I've never seen such a ridiculous looking outfit in my entire life. I couldn't believe they were serious when they showed me the pattern sketches!"

"After five thousand years, court fashion has tried out pretty much all the variations," Zindel said. "There's not much new they can do to us, so they have these periodic spasms of 'historical inspiration' when they go back and reinterpret famous periods of the past. If I remember correctly, the inspiration for our current . . . costumes was the period of Wailyana the Great. Which, if you're familiar with your Ternathian history, was just over nine hundred years ago. Of course, according to my own research, *Wailyana's* tailors were inspired by the Time of Conquest, which technically ended about six hundred years before *her* time."

Kinlafia looked into the Emperor's eyes. For a moment, he was certain Zindel had to be putting him on, but—

<Oh, no, he isn't,> Alazon Told him. *<There are some disadvantages to being the descendents of the*

oldest imperial dynasty in Sharonian history, you know.>

"I hadn't realized their . . . lineage was quite so distinguished, Your Majesty," he told Zindel. "And I hope I'm not going to poke anyone's eye out with that ridiculous rapier Privy Voice Yanamar insists that I really do have to wear. But, to be totally honest, what truly astounded me was their promise to have the entire outfit ready for final fitting before lunch tomorrow."

"Our staff, unfortunately, has had entirely too much experience meeting impossible deadlines, I'm afraid," Empress Varena said with a slight smile. "Mind you, we take shameless advantage of that experience!"

"Yes, we do," her husband agreed. "In fact, I—"

Zindel broke off as a side door opened to admit the imperial daughters. Kinlafia turned towards the new arrivals, one eyebrow rising, then, for the second time in a single day, froze as if he'd just been punched squarely between the eyes.

He recognized all of them. He would have been able to put names with faces just on the basis of all of the recent newspaper coverage. Gods knew their photographs and sketches had been everywhere in the papers he'd been devouring ever since he'd reached civilized universes once more! But this wasn't simply a matter of identifying them from their pictures. He *recognized* them.

Anbessa, the youngest. The willful, eleven-year-old, golden-haired whirlwind of energy. A little terror, with all of her family's determination but without the rough edges-smoothing experience of maturity. Who, if she'd only realized, held her father's heart in her often grubby little hands.

Razial, the middle daughter. Dark-haired, like her father, but without the golden highlights. Taller than Anbessa, at fifteen, with the awkward coltishness of adolescence and all the tempestuous passion of her raging hormones, all undergirt with an astounding sensitivity and gifted ear for the beauty of language. The painter whose landscapes decorated her father's study wall, and the daughter whose desk drawer was stuffed with poetry which could have made a statue laugh or a boulder weep.

And Andrin. Tall, quiet Andrin, of the unquiet, knowledge-shadowed sea-gray eyes of her father and her brother. Of the gold-shot black hair of the Caliraths and the haunted soul of the Calirath Talent. Of the sword-straight spine. Andrin, who never recognized the grace of her own carriage, the strength and character already so plain for those with eyes or Talent to see, despite her youth.

Andrin . . . whose presence reached out and took Darcel Kinlafia by the throat.

He stood there, unable to move, while the images roared through him. Andrin, standing tall and straight, face white and strained with grief but with eyes that flashed defiance, as she faced tier upon tier of seated men and women in a magnificent chamber somewhere which Kinlafia had never seen. Andrin, weeping like a broken child. Andrin alight with laughter, launching a falcon from her wrist like an ivory thunderbolt. Andrin, in a torn gown, with a smoking revolver in her hand and murder in her eyes. Andrin, standing before the high priests of the Triad as she laid her hand upon the *Book of the Double-Three* to swear some high and solemn oath.

They ripped through his mind, those images, those visions. None of them had happened yet, and yet he knew—he *knew*—that every single one would come inevitably to pass. And as he Saw them, he Saw himself. Saw himself with his arms about her, holding her as she sobbed upon his shoulder. Saw himself standing at *her* shoulder. She was older now, and she turned to look at him, her eyes grim, as he passed her a document of some sort. He Saw himself recognizing in her a daughter. Not simply the daughter of Zindel and Varena Calirath, but *his* daughter. The daughter of his heart, as surely as if she had been born of his own flesh and bone.

This is why Janaki wanted him here!

The thought flared like an explosion, and in that instant, Darcel Kinlafia realized what was happening. This knowledge, those visions, those recognitions, weren't his. Or, rather, they weren't *solely* his. In that chaotic, stunned instant, he knew precisely what it was to have the Calirath Talent, for in that moment, he shared it with the Emperor of Ternathia. It was *Zindel's* vision, his recognition of his daughters, roaring through Kinlafia's Voice Talent, like a flash of lightning bridging the gap between two pylons of the Ylani Strait suspension bridge.

And in that recognition, Kinlafia discovered the true curse of the Calirath Talent. For all their clarity, all the iron certitude that they would someday come to pass, those visions were isolated from one another. There was no continuity, no thread to tie them together, to tell him *why* Andrin wept, or who she stood to face in such splendid defiance. No calendar to tell him when he handed her that document, or where, or why.

Kinlafia stood there for an eternity, frozen, realizing that he'd been right to suspect that Janaki had more reasons than he'd shared for sending him to Tajvana. And he also realized why Janaki hadn't shared those other reasons. Not out of dishonesty, not out of any intent to deceive or mislead, but because without this moment of fusion, Kinlafia could not possibly have understood any explanation Janaki might have offered.

And then, as abruptly as it had struck, the moment of almost unendurable vision ended. Ended in the tick between one second and the next. That was all the time it had truly taken—no longer than the time between two heartbeats—to change Darcel Kinlafia's life and future forever.

He blinked, and the world about him flashed back into focus. He sensed Alazon's concern and realized that even though she hadn't shared the vision of Zindel's Glimpse, she'd Felt its impact upon him. He wanted to tell her not to worry, that everything was all right. But he couldn't, because he didn't know if things *were* "all right" . . . or if they ever would be again. All he knew was the way things had to be.

And it was knowledge that only he and Zindel shared. Knowledge which could not be—*must* not be—shared with anyone else. Especially not with Andrin. Not yet. Perhaps never.

"And these are our daughters," he heard Zindel chan Calirath's deep, calm voice say. "Girls, come meet Voice Kinlafia. I suspect—" Kinlafia turned his head and looked into those steady gray, Calirath eyes with their burden of ghosts yet to come "—that we'll be seeing quite a bit of him in the future."

CHAPTER TWELVE

ERTHEK VARDAN TIPPED his chair back. He balanced it on its rear legs, with the top of its back braced against the wall, while he held the book tilted so that the ceiling-hung kerosene lamp's light spilled over the pages.

The wall behind him was made of logs notched and laid into place, then chinked with clay. It was rough and ready looking, but it was also solid and, like the steeply-pitched rain-shedding roof, it was definitely weatherproof. The weather was still warm enough that the fire crackling on the hearth wasn't really needed for heat, yet it was a welcome relief against the omnipresent, damp chill. Coupled with the sound of rain pattering against the roof overhead, it produced an oasis of welcoming comfort which was almost enough to make a man forget that he'd been stationed at the ragged edge of the known multiverse.

Personally, Erthek wasn't likely to be that forgetful.

Grateful as he was for the stout roof and the fire, he missed things like the theater, hot baths that didn't have to be laboriously heated, bucket-by-bucket, and restaurants. No one would have called him a hedonist, but he hadn't quite counted on conditions this primitive when he volunteered for three years' Portal Authority service as a way to earn money for college.

Still, he knew he'd been lucky, in a horrid sort of way, to have drawn this particular posting at this particular time.

What had happened to the Chalgyn Consortium's survey crew was horrible, but the PAAF had shown these "Arcanan" barbarians that they didn't want to confront Sharonian *soldiers*, whatever they might have done to a surprised, vastly outnumbered party of civilians.

Erthek himself was no soldier, of course. In fact, he was a civilian employee of the Portal Authority on his very first assignment. He was also less than twenty-one years old, and he suspected that he'd been originally earmarked for this particular relay post because his superiors figured that he, unlike some old fogy in his thirties, had the youthful resilience to survive it. Or it might be simpler than that. In fact, it almost certainly was. After all, he was probably the most junior Voice in the Authority's employ, and when he'd first been assigned to Thermyn, no one had had any reason to suspect the existence of Hell's Gate, far less what was going to happen on its other side. At that point, this had simply been what had to have been the least desirable Voice posting of them all, so it had made sense to hand it to the most junior Voice of them all.

But the choice to assign him here had virtually guaranteed Erthek's later career. No one was going to forget his part in passing the critical message traffic from Hell's Gate back and forth along the Voicenet. Erthek Vardan was going into the history books, and wasn't that an amazing thing? The notion amused him, and yet there was something else under the amusement. A hard, vengeful something that found grim satisfaction in serving as one of Sharona's messengers in the confrontation with the murderers of Shaylar Nargra-Kolmayr and her companions.

He'd never expected to find himself doing something *that* important this early in his Authority service. And, truth to tell, he was grateful that Petty-Captain Waird chan Lyrosk had finally reached Fort Brithik. Chan Lyrosk was a Ternathian, on loan to the PAAF, which made him not simply senior to Erthek in the Authority's service, but an army officer, as well. Erthek knew he'd miss the independence he'd enjoyed as the only Voice available to Company-Captain chan Robarik, Fort Brithik's CO . . . but any disappointment on that side was more than outweighed by the relief he'd feel when someone else became officially responsible for this critical Voice relay tomorrow morning.

He grimaced at the thought, then looked up from his book at the clock ticking away on the mantelpiece. A fresh gust of raindrops pattered noisily across the roof and made him even more grateful for the fire of split logs. But under his gratitude, there was a growing flicker of concern. It certainly wasn't anything strong enough to call *fear*, but it was more than simple uneasiness. There hadn't been anything scheduled, but it was unusual for a full day to pass without any Voice transmission from Shansair Baulwan. If nothing else, Shansair usually made a conscientious effort to tell Erthek when he was shutting down for the evening so that Erthek could shut down himself, instead of maintaining his Listening schedule.

Well, he told himself, *if I haven't Heard anything from him in the next hour and a half, then I'm just going to have to send him a message and ask if it's okay for me to go ahead and turn in. He ought to be able to Hear me, even if I can't Hear him without trancing. In the meantime . . . .*

One of the chickens in the hencoop built onto the side of the relay station stirred, clucking loudly as something disturbed it. Erthek listened for a moment—they'd had problems with a persistent bobcat, and he started to reach for the shotgun racked on the wall above him. But the hen in question sounded more querulous than frightened. An approaching bobcat would have led to something more strenuous, and Erthek chuckled. Probably that last gust of rain had blown in through the coop's wire side and the chicken was merely letting the world know how irritating it had found the experience.

Still, the sound was almost like a reminder, he thought, glancing at the clock once more. Then he slipped a bookmark between the pages of his novel, closed the book, and laid it in his lap as he closed his eyes and settled into the upper stages of a trained Voice's trance. It increased his sensitivity and extended his reception range considerably, and he reached out, Listening for all he was worth for any hint of transmission from Petty-Captain Baulwan. There was nothing, and he frowned slightly as he started to—

* * *

Commander of Fifty Iftar Halesak, CO, Second Platoon, Able Company, Second Andaran Temporal Scouts, moved through the wet, rainy dark with a serpent's silence. He hadn't asked for this assignment, but that was only because he hadn't known it would exist. And if he had known, he would have assumed it was the sort of thing Special Operations would have handled. Unfortunately, it would appear that Two Thousand Harshu was a bit short in the SpecOps department. No doubt the expeditionary force commander found that highly irritating, but Halesak didn't. He was too busy being fiercely glad that *he'd* gotten it to spare much sympathy for his commanding officer's dilemmas.

As an officer of the Second Andaran Scouts, Halesak would have wanted vengeance for what had happened to the Second Andarans' Charlie Company when the Sharonians massacred them, no matter what else might have happened. He'd known some of those men for upwards of ten years, and all of them had been his brothers in arms, his *family*. Indeed, one of those massacred men had been his brother-in-law. Yet there was a part of him that was almost ashamed by how little Charlie Company's complete destruction actually meant to him . . . compared to what else had happened. As one of the very few *garthan* officers in the Union Army, Iftar Halesak's heart filled with a white, blinding fury whenever he thought of the way the Sharonian butchers had shot down Magister Halathyn vos Dulainah as if he'd been no more than a stray dog.

Halesak hated the *shakira* and the entire perverted, vicious caste system they called a society with a pure and burning passion. He'd been luckier than many, because his father had possessed the determination and the courage to break free of Mythal before Iftar had ever been born. It was as well he had, too, for Iftar had been born with the Gift his father had not. It wasn't an especially powerful Gift, but it would have been enough, back in Mythal, for the *shakira* to have taken Iftar away from his parents and placed him with a *shakira* family to be raised.

But if Fifty Halesak and his two sisters had never personally lived under the crushing weight of *shakira* oppression, all too many other members of his family had, and so had his wife, when she'd been a child. And because those others who meant so much to him had, he'd understood on a deep, emotional level what all too many of his fellow Andaran citizens grasped only intellectually. He'd understood that Mythal's chosen society wasn't simply wrong, it was *evil*. Which meant he'd understood just how special Halathyn vos Dulainah had truly been. What it had taken for the man whose Gift and intellect had made him the crowning jewel of the *shakira*'s magic-wielding establishment to turn his back on all of the power, prestige, privilege, and family prominence which had been his simply because his own fierce sense of right and wrong had left him no choice.

In his entire life, Iftar Halesak had never personally known a single *shakira* worth the effort to snuff out his miserable life. But every *garthan* had known of Halathyn vos Dulainah and the way he had made their cause his own. And now that man had been slaughtered. There was not a *garthan* in any Arcanan-claimed universe who would ever forgive these "Sharonians" for that, and Fifty Halesak knew he carried all of those other *garthan*'s hopes, desires, and anger with him as he made his careful, quiet way through the darkness.

He and his men had spent the last twenty-one hours hidden in the sopping wet trees around the Voice's cabin's clearing. They'd had to be cautious, of course, but it really hadn't been that great a challenge for someone with the Andaran Scouts' training. Now, if everything went according to plan, Able Company *first* platoon was about to hit the next Voice relay *after* Fort Brithik at this same, exact moment.

He eased to a halt, raising his left arm to signal the other men of his platoon, as a chicken clucked loudly from the coop beside the relay station. He stood waiting patiently in the breezy rain, despite the fire blazing within him, until the noisy fowl had settled back again. It didn't take very long, and he used the time comparing what he'd seen with his own eyes so far to the briefing Five Hundred Neshok had provided. It was amazing how accurate the five hundred's information had turned out to be, he thought, and then, as the chicken quieted, he started forward once more.

The daggerstone in his hand seemed absurdly light in comparison to the dragoon arbalest he normally carried. Many Gifted Arcanan soldiers carried daggerstones as personal, backup weapons, but they were seldom used offensively. They were too short-ranged for normal battlefield use, and if they were loaded with fireballs—the most common spell loading—they weren't exactly precision weapons. Most troopers considered getting caught in the fringe of their own fireballs to be a Bad Thing, after all. Besides, they were too readily detected, too likely to betray a man's position to any Gifted adversary, to be carried on most scouting or covert operations. But he'd already determined that the log-built relay station had no windows to let out any betraying flashes of light, and worries about detectability didn't loom so large against murderous barbarians who hadn't even known magic existed three months before, he told himself with a thin smile.

He and his point squad reached the front of the relay building. He really should have delegated this particular task to his platoon sword, he knew, and perhaps he would the next time. But not tonight. Oh, no, not tonight.

He took time for one more quick, sweeping glance around. Then he laid his left hand on the door latch and drew a deep breath. The door was unlocked, the latch turned easily under his hand, and he slammed forward, driving his shoulder into the heavy wooden panel. It exploded open, and he erupted into the room beyond it.

According to Five Hundred Neshok's information, there were only three men permanently housed in this relay station, and only one of them was a Voice. Halesak had expected that information to prove as accurate as everything else Neshok had told him, but he hadn't expected to come face-to-face with the Voice so quickly. For a moment, he refused to believe he had, that things could possibly have gone *that* well. But then he saw the bronze falcon badge on the other man's civilian tunic.

* * *

Erthek Vardan's head jerked up, and his eyes snapped open. He had no idea what was happening. He didn't even know the origin of the sound which had yanked him so brutally up out of his light trance.

Nor did he ever find out.

His eyes might have opened, but they still hadn't focused when Iftar Halesak raised his daggerstone and triggered the first of its stored spells. The spell ripped across the relay station's main room in a bar of quasi-solid lightning. It struck Erthek square in the chest, and his heart and lungs literally exploded inside the ribs which had been no protection at all against that spell.

He was dead before he ever truly saw the man killing him.

* * *

Acrid, throat-catching smoke still poured up into the early morning sky from the smoldering ruins of the Sharonian fort which had once guarded the portal between New Uromath and Thermyn as the first Sharonian prisoners were hustled back across into New Uromath.

Alivar Neshok stood outside the captured Voice relay station, watching critically, and hoped his strategy for crippling the Sharonian Voices' ability to warn their superiors had continued to work as effectively as he'd assured Two Thousand Harshu it would. So far, at least, things seemed to be going well, and he intended to keep it that way.

He wasn't positive, but he strongly suspected that someone had probably complained to Thousand Carthos or Thousand Toralk about his methods by now. Five Hundred Vaynair, for example, had made his own feelings about those methods abundantly clear to Neshok. But if the medical officer had taken his protests higher, as Neshok was virtually certain he had, they'd clearly fallen upon deaf ears.

More likely, someone told the asshole to take a hike, Neshok told himself with a certain undeniable smugness.

But his satisfaction faded back into concentration as his assigned troopers kicked and prodded the newest batch of captured Sharonians back through the portal. There were more prisoners this time. Fort Brithik had boasted a larger garrison, and more of them had been indoors, under cover, when the attack came in. For that matter, Two Thousand Harshu had decided to take a chance on Neshok's success to date. The expeditionary force had taken the defenders totally by surprise, thanks to Fifty Halesak's successful neutralization of the Voice on the New Uromath side of the portal.

In theory, the next relay station *beyond* Brithik had also been reached and neutralized. That was a little more problematical, though, because Neshok's interrogations hadn't been able to fix that station's position with the same degree of accuracy. Still, they'd known approximately where to look, and under the circumstances, Neshok had felt justified in urging Thousand Toralk to forgo the yellows' attack in this instance. As Neshok had pointed out, there wasn't supposed to be a Voice inside the fort at all, and they needed still more prisoners. And even if it turned out that there was a Voice inside Fort Brithik after all, the next link in the Voice chain had almost certainly been successfully severed. The thousand obviously didn't much like Neshok, but he'd had to admit that this was probably their best chance to secure a sizable number of prisoners for future interrogation.

So the battle dragons had come sweeping down out of the darkness and filled the night with fury. Even without the yellows' poisonous vapors, the reds had killed well over two-thirds of Fort Brithik's garrison. That still left the next best thing to a hundred and sixty fresh prisoners, however, and Neshok was determined to get them back to the other side of the portal before any Voices among them could contact anyone else if it should turn out that he was wrong about whether or not the Voice network had already been severed up-chain from them.

If that arrogant little bitch had been telling the truth about portals cutting off Voice transmissions the same way they affected spells, then any Voice they got back to New Uromath should—theoretically, at least—be effectively silenced.

As if the little slut would've told the truth about anything *if she'd had a choice! Hells, I wouldn't believe her if she told me the sun was going to rise in the east tomorrow morning! That frigging idiot Olderhan can believe whatever he wants about his precious* "shardonai," *but I'm not going to risk the security of this entire expeditionary force on his fucking stupidity!*

His lip curled contemptuously at the thought of the commander of one hundred whose utter and complete incompetence had created this entire war. Then he shook himself and started grimly forward to where his subordinates were sorting out the prisoners on this side of the portal.

"Five Hundred!" Javelin Porath barked, snapping to attention as Neshok appeared out of the predawn dimness, and the Intelligence officer smiled.

Porath had continued to demonstrate a consistent enthusiasm, as well as ability, ever since that first session at Fort Shaylar. Several of the men who'd been assigned to Neshok had turned out quite well, actually, although there'd been a few disappointments. But Porath was the very best of the lot, and the acting five hundred already had the javelin earmarked for a formal transfer to Intelligence, where his talents could be most effectively utilized.

"As you were, Lisaro," he said now.

"Yes, Sir!" the javelin acknowledged.

"And what do we have here?" Neshok continued, folding his hands behind him as he turned to survey the fresh clutch of shocked, bewildered prisoners. Most of them were only partially dressed, since they'd been in bed when the attack hammered over them, but a few wore more or less complete uniforms. No doubt they'd had the duty . . . or been about to go *on* duty, he thought. Now all of them looked back at him, with the mixture of defiance and fear with which he'd become increasingly familiar.

"Well, Sir," Porath said, "I'm afraid I did find this."

He held out his hand, and Neshok frowned as he took the small, bronze falcon pin. For just a moment, his belly tightened as he realized the information from his previous interrogations hadn't been completely accurate, after all. He looked down at it, weighing it in his palm for a moment or two, then snorted. He'd already known the Sharonians were scrambling to push the necessary personnel forward as quickly as possible. Apparently, they'd managed to get at least some of those personnel *almost* into position in time.

"I don't suppose you found someone actually wearing it, did you, Javelin?" he asked, smiling thinly.

"No, Sir. But I *did* find it—or, rather, one of my troopers found it—on the trail between here and the fort."

"Which would tend to suggest that someone took it off and tried to lose it, is that what you're saying, Javelin?" Neshok inquired genially.

"Yes, Sir. That's exactly what I think happened."

"Well, I'm inclined to agree with you." Neshok tossed the pin into the air and caught it two or three times, then turned to face the prisoners directly.

"I'm perfectly well aware of what this means," he said through the translation spellware, holding up the pin. "At least one of you is what your people call a 'Voice.' I want to know how many of you are, and who you are."

No one responded, and Neshok bared his teeth. Whoever the Voice—or Voices—might be, he was clearly a quicker thinker than most. He couldn't have known what technique Neshok had developed for dealing with his kind, but he'd obviously recognized at least the possibility that the Arcanans might have figured out what that little bronze pin meant.

"I've asked pleasantly once," the acting five hundred said. "I'm not going to ask politely again."

Still no one responded, and Neshok's smile grew a bit broader. On the one hand, assuming Shaylar *had* been anything remotely like truthful, the hidden Voice had been neutralized by the simple act of bringing him to this side of the portal. On the other hand, Shaylar had probably been lying about anything she thought she could get away with. Which, given Olderhan's stupidity, had probably been just about everything. And even if she hadn't been lying about that, Neshok wasn't exactly brokenhearted by the opportunity to begin creating the proper psychological impact.

Besides, his encounter with her hadn't exactly left him feeling very well inclined towards *other* Voices.

"Javelin Porath?" he said, and held out his hand.

Porath handed him one of the hand weapons—the "revolvers"—which had been captured from the enemy. Neshok didn't much like the thing. The recoil was painful (and, little though he liked admitting it, frightening), and he'd found it very difficult to adjust to the incredible noisiness and brilliant flash when it was fired. Still, he'd forced himself to acquire at least some proficiency with it—although, in his more honest moments, he rather doubted that he could have expected to hit anything at much more than arm's length—because he'd wanted a weapon his prisoners were going to recognize as such. Now he nodded to Porath, and the javelin reached out and grabbed a randomly selected prisoner by the front of his tunic. With his hands manacled behind him, the Sharonian had no choice but to stumble forward, and Porath hauled him over to Neshok.

"Would the Voice care to identify himself now?" the Intelligence officer inquired, pressing the muzzle of the captured weapon against the prisoner's temple and cocking it.

Still no one spoke, and Neshok shrugged.

"Suit yourself," he said softly, and squeezed the trigger.

It was the first time he'd actually used a "revolver" for its designed function. The recoil was as unpleasant as ever, but he'd allowed for that. What he *hadn't* quite allowed for was the way the prisoner's head *splashed* as the heavy bullet blew it apart. Blood and bits of tissue erupted across Neshok, but he managed not to flinch as the corpse flipped backwards and thudded to the ground.

The other Sharonians stared at him. Clearly, they hadn't believe he'd actually shoot one of them in cold blood.

Well, he thought, *at least we've established now that I will. That's worthwhile in its own right.*

"Would the Voice care to reconsider his position?" he asked, watching Porath choose yet another prisoner, once more at random.

The second Sharonian stumbled forward, his face white and strained. He tried to dig his heels in, but without the use of his hands, resistance was ultimately futile. Porath dragged him over to stand where the first prisoner had died, and Neshok pressed the muzzle against his head, in turn.

"Wait!" a Sharonian voice called.

Neshok turned his head, quirking one eyebrow, and gazed interrogatively at the speaker. The Sharonian looked to be a bit older than most of the prisoners, and he wore only a sleeveless undershirt of some sort above the waist, which meant he wasn't displaying any rank insignia. But there was something about his eyes—a hard, challenging something, like the eyes of that wiry little senior-armsman back at Fort Shaylar.

"I'm the Voice," the Sharonian said.

"Are you?" Neshok considered the other man for a moment, then shrugged and beckoned the one Porath had chosen back in among the others. "Come here."

The man who'd identified himself walked across to face Neshok.

"So, you're the Voice?"

"Yes," the Sharonian said, but Neshok shook his head and held up his personal crystal. A bright red light strobed down inside it, and the Intelligence officer sighed.

"I'm afraid you're not," he said. "This is a truth spell. And according to it, you've just lied to me."

"I don't care what your rock says," the prisoner replied. "You wanted the Voice. You've got me."

"Yes, I have, but you're *not* a Voice. And I've decided I don't like people who lie to me."

The second shot was just as noisy as the first one, and the second Sharonian fell diagonally across the body of the first.

"We can keep this up as long as you like," Neshok told the remaining prisoners, and nodded to Porath again.

"That won't be necessary," another Sharonian said. His face was hard with hatred, and he stepped forward on his own. "I'm the Voice."

Neshok looked at him for a moment, then glanced down at his PC again. This time, the crystal showed no flashing red, and he nodded slightly.

"And would you happen to be the *only* Voice?" he asked calmly, still watching the crystal.

"As far as I know, I'm the only one still alive, at any rate," the Voice said harshly, and once again the crystal remained clear.

"And who would this fellow have been?" Neshok said, nodding his head at the second dead man.

"Company-Captain chan Robarik," the Voice grated, and Neshok just managed not to curse. Just his luck. They'd actually managed to take the fort's commanding officer alive, only to have him get himself killed out of sheer stupidity.

"It's too bad *you* didn't step forward soon enough to keep him alive," he told the Voice.

"No Sharonian made you pull that trigger," the Voice said.

"You may have a point," Neshok conceded, then cocked his head. "Tell me, is it true that no Voice can communicate with another one *through* a portal?"

"Of course it is," the Sharonian replied.

"So you all keep telling me, and I suppose I have to believe you," Neshok said, glancing back down at his PC once more. "Still, it's probably best not to take any chances, don't you think?"

The Voice only glared at him, and Neshok shrugged. Then he raised the revolver again.

"Now," he told the other prisoners a moment later,

his own voice sounding strangely far away and tinny through the ringing in his ears, "I trust the rest of you will see the wisdom of answering my questions promptly and thoroughly. If you don't—" he looked down at the three bodies sprawled grotesquely across the ground "—I'm afraid I'm going to have to reload, aren't I?"

CHAPTER THIRTEEN

THE PARADE, KINLAFIA decided, was going to be just as incredibly gaudy as the Emperor had promised.

And my own modest appearance definitely contributes to the overall gaudiness.

He looked down at the sleeve of his coat and grimaced. The skintight trousers—only the tailors and the incredibly polite (if not overly impressed) valet had told him they were properly called "pantaloons"—looked (and felt) as if they'd been sprayed on. He could see why that style had gone out of fashion so many centuries ago; what he *couldn't* see was what lunacy had ever brought it back *into* fashion. At least the rigorous lifestyle of a Portal Authority Voice assigned to survey duty had kept him reasonably fit . . . unlike some of the courtiers and politicians, who looked remarkably like sausages stuffed into too-tight skins.

The boots weren't *too* bad, although he'd had no time to break them in properly and the gilded tassels with the diamond sets were a bit much. Then there was the single, elaborately engraved silver spur mounted on his right heel. And the full-sleeved silk shirt with enough ruffles and lace to have made him look like an irritated pigeon if not for the coat's confinement. Ah, yes, the coat. The thing had to weigh at least thirty pounds, and at least half that poundage was consumed by the layer upon layer of scallop-cut silk fluttering from his shoulders. Alazon had informed him that they were properly called "capelets," and he supposed he could understand why they were. Why anyone wanted to waste that much perfectly good—and hideously expensive—fabric on them was something else, however.

And then, as the crowning touch, there was the rapier. The never-to-be-sufficiently-damned rapier. Not only was the accursed thing a good four feet long, but it was also a genuine, tempered steel blade which dragged at his left side like an anchor and waggled around behind him like . . . like . . .

Actually, he couldn't think of a good way to describe it, he decided disgustedly. He didn't know enough cuss words.

One of the things he'd liked best about his survey crew duties was the fact that he'd never had to worry about formal clothing very much out in the wilderness. Sturdy denim trousers, boots, and a serviceable shirt—plus, of course, the pistol belt which was an essential fashion accessory—pretty much took care of the sartorial problem. Not only that, it kept him from feeling like a circus clown.

Unfortunately, his normal outfits would have been completely unacceptable today. Which, in his considered opinion, said something unhealthy about the mentality of high-fashion designers. But he was trapped on their turf, and his total lack of experience left him with no option but to rely entirely on the judgment of others. It was, he'd discovered, an uncomfortable feeling. Fortunately, he'd had Alazon to look out for him, and he had to admit that the tawny, almost amber-colored silk she'd chosen for his ridiculous coat was just as striking with the black "pantaloons" and gleaming boots as she and the imperial tailors had promised it would be. Now if only he could figure out what to do with the elaborate fall of capelets, the ridiculous rapier, and the ludicrous confection of silk, fur trim, sequins, and feathers which shared some distant ancestor with a Bernithian Highland bonnet.

<*Oh, come now, Darcel!*> a richly melodious Voice laughed. <*It's not* that *bad. Besides,*> the Voice turned suddenly more serious, with an undertone of warmth and a pleasant, furry little edge of desire, <*unlike most of these poor people, you've actually got the physique and the coloring for it. In fact, you're probably the best looking male present.*>

<*I'm glad you think so,*> he replied. <*Even if it does just go to prove how hopelessly biased you are in my case.*>

<*Nonsense. Oh, I'm sure I am biased, but you're not exactly the best judge of your own handsomeness, either. I believe the exact phrase I'm looking for is "You clean up pretty." Besides, you've got a really nice backside, and those pantaloons show it off so well!*>

He snorted a laugh and shook his head.

<*Where are you?*>

<*We're just coming down now,*> she assured him, and he turned towards the stair behind him.

Alazon's position as Zindel's political chief of staff had turned her into a sort of auxiliary parade marshal.

She'd been incredibly busy with last-minute details all morning, although two Voices could at least manage to keep track of one another much better than other people might have. In fact, Kinlafia had discovered that he always knew exactly where Alazon was, just as she knew where he was. That was one aspect of the bond which had leapt upon them so unexpectedly that had surprised them both. Indeed, both of them were still just a bit bemused by its strength and depth, and he knew it was going to take a *lot* of getting used to.

Kinlafia had always envied his married friends for the strength of their marriage bond. The one between Jathmar and Shaylar had been particularly rich, as any Voice would have recognized. But he already knew the one between him and Alazon would be even deeper, even more richly textured, for *both* of them were Voices, and he felt a tiny stab of something that was almost guilt as he thought about his murdered friends. It seemed . . . wrong, somehow, that their deaths had brought him and Alazon together.

<I never met Shaylar or Jathmar, love,> Alazon Said gently. *<But I did See and Hear the message you relayed from her. You may not realize just how much side trace came along with it, from both of you. Trust me. People you loved that much—and who loved you that much—would never begrudge us our happiness.>*

<I never said I was a particularly rational person,> he Told her.

< No, I've noticed that about you. You do *appear to do things rather . . . impulsively, don't you?>*

<Only when it comes to falling in love with beautiful women.>

He Heard her mental gurgle of laughter and smiled. But then the smile vanished as she appeared at the top of the stair.

<*My gods. You* are *beautiful.*>

She paused in midstride, her head coming up, and he saw the color rising to her cheeks.

<*How did someone that nearsighted get approved for survey crew duty?*>

<*I'll have you know my vision is perfect, My Lady,*> he replied as lightly as he could when his heart seemed to have soared into his throat.

She shook her head and continued down the stair to him, and he never even saw Ulantha Jastyr or the other four people with her.

Whatever idiot had set the rules for designing male apparel for Empress Wailyana, someone else had obviously been in charge of designing female fashions. Or perhaps the empress had simply kept lopping off heads until she got a designer she liked. However it had happened, Darcel Kinlafia, for one, wholeheartedly approved the result.

Alazon was gowned in a deep, rich green which perfectly complemented her midnight hair and dusky-ivory complexion. It was an off-the-shoulder design, which emphasized her upthrust bosom and drew attention to her shapely shoulders and long, slender neck. A beautiful emerald necklace, with matching earrings and bracelet, glittered in the sunlight, the floor-length skirt was light and flowing enough to swirl around her long, shapely legs whenever she moved, and the gown was cut to highlight her tiny waist. Golden combs, set with more small emeralds, swept her hair back in a coiffure which managed to be simultaneously formal and yet gracefully natural, unlike most of the far more elaborate confections Kinlafia had already seen.

She reached the final step and crossed the marble palace sidewalk to him, holding out both hands. He took them, and discovered that the high heels of her court shoes canceled the usual difference in their heights. He found himself gazing deep into her gray eyes . . . which, he realized, was a dangerous thing for him to be doing if they were going to keep to the parade's rigorously planned schedule.

"Your vision *can't* be anything remotely like perfect," she said, freeing one hand to reach up and touch him on the cheek. "Your *appearance*, on the other hand, is. Perfect, I mean."

"And you think I have problems with *my* eyes?" He shook his head, smiling. "And even if you think I 'clean up pretty,' you'd better be ready to give me some advice."

"What sort of advice?"

"Like telling me how in all the Arpathian hells I *walk* with this thing!" He indicated the long, thin rapier sheathed at his side. "I've already tangled myself up in it at least two dozen times, stabbed a hole in the upholstery, eviscerated a couch pillow, and sent two underfootmen to the infirmary."

"You *didn't*!" she laughed, eyes dancing.

"Well, I'm not *sure* about the underfootmen," he conceded. "They might have hobbled off to heal on their own somewhere. But there are feathers all over my apartment, if you don't believe I've heroically slain that dastardly pillow."

He smiled back at her, then shook his head.

"Seriously. How *do* people manage these things?"

"Oh, Darcel, you poor man. We don't have time for deportment lessons. Let me see . . . oh, dear. Hmmm . . . All right, when you walk, you have to keep your left arm sort of clamped, like this."

She touched his wrist to move his arm into position, and a pleasant tingle seemed to radiate from her fingers. One which both of them resolutely ignored . . . for the moment.

"There. You keep this arm cocked, and that contains the capelets . . . unless the wind gets up, at least." She smiled and reached up to twitch the multiple layers of silk into order. "Then this piece goes like so, over this shoulder." She adjusted the richly embroidered sword sling over his left shoulder. "That helps with the capelets, too, and lets you tuck the sword hilt under this chain and keep it out of the way. You'll just have to pay attention to where the end of the scabbard is behind you, I'm afraid."

"Lovely. I'll probably rap an empress or a duke or president across the knees. Better yet, I'll get it tangled between their ankles and send them sprawling. *That* should be an impressive start to this new political career of mine!"

She spluttered with laughter again, then shook her head.

"I'm sorry, Darcel. I don't mean to laugh at you. I mean, I *do*, but—" She shook her head again. "It's just that most of the courtiers positively preen on occasions like this. They can't wait to get into fancy costume and show it off. And Earl Ilforth makes preening in *his* finery a permanent pastime. That's why it's so refreshing to find someone who actually hates court dress as much as I do."

His eyes widened.

"Why in the multiverse would you hate wearing a gown that makes you look like a goddess?" he demanded, and her entire face flamed at his simple sincerity. Then she surprised him with a tart rejoinder.

"Because it weighs about sixty pounds, the corset is made of steel, these stiletto-heeled shoes pinch my feet and make my calves scream, and the trailing skirts and these ridiculous, yard-long sleeves tend to snag on things—like other people's swords, three thousand year-old statuary, and the occasional rosebush."

"Oh." It was his turn to laugh. "Oh, dear. How are we going to get through the day in these things?"

"By gritting our teeth, smiling, and thinking very hard about long, hot baths and witch hazel for the chafed spots and bruises."

"Bruises?"

"You don't want to know," she assured him. "I did mention that the corset is made out of steel, didn't I?" She gave him a bright smile. "Still, at least we both have the comfort of someone to commiserate with now. And, speaking of 'now,' we really must get moving. The marshal's reserved a place of honor for you."

She hadn't been joking about his position in the parade, he discovered when they arrived at the designated float. The bunting-draped vehicle, drawn by a beautifully matched pair of gray Shikowr geldings, was smaller than many of the others . . . but it was also sandwiched between those of the Portal Authority's first director and the imperial family.

And, unlike First Director Limana or the Emperor's family, he had *his* float all to himself.

He turned towards Alazon and opened his mouth, but she spoke before he could.

"First," she said firmly, "it's far too late for us to be changing the order of the parade now. You're stuck with this one. Second, it was First Director Limana's suggestion that you be assigned your own float, and I think his instincts were right. And third, His Majesty wants your political career properly launched. In other words, there's no way out, so you might as well just climb up there, smile, and pretend you like it."

He almost argued anyway. Fortunately, his own sense of the ridiculous came to his rescue before he completed the process of making a fool out of himself, and he bent his head in submission.

"Yes, ma'am," he said meekly.

"Good. Now, get!"

She made shooing motions with both hands, and after making certain he had the rapier throttled into at least temporary submission, he started obediently up the short, steep ladder.

He managed to make it to the top without killing himself or any innocent passersby, and settled himself into the surprisingly comfortable seat. For all intents and purposes, the thing Alazon had insisted upon calling a "float," was simply an unusually impractical and unstable carriage. Despite her assurances that even the two-wheeled floats like his "almost *never* fall over," Kinlafia felt more than a little insecure as he surveyed the world from his high perch. The fact that the float came equipped with a seat belt didn't exactly inspire him with confidence, either, although he felt profoundly grateful for its presence as he strapped himself securely in.

Once he was reasonably confident that he wasn't about to plummet to his doom, he drew a deep breath and looked around him at the assembling spectacle.

Since the still officially independent Kingdom of Othmaliz was this afternoon's host, the Othmalizi Army's marching band formed the parade's vanguard. A troop of the Seneschal's Own Dragoons followed, and was followed in turn by a company of Imperial Ternathian Marines, then a company of Uromathian infantry, one of Farnalian cavalry, and on and on.

The "floats" were interspersed among the marching and mounted formations, and the imperial family's was actually rather near the end of the entire procession. In fact, despite the ruler-straightness of Emperor Daerha Boulevard, the official parade route, Kinlafia (whose vision really was as good as he'd told Alazon it was) found it almost impossible to make out details of the leading formations simply because of the sheer distance involved.

The floats also varied widely in size. Kinlafia's was one of the smallest; the imperial family's was undoubtedly the largest. Where his had only two wheels and was towed by a single pair of Shikowrs, the Emperor's float was a six-wheeled, articulated wagon towed by an entire six-horse team of tall, black Chinthai. The massive draft animals, descended from ancient heavy cavalry mounts, were taller at the shoulder than Kinlafia, and their flowing manes and tails had been elaborately braided and threaded with silken streamers in the green and gold of the House of Calirath.

Zindel chan Calirath himself sat on a throne which rose considerably higher than Kinlafia's, although the broader vehicle at its base promised greater stability. At least, Kinlafia certainly hoped it did. The thought of watching the future Emperor of Sharona plunge to his doom from a parade float left a little something to be desired from a public relations viewpoint.

Empress Varena sat beside him, on an equally elevated throne, and all three of their daughters were grouped around them on thrones of their own. It was fairly obvious from where Kinlafia sat that young Anbessa wasn't exactly enthralled, but it was equally obvious that her mother had "reasoned" with her to good effect. Razial, on the other hand, seemed excited, eager for the spectacle to begin.

And then there was Andrin. Kinlafia gazed at her for several seconds, trying to gauge her emotions from the set of her shoulders, the angle of her head. He couldn't. And yet, he *could*.

He grimaced and shook his own head. Was he really interpreting her emotions correctly? Or did he just think he was? How much of what he *thought* she was feeling was real, and how much was simply an echo of that devastating moment in which he had shared the Emperor's Glimpse?

No one could claim that your life's been exactly boring for the last two or three months, Darcel, he told himself. *But the last thirty-six hours have to have established a new all-time record, even for you. A private audience with the Emperor, Alazon, an invitation to a quiet little supper with the entire imperial family, and then Her Imperial Highness Grand Princess Andrin.*

It didn't seem possible. Still, at least it had all come at him so quickly he hadn't really had time to come to grips with it. That was good, because he rather suspected that when he finally did have the opportunity to sit down and think about it, it was going to scare the holy living hells out of him. It was one thing to think about running for office, about the probably mundane career of a mere Parliamentary Representative. It was quite another to discover that he—Darcel Kinlafia, from a sleepy little university town in the pampas of New Farnal—had a fate which was somehow bound up with that of the heir-secondary to the Winged Crown of Ternathia . . . and now of all Sharona.

Somehow, he didn't think his life was *ever* going to be "boring" again.

* * *

Andrin made a soft, soothing sound to Finena as the falcon shifted uneasily on the back of her elaborate chair. The sound itself was all but inaudible against the surf of background voices, but the falcon didn't have to physically hear it to recognize it. Her head bent, and the razor-sharp beak stroked gently against the side of Andrin's neck. Then the bird straightened once again, standing proud and motionless on her perch.

The good news was that Finena had already endured a half-dozen parades back home in Ternathia. The bad news was that none of them had been even remotely like *this* one was going to be. The rumble of voices which was making Finena nervous came almost entirely from the Calirath Palace staff—of which, admittedly, there seemed to be somewhere in the vicinity of fourteen million, she thought wryly—and her family's personal retainers. Once they began moving out of the palace gates and down the formal parade route, and the thousands upon thousands of spectators began to cheer, it was going to get infinitely worse.

"There," she murmured, reaching up to stroke Finena's folded wings comfortingly. "There, love. If it gets too bad, you can always fly back to the Palace." She smiled crookedly. "I wish *I* could," she added.

Her father glanced at her as if he'd heard her. He

hadn't, of course—not as quietly as she'd spoken, and not through all the background noise. But he hadn't really had to. She'd realized, over the last several weeks, that her father actually knew her even better than she'd ever thought that he did. She'd never doubted his love, the time that he always somehow saved for his children. But since the disaster at Hell's Gate, he'd shown an almost terrifying awareness of what was inside her. What she felt, what she feared, what she dreamed of and about as all of them swept inexorably into the future. It was immensely comforting and simultaneously frightening, in an obscure sort of way.

Don't be silly, she scolded herself. *And don't be a coward, either. You* know *why it's scaring the daylights out of you!*

And she *did* know. It frightened her because she knew too much about the Calirath Talent. She knew how hard and fast the Glimpses were falling upon her father, because they were falling upon her, too. Yet there was one enormous difference between her Glimpses and his.

Those gifted—or cursed—with the Calirath Talent were not given the ability to Glimpse events in their own lives. There were times—many of them, in fact—when a Calirath's Glimpse *did* tell that person a great deal about what was going to happen to him or her. But even when that happened, there was almost always a . . . blind spot. A blankness. A cutout in the vision where the person whose Glimpse it was ought to have been and which kept him from Seeing himself, *his* actions . . . his fate. No one knew why that was, yet it was true. With one exception.

There was one Glimpse that *was* given to most of those who carried the activated Calirath Talent, and cold comfort it was. It was the Glimpse of their own violent deaths. Not in accidents, or of disease, because the Calirath Talent didn't work that way. A Glimpse revealed the consequences of *human* actions, human events, not the simple workings of fate or chance. That was one reason there'd been so few successful assassinations of Caliraths over the millennia. It was *hard* for a killer to sneak up on someone who was able to Glimpse the moment of his or her own murder, after all. Not impossible, as history had unfortunately demonstrated, but difficult.

Andrin wasn't concerned about her own impending demise. She was worried—deeply and desperately—over the continuous flickers of Glimpses about Janaki. She longed to be able to nail those down. To choke the truth out of them. But there were too many other people tied up in them, too much violence, too many images which made no *sense*.

Yet what frightened her even more than that was the possibility that her father's understanding, his obvious concern for her, meant he was Glimpsing something about *her* future that worried him deeply. She knew her father would face anything to protect her and her sisters. What frightened her was her growing suspicion that he was afraid of something not even he could protect her from.

And how does Voice Kinlafia figure in all of that? she wondered, turning to gaze back over her shoulder at the handsome, brown-haired man perched in the one-person float behind her. She knew he had to be scared to death. Triad knew there were enough butterflies dancing in *her* middle, and she'd been riding in parades like this since she was younger than Anbessa! But if he was anxious, he was concealing it well.

That was good. Andrin had already discovered how frequently famous or important people failed to to measure up to others' expectations. She couldn't say Kinlafia was exactly what she'd expected from the power and the anguish and the clarity of the Voice transmission SUNN had broadcast throughout all of Sharona. She'd expected someone taller, bigger than life, with a granite chin and piercing eyes.

What she'd gotten was a man who needed no steely jaw or granite chin. A man whose brown eyes were wounded, not piercing, yet still remained warm and compassionate. A man whose heart had taken savage wounds, yet refused to close inward upon its pain. A man who was not yet fully aware of his own strength. She wondered if she were catching just a faint echo of the Glimpse her father had obviously experienced when she and voice Kinlafia first came face-to-face.

I don't know you . . . yet, she thought, glancing back over her shoulder at him again. *But I will. I know I will . . . and that my father approves of whatever will happen when I do. But Glimpses never show gentle, happy things, do they, Voice Kinlafia? So how much pain, how many tears, are waiting for you and me? And will you someday curse the day you first became entangled in the Calirath destiny?*

She didn't know, and as the parade to began to move at last, she turned unquiet sea-gray eyes away from the man behind her with a silent prayer to any god who might be listening.

He's lost enough already, she told whoever might hear. *Don't let me cost him even more. Please. Spare me that debt, at least.*

CHAPTER FOURTEEN

SHAYLAR NARGRA-KOLMAYR closed the book in her lap, leaned back with a sigh, and glanced back out the window.

"Tired, love?" a voice asked, and she looked across the small compartment at her husband, Jathmar, and smiled slightly.

"Not physically," she said, knowing that he didn't really need a verbal answer, given what he could sense through their marriage bond. "Not at the moment, anyway. But I think my soul's feeling the wear and tear."

"I suppose that's a pretty fair way to describe it, at that," Jathmar acknowledged. "After all, we're farther away from home than any Sharonian's ever been before, aren't we?"

Shaylar's mouth tightened briefly, then she shrugged.

Jathmar was right, of course. They'd already traveled to the very end of the explored multiverse before they ever discovered the huge portal which had led them into such disastrous contact with the Arcanan Army. It was hard to believe that in barely two months, they'd already traveled the better part of twenty-nine *thousand* miles since their capture . . . or that they were still just under a third of the way from the universe Arcana had named Mahritha to their destination in New Arcana. According to the maps their captors had shown them, they were currently in a universe called Mountain Spine, speeding rapidly along a narrow, canyonlike roadway cut through a humid stretch of jungle in what a Sharonian would have called the Sunhold of Garmoy in southeastern Uromathia.

"I know we both wanted to see the multiverse," she said wryly, after a moment, and waved out the window at the terrain rushing by as evening came on, "but this is a bit more of it than *I* had in mind, at any rate. Even if we are seeing it in indecent comfort, at the moment."

The thing the Arcanans called a "slider" was a bit like a Sharonian railroad . . . but only a bit. They'd first boarded the slider almost a thousand miles ago, in the universe of Ucala, and it was an enormous improvement over riding the backs of transport dragons. True, there was still a certain sense of wondrous disbelief about dragon flight, even after so many wearisome thousands of miles of it, but the deeply, comfortably cushioned seats and sleeping berths of the slider were an unspeakable luxury.

In most ways, the slider was like a first-class railway car, yet the differences between it and any railroad Shaylar or Jathmar had ever seen only stood out even more starkly because of the surface similarities.

For one thing, the slider car was a self-contained unit. They'd seen several "trains" of sliders, proceeding together, but that was simply because of routing considerations. There was no such thing as a slider "locomotive"; instead, each slider contained its own spell accumulator, and that spell accumulator moved that slider car—and only that slider car—along the slider track. Except, of course, that it wasn't really a "track" at all, in the Sharonian sense of the word. It was only a series of nodes, arcanely anchored to the bedrock beneath them, which served the sliders' motivating spells as guides. The slider itself whizzed along a rock-steady eighteen inches above the graded right-of-way at a speed of about fifty miles per hour. If two sliders should meet one another headed in opposite directions, they simply slid to the side to let each other past, then moved back into the center of the roadbed and continued on their separate ways.

Any slider had to slow down occasionally, of course. Not even magic, it appeared, could avoid the occasional tortuous switchback or necessary tunnel when it came to staking out rights-of-way over literally thousands of miles. In fact, Shaylar suspected that it was probably no faster, over an average distance, than one of the Trans-Temporal Express's passenger or freight trains. But its silence, smoothness, and flexibility were yet another proof of how incredibly different the "technology" of Arcana was from that of Sharona.

"At least we're still alive, Shay." Jathmar's soft voice summoned her back from her wandering thoughts. "And we're still together. And," his voice changed subtly as an almost grudging edge crept into it, "whatever else, we're damned lucky Jasak is such a fundamentally decent sort."

"Yes, we are." Shaylar's dark, beautiful eyes warmed with deep approval as she gazed at him. Jathmar felt that approval through the marriage bond, and acknowledged it with a crooked smile of his own.

"I am *trying*, love."

"Oh, I know," Shaylar said. "Believe me, Jath, I know."

And she did. She not only knew, but she understood exactly why Jathmar's feelings where Sir Jasak Olderhan were concerned remained . . . complex, to put it as tactfully as possible. Gadrial Kelbryan—*Magister* Gadrial Kelbryan—had shared a term to describe both Jathmar and Jasak. It wasn't one Shaylar had ever heard before, but once Gadrial explained its meaning, she'd had to agree that it was a perfect fit for both of them. The term was "alpha male," and she and Gadrial had watched with a mixture of apprehension, frustration, impatience, and genuine amusement as the two men tried to come to some sort of understanding of their mutual roles.

It wasn't an easy task. Of course, it wouldn't have been an *easy* task for anyone, whatever sort of alpha or beta male they might have been.

No one could possibly expect Jathmar to forget that it was the men of Jasak Olderhan's company who had killed every other member of their survey crew. Who had come literally within a hair's breadth of killing *Shaylar*, as well—and even closer than that to killing him. In fact, without Gadrial Kelbryan's minor Gift for Healing, Jathmar, at least, *would* have died, and it was highly probable that Shaylar would have followed him.

No, no one could reasonably have faulted Jathmar for hating the very ground Jasak walked upon, or feeling a fierce, savagely satisfied sense of vengeance when Sharonian troops virtually annihilated Jasak's command after Hundred Hadrign Thalmayr relieved him of command. One thing was certain—*Jasak* had never blamed Jathmar for feeling that way.

But Shaylar was a Voice, with the perfect recall and gift for languages which accompanied her Talent. Since her capture, she'd acquired a native's fluency in Andaran, the common language of the Union of Arcana's Army. Which was the reason she knew that Jasak had never intended for anyone to die. That what she'd thought at the time was the order to open fire had, in fact, been Jasak's voice shouting the order *not* to fire.

The order one of his subordinates, whose stupidity had apparently been exceeded only by his arrant cowardice, had disobeyed.

Jasak had been even more horrified than Shaylar and Jathmar, in some ways, when Shevan Garlath shot down Ghartoun chan Hagrahyl while the survey crew's leader stood there with empty hands, trying to talk. But when the infuriated Sharonians responded to chan Hagrahyl's murder by opening fire with the rifles no Arcanan had ever even imagined might exist, Jasak had found himself with no option but to fight the battle no one had wanted. So he had . . . and at the end of it, Shaylar and a savagely wounded Jathmar had been the only Sharonian survivors.

"We really are lucky he and Gadrial are *both* such decent people," she told her husband now. "And that he's an Andaran."

"And that he's some sort of an anachronistic throwback, too," another voice said.

Shaylar and Jathmar's heads turned as another woman—a little older than Shaylar, and a little taller (*everyone* was at least a "little taller" than Shaylar)—appeared in the compartment door.

"Sorry," the newcomer said. "I didn't mean to intrude, but it's getting towards suppertime. I'm sure Jasak and

Chief Sword Threbuch have the stewards setting up in the dining compartment by now. Would you two care to join us?"

"As a matter of fact, I'm starved," Shaylar said. "I don't really understand why. It's not like we've been burning off a lot of energy traveling for the last few days."

"No, we haven't," Gadrial Kelbryan agreed. "I'm hungry enough to eat a dragon myself, though. I wonder if it's because we're all finally in a position to take it a bit easier and pay more attention to little things like starvation?"

Her wry smile was almost impish, and Shaylar snorted in a combination of amusement and frustration.

Gadrial was a Ransaran, which meant she came from the Arcanan equivalent of Uromathia, but Ransar was *very* unlike the Uromathian Empire. Ransarans were much more like Ternathians—or even New Farnalians, like Darcel Kinlafia—than Uromathians, with a fervor for freedom and the rights of individuals which sometimes seemed to Shaylar's Shurkhali sensibilities to border on the fanatical, or the obsessional, at least. Not that Shaylar had any intention of complaining. She owed Jathmar's very life to the Ransaran . . . sorceress, for want of a better term, and despite the unmitigated horror of the circumstances which had brought them together, Gadrial had become one of the closest non-Talented friends Shaylar had ever had.

But, for all of that, the slim, powerfully-Gifted magister was also one of her jailers. The fact that Gadrial was also a potent protector, one who'd demonstrated her willingness to literally step between Shaylar and a furious dragon, only made their relationship still more . . . complicated. And the emotions Shaylar could sense out of Gadrial whenever the other woman looked at Sir Jasak Olderhan added their own unique strand to the impossibly tangled knot into which the gods had decided to weave all four of their fates.

"He *is* a throwback, you know," Gadrial said as the three of them left the passenger compartment and started down the carpeted hallway towards the luxury slider's dining compartment.

"Jasak?" Jathmar asked.

"No, Chief Sword Threbuch," Gadrial replied with a grimace. "Of course I mean Jasak!"

"It was intended as a simple expression of interest," Jathmar said with dignity. His own Andaran was improving steadily, although he remained substantially less fluent in it than his wife. Given her utterly non-Andaran sandalwood complexion, flashing dark eyes, glorious midnight hair, and exotically musical accent, Shaylar could never have passed as a native Andaran-speaker, but her command of the language was at least as good as Gadrial's own.

"She knew that, Jath!" Shaylar scolded now, poking him sharply in the ribs with a jabbing index finger. Then she looked at the other woman. "I think I agree with you, Gadrial, but exactly how do you mean that?"

"I sometimes think Jasak thinks he's living back during the days of Melwain the Great," the magister replied. Her tone was light, almost jesting, but Shaylar sensed a core of genuine concern under the amusement.

"'Melwain the Great'?" she repeated, and Gadrial shrugged.

"Melwain was an Andaran king who lived well over a thousand years ago. By now, the legends crusted around him are so thick that no one really knows how much of his story is historical and how much is invented, but it doesn't really matter. He's become almost the patron saint of Andara because he lived such an unbelievably honorable life."

Gadrial rolled her eyes with such a fundamentally Ransaran combination of emphasis and resignation that Shaylar giggled.

"All very well for *you*," Gadrial said severely. "You didn't grow up living in the same universe as Andara! Those people—!"

She shook her head again, and Jathmar's deeper chuckle joined Shaylar's amusement.

"Actually," Gadrial continued after a moment, her voice and expression both considerably more serious, "most non-Andarans really do find Jasak's people a bit hard to understand. Mythalans don't believe the concept of 'honor'—to the extent that they're even capable of visualizing the concept, at least—extends to anyone outside the *shakira* and *multhari* castes. And my own people spend a lot of their time scratching their heads and trying to figure out how anyone could define so much of who and what they are on the basis of an honor code that goes back well over a millennium and seems to consist primarily of accepting an endless series of obligations simply because of who you chose as parents. But there they are. They really still exist—some of them, at least."

"Not all of them seem to share Jasak's view of exactly what honor requires, though," Jathmar said more darkly, and Gadrial nodded.

"That's what I meant when I called him a throwback. Don't get me wrong, he's not unique. There are a lot of Andaran throwbacks, and I'm still a bit surprised by just how grateful for that fact I've become over the last couple of months. But there's what I guess you could call a 'new generation' of Andarans, as well. People like that poisonous little toad Neshok we met in Erthos, or even Five Hundred Grantyl, back at Fort Wyvern. Neshok couldn't care less about Andaran honor codes—he probably thinks they're all hopelessly obsolete, at best, and an object for contempt, at worst. Five Hundred Grantyl, on the other hand, just thinks they're old-fashioned. He's willing to accept that a lot of people still believe in them, and that, because of that, he has to put up with what those people believe they require, but it's all part of the fading past, not the future, as far as he's concerned.

"Jasak doesn't think that way. Neither does his father, from what I've seen and heard about the Duke. They both *believe*, Jathmar, and they'll do whatever honor requires of them, and damn the cost. It's what makes them who they are, and, to be honest, it's part of what makes the Duke's political base so strong. Even Andarans who are no longer prepared to subjugate their own lives to the requirements of traditional honor codes deeply respect people who are prepared to. People who *demonstrate* that they're prepared to . . . and to accept whatever it costs them."

"Gadrial," Shaylar paused between steps and hooked one hand into Gadrial's elbow, stopping the other woman and turning Gadrial to face her, "you're worried. Why? You told us Jasak's father is the most powerful of all the Andaran noblemen."

"He is." Gadrial looked out the window for a moment, then back at Shaylar. "He is," she repeated, "and I know he'll accept Jasak's decision to declare you his *shardonai*. He'll protect you as he would the members of his own family—for that matter, you *are* members of his own family now—and he'll agree with Jasak's reasons for making you Olderhan *shardonai*. But what he won't do, what he *can't* do under that same honor code, is use the power of his office and his title to save Jasak's career or quash any court-martial Jasak may face."

"Court-martial?" Jathmar repeated sharply.

"Do you really think the politicians and the most senior officers of the Union's military aren't going to be looking for a scapegoat if all of this goes as badly as it well might?" Gadrial asked bitterly. "Jasak hasn't discussed it with me—not in so many words—but he doesn't really have to. Someone's going to be blamed for what happened to your people, Jathmar. And if there *is* a war, someone's going to be blamed for starting it. And who's going to be an easier—or, for that matter, more reasonable—scapegoat than the man who was in command of the troops who wiped out the rest of your survey crew?"

"But—" Jathmar began, then chopped himself off, wrestling with his own complex feelings.

A part of him still couldn't forgive Jasak for what had happened to his friends. He suspected that whatever else might happen in his life, however his feelings might change in other respects, there would still be that small, bitter core where all the pain, fear, and loss was distilled down into a cold, dark canker. And that part was perfectly prepared to see Sir Jasak Olderhan pay the price for what had happened to his crewmates, to himself, to his wife.

Yet the rest of him knew Jasak was a decent, caring,

honorable man who'd done everything he could to prevent that massacre. True, he'd made the mistake of doing what his own military's regulations required of him instead of relieving Shevan Garlath of command of his platoon, and he would never forgive himself for that. But after that mistake, he'd done everything humanly possible to stop the killing, and Jathmar and Shaylar were alive and as close to free as they were solely because of Jasak Olderhan. If there was a single human being on the Arcanan side who had consistently acted honorably and honestly throughout this entire debacle, it was Jasak.

"But that's wrong," Jathmar heard himself saying quietly, almost plaintively.

"Of course it is. I see that, you see that, Shaylar sees that. *Everyone* sees that . . . except for Jasak." Gadrial threw up her hands in frustration. "He certainly knows *I* don't agree with him—that's why he won't talk to me about it. He only shrugs when I try to get him to. I've even accused him of masochism, of *wanting* to be punished for what happened to you and the rest of your people. But that's not it either, and he knows I know that as well as he does. He doesn't want to be court-martialed, doesn't *want* to be saddled with responsibility for the first inter-universal war in history. He just refuses to even try to run away from it, just as his father is going to refuse to use his political power and prestige to save him from facing it. The Duke will do everything in his power to help *defend* Jasak if a court-martial's impaneled, but he won't step a single inch over the line to *stop* one, even to save his own son."

"Gadrial, I—"

"No, Shaylar." Gadrial shook her head. "Don't say it.

Jasak doesn't blame you or Jathmar at all. Neither do I, and neither will any member of his family. It's just the way Andarans—*some* Andarans, at least—are." Her expression was an odd mixture of sorrow, exasperation, and a curious, almost forlorn sort of pride. "You can't change them. And if you could, they—he—wouldn't be the people they are, now would they?"

"I suppose not."

"But what I meant before, about Jasak and the Duke being throwbacks," Gadrial said, "is that it's exactly that same stubborn, bullheaded, obsolete, hopelessly romantic sense of honor which absolutely guarantees that the Duke of Garth Showma will protect his son's *shardonai* with his very life, no matter what else may happen."

CHAPTER FIFTEEN

"GOOD EVENING, YOUR MAJESTY," His Crowned Eminence, the Seneschal of Othmaliz, said as his visitor was shown into his private apartment in what had, until a very few weeks before, been known as the Great Palace.

"Good evening, Your Eminence," Chava Busar, Emperor of Uromathia, replied.

The two men were a study in contrasts.

The seneschal was a short, round man, addicted to decorating his already colorful religious robes with additional jewels, bullion embroidery, lace, and pearls, while rings dripped from his fingers. He literally glittered when he walked, and the beautiful little silver bells which adorned his unique, stovepipe-shaped, gold-encrusted religious headgear jingled musically with every movement.

Chava Busar was also short. That, however, was the only real similarity between them. Where the seneschal was so obese that he seemed to roll along, rather than walk, Chava was lean and athletic, especially for a man in his late fifties. Unlike the clean-shaven, moon-faced seneschal, the emperor favored a neatly trimmed, dramatically shaped dagger beard, and his eyebrows—bushy for a Uromathian—floated above almond-shaped eyes dark as still water on a moonless night. There was a hardness in those eyes, as well, like a shelf of obsidian just under the water's surface. For his height, he was broad shouldered and powerfully built, and where the seneschal seemed to roll into a room, Chava strode purposely forward into a universe which belonged—or *ought* to have belonged, at any rate—exclusively to him.

Yet for all the physical contrasts between them, there were similarities under the skin, as well, and it was those similarities which had brought the emperor to this very private meeting. Indeed, a meeting so private that not a single advisor—or bodyguard—was in sight. In fact, none of the servants with whom the seneschal routinely surrounded himself was present, either.

"Please, Your Majesty," the seneschal invited, gesturing to the two comfortable chairs placed to face one another in front of the enormous portrait of Bergahl in glory which dominated the main room of the seneschal's suite. "Be seated."

"Thank you."

Chava accepted the invitation, sitting regally in the indicated chair. Both chairs were more than a little thronelike, he noted, although the seneschal's was fractionally larger and ever so slightly more richly carved, and his lips twitched ever so minutely at the observation. *How very like the Seneschal*, the emperor thought.

The seneschal waited until his guest had settled into place, then took the facing chair. A small table, with a bottle of wine, pastry cakes decorated with sesame seed, and a platter of delicate sandwiches sat conveniently placed for both of them, and he smiled at the emperor as he personally poured wine into the waiting crystal glasses.

"I think you'll find this palatable, Your Majesty." He smiled. "It comes from one of my own vineyards. I'm quite proud of it, actually."

"Thank you," Chava repeated as he accepted the glass and sipped delicately. His bushy eyebrows rose, and he nodded in approval. "You're quite right, Your Eminence. It's very good."

"I'm glad you approve." The seneschal smiled again, and this time his smile was as tart as alum. "It's always a pleasure to entertain a guest who appreciates what small comforts one can offer him."

"Oh, I most definitely agree, Your Eminence." Chava's smile just showed the tips of his teeth. "Indeed, to be totally frank, I find myself amazed at your tolerance and forbearance in the face of having your entire city turned topsy-turvy by this Conclave." He shook his head. "To find oneself suddenly and unexpectedly playing host to the rulers of every land of Sharona must pose extraordinary hardships. Particularly upon such short notice."

"One cannot pretend that the entire affair has not created great difficulties—*great* difficulties," the seneschal agreed gravely. "The dislocation of the capital's normal business has, of course, been extreme. It will take quite some time for the proper administrative agencies to reassert an orderly control over many aspects of it."

"Not to mention the . . . disruptions here in your own home," Chava observed, and watched with amused satisfaction as the seneschal's fat face darkened.

"I am only the Seneschal of the Order of Bergahl,"

he said after a moment. "The Great Palace is not *my* home, but the home of the Order itself, as symbolized by the man chosen by the Order as its head. Nonetheless," he inhaled deeply, "I must confess that arranging to house so many prominent and powerful political figures has, indeed, led to significant disruptions here in the Palace."

Chava nodded sympathetically. Both of them knew the true nature of the "disruptions" to which the seneschal took such exception. Prior to Zindel chan Calirath's arrival with his wife and daughters, the seneschal had been housed in the Emperor's Wing of the palace. The decision by the Emperor to return to his ancestral home—and to the building which, however little public recognition the fact had received, still belonged to him—had placed the seneschal in a most difficult position. In the end, he'd decided he dared not refuse to move out of what had been the House of Calirath's family living space by a tradition literally millennia long. His present suite of rooms were luxurious to the point of opulence, and decorated with priceless artworks, but they were no longer in the Emperor's Wing, and his resentment was only too apparent.

"I was particularly impressed, Your Eminence, by how gracefully you and the Order have dealt with this situation," Chava said after a moment. "It must have been particularly difficult, after more than two centuries of independence, to find oneself face-to-face with the Emperor of Ternathia. I've often thought that the Caliraths simply don't realize how . . . instinctively patronizing they are." He smiled again, briefly. "It's hard to blame them, I suppose. They are, after all, the oldest dynasty in the history of Sharona. It would probably be unfair to expect them to realize how hard—and often—they step on so many people's toes because they simply assume the precedence so many *other* people automatically grant them."

"Indeed," the seneschal agreed. He sipped his own wine, then lowered the glass and regarded the emperor levelly.

"One is, of course, always gratified by the sympathetic understanding of a ruler as powerful as the Emperor of Uromathia. Still, it occurs to me that this meeting wasn't arranged solely so that you might commiserate with me on the dislocation of my capital, Your Majesty."

"No, of course it wasn't," Chava acknowledged, and reminded himself that however fat and ridiculous the seneschal might appear—might actually be, for that matter—he, unlike Chava, had not inherited his power. The man who had been born Faroayn Raynarg, the next-to-youngest son of a dune-treader merchant who had spent much of young Faroayn's boyhood jailed for dealing in stolen dune-treaders, had made his way to the top of a religious order in which it was not unheard of for fatal accidents to overtake one's rivals. That might have been many years ago, and it was entirely probable that the years the lean and hungry "Father Faroayn" had spent as His Crowned Eminence had softened his steel even as they had expanded his waistline. But it would be best to remember that he was not truly—or, at any rate, had not always been—the petty little buffoon who'd humiliated himself so on the day of Zindel chan Calirath's arrival in Tajvana.

"Actually, Your Eminence," the Uromathian continued after a moment, "I requested this meeting because it occurred to me that it's been many fine centuries since an Emperor of Uromathia last spoke to a Seneschal of Bergahl as one ruler to another."

The seneschal stiffened in his chair, and his round face hardened at the words "many fine centuries." Anger flickered in the backs of the small eyes, half-hidden in pouches of fat, and Chava recognized it with quiet satisfaction. At the moment, it was quite probable that at least some of that anger was directed at him, for reminding the seneschal of his self-inflicted humiliation. But that was all right with Chava, because there was so very *much* of it . . . and most of it was certainly directed where he wanted it.

I wonder if the fat fool truly thought only he and the Ternathians would understand that particular challenge? the emperor thought sardonically. *What? He thinks I have no historians—no spies? That Uromathia forgets its tools simply because we haven't used them in two or three centuries?*

Still, he reminded himself, in fairness to the seneschal, the episode really wasn't well known, and the pretense of friendship between the Order of Bergahl and the departed Calirath Dynasty had helped bury it deep. But Chava knew about the confrontation between the last Ternathian Emperor to rule from Tajvana and the then-current Seneschal of Bergahl.

Emperor Gariyan VII hadn't much cared for the Order of Bergahl. Indeed, he'd distrusted it deeply after watching it cater to the more restive elements of his imperial capital's population for decades. The Empire had been in a state of ferment. Not disruption, really, and not rebelliousness, but of . . . uncertainty. No one really knew exactly what had inspired Gariyan's father to begin the phased reduction of the Empire. The argument that the imperial infrastructure had become too expensive to maintain made a certain degree of sense on the surface, yet it had never withstood serious scrutiny very well. Imperial taxes had been ludicrously low; it wouldn't have been impossible, or even significantly difficult, for that tax structure to be adjusted to provide the necessary funding.

Yet no one had a better reason for Gariyan VI's decision to abandon—or emancipate, depending upon one's viewpoint—the eastern portions of his sprawling empire. Certainly there'd been no organized resistance to "tyrannical" Ternathian rule, despite the isolated cases of nationalistic resentment Chava had managed to dredge up during the debate on the Act of Unification. Indeed, there had been significant elements in almost all of the pre-withdrawal provinces which had spoken out strongly in favor of remaining under the Winged Crown. In the end, however, those arguing in favor of continuing as Ternathian subjects had found themselves outnumbered by a combination of their fellow citizens who preferred freedom to increased tax burdens, and those who had truly found themselves unhappy under "foreign domination" for so many centuries.

And so, over a period of two generations, Ternathia's frontiers had withdrawn over three thousand miles to the west, and a sizable percentage of the world's population had spent the last two or three centuries as independent states.

Yet Gariyan VII clearly had entertained few illusions about who was likely to emerge as the dominant political faction in Othmaliz. Indeed, he'd almost certainly known that Uromathian money had been subsidizing the Order of Bergahl's ambitions for power in Othmaliz, and he had summoned the then-current seneschal to Calirath Palace before his family departed—for all time, most had expected—to Estafel and Hawkwing Palace.

There were disputes, even between the reports Chava had access to, of exactly what had passed between the departing emperor and the politically powerful priest already maneuvering to assert his Order's control of Othmaliz. Most of them agreed, however, that Gariyan had pulled no punches in its course, and *all* of them agreed that it was at that point that the seneschal had first discovered that the Caliraths had no intention of passing ownership of Calirath Palace to the newly created Kingdom of Othmaliz.

He had not, apparently, reacted well to that information. After all, like the current seneschal, he'd undoubtedly been looking forward to easing his own posterior onto a throne in the Grand Throne Chamber from which so much of the world had been ruled for so long. When Gariyan informed him that the Caliraths intended to remain the palace's landlords, the seneschal had threatened to nationalize it, even against their wishes. Not even Chava knew precisely what . . . argument Gariyan had presented to discourage such precipitous action, but it had obviously worked for the better part of three centuries.

Yet if the Order of Bergahl had never quite found the nerve to test the temper of the Calirath determination to retain ownership of the palace, that long ago seneschal had still found himself in a white-hot rage. The conversation had been one of ice from Gariyan's side and blast furnace-fury from the seneschal's. And it was in the course of that . . . discussion, just before he stormed out of the audience chamber, that the seneschal had uttered what any reasonable sort might have construed as a threat.

"It will be many fine centuries before a Calirath returns to this city to enjoy this Palace," he had said, "for the Daggers of Bergahl are sharp, and the memories of his priests are long!"

It had not, perhaps, been excessively politic of the current seneschal to remind Zindel chan Calirath of that long ago predecessor's comment, Chava Busar reflected. Of course, the weeks of semi-hysterical pro-Calirath rallies which had preceded Zindel's arrival would have been enough to flick any ruler on the raw, especially here, in this particular city. And the possible consequences of a third-party investigation of a regime as corrupt as that of the current seneschal's might very well prove dire, which couldn't have improved the seneschal's reaction to all those frothing rallies and Ternathian flag-bestrewn demonstrations. Desperation could make even a normally prudent man do foolish things, Chava conceded charitably. Of course few people would have called the Seneschal of Othmaliz particularly prudent these days, but perhaps the seneschal had actually believed Zindel would recognize the implied threat and be cowed by it. Or, at least, sufficiently . . . chastened to declare a quiet moratorium on any potentially embarrassing audits, at any rate.

If so, however, he'd been either an idiot or incredibly ill-served by the spies who should have given him an accurate appreciation of Zindel chan Calirath's character. Chava hated the Ternathian Emperor with a passion so pure it was almost sublime, yet he'd never made the mistake of underestimating his opponent.

"Yes," the seneschal said finally, "it has been too long

since a seneschal discussed the burdens and difficulties of rulership with an Emperor of Uromathia."

He smiled thinly, then paused, sipping wine once again, before he lowered the glass once more and cocked his head to one side.

"Am I, by any chance, correct in assuming that it's those burdens and difficulties which you wish to discuss with me this evening, Your Majesty?"

"In many ways," Chava acknowledged. He sat back in his own chair, his elbows on the armrests, his fingers steepled across his chest as he crossed his legs and regarded the seneschal thoughtfully.

"It occurs to me, Your Eminence, that you and I are among the unfortunately small number of delegates to the Conclave who truly recognize what's at stake here. It's regrettable that so many of our . . . colleagues are obviously blind to that reality."

"Indeed." The seneschal sat back, as well, his expression thoughtful. "Precisely which aspects of that 'reality' did you wish to discuss, Your Majesty?"

"It's obvious to me," Chava replied, "that in many respects, this Conclave has been a farce—a façade—from the very first moment. On the surface, it represents an emergency gathering of rulers and heads of state in the face of a potentially deadly inter-universal threat. A spontaneous decision on the part of First Director Limana and the Portal Authority. But you and I aren't children, Your Eminence, to be so easily misled when it comes to the true exercise of power."

"Indeed?" the seneschal inquired politely.

"Your Eminence," Chava said chidingly, shaking his head with a small, world-weary smile, "the point of contact with these 'Arcanans' is forty-eight *thousand* miles from Sharona. And so far, what have we seen out of them in terms of any significant military threat? Crossbows? *Swords*?"

The emperor laughed scornfully.

"Oh," he waved one hand in a dismissive gesture, "we've heard about their 'fire-throwers,' and their 'lightning-throwers,' but what happened when the Portal Authority's regular troops finally encountered them? Did those 'magical' weapons of theirs help them then? Could they match the effectiveness of rifles, machine guns, and mortars? Of course not! And since these negotiations have begun, what new terrible threats have they produced? Floating tables? *Talking rocks?*" He snorted. "Are we infants to be terrified by such parlor tricks? Useful, I'll grant you that, but if they truly had weapons as threatening as those certain delegates to this Conclave had imputed to them, why would they be *negotiating* with us in the first place? I believe it's obvious, especially in light of the ludicrous ease with which they were bested by properly led and armed regular troops, that they pose no true military threat to us. Indeed, *they* recognize that they don't. What other reason could they have for negotiating with us over the possession of a cluster of portals of such value as Hell's Gate? Would *you* have chosen to negotiate in such a case with someone you regarded as your military *inferior*, Your Eminence?"

The seneschal looked at him for a long, thoughtful moment, then shook his head.

"Of course you wouldn't have!" Chava snorted again, more scornfully even than before. "When the prize is as great as this one, when one's responsibility to secure it for one's own nation is so overriding, a man with *strength* takes what he must. There will always be time for the diplomats to make everything neat and tidy, but that time comes later, not when the opportunity and responsibility alike lie in the palm of a man's hand!

"But these Arcanans *have* chosen to negotiate, which tells us a great deal about their perception of our relative military strengths. And yet, this Conclave continues to be driven by panic-mongers. By men—and women—who seek to use the pretext of this somehow imminent threat, despite the forty-eight thousand miles between it and us, to justify a mad rush into some sort of a world empire. I find it remarkably convenient that the Portal Authority, which has always adopted Ternathian models, and which—as you and I both surely know—came into existence in the first place only at the insistence of Ternathia, has charged headlong into this emergency Conclave at which one of its own directors proposed that *Ternathia* become the lord and master of us all. Of course, Director Kinshe was *officially* speaking as a parliamentary representative from Shurkhal, wasn't he? And who could possibly doubt the towering honesty of these Glimpses, these visions of dreadful threats and savage destruction, which, of course, *only* a Calirath can See? Or the '*spontaneity*' of the Farnalians' and the Bolakini's rush to second that so-convenient Shurkhali motion to put a crown on the head of one of those same Caliraths?"

Chava's voice dripped derision, and the seneschal's jaw tightened once more. Othmaliz had long coveted Shurkhal, not least because of the Grand Ternathian Canal. Long before the canal's eventual construction, the possibilities it had raised—particularly in conjunction with control of Tajvana itself and the Ibral Strait—had been obvious to everyone . . . including several generations of seneschals. The relatively sparse Shurkhali population had made the notion of a quick, tidy little war of conquest appealing. In fact, that conquest had been attempted on two separate occasions, with a notable lack of success—a fact which went far towards explaining the long-standing hostility between Othmaliz and the desert kingdom.

"I cannot disagree with you, Your Majesty," the seneschal said finally. "Unfortunately, it would appear to be a little too late to rectify the situation at this time. The Act of Unification has already been ratified, and while it might be possible for *you* to decline to conform with its terms, I, unfortunately, have a parliament to which I must answer."

And very irritating it must be, too, Chava thought sardonically. *Especially after so many years of having it automatically rubberstamp any proposal you chose to have your mouthpieces put before it.*

"Oh, I agree—both that it's too late, and that it's unfortunate that should be the case," he said aloud. "Nonetheless, as men with responsibilities to those they govern, it behooves us to do what we may to restrain the excesses of the panic-mongers. And while one would never suggest or encourage the adoption of extralegal resistance of what, after all, will be a legitimate, properly approved world government, it also behooves us to resist the potential abuse of power by the cabal which has obviously come together to secure the Ternathian domination of the entire explored multiverse."

"I thoroughly agree that one should eschew 'extralegal' measures," the seneschal replied. "Even when they succeed, they tend to undermine the legitimacy of anyone willing to embrace them. After all, if one is willing to step outside the law in pursuit of one's own goals, then how can one legitimately argue that others are not fully justified in doing the same thing if their interests conflict with one's own? Of course," he looked directly into Chava's eyes, "that assumes such measures become public knowledge, does it not?"

Chava arched a mental eyebrow. So, the seneschal knew about the covert activities of his own secret police, did he? Well, it had always been unlikely those activities could escape scrutiny forever.

"I'm sure it would . . . assuming, of course, that one had any inclination to resort to them in the first place," he said piously.

"Assuming that, of course," the seneschal agreed politely. Then he pursed his lips thoughtfully.

"Your Majesty, I've greatly enjoyed our conversation, and I appreciate the candor with which you've addressed our common concerns. Still, it occurs to me that you, at least, are in a position from which you will eventually see your grandchild on the throne of that same world-empire. In light of that, it would appear to me that the degree to which our two peoples are likely to suffer under its dominion aren't precisely *equal*, shall we say?"

"Yes, and no, Your Eminence." Chava sighed. "One would like to think your analysis would be accurate. However, while I would regard any child of this proposed union as *my* grandchild, Zindel chan Calirath will almost certainly regard that child as *his* grandchild. And given that the crown will be placed upon Zindel's head, not mine, I greatly fear that under normal circumstances, that grandchild will grow up under Ternathian influence.

It may be a child of my blood, Your Eminence, but it will regard Uromathia through Ternathian eyes."

"If that should happen, I would grieve for you, Your Majesty. In the meantime, of course, I will pray to Bergahl on your behalf. He is, after all, a god of justice, and if there is any justice, Zindel's blatant manipulation of this crisis to his own advantage will not prosper."

"I thank you for your prayers, Your Eminence. And I fear you're probably correct—it would take the intervention of the gods themselves to thwart the ambitions Zindel has obviously cherished since well before these 'Arcanans' turned up to provide him with the pretext he required."

"Perhaps so," the seneschal agreed.

"Still," Chava straightened in his chair, smiling brightly, with the air of a man determined to find a bright side so that he could look upon it, "one ought to be willing to extend at least a little trust and faith that the gods *will* intervene on the side of right. And, of course, it's also possible I'm being unduly pessimistic about how the child of any union between Prince Janaki and one of my daughters would be reared. There could be many influences in such a child's life, after all. That's a point we would all do well to remember. Indeed, it's in my mind that should my daughter become pregnant, and should the child be born whole and healthy, fit to take up the burden of the crown of Sharona in the fullness of time, it would be only fitting for me to make a substantial offering to the gods, both in gratitude for the birth and to petition the gods to keep that child safe and raise him—or her—free of pernicious influences."

"Indeed, Your Majesty," the seneschal agreed once again.

"In fact," Chava continued, obviously warming to his theme, "it would be appropriate, I think, for me to make that offering not simply to Dosaru, but to other gods of justice, as well. After all, that child will one day govern all of us, so surely it wouldn't be amiss to petition all of the gods whose worshipers will be his subjects."

"I would think such a gesture of largess on your part would be deeply appreciated by pious people everywhere, Your Majesty," the seneschal said warmly.

"Well, in that case," Chava's eyes narrowed as they bored into the seneschal's, "I imagine Bergahl's Comforters would undoubtedly receive a significant contribution at such time as that child was declared healthy and fit to rule."

The seneschal's face was very still for a heartbeat or two. Then he nodded slowly.

"I think that would be most appropriate, Your Majesty," he said. "Most appropriate, indeed."

CHAPTER SIXTEEN

"SIT DOWN. SIT DOWN, Klayrman!"

Commander of One Thousand Toralk obeyed Commander of Two Thousand Harshu's ebullient invitation and seated himself across the snow-white tablecloth from him. Harshu's command tent was pitched upwind of the smoke—and smell of seared flesh—rising from what had once been Fort Brithik, but occasional tendrils of that smoke still reached it, and the silver, china, and crystal glittering on the table under the accumulator-powered light globe seemed almost . . . bizarre to the Air Force officer.

"Wine?" Harshu invited, and beckoned to his orderly before Toralk could reply. The orderly poured ruby-colored wine from a bottle whose label had never been printed in Arcana into Toralk's glass, and Harshu smiled.

"Whatever else we might want to say about these people, they seem to be excellent vintners," he observed. "Try it. I think you'll like it."

Toralk sipped obediently, then nodded. It *was* excellent, rather like one of the better Hilmaran reds.

"It's good, Sir," he said, and Harshu chuckled.

" 'Good'?" The two thousand shook his head. "And here

I thought all Air Force officers had an appreciation for the finer things in life! Oh, well, I suppose I can't have everything. I'll just have to settle for the frankly remarkable job you've been doing managing this advance, Klayrman."

"I'm glad you're satisfied, Sir," Toralk replied.

"I'm a lot more than just 'satisfied,'" Harshu told him. "So far, you've hit every objective ahead of schedule. Your SpecOps teams have done a remarkable job of cutting the Voice chain ahead of our attacks, and we haven't lost a battle dragon since the swamp portal. I'm very pleased, Klayrman. Very pleased."

"Thank you, Sir."

Toralk started to say something else, then stopped and sipped more wine instead.

"Something troubling you, Klayrman?" Harshu asked, and the Air Force thousand looked up. He'd hoped Harshu hadn't noticed his hesitation, but he should have remembered just how sharp, how observant, the two thousand was.

"Well, as a matter of fact, Sir, there *are* a couple of things that . . . concern me," Toralk admitted.

"Spit them out, then," Harshu invited, and snorted a chuckle. "You've got a lot of capital with me just now, Klayrman. You might as well use some of it, so trot out whatever's on your mind."

"Sir, it's just that I'm not . . . entirely comfortable about some rumors I'm hearing. Rumors about POW treatment."

Toralk met the two thousand's eyes levelly, and Harshu frowned ever so slightly.

"I assume you're referring to Five Hundred Neshok," the expeditionary force commander said after a moment.

"His name *has* come up in some of the rumors that

concern me. On the other hand, it isn't the only name that's been mentioned to me, Sir."

"What kind of rumors are we talking about, exactly?" Harshu asked, then sipped from his own wineglass.

"From what I've been hearing, Sir, I'm afraid we're having a lot of Kerellian Accord violations. I'm hearing about prisoners who never make it back into confinement. Who 'mysteriously disappear' between the point of their capture and the POW cage they're supposed to be marched off to. And I'm hearing about other prisoners who are badly beaten, systematically, by their guards. A lot of it, I think, is the result of the stories about what happened to Magister Halathyn. The fact that Intelligence hasn't been able to confirm or deny those stories bothers me, Sir. It bothers me a lot. And in addition to that . . . inability—" Toralk met Harshu's eyes again "—there are those rumors about Five Hundred Neshok and his . . . mistreatment of prisoners undergoing interrogation."

The Air Force officer sat back in his chair, waiting, and Harshu turned his wineglass under the light, gazing into its crimson heart as if it were a scrying crystal. He stayed that way for several moments, then returned his attention to Toralk.

"I've heard some of those same rumors," he said finally, his voice quieter and less ebullient than it had been. "Some of that, I imagine, is inevitable. And, to be completely honest, I'd rather see that than a reluctance to engage the enemy. But I have to agree that from what I've heard from certain sources, there have been significant violations of the Kerellian Accords."

Toralk started to say something, then made himself sit silently, waiting, and Harshu shrugged.

"I don't like the thought of casually mistreating prisoners of war, Klayrman. It's a violation of the Articles of War, it's conduct unbecoming the Arcanan armed forces, and—ultimately—it's prejudicial to good discipline. Nothing turns first-line soldiers into their own worst enemies quicker than developing a taste for atrocities.

"But we're in a peculiar position right now," the two thousand continued. "We don't really know these people, and they don't know us. We don't know what their equivalent of the Kerellian Accords may be. And we still don't know how deep we have to go to find the sort of readily held bottleneck we need to provide defensive depth for Hell's Gate."

"But, Sir," Toralk said quietly when the two thousand paused, "if we don't know what their equivalent of the Kerellian Accords are, then wouldn't it be wiser of us to be sure that we adhere as closely as possible to *our* version? As you say, we don't know how deep we have to go, or how long we may end up fighting these people. In the long run, isn't it important for us to establish from the beginning that we're not going to be responsible for—or permit—any 'atrocities' from our side, if we expect to avoid any from *their* side?"

"There's some of this in any war, whatever we might wish, or whatever the Articles of War or some neatly sanitized history might suggest to the contrary," Harshu said. "It *always* happens, Klayrman, even with the best troops. And at the moment, given the fact that we've attacked them while we were still negotiating with them, I doubt very much that we're likely to find any Sharonians cherishing warm and fuzzy thoughts where we're concerned, however closely we might adhere to the Accords."

"I'm sure you're right, Sir." In fact, that had been the basis for Toralk's greatest reservation about the wisdom of this entire operation from the outset. "But eventually we're going to have to get past that, unless we're planning on remaining at war with these people forever. And, forgive me, Sir, but sooner or later they're going to have Arcanan prisoners of their own. It seems to me that the way we treat their people when we capture them is going to have a significant impact on how they treat our people."

"No doubt it will. To be honest, though, I'm inclined to cross that bridge when we reach it. At some point, this front is going to stabilize. Frankly, I intend to get quite a bit deeper into their rear areas before that happens, but it *is* going to happen, Klayrman. When it does, we're going to be looking at new negotiations, probably debates on prisoner exchanges, and quite probably demands—from both sides, I imagine—that those responsible for the deliberate abuse of POWs face punishment. Exactly how all of that will play out is more than I'm prepared to speculate upon at this point. One thing I do know, though, is that no matter how angry one side or the other may be, *everything* is going to be subject to reinterpretation and negotiation when that time comes. They may be as angry with us as they like, may distrust us as deeply as they please, but sooner or later, we're still going to have to talk to each other, and we will. Whatever's happened between us, we will."

"Sir, are you saying that the mistreatment of POWs by Arcanan personnel doesn't *matter*?" Toralk asked carefully.

"No, I'm not," Harshu replied just a bit frostily. "I'm

saying that, at the moment, there are aspects of our situation and our mission requirements which concern me more than the rumors—no, let's be honest and call them what they are, the *reports*—you're referring to.

"We're flying completely blind out here, Klayrman. We don't know *squat* about these people. Oh, we've captured quite a stack of maps and other information, but unfortunately, our translation spellware doesn't let us read written documents just yet. It's not going to for at least several more weeks, according to the Intelligence people, either. From the maps we've found so far, this Sharona's explored territory doesn't appear to be anywhere near the size of our own, but we can't be certain of that. And I've *got* to know what's out there in front of us if we're going to continue to advance without heavy losses. And we can't *afford* heavy losses, since there's nothing immediately behind us to hold any Sharonian counterattack that gets by us.

"Those are the concerns which are floating around the front of *my* brain, Klayrman."

Toralk looked at his commanding officer for several seconds which seemed like minor eternities.

"Sir," he said finally, quietly, "if you don't stop this, and stop it quickly, it's going to stick to your name, your reputation, forever."

"Fuck my reputation," Harshu said flatly. Toralk's eyes widened in astonishment, and the two thousand snorted in harsh amusement. "Oh, I won't pretend I'm not as vain as anyone you're likely to meet. Hells, I'll go further than that—I've got an ego big enough for any three other men I know! So what? Reputation isn't worth a fart in a windstorm—not when it gets in the way of the mission. I've got fourteen thousand men out here with us or spread out behind us. My responsibility is to them and to the mission. I *need* the information that little bastard Neshok is bringing me if I'm going to keep as many as possible of those men alive and accomplish what we're out here to do."

So there it is, Toralk thought. *You know exactly what I'm talking about, exactly who it is that worries me, and you're willing to accept it in the name of expediency.*

The thousand knew he wasn't being entirely fair. "Expediency" was an ugly word, but what Harshu had said about keeping his men alive was also true. And the fame-seeking two thousand's indifference to what posterity made of him was what had surprised the Air Force officer so deeply.

"Sir," Toralk said after a moment, "I'm not sure I can agree with you. I don't mean that I disagree with anything you've said about the responsibility to our men, or even the importance of our mission, now that we're out here and engaged on active operations. But I'm worried about what simply ignoring violations of the Accords is going to do to *us*, not what it's going to do to the enemy. We do have a moral responsibility where the treatment of the Sharonians is concerned, and if we shirk it, it's going to poison us."

There was a long silence, then Harshu inhaled deeply.

"You may be right, Klayrman. In fact, you probably are."

He paused for another long moment, then shrugged ever so slightly.

"Actually, as I suspect you realized perfectly well before you broached the subject, there's not really all that much . . . free enterprise prisoner abuse going on.

There is some of it, I'll grant you, but it's small beer compared to the other concerns you've raised. It's also in direct contravention of my standing orders where the Kerellian Accords are concerned, so if you want to talk to the MPs about it, point out to them that abusing prisoners is against the rules and kick them in the arse until they do something about it, I have absolutely no objection.

"On the other hand, let's not pretend we don't both know exactly who really concerns you tonight. It speaks well of you, as an officer and a man, that it concerns you enough you were actually willing to call me on it. I respect you for that. But I've still got to have that intelligence. We can't read their documentation, but interrogation is telling us enough for us to make some pretty solid interpretations of the maps we've captured. I'd be happier if we could orient them properly to our own maps and feel confident that we're reading the scales accurately. I'd especially prefer to be able to do that without prisoner interrogation. I can't do any of those things yet, though, which makes what Neshok is bringing me the closest I can come to solid planning information. For example, we know now that this chain splits—that it comes back together again at some place called Traisum, and that something called a 'railroad' that sounds a lot like our sliders has been extended to that point from their own home world. We know there are only very weak forces along the other side of this split chain, and we have the critical information we need for your SpecOps teams to find the next links in the Voice chain.

"I *need* that kind of intelligence, and I'll do what I have to to get it."

The two thousand's voice was flat, inflexible, and Toralk sat very still. Then, finally, he cleared his throat.

"And what happens to the people who get it for you in the end, Sir?" he asked softly.

"In the end?" Harshu smiled bleakly. "I'm sure Five Hundred Neshok has visions of promotion, of power. I'm sure he probably thinks *I'm* going to be promoted for my glorious victories out here. No doubt he expects the patronage of such a rapidly rising star to pull him up in the wake of my own meteoric elevation. But that's not going to happen. I suppose it's possible I *will* be promoted, and even that I'll garner all sorts of public testimonials and praise . . . in the short term, at least. In the end, though, Klayrman, people are going to start asking the questions you've had the guts and integrity to start asking already. They're going to look at how I got the intelligence I needed, and after that, I don't think there'll be that many more promotions, that many more field commands. Not for the commanding officer who winked at his subordinates' use of torture and even murder."

"And Neshok, Sir?" Toralk asked in an even softer voice.

"And Neshok, Klayrman," Harshu's bleak smile turned terrible, "is going to discover that I never authorized a single thing he's done outside the Accords. That's not going to save me from whatever happens, but it's not going to save *him*, either. There won't be any orders he can use for cover, no way he can say 'I was just following instructions,' or 'Everything I did was in policy.' You said the Sharonians are going to demand punishment for anyone who's abused their POWs? Well, who do you think they're going to punish? I know why Neshok thinks he reports directly to me, why there's no one in the chain of authority between him and me. But why do *you* think it's that way, Klayrman?"

Vothon, Toralk thought. *You've been planning this all along. You're* using *Neshok, and you're making sure that when he finally goes down, he can't take anyone else—except maybe* you*—with him.*

"Sir—"

"No, Klayrman. We're not going to discuss this any more. Not tonight, at any rate. Tonight, we're going to have supper together, and we're going to discuss the latest intelligence data from Five Hundred Neshok and how it affects our future planning.

"I've decided we're going to have to split our forces. We can't afford to leave this other sub-chain just sitting there, waiting to serve as a conduit into our own rear areas, especially if we don't manage to punch out Traisum cleanly, after all. So, I'm going to send Carthos up the other branch first thing in the morning. He'll have four universes to cross before he gets to Traisum, whereas we'll only have two more, but according to the Five Hundred's reports—" the two thousand showed his teeth in a cold, humorless smile "—those are very recently discovered universes, compared to the ones along the other route, and they're covered only by very light forces. I'm not that worried about the opposition he might hit, but it's also a lot longer route, almost twice as long as the shorter, better-explored one. Even with dragons, it's going to be a long, bitter haul, and it will be even worse for the other side if they hold us short of Traisum and try to exploit the other sub-chain to get at our rear. That means it's going to be a secondary theater for both sides, and that we're a lot more likely to hit serious resistance in Failcham and Karys than he is on his axis of advance.

"And that, in turn, means I'm going to need my best Air Force commander here, so I'm keeping you on this side. I'm afraid you'll be acting under my direct orders, while Carthos gets a more independent command." The two thousand met Toralk's gaze levelly. "I'm sorry about that. It means he'll get more credit for making the decisions about everything, ranging from tactics to supply considerations . . . even methods of intelligence-gathering. I'm afraid no one's going to give *you* a lot of credit for any decisions like that which have to be made during our own advance."

Toralk looked back at his commanding officer and realized what Harshu was truly saying.

I shouldn't, he thought. *I shouldn't let him do this. I should either support his decisions, his policies, openly, or else ask to be relieved, not let him cover me while he throws Carthos and Neshok to the dragons . . . along with himself.*

For a long, quivering instant, he hung on the brink of saying that out loud. But then—

"That's all right, Sir. I won't pretend I'm happy about everything you've just said, but you're right about at least one thing. We do have a job to do out here, and I suppose it's time we rolled up our sleeves and got on with it."

* * *

Division-Captain Arlos chan Geraith stepped out of the comfortably heated car onto the rear platform. The noise of steel wheels drumming along steel rails, the hammer of wind, the vibrating rattle of fittings and glass windows, filled his ears, and it was bitterly cold (although not nearly so cold as it would get in a few more weeks) as the enormous train rushed through the night.

The vast breadth of the Grocyran Plain stretched away to the north and east, an endless land of swamps, birch forests, and conifers in the center of the vast continent of Chairifon. The double strand of rails stretched thirty-nine hundred miles, as a bird might fly, from this universe's Lake Arau in the eastern foothills of the Arau Mountains to the southwestern mountains of Harkala, close to the ancient city of Aeravas. But this massive train, loaded with the men, horses, vehicles, and artillery of the First Brigade of his Third Dragoon Division of the Imperial Ternathian Army was no bird. The compromises forced upon the Trans-Temporal Express's construction engineers by uncooperative terrain had added at least seven hundred miles to that theoretical straight-line distance.

They were less than halfway across the universe of Faryika, pounding furiously down-chain towards Traisum, with almost nine thousand miles still to go. The good news was that there was only one more water gap to be crossed; the bad news was that the gap was over a thousand miles wide and that shipping would be agonizingly hard to come by in the thinly inhabited universe of Salym. It was going to take time to get his men and equipment across that stretch of saltwater.

Time, he thought. *Please, Vothan give me the time! It's not supposed to take* months *just to get my troops into the likely theatre of operations! The War College never prepared any of us for a move like this one. Or,* his thought turned grimmer, *a war like this one could turn into.*

He unbuttoned the top button of his coat and took

the flat, thin case from an inside pocket. He opened it and extracted one of the long, slender, handrolled New Ternath cigars, then returned the case to his pocket. He took a moment to savor the rich smell of the tobacco, passing it slowly under his nose, then clipped the end, put it in his mouth, and struck a match. He shielded the fragile flame in his cupped palms until it had burned away the last of the chemical taste, then lit the cigar slowly and carefully, turning the tip in the match flame until it was evenly alight. Then he tossed the match from the platform and watched it arc out into the carriage's slipstream like a short-lived comet, snuffed out the instant it left the wind-shadow of the platform.

He stepped to the right side of the platform and leaned on the rail as he gazed out westward across the plains. Thick stands of birch, trunks gleaming silver-white in the moonlight, stretched away on either side of the right-of-way, interspersed with equally thick stands of evergreens. The reflected light from the coach windows raced along the ground, keeping pace with the train, flickering hugely as it crossed boulders or the sides of the occasional rail cutting. Stars gleamed overhead, and a halo of ice crystals encircled the high, white moon as it floated in a sky of midnight blue. Far ahead, invisible from chan Geraith's position on the platform, three powerful engines thundered down a diamond cavern, carved through the darkness by the lead engine's powerful headlamp, and a thick streamer of funnel smoke trailed back from them like a twisted banner, shot silver and black with moonlight.

They were the only bubble of life and light—of *human* life, at least—for literally thousands of miles. The permanent human population of this entire universe was less than twenty thousand, which meant First Brigade's three thousand men had increased it by over fifteen percent. And it also meant that those less than twenty thousand human souls were a tiny, tiny presence on this vast and empty world.

They'd had to leave the mighty Paladins of their original train behind. None of the immediately available heavylift freighters had boasted the capacity to carry those enormous locomotives across the water gap in Haysam. Besides, they'd been too badly needed for the Sharona to Haysam run. Hayrdar Sheltim, chan Geraith's train master, had needed three of the Norgamar Works' individually smaller and less powerful Windcleaver-J 2-8-4 locomotives to replace the pair of Paladins, but it was probably just as well. The Windcleavers were nimbler than their larger cousins, better suited to the mountainous terrain between them and Harkala.

He drew heavily on the cigar, watching its tip glow brightly, savoring the moment of privacy and the pristine beauty of the world racing past him at least as much as he savored the rich taste of the smoke. He treasured moments like this. Moments when he could step away from his staff, his unit commanders. When he could take off the persona of a division commander, allow himself to step off the stage where his performance must engender confidence and determination.

I suppose it's sort of sad that I have to stand out here freezing my posterior off to find what Misanya calls my "comfort zone."

He smiled at the thought of his wife. She was a soldier's daughter, as well as a soldier's wife, and she understood what that meant, how their joint lives must be subordinated to the sometimes harsh demands of his chosen profession. But it had also left her with a refreshing irreverence for the sort of posturing and grand tragedy that certain soldiers of their acquaintance liked to embrace. She was quick to exterminate any tendencies in that direction in her own husband, at least, for which chan Geraith was profoundly thankful.

Then his smile faded as he reflected upon how many weary thousands of miles behind him Misanya was.

Stop that! he scolded himself. *You're not the only soldier who's missing his wife tonight, Arlos!*

Which was true enough. And it wasn't as if he didn't have enough other things to worry about. He particularly disliked what Company-Captain Lisar chan Korthal, his staff Voice, had been reporting from the negotiations at Hell's Gate. The obstructionism Platoon-Captain chan Baskay's messages described made no more sense to chan Geraith than it did to chan Baskay himself. Nor had the division-captain much cared for the suspicions chan Baskay and Arthag had reported up the chain.

The bastards are up to something, he thought moodily. *It's not just my ingrained paranoia, either. I just don't know* what *they're up to . . . but I'm afraid we may all be going to find out.*

He took the cigar out of his mouth long enough to grimace properly, then put it back.

At least chan Tesh and chan Baskay haven't sent any more bad news our way in the last couple of days. That's something. And the fact that these godsdamned Arcanans don't have a clue how much firepower an entire dragoon brigade represents is another something. Of course, I *don't have a clue what else* they *may have available, now do I?*

He snorted at the thought. It wasn't precisely the

first time he'd had it, and he suspected it wouldn't be the last.

In fact, I'm going to go right on wondering about that until—and unless—I find out. And if I do *find out, it's going to be because everything's fallen straight into the shitter. So I suppose it's actually one of those little mysteries of the multiverse I'd really rather not solve, if it's all the same to the Triad.*

He shook his head and stood, gazing out at the untouched beauty of the moon and stars, and wondered how long he could last tonight before the chill finally drove him back inside.

CHAPTER SEVENTEEN

NITH MUL GURTHAK closed his office door carefully, then crossed to his desk and seated himself behind it. Outside his windows, a chill, moonless night wrapped itself about Fort Talon, and he smiled crookedly. There was no reason he *had* to do this during the hours of darkness, yet it always felt curiously satisfying.

Conspiracies ought to be worked upon in darkness, however justified their objectives, he thought as he reached for the ornamental *rankadi* knife on his blotter.

He picked it up, closed his eyes, and reached out once more—not with his hands, this time, but with his Gift. His very powerful Gift, which no one outside the Council of Twelve and his own immediate line family suspected that he had.

It hadn't been easy, putting that Gift aside. Denying himself its use as he fitted himself into the narrow template of an officer in the Union of Arcana's Army. Nith mul Gurthak had been born Nith vos and mul Gurthak, of high *shakira* caste, as well as one of the traditional military families of Mythal. But he had systematically concealed the strength of his Gift, starting in early boyhood. Private tutors had trained him in its use with brutally merciless rigor, beginning years earlier than even *shakira* youths normally began their schooling. There had been more times than he could count when young Nith had wept himself to sleep at night, but he had never complained, never even considered shirking his responsibilities. He had been selected for his role, his duty to the caste, even before he had been born, on the day when the marriage between his *shakira* father and *multhari* mother was first arranged, and that was an honor no *shakira* worthy of his caste could possibly have rejected. The strength of his Gift, and the skill with which he had learned not simply to use it, but to *conceal* it, as well, had only justified that choosing.

Now his shoulders relaxed, ever so slightly, as his questing Gift confirmed that the privacy spells about his office were all in place, up, and running. There was nothing particularly spectacular about those spells; they were standard, Army-issue spellware, supplied by the Union of Arcana to ensure its military officers' security in the execution of their duties. That was just fine with mul Gurthak. No one else in Fort Talon—or, for that matter, the entire universe of Erthos—could match the strength of the Gift no one knew he had, and it would have taken hours of preparation for *him* to penetrate those privacy spells. No one else could have hoped to do that without alerting him to the security breach in ample time to deal with it.

Satisfied that no one could possibly observe him, he rolled up the left sleeve of his uniform blouse and drew the gleaming, razor-sharp *rankadi* blade. He held it under the light, before his eyes, clearing his mind of extraneous thoughts as he focused upon that glittering steel. The steel which had been used no less than eleven times to cleanse his bloodline of weakness and failure. The steel which was consecrated to the Great Task of the *shakira* by the blood it had shed, the honor it had preserved.

He felt his heart and mind fall into shared focus, settle into the perfect balance of thought and emotion appropriate to his sacred purpose, and a serene smile touched his mouth as he closed his eyes. He held the blade across his forehead with both hands while he murmured the words of the second verse of the fourth chapter of the *Book of Secrets*, and then, without opening his eyes, pressed the blade's wickedly sharp edge against the inside of his left forearm. A line of blood sprang up against his dark skin, and he moved forearm and dagger carefully, with the smoothness of long practice, to gather that blood on the flat of the blade.

He opened his eyes once again and maneuvered the *rankadi* blade over the personal crystal sitting on the blotter of his desk. He spoke a single word in ancient Mythalan, then tilted his right wrist carefully and watched as a single drop of his blood fell from the dagger's tip to the fist-sized crystal. It glittered there, like a fallen ruby, for perhaps ten seconds. Then, without fuss, fanfare, or any spectacular glow and flash of arcane power, it simply disappeared . . . and the PC flickered alight.

Mul Gurthak inhaled deeply as he saw the brief menu of commands. He'd done this any number of times, especially once he'd begun rising in rank within the Union Army, and yet there was always that moment of tension, that anticipation, almost as if somewhere deep inside he truly believed the carefully crafted spellware might have somehow failed since its last use. Which was ridiculous, of course. Spells researched and developed at the Mythal Falls Academy simply didn't fail.

He picked up his stylus and tapped the menu entry he needed. Then he sat back in his seat, raised both hands to cover his eyes, and bent his head in ritual submission and greeting.

"Mightiest Lords," he said in a dialect so ancient that no more than a handful of people in the entire multiverse would have understood it, "the least of your servants begs you to receive his report and consider his actions, that they may redound to the glory of the *shakira* and the high holiness of their purpose and the completion of the Great Task."

He waited, head still bent, for a full ninety seconds before he allowed his hands to fall to the blotter and his spine to straighten. Then he cleared his throat and began to speak once more, this time in modern Mythalan.

"Mightiest Lords, I trust that by now you have received my earlier messages. I will endeavor to be as brief as possible in updating you upon my progress in the service of the Great Task. As always, I await any instructions from you."

Should anyone outside the most trusted servants of the Council of Twelve ever gain access to the messages he had recorded over the years and decades of reports to the Council and its members, the consequences would have been disastrous. The damage to the Great Task would have been incalculable, and the consequences to mul Gurthak himself would have been far worse than merely fatal, but the commander of two thousand had never worried about the security of his messages.

The spellware which supported and protected them

was the very finest in the entire multiverse . . . and no one outside the Council even suspected that it existed. Without mentioning it to anyone else, the researchers at Mythal Falls Academy had perfected a technique which archived material at a compression rate of over five hundred thousand-to-one. A single second of crystal recording could contain the equivalent of no less than a hundred and forty *hours* of normally recorded data or imagery. The messages which mul Gurthak routinely sent in would be less than a flicker in the stream of a normal crystal recording, imperceptible to anyone who lacked the special spellware required to strain them back out of the flow once more, and Mul Gurthak's reports had all been carefully hidden away in the long, chatty letters he routinely recorded and sent to his brother-in-law. His third sister's husband had no idea of mul Gurthak's actual duties, much less of the power of the two thousand's Gift. Nor did he have any idea that mul Gurthak's letters to him were routinely intercepted by the Mythalan postal service and routed very quietly to agents of the Council of Twelve to be scanned for messages from the two thousand before they were passed on to him.

The transmission pipeline itself was as close to perfectly secure as fallible mortal beings could hope to come, yet the Council hadn't stopped there. Even if the message could have been detected and recovered by anyone else, it could not have been read. The encryption program, like the compression spellware itself, was the product of secret research at the Academy. It was unique in that there was no encryption key anyone could enter. The encryption was embedded in the sarkolis of the originating PC itself, and only two other PCs in the multiverse could decrypt it. All three of them had been enspelled simultaneously, and one of them had then been issued to mul Gurthak, while the others had been placed in the care of two separate members of the Council of Twelve. Those three PCs, and *only* those three PCs, could read material generated from the secret spellware concealed behind the activating cantrip mul Gurthak had just used, and no one could activate—or even detect—that spellware without both the blood of the PC's proper owner and the proper ritual to control its shedding.

Should the existence of that elaborate encryption program ever come to the attention of mul Gurthak's non-Mythalan superiors, questions would undoubtedly be asked. Unfortunately for those superiors' curiosity, mul Gurthak would have been under no legal obligation to answer their possible questions. The two thousand found that deliciously ironic, since it was the Ransaran insistence on a citizen's right to privacy which had deprived military and law enforcement agencies of the police power to legally demand access to private encryption spellware or the personal messages it protected.

"As I've already reported," he continued, refocusing his thoughts and attention on the task in hand, "the sudden appearance of these 'Sharonians' and Olderhan's involvement in the first contact, not to mention the incredible ineptitude of Bok vos Hoven, left me with no option but to improvise."

He might, he reflected, be taking a not-insignificant risk in his characterization of vos Hoven. The incompetent idiot's family connections were just as exalted as he'd claimed, and making enemies that highly placed could be . . . prejudicial to a man's life expectancy. By the same token, though, mul Gurthak had amply demonstrated his own competence, judgment, and value in the Council's service over the past twenty-plus years. He had patrons of his own, at least as highly placed as vos Hoven's relatives, and even if he hadn't had them, the recognition, identification, and repair of flaws in the Great Task's execution was a critical component of the mission he'd been assigned. Any attempt to sugarcoat vos Hoven's shortcomings would have been a betrayal of his duty to the caste.

"I believe that, so far at least, events are transpiring much as I had hoped they might. It was fortunate the members of the Council had seen fit to arrange to provide me with significant assets in my area of responsibility, despite its distance from Arcana. This gave me far more influence at critical points than would have been the case without them. By the same token, however, I've been required to commit all of them, and I fear that few of them will survive. Indeed, it seems increasingly likely that their continued survival beyond the end of their immediate usefulness would, in itself, pose a considerable threat to the Great Task.

"According to my most recent dispatches from Two Thousand Harshu, Rithmar Skirvon has disappeared. Either he was killed in the otherwise successful Special Operations mission which clearly managed to kill the Sharonians' Voice at Fallen Timbers, or else he was captured and is currently the prisoner of the handful of Sharonians who appear to have so far evaded capture themselves. I have little doubt that he will have told them anything he knows by now. Fortunately, his actual knowledge is strictly limited, and the possibility that his captors will be in any position to utilize what he may have told them is slight. Nonetheless, it would be prudent, in my judgment, to make arrangements for his elimination as soon as possible after his recovery by our own forces. Indeed, the best resolution would be for him to be killed in the crossfire when our troops attempt to rescue him, and I am cautiously exploring possible avenues for arranging that outcome.

"Thousand Carthos, on the other hand, has now been placed in command of an independent advance up a second line of universes. While this deprives him of further opportunity to shape the main thrust to our liking, it also means he no longer has Harshu or Toralk looking over his shoulder, and his natural attitude towards these Sharonians is much closer to our own than either Harshu's or Toralk's. I feel confident that we could have relied upon him to generate a significant number of 'atrocities' in his own command area even without my . . . instructions to him.

"Two Thousand Harshu is proving rather more . . . problematical than I'd originally hoped," mul Gurthak admitted. "Unfortunately, his seniority made him the only choice, other than myself, to command the expeditionary force. The good news is that he's reacted very much as I anticipated to the 'discretionary instructions' I sent him. I believe you will have discovered by now, from the copy of my instructions to him which I appended to my last report, that it must be crystal clear to any impartial reading that I never ordered him to launch this attack. Indeed, I intend in the next few days to send him dispatches admonishing him for having taken too much upon himself in launching any offensive beyond the Hell's Gate universe itself. I will also be sending copies of those dispatches up the official communications pipeline to the High Commandery. Of course, now that he's committed us to actual operations, I have no option but to support him to the very best of my ability in order to ensure that those operations succeed."

Mul Gurthak paused the recording and leaned back in his chair, interlacing his fingers across his chest while he considered what he'd already recorded. He thought about it for several seconds, then straightened and resumed.

"The bad news is that Harshu is clearly up to something. At this time, I'm not certain exactly what, but I suspect he's more of a throwback to the old Andaran honor code than I'd believed. If my suspicions are accurate, he's deliberately engineering a situation in which any blame for atrocities and excesses committed in the course of this expedition will be seen as his, and *only* his, personal responsibility. Should he succeed in doing so, it will almost certainly result in at least some mitigation of the consequences of those excesses upon public opinion.

"Despite that, I believe the basic objectives will still be attained. Five Hundred Neshok, in particular, is working out very well. His personality is just as sociopathic as our evaluating spellware suggested, and his violations of the Kerellian Accords continue to mount steadily. No matter what Harshu may want, Neshok's actions are going to have a huge impact on public opinion in the home universe. The Ransarans' repugnance will be impossible to overstate, and the more traditional elements of Andara will be equally horrified. The fact that Neshok, Carthos, and Harshu are all Andarans themselves will, of course, fasten responsibility for this entire fiasco upon Andara and the Andaran officer corps.

It was an Andaran—Harshu—who launched the attack in an excess of militarism and personal ambition which far exceeded my instructions to him. And it was two other Andarans—Neshok and Carthos—who proved themselves to be merciless butchers and sadists.

"I was unable to be too explicit in my suggestions to Neshok about the best way to use the traitor vos Dulainah's death to further our objectives. It's become clear, though, that he understood the concept quite well. He's also been rather more subtle than I anticipated by insisting that his briefings on vos Dulainah's death are a 'best guess reconstruction of events' based on 'reports which cannot be substantiated at this time.' That gives him—and, indirectly, me—a certain degree of insulation. Despite those qualifications, however, they've spawned dozens of independent atrocities—all of which appear to have been committed either by Andarans or by runaway *garthan*—which will further blacken Andara's reputation, especially in Ransaran eyes."

He paused once more, his face carefully expressionless despite the malicious glee that bubbled deep inside at the thought of using the traitor Halathyn vos Dulainah's death to finally smash Andara's grip upon the High Commandery. The fact that the atrocities his supposed murder at Sharonian hands was spawning among the Andarans and fugitive *garthan* who had idolized the senile old lunatic would hammer a wedge between the components of the Andaran-Ransaran political alliance which had always frustrated Mythal's objectives, as well, only made it even sweeter to contemplate.

"The fact that I was forced to improvise with so little warning has forced me to run certain risks," he continued after a moment. "The connection between us—specifically, between myself, the Central Bank, and Carthos—is particularly worrisome. In addition, both Neshok and Five Hundred Klian represent lesser risks.

"Neshok will cease to be a problem as soon as I decide his usefulness is at an end. He's unaware that one of the troopers assigned to his intelligence section has very specific . . . instructions where he's concerned."

Mul Gurthak allowed himself a thin smile. Of course Neshok was "unaware" of those "instructions," since Javelin Lisaro Porath was unaware of them himself. Nor was there any reason for Neshok to suspect anything of the sort was even possible. The technique mul Gurthak had used to implant them required someone with a Gift vastly stronger than the one anyone outside the Council of Twelve knew mul Gurthak possessed. It also happened to have been proscribed, along with all other mind-ripping spellware, at the time the Union of Arcana was formally ratified. Unfortunately for the demands of the pious Ransaran reformers, the Council of Twelve had already been in existence for centuries at that time, and the Councilors had taken steps to preserve the knowledge which so many others—including so many *shakira*, who ought to have known better—had been prepared to simply throw away.

When Porath received the activation signal from mul Gurthak, he would obey the commands the two thousand had imprinted. Alivar Neshok would die quickly, before Porath—in an obvious paroxysm of guilt over the hideous crimes he had committed under Neshok's orders—hanged himself. And the most amusing aspect of the entire thing, as far as mul Gurthak was concerned, was that the signal would be a routine dispatch from him promoting Porath from javelin to sword on the basis of Neshok's glowing reports.

"Carthos, however, is beyond my immediate reach, as is Harshu," the two thousand continued. "We can always hope that one or both of them might become casualties once Sharonian resistance finally begins to solidify. We obviously cannot *count* upon that happy outcome, however. I believe that ultimately, Harshu will be almost as useful to our purposes alive as he would be dead. In a best-case scenario, his court-martial for permitting and condoning violations of the Kerellian Accords should constitute a significant self-inflicted wound for Andara.

"If not for Carthos' links to myself and the CBM, *his* court-martial—or disgrace, at least—would probably prove almost equally useful. In his case, however, any investigation by the Inspector General's Office would be entirely too likely to discover those links. For that matter, Carthos himself might well reveal them—and the 'suggestions' I gave him before sending him out to join Harshu's command—in return for being permitted to plead guilty to some lesser offense. As a consequence, I believe his removal to be imperative. Unless otherwise instructed, I intend to use the Gorhadyn Protocol to terminate him at the appropriate moment."

The beauty of the Gorhadyn Protocol—aside from the fact that no one outside the Council of Twelve even suspected its existence—was that its effects were virtually impossible to distinguish from a natural stroke. Only a powerfully Gifted magistron who already suspected what had happened could possibly detect it, and even then only if the autopsy were performed within no more than twelve to eighteen hours of the moment of death.

The drawback to using the Gorhadyn Protocol, of course, was that having too many people drop dead of convenient strokes at convenient moments was likely to raise a few eyebrows, at the very least.

"I've already reported my proposal for dealing with Hundred Olderhan and his family," mul Gurthak went on, "and if the Council approves my proposed strategy, it will be necessary for Five Hundred Klian to be removed, as well. Even if the Council rejects my proposal, however, Klian's death will hurt nothing and will further reduce the handful of people who know how vos Dulainah actually died. I therefore intend to deal with him at an appropriate moment. At this time, I'm looking for some means other than the Gorhadyn Protocol for accomplishing that portion of the operation. From the prospect of continuing to safeguard the Protocol's existence, I believe it would be wiser to find some other way to eliminate him. At the same time, it might well be that our agents in Arcana and New Arcana would be able to spin the similarity of his and Carthos' deaths into a suspicion that highly placed Andarans ordered their removal in an effort to shut their mouths about the 'truth' of Andaran mismanagement, arrogance, and atrocities, beginning with young Olderhan's wanton slaughter of the Sharonian civilians. Please advise me as to your feelings in this regard. Although the message turnaround time will probably preclude the arrival of any advice from you before I'm forced to act in Klian's case, I will, of course, obey your instructions to the very best of my ability, should it be possible for them to reach me before that time."

He paused once more, considering all he'd already said. As always, he would play the entire message back at least once before he actually compressed it and embedded the encrypted file in his next letter to his brother-in-law. It was unlikely he'd be making very many changes, however, and he allowed himself a modest glow of pride. Given the disastrous effect of the Sharonians' sudden appearance and, especially, of Bok vos Hoven's incredible incompetence on the long-standing strategy of the Great Task, the job he'd done picking up the pieces and starting over again was nothing short of brilliant, and he knew it. False modesty was not a *shakira* vice, and mul Gurthak had no doubt that his performance in this emergency would be noted by the Council.

There might still be a few minor details in what he'd already recorded which needed a certain fleshing out, but he could always attend to that later. For now, it was time to shift gears and bring the Council fully up to date on what they had learned so far about the Sharonians and their "Talents."

"In addition to the purely military information which Neshok has obtained for Harshu," he began, "we've learned quite a bit more about the Sharonians.

"It would appear that at least traces of these 'Talents' of theirs are considerably more widespread in their population than trace Gifts are in our own. However, the strongly 'Talented' appear to be no more numerous than our own strongly Gifted. Moreover, the Sharonians' Talents are less flexible than our Gifts. From everything Neshok has been able to discover so far, it's extremely unusual for any Sharonian to have more than one or two Talents, and however powerful those Talents may be, they represent all the Sharonian in question can do. Whereas someone with a Gift can utilize almost any piece of spellware, Sharonians with Talents can do only the one or two things their Talent—or Talents—permit.

"On the basis of this, I believe that . . ."

The man who never thought of himself as Nith vos Gurthak except at very private moments, like this one, sat in his office, cradled in the heart of darkness, and continued his report quietly.

CHAPTER EIGHTEEN

SIR JASAK OLDERHAN sat backward in the pedestal-mounted swivel chair, resting his crossed forearms on the top of the chair back, and leaned his chin pensively into the cushion they provided. Outside the observation dome, the virgin forests of the universe called Dystria flowed past. It was early morning, and the humid air of the Kythian lowlands hung in a sort of translucent golden haze as the slider rushed towards the coast and the passenger ship waiting to transport them across the fifteen hundred miles of saltwater to the next portal in Paerystia.

Thirty-five thousand miles, he thought. That was how far he'd traveled with his *shardonai* and Gadrial Kelbryan in the last two months. *And we're still less than halfway to New Andara. I wonder if—*

His musing thoughts broke off as he heard feet on the steps behind him. He looked back over his shoulder, and his eyes brightened as he saw Gadrial climbing up them from the lounge level.

"So *here* you are," she said. "We missed you at breakfast, you know."

"Sorry." He smiled briefly. "I wasn't very hungry this morning."

"So we all surmised. The question, of course, is why not?"

Jasak wondered for a moment if she realized just how scolding her tone sounded. There was a gleam in her dark eyes as she folded her arms across her chest and cocked her head to one side. She looked for all the world like a nanny waiting for her obstreperous charge's latest excuse, he thought with an inner smile. Then the temptation to smile faded, and he shrugged very slightly.

"By my calculations, Five Hundred Klian's initial dispatch got to New Andara somewhere around four o'clock this morning, our time," he said.

Gadrial's eyes darkened, losing their glint of amusement, and she unfolded her arms to touch him lightly on the shoulder.

"I hadn't even thought about that," she said quietly.

"I'm not surprised." He smiled crookedly at her. "We're still barely forty percent of the way home, and it feels like we've been traveling forever. Sometimes, I think 'home' doesn't really exist, you know. There's only this bubble around us, filled up with dragons and slider cars and passenger cabins aboard ships. We just *think* there's anything else out there."

"It *is* strange," she agreed. "I know it took just as long to get to Mahritha as it's going to take to get home again, but you're right. Somehow, I do feel less . . . connected with everything around us than I did on the way out."

"Because it was all new on the way out?"

"That may have been part of it, but I don't think it's the real reason for the difference."

Gadrial frowned, gazing out the observation dome's windows and apparently forgetting about the slim, fine-boned hand still resting lightly on his shoulder.

"I think the real difference is the reason we're making this trip," she said slowly after several seconds, and he nodded.

"Of course it is. And, to be honest, a part of me wishes we could just stay inside my nice, safe bubble. But we can't, can we?"

"I'm afraid not." Her hand squeezed his shoulder for a moment, and her own smile was sad. "Sooner or later, we're going to get home, whatever it may feel like now. And what happens then?"

"I don't know," he admitted. "We'll find out in another couple of months, I suppose. At the moment, to be honest, I'm more concerned about how my mother and father felt when the hummer finally arrived."

Gadrial nodded slowly. With no equivalent of the Sharonians' Voicenet, the Union of Arcana had to rely on the arcanely augmented, specially bred "hummers" for quick long-distance communication. But "quick," she had discovered, was a relative term. From what Shaylar and Jathmar had said so far, it would have taken Shaylar's original message less than two weeks to reach their own home universe. Exactly how much distance that represented was one of the questions they'd declined to answer, for which neither Gadrial nor Jasak blamed them. From several things they'd let drop, however, Gadrial was convinced that the total distance was substantially less than the distance between Mahritha and New Andara. Still, that had to be a very different thing from "short," given how long Shaylar's message—which unlike Five Hundred Klian's, had moved literally at the speed of thought, except when it had to slow down to cross the occasional water gap—had taken to cross it.

But however great the distance might be, the communications loop between the swamp portal and Sharona was eighty percent shorter than the one between Fort Rycharn and New Andara. Gadrial was no soldier, but even she could see the military implications of that sort of advantage.

Not that those implications were foremost in her mind at that instant.

"I know you're worried about your parents," she said after a moment. "I don't blame you. But I've learned a little bit about the Duke during my years in Garth Showma. And I've learned quite a bit more from you."

He turned his head to quirk an eyebrow at her, and she snorted quietly.

"You don't exactly run on and on about them, Jasak, but when you do talk about them, I hear an awful lot of love . . . and trust. And just from watching you in action with Shaylar and Jathmar, I've learned a lot about the values they thought were important enough to teach their son. So I know they're going to be worried, and they're going to be upset, but they're also going to understand what you did and why you did it."

"I know." He inhaled deeply. "I really do know. Unfortunately, that doesn't keep me from wishing that if they'd had to hear about something like this, I'd been able to tell them in person."

"Maybe not, but look at it this way. This way, at least they're going to have had a couple of months to begin coping with it before they actually see you. And unless I miss my guess, your father's going to have been using that time to very good purpose."

"Gods, I hope so," Jasak said softly, and Gadrial squeezed his shoulder once more.

She started to say something, then stopped and shifted mental gears. Jasak had already made it abundantly clear that he didn't want to discuss the board of inquiry he would certainly face, or the court-martial which might very well follow close upon its heels.

"How do you think Parliament is going to react?" she asked instead.

"I think it's going to be a godsdamned mess," he replied flatly. "The Mythalans, at the very least, are going to go absolutely berserk, and I'm afraid at least a chunk of the Andaran MPs are going to find themselves in at least limited agreement this time around."

"Really?"

"Not for the same reasons." Jasak shook his head quickly. "We Andarans don't go in much for xenophobia for xenophobia's sake, and I don't imagine most of us are going to hold the fact that Sharonians don't know anything at all about magic against them. But what they did to Thalmayr when they punched out the portal . . . *that's* going to really, really worry a lot of Andarans."

"I can see that, I suppose. But is it going to make them more cautious, or is the perceived threat going to make them more belligerent?"

"That I couldn't begin to tell you," Jasak said frankly. "I'd prefer to see more caution, but I'm afraid the opposite is probably at least as likely. To be honest, an awful lot is going to depend on what else has happened out there in Mahritha."

"And no one in Parliament is going to be able to affect that very much either way, are they?"

"No, and that's one of the things that worries me

most," Jasak admitted. "Even if Parliament does its dead level best to put the brakes on the situation—and I know that's what Father, for one, is going to be recommending—it's still at the end of a four-month two-way communications loop. Which means that whatever happens out there is really in the hands of the local command structure and likely to remain there."

"You're thinking about Two Thousand mul Gurthak, aren't you?"

"Yes." Jasak pursed his lips and exhaled noisily. "The more I think about it, the more I wonder exactly why he wanted me out of his office before he talked things over with that diplomat, Skirvon. I keep trying to tell myself I'm just being paranoid, pessimistic. But I keep coming back to it."

"Why?"

"Because he knows who my father is, and he knows where we're headed. What if he wanted me out of that office because he didn't want me to know what his plans really are?"

Gadrial turned back from the windows, her eyes narrowing.

"I don't much care for Mythalans either, you know," she said with truly massive understatement, "but why would he want that?"

"I did say I know it sounds paranoid," Jasak reminded her. "But if *I'd* been the local senior officer, and if I'd known that someone with a close, personal connection to the Duke of Garth Showma was headed directly back to New Andara, I'd have done my damnedest to make sure he carried with him the clearest possible statement of my intentions. I'm not talking about dispatches, Gadrial. I'm talking about the sort of face-to-face conversation where the real explanations get made. The opportunity to use me as his go-between to Father. Unless, of course, for some reason he didn't *want* Father to know what he's really up to."

Gadrial started to tell him he truly did sound more than a bit paranoid. But then she stopped. Maybe he did, but as one of her research team members in Garth Showma was fond of pointing out, even paranoiacs sometimes had real enemies.

And mul Gurthak is *Mythalan*, she reminded herself.

"What do you think he might not want your father to know about?" she asked instead.

"I don't know."

"But you obviously suspect that there's *something*, or you wouldn't be worrying about it this way."

"I just can't quite understand why he'd want to discuss his instructions to his diplomats in such . . . privacy. Not under these circumstances, anyway."

"Maybe he just felt he could speak to them more freely without you," she pointed out. "You were the officer in command during the initial incident. Maybe he felt they'd be more frank about discussing options and possibilities—or the consequences of the incident—without you. And you said you didn't think he was very happy about your decision to make Shaylar and Jathmar your *shardonai*. Maybe he was afraid they really have managed to influence you—us—somehow, and he wanted to minimize any secondhand impact that might have had on what Skirvon might say or think."

"That's certainly possible. And, for that matter, he's a commander of two thousand, and I'm only a lowly little commander of one hundred . . . for now, at least." His mouth tightened briefly, and Gadrial's eyes flickered.

Those last four words were about as close as he'd allowed himself to come yet to admitting his worry about the probable consequences for his military career. "But none of that changes the fact that I was absolutely the closest thing he had to some sort of expert—or informed opinion, at least—on the people he was sending Skirvon off to talk to. Even if he didn't want me sitting in on that discussion, why didn't he send Skirvon to pick my brain for additional information before sending him off to talk to Shaylar's people? Sure, they had my written report—and yours. But if I'd been a diplomat setting off to talk to a completely unknown civilization, I'd have wanted every scrap of information or firsthand impression I could possibly get."

"You're beginning to make me very nervous," Gadrial said slowly. "Are you suggesting mul Gurthak said something to them in private, gave them some kind of secret orders, he doesn't want anyone else to know about?"

"I'm afraid that *might* be what happened," he admitted.

"But what kind of orders?"

"I don't know," he said again. "On the other hand, there is that Mythalan xenophobia to think about."

"Surely you don't think he wants—?"

Gadrial broke off, unable—or unwilling—to complete the question, and Jasak grimaced.

"I can't believe that even a Mythalan would actually want a war, especially with someone who's already revealed the combat capability these people have. At least, I don't think I can. But I do worry about just how hardline he may have wanted them to be. We're the ones who were in the wrong initially. What if he's unwilling to admit that? What if he's decided to draw his own line in the mud, like Hundred Thalmayr?"

Gadrial nodded very slowly, her expressive eyes dark and shadowed with worry. Hadrign Thalmayr had been a complete and total idiot, but at least his mental processes—such as they were and what there'd been of them—had been straightforward and almost agonizingly clear. He'd been arrogant, stupid, and far too conscious of the "military honor" of Arcana in general and himself in particular, but Gadrial doubted that there'd been a single subtle bone in his entire body. Certainly there'd been an acute shortage of *brain cells*, at any rate!

Nith mul Gurthak was something else entirely. Everything she'd heard about him suggested he was anything but an idiot. Which, unfortunately, might not be as good a thing as she'd been assuming it was. Given the typical Mythalan attitude towards the non-Gifted, and given the almost inevitable Mythalan revulsion at the very concept of someone whose very different Talents might challenge the primacy of the Gifted, "xenophobia" might actually be too pale a word for his reaction to the Sharonians' sudden appearance. If he'd opted to respond as a *Mythalan*, rather than as an officer of the Union Army, then he very well might have issued far harsher and less accommodating instructions to Rithmar Skirvon than he'd admitted.

"You're definitely making me nervous now." She balled the hand on his shoulder into a small fist and smacked him lightly on top of the head with it. "I'll have to think of some way to *thank* you for convincing me to share your paranoia."

"Sorry." He caught her wrist and looked up at her. Even with him seated in the chair and her standing beside it, he didn't have to look up very far, and something deep inside her tingled at the warmth in his eyes.

He, on the other hand, seemed completely oblivious to his own expression, she thought, with more than a hint of frustration.

"Have you sent a letter ahead to your father to tell him about your suspicions?" she asked after a moment.

"Not yet. I've been turning it over in my mind. But I probably will send word ahead by hummer after we dock in Paerystia." He twitched his shoulders. "Actually, I wanted to talk to you about it before I wrote to him. I kind of hoped you'd just tell me I was crazy."

"I wish I could—tell you that, I mean. But even though you may be *wrong*, I don't think you're crazy. And the truth is, I'm afraid you're not wrong, either."

"Great."

Jasak's spine slumped just a bit, and he shook his head with a deep, heartfelt sigh.

"I'll go ahead and write. In the meantime, though, I don't think this is anything we need to discuss with Shaylar and Jathmar."

"Rahil, no!" Gadrial shook her head quickly, emphatically. "There's nothing anyone could do about it at this point, and there's absolutely no reason to worry them any more than they're already worried, Jasak!"

"That's exactly what I was thinking."

He pushed himself up out of the chair and took the hand which had rested on his shoulder in both of his. He held it for just a moment, smiling at her, and then drew himself up to his full towering height.

"And now that you've come and rousted me out of my hiding place up here, I've discovered that I'm actually hungry, after all. Would you care to come down to the dining compartment and share a cup of tea with me while I irritate the stewards into finding me something to eat?"

* * *

"Where did Gadrial go?" Shaylar asked.

"I think she went up to the observation dome looking for Jasak," Jathmar replied, looking up from the book in his lap. Then he straightened, and his eyebrows rose as he sensed her quiet consternation through their marriage bond. "Why?"

"I need—*we* need—to talk to her, Jath."

Shaylar's magnificent brown eyes were worried, and Jathmar laid the book aside and stood to take her in his arms.

"What is it?" he asked. She leaned back in his embrace, looking up at him, and he shrugged. "I've been able to tell that you were worrying about something for several days now, love. I just haven't been able to figure out what it was. I've been assuming you'd tell me about it in your own good time. So, is that time now?"

"I don't know if it's a 'good time' or not, but I'm afraid it is something we need to talk about," she said unhappily. "And, frankly, the fact that you haven't been able to figure out what's bothering me is part of the problem."

"What?" He couldn't quite keep an edge of hurt out of his tone, and she squeezed him quickly.

"That's not how I meant it!" she told him quickly. "What I meant was that we've always been so sensitive to one another because of our marriage bond that each of us has almost always been able to figure out what's bothering the other one, when something is. But this time, you haven't been, have you?"

"Well, I didn't want to *push* you . . ."

"Of course you didn't. But that's not my point, either."

"In that case, what *is* your point?" he asked with an unusual sense of frustration.

"It's about our bond, Jathmar," she said softly, her eyes anxious.

"What about it?" His expression was perplexed, and she sighed.

"You're not a Voice," she said. "Maybe that's why you haven't noticed."

"Noticed *what*?"

"It's weaker, Jath," she said very softly. "It's weaker."

"*What?*" He stared at her in consternation.

"It's weaker," she repeated. "Oh, it's not like it was when I had that head injury. It went away practically entirely then. This is different. It's . . . it's like we're losing some of our connections. When Voices Speak to one another, there are all sorts of side traces—emotional overtones, thoughts which aren't fully articulated but still transmitted, traces of memory. We're trained to filter those out when we're working to pass on messages, but they're always there. Well, marriage bonds are like that, especially when they are as strong as ours has always been."

"I've never really noticed it," he said slowly. "Not the way you're describing it right now, at least."

"Yes, you have," she disagreed. "But because you're not a Voice, you haven't realized they were all there, deepening and enriching the way our feelings flow back and forth. I *am* a Voice, though. I've always been aware of them. And now, for some reason, they're . . . weakening."

"What do you mean?" For the first time since the conversation had begun, he felt truly frightened by where she seemed to be going. "You mean we're *losing* our bond, somehow?"

"I don't *know*. I wish I did. All I know right now, though, is that we started losing those side trace elements a universe or two back. I don't have any idea why, and I don't have any idea how far it's likely to go. I've never heard of anything like it, so I don't have any way to hazard a guess about any of those questions."

"Then what do we do, love?" Jathmar hugged her tightly.

"I don't know," she repeated yet again. Then she looked up at him again.

"Have you tried using your Talent lately?"

"Not really," he replied slowly. "We haven't really stopped anywhere long enough for me to get a clear Look at things."

"Well, maybe the next time we stop, you should try," she suggested. "I'm the only Voice in this entire universe. I don't have anyone else to test my Talent with, but you don't need another Mapper."

"I don't think I like where you're going with this one, love," he said unhappily.

"*I* don't like where I might be going with it," she told him.

"Do you really think we should discuss it with Gadrial?" he asked her after a moment, trying to ignore the sick look in her eyes which he knew was mirrored in his own.

"I can't think of anyone else to discuss it with," Shaylar replied with a small, wan smile. "There's no one else with a Talent in the vicinity, that's for sure. She might have at least some suggestion about what could be causing it. Even if she can't come up with an answer, she might start us thinking in the direction of one."

"But then she'd also know about the problem."

Shaylar's eyes narrowed as she tasted the suddenly darker tinge of his emotions.

"Of course she would. Why?"

"Shaylar, I know Gadrial is our friend. And," he added a bit more reluctantly, "I know Jasak will do everything in his and his family's power to protect us. But unless these negotiations of theirs actually produce some sort of peaceful resolution, without anyone else getting killed, they're still going to be the enemy, love. Maybe not of us personally, but of Sharona. And both of them are honorable people who take their obligations seriously. If there is something happening to our marriage bond, to our Talents—possibly because we're spending so much time in proximity to someone who's Gifted, for all I know—do we really want to let the enemy know? Even if they would never do anything to hurt either of us, if it turns out to be something they could use against other people's Talents, you know that Jasak, for sure, and Gadrial almost equally for sure, would feel compelled to pass it along."

"But if we can't even ask Gadrial about it, then who *can* we ask?" Shaylar asked in a tiny voice.

"I don't know, love." Jathmar said softly. "I don't know."

CHAPTER NINETEEN

"SO, HOW'S YOUR problem patient *this* week?" Regiment-Captain Namir Velvelig asked, turning from the office window through which he had been contemplating Fort Ghartoun's parade ground as Company-Captain Golvar Silkash completed the rest of the semi-weekly sick report.

"The esteemed Hadrign Thalmayr?" Fort Ghartoun's senior medical officer grimaced. Then he shrugged with a combination of helplessness, irritation, and smoldering frustration.

"The truth is, Sir," he continued, "that Tobis is more and more convinced the man's strongly Talented himself. Which, if you'll pardon my saying so, would be a dead waste of a Talent even if Thalmayr had the least clue of what a Talent was, in light of his total and invincible stupidity."

"Now, now, Silky," Velvelig admonished gently. "We've known one another a long time. There's no need for you to indulge in all these euphemisms to hide your true opinion of our guest."

Despite the sourness of his expression, Silkash made

a sound that was halfway between a snort and chuckle. Any temptation towards amusement vanished quickly, however, and he shook his head.

"Honestly, Sir, Thalmayr is a disaster. I don't know what we're going to do with him. As nearly as Tobis—" Platoon-Captain Tobis Makree was the un-Talented Silkash's strongly Talented assistant surgeon "—and I can tell, he's convinced himself our efforts to Heal him are actually some sort of insidious brainwashing or mental torture."

"You're saying he's a lunatic, as well as an idiot?"

"I wish I could dismiss it quite that easily, actually." Silkash shook his head again. "The thing is, the Talent he's got is sufficient, even without his having any idea in the world what it is, to throw up a mighty tough block. So he managed to tremendously limit what Tobis could do to control his pain. He even managed to limit the speed of the physical Healing we could encourage. And that same block made it all but impossible for Tobis to get through to those suicidal urges of his, and *that*—"

"Don't tell me," Velvelig interrupted. "Because he made it so hard to get through, Tobis had to adopt a brute force approach, and that only made things worse. Right?"

"Exactly right," Silkash agreed. "We didn't have a choice if we were going to keep him alive. We *had* to get through to him, so Tobis did . . . despite the fact that Thalmayr was fighting him every inch of the way. And despite the fact that Thalmayr's resistance really did turn the entire effort into something that could be readily mistaken by the uninformed for the 'mental torture' he thinks we were out to inflict in the first place!"

"Wonderful." Velvelig pursed his lips and looked back out the window.

Frankly, he could have gotten along just fine indefinitely without having Hadrign Thalmayr dumped on him. The regiment-captain wasn't much given to coddling weakness. That wasn't part of any Arpathian's cultural baggage, and in this case, Velvelig's contempt for Thalmayr's indescribably wretched performance as a military officer left him even less inclined to pity the Arcanan.

Which, unfortunately, did nothing to absolve him of his responsibility to see to it that the medical needs of any POW in his care were met.

Assuming the camel-fucking idiot will let *us meet them!* he thought sourly.

"Is there anything we can do about that situation?" he asked aloud.

"At this point?" Silkash shrugged. "Probably not. In fact, I've come to the conclusion that the best thing we can do, for the next few weeks, at least, is to pretty much leave him alone. Physically, he's close to fully recovered—or as close to it as a man who'll never walk again is going to get. The discomfort he's still experiencing can probably be treated by an herbalist almost as well as by a Healer at this point. We'll keep Tobis away from him for a while, see if he settles down if we stick to a purely physical nursing regimen."

"You really think that will help?"

"I don't know. Actually, I'm inclined to doubt it, as deeply as the idiot's dug himself in. I just don't see any other practical approach. If we can't find some way to get through to him soon, though, I'm going to recommend sending him on up-chain. Tobis is good, and with all due modesty, I'm a pretty fair surgeon myself, but let's not fool ourselves. There are hospitals closer to Sharona which are undoubtedly far better qualified to deal with something like this."

"I see."

Velvelig clasped his hands behind him and bounced gently up and down on the balls of his feet for a moment, then nodded to himself.

"Very well," he said, turning back from the window once more. "Write it up as a formal recommendation, and I'll approve it. To be honest, I'll be relieved to see his back!"

"I don't think you'll get an argument from anyone over in *my* shop," Silkash assured him.

"Good. In that case—"

"You wanted to see me, Sir?"

Velvelig broke off in midsentence as Senior-Armsman Folsar chan Tergis poked his head through the door behind the seated Silkash. The senior-armsman seemed blissfully unaware that interrupting his commanding officer was a military *faux pas*. Just as he seemed unaware that even the most rudimentary military courtesy would have required him to at least knock before opening the regiment-captain's office door unannounced.

Judging from his expression, Company-Captain Silkash obviously *was* aware of those minor points of military etiquette. Either that, or he'd just swallowed a spider, since he appeared to be experiencing some difficulty with his breathing.

Velvelig's own expression remained commendably grave—Arpathian septmen's faces tended to do that—despite the mental snort of amusement chan Tergis almost always managed to evoke. The senior-armsman might not have struck most people as particularly hilarious, but Velvelig had never been able to imagine anyone more unlike most people's concept of a professional military man. Which was fair enough; despite the "chan" in front of his surname, chan Tergis had never set out to pursue a military career.

The Ternathian was short (for a Ternathian, at any rate), sturdy, and undeniably plump. He had a round, guileless face, with blue eyes, both of which never quite seemed to focus on the same object at the same time. His straw-colored hair always looked at least a week overdue for a cutting, even if he'd only left the barber fifteen minutes before. And, unlike almost any other Voice Velvelig had ever known, chan Tergis had a distinct weakness for the bottle. Not only that, but on those occasions when he succumbed to that weakness, his normally pacific disposition tended to transform itself into a not particularly skilled but highly enthusiastic pugilism which rather reminded Velvelig of the old cliché about the bison in the glassworks.

It was those last two character traits which explained what he was doing in PAAF uniform and assigned to Fort Ghartoun. Inebriation had played a major role in getting his signature onto the enlistment form in the first place, and a series of less than felicitous encounters with various MPs in a wide selection of drinking establishments had led him to assignments like Fort Ghartoun, located about as far from Sharona as it was possible to get.

Yet despite his character flaws, which the gods knew were legion, he'd retained his noncom's rank for two reasons. First, when he was sober (which, to be fair, was most of the time), he was as hard-working, punctual, and reliable as anyone could ask. Second, despite the effect prolonged abuse of alcohol normally had on any Talent, chan Tergis' Voice remained incredibly strong and clear.

But no matter how strong his Talent, dozens of COs had despaired of ever transforming him into a neatly turned out exemplar of proper military appearance. Or behavior. It was simply impossible to get him to understand—or, at least, to observe—more than the bare minimum of the principles of proper military procedure and courtesy.

"Yes, Senior-Armsman, I did want to see you," Velvelig said, and chan Tergis nodded and cocked his head.

He can't really *be that totally clueless*, the regiment-captain told himself for far from the first time. *No one could possibly be as smart as I know he is and not be able to figure it out eventually. Unless they* choose *not to, of course.*

If he'd thought it would do one bit of good, he would cheerfully have hammered chan Tergis to encourage him to figure it out. Unfortunately, the senior-armsman's determination to remain the squarest peg in a round hole that anyone could possibly be was invincible. Besides, much as he sometimes irritated Velvelig, the Voice was rather charming in his own thankfully inimitable fashion.

"What was it you wanted to say to me, Sir?" chan Tergis inquired after a couple of seconds.

"If you'll give me a moment, I'll be right with you," Velvelig told him, and looked at Silkash. The company-captain's spider was doing its best to crawl back up through his nose, judging from his face's alarming color and the wheezing sounds he was making.

"If you'll excuse me, Company-Captain," Velvelig said with admirable gravity, in a voice which scarcely quivered at all, "I believe the Senior-Armsman requires a moment of my time."

"Of course, Sir," Silkash managed to get out. He stood. "With your permission, Sir?" he added in somewhat breathless tones, and Velvelig nodded.

"Dismissed, Company-Captain," he said, and Silkash departed. In fact, he actually managed to get through the office door and close it behind him before the laughter he'd valiantly suppressed broke free.

Velvelig shook his head slightly as he listened to the whoops coming from the hallway outside, then returned his attention to chan Tergis.

"So, here you are," he said. The senior-armsman simply nodded, and Velvelig gazed at him for a moment. Then the regiment-captain walked across to seat himself behind his desk, and the amusement he'd felt only moments ago had disappeared by the time he leaned back in his chair.

"I'm getting a little nervous," he told chan Tergis then.

"Nervous, Sir?" the Ternathian repeated.

"Yes. How long has it been now since your last Voice transmission from Company-Captain chan Tesh?"

"Seventy-six hours and—" chan Tergis pulled out his watch and opened it "—and forty-three minutes, Sir."

"I see." Velvelig cocked his head, lips ever so slightly pursed. Obviously, chan Tergis had been doing a little worrying of his own.

"Have you attempted to reach Petty-Captain Baulwan or Petty-Captain Traygan?" the regiment-captain asked.

"As a matter of fact," chan Tergis said slowly, snapping his watch closed once more and returning it to his pocket, "I have. Of course, I'd actually have to go through Lamir Ilthyr to relay to Erthek Vardan or Petty-Captain chan Lyrosk at Fort Brithik."

"And you haven't been able to raise them, either?" Velvelig's voice was just a shade sharper than it had been.

"No, Sir." Chan Tergis' blue eyes had sharpened into unusually clear focus, and he shook his head. "Of course, to be fair, it wouldn't be the first time we've had trouble getting Lamir to Hear one of us," he added. "He's not a lot older than Erthek, and he's considerably weaker than either Petty-Captain Baulwan or Petty-Captain Traygan—or Erthek, for that matter—and to be completely frank, we've got him covering too wide a gap." He shrugged. "You know how thin we're always stretched out here, Sir. When it was decided that we had to have our stronger voice assigned to Company-Captain Halifu, Petty-Captain Baulwan was sent on ahead from Fort Brithik, but we all knew there were going to be occasional glitches, especially once the decision was made to send chan Lyrosk to Brithik to work with Erthek Vardon. That left Lamir all alone to hold the relay between us and Brithik, and even though he's as disciplined and conscientious as anyone could ask, the fact that he's still young means his Talent still has a bit of growing to do. The truth is, the stretch he's responsible for covering is wide enough that even something as minor as an allergy attack could create a problem, which is the main reason we've been planning on recalling Erthek from Fort Brithik, now that chan Lyrosk is there, and assigning him to the same relay station as Lamir. Neither of them is all that strong, but together, they'd give us enough redundancy to feel comfortable about keeping the gap closed."

"But you aren't comfortable in your mind about any 'allergy attack' in this case," Velvelig said shrewdly, and chan Tergis shook his head again.

"No, Sir, I'm not," he admitted. "Lamir's receiving range is shorter than his transmission range, that's why he's closer to Fort Brithik than to us. He'd have to be seriously ill to be unable to reach me with a transmission from his end, especially if he tranced to do it. And he's never let better than three days go by without sending at least a test message."

"Is it possible he's come down with something a bit more serious than an allergy attack? Something that came on quickly enough that he didn't realize he needed to get a message off to you before it put him out of commission?"

"Certainly it's *possible*. Probable, though?" Chan Tergis shrugged. "I'd have to say I don't think it's very likely."

"I see," Velvelig said again.

"This is a prime example of why we shouldn't have Voice relay stations with only single Voices assigned to them," chan Tergis said. "If one Voice goes down, for any reason, there ought to be another one ready to back him up the way they do in the inner and middle rings. And we wouldn't have had to play musical chairs with Baulwan and chan Lyrosk this way, either. To be honest, we've virtually built communications breakdowns into the system ourselves simply by stretching our supply of Voices so thin."

"I agree with you, Senior-Armsman," Velvelig said

dryly. "Unfortunately, there are those nasty budgetary considerations. And, let's face it, the supply of Voices willing to go haring off into the wilderness is limited—very limited."

"I realize that, Sir." Chan Tergis' tone held a hint of what might almost have been apology, and Velvelig's use of his own rank had apparently jogged his mental elbow into remembering the proper form of military address when speaking to a superior . . . for the moment, at least. But his expression was also stubborn.

"I'm not saying there weren't what seemed to be perfectly good reasons for accepting the kind of stretch we're working with out here," he continued. "I'm only saying that we've just found out why what looked like good reasons really weren't. Not now."

"A point which I'm quite sure hasn't been lost on First Director Limana and the rest of the Portal Authority," Velvelig said. "In the meantime, we're still left with our uncertainty about the reasons for the silence coming from down-chain."

Chan Tergis nodded, and Velvelig inhaled deeply.

"Very well, Senior-Armsman. I want you to continue trying to reach Voice Ilthyr. But I also want you to send a message up-chain. I want higher authority informed about this."

"You think something serious is wrong?" Chan Tergis' question came out sounding remarkably like a statement, Velvelig thought, and shrugged.

"I don't know that I'd say I think something *is* seriously wrong. But I'm certainly open to the possibility that something *may* be wrong. It's hard for me to visualize something that could have kept any warning from getting out to us, but in light of what chan Tesh and chan Baskay have been saying, I'm not going to rule anything out, either."

"I'm not exactly in favor of taking any chances, either, Sir, but it's almost three hundred miles from Fort Shaylar to Fort Brithik, and it's another twelve hundred miles from Fort Brithik to Fort Ghartoun. That's the next best thing to sixteen hundred miles of nothing but horse trails and wilderness, and Lamir's relay station is five hundred miles *this* side of Brithik. I can't think of anything that could cover that much ground in just three days!"

"Neither can I," Velvelig said mildly. "On the other hand, two months ago I couldn't have imagined anything that threw honest-to-gods fireballs or lightning bolts, either. Under the circumstances, it probably wouldn't be a bad idea to accustom ourselves to stretching our mental horizons, don't you think? And if it should happen that for some strange reason *we* drop off the Voicenet, I'd like to think someone might notice."

"Yes, Sir. I understand."

"Good, Senior-Armsman. Now—" Velvelig made a shooing motion with his right hand "—go do it."

CHAPTER TWENTY

"NOW *that's* A sight for sore eyes, Sir. If you don't mind my saying so."

Platoon-Captain His Grand Imperial Highness Janaki chan Calirath drew rein as they topped out across the modest ridge line, then looked across at Chief-Armsman Lorash chan Braikal with a quizzical expression.

"I don't mind at all, Chief," he said mildly. "In fact, I agree. Although, to be honest, it's not my sore *eyes* I'm thinking about."

The chief-armsman's mouth twitched, but he'd been an Imperial Marine for seventeen years, and his expression had learned to behave itself . . . more or less.

"As the Platoon-Captain says, of course, Sir," chan Braikal responded after a moment. "Far be it from me to confuse the Platoon-Captain's anatomical parts."

"I should certainly hope not, Chief." Janaki's voice was admirably severe, but his eyes twinkled, and chan Braikal snorted. Then the noncom's expression turned more serious.

"All joking aside, Sir, I really am glad to see that," he said, waving one hand at the incredible energy raising the thick clouds of dust under the baking sun of the Queriz Depression. Black banners of smoke from the funnels of steam shovels and bulldozers mingled with the dust, hanging in a lung-clogging pall, and they could see the long, gleaming line of steel rails stretching out towards the southern horizon beyond it.

"I am, too," Janaki agreed, and uncased his binoculars. He raised them to his eyes, and the distant scene jumped into sharp focus as he turned the adjusting knob.

There had to be at least a thousand workers immediately visible down there, he reflected, and every one of them was as busy as an entire clan of beavers. Bulldozers and shovels chewed the roadbed out of the bone-dry, mostly flat terrain, rampaging through their self-induced fog of dust like steam- and smoke-snorting monsters. Steam-powered tractors followed along behind them on caterpillar treads, dumping heavy loads of gravel for more bulldozers, scrapers, and steamrollers to level into place and tamp firmly. Then more tractors followed behind, hauling heavy trailers stacked high with railroad ties and rails. Workers balanced precariously atop the loads tossed ties and rails over the trailers' sides with the easy rhythm of long practice, and each balk of timber, each gleaming length of steel, landed precisely where it was supposed to be.

More workers moved forward, adjusting the ties, setting them into the waiting gravel ballast of the steadily advancing roadbed. Gangs of track-layers followed them, lifting the rails, swinging them into place on the heavy, creosote-soaked ties, holding them there while plate men fished the rail ends, then stood aside while flashing hammers drove the spikes.

The Crown Prince of Ternathia—who was well on his

way to becoming the crown prince of all of Sharona—lowered the binoculars and shook his head. This was scarcely the first Trans-Temporal Express railhead he'd ever watched advancing across a virgin universe, but right off the top of his head, he couldn't remember ever seeing such a focused, frenzied, carefully choreographed boil of energy.

And just why should you find that particularly surprising, Janaki? he asked himself sardonically. *You've never seen them laying track towards something that looks entirely too much like an inter-universal* war, *either, have you?*

"That sore part of me that isn't eyes is really looking forward to parking itself in a passenger car's seat," he informed chan Braikal as he returned his binoculars to their case. "Of course, after this long in the saddle, my memory of what passenger cars are like has become a bit vague."

"I'm sure it will all come back to the Platoon-Captain," chan Braikal said. "And I hope you won't take this wrongly, Sir, but the main reason *I'll* be glad to see those passenger cars has more to do with speed than places to sit. The farther and faster towards the rear we get these prisoners—and you—the better I'll like it."

Janaki grimaced and started to say something, then stopped himself and looked away once more. His own feelings at being bundled safely off to the rear, however important the job they'd found to give him as part of the bundling process, remained profoundly ambiguous. The part of him which had been trained as his father's heir recognized the logic in Company-Captain chan Tesh's decision to send him back to Sharona. Indeed, that intellectual part of him recognized that it would have been the height of insanity for chan Tesh to do anything else. But what his intellect recognized as sanity and what his emotions insisted he ought to be doing were two quite different things.

"Sir," chan Braikal said quietly, "I know this isn't really what you want, but you know it's the *right* thing for you to be doing."

Janaki looked back at the older man, and chan Braikal smiled sadly.

"You'd have done just fine, Sir," the chief-armsman told him. "I've seen quite a few platoon-captains in my time. Brought along my share of 'em, for that matter, if you'll pardon my saying so. Some of them, to be honest, scared the shit out of me. Others . . . well, let's just say I wasn't too sure where I'd find them standing on the day it finally fell into the crapper on us. But you?" He shook his head. "You might've ended up screwing up—I don't think you would have, but anybody can. But if you had, at least I'm pretty sure all of the holes would've been in the front."

"Thanks, Chief . . . I think," Janaki said wryly.

"Don't mention it, Sir." Chan Braikal grinned at him, and Janaki snorted.

"Well, however that might be, I suppose we should get this show back on the road."

"Yes, Sir."

The chief-armsman turned in the saddle to bawl a few pithy suggestions to the other men of Janaki's platoon. The recipients of his requests responded promptly, and the ambulances containing the Arcanan POWs Janaki was responsible for escorting to the rear moved briskly forward.

Janaki watched them roll past him behind their double

teams of mules, each ambulance flanked by its pair of assigned, watchful mounted Marines, and admitted to himself that he felt a profound sense of relief. Despite any ambiguity (and he was honest enough with himself to realize chan Braikal had put his finger squarely on the question which bothered him the most), he would be overjoyed to get those prisoners back to Sharona. And not just because he knew how vital their interrogation was likely to prove, either. From the reports he'd received down the Voicenet, it sounded as if his father had more than enough forest fires to put out. No doubt Emperor Zindel could find any number of useful things for his heir apparent to be doing as part of the extinguishing process. And according to those same reports, his sister Andrin had been forced to shoulder a huge share of the heir's responsibilities in his absence . . . and she wasn't even eighteen yet. It was time he got home and took that off her shoulders.

Of course, there *was* that bit about marriages.

Janaki grimaced. He'd never doubted that his eventual marriage would be carefully considered and weighed. It couldn't have been any other way for the heir to the Winged Crown of Ternathia, and there'd been no point pretending it could have been or whining about the fact that it wasn't. But given the . . . testy relations between Ternathia and Uromathia, he'd never anticipated being required to marry into the family of *Chava Busar*, and he couldn't say he found the idea very appealing.

The Voice reports he'd been able to monitor had been fragmentary and disjointed. He didn't have a Voice actually assigned to his platoon, and the Voice relay stations tended to be far enough apart to make it all but impossible for travelers passing between them to stay in any sort of steady touch, unless they were Voices themselves. From what he *had* Heard and Seen, though, it didn't sound as if his father was any happier about the prospect than Janaki himself was. Not that his father's unhappiness would change anything any more than Janaki's might have. They were both Caliraths, after all, and Janaki felt an odd sort of pride in the realization that his father would make the decision on the basis of what had to be done, regardless of any personal costs, in the full confidence that Janaki would understand.

He looked up at the graceful speck circling lazily against the blazing sky and raised his gauntleted left hand, then whistled shrilly. He rather doubted that the circling peregrine falcon could possibly have physically heard anything, but Taleena didn't need to. She caught the thought he'd sent with the whistle and folded her wings.

He watched the magnificent bird streak down out of the heavens, rocketing towards him, touched with the reflected fire of the sun. Then she struck his gauntlet with all the power and control of her breed. He lowered his hand, and she hopped from his leather-protected wrist to the frame mounted on his saddle, pausing only to press her wickedly sharp beak gently and affectionately against his cheek.

Janaki chuckled softly, stroking the sleek head with an equally gentle fingertip, and crooned to her.

"There, dear heart," he murmured. "Wouldn't want to lose *you*, would I?"

Taleena ignored the comment, just as it deserved to be ignored, Janaki thought with a smile. Imperial Ternathian falcons didn't get "lost."

Which is just as well, he thought as he urged his blue roan Shikowr forward after the last ambulance. *And if she doesn't get lost, I don't suppose* I *can, either. However tempting it might be. And I suppose the truth is that I'm still anxious to get home, marriage or no marriage. Whatever else happens*—he snorted in amusement—*I should at least get a long, hot bath out of it. Two or three days' worth of soaking ought to be just about right, and the way I feel right now, that would be worth even having Chava Busar as a father-in-law!*

* * *

Tayrgal Carthos watched the smoke curling up from the bonfire which had once been a pathetic excuse for a portal fort and tried to decide whether he felt more satisfaction or irritation.

It was a hard call to make, he reflected as his command dragon came in to a relatively smooth landing. On the one hand, he'd been given independent command of one arm of the pincer punching into Sharonian-held territory. On the other hand, it was definitely the secondary arm, and he and the relatively light forces Two Thousand Harshu had seen fit to assign to him (little more than three thousand men and barely enough transports to move them) had an enormous journey ahead of them—a point the extensive flight they'd had to undertake just to get to their next staging point underscored quite nicely, he thought grumpily.

The portal between the previously Sharonian-claimed universes of New Uromath and Thermyn was located in the flat plains of northwestern Elath in Central Andara, but the portal between Thermyn and Nairsom lay a good twelve hundred miles south of there. That put it in a deep, narrow, inconveniently placed valley in the mountains near what should have been the city of Gerynth in the Kingdom of Yanko, where the connection between the continents of Andara and Hilmar began to neck down. And once he'd finished moving his entire command that far (and resting his dragons before beginning the next stage) he'd moved through into Nairsom only to discover that he'd also moved from the heat of Gerynth back into the late autumn chill of Elath within fifty miles of the city of Drekon, barely three hundred miles from his Thermyn starting point at Fort Brithik.

The good news was that it was only a little more than six hundred miles from Drekon to his next portal, located in the Kingdom of Lokan's Duchy of Kanaiya. The bad news was that it lay at the northern tip of Lake Kanaiya, and while the weather at Drekon was only pleasantly crisp, the temperature in Kanaiya was going to be quite another matter. And from Five Hundred Neshok's prisoner interrogation, it looked like a leg of well over *three thousand* miles once he'd crossed over from Nairsom to Resym.

Yet those were merely logistical details, to be taken in stride, he reminded himself as he climbed down from the dragon. To be sure, those "details" meant there was no way in any world that he could possibly hope to reach Traisum before Harshu. He'd simply had to accept that he'd been turfed out of any of the glory for the conquest of that universe and that that miserable Air Force puke Toralk was going to get credit for it, instead. Still, by the same token, *he'd* been given an independent command, whereas Toralk was going to be right under Harshu's eagle eye.

The question in his mind was why Harshu had

arranged things that way. Several hypotheses suggested themselves to him, ranging from the possibility that Harshu had such unbridled trust in him that he was the only man suitable for the task (which Carthos rated as only a little less likely than holding the winning ticket in the All-Arcana Sweepstakes) to the possibility that Harshu had discovered just how deeply in debt to Two Thousand mul Gurthak Carthos actually was.

That was the possibility that worried the thousand. On the face of things, it wasn't very likely anyone knew, given how carefully both he and mul Gurthak had covered their tracks. But if Harshu *had* figured it out before he decided to send Carthos clear out here on the "flanking sweep," as he'd called it in his orders, then several thoroughly unpleasant possible futures presented themselves to Carthos' scrutiny.

The fact that it was illegal for a senior officer to cosign a loan for one of his subordinates could lead to ugly repercussions if Harshu reported it to the Inspector General. It happened from time to time, anyway, as everyone perfectly understood, but seldom if ever on the scale of Carthos' dealings with mul Gurthak. Or, rather, with the Central Bank of Mythal, upon whose Loan Board one of mul Gurthak's innumerable cousins happened to hold a permanent seat. CBM was the largest, wealthiest, and most powerful of all the Mythalan banks, as befitted the official state bank of the Mythalan Hegemony. It must hold literally millions of loans. But very few of them had been granted on such favorable terms or secured by such threadbare collateral, and the fact that CBM had been remarkably patient with his . . . spotty repayment record would also interest the IG, Carthos felt quite sure.

If it came to a formal investigation, Carthos would be lucky if he was allowed to resign his commission without additional (and probably painful) disciplinary action. Even prison time was entirely likely, if only as a horrible example to discourage others from following in his footsteps. He knew that. But what worried him even more than that was the possibility that a *thorough* investigation would also discover all the small favors he'd done mul Gurthak over the last few years. Although there'd never been anything quite so crude as an openly demanded *quid pro quo*, there'd also never been any question in Carthos' own mind that those "favors" constituted the true interest on his past-due loans. He was quite certain the IG would see it that way, at any rate. And if the private memos mul Gurthak had sent to him at the same time the Mythalan two thousand had ordered him forward to join Harshu ever came under public scrutiny, things would get very, *very* ugly.

And if *Harshu* had already become aware of them . . .

Stop it, Tayrgal! the thousand told himself sharply. *If he knows, he knows. And if he* did *know, he probably wouldn't have settled for just sending you off to the backside of nowhere.*

"Sir! Welcome to Nairsom!"

"Thank you, Five Hundred Eswayr." Carthos returned Commander of Five Hundred Pahkrys Eswayr's salute. Eswayr—a wiry, fair-haired Inkaran—was his senior ground forces battalion commander. Carthos found his accent rather hard to follow (the islanders seemed to take a perverse delight in massacring the pronunciation of Andaran), but the five hundred seemed a reasonably competent sort, if a bit on the overenthusiastic side.

"I see Hundred Helika's reds were reasonably effective," Carthos continued dryly, looking past Eswayr at the blazing wreckage Commander of One Hundred Faryx Helika's 5001st Strike had left where the small Sharonian portal fort used to be.

"Yes, Sir." Eswayr turned to survey the same scene, and grimaced. "I know you wanted it intact, Thousand. I'm afraid it was just a bit more flammable than our pilots assumed it would be."

"I see." Carthos hid a grimace of his own. Somehow, he doubted the Air Force would have made the same mistake if Toralk had been here to ride herd on them. On the other hand, to be fair (not that he particularly wanted to be), Carthos himself had emphasized to Five Hundred Karth Mala, his senior Air Force officer, that it was essential that the fort be taken out fast and hard. And since Harshu had retained both of Toralk's yellows . . .

"May I assume the Voice chain has been cut?" the thousand asked after a moment.

"Yes, Sir. The strike teams located the relay station and took it out last night. And it appears that the portal Voice was killed in the initial strike on the fort."

"So there's something to be said for overkill, after all," Carthos observed with a desert-dry smile. Then he shrugged. "To be honest, Pahkrys, I'm just as glad Hundred Halika's opening strike leveled the place." He twitched his head at the demolished fort. "I was never too happy about the distance to the next portal. I know there was a relay station, but it's only about six hundred miles. If the information we have on these Voices is accurate, quite a few of them could reach that far without a relay."

"I know, Sir." Eswayr seemed to relax just a little.

"Well, then!" Carthos said, straightening briskly and planting his hands on his hips. "I suppose it's time I had a few words with Five Hundred Mala and we started getting the troops forward again."

"Yes, Sir," Eswayr said once more. Then he seemed to hesitate for a moment. "Uh, Sir, I did have one other question."

"Question?" Carthos looked back at the infantry officer, one eyebrow arched.

"Yes, Sir. We have a few prisoners, Sir. I was just wondering what you wanted me to do about them."

"Prisoners?" Carthos repeated with a frown. "What sort of prisoners? How many of them?"

"There are only about fifteen of them," Eswayr said. "Three of them are pretty badly burned."

"Any officers?"

"No, Sir. Mostly enlisted, with a couple of noncoms."

"I see." Carthos gazed unseeingly into the crackling flames consuming the fort for several heartbeats, then returned his gaze to Eswayr.

"Has anyone questioned them?"

"Yes, Sir. They . . . didn't seem to know very much."

"And you believed them?"

"According to the verifier spells they were telling the truth, Sir."

"Then they're not very useful, are they?" Carthos observed.

"Apparently not," Eswayr agreed. "On the other hand, Five Hundred Neshok might be able to get more out of them by asking the right questions."

"But Five Hundred Neshok is the better part of three thousand miles from here with Two Thousand

Harshu," Carthos pointed out. "It would take us just a while to get the prisoners to him. And by the time any information he got out of them got back to us, it would probably be hopelessly out of date."

Eswayr nodded, and Carthos' nostrils flared. He didn't much care for these Sharonians. He wouldn't have under any circumstances, but even if he'd been inclined to, there were those memos from mul Gurthak to consider.

"I don't see any point tying up a transport on that sort of useless shuttle mission, Five Hundred," he said. "It's not like we have all that many of them to spare, after all."

"No, Sir," Eswayr agreed.

"And if they don't have any useful information for us, then I don't really see much point in hauling them along with us, either."

Carthos looked levelly into Eswayr's eyes. For a moment, he thought the five hundred was going to balk. But then the Inkaran drew a deep breath.

"Yes, Sir. I'll . . . take care of it."

"Good." Carthos patted the smaller man on the shoulder with a smile. "I'll leave it in your hands, then. Now, where can I find Five Hundred Mala?"

CHAPTER TWENTY-ONE

"COME IN KLAYRMAN! Come in."

Klayrman Toralk obeyed the invitation and stepped into Two Thousand Harshu's command tent. He'd half-expected a summons like this one. In fact, he wondered what had taken so long. More than two days had passed since the revelations of his supper with Harshu. Tayrgal Carthos had been sent upon his way forty-eight hours previously, but Harshu had yet to move towards his own next objective, and so far, at least, Toralk had no idea why he hadn't.

Hopefully, that's about to change, he told himself as he approached the map table floating in midair at the center of the outsized tent.

Aside from himself and Harshu, the only other person present was Commander of Five Hundred Herak Mahrkrai, Harshu's chief of staff. Mahrkrai—old for his rank, with iron-gray hair and oddly colorless eyes—was the sort of officer who seemed to have specialized in unobtrusiveness throughout his entire career. Toralk had worked with him enough in planning the Expeditionary Force's operations to know he was a highly competent, even an imaginative man, but he didn't *project* that. His apparent . . . blandness, for want of a better word, was the most striking thing about him, and Toralk wondered why. He supposed it might have owed something to the fact that Mahrkrai's less showy personality was simply lost in the shadow of Harshu's far more extroverted and aggressive impact on everyone about him.

Of course, it's always possible Harshu picked him expressly because *he has that sort of personality. But if he did, the question is whether it was because Harshu was smart enough to know he needed a balance wheel like Mahrkrai? Or was it because he wanted to make sure his chief of staff wouldn't challenge him for the spotlight?*

"Thank you for getting here so promptly, Klayrman," Harshu continued, reaching out to offer the Air Force officer his hand.

"I'd say you were welcome, if there were any particular reason why I *shouldn't* have come promptly, Sir," Toralk replied, and Harshu snorted.

"What a polite way of saying we've been sitting here on our arses too long!" the two thousand said. Toralk opened his mouth, but Harshu shook his head before he could speak. "No, that's a perfectly reasonable thing for you to be thinking, actually. Especially given how heavily all of our preliminary planning emphasized the need to move quickly once we got through the initial Sharonian defenses. Unfortunately, Five Hundred Neshok has turned up some intelligence which Herak and I have been kicking around for the better part of twelve hours now."

"What sort of intelligence, Sir, if I may ask?" Toralk said cautiously.

"According to two or three of our prisoners, there are Arcanan prisoners being held in our next objective, Sir," Five Hundred Mahrkrai answered for his boss.

"What?" Astonishment startled the question out of Toralk. The instant it was out of his mouth, though, he wondered just why he was surprised. They'd known all along that the survivors of the Second Andarans had been taken prisoner, which meant, logically, that they had to be being held somewhere.

I suppose I simply assumed they'd have done the same things with their prisoners that we did with ours—gotten them moved to the rear for proper interrogation as quickly as possible. Except, of course, that we *haven't* *been doing that since we launched this attack, have we?*

That last thought suggested some potentially grim reasons for holding prisoners closer to the front, so he decided not to think about it any more just at the moment.

"We've confirmed it," Harshu told him. "At least, the verifier spells have confirmed that the prisoners giving us the information believe it's accurate. According to the best information Neshok's been able to put together, the worst wounded of our people were held at this Fort Ghartoun, or Fort Raylthar, or whatever the hells it's named these days."

"It makes sense, Sir," Mahrkrai put in. "As far as we can tell, they don't have anything like our magistrons. They're pretty much limited to natural healing times, and transporting badly wounded men without even dragons must be a nightmare. So they probably parked the most badly hurt of our people at this Fort Ghartoun. Since they didn't know a thing about our aerial capability, they must have figured Ghartoun was far enough from our point of contact to be secure."

"But you see our problem, don't you, Klayrman?" Harshu said, waving one hand at the sketch map on the table. "We can't exactly use the yellows—or even the reds—in a surprise attack if our own people are being held inside the fort."

"No, we can't, Sir," Toralk agreed, stepping closer to the table and gazing down at the map.

"At least it's on this side of the next portal," Harshu pointed out. "As long as we exercise a little caution, there's not too much chance of anyone spotting us moving into attack position."

"I'm not sure how significant that really is, Sir," Toralk replied. Harshu raised an eyebrow, and the Air Force thousand shrugged. "Obviously, there's always a greater chance of being spotted moving through a portal—one of the more irritating things about them is the way they bottleneck your movement options to at least some extent, after all. But we've pretty much swept the area between here and the next portal. There weren't any civilian settlements—" *thank the gods*, he very carefully did not say aloud, thinking about Neshok "—and we'd neutralized the Voice relay even before we hit Fort Brithik. So we can move with virtual impunity right up until the instant we jump off for the attack. All of that's true. But from the outset, one of our primary planning considerations has been the neutralization of their Voice chain's *next* link, the one immediately beyond whatever might be our current objective. So we're still going to have to get our long-range penetration teams through the portal before the attack, which is going to take us right back to that bottleneck situation."

"Maybe not, Sir," Mahrkrai put in diffidently. He tapped the sketch map. "From this, it looks as if their fort is a good mile or mile-and-a-half inside the portal. If we can get people on the ground, maybe a talon or two of dragons in the air, between the fort and the portal, they won't be able to get a Voice through to the other side. Not, at least, until we can get our people through to take their next Voice relay station."

"And you know roughly where that is?" Toralk asked.

"Yes, Sir. We do."

"I see."

Toralk fell silent, pursing his lips as he moved his gaze to the sketched floor plan pinned to the table beside the map. He wasn't about to invest too much confidence in that sketch's accuracy—not knowing how Neshok obtained his information. Still, it was probably fairly close. The Sharonians, like the Union of Arcana itself, seemed to stick to fairly standardized designs for things like portal forts.

He ran a fingertip across the sketch, thinking hard, then looked back up at Harshu.

"I could wish we had some SpecOps troopers to spearhead this thing, Sir. Still, I think we could probably do it without an opening air strike. Assuming, of course, that we still have the advantage of surprise." His expression was sober, and his voice took on a warning note as he continued. "With their weapons, if they figure out we're coming and get themselves stood-to in time, even a relatively small garrison is going to inflict heavy casualties if we don't hammer them with a surprise air strike first."

"Understood." Harshu stepped over close beside the Air Force officer, gazing at the same sketch.

"To be honest," the two thousand went on, after a moment, "I never expected that we'd get much farther than we already have without taking substantial casualties of our own. I'm inclined to think now that I was overly pessimistic in that respect, given how decisively your combat strikes have been shutting them down before we ever have to go in on the ground. I don't really want to do anything to change that, like sending in some sort of conventional assault instead. But if they *do* have any of our people inside, then we can't justify not trying to get them out—or, even worse, possibly killing them ourselves—simply because we might risk a few more casualties in a rescue attempt."

"I agree, Sir," Toralk said firmly, although he was strongly tempted to point out that even if they hadn't suffered very many casualties in human terms, the *dragons* they'd lost had been more than merely painful. The diversion of both transports and battle dragons he'd been forced to make to Five Hundred Mala to support Carthos' independent advance hadn't helped his force availability any either, of course.

"How soon can you give me an operations plan?" Harshu asked.

"Probably by lunchtime, Sir." Toralk shrugged. "As I say, I'd feel better with a SpecOps company to lead the way, but this is a fairly standard scenario. We spend a lot of time planning and executing these on the fly in our normal training exercises, and we've learned a lot about these people, too."

"Good. It's going to take us a full day to get our transports moved into striking range and rested, anyway. Can you do your planning while we're actually in the air?"

"No, Sir," Toralk said with fairly massive understatement. "But what I *can* do is hold a small planning staff right where we are while we put the ops plan together. Then I can load them all onto a single transport and catch up with you sometime this evening. We'll have to leave the transport behind to rest while the rest of the attack kicks off, but the availability of a single transport dragon either way isn't going to make or break the op."

"Good," Harshu repeated. "Good! I'll be looking forward to seeing your plan."

* * *

<Good, Syrail. Good!> Folsar chan Tergis Said enthusiastically as he Watched the crystal-clear imagery of something physically seen through someone else's eyes. *<I've known Voices three times your age who wouldn't have gotten it that clear. I think you're finally getting the hang of it.>*

The Fort Ghartoun Voice could Feel Syrail Targal's pleasure at the compliment. A pleasure due in no small part to the fact that the thirteen-year-old boy knew that it was deserved.

<You know, Folsar,> Syrail Said back, *<you really are a pretty good teacher.>*

<Am I?> chan Tergis chuckled. *<Just between you and me? I'd rather be sitting in a school somewhere a lot closer to Sharona than being stuck out here.>*

<Well, I'm just as happy you're here.>

<Thanks . . . I think,> chan Tergis Said dryly.

The truth was that chan Tergis *had* been a teacher—and a good one—in one of the private Talent academies before his weakness for distilled grain products landed him in the uniform of the PAAF. He wasn't above occasionally bewailing the change in his fortunes, although—while he wasn't prepared to admit it to anyone (including himself, most of the time)—he actually rather enjoyed his present life. Oh, he really did miss the amenities of the home universe or the more developed of the colonized universes. But he also knew that his drinking problem—and the fact that it *was* a problem simply could not be denied—was far more difficult for him to deal with in those universes.

Funny, he thought on a level carefully shielded from young Syrail. *Two-thirds of the drinking problems in the military happen out here in one of the frontier postings. I guess some folks miss the bright lights enough that sheer boredom gets them. Me, I think seeing all this empty, unspoiled breathing space takes the pressure off, somehow.*

He didn't know if that was the truth, or if he was fooling himself, and it didn't really matter. He'd been sober for almost a full year this time, and he'd discovered that he really liked Regiment-Captain Velvelig. There was a lot more humor and warmth hidden behind that Arpathian façade than most people would ever realize. Besides, the "can't-make-*me*-a-soldier" game was ever so much more fun with a CO who understood the rules!

<*Mom's calling me, Folsar,*> Syrail Said, and the imagery of the view from his window which he'd been sending to chan Tergis disappeared abruptly. <*I think I may have left a few chores undone this morning.*>

<*Haven't you figured out yet that you can't fib to another Voice?*> chan Tergis replied with a chuckle. <*You don't just* think *you left them undone.*>

<*Well, maybe not,*> Syrail admitted sheepishly. <*Bye!*>

The boy withdrew, and chan Tergis sat up in the straight-backed chair beside his small desk and opened his eyes.

Syrail was a good kid. He reminded chan Tergis of his own youngest cousin, as a matter of fact, although Syrail's Talent was considerably stronger. In fact, it was a shame, bordering on something worse than that, that he was stuck out here in Thermyn. There weren't more than a couple of thousand people in and around Fort Ghartoun and the surrounding countryside. No one—unless it was Regiment-Captain Velvelig—had any hard and fast official numbers for Thermyn's population, but however many people there were, there weren't enough to have a proper Talent academy, and Syrail's Voice really needed training.

Fortunately, the boy's family's cabin was less than thirty miles from Fort Ghartoun. That was close enough that chan Tergis had caught the telltale involuntary Voice transmissions of an extraordinarily powerful Talent just coming into its own. It hadn't taken him long to track down the source, although he had been a bit surprised by Syrail's youth. Generally, a Talent as strong as Syrail's didn't truly begin manifesting until its possessor was at least fifteen or sixteen years old. Which probably explained why his parents hadn't worried about having him tested for Talent before they headed out to Thermyn. After all, Syrail had been only twelve when they set out, and they were due to return to Sharona in only a few more months.

Syrail's father, who was also named Syrail, although he usually went by his nickname, "Kersai," which meant "redhead" in his native Tathewinan, was a geologist, employed by the Fairnos Consortium, who'd been assigned to the preliminary survey of the Sky Blood Lode in Thermyn. Even though the basic geology was identical in every universe, there were almost always minor variations. Landslides limited to individual universes, or forest fires, or floods, or any number of purely local factors could affect plans to develop something like the huge silver deposits.

In this case, the altitude differential between the Thermyn and Failcham sides of the portal had produced more of that than usual. It was fortunate that this portal had obviously been here literally for centuries, if not longer. There were ample clues as to what must have happened to the local geography and flora and fauna when that savage tidal bore of furnace-hot, kiln-dry wind from the Ricathian Desert came ripping through it and blasted straight into the western face of the Sky Blood Mountains. The local plant life had recovered, masking the worst of the inter-universal sandblasting under fully mature forest, but there were still spectacular expanses of naked, wind-blasted rock where the lash of the portal blast had scourged the flesh from the mountains' bones.

Kersai was young for the responsibility of dealing with that sort of "minor variation," but he was also smart and hardworking, and from everything chan Tergis had been able to discern, he'd done a first-rate job. In fact, he, his wife Raysith, and Syrail were going to be heading back to Sharona in just a few days, at least three months ahead of their original schedule, for a well-deserved vacation and promotion. Chan Tergis had already discussed young Syrail's need for additional training with his parents, and although neither Kersai nor Raysith was very strongly Talented, they were obviously delighted by his enthusiastic praise for what Syrail had already accomplished.

Chan Tergis was glad. The truth was that he was going to miss the boy, and he'd given the lad his own bronze falcon badge as a going-away gift. Technically, Syrail wouldn't be allowed to wear it until he'd passed at least his second-stage training and been certified, but chan Tergis had a spare, and he'd known it would be the perfect gift even before he watched those brown eyes go huge and round with delight.

And I can use anything good that happens these days, he told himself.

His expression tightened at the reflection. There was *still* no word from Rokam Traygan or Shansair Baulwan. In fact, there was still no word from Lamir Ilthyr, for that matter, and there damned well ought to have been by now. He knew Regiment-Captain Velvelig was more perturbed by the ongoing silence than he'd chosen to let on, and so was chan Tergis. Truth to tell, he was beginning to wonder if something rather more serious hadn't happened to Ilthyr. Fatal accidents were scarcely unknown out here on the frontier, where a man might be bitten by a snake, mauled by a bear, break his neck in a fall, or be crushed when a falling horse rolled over on him. True, things like that happened rather less frequently to Voices than to others, given the (relatively) sedentary nature of their duties, but they could still happen. And he was becoming unhappily certain that he was going to discover that something a lot more serious than a simple allergy or the flu had happened to young Lamir.

Stop borrowing trouble! he scolded himself. *If you find out it was nothing serious after all, think how stupid you're going to feel.*

* * *

Janaki chan Calirath straightened in his seat and stretched hugely as the abbreviated, shabby train hissed and banged to a halt at the Fort Salby station. The standard seats in the Trans-Temporal Express's third-class carriages hadn't been designed to fit Caliraths. And the seats the coin-counters in the TTE home offices had seen fit to put into the carriages on their work trains made third-class carriages seem palatial by comparison. Still, as he and Chief-Armsman chan Braikal had already agreed, even this beat the hell out of a saddle.

He snorted with amusement at the thought, then glanced at chan Braikal.

"Go ahead and get them organized to detrain, Chief. I'll find out where we need to put them."

"Yes, Sir."

Janaki left that task in chan Braikal's more than capable hands and climbed down onto the sun-blasted boardwalk of the Fort Salby rail station. It wasn't the first time he'd been here, but the place hadn't gotten much cooler between visits.

There *was* one notable change, he noticed, and he was glad he'd been warned about it before he saw the Uromathian cavalry standard for the first time. Given the traditional relationship between Ternathia and Uromathia—and his own . . . unanticipated marital prospects—he wasn't overjoyed to see the crossed crimson sabers on a black field flying from one of the flagpoles on Salby's parade ground.

"Platoon-Captain chan Calirath?" a voice said, and he turned towards the speaker.

"Yes, Sir!" he said crisply, coming to attention and saluting the dark-complexioned company-captain with the pronounced Shurkhali accent.

"Stand easy, Platoon-Captain," the company-captain said dryly and extended a hand. "I'm Orkam Vargan, the XO. And I'm glad to see you, for several reasons. One of which, I don't imagine *you're* going to like very much."

"Sir?" Janaki said a bit warily, and Vargan gave him a lopsided smile, dark eyes sympathetic.

"I'm afraid there have been some changes in your orders. I know you were supposed to be their military escort all the way back to Sharona, but given what's been going on in Tajvana, the Powers That Be have decided they need you home as quickly as possible, and not as just one more platoon-captain. Which means, I'm sorry to say, that delivering these prisoners to Salby is the last thing you're going to do as an Imperial Marine . . . Your Highness."

Janaki had guessed where Vargan was headed, and he'd been prepared to protest. But he didn't. He didn't because even as Vargan spoke, a lightning bolt seemed to stab through his brain. It hit so hard, so suddenly, his breath actually caught.

The Glimpse made no sense. Not yet. Regiment-Captain Velvelig had told him about the warning his father had sent down-chain after the Emperor and Andrin had experienced their initial Glimpses. Unfortunately, the warning hadn't come with a great deal of detail—not unusual, as Janaki knew only too well, where Glimpses were concerned. Yet the little bit Velvelig had been able to tell him resonated strongly with the images of fire and explosions, the sound of screams and the thunder of weapons, ripping through him now.

Janaki's Talent had never been remotely as strong as his sister's. In fact, he'd always been rather guiltily thankful that it wasn't. He'd watched his father and Andrin dealing with the . . . discomfort of their Glimpses, and he'd been glad his own Glimpses had never hit him that hard.

Today, though, he longed for a bit more of Andrin's sensitivity. Chan Braikal had told him about the Glimpse he'd experienced on their march to Hell's Gate, but Janaki himself remembered nothing from it. That was more than merely frustrating, although he'd been able to guess—given the fact that the Chalgyn Consortium crew had been massacred only a very few hours after he'd experienced it—what it must have been about. But from the physical reactions chan Braikal had described, it was obvious that it must have been a very powerful Glimpse, much more powerful than he'd ever had before. And because no one had ever expected him to have a Glimpse of that strength, his training in how to dig it back out of his subconscious was nowhere near as good as his sister's.

"Are you all right, Your Highness?"

He heard Vargan's voice echoing weirdly through the power of his Glimpse and tried to force his eyes to focus on the company-captain. For a second or two—possibly even a little longer—they flatly refused. They were . . . somewhere else. Somewhere dark and frightening.

Then they did focus, and Janaki sucked in a deep, sudden breath.

"Your Highness?" Vargan repeated, and this time there was genuine concern in his voice.

"I'm sorry, Company-Captain," Janaki said, shaking himself vigorously. "I . . . guess I really didn't want to hear that."

"I wish I hadn't had to tell you," Vargan admitted.

"Well, I hope all of this enthusiasm to get me home doesn't mean I have to leap right on the next train." Janaki prayed that his smile didn't look as forced as it felt. "I've been doing nothing but traveling for the best part of four months now—first *to* Hell's Gate, and then straight back home *from* Hell's Gate. I'd really, really like to spend one day or so sitting still. Preferably in a deep, hot bathtub somewhere."

"They said they want your return expedited," Vargan said slowly. "Still, it's going to take us most of a day just to figure out the train schedule, given the way the Third Dragoons' movement is screwing up the TTE's timetables. I can't guarantee anything, but I suspect Regiment-Captain chan Skrithik could see his way to letting you have twenty-four hours. Maybe even forty-eight."

"I'd like that, Sir."

"We'll see what we can do, Your Highness. I promise."

"Thank you, Sir."

"And now," Vargan continued, "let's get these POWs of yours off the train. I've arranged suitable—and secure—quarters for them while they're our . . . guests."

Janaki nodded and followed Vargan as the company-captain strode briskly over to the train, but the crown prince's thoughts were somewhere else entirely. He hoped Vargan was right about chan Skrithik. If the company-captain wasn't, then it was going to be up to Janaki to find some way to change the regiment-captain's mind. Janaki *needed* that time here at Fort Salby, and not just for a bath, however sensually seductive hot water and soap might be.

Whatever he'd just Glimpsed, it was going to happen

here—*right* here, at Salby, and physical proximity to a Glimpse's locus had a powerful sharpening, focusing effect on the Glimpse itself, even for someone whose Talent was as erratic as Janaki's. So he needed to be here, if he was going to figure out what that Glimpse truly meant. But the one thing he knew with absolute certainty was that if he explained what he'd already Seen to chan Skrithik, he'd never be given the opportunity. The Fort Salby CO would literally throw him onto the next train—and, in the absence of trains, onto horseback—to get him as far away as possible if Janaki told him the one crystal-clear image he'd brought back from his Glimpse in the instant his eyes refocused.

The image of Company-Captain Orkam Vargan's decapitated body sprawled across torn, corpse-strewn ground while his blood soaked into Fort Salby's parade ground.

CHAPTER TWENTY-TWO

COMMANDER OF FIFTY Halesak reminded himself that he was going to need the use of his hands soon. Which would be a bit of the problem if he insisted on clinging to the rope so tightly that the hands in question were numb.

He forced himself to loosen his grip—a little—and pressed his face against the side of the transport dragon's freight platform. Even with the Air Force-style face shield on his helmet, the wind of the mighty beast's passage threatened to suck the breath right out of his lungs. He felt every prodigious sweep of the dragon's pinions, the pounding of its vast heart, and the night wind battering past him was cold even through his heavy clothing and thick gloves, also Air Force-supplied, at an altitude of almost six thousand feet.

All of that was true—and none of it mattered at all. Not tonight. Tonight was even more important than silencing the relays in the Voice chain. Tonight they brought some of their people home again, and no one—*no one*—was going to do that without the Second Andarans.

The dragon slowed abruptly, and Halesak's nerves

tightened as the cargo-master slapped him on the shoulder in warning. The commander of fifty pulled his head back as the slipstream weakened. He looked down, and saw their objective.

Timing for this operation had been tricky. Halesak wasn't sure exactly where the other side of this portal was located, but it had to be at least seven or eight thousand miles further east in its own universe, given the obvious ten-hour or so time difference between the two aspects of the portal. Personally, he suspected that was one reason the Sharonians had located their portal fort in the lee of a steep ridgeline. The last thing someone needed in the middle of *his* night was to have a miles-wide half-disk of noonday brightness streaming in through the window. To be sure, it was undoubtedly a spectacular sight when that flaming sun and hot, bright sky carved themselves out of a sky dusted with winter constellations. Halesak had watched the same sort of thing himself, with an unfailing sense of awe . . . and knew how fervently he and his fellow troopers would have bitched if it had been shining in through *their* windows.

From all the reports, the far side of the portal also had to be substantially lower in altitude. There'd been ample signs of the kind of damage that sort of differential produced, although it had obviously happened a long, long time ago. That damage had complicated things a bit when it came to picking the path for the ground element, too. In the end, they'd had to take a chance on sending in a high-altitude recon gryphon and generating detailed topographic maps from the imagery its crystal had captured.

Fortunately, no one on the ground seemed to have noticed the unusually large eagle circling over their fort.

Ideally, the planners would have liked to hit Ghartoun in full darkness. Thanks to the portal, however, there *was* no full darkness for this particular objective. The best they'd been able to do was to schedule the attack for roughly five o'clock in the morning, local time. At this time of year, that would still be about thirty minutes before local sunrise, and about thirty minutes *after* sunset on the other side of the portal. It wouldn't be true full dark on either side, but at least the portal was east of their objective. That meant all of the available light would be coming from the same direction, which would let them approach out of the darker western sky above the Cratak Mountains. Personally, Halesak would have preferred some heavy cloud cover, but that wasn't going to happen here.

The cargo-master slapped his shoulder again, harder this time, and Halesak nodded vigorously. Then the dragon swept over the parapet of the fort, clearing it by barely fifty feet, and braked into an abrupt hover as the Gifted cargo-master activated the levitation spell.

The spell wouldn't support the dragon's heavy bulk for more than a very few minutes, but that was all the time in this universe—or any other—Iftar Halesak and his men needed.

* * *

Under-Armsman Lyntail chan Turkan hated the dawn watch.

Chan Turkan was what was technically known in the PAAF as "a screwup." Actually, Master-Armsman Karuk, Fort Ghartoun's senior noncom, was prone to use a rather more pithy and less polite term in his own native Arpathian on the many occasions when he . . . counseled chan Turkan. Which was one reason chan Turkan tended to draw the dawn watch as often as he did, given that Karuk was a great believer in using unpleasant duty as a gentle spur to encourage better performance. And when Regiment-Captain Velvelig decided to double the sentries on each watch for reasons best known only to himself, chan Turkan had been the inevitable candidate for his present duty.

After almost eight months of attempting to encourage better performance, however, even someone as formidable as Master-Armsman Karuk might be excused for beginning to feel the first, faint outriders of despair where chan Turkan was concerned.

The master-armsman might not have despaired, but he was showing clear signs of deciding the time had come for more drastic measures. Chan Turkan had no idea what those "more drastic measures" might be, but as he stood on Fort Ghartoun's parapet, gazing at the portal and the dawn slowly strengthening beyond the crest of the eastern ridges, he was glumly certain he'd be finding out shortly.

As it happened, he was wrong.

Something made him turn around. It might have been a sound, it might have been something else. Either way, he didn't have time to figure out what it was.

His jaw dropped in total disbelief as . . . *something* came hurtling over the fort's western parapet. Whatever it was, chan Turkan had never seen anything like it before. It was an impossible fusion of improbable creatures—something with the head of a huge bird of prey, the hindquarters of a lion, feathered forelegs that ended in monstrous talons, and *wings*.

It came over the wall, bursting out of the predawn darkness of the western sky without a sound, and the

PAAF trooper on the northwestern tower never had a chance to scream. The terrifying apparition swooped down upon him. The clawed talons snatched him up by the shoulders; the clawed rear feet ripped out, raking him from chest to abdomen in a dreadful disemboweling stroke; and the terrible, metallically glinting beak snapped once. The severed head flew in one direction and the discarded, mutilated body tumbled to the parade ground in a shower of blood and other body fluids as the impossible killer rocketed back upwards.

Chan Turkan was frozen, unable to believe—to *comprehend*—what was happening as more and more of the murderous creatures came streaking over the fort's walls.

Some of the sentries had time to scream as the fresh wave of death swept over them. Someone actually even had time and the presence of mind to start ringing the alarm bell, but it tolled only twice before one of the monstrosities pounced on whoever it was. Chan Turkan heard the screams, heard the high, wailing hunting shrieks of the no-longer-silent killers. Somewhere a rifle or pistol cracked as one of the sentries somehow got a shot off, and chan Turkan found his own hands suddenly scrabbling frantically at the leather rifle sling on his own shoulder.

He was still scrabbling at it when one of the second-wave gryphons struck him from behind, like a falcon striking a hare, and snapped his neck instantly.

* * *

As the transport dragon came over the palisade and went into its hover, Halesak watched the opening gryphon strike swarm over the defenders.

He'd always hated the strike gryphons. The recon

gryphons were something quite different. First, they were almost always female, whereas every strike gryphon was a male, although that was less important than their other differences. The recon gryphons were also bigger, stronger, less maneuverable, smarter . . . and much, much more biddable. Some of them were actually affectionate, and became quite devoted to their handlers.

So far as Halesak was aware, no strike gryphon had ever been devoted to *anyone*. Their designers had built them around an almost insane territoriality, a vicious temper, and a voracious hunger. They had one and only one function: to kill anything in their programmed area of attack. Strike gryphons were never trained for their missions, the way recon gryphons often were. Instead, their handlers relied completely on the compulsion spells laid into the creatures' hate-filled brains through the sarkolis chips surgically implanted in the young no more than four or five days after hatching. That was one reason Halesak hated them. There was always the possibility that those compulsion spells might fail, and the last thing any semi-sane soldier wanted was to have a theoretically "friendly" rogue gryphon rampaging through his formation in a killing frenzy.

At least this time the spells seemed to be holding, and it was obvious the Sharonian sentries had never had a clue the attack was coming. Most of them were caught with their shoulder weapons still slung, and very few of them had time to do anything about that.

In fact, very few of them had time to do anything but die.

* * *

Namir Velvelig's bare feet hit the floor as the cacophony of screams, shots, and a strange, high-pitched wailing sound yanked him brutally up out of dreamless sleep. He seized his pistol belt, slung it about his waist without even considering trousers or blouse, and raced out of his quarters to the office window which overlooked the parade ground.

At the moment, that parade ground was a scene of barely predawn nightmare.

He saw the hawk-headed monsters ripping and tearing at his sentries, saw the mutilated bodies of his men strewn across the interior of the fort where their killers had dropped them like so much garbage. And he saw those same killers sweeping back, circling above the barracks where most of the rest of his men were quartered.

Velvelig was an Arpathian. Despite his thoroughly modern education, despite his years as a professional soldier in a modern army, the shamans' tales had prepared him for devils and demons in a way most Sharonians would no longer have understood. His forebrain could only stare in disbelief at the slaughter outside his window. Deep down inside, though, those shamans' tales took over. He didn't have to *think* to know what a man did about demons, and that part of him instantly determined that his revolver was not the best possible tool for his requirements.

He whirled away from the window. He didn't have the key which was still in the pocket of the trousers he wasn't wearing, and there was no time to worry about niceties. A single shot from his H&W blew the lock off the chain through the trigger guards of the racked shotguns.

Velvelig's hands moved with flashing speed as he scooped up one of the weapons. The Model 7 combat shotgun was a purely military weapon, a slide-action weapon with a five-round detachable box magazine and a bayonet lug, and designed to fire brass-cased ammunition which was much more powerful than the standard civilian loads. It was heavy, ugly, and a brute to fire, but it was as lethal as it was unlovely, and there were twenty-four preloaded magazines of double ought buckshot on the shelf across the bottom of the weapons rack. Each cartridge contained ten pellets, each of them the size of a Polshana .36-caliber bullet, and Velvelig racked the action open, slid a loose round into the chamber and closed it, then slapped in a magazine. He had few illusions about what was about to happen, but he took long enough to sweep half a dozen more magazines into a canvas ammunition carrier and slung it over his shoulder.

Then he stepped out onto the planked walkway in front of his office.

* * *

Halesak grunted as he fast-roped down from the transport and his heels thumped on the firing step inside the fort wall. He started to bark the order for his men to assemble on him, then ducked as another gryphon came slicing in just above his head.

Something exploded down below him. His ears classified it instantly as the sound of one of the Sharonian weapons, but this one sounded slightly different, somehow. He whirled towards the noise and saw a single man, naked but for a loose white pair of skivvies and a weapons belt, standing on the veranda across the front of what Neshok's sketch map called the office block. He had what looked like one of the standard shoulder weapons, but as Halesak watched the man fired again, and a second gryphon shrieked and collapsed in midair as if it had just flown headlong into a wall. It slammed into the ground in a broken ball of fur and feathers, and the single defender's left hand stroked back under his weapon's barrel and he fired again.

A *third* gryphon went down, and the man who'd killed it cycled his weapon once more and tracked smoothly, almost unhurriedly, onto a fourth target.

*   *   *

Velvelig had a vague impression of something huge and dark hovering just above the wall. Whatever it was, there wasn't anything he could do about it at the moment, and he was totally focused on the task he *could* do something about. The veranda roof gave him overhead cover, and he had an excellent view of the monster-besieged barracks. He'd always been a superior wing shot, and these things—whatever the hells they were—were bigger than deer, not doves. He squeezed the trigger, the shotgun's buttplate hammered his shoulder, and a fourth monster smashed into the barracks wall like two hundred pounds of dead meat.

He swung onto a fifth creature and fired. Then a sixth.

Half a dozen of the murderous beasts were down, and he pressed the magazine release. The empty magazine thumped to the veranda floor, and he slammed in another, worked the slide, and brought down a seventh target.

*   *   *

Nothing could ever let Iftar Halesak forget that the Sharonian butchers had murdered one of the greatest men in Arcana's history in cold blood. The hatred that had kindled in his heart was something perhaps only another *garthan* could truly have understood. Yet as he saw that single defender, standing his ground, firing with such cool, steady precision, he felt an unwilling surge of admiration. It wasn't just the other man's courage, though gods alone knew how much raw nerve it must take for someone who'd never even suspected that gryphons existed to face them with such steadiness. No, it was the other's obvious sense of duty . . . and his effectiveness.

Even as Halesak watched, that single Sharonian brought down a seventh and an eighth gryphon. The fact that the attacking predators were so focused on the targets designated by the combination of their controlling spellware and their own natural viciousness meant they paid the man killing them almost no attention at all. They were so totally committed to neutralizing the barracks, keeping anyone from getting out of *them*, as their pre-attack command programming required, that they never noticed the single man outside the *office* block.

"Yirman!" the commander of fifty barked. "Get the gates open! The rest of you, on me!"

Lance Yirman Farl and the two other men assigned to help him went thundering down the nearest stair to the parade ground below. The rest followed Halesak as he went scurrying along the firing step, looking for a clear firing angle.

* * *

Velvelig brought down yet another gryphon, and his second magazine was empty. He dropped it out of the magazine well and reached into the carrier at his side for a third.

That was when the crossbow bolt hit him.

It slammed into his right hip like an incandescent spike, and he grunted explosively at the raw, brutal stab of agony. The sheer sledgehammer impact was enough to knock him backward, off his feet, and he went down, losing his shotgun as he landed. His left hand went to the stubby, thumb-thick steel shaft driven deep into his pelvis, but his right swept down to his holster and the heavy, familiar weight of his H&W revolver fell into his palm.

The monsters swarming around the barracks had noticed him at last, and one of them came straight at him. He brought the revolver up, tracking the incoming nightmare with a rock-steady muzzle, and fired.

The hollow-nosed .46-caliber slug hit the gryphon in the left eye at a range of little more than fifteen feet. The creature's head snapped up under the brutal impact, but momentum kept it coming, and Namir Velvelig's world went black as the plummeting body smashed into him.

* * *

Iftar Halesak stood in the center of the captured fort's parade ground, looking about him at the litter of bodies—and body parts—sprawled across the gore-splashed dirt. In some ways, the carnage was even worse than he'd seen at Fort Shaylar and Fort Brithik. The bodies there hadn't been this mangled. This . . . shredded. True, many of them had been so burned and shriveled as to no longer look human, but in some ways that had actually lessened the impact. It had been hard to think of them as anything which had ever *been* human, while those killed by the yellows had at least been intact. These bodies were not. In fact, they looked exactly like what they were—the brutally mutilated corpses of men who had been literally torn to pieces by vicious, ravening predators bigger than most of them had been.

So what? he demanded of himself harshly. *Dead is dead, however you get that way. Besides, at least it's pretty quick when a gryphon gets hold of you! And none of these bastards was an old, gentle* civilian *who got murdered* after *he'd surrendered.*

A stubborn little voice buried deep in the back of his brain stirred uneasily at that last statement. He felt it there, but he crushed it ruthlessly back into silence. Whatever might be happening to surrendered Sharonian POWs, he and his men hadn't had anything to do with it. And none of it could change what the butchers had done to Magister Halathyn.

He watched the dismounted unicorn cavalry troopers spreading out to relieve the initial infantry assault force. He and the other air-dropped infantry had opened the gates and held them until the cavalry could arrive against the disjointed efforts of the dozen or so Sharonians who'd been outside the barracks and somehow evaded destruction by the gryphons. He'd lost three of his own men, but the defenders had been so stunned, so shocked, by what had happened to them that they'd had virtually no unit organization at all. Their counterattacks had been determined, but they'd been launched in ones and twos, without sufficient strength—even with their infantry weapons—to break through the defensive fire of Halesak's arbalests and infantry-dragons.

Most of those who'd tried to retake the gate were just as dead as the ones the gryphons had ripped apart, and—

"Sir! Fifty Halesak!"

Halesak turned and found Yirman Farl pelting across the parade ground towards him.

"What is it?" the officer asked sharply.

"We've found the POWs!" Farl announced excitedly. "One of them's asking for *you*, Sir!"

"For me?" Halesak blinked.

"Yes, Sir!" Farl's smile looked like it was about to split his face in half. "It's Fifty Ulthar!"

"*Ulthar?*" Halesak repeated sharply. "Where?"

"Over here, Sir!"

Halesak followed the lance quickly through the carnage to what was obviously the fort's brig. There were perhaps a dozen men locked into its cells. The early morning light pouring in through the outer barred windows showed that the cells weren't particularly crowded, and that they'd been provided with ample bedding. That registered peripherally with Halesak, but his attention was locked on the tallish, wiry, red-haired Andaran who had a cell entirely to himself.

"Therman!" Halesak seized his brother-in-law's good hand as Fifty Ulthar reached it through the bars to him. "Gods, man! We thought you were *dead!*"

"Not quite." Ulthar was paler than ever, Halesak thought, and noticed the awkward way the other man stood, with his left arm in a sling. The shoulder on that side was oddly hunched and swollen, as if there might be multiple layers of bandage under his blouse, and his face was grooved with pain lines which hadn't been there the last time Halesak had seen him.

"I took a hit through the shoulder," Ulthar explained as he saw the direction of Halesak's gaze. "Tore the hell out of it, actually, and these people don't have healers. Not like ours, anyway. They did their best, but . . ."

He shrugged his good shoulder, and Halesak's jaw tightened.

"If they did, it's the *only* time they did," he grated, and Ulthar's eyebrows rose.

"What's that mean?" he asked. Halesak looked at him in surprise, and Ulthar smiled crookedly. "I know you better than that, Iftar. It's not like you to leap to conclusions, and I'm a bit at a loss to understand how you'd know anything about how they've been treating us since they captured us."

"I don't have to know about that to know what sort of butchers these people are," Halesak said harshly. Ulthar's surprise was obvious, and Halesak's lips drew back in a snarl. "The fact that they shot Magister Halathyn down like a dog after he surrendered is all *I* need to know, Therman!"

"Shot Magister Halathyn?" Ulthar's surprise had segued into confusion. "What're you talking about? *They* didn't kill Magister Halathyn!"

"*What?!*" Halesak stared at him in disbelief. For an instant or two, the ex-*garthan*'s brain simply refused to process information. Then he shook himself violently. "But the Intelligence reports . . . the briefings—"

"I'm telling you, they didn't do it," Ulthar said. "They *couldn't* have. It wasn't one of their weapons—it was one of ours. An infantry-dragon. A lightning-thrower."

"Are you sure, Therman? Are you *positive?*"

"Damned right I'm sure," Ulthar said grimly. "They allowed us funeral rites when they buried the dead. I saw Magister Halathyn's body with my own eyes, Iftar. He'd been wounded in one arm, probably by one of their hand weapons, during the attack, yes. But it was the lightning that killed him."

"Oh my gods," Halesak whispered, remembering the

hatred, the fury which had impelled him. "They said they couldn't *confirm* it, but . . ."

"I don't know what 'they' told you," Ulthar said, "but as far as I can tell, these people have treated all of their prisoners—including me, Iftar—with respect. I haven't seen one bit of casual brutality, and their healers—such as they are—have done everything they could for our wounded. Despite the fact that *we* shot at *them* first."

"We shot first?" Halesak parroted.

"Of course we did!" Ulthar's voice was suddenly harsh and bitter. "Hundred Olderhan was right. He wanted us pulled back, away from the portal until we could sort out how to manage a *peaceful* contact, but Hundred Thalmayr had other ideas. I talked to one of the sentries he ordered to open fire on the single cavalry trooper they sent forward to talk to us. To *talk* to us, Iftar!"

Halesak's mind was working overtime, putting bits and pieces together, remembering the rumors about how Five Hundred Neshok went about "interrogating" captured Sharonians . . . and remembering that Two Thousand Harshu hadn't done a thing to stop him.

"Listen, Therman," he said quickly, urgently, leaning closer to the bars and keeping his voice low, "can you prove we didn't kill Magister Halathyn?"

"Prove it?" Ulthar's confusion was obvious, and Halesak shook his head hard.

"All our intelligence briefings have . . . strongly suggested that the Sharonians murdered Magister Halathyn after he surrendered. I didn't have any more reason to question that than anyone else did. Not till now. Now I do, and I have to wonder *why* they've gone out of their way to 'suggest' to all of us that that's what happened."

Ulthar stared at him for a moment, then grimaced. "Magister Halathyn's been buried for three months now, Iftar. In a grave in a swamp, without any sort of preservation spell. I don't know if *anyone* could prove exactly how he died at this point. I know *I* saw his body, and I think at least one or two of the others did, but I can't *prove* anything."

"And can anyone else confirm that we shot first?" Halesak pressed.

"I don't know," Ulthar said slowly. "The man I spoke to—Lance Tiris—died shortly after we were captured. Their healers tried, but they couldn't save him."

"Damn," Halesak murmured, and Ulthar cocked his head, blue eyes intense.

"What the hells is going on here, Iftar?"

"Look," Halesak said, even more quietly than before, "I don't know for sure what's going on. We were told *they* started it both times. And we were told there were those 'unconfirmed reports' that Magister Halathyn was murdered after he surrendered. Plus the rumors—I don't know exactly who started them—that they shot our wounded after they surrendered."

"That's bullshit!" Ulthar exploded. "That's—"

"Shut up!" Halesak hissed. "Shut up and *listen* to me!"

Ulthar spluttered to a stop and Halesak drew a deep breath.

"That's better," he said, then paused, trying to decide how to say what needed saying.

"Look," he said again, finally, "you're my sister's husband, my daughter's uncle. I don't want to go home and explain to either of them that something happened to you after I found you alive!"

"But—"

"I'm telling you, we wouldn't have been told what we were told as often as we were told it before this op kicked off unless somebody had decided it was what we *needed* to be told. And if that *was* what happened, it fucking worked." He smiled grimly. "Believe me, Therman, you don't want to know the things *I've* been contemplating since they told me how Magister Halathyn is supposed to have died, and I am sure as hells not alone in that.

"But if I'm right, if it was done on purpose, how do you think they're going to react if you insist on telling them we've all been lied to?"

"If you've been lied to, then it's my duty to tell people the truth." The familiar stubborn look in Ulthar's blue eyes made Halesak's stomach clench painfully, and he fought a sudden urge to seize his less massively built brother-in-law by the front of his uniform blouse and shake some sense into him.

"Godsdamn it, you *listen* to me this time, Therman Ulthar," he said instead, a whetstone of passion sharpening the edge of his intense voice. "I'm a *garthan*. My people—*your* people now, damn it—know all about being lied to and manipulated. Gods, man! Those bastard *shakira* have been doing it for thousands of years! And given what you've just told me, I smell the mother of all lies. Don't you think for one moment that whoever's responsible for it wouldn't be perfectly willing to 'disappear' a single inconvenient commander of fifty who can't even substantiate his 'preposterous claims.'"

"That kind of thing may go on in Mythal," Ulthar said sharply, "but this is the *Union* Army, godsdamn it!"

"And I'm not telling you to keep your mouth shut forever," Halesak shot back. "I'm telling you to keep your mouth closed and your head down until you know for absolute, fucking certain that the senior officer you're telling about it isn't part of a deliberate campaign to change the truth. Do you understand me, Therman? I'm not going home to tell Arylis that you got your stupid self killed playing Andaran honor games with somebody you shouldn't have trusted!"

Ulthar glared at him, but then, slowly, drop by drop, the anger flowed out of his blue eyes to be replaced by something else.

"I'm sorry, Ulthar," Halesak said more gently, meeting that blue gaze of bitter disillusion. "I'm sorrier than I can say. And I agree with you. The truth has to be gotten out eventually. But for that to happen, you have to be alive to do the getting, and I am *not* going to lose you when I just got you back from the dead. Do you read me on this one?"

Ulthar looked at him for long, long moment of silence. And then, finally, nodded slowly.

"Good," Halesak said quietly, reaching through the bars to squeeze his brother-in-law's sound shoulder. "Good."

CHAPTER TWENTY-THREE

"WELL, WELL, WELL," Alivar Neshok murmured as he walked down the line of sullen-faced Sharonian prisoners assembled on the captured fort's body-strewn parade ground. Some of them were lightly wounded; all of them had their hands manacled behind them; and if the look of anyone except a combat-trained magister could have killed, Neshok would have been a smoldering corpse.

The thought rather amused him, actually.

"Those five," he told Javelin Porath. "And . . . that one," he added, pointing at an overweight, blue-eyed senior-armsman.

"Yes, Sir!"

Neshok nodded and walked off, hands clasped behind him, whistling softly. He knew he could count on Porath to deliver the selected prisoners suitably.

His whistling faded as the one major flaw in his present sense of satisfaction floated to the top of his mind once again. The fact that his interrogations had revealed the presence of Arcanan POWs here at Fort Ghartoun was going to be a major feather in his cap, since that was the only reason they hadn't been killed right along with their captors instead of being liberated. But the fact that the attack had gone in on the ground to rescue them meant the Intelligence section had gotten in further behind the lead combat elements than they had during the previous operations.

Which meant the fort's badly wounded Sharonian commander was out of Neshok's reach . . . for the moment, at least.

Neshok growled a mental curse at the thought. Commander of Five Hundred Vaynair had the bastard safely squirreled away in the casualty queue over at the field hospital. Personally, Neshok would have preferred to let the son-of-a-bitch die from his wounds—which he certainly would have done, probably fairly quickly, without Gifted healing—as an example to the rest of the prisoners. Or, failing that, Neshok could at least have shot him himself for the same purpose. Vaynair wasn't going to let that happen, though, and Neshok spared another mental curse for the officious Andaran Scouts commander of fifty who'd hustled the wounded Sharonian off to the healers before Neshok could get his hands on him.

Well, I'll just have to do the best I can with what I still have to work with and settle up with the troublemakers later, he told himself. *And at least this time around, I've got a lot more people to get answers out of.*

He stepped into his chosen interrogation site. It had been a stable, but the unaugmented horses who had been housed here no longer required its stalls. Dragons and gryphons—especially *battle* dragons and gryphons—had active metabolisms, and horses and mules tasted just as good as cattle and sheep as far as they were concerned.

And watching gryphons and dragons feed was probably an eye-opener for the Sharonians, especially after what the gryphons did to so many of their buddies. He chuckled nastily to himself. *That alone ought to loosen a few tongues.*

He strolled across the front of the stable, considering the stalls. They'd do as holding cages if he needed them, he decided, while the tack room he'd had cleared would give him the sort of privacy and . . . intimacy he'd found so effective in the past.

He glanced up as Porath and two other troopers kicked and cuffed their prisoners into the tack room.

"Now, now, Lance Porath," he chided gently, following them inside. "Surely there's no need for all that roughness . . . yet, at least."

"Yes, Sir. Whatever you say," Porath replied with exactly the right edge of disappointment, and the five hundred shook his head and wagged one finger admonishingly. Then he turned his attention to the Sharonians.

"Now then," he continued, addressing them through his translating PC. "My name is Neshok, Five Hundred Neshok of the Army of the Union of Arcana. You and I are going to become very well acquainted, and in the process, you're going to tell me exactly what I want to know."

None of the Sharonians replied, of course, and Neshok smiled thinly.

"You may not think at this moment that you will," he told them, "but if you do, you're wrong. Trust me, you're wrong."

* * *

Folsar chan Tergis looked at the smiling, thin-faced Arcanan and felt a cold stab of terror. This Neshok was radiating his emotions so powerfully that even a half-Deaf Voice—and chan Tergis was anything but half-Deaf—couldn't help picking them up, physical contact or no.

Not any more than he could help realizing that the Arcanan was the next best thing to certifiably insane.

He's enjoying this, chan Tergis thought. *Really,* really *enjoying it. It's not just about power for him; there's something almost erotic about it as far as he's concerned, and he's looking* forward *to killing. Triad, how many more of these people are just like him?!*

"Now," the smiling lunatic's voice was almost caressing, "suppose one of you tells me who your assigned Voice might be?"

Chan Tergis' blood seemed to freeze in his veins, but his brain raced with feverish speed. Obviously, these people knew a lot more about Sharonian Talents than anyone had thought they might. Which made the reason for the silence from the down-chain Voices suddenly and terrifyingly easy to understand.

In that moment, Folsar chan Tergis could see what was going to happen as clearly as any Calirath, and a fresh thought hammered through him. He hadn't made any secret of Syrail Targal's awakening Talent. Indeed, he'd been proud of the boy, bragged about the strength of his Voice. If this Neshok was as . . . thorough as chan Tergis was afraid he might prove, someone who knew about Syrail was going to break and tell him. And when that happened . . . .

<*Syrail!*> he Shouted. <*Syrail, Listen to me!*>

For an instant, there was no response. Then he Saw a flash of vision, someone else's hands scooping sweet feed from a burlap bag for eager, velvet-nosed horses.

<*Folsar?*> Syrail's Voice came back as the vision disappeared. The boy sounded startled, and more than a little apprehensive. Obviously, more of chan Tergis' side trace emotions were coming through than he'd intended, but maybe that was a good thing. <*What is it? What's wrong?*>

<*It's the Arcanans,*> chan Tergis Said urgently. <*They've taken the fort.*>

He sent flashing mental images—horrific images, of the striking gryphons, the horned, lynx-eared unicorns, and the terrifyingly enormous dragons—with the speed and completeness possible only for a highly trained Voice. The thirteen-year-old at the other end of the Voice link gasped at the raw brutality of everything he was Seeing and Hearing, and chan Tergis allowed himself a moment of bitter regret for having inflicted that upon him. But someone had to know.

He felt a brief instant of stunned silence, of shock so profound he was afraid the boy was going to withdraw entirely. He wouldn't have blamed Syrail a bit if he had, but the boy was made of sterner stuff than many an adult chan Tergis had known.

<*What's happening now?*> he Asked after a moment, his Voice amazingly steady. <*What do you want me to do?*>

<*For right now, just hold the link open,*> chan Tergis Said. <*Listen and Watch.*>

<*Do you want me to try and get through the portal? Contact the Failcham relay station?*>

<*No!*> chan Tergis practically shouted the single

word. Then he shook himself mentally, managing somehow to keep his expression from revealing what was going on inside his—and Syrail's—heads. <*If they've gotten this far up-chain without anyone getting a warning out, then they've been taking out the Voices as they come,*> he went on in a calmer, more normal Voice. <*That means they know what to look out for, and it probably means they're going to take pains to locate that relay station. If you try to get across the portal and contact anyone, it's just going to draw their attention, and that's the* last *thing you need to do. Believe me, Syrail.*>

<*All right.*> Syrail sounded much more subdued, even frightened, and chan Tergis' jaw tightened as he realized the boy's fear wasn't for himself. He wanted to tell Syrail how proud he was of him, how much the boy had come to mean to him, but there wasn't time. Nor was there really any need—not for two Voices as deeply linked as they were in this moment.

<*It's going to be—*> chan Tergis began, then broke off as the man who'd introduced himself as Alivar Neshok walked over to stand four feet in front of the line of prisoners.

* * *

"It may be," Neshok said reasonably, "that some of you—maybe even all of you, at this point—don't believe me. Perhaps you believe that by keeping your mouths shut you'll manage to deprive us of some critical piece of information. But, you see, there's a problem with that particular line of logic. We've captured quite a few of you this time. Believe me, even if *you* manage not to tell me something when I ask, someone else will answer the same question before it's over. Someone else *always* will. It's just a matter of how many people get hurt first."

None of the Sharonians replied, and something inside Neshok purred like a huge, hunting cat.

He clasped his hands behind himself again, letting himself bob gently up and down on the balls of his feet as he studied their expressions. They seemed less shaken than most of his earlier interrogation subjects had been, he decided. That was interesting, something to bear in mind. Apparently seeing their fellows ripped apart by gryphons was a less shattering experience than being strafed with fireballs or strangled in a cloud of gas. Our perhaps it was simply that the casualty count had been so much lower this time?

"Come now," he told them almost caressingly. "Don't pretend you don't understand what I'm telling you. And think about this. You six have the unfortunate privilege of being the first people I'm going to be asking these questions. There are a lot more where you came from, and, the truth is that you'll be almost as useful as . . . examples, shall we say, as you'll be as information sources. To be perfectly frank, I don't really care whether *you* answer my questions or not."

Still no one spoke, and Neshok unclasped his hands to reach out and take the Sharonian revolver from Porath.

"Now to return to my first question," he said with a bright, friendly smile. "Who's your assigned Voice?"

* * *

Chan Tergis' spine stiffened. He didn't even have to turn his head to know that none of his fellow prisoners as much as glanced in his direction. All of them stared straight ahead, jaws clenched.

"Perhaps you think I'm joking about the consequences of refusing to answer my questions," the Arcanan said. He raised the H&W with the air of a man who knew how to use it and aimed it at the forehead of Petty-Armsman Erkam Varla, the prisoner at the far end of the line. "Trust me," he cocked the hammer, "I'm not."

Sweat beaded Varla's forehead, but he only pressed his lips more tightly together, and Neshok began to squeeze the trigger. There was no hesitation in him. The emotional aura blasting across the tack room battered chan Tergis like waves driven by a winter gale, and the Voice *knew* beyond a doubt that the Arcanan was going to fire.

"Stop!"

Neshok paused, one eyebrow arching, and glanced sideways at chan Tergis.

"You had something you wished to say?" he said politely.

"I'm the Voice," chan Tergis said hoarsely.

<No, Folsar!> Syrail cried in the back of his brain, but chan Tergis' eyes never even flickered from Neshok's face.

"Are you, now?" The Arcanan glanced at the crystal which had been translating. It glowed with a steady blue, and he nodded. "Yes, you are," he said. "How convenient. I expected it was going to take longer to find you."

Chan Tergis said nothing, only looked at him, and Neshok smiled.

"Now, the next question, I suppose, is whether or not you're the *only* Voice here or in the local settlements. Are you?"

Chan Tergis' mind seemed to be speeding faster than ever. The way the Arcanan had checked his crystal suggested it was somehow capable of telling him whether or not chan Tergis was lying. It must be one of these people's preposterous "spells" which somehow duplicated a Sifter's Talent. But how literal-minded was it?

"I'm the only Voice Regiment-Captain Velvelig has," he said in flat, hard tones, and the crystal glowed blue again.

"So you are," Neshok said, and chan Tergis Felt Syrail's whirling emotions from the other end of their link as the boy tasted his own fierce determination to protect him.

"I'm afraid," Neshok continued, "that we've only been able to come up with one way to make certain you Voices don't go chattering away to one another."

Chan Tergis felt his facial muscles tighten, but it was scarcely a surprise. Not given the emotions he'd already sensed from this smiling, purring butcher.

"I'm sure you'll understand," the Arcanan continued, moving the revolver from Varla's forehead to chan Tergis'.

<*Folsar!*> Syrail cried. <*You can't—*>

<*There's no more time, Syrail,*> chan Tergis Said, and his Voice was almost calm. <*I'm sorry. Tell your parents. Tell them someone else here at the fort may remember how I've bragged about you, may tell them about you. You've got to run. Hide. Don't let them—*>

The blinding brilliance of the muzzle flash silenced his Voice forever.

* * *

"I've got the intelligence summaries for your next couple of objectives Klayrman," Two Thousand Harshu told Thousand Toralk that evening. "From what we've been able to put together so far, the next stop—the one in the universe they call 'Karys' should be easy. But the one after that, in 'Traisum'—that one's going to be the hardest nut to crack yet."

"Really, Sir?" Toralk tried very hard not to let his distaste for the way that "intelligence summary" had been assembled show. Harshu obviously saw it anyway, and gave his head an impatient shake.

"I know how you feel about Neshok, Klayrman. And, to be honest, it's time I started reining him in. In fact, I *have* started. I've removed our prisoners from his control, and I've approved Five Hundred Vaynair's refusal to release the wounded to him."

"May I ask why, Sir?" Toralk inquired very carefully.

"Mostly because we're starting to hit more heavily settled universes, according to what we've already learned. Or we will be shortly, at any rate. Fort Mosanik in Karys isn't much. Your yellows should be able to deal with it without any trouble. But somewhere on the other side of it, we're going to encounter this 'railroad' of theirs. Apparently they've got quite a large work crew pushing it down-chain as quickly as they can, and it's undoubtedly got one of these Voices of its own assigned to it.

"That's going to make problems enough all by itself. But once we get past *that*, there's this Fort Salby in Traisum. I think you'll find the information on the portal itself fascinating reading. Then, once we get past that, there's the fort and a substantial settlement around it. In addition, it appears that there are quite a few farming and ranching villages and homesteads stretched out along the route from Fort Salby to the next universe. With that many people mucking about, it's highly unlikely that we're going to be able to continue to . . . neutralize this Voicenet of theirs. There's too much chance of missing a Voice hiding in the underbrush, as it were. That means we're going to lose the advantage of surprise, which is going to make any real advance beyond Fort Salby problematical, at best.

"But that's all right, actually. As you know, we've captured quite a few of their maps intact. We still can't read their language, but a couple of my bright young staff officers have been fooling around with our standard recon image-intepreting spellware, and they've found a way to adapt it. They're scanning the captured maps into their PCs, and then using the interpreting spellware to compare them to *our* maps and look for terrain feature matches. Once they find one, the spellware automatically orients the Sharonian maps to ours and scales them accurately, using ours as a base. We may not know how to read any of the names on their maps, but we're able to make some detailed appreciations of the *terrain* on them now. Which means we know what the rest of this portal chain looks like, although I could wish we knew more about the rest of their explored chains. At any rate, the maps all confirm what the prisoners say. The Traisum portal is definitely going to be the chokepoint we've been looking for. For a lot of reasons."

"Really, Sir?"

"Oh, yes." Harshu smiled thinly. "As I say, I think you'll be impressed. The portal itself would be a nightmare for anyone without dragon capability, and the *approaches* to the portal in Traisum itself are almost as bad. The only ground access to the portal is by way of a valley which is dominated by this Fort Salby. That's one reason I want Salby so badly. I want to be able to control that valley, keep them penned up in it where we can pound them hard, bleed any effort just to reach the portal. Given their lack of any aerial capability, we should always be able to break off and fall back through the portal if they start pushing us too hard."

"Excuse me, Sir, but if the portal is as defensible as you seem to be suggesting, why should we move beyond it?"

"There seems to be substantial agreement among our current prisoners that the reinforcements their swamp portal commander was anticipating will probably be no more than a week or so out from Fort Salby by the time we can reach the portal. If I were their commander, and if I didn't have transports, then I'd probably think long and hard before even contemplating fighting my way through the portal from Traisum to Karys. On the other hand, we still haven't seen these people's heavy weapons, and we don't have any way of predicting the actual combat power of this reinforcement they're expecting. They may think they *can* force the portal. They might even be right.

"By taking Salby and controlling the approach valley, we'll be able to start hitting them early. Hopefully, we'll have a chance to get a feel for how their combat capabilities differ from those we've already encountered. I want that feel before it comes down to a toe-to-toe fight for the actual portal. If, on the other hand, their basic combat power is as outclassed as our more optimistic junior officers prefer to assume, they may never get past us to the portal in the first place. At any rate, from the topography on these maps, it looks like whoever selected the site for Fort Salby had an excellent eye for terrain.

They've definitely put the plug into this valley at its most defensible point, which means it's the logical anchor for us to hang our own defensive positions on.

"In any case, I'm assuming that once we hit the fort itself, word of our presence is going to get out. We won't be able to keep it from spreading up-chain from Traisum, no matter what we do. And I'm not planning on advancing any farther than Traisum, anyway."

The two thousand shrugged.

"In light of all that, the intelligence value of anything more Neshok could extract from his prisoners has got to be of strictly limited utility. And, quite frankly, I'm delighted that that's the way it is." For just a moment, a haunted, almost haggard, expression flickered across Harshu's face. Then he met Toralk's eyes levelly. "I can't justify continuing to allow him to do the things he's been doing unless he's in a position to provide me with genuinely critical information, and that's not going to be the case any longer."

"I can't pretend I'm not . . . very relieved to hear that, Sir," Toralk told him after a moment.

"I know you are, Klayrman." Harshu reached across the floating map table in his command tent and patted the Air Force officer's forearm gently. "I know you are."

There was silence for a moment. Then Harshu inhaled sharply and handed Toralk his copy of the current intelligence summary.

"When you look this over, I think you'll see why this Fort Salby's going to be tough," he said much more briskly. "I'll be interested to see if you come to the same conclusions I did about the most effective approach. I don't want to prejudice your thinking, but as you look through the summary, I'd like you to consider—"

* * *

"My gods, Sir! I thought you were dead!"

"As you can see, Silky, we Arpathians are even tougher than you knew." Namir Velvelig's eyes were darker and bleaker than Company-Captain Silkash had ever before seen them, yet his voice held a ghost of genuine amusement.

"No one's *that* tough," Silkash said flatly. "Remember, I'm the one who triaged you in the first place."

"You did?" Velvelig cocked his head to one side. "Odd. I don't recall it."

"I imagine that's because you were unconscious, almost out of blood, and had serious cranial injuries, not to mention a badly shattered hip and what I'm almost certain was at least one spinal fracture," Silkash told him. The surgeon's face twisted with bitter memory. "I black-tagged you."

"I see."

Velvelig reached out and squeezed his friend's shoulder. He understood now why Silkash looked the way he did. A black tag indicated that there was no point trying to save the patient. That it was time to let him go and concentrate on saving those who might live, instead.

"I don't think your judgment was in error, if that's what's bothering you, Silky," the regiment-captain said after a moment. Silkash looked skeptical, and Velvelig snorted. "Look, don't forget that these people can work magic. *Magic*, Silky. And apparently it's not limited solely to better ways to kill people, either. You wouldn't believe what I saw their healers doing before they decided I was fit enough to go to jail with the rest of you."

"If they could fix everything that was wrong with you, they really *are* wizards," Silkash said. Then he grimaced.

"What?"

"I was just thinking. If they could fix you up, as badly hurt as you were, and do it this quickly, no wonder an idiot like Thalmayr didn't understand what *we* were doing! I'll bet you they don't use surgery at all."

"I don't know about that." Velvelig shook his head. "I saw them doing some surgery, but I'd say they only do it for relatively minor injuries. I'm guessing there's some kind of limit on how much healing they can do at any one time with these spells of theirs, so they probably handle the little stuff the hard way and save the 'magic' for really serious problems. But I think you're probably right about Thalmayr . . . since I saw him walking out of their medical tent unassisted."

He and Silkash looked at one another, and Velvelig saw the mirror of his own response to the sight of a magically—literally—restored Hadrign Thalmayr walking around Fort Ghartoun. Of course, it was probably even more complex for Silkash than it was for Velvelig. After all, the surgeon was a Healer even if he lacked the Talent for it. His oath, as well as his natural personality, required him to want to see any of his patients fully recovered.

However stupid, frustrating, detestable, and just plain infuriating the patient in question might be.

"Well, that's certainly interesting," Silkash said after a moment.

"That's one way to put it. On the other hand, I'm considerably less interested in Thalmayr than I am in what else has been going on."

"I don't know everything that's happened," Silkash replied slowly, and Velvelig's spine stiffened at the bleakness which suddenly infused the surgeon's voice. "What I *do* know hasn't been good, though."

"In that case," Velvelig said, in a tone whose evenness might have deceived anyone who didn't know Arpathians, "I suppose you'd better tell me about it."

* * *

"I'm worried about the horses, Dad," Syrail Targal said.

"So am I," his father said, patting him on the shoulder. "They'll just have to look after themselves for a while, though. Just like we will."

Syrail nodded, and his father ruffled his hair the way he'd done when Syrail was much younger. The youngster managed a smile, and Kersai gave him a gentle nudge in the direction of the carefully hidden tent.

"Go help your mother with supper," he said quietly.

"Yes, sir." Syrail nodded again and headed obediently towards the assigned chore.

His father watched him go, doing his best to hide the depth of his own concern. It had been just over twelve hours since the fall of Fort Ghartoun, and given the strength of the Voice Talent Syrail had been showing for the last several months, there wouldn't have been a lot of point trying to deceive the boy into thinking his parents weren't frightened. But no father wanted to add to his child's fears. Especially, Kersai thought, his expression turning hard and bleak, when that child had already Seen what Syrail had Seen in Folsar chan Tergis' last moments of life.

A part of the worried father was furious at the Fort Ghartoun Voice for inflicting that sort of trauma on his son. And an ignoble part of him was even angrier at chan Tergis for having bragged about Syrail's remarkable Talent to other members of the fort's garrison. If the Voice had just kept his big mouth *shut*, then Kersai

Targal wouldn't be hiding in the early-winter woods praying that the cold-blooded butchers who shot Voices out of hand wouldn't catch up with his son!

But most of him knew it was totally irrational to be angry with chan Tergis. There had been no possible way for the Voice to anticipate what had happened, to even guess that his pride in his protégé might prove dangerous to Syrail. And if his final Voice message to Syrail had been traumatic, it had also been the only thing that had warned Kersai and Raysith to flee.

The man warned us with literally the last seconds of his life. Told Syrail to run and hide when he knew *he was about to be murdered*, Kersai thought. *Gods—while he was* being *murdered! How could anyone be* angry *with someone who did that?*

He knew all of that intellectually; it was just his emotions which couldn't quite catch up with the knowledge. Which was stupid . . . which, in turn, was one reason he was as irritated with himself as he was. He could actually understand that, although there wasn't anything he could do about it. Not yet. Not when his son might very well already be under sentence of death by the same barbarian butchers who had massacred the Chalgyn Consortium crew and now, apparently, launched a vicious, unprovoked attack on *all* Sharonians even while they were officially "negotiating for peace."

He grimaced, gazing up at the sky, wondering if one of those eagle-lions Syrail had tried to describe to him might already be circling high overhead, spying on them. He'd hidden his encampment as carefully as he could, and he'd used his surveys of the surrounding terrain to pick a spot which offered at least three separate avenues of escape. But if these bastards could literally *fly* . . .

He grimaced again and reached into his coat pocket to squeeze the bronze falcon he'd taken out of Syrail's dresser drawer. Then he turned and made his own way towards the tent.

CHAPTER TWENTY-FOUR

SENIOR SWORD BARCAN KALCYR pulled out his navigation unit and glowered at it as his unicorn picked its way through the unforgiving terrain.

The hammering these mountains had taken when this universe's portal formed was more extreme than most. It must have been exciting as hell, but Kalcyr was delighted he hadn't been here to see it. The way it had battered the mountainsides, stripping away trees and soil, leaving naked stone cliffs which rose like ramparts and piling up the wind-driven equivalent of silt behind any sheltering windbreak, had made a complete farce out of the normal maps for this particular piece of terrain. And the fact that the tree cover had been given time to fill back in after the carnage finally tapered off only made things even worse. Or that was the way it seemed to Barcan Kalcyr, at least.

Remember to thank Hundred Worka for this when we get back to base, he told himself.

The navigation unit took a moment to think about his demands. It usually did when it had to coordinate itself with the take from a gryphon-borne recon crystal. The spellware that translated the airborne reconnaissance data for a ground-based unit's navigation requirements always seemed to have a glitch or two running around in it. After a few moments, though, the display settled itself, and he snorted with a certain degree of sour amusement.

So, there you are. Or there you were, *at least,* he thought at the red icon glowing in the the display's depths.

He wished—not for the first time—that there were some way to send the recon crystal's imagery direct from a gryphon to a ground unit while the gryphon was still in the air. Unfortunately, no one had ever come up with one. The gryphon still had to return to base, the crystal had to be extracted from its harness, and then whatever had been recorded had to be downloaded to the units which actually needed it, which meant it was always at least a little out of date by the time it got to the sharp end.

Still, it's one hell of a lot better than anything these Sharonians have, he reminded himself, and his mouth tightened.

He hadn't much cared for anything about the Sharonians even before the invasion actually kicked off. Just listening to the intelligence briefings had told him what sort of barbarians they were, and then there was Magister Halathyn's cold-blooded murder. That was one crime no one was ever going to forgive, and Kalcyr's attitude towards Sharona hadn't gotten one bit better when they found the seared and burned bodies of Fifty Narshu and his men. He *knew* Narshu had to have gotten at least a few of the other side, but there'd been no sign of any Sharonian bodies.

Left our men to fry in their own fat while they took theirs with them.

Kalcyr felt a familiar stir of rage and clamped his jaws tight. It had taken the healers quite some time to identify Uthik Dastiri's half-consumed body. When they finally did, though, it was obvious he'd been shot right between the eyes at very close range before his body was left for the flames like so much garbage. Clearly, the Sharonians had continued their practice of shooting their prisoners out of hand.

Kalcyr's teeth grated, and he forced himself to make his jaw muscles relax. It wasn't easy. It especially wasn't easy when he found himself wondering what the Sharonians had done—or, perhaps, were even now continuing to do—to Rithmar Skirvon and the two missing members of his military escort.

Well, they made the rules, Senior Sword Kalcyr told himself grimly. *Now they can just take the consequences*.

"All right," he told the rest of the half-troop of cavalry Hundred Worka had assigned to him. "According to this," he waved the navigation unit at them, "we're getting damned close. In fact, I think they're probably up there, under that overhang."

* * *

Kersai Targal swallowed a curse.

He'd hoped to escape discovery entirely, but it didn't look like things were going to work out that way.

One of those godsdamned eagle-lions Syrail was talking about, I'll bet, he thought bleakly.

It wasn't a happy thought, and watching the speed and nimbleness of the weird-looking, horned horses under the Arcanans searching for them didn't make it any happier.

The way those things covered ground made it obvious that Raysith, Syrail, and he could never hope to stay away from them on foot. Not when they had airborne spies to tell them exactly where their prey had gone.

Kersai looked down at the rifle in his hands. He was tempted—*so* tempted—to use it, but there were at least fourteen or fifteen of them. He probably could have picked off several of them, but he'd never get them all, and if *he* started the shooting, there could be only one possible outcome.

"Syrail," he said quietly.

"Yes, sir?"

"Take the rifle. Then I want you and your mother to go hide up at the top of the ravine."

"But—"

"Don't *argue*, Syrail. There's no time for it." Kersai turned his head and looked at his son, there in the windy, sun-dappled afternoon, and wished there *were* time. Wished he didn't have to be brusque with the boy he loved so much on this, of all days.

"You have to go now, son," he said more gently. "I need you up there looking after your mother. Now, go. Take care of her, understand?"

"Yes, Dad." Syrail's voice was low, wavering around the edges despite his effort to keep it steady, and Kersai put an arm around him and hugged him tightly.

"I love you, Syrail. I love you very much."

The boy looked back at him, mouth working, unable to speak at all this time, and Kersai gave him one last squeeze.

"Now go," he said softly, and Syrail obeyed him.

Kersai watched him go, then looked back down at the horsemen—if that was the right term for someone mounted on such preposterous creatures—advancing steadily towards his position. He needed a little more time for Syrail and Raysith to reach the next hiding spot he'd picked out for them. Besides, he wasn't in any great hurry for what he knew he needed to do.

He lay there, stretched out on the rock, savoring the caress of the surprisingly warm sun on his shoulders, and waited.

* * *

Kalcyr and his mounted troopers had almost reached the coordinates from the recon gryphon's overflight when a man stood up in front of them.

Kalcyr reined in his unicorn so abruptly the beast snorted and tossed its head in protest, and his eyes flitted about. The single Sharonian standing in front of him wore civilian clothes, and Kalcyr didn't see any sign of a revolver or a rifle. That didn't mean much, though. There could have been half a dozen more of them hidden away in the rocks and trees, every one of them with one of those accursed rifles waiting to blow him and his men out of their saddles.

The Sharonian—a youngish, red-haired fellow—kept his hands in plain sight and just stood there, watching Kalcyr. His expression was remarkably calm, but Kalcyr could see the tension hovering in his tight shoulders, in the way he held himself absolutely motionless.

Good, the senior sword thought harshly. *Go ahead and* sweat, *you bastard!*

Finally, the Sharonian spoke. It was only so much gibberish, and Kalcyr reached into a cargo pocket and extracted the PC loaded with Five Hundred Neshok's translation spellware.

"What?" he barked. "What did you say?"

* * *

Folsar chan Tergis had kept Syrail informed on all of the nonclassified details of the Fallen Timbers negotiations, and Syrail had shared those reports with his parents. So Kersai had at least heard about the Arcanans' magical translating rocks. Even so, actually seeing and hearing one came as more of a surprise than he'd expected. Still, it wasn't as if it had come at him completely cold, and he drew a deep breath.

"I asked you what you want," he repeated in the steadiest voice he could manage.

"What do you *think* we want?" the man who seemed to be in charge shot back. He sounded angry, and Kersai hoped that was only a trick of the translating magic.

"I don't know," he said as reasonably as he could. "You're obviously soldiers. I'm not. And, as you can see, I'm not even armed."

He opened his coat carefully, aware of the dozen or so crossbows aimed straight at him. He held it open, letting them see that the garment had concealed no shoulder holster or other hidden weapon.

"So, you're not a soldier, hey?" the mounted man said with a scornful expression.

"No, of course not," Kersai replied.

"So, if you're not a soldier, why are you hiding out here?"

"Why?" This time Kersai let a little incredulity into his tone. "You've *invaded* us. As far as I can see, it only makes sense to stay out of your way."

* * *

Kalcyr had to admit the other man had a point. In fact, he had a better point then he knew.

One of the troopers behind him stirred uneasily.

Kalcyr sensed the motion and turned his head to give the offender a savage glare, and the man froze.

Lily-livered bastard, Kalcyr thought. *Probably one of those pricks who stays up at night moaning over the Kerellian Accords. These bastards started the massacring, and Five Hundred Neshok's right about taking chances with these 'Talents' of theirs.*

"So, 'civilian,'" he said. "What's your name?"

* * *

Kersai looked up at the cavalry commander. The Arcanan wasn't looking back at him; instead, his attention appeared to be focused on the crystal in his hand, and Kersai's eyes narrowed as he remembered what Syrail had told him about chan Tergis' last transmission. About the crystal which had flashed blue like some sort of inanimate Sifter.

"Syrail," he said quietly—and truthfully. "Syrail Targal."

* * *

Kalcyr grunted in satisfaction as the verifier spell in the PC blinked with blue confirmation. The Sharonian looked older than he'd expected, but then again, the man who'd given the name to Five Hundred Neshok probably hadn't been in the best possible condition when he'd done so. Besides, nobody at the fort, except for the military Voice assigned to it, had ever actually met this Syrail, as far as anyone knew.

"Stand where you are," he commanded, then nodded to two of his men.

"Take a look," he said.

The selected troopers climbed down, passing their reins to one of their fellows, and advanced on the Sharonian. The PC had translated Kalcyr's order to them into Sharonian, as well, and the civilian obviously knew what was coming. He made no effort to resist, although Kalcyr's men were no gentler than they had to be. They were, however, thorough, and one of them grimaced, then waved a small, bronze falcon-shaped badge triumphantly.

Kalcyr reached down and took it, letting it lie in his palm. Then he looked back at the man from whom it had been taken.

"So, you're a Voice."

* * *

Kersai kept his mouth shut.

It wasn't easy. His heart raced, and he could feel the air fluttering in and out of his lungs. He knew now what was coming, and he felt the sweat beading on his brow.

A part of him wanted desperately to answer the Arcanan's questions truthfully. Another part wanted even more desperately to lie. But the truth would probably have been useless . . . and the lie would probably have been detected.

He clenched his fists at his side, standing between the two men who had searched him and who still held his elbows. There was a reason he'd brought that badge along. He'd hoped it would never be needed, that this moment would never come. But the moment *had* come, and he found himself clinging to his love for his son and his wife as he gazed silently up at the hard-faced, hard-eyed Arcanan.

* * *

"So, the gryphon's got your tongue, has it, '*civilian*'?" Kalcyr demanded. The Sharonian only looked back up at him, and the senior sword felt a cold, hard sense of satisfaction. The man's very silence was proof he was exactly what Kalcyr had been sent out here to find. Not that denying the truth would have done him any good in the face of the verifier spells Five Hundred Neshok had loaded to Kalcyr's crystal.

"Not so talkative now, I see," he said, sliding the PC back into his pocket now that it was no longer needed. Still the Sharonian only looked at him, and Kalcyr shrugged.

The senior sword wasn't going to shed any tears over what needed to be done. For that matter, he wasn't going to pretend he didn't take an intense, personal satisfaction out of it. But unlike the Sharonians who'd murdered their Arcanan prisoners, Kalcyr saw no need for brutality.

He looked at the two men flanking their prisoner and nodded.

Quick and clean, he thought approvingly as the blood fountained from the Voice's slashed throat. *Quick and clean.*

He looked down at the crumpled body, which seemed smaller, the way dead men almost always did, then looked up at the sky, remembering another day, other bodies.

"Leave him. Mount up," he said flatly, and the dismounted troopers hesitated only for a moment before they obeyed. Kalcyr gave the corpse one more look, then reined his unicorn's head around and started back the way they'd come, leaving the body for the buzzards.

If it was good enough for Fifty Narshu and his men, it's good enough for that bastard, he thought, and never looked back even once.

* * *

"Overall, I like your attack plan, Klayrman," Two Thousand Harshu said. "The only thing I wonder about is whether it wouldn't be better to go ahead and commit the gryphons first. They were certainly effective enough at Fort Ghartoun."

"Yes, they were, Sir," Toralk agreed. "But we also lost over a dozen of them."

"Practically all to that one damned lunatic with the—the what-do-you-call-it? The *shotgun*," Harshu pointed out.

"True." Toralk nodded. "Still, it did cost us ten percent of our total gryphon strength. I'd like to conserve that, especially if we end up needing it for Fort Salby."

Harshu cocked his head, then frowned slightly while the command tent's canvas flapped gently in the brisk early afternoon breeze.

"That's a logical argument, Klayrman. Why do I think it's not the only one?"

"There is one other thing," Toralk admitted slowly, reminding himself once again that there was a keenly intelligent, highly observant brain behind those intense eyes. "I wouldn't call it a 'logical argument,' exactly, but it is causing me a little concern."

"Well? What is it?"

"It's just that some of the gryphon-handlers are reporting that the compulsion spells don't seem to be working with one hundred percent effectiveness."

"What?" Harshu's eyes narrowed. "What do they mean?"

"That's just it, Sir. They don't seem able to point to any one area in which the spells are malfunctioning. In fact, it's more of a . . . a *feeling*, I guess you'd say, than anything else."

Harshu looked more than mildly incredulous, and Toralk shrugged.

"I didn't say *I'd* observed any problems, Sir. I just said the gryphon-handlers are expressing concerns. Some of them, at any rate. And, to be completely honest, I've never been a gryphon-handler. I know that anyone who does that job successfully for very long has to develop particularly acute instincts where the gryphons are concerned, though, so they could well be seeing something I'm not. Whatever's happening, it's making them a bit worried. Let's face it, Sir—it's not exactly a safe job."

This time, Harshu nodded slowly. In fact, gryphon-handling was one of the more dangerous Air Force specializations. Not a year went by that at least one gryphon-handler wasn't turned upon by his attack-gryphons. People who did the job for very long had to develop a feel for when one of the hyper-aggressive creatures was hovering on the brink of breaking the compulsion spells which normally kept its ferocity under control.

"Do you think there really *is* a problem?" the two thousand asked. "Or do they just *think* there is?"

"Honestly, Sir, I don't know. I only know there's a certain level of anxiety, and I'd just as soon let them stay where they are for right now. If we need them, we can use them, but if we don't need them, then why not let the handlers settle down a bit before we have to commit them somewhere else?"

"I don't suppose I can argue with that," Harshu conceded. "Especially when the fellow arguing in favor of it is the one who's successfully punched out every fort we've encountered so far."

Toralk nodded slightly at the implied compliment, then waved one hand at the map on the table.

"As you see," he said, indicating a red push pin, "our advance party's located an appropriate oasis for our forward staging point. We're still going to have to fly in a lot of water, though, Sir. That's going to cut into our total lift capability. That's why my assault plan calls for leaving the heavy cavalry behind, at least temporarily. They're going to be of limited utility in taking out the fort itself, under the proposed operations plan, and leaving the heavy cav behind gives us the best trade-off for hauling water."

"Agreed." Harshu nodded.

"It's going to cost us a couple of days before we can move on Fort Salby, you understand, Sir? We're going to have to use up some additional transport flights leapfrogging them forward to Fort Mosanik before we can ship them the rest of the way to Traisum."

"Understood," Harshu said.

"Then that only leaves the question of exactly what we do about this after we punch out Mosanik." Harshu tapped another push pin, then looked up at his commanding officer. "I've viewed the imagery from the recon-gryphons, Sir. These people may not have magic, but seeing the kind of engineering they're capable of is . . . well, it's impressive as hell, is what it is, Sir. I'd like your guidance on exactly how we want to approach it."

* * *

"I wish I were going with you, Iftar," Therman Ulthar said quietly as he watched his brother-in-law strapping up his backpack.

"Don't be silly." Iftar Halesak looked up at him and shook his head. "You've sure as hell earned a little more rest, Therman!"

"Maybe."

Ulthar moved his newly healed shoulder gingerly. His stint as a prisoner of war of people who didn't have magistrons had given him a whole new appreciation for modern medicine. The fact that he'd recovered the shoulder's full range of motion literally overnight would have been wonderful enough, but it was also the first time he'd been truly pain-free in literally months. He luxuriated in the sensation, but even as he delighted in the absence of pain, that very delight brought home the thing that most concerned him.

"It's not the rest I'm worried about," he admitted, and Halesak frowned.

"What *is* worrying you?" the *garthan* asked. "You're not still feeling guilty over what that bastard Neshok did, are you?"

"Actually, I am." Ulthar's expression was profoundly unhappy. "I should have said something, stopped him—"

"By the time you were out of the healers' hands and knew what the hell was going on, Two Thousand Harshu and Thousand Toralk had already put a stop to it," Halesak pointed out. "This time, at least," he added.

Ulthar's mouth tightened, and Halesak shook his head.

"I'm telling you, Therman. Let it lie, for now, at least. I don't know what else is going on, but it looks to me like the Two Thousand's decided to put a muzzle on Neshok. If that's the case, then he's not going to be torturing or murdering any more POWs. Which means you don't have to play the noble Andaran paladin in shining armor and maybe get your fool self killed trying to stop it."

"Not trying to stop *Neshok*, anyway," Ulthar muttered.

"And what does that mean?" Halesak demanded.

"They're leaving Thalmayr in command here."

"Thalmayr?" Halesak frowned in surprise. "Who had that brainstorm?"

"I think it was Five Hundred Isrian."

"Oh, *wonderful*." Halesak looked as disgusted as he sounded. Chalbos Isrian was one of Two Thousand Harshu's senior battalion commanders. He was also one of the officers who'd argued most forcefully in support of Neshok's plan for dealing with the Voicenet.

"Exactly."

"It may not be that bad," Halesak said, but he sounded as if he were arguing with himself, not his brother-in-law, and he knew it.

"I hope not," Ulthar said bleakly. "But the fact is, Thalmayr is a frigging idiot at the best of times. And I've got a feeling—a really *bad* feeling, Iftar—that he's just been biding his time. He blames the Sharonians for what happened to us, instead of blaming his own stupidity. And I think—"

He broke off with a shrug.

"You think what?" Halesak asked sharply.

"I think he'll never believe the Sharonians were really trying to help him. I know their healers testified that they were under verifier, and as far as I know, no one's ever been able to fool the verification spells. I know I'm convinced they were doing their best to help *me*. But I don't think there's enough evidence in the multiverse to convince *Thalmayr* of that. And what really scares me is how stupid he proved he could be *before* he was wounded. Gods alone know how much stupider he's capable of being now!"

"Wonderful," Halesak repeated with a sigh, then shook

his head. "Thanks a lot, Therman. Now you've almost got *me* wishing you were coming along with us!"

* * *

"All right," Commander of Five Hundred Cerlohs Myr said, looking around the briefing tent at the circle of faces one last time. It was pitch black outside the tent's canvas walls, but the spell-powered light globes illuminated its interior brilliantly. "All of you know what you're supposed to do. Now, let's go get the job done. Right?"

"Right!"

The one-word response came back in a strong, confident rumble of voices, and Myr nodded in satisfaction . . . mostly.

He looked around at his flight and strike commanders. Their losses in the first attack had come as a shock to all of them, but since then, they'd scored an unbroken string of successes and advanced the better part of three thousand miles in barely eleven days without the loss of a single additional dragon. It was the sort of operation they'd trained at in maneuvers for years and never really expected to have the opportunity to mount, and they knew they'd performed brilliantly so far. Which explained why their faith in themselves went far beyond mere confidence now. They viewed themselves as an elite, and there was a brashness, a swagger in them.

That's good, Myr told himself. *Dragon pilots are* supposed *to know they have big brass ones. That they're the best of the best.*

But there was still that tiny, tiny flaw in his satisfaction. That sense that too much faith in themselves might still lead them to take one chance too many. To push that little bit too hard.

And just what do you want to do about it, Cerlohs? he asked himself. *You want to make them* less *confident before you send them out on an op?*

There could be only one answer to *that* question, he reflected, and had to smile at his own perversity.

It's just your own crossgrained cussedness, he scolded himself. *You'd find something to be upset about even if you fell into a vat of beer!*

"All right," he repeated again. "We've got another fort to burn. Let's get them in the air, gentlemen!"

CHAPTER TWENTY-FIVE

JANAKI CHAN CALIRATH sat in the tiny sitting room attached to his quarters and gazed out at the salmon-colored sky as dawn came to Fort Salby.

The lack of handy trees had enforced a different building plan on Fort Salby, and the time—and the presence of the TTE construction crews—which had been required for the Traisum Cut had provided the labor force and materials to execute that plan. Instead of the wooden palisades which surrounded most portal forts, at least until permanent long-term settlements went in, Salby had been built from a combination of stone and adobe. It had also been built on a considerably larger scale, since it was intended from the outset to be the permanent administrative center for this portal. Its walls—and those of its internal structures—were not only tougher, they were also considerably thicker than those of most portal forts, as well, which helped their interiors stay cooler during the worst of the day's heat.

And it also makes them a hell of a lot tougher, the crown prince thought almost calmly. Almost.

The morning was still cool, chill, as the dry semi-desert air waited for the sun's heat. It was very quiet, and the calm tranquility swept over him, made even stiller and calmer somehow by the chaos swirling within him.

Taleena slept on the perch stand just inside the window, and his eyes lingered on her. There were ghosts in those gray eyes. Ghosts which hadn't been there the day before. The same ghosts which had haunted many a Calirath's eyes over the millennia.

I guess there's no such thing as a weak Calirath Talent, after all, under the right circumstances . . . or the wrong ones, he thought. *Too bad. There are some things I'd really rather not know about.*

The Glimpse wasn't entirely clear yet, but it was becoming that way, and as it clarified, dropped into focus, he understood exactly why it had been so strong in the first place.

I need to tell Regiment-Captain chan Skrithik. But if I do . . .

Janaki grimaced. The problem was that he couldn't just tell the regiment-captain. Certainly, he couldn't tell chan Skrithik *everything*. There was still more he had to find out, more he had to squeeze out of the Glimpse, and there was only one way he could do that.

He stood and walked to the window, leaning on the thick sill, and his face was grim.

What have they done to you, Sir?

He sent the question out into the shadows of his mind. There was no answer, of course, and he closed his eyes against a brief, sharp stab of pain. If what he'd already Glimpsed was true, there was no point trying to send a warning to Regiment-Captain Velvelig. Not now. If he'd only had it a few days—maybe even *one* day—sooner, then maybe he could have alerted Fort Ghartoun. Done *something* different.

But he hadn't had it soon enough, and now there was nothing he could do. Not for Velvelig and Fort Ghartoun, at any rate. Or, for that matter, Fort Mosanik. And perhaps it had had to be that way all along.

He gave himself a shake, sucked in a huge lungful of the cool air, and straightened his shoulders.

"Go ahead and sleep, dear heart," he murmured, touching the sleeping falcon's folded wings ever so lightly. "I've got to go talk to someone."

* * *

Rof chan Skrithik was not amused.

Technically, he supposed, it might be argued, in light of the extraordinary orders he'd received, that his early-morning caller was no longer a platoon-captain, in which case he had to be considered the Crown Prince of Ternathia. Actually, of all of Sharona, although his father's formal coronation wasn't due for almost two weeks yet. But whatever the young man's official status might be, having someone knock on the front door of his quarters before he'd had time for breakfast—or even the strong cup of coffee it took to start his mental processes every morning—was . . . irritating.

"I'm sorry to intrude so early, Sir," Janaki chan Calirath said, almost as if he'd read chan Skrithik's mind. "I wouldn't have, if it weren't vital that I speak to you as soon as possible."

"About what?" Chan Skrithik managed to keep the bite out of his tone somehow.

"Sir," Janaki inhaled deeply, "I have to tell you that I've experienced a Glimpse. A *major* Glimpse."

Chan Skrithik's irritation vanished instantly, snuffed by an arctic wind as he looked into Janaki' gray eyes.

"What sort of Glimpse, Your Highness?" he asked in a totally different voice.

"It's not complete yet, Sir," Janaki said with a grimace of frustration. "To be honest, my Talent isn't as strong as Father's—and it's a *lot* weaker than my sister Andrin's. It's still coming into focus, and it's going to take a while longer before it comes clear. Or as clear as it's *going* to come, at any rate. I'm afraid Glimpses aren't quite as cut and dried as a normal Precog."

"I understand that, Your Highness. At the same time," chan Skrithik managed a tight smile, "I don't imagine you'd be telling me about it at this point if you didn't at least have a pretty shrewd notion of where it was headed. And," the regiment-captain's eyes sharpened, "unless it concerned Fort Salby or something else along those lines."

"You're right, Sir. It does—concern Fort Salby, I mean." Janaki's nostrils flared. "I know this is going to sound preposterous, at least at first, but, well, Fort Salby is going to be attacked."

"What?" Despite his total faith in the power of the Calirath Talent, Rof chan Skrithik felt a moment of sheer incredulity. Janaki couldn't be serious! But when he looked into that young face, so much like a younger version of the official portrait of Emperor Zindel hanging in his office, any temptation towards disbelief vanished.

"Attacked by whom, Your Highness?" he asked instead. Then he shook his head in irritation. "That's a stupid question, I suppose, isn't it? Who else could it be?"

"I know it sounds crazy, Sir," Janaki said, "but some of the details I've managed to strain out of the Glimpse might explain how they could get this far up-chain this quickly. Mind you, I don't know how they did it without any sort of warning getting out, but the short version is that they've got something I can only describe as . . . dragons."

"Dragons?" chan Skrithik repeated very carefully, and Janaki snorted a humorless laugh.

"I did mention that I knew it was going to sound crazy," he reminded Fort Salby's commanding officer. "Unfortunately, I don't know what else to call them. They're big—in fact, they're godsdamned *huge*, from what I've Glimpsed so far—and they fly. Not only that, they breathe fire and . . . other things."

Chan Skrithik sat back in his chair, examining his future emperor's face very carefully. Then he drew a deep breath of his own and pointed at the chair on the other side of the table.

"If you'll forgive me, Your Highness, I haven't eaten yet this morning, and my brain doesn't work very well without its morning infusion of caffeine. Why don't you join me for breakfast and tell me just what in Vothan's name is going on?"

* * *

". . . sometime within the next few days, Company-Captain," Janaki said a couple of hours later. "I wish I could be more specific than that, but that's not the way Glimpses work. Not for me, at any rate. I only know it's coming and that they've somehow kept any advance warning from getting out. And that Petty-Captain chan Darma—" he nodded at the only officer present who was even more junior than he was "—has been unable to raise Fort Mosanik's Voice this morning."

"I see." Company-Captain Vargan frowned thoughtfully, then shrugged. "No one can have everything, Your Highness. The fact that we know they're coming at all is more than we really had any right to expect."

Regiment-Captain chan Skrithik nodded in agreement. He, Vargan, Petty-Captain Kaliya chan Darma, chan Skrithik's assigned Voice, and Sunlord Markan sat in a row of chairs, facing Janaki as he stood in front of a large-scale, detailed topographical map of Fort Salby and the surrounding territory. Janaki felt remarkably like a junior student, called upon to read his latest research paper aloud to a visiting delegation of department heads.

Not all of whom seemed particularly enthralled by his presentation.

"As Company-Captain Vargan says, we are fortunate to know as much as we do," Sunlord Markan agreed after a moment, but the Uromathian cavalry commander's expression was more shuttered than the Shurkhali's. He gazed at Janaki with cool, thoughtful eyes, then cocked his head. "Forgive me . . . Your Highness, but I appear to be somewhat less familiar with the nature of your family's Talent than my colleagues are. Or, perhaps, I should say that I am less familiar with its limitations. May I ask a question or two?"

"Of course, Lord of Horse," Janaki replied.

This entire briefing felt awkward. Partly, that was the inevitable result of the fact that his Glimpse remained less than complete at this point. Partly it was because despite his official separation from PAAF service, he still wore the uniform of the Imperial Ternathian Marines (and would continue to do so until he reached home and formally mustered out), which made him the most junior officer in the room, despite his exalted birth. And partly it was because Markan's ambivalent feelings where he was concerned had been evident from the very beginning. The sunlord seemed inclined towards skepticism, as if he suspected Janaki, as the heir to the throne which Uromathia had never quite managed to best (or equal), of trying to use and manipulate him. Janaki didn't like that last point very much, but there was no use pretending it wasn't true. Or, for that matter, pretending it would have been reasonable to expect any other response out of a senior noble of the Ternathian Empire's greatest rival.

"You say that your Glimpse indicates we will be attacked here shortly," Markan said in excellent, although accented and somewhat overly formal, Ternathian. "I understand that you can not tell us exactly when—not yet, at any rate. But the question in my mind is whether the fact that you have warned us at all will not alter the events you have Glimpsed, and so invalidate the entire Glimpse, in part or in whole?"

"I see what you're asking, Sunlord." Janaki gazed at the Uromathian for a second or two while he considered how best to answer the question.

"First, anything that might be altered would happen . . . downstream from the initial attack itself," he said then. "The Arcanans' decision to attack us, the approach route they're likely to take, the timing of the attack—all of those are governed by circumstances which almost certainly can't and won't be changed by any actions we might take prior to their arrival here in response to my Glimpse. That's not absolutely guaranteed, of course, but it's very, very likely.

"Second, Glimpses are never as clear as straight

Precognition. Because they relate to the actions and decisions of human beings, they're more . . . flexible. More 'amorphous,' I suppose. Any Glimpse is in a state of flux right up to the moment the events it concerns actually occur. That's one reason they're sometimes so difficult to interpret or describe to anyone else. Some aspects are very clear, and tend to remain that way. Those are what we think of as the 'core aspects' of a Glimpse. According to the latest theory on how Glimpses work, what someone with my Talent actually Sees is the most likely outcome of human actions and decisions from a potentially huge number of closely parallel universes." He shrugged. "I'm not positive the theory is accurate, but it *seems* to hold up, and according to it, those 'core aspects' represent the points in a Glimpse at which the decision trees of all those universes flow together most strongly, where the outcomes we See are most statistically likely to occur. The *less* clear aspects are the ones in which the decision trees have greater numbers of branches, so there's less certainty as to which ones are going to be chosen."

He paused again, watching Markan's face. After a few moments, the Uromathian nodded in understanding, and Janaki continued.

"Up until the moment this attack actually begins, the decision trees are already pretty well set. Oh, it's possible that if we do something in preparation and *they* find out about it, they might alter their plans as a result. It's unlikely, though, and I don't expect any pre-attack portions of my Glimpse to change very much. Once the attack does begin, things get more complicated, and at that point what we do to meet the attack is definitely going to affect the possible decisions and actions of our adversaries as they respond to *our* responses. However, that's where what we refer to as the 'fugue state' of my family's Talent comes into play."

Rof chan Skrithik shifted slightly in his chair. He seemed about to say something, but Janaki gave him the sort of look platoon-captains weren't supposed to give regiment-captains, and the fort's commander kept his mouth firmly shut. He still looked more than a little unhappy, though, and Janaki understood why. Some aspects of the Calirath Talent were carefully not talked about. Including this one.

"'Fugue state,' Your Highness?" Markan repeated. From his tone, which was no more than politely inquiring, one might have been fooled into thinking he'd failed to notice chan Skrithik's unhappiness, Janaki thought with a wry mental smile.

"No one can deliberately summon or induce a Glimpse, Sunlord. Although my family's obviously been experiencing them for a long time, there are some things about Glimpses no one has ever been able to explain satisfactorily, and we've never been able to make our Talent perform to order, as it were. There are certain sets of circumstances which seem more likely to trigger Glimpses, but no one's ever been able to find a way to do it at will. One thing we do know, though, is that once someone with the Talent experiences a major Glimpse, that person almost always finds himself experiencing a sort of . . . continuous Glimpse if he himself is directly involved in the events as they occur."

Markan's eyes sharpened in sudden, intense speculation, and Janaki smiled again, a bit more tartly.

"That's right, Sunlord," he confirmed. "That's why

battlefield Glimpses have served my family so well upon occasion. It doesn't always happen. For that matter, the occasions on which someone finds himself an actual participant in his own Glimpse are rare, to say the very least. But the odds are very good that my own involvement in whatever happens here will trigger the fugue state, in which case I'll be able to predict—probably at least several minutes ahead of time, and possibly quite a bit better than that—how events are going to depart from my original Glimpse."

"With all due respect, Your Highness," chan Skrithik began, "I don't think having you—"

"Regiment-Captain." Janaki's quiet voice cut chan Skrithik off like a knife. Fort Salby's commander looked at him, and Janaki looked back.

"Even with Sunlord Markan's men added to your own, you have fewer than four thousand men," the Crown Prince of Ternathia said, "and you've got better than two thousand civilians to protect right here at Salby. Then there're the TTE work crews out at the railhead."

"And, Your Highness?" chan Skrithik prompted when Janaki paused.

"And you've got at least eight to ten thousand men coming at you, Sir," Janaki said flatly. "With dragons, and those lion-eagle things, and the gods alone know what other 'magic' weapons. If you're going to hold your position and protect the people around you—the Sharonian *civilians* around you—then you're going to need me right here."

"But—"

"We're not going to argue about this, Regiment-Captain." Janaki looked chan Skrithik straight in the eye.

"It's the job of an Imperial Marine to protect civilians. It's the job of any member of the Empire's nobility to protect civilians. And it's the job of a Calirath to protect civilians. Who those civilians are, where they came from, and how many of them there may be is beside the point."

Chan Skrithik looked prepared to go right on arguing, but then he stopped. He gazed at Janaki for several seconds, and Janaki wondered exactly what the regiment-captain was seeing in that moment. In one sense, he was clearly chan Skrithik's subordinate, a junior officer the regiment-captain had every right to order to the rear, if he so chose. But he was also the Crown Prince of Ternathia, the Crown Prince of Sharona, elect. And what he'd just said had been the tradition of the Calirath Dynasty literally for millennia.

It was that long, dusty line of ancestors chan Skrithik saw standing behind him, Janaki decided. There were times when being the heir to the oldest ruling family in the history of mankind had its advantages.

"Granting what you've just said, Your Highness," the regiment-captain said instead of whatever he'd been *about* to say, "the fact remains that you can't be positive your participation will trigger fugue state. If it doesn't, then having you here would be a pointless, and potentially very expensive, mistake."

"I agree," Janaki replied steadily. "And, as I say, I can't guarantee it will happen. But what I've already Glimpsed includes Seeing myself in fugue state." He *really* didn't like admitting that bit, but it was the best way to convince chan Skrithik. "That's why I think it's a virtual certainty that it will happen. And the same bits and pieces of Glimpse in which I've Seen that have also shown me that you're going to need me if you hope to hold this position."

Chan Skrithik flinched slightly. Then, slowly and manifestly unhappily, he nodded.

Janaki nodded back, grateful that some of the aspects of the Calirath Talent were so closely held. It would never have done for chan Skrithik to truly understand what Janaki had just told him.

"Assuming that His Highness' Glimpse is indeed accurate," Markan said after a moment, "then it's obvious we must warn higher authority and inform them of what must already have transpired down-chain from here."

"Agreed, Sunlord," chan Skrithik said, glancing at chan Darma. "And we need to warn Olvyr Banchu and the rest of his work crew."

"We need to do more than just warn them, Sir," Vargan said. "There's no way we could pull all of them back to safety in the time we appear to have. To my mind, that suggests we have to send a detachment forward to help defend them."

"But if they are too obviously anticipating attack," Markan pointed out in a completely neutral tone, "and if the Arcanans realize that, then are they not likely to alter the attack plan His Highness has Glimpsed?"

Vargan's expression tightened, but Janaki raised one hand before the company-captain could speak.

"I'm afraid the Sunlord has a valid point, Company-Captain. On the other hand, there are some fragmentary bits and pieces of Glimpse which suggest pretty strongly that the Arcanans aren't planning to attack the railhead itself until after they've dealt with Fort Salby."

"With your permission, Your Highness?" Petty-Captain chan Darma said before Vargan could respond.

"Yes?"

"What you've just said makes a lot of sense, actually."

"It does?" Vargan looked skeptical, and chan Darma shrugged slightly, his expression grim.

"As His Highness has already pointed out, somehow they've kept any hint of warning from reaching us, Sir. They couldn't have done that by accident. That means they have to know about the Voicenet . . . and that they've somehow been eliminating, or at least silencing, the links in the chain as they advance. If that's the case, though, then when they see a labor force as large as the one Engineer Banchu has out there, they're going to have to anticipate that there's a Voice assigned to it. And I doubt very much that they could believe it would be possible to completely take out that many people, that widely dispersed, before the Voice in question got a warning off."

"He's right, Orkam," chan Skrithik said. "They'll probably count on cutting the Voicenet chain here at Salby, or else slipping a raiding force past us to find and take out the next relay station up-chain. But they're not going to want to risk the construction crew's warning *us* that they're coming before they get here."

"I still think we should beef up their security, Sir," Vargan said after a few moments. "I know most of them already have their personal weapons, and gods know they've got enough heavy equipment to dig themselves in deep. For that matter, a lot of them are veterans. But most of them are still *civilians*."

"I'd certainly be willing to do that," chan Skrithik agreed. Then he smiled nastily. "Suppose we mount a couple of Yerthaks on flatcars and send them down to Banchu? We could send along a rifle company to back them up, of course. And what about sending along Platoon-Captain chan Morak, as well?"

Vargan considered the suggestion. Platoon-Captain Harek chan Morak was Company-Captain Meris Nalkhar's senior assistant, and Nalkhar was Fort Salby's senior combat engineer officer.

"I think that would be a very good idea, Sir," he said after a moment.

"Good," chan Skrithik said, then turned his attention back to Janaki. The regiment-captain remained obviously unhappy about the notion of Janaki's remaining at Fort Salby, but he equally obviously knew it was going to happen anyway, which meant it was time to make the best possible use of the resource Janaki represented.

"Very well, Your Highness. What can your Glimpse tell us about their probable attack plan?"

"Well, Regiment-Captain, from what I've Seen so far, they'll open the attack with a strike by those 'dragons' of theirs. They'll come in this way," he turned to trace a line from the Traisum-Karys portal through the mountainous terrain to Fort Salby, "and apparently the range of their . . . breath weapons, for want of a better term, is fairly limited. They have to get in close, so I'd say they're going to go for surprise. Which means . . ."

He went on talking, outlining what he already knew, and even as he spoke, other bits and pieces of Glimpses roiled through the back of his brain like unquiet ghosts.

Be patient, he told those ghosts. *Be patient . . . I'll be with you soon enough.*

CHAPTER TWENTY-SIX

"SIR! SIR, WAKE UP, please!"

Division-Captain chan Geraith twitched awake. His eyes snapped open, and his right hand reached up and closed on the wrist of the hand which had been gently but insistently shaking his shoulder.

"What?"

He blinked, summoning himself back from the depths of sleep, then sat up quickly, eyes narrowing, as he realized he'd been awakened not by his batman, but by Company-Captain chan Korthal.

"What is it?" he asked his staff Voice more sharply.

"Sir, I've just received an urgent message. It's for you—from Crown Prince Janaki."

Chan Geraith's expression didn't even flicker, but he twitched internally in surprise.

"From the Crown Prince?" he repeated in the tone of someone who wanted to be absolutely certain he'd understood correctly. "Not from His Majesty?"

"That's correct, Sir." Chan Korthal's expression, chan Geraith noticed, was tight and worried, and his own inner tension clicked up another notch.

He started to reach for the bedside lamp to turn up the wick, then snorted and diverted his hand to the window shade above his berth, instead.

Like most trans-universal travelers embarked on a lengthy journey by rail, the men of chan Geraith's division hadn't bothered to reset their watches or readjust their internal clocks. They weren't spending long enough in any one universe to even try to acclimate themselves to local time zones, so they might as well wait for that until they reached their destination. Which meant that it was the middle of the night by chan Geraith's body's time sense, but brilliant sunlight was leaking in around the edges of the window shade as it swayed and bounced gently with the staff car's movement.

He raised it a fraction of an inch, letting natural light illuminate his sleeping compartment, then stood. After so long, he thought as he shrugged into the robe his batman had left ready on the bedside chair, it would have felt unnatural not to have the floor vibrating and swaying underfoot. He belted the robe, then turned back to chan Korthal.

"All right, Lisar. What's this message?"

Chan Korthal looked at him for a moment, then closed his eyes. Because chan Geraith had no Talent at all, he required the services of a particularly competent Voice, and Lisar chan Korthal filled that requirement admirably. When he began to speak a heartbeat later, it was not his voice chan Geraith heard; it was the voice of his future emperor, perfectly reproduced.

That was chan Geraith's first thought. Then the words chan Korthal was relaying so perfectly registered, and Arlos chan Geraith's face froze almost as solid as the ice forming in his veins.

* * *

". . . so that's the situation, Division-Captain," Janaki chan Calirath said through chan Korthal's mouth the better part of fifteen minutes later. "What I've Seen so far explains a lot about the Arcanans' transport and combat capabilities, but I still don't have a clue *why* they're doing this. The fact that we haven't heard a word from Company-Captain chan Tesh, Regiment-Captain Velvelig, or any of our other outposts seems to me to represent clear proof that this is a carefully planned, well thought out offensive which they must have been putting together the entire time they've been ostensibly negotiating with us. What that says about their ambitions and ultimate intentions—much less about whether or not there's any point even attempting to treat with them—is more than I'm prepared to speculate about at this point.

"I've relayed as many details of my Glimpses to your staff Voice as I could. Unfortunately, those Glimpses are not yet complete. If and as the opportunity arises, I'll send additional details. At this time, my best estimate is that we'll be attacked here within no more than forty-eight hours, and probably sooner than that. Preparations to meet that attack are underway. In my judgment, my presence here will be necessary if that attack is to be successfully resisted."

Chan Geraith's face was carved from stone. The young man who had sent him this warning was vital to the successful unification of his planet. His life, his *function* in that unification process, were vastly more important than the defense of a single portal fortress and the town about it. There was absolutely no question in Arlos chan Geraith's mind on that point, and unlike Regiment-Captain chan Skrithik, he was a full division-captain, so—

"That's all I can tell you right now, Sir," Janaki said. "Except to add this. *Chunika s'hari, Halian. Sho warak.*"

The division-captain's eyes closed, and the stone of his face twisted. For an instant, he looked twenty years older. Then he inhaled deeply, and nodded.

"*Sho warak*, Your Highness," he murmured.

Chan Korthal's eyes opened. Like any Voice with the monumentally high security clearance the company-captain had to carry in order to serve as chan Geraith's staff Voice, he knew there were questions which would never be answered. That he would transmit information again and again which meant a great deal to its recipients, but nothing at all to him. As chan Geraith looked into the younger man's eyes, he saw chan Korthal's curiosity . . . and his awareness that this was going to be one of those times.

And he was right.

"Thank you, Lisar," the division-captain said quietly. "Please ask Regiment-Captain chan Isail to wake the staff. And have him include Brigade-Captain chan Quay in his wakeup call."

"Yes, Sir," chan Korthal replied, equally quietly, and withdrew from the sleeping compartment.

Chan Geraith contemplated the door which had closed behind the Voice, but his thoughts were far away. They were with the young man who had sent him that final message in a language so ancient that probably no more than a handful of people in all of Sharona would have understood it.

Chunika s'hari, Halian. Sho warak.

"I am your son, Halian. I remember."

Chan Geraith closed his eyes once more, and let those words toll through him. The words which absolutely precluded him from ordering Janaki chan Calirath out of Fort Salby before the hammer blow landed.

"*Sho warak*," the division-captain murmured one more time. Then he straightened his shoulders and pressed the button to summon his batman with his uniform.

* * *

Alivar Neshok sat in his tent, glaring at the words of the report floating in his personal crystal. Outside the tent, the Expeditionary Force's encampment swarmed with activity. The follow-on echelons of transports bringing up the heavy cavalry which had been left behind weren't due to arrive for another several hours, but the preparations for the attack on Fort Salby were moving ahead already.

Moving ahead based on the information I *got for them*, Neshok told himself bitterly. *Moving ahead at the end of an entire advance that's only been possible at all because of the information* I *got for them!*

He managed to keep his teeth from grinding together, but it wasn't the easiest thing he'd ever done. He knew who he had to thank for Two Thousand Harshu's abrupt decision to "relieve you of the stress of the duties you have performed so outstandingly," as Harshu's memo had so cloyingly put it. Thousand Toralk and that sanctimonious prick of a Healer, Vaynair. *They* were the ones.

Well, we'll see just how well their godsdamned offensives go without me holding their hands and wiping their arses for them!

His nostrils flared, but even as he told himself that,

deep down inside of him a tiny voice told him he should have seen this coming long ago. That in the end, it was Harshu, not Toralk or Vaynair. That the two thousand had used him to do a dirty job that needed doing without getting any of the dirt on his own lily-white hands, and that now Harshu had decided to discard him. That the gratitude, the patronage, Neshok had anticipated were going to turn out to be very different things, indeed, as far as Harshu, that "noble" Andaran, was concerned.

But that was all right, he told that tiny voice right back. He had another patron, one senior to Harshu, and Two Thousand mul Gurthak would appreciate and remember his efforts on mul Gurthak's part.

He'd better, anyway, Neshok told himself grimly. *If he doesn't—if* he *tries to send me for the long drop, too—he won't like what I have to say to the Inspector General. Not one little bit, he won't like it.*

A raised voice shouted orders outside his tent, a squad of infantry doubled past, equipment clattering, and somewhere on the far side of the hot, dusty encampment he heard the rumbling grumbles of irritated dragons growing impatient for their meal. Everyone else was so busy, so focused, and here he sat, finishing up his routine paperwork like a good little clerk in a forgotten corner. Tidying up his reports, making sure all the blanks were filled in. And, while he was at it, doing some careful editing about his exact interrogation techniques, as well.

He glowered down at the crystal for several more seconds, then drew a deep breath and got back to work.

* * *

"This," Under-Armsman Kardan Verais muttered under his breath, "is a godsdamned pain in the arse!"

It became evident that he hadn't spoken quite as

much under his breath as he'd thought he had when Junior-Armsman Paras chan Barsak slapped him across the back of his pith helmet.

"Less bitching, more digging," chan Barsak told him. The junior-armsman was noted for a certain lack of understanding for anyone who gave less than his full effort to the task at hand, but Verais wasn't particularly worried. Given how liberally coated his shirtless torso was with a pasty skim of dust, dirt, and sweat, even chan Barsak had to be relatively satisfied with his efforts.

Of course, Verais reflected, "relatively satisfied" wasn't quite the same thing as "completely satisfied."

"I don't mind digging. It's prying out the godsdamned *rocks* I hate," he said with a grunt as he heaved another head-sized hunk of stone to one side. "Besides, this is a stupid place to be digging a hole anyway."

"Oh, you think so?" Chan Barsak was just as filthy as Verais—not surprisingly, since he'd been the one doing the digging until they'd changed off again ten minutes ago. "You don't like the field of fire?"

"I like the field of fire just fine . . . I guess." Verais dragged a forearm across his sweaty face, then spat and watched the tawny, dust-darkened spittle disappear over the lip of the nearly vertical slope in front of them. "We're a long way from the road, but I guess we can reach it from here. But we could've covered it better from closer, and without having to hump the guns and ammo all the fucking way up here! Not to mention—" he started swinging the mattock again, grunting the words between swings "—being a hells of a lot easier to dig in!"

"Yeah?" Chan Barsak looked over the other PAAF troopers working to prepare the squad's position. Most of them were stripped to the waist, like Verais. Over half of them were digging in the hard, rocky, sunbaked mountainside, hacking out weapons pits that were going to be shallower than The Book wanted no matter how hard they tried. Most of the rest were shoveling the spoil from the pits into the sandbags that were going to go on top of those holes when they were done. All of them were sweating hard under the brutal sun, and unlike chan Barsak, the majority of them weren't Ternathians.

"Look," the junior-armsman said, searching for the best way to explain to a non-Ternathian, "if Crown Prince Janaki says a shit storm's coming, then you better believe it's coming and the crap is gonna be really, really deep. Trust me on this. What? You think maybe his family's been doing what it does for so long without figuring out how to get its shit straight?"

"Yeah, but—"

"'But' nothing," chan Barsak interrupted. "If the Regiment-captain wants us up here after talking to the Prince, there's no way in hell—*anyone's* hell—*I'm* going to argue with them. And if I'm not gonna argue with them, then *you* aren't going to."

"Yeah. Yeah, yeah, yeah. I got it. I got it!" Verais grumbled, swinging the mattock still harder.

"Good."

* * *

Andrin Calirath jerked upright in her bed so quickly that Finena reared up on her bedside perch, mantling instinctively.

Andrin never even noticed her beloved falcon. Her sea-gray eyes were wide, unseeing, as she Saw with other senses, another Talent.

How long she sat there, frozen, Watching the horrifying images and sounds rolling through her brain, she never knew. But then, finally, she closed those haunted eyes once more. She sat very still, unmoving in the hushed, comforting midnight silence of Calirath Palace, and her face was white and strained.

"Janaki," she whispered. "Oh, *Janaki.*"

* * *

"Are you sure about this, Platoon-Cap—I mean, are you sure about this, Your Highness?" Company-Captain Lorvam Mesaion asked.

Fort Salby's senior artillerist stood on the fort's western fighting step, watching as fatigue parties, reinforced by almost every male civilian above the age of twelve, worked with focused, purposeful intensity.

"Sure about what, Sir?" Janaki asked.

He'd come up to the stretch of wall between the two out-thrust bastions which flanked the main gates and climbed up onto an empty gun platform to gaze out towards the portal. Mesaion wasn't sure exactly what kept bringing the Ternathian crown prince back to this position again and again. From his own perspective, it was the ideal place to keep an eye on the preparations for which he personally was responsible, but he knew Regiment-Captain chan Skrithik had been keeping Janaki extraordinarily busy. Too busy, the company-captain would have thought to be making his way up here every hour or so.

"Sure about putting those things up here," Mesaion said, jerking his head at the sweating, grunting PAAF troopers with sledgehammers who were busy spiking the base plates of ten Yerthak pedestal guns' mounts into the solid tops of the towers and bastions. Well, the *reasonably* solid tops of the towers and bastions; Mesaion had a few private reservations about how well they were going to stand the recoil of any sustained firing. The half-ton weapons themselves sat to one side, and getting those pigs up to the tops of the towers had been anything but easy. In fact, in the end they'd had to move most of them by brute force and human muscle power.

Mesaion just hoped it was all going to be worth it. And that they were going to get off more than a few shots per gun before the masonry's solidity or the crude modifications they'd made to the mountings themselves betrayed them.

Now Janaki glanced at the guns, then arched an eyebrow at the artillerist, and Mesaion shrugged.

"They'll have the reach to cover the approaches from *this* wall, and from the western towers, Your Highness," he pointed out. "But if you're right about where their attack's going to be coming from, the ones on the *eastern* wall aren't going to be much help."

"Not against *ground* targets, no," Janaki conceded.

Mesaion opened his mouth, then closed it again. Although he was from New Farnal, not Ternathia, he'd read enough history to know how well the Calirath Talent had served the Empire over the millennia. Still . . . *dragons?* Flying monsters with the heads and wings of eagles and lions' bodies?

"I know it sounds crazy, Company-Captain," Janaki said with a tired smile. "Just humor me."

"If you say so, Your Highness," Mesaion replied after a moment.

"How are the rest of your positions coming along, Sir, if I may ask?"

"They won't be ready before dawn, if that's what you mean, Your Highness. Aside from that, they're coming along pretty well."

"Good, Sir. That's good."

Janaki nodded to Mesaion and stepped closer to the parapet and leaned his elbows on it, gazing out across the town of Salby and up at the looming portal. Chan Skrithik had loaded up all the women and children he could cram onto the available railroad cars and sent them steaming off towards Salym. Unfortunately, he'd had space for less than eight hundred civilians, and sheltering the rest was going to pack the fort to the bursting point. Still, that would be far better than leaving them to face the oncoming storm unprotected.

Assuming, of course, that they managed to keep the Arcanans' monstrous winged beasts from turning the fort into nothing more than a conveniently concentrated slaughtering pen.

Janaki's mouth tightened as he contemplated the unspeakable casualties which still might all too readily be inflicted upon people for whose protection he and his family were responsible. Then he made himself relax as he looked down at the dust rising from either side of the ribbon of railroad that reached along the valley floor below towards the portal.

Company-Captain Mesaion might have his doubts about some of the artillery deployments Regiment-Captain chan Skrithik had ordered on the basis of Platoon-Captain chan Calirath's Glimpse, but that hadn't prevented the artillery officer from getting the guns deployed as quickly as possible. Unfortunately, Fort Salby, despite the thickness of its walls, hadn't really been intended to be defended against an attack by modern heavy weapons. The fighting steps simply weren't deep enough to mount true artillery—especially not artillery on field carriages, instead of fortress carriages—and the gun platforms had never been intended for anything heavier than machine guns, so Mesaion's field artillery had to be deployed outside the walls, along the foot of the stair-steplike bluff upon which Salby stood, if the guns were going to be used at all.

That explained a lot of the dust Janaki gazed down upon. The gun pits were going to be only a bit deeper than usual, but chan Skrithik—or, rather, Janaki, to be scrupulously honest—had insisted upon the thickest possible overhead cover. Firing a four-inch breechloader, or one of the three-point-four-inch quick-firers, with a roof of heavy sandbags only a few feet over the gunners' heads promised to be . . . exciting. But not as "exciting" as things might have been with dragons raining fire or lightning into the gun pits with them.

Janaki wished chan Skrithik had had more field guns available. Even with the light horse guns Sunlord Markan and Windlord Garsal had brought along, though, the regiment-captain had little more than a dozen pieces. He and Janaki had spent an arduous couple of hours bent over the map table, matching terrain against Janaki's fragmentary Glimpses, to pick the best places to put the guns he did have, but neither of them was happy about the total numbers they had to deploy.

The single three-gun section of 4.3-inch howitzers and the nine heavy mortars Mesaion had available could probably take up at least some of the slack. They, however, couldn't be used from positions with overhead cover, which was why they'd been deployed inside the fort itself. From their position on the parade ground they were protected from direct counter-fire and had excellent three-hundred-sixty-degree command, as long as the targets were far enough away for their high-trajectory fire to clear the walls.

Of course, if the Arcanans' dragons got through to the fort . . . .

Tin roofs, laid over appropriated railroad ties and covered with layered sandbags, were going up all along the fort walls' fighting steps, as well. They weren't as sturdy as Janaki would have preferred, but they were a hells of a lot better than nothing, and they should offer significant protection against plunging dragons' breath. He hoped so, anyway.

Covered rifle pits were also springing up outside the walls, placed to cover the artillerists as well as to protect the ground-level approaches to the fort, and there were quite a few cavalry troopers wielding shovels, picks, and axes out there.

Sunlord Markan and Company-Captain Vargan, in a rare bout of agreement which had probably surprised them even more than it had chan Skrithik, had both looked more than a little affronted at how emphatically Janaki had informed them that Sharonian cavalry had no business at all on the same battlefield as *Arcanan* cavalry. Actually, they'd been even more affronted because of the Arcanans' lack of modern small arms. Only fools—which neither Markan nor Vargan were, however little they might care for one another—would have even contemplated committing cavalry against dug-in riflemen, machine guns, and field guns, but both Markan and Vargan were cavalry troopers of the old school. Against *crossbows* the possibility of one last, anachronistic, glorious charge had suggested itself to both of them, which had turned them into unlikely allies in this one case.

Janaki had used both booted heels to stamp on *that* notion just as hard as he could. Vargan had accepted the veto with something which might have been described as good grace by a sufficiently charitable observer. Markan, on the other hand, had accepted it with scrupulous, icy courtesy. Of the two, Janaki considerably preferred Vargan's reaction.

Still, the sunlord had agreed that under the circumstances his precious cavalry horses were less important than human lives. Fort Salby's stables had been emptied of their intended occupants, and all of the command's horses had been moved down to the paddocks built around the oasis some several miles east of the fort to make room to pack in still more civilians. The men who might otherwise have ridden those horses were out there behind those shovels, digging in as riflemen, instead. And Janaki had to admit that however much Markan might have longed for one final charge, he'd turned energetically to the task of integrating his troopers into chan Skrithik's defensive plan when that charge was denied him.

Now we just have to see whether or not it does any good, Janaki thought grimly.

* * *

"I'd be happier if we could hit them earlier, Sir," Commander of Five Hundred Myr said.

He and Klayrman Toralk stood outside the Operations tent, looking out across the improvised dragonfield. The transports were beginning to show signs of accumulating fatigue, Toralk noted, and several of the battle dragons were showing fatigue in their own fashion. Which, unfortunately, consisted of being even more irritable than usual.

"I can understand that," Toralk agreed, and he could. But even dragons' eyes needed some light. This Fort Salby had the potential to turn into a nasty handful, and this time the approach was going to be tricky enough all by itself. It was no time for battle dragons and their pilots to fly into hillsides they couldn't quite see in time . . . or discover that not even dragon eyes had enough light to pick out their targets accurately.

"It's not another damned wooden fort with just a handful of men in it, Sir," Myr pointed out in what Toralk couldn't quite call a wheedling tone. "You've seen the plans."

"Yes, I have," Toralk agreed once again.

The detailed maps of this portal chain which they'd captured at Fort Ghartoun included one of Traisum, and the modified image-interpreting spellware had worked perfectly. They knew precisely where Fort Salby was, and exactly what the terrain around it looked like. They'd even found what one of their prisoners had identified as a map of Fort Salby itself, and "tougher nut" was a grossly inadequate way to describe the difference between it and something like Fort Ghartoun.

Salby's walls were taller, thicker, and stronger. They were also going to be far more resistant to fire, and the buildings inside the fort were made of the same materials, which would make the reds' breath weapons much less effective. If taking those walls and those internal structures turned into any sort of hand-to-hand fight, it was going to be bloody. *Very* bloody.

One thing the map *didn't* show was what sort of cellars or underground passages might be integrated into the fort. There had to be some, and they were going to pose problems of their own, however the expeditionary force went about attacking the place.

"Listen, Cerlohs," Toralk said, turning to face his Talon commander fully, "I understand what you're saying. And I agree that our chances of taking them completely by surprise would be better if we hit them in the dark. But your chances of losing a dragon—or two or three of them—on the approach would also be a lot higher."

Myr looked unhappy, but he couldn't really argue that point. The approach route they'd selected took advantage of the mountainous terrain between the portal and their objective, using it to screen and conceal the incoming strike until the very last minute. But while battle dragons were trained for nap-of-the-earth flight, threading the needle of the valley which would lead them to Fort Salby wasn't something to try in pitch blackness.

"Assuming all your dragons survive the approach," Toralk continued, "you've still got the problem that, as you just pointed out, this is going to be a really hard target, and it's got a garrison at least four or five times as big as anything we've hit so far, with artillery and more of those damned 'machine gun' things of theirs. If they have time to get their heavy weapons into action, we're going to get hurt. Remember what happened to your reds at the swamp portal."

"That's exactly what I am remembering, Sir," Myr replied. "If we hit them fast enough, with enough surprise, we'll be on top of them and knock those weapons out before they even know we're coming. They won't get a chance to bring them into action at all, and, frankly, I'd like that one hells of a lot better than the alternative!"

"But to do that you have to actually *hit* them," Toralk pointed out. "And to do that, the dragons have to be able to *see* them."

Myr started to open his mouth again, but Toralk shook his head.

"I understand what you're saying, Cerlohs. But look at it this way. As far as we can tell, they still haven't gotten any messages out. And because of the captured maps we can finally actually read reliably, we haven't even had to send in a recon flight, so they can't know we're coming."

For a moment, Myr looked as if he might argue that point, but then he grimaced and shook his head. Although no gryphons had been sent through into Traisum, a very high altitude gryphon had overflown the Sharonians' "railhead," barely three hundred miles up-chain from the ruins of what had been Fort Mosanik. The image interpreters were still trying to make sense out of the take from the recon crystal, still trying to figure out what some of the huge, complicated, awkward-looking machinery was for, but the fact that all those workers were still out there, still working, was the clearest possible proof the Arcanans' presence at Fort Mosanik remained undetected.

"Since they don't know we're coming, anyway, and since these people won't know any more about dragons or gryphons than any of the people we've already hit, you're still going to have what amounts to complete tactical surprise," Toralk continued. "Maybe they'll have a few seconds, even a few minutes, to see you coming, but even if they do, how much good is it going to do them? As far as they know, they're still at peace, so they're going to be maintaining a peacetime routine. It'll take time for them to get from that mindset into putting up any sort of effective resistance. Do you really think they're going to manage to do that, to break their heavy weapons out of storage, *and* get them into action, before you can get in at least two or three passes with your yellows?"

Myr shook his head, and Toralk snorted.

"I don't think so, either. But for those passes to be effective, you've got to have the light for targeting. If you don't, if you miss on the first pass, then you're likely to have to come back through much heavier fire, and even their rifles may get lucky."

"All right, Sir." Myr smiled crookedly. "You've made your point. For that matter, it was *my* people who came up with the timing in the first place! Just put it down to opening-night jitters, I suppose."

"Don't think you're the only one feeling them," Toralk said dryly. "Frankly, I'll be happier when we're able to settle in on the defensive instead of advancing further and further into the unknown this way. I know no thrusting, offense-minded Air Force officer is supposed to admit that, especially where a ground-pounder might overhear him. But you know what? I'm feeling sort of lonely all the way out here at the end of our advance."

CHAPTER TWENTY-SEVEN

COMPANY-CAPTAIN SILKASH tried to conceal his anxiety as the pair of hard-faced Arcanan guards marched him across Fort Ghartoun's parade ground. The surgeon's eyes flitted around busily, taking in everything he could see, and the mind behind those eyes was equally busy.

The Arcanans had decided to use the stables as an improvised holding area for the bulk of their prisoners. Despite the heavy casualties the eagle-lions had inflicted, there were well over four hundred of those prisoners, and finding a place to put them all obviously hadn't been easy. Silkash wouldn't normally have considered a stable a very secure prison, but the Arcanans had come prepared. The surgeon still had no idea how this "magic" of theirs worked, but the gleaming web which had been stretched across every opening in the stable buildings looked depressingly effective. It was clearly visible even in full daylight, and the Arcanans had completely ringed the stable with the glittering tubes of their fireball-throwers as a pointed warning to any Sharonians who might have entertained notions about somehow finding a way through its close-meshed glow.

The officers, on the other hand, had been kept separate from the enlisted and the noncoms. Which, Silkash reflected wryly, had given them an unanticipated opportunity to experience Fort Ghartoun's hospitality from the same perspective as their recent "guests," although they were packed considerably tighter in the cells than their Arcanan POWs had been.

Of course, his eyes darkened, there had been a few other differences between their own experiences and those of their Arcanan POWs.

Anger smoldered like slow lava down inside the medical officer. There'd been no opportunity for anyone to make any formal reports to him or to Regiment-Captain Velvelig, but there'd been at least some contact with some of the non-officer prisoners. They'd heard what had happened to chan Tergis, and the Voice wasn't the only Sharonian who'd been killed in cold blood after surrendering. To have his men treated that way, especially after Velvelig had been so insistent upon treating *his* prisoners with respect and dignity, had filled the Arpathian with a white-hot rage. Despite the regiment-captain's self-control, Silkash had literally felt the heat of that anger radiating from the other man.

And then, as suddenly as it had begun, the brutality had ended. It hadn't tapered off, it had simply *stopped*, like a locomotive when the steam was turned off. Silkash hoped that indicated that the savagery had never been authorized and had stopped as soon as higher authority learned about it, but he wasn't quite prepared to conclude that that was what had actually happened.

In the meantime, the main body of the invaders had

clearly moved on. Which, he thought glumly, probably meant they'd already attacked Fort Mosanik by this time. It still seemed impossible, but if they'd managed to get from Hell's Gate to Fort Ghartoun as quickly as they had . . . .

His thoughts shifted focus abruptly as his guards pushed him up the steps to the veranda of the office block. They weren't particularly gentle about it, and the manacles holding his hands behind him made him awkward. He thought about registering some sort of protest, then decided that might not be the very smartest thing he could do.

They thrust him into the building, and he found himself being marched down the short hallway to what had been Velvelig's office. They opened the door and shoved him through it, and Silkash's lips tightened involuntarily as he saw Hadrign Thalmayr sitting behind Velvelig's desk.

The two guards withdrew, leaving Silkash standing in front of the desk. Thalmayr pointedly ignored him, keeping his attention on one of the omnipresent crystals these people seemed to take with them everywhere. This particular crystal was filled with floating words and letters in the Arcanan alphabet, and Silkash wondered what Thalmayr was studying so intently in order to emphasize his prisoner's total lack of importance.

Probably a laundry list, the surgeon told himself sourly. *He's not smart enough for it to be anything more complicated than that!*

He knew the sarcasm was nothing more than a defensive mechanism, the only shield against the uncertainty and fear simmering deep inside him he could come up with under the circumstances. To his surprise, it was rather comforting, anyway.

He stood there for several minutes. Then the door opened again, and Silkash's belly muscles tightened as Platoon-Captain Tobis Makree was shoved through it. This time, the guards didn't withdraw again, either. Instead, they stood back against the wall behind the prisoners, and Silkash's heart sank as he noted the heavy truncheons at their sides.

Thalmayr let the two Sharonians wait for at least another five minutes before he finally looked up from his crystal. Then he leaned back in Velvelig's chair, and his smile was thin and ugly.

"Well, well," he said after a moment. Or, at least, that was what the crystal on his desk said as it translated for him. Somehow, Silkash thought sinkingly, the fact that he was finally able and willing to communicate with them wasn't particularly reassuring.

"So, here we are," he continued after a heartbeat or two. "I've been looking forward to this morning. Do you know why?"

Neither Sharonian answered, and Thalmayr's smile grew even thinner. Then he nodded briefly to the guards, and Silkash cried out involuntarily as a heavy truncheon smashed into his kidneys from behind and the pain hammered him to his knees.

"I asked you a question," Thalmayr said. "Do you know why I've been looking forward to this morning?"

Silkash looked up at him through a haze of sudden agony, then grunted as a heavy boot slammed into his ribs. He went down, trying to curl into a protective knot, and the boot crunched into him again. And again.

"No!" he heard Makree shout. "We don't know!"

"Really?" The amusement in Thalmayr's voice was as hungry as it was ugly, but at least the boots stopped hammering Silkash. "I'm astonished," the Arcanan continued. "The two of you, such conscientious *'healers.'* So concerned about my well-being, so desperate to save my life, to cure my wounds. I can't believe such perceptive, compassionate people couldn't guess why I've been feeling so much anticipation all morning."

Thalmayr's voice seemed to be coming from a long way away as Silkash forced himself not to whimper around the waves of pain rolling through him.

"Well," Thalmayr said, and the chair scraped across the floor as he stood, stretching hugely to draw deliberate attention to his restored mobility, "the answer is simple enough. Although I wasn't aware of it at the time, you *gentlemen* did your very best to help me. It embarrasses me deeply that I didn't realize that at the time. Fortunately, it's been explained to me since, and, I assure you, I'm more grateful for your efforts than I could ever possibly express."

The Arcanan's eyes were ugly, and he slowly and carefully pulled on a pair of thin leather gloves.

"I've thought and thought about how I might be able to express my gratitude to you," he continued as he smoothed the leather across the backs of his hands. "Unfortunately, even with the assistance of my PC here, I don't think I have the words. So I've decided the best way to tell you—" he held out one gloved hand, and the nearer guard handed him his truncheon "—is to *show* you."

* * *

Hundred Geyrsof's fingers were steady in the control grooves as Graycloud led the 3012th Strike through the portal.

The yellow dragon flew strongly, steadily, sharing

his pilot's eagerness as Geyrsof lay stretched out in the cockpit, watching the imagery displayed on his helmet's visor. Ahead of them, the eastern sky glowed with the approach of dawn, but the shadows shrouding the ground below was were still dense enough to make him a tiny bit nervous. The mountains about them weren't all that high, compared to many another, more impressive range, but he'd been impressed—almost awed—by the incredible cliffs his dragons had been forced to climb over just to get here. And if there were taller mountains in the multiverse, the rugged slopes of *these* mountains were more than solid enough to flatten any dragon careless enough to fly into them.

The mission planners were right to insist on waiting for dawn. The thought ran below the surface of Geyrsof's concentration on the steep, barren, poorly visible mountainsides streaking past beyond Graycloud's wingtips. *We probably could have done this with less light . . . but I wouldn't have enjoyed it!*

The old cliché about the dearth of "old, bold pilots" flickered in the back of his brain. Then he felt himself tightening inside as they reached the last waypoint and turned onto their final approach.

There! Geyrsof's eyes narrowed behind his visor as he saw the fort lying ahead of him, exactly where the maps said it should be. He looked through Graycloud's eyes, moving the crosshair while he prepared to climb high enough to gain a clear line of fire onto the fort's parade ground. But then something jabbed at the corner of his attention, and his eyes moved back to the shadows below the fort's wall.

What the hells? That's not supposed to be there . . . whatever the hells it is. It's—

He was still peering into the shadows, using Graycloud's vision to try to figure out what those dimly visible shapes and scars on the earth were, as the two yellows and their accompanying reds entered the final stretch of their approach valley . . . and the four Faraika II machine guns dug in on either side, just below the summit, opened fire.

* * *

Janaki chan Calirath had been standing on the raised gun platform between the gate bastions with Taleena on his shoulder for the last two hours. He'd stood there, almost motionless, gazing steadily into the west, and Rof chan Skrithik had stood equally silent at his other shoulder, with Senior-Armsman Orek Isia, Fort Salby's senior Flicker, by his side.

The regiment-captain felt . . . uncomfortable. Which, he reflected, was a pitifully pale word to describe his emotions at this moment. Part of him wished desperately that he'd gone ahead and ordered Janaki to the rear. Another part of him—the part charged with defending twelve hundred civilians, including his own wife—was desperately glad the prince and his Talent were here. And yet another part wondered if Janaki would have gone, even if he'd been ordered to.

And just who the hells would you have used to make *him go if he'd refused, Rof?* he asked himself wryly, glancing at the Marine standing respectfully behind the two officers. Chief-Armsman chan Braikal looked most unhappy, but chan Skrithik had no doubt whose orders the Marine would have followed if it had come to a choice between him and the Crown Prince of Ternathia.

Besides, when it came right down to it, Rof chan Skrithik was a Ternathian himself. He knew how valuable

Janaki's life was. He also recalled the Caliraths' motto . . . and the quotation attributed to Emperor Halian over fifteen hundred years ago, when he'd rejected all of the arguments in favor of withdrawing from the defense of his Bolakini allies.

"It takes twenty years to make an Emperor," Halian had said. "It takes twenty *centuries* to make an Empire the world can trust."

Janaki chan Calirath understood what his ancestor had said all those centuries ago, chan Skrithik thought.

"What's that?" chan Braikal said suddenly. "There—above the southern hilltop?"

Chan Skrithik couldn't make out what the Marine was talking about, but Janaki answered him. The prince didn't even turn his head to look. He didn't have to . . . just as chan Skrithik didn't have to look into Janaki's gray eyes to see the shadows moving in their depths.

"It's starting, Chief," the crown prince said quietly.

* * *

"Still think it's a stupid place to put a machine gun?!" Paras chan Barsak shouted in Kardan Verais' right ear.

"Fuck, *no!*" Verais shouted back.

They had to shout, even though their heads were barely a foot apart, and even then they could scarcely hear one another. The cacophonous bellow of four .54-caliber machine guns tended to make it difficult to carry on a conversation. The heavy Faraikas couldn't sustain maximum-rate fire for very long without overheating catastrophically, but they didn't have to, either.

Each of the four machine-gun emplacements on each side of the valley poured at least two hundred rounds at the monstrous beasts leading that airborne onslaught, and none of their targets even tried to dodge.

* * *

Cerlohs Myr watched in utter horror as *both* his remaining yellows ran straight into the massed fire of the Sharonian weapons which shouldn't have been there. Geyrsof and his wingman had been concentrating on their assigned target, not looking for machine guns on the tops of mountains a good mile and a half *short* of the target that didn't know they were coming. Myr had no idea what those guns were doing there. Indeed, he could hardly even *find* them! The brilliant flames of their muzzle flashes illuminated the shadows wrapped around their positions like chain-lightning, but they were so solidly dug-in, with so many sandbags and so much earth piled on top of their positions, that the muzzle flashes were *all* he could see.

Well, that and the consequences of those muzzle flashes.

Graycloud and Skykill seemed to stagger in midair. The fire wasn't even coming in from below, where their scales were thickest, and the massive bullets punched through their sides like white-hot awls. One of them—Myr had no idea which—managed to scream in mortal agony, and then both of them went smashing down out of the heavens in bloody, shattered ruins that bounced and skidded onward along the valley floor like toys that flailed broken wings like pitiful, tattered banners.

The three reds behind them went the same way before their pilots could react. The rest of the attack flight responded instinctively, rocketing steeply upward. But the deadly flanking fire tracked them as they climbed, and another red and one of the blacks went down, as well, before they could clear the threat zone.

Myr looked back from his own dragon as Razorwing

bounded upward, and saw the broken bodies of seven—*seven!*—of his precious dragons and their pilots sprawled grotesquely across the valley floor.

* * *

The cheers were deafening.

Rof chan Skrithik found himself shouting right along with the rest of his men, bellowing his triumph, and he knew he was shouting even louder because of his reaction to the sheer size of the Arcanans' winged monstrosities.

But Janaki wasn't cheering.

The crown prince reached out and caught chan Skrithik by the front of his uniform tunic. The regiment-captain's eyes widened in surprise at the strength with which Janaki grabbed him and literally yanked him forward. He started to say something, but then Janaki turned his head to look at him, and chan Skrithik's mouth closed with a click.

He'd thought there were ghosts in his crown prince's gray gaze before; now he saw the reality.

Janaki's eyes were huge, the pupils far too dilated for the strengthening morning light, unfocused on anything of this world. They didn't seem to be looking at anything about him, and yet chan Skrithik had the eerie sensation that Janaki didn't simply see him; he Saw right *through* him.

"They aren't going to give up that easily," the Crown Prince of Ternathia said in the clear, distant voice of a Calirath in fugue state. "They'll be back—soon." He pointed directly overhead. "There."

Chan Skrithik nodded, and looked at Senior-Armsman Isia.

"Overhead watch," he said harshly. "Alert everyone."

"Yes, Sir!"

Isia saluted sharply, then closed his eyes, and one of the small stacks of message canisters on the parapet beside him began to disappear with the preplanned dispatches, written well ahead of time against this very moment.

Almost simultaneously, the canisters began to appear at their destinations. Company-Captain Mesaion glanced at his copy, and began shouting orders of his own.

* * *

Cerlohs Myr counted noses with a sense of total disbelief as his remaining dragons circled well to the west of those murderous machine guns.

After transfers and rearrangements to make up for his earlier losses, the 3012th had headed into action this morning with eleven dragons. Now it had only four . . . and both of his precious yellows were gone, simply blotted away.

He lay in his cockpit, forcing himself to think as clearly as possible despite the shock and white-hot rage blazing within him. The loss of seven battle dragons—*seven!*—before any of them had even fired a shot was far worse than merely devastating. It represented almost half of his total available combat strength . . . and a third of all the battle dragons deployed to this entire chain.

The long-term implications of that level of losses, especially in light of the Air Force's low total inventory of battle dragons, were something he resolutely refused to contemplate. Not yet. There would be time to think about that later, and he wasn't looking forward to it.

The *short-term* implications were something he couldn't avoid thinking about, however. His entire battle plan had been built around bringing the maximum possible weight of fire to bear on Fort Salby as quickly as possible. The yellows were supposed to have been the opening salvo, blanketing any exposed defenders in a lethal, saturating canopy of gas. Had they somehow missed their mark, their escorting reds had been supposed to sweep the fort's exposed interior with fireballs while the yellows looped back for a second pass. Now, with Hundred Helika's 5001st, Myr's weakest strike, detached to support Thousand Carthos' secondary advance, he had only the four shocked survivors of Geyrsof's 3012th—all of them blacks—and the six reds and four blacks of Commander of One Hundred Sahlis Desmar's 2029th Strike.

Part of his brain argued that he had to break off and pull back. That the losses he'd already taken were heavier than the conquest of one more Sharonian portal fort could possibly justify. But this wasn't just one more portal fort; it was the perfect forward defensive position Two Thousand Harshu had been looking for from the moment the Expeditionary Force began its advance. Besides, he *wanted* these people.

He didn't know why they'd put machine guns in such an unlikely spot. From test firings with captured weapons, Intelligence had determined the approximate range of the Sharonians' heavy automatic weapons, so he knew they had the *reach* from those positions to cover the railroad and road which connected the portal to the fort and its small, surrounding town. And he supposed that given the initial hostile contact between Arcana and the Sharonians, it would have made sense to devote at least a little attention to defending the approaches from the direction of Hell's Gate. But he also knew how heavy those large-caliber machine guns were, and getting them into position—or just keeping them supplied with ammunition and getting their gun crews up-and-down those mountainsides, for that matter, especially without dragons—must have been an unmitigated pain in the arse.

The elevation damned well gives them good command of the surrounding area, I suppose, Myr thought harshly. *But why here and nowhere else?*

Another possibility suggested itself to him, but that was ridiculous. If these people had had *any* idea an Arcanan invasion force was this close to Traisum, they would never have left those work crews and all of that heavy equipment exposed on Fort Mosanik's very doorstep! And even if they had known, how could they possibly have placed those weapons so perfectly? Given all of the possible lines of approach, how could they have picked *exactly* the right one to cover?

No way! He shook his helmeted head. *However it happened, the bastards have to have just lucked out. Well,* his mouth twisted grimly, *I suppose things have gone so well this far that it's about time* we *had a little bad luck, too. But these fuckers are* not *going to get away with massacring* my *people this way!*

He used his helmet spellware to trigger the combination of a white and an amber flare, and one of Geyrsof's surviving blacks climbed obediently up to his level. The pilot looked over at him, and Myr used dragon-pilot hand signs to order the other dragon back to report to Thousand Toralk and Two Thousand Harshu.

The pilot nodded, and his beast banked away. Myr watched him go, then turned grimly back to the task at hand. No doubt Toralk and Harshu would have their own thoughts about his fiasco, and he wasn't exactly looking forward to hearing them. But by the time his superiors got around to sharing their impressions of his most recent operation with him, that fort was going to be a smoking, smoldering ruin.

Cerlohs Myr owed the First Provisional Talon—and the 3012th Strike—that much.

* * *

Company-Captain Mesaion stood tautly in his position, field glasses glued to his eyes, staring up into the early morning sky above Fort Salby.

Chief-Armsman Wesiar chan Forcal stood beside him, but unlike Mesaion, chan Forcal was parked under the very best overhead cover they could give him. The supporting structure above him was made of two crossed layers of railroad ties, thickly buttressed by sandbags. The western side of his personal bunker was the parapet of the fighting step itself, and the northern side was the equally solid adobe and stone of one of the gate bastions. The southern side was a wall of sandbags stacked two-wide at the top and four-wide at the bottom. In fact, only the eastern side was open, and that only so that he could communicate with Mesaion.

There was a reason for how elaborately the chief-armsman was protected while his superior was so exposed. Unlike Company-Captain Mesaion, Chief-Armsman chan Forcal didn't need field glasses as he stood there with his eyes tightly closed and his head cocked in an attitude of intense concentration. He was one of the most precious commodities any artillery commander could have: a highly trained, highly experienced predictive Distance Viewer.

"Coming in!" he announced suddenly. "Circling to the north, and climbing!"

Mesaion swung his glasses onto the indicated bearing and saw a swarm of distant black dots climbing in a tight corkscrew, wings laboring. Even with the glasses, he couldn't make out a great many details at that range, but he didn't really need to, either.

Sorry I ever doubted you, Your Highness, the artillerist found himself thinking. Then he lowered the glasses.

"Keep your head down Wesiar," he said. "We can't have anything happening to it, now can we?"

He smiled tightly at the Distance Viewer, then turned his own head to look at the crews assigned to the pedestal guns and machine guns mounted atop the walls.

"Okay, boys! The Prince put you right where you need to be! And in just a minute, it's going to be time to show these bastards why!"

* * *

Hundred Myr's lips skinned back as the 2029th reached its designated pushover altitude. He'd been right. They might have placed outlying machine guns to cover the railroad and the ground approaches, but they hadn't bothered to put any of them out here in these barren, totally uninhabited mountains. Now, safely above the reach of their godsdamned weapons, he and his dragons headed out towards their objective.

Myr gazed down through Razorwing's vision, examining the fort they'd come to burn, and grimaced.

I shouldn't have argued against sending in the recon gryphons, he told himself bitterly. *Obviously,* they *don't think of this thing as "just one more portal fort," do they? They must have a dozen of those machine guns up there on the walls.*

His belly muscles tightened at the thought, but his

fingers were sure and confident in the control grooves. Yes, they had a lot of firepower down there, and no one was going to dismiss the threat—not after what had happened to the 3012th. But this wasn't going to be broadside shots into unsuspecting beasts moving on steady, predictable courses. No. *These* defenders were going to have to fire directly upward, into the teeth of a dozen thirty- or forty-ton battle dragons, flying straight at them and belching fire and lightning bolts as they came.

And that, my fine Sharonian friends, Myr thought savagely, *is a very different dragon fight, indeed.*

* * *

"Steady," Mesaion murmured to himself, far too low for any of his gunners to have heard. "Steady . . . steady . . . *steeeady.* . . ."

The dragons were almost directly overhead now. Surely they would have to begin their attack dive soon.

The artillerist spared one precious moment to look over his shoulder to where Crown Prince Janaki stood on the parapet-level gun platform beside Regiment-Captain chan Skrithik. The prince wasn't looking his way, which was a pity. Mesaion would have liked to have at least nodded to Janaki in appreciation.

The Yerthak pedestal gun was essentially a naval weapon which had been around for decades. In fact, it had slipped over into obsolescence these days, and it was being steadily phased out of naval service in favor of light quick-firing weapons, like the ship-mounted version of the field artillery's three-point-four-inch quick-firer, because its shells simply were no longer heavy enough for its original design function. But it remained an effective weapon for many other purposes, and the decision to upgrade the Imperial Navy's tertiary armament meant that a largish number of Yerthaks which had become suddenly surplus to the Navy's needs were finding their way into Customs Service or PAAF use.

In many ways, it was similar to the Faraika, but instead of two to four barrels in a single, fixed sleeve, the Yerthak—depending upon its caliber—had from four to six barrels arranged to rotate around a central axis in a circular motion. Instead of belted ammunition, they fired rounds from huge clips, like oversized rifle magazines, with each barrel firing as it reached the highest point of its circular path. A pedestal gun's sustained rate of fire was lower than that of the lighter Faraika, and it could maintain maximum-rate fire only briefly, but that was fine with Mesaion. Because, unlike the Faraika, the Yerthak was a genuine artillery piece.

The Yerthak Works had produced the weapon in several calibers. The most common were the one-point-five-inch and two-point-five-inch versions. The two-point-five, like the ones on Fort Salby's walls, came with four barrels and had a muzzle velocity of almost sixteen hundred feet per second and a maximum range of just over six thousand yards with the new "smokeless powder" rounds. And, unlike the one-point five-inch, it was capable of firing shrapnel rounds, not simply high-explosive or solid ammunition.

They had been intended for relatively short range actions, meant to smother light torpedo craft in a torrent of high-explosive. As such, their designed elevation was strictly limited. But thanks to Janaki's warning, the available guns were deployed in a wide ring and mounted on firing platforms wide enough to allow the weapons to be traversed through three hundred and sixty degrees. Elevation was still limited, but the Fort Salby machinsts had torched off the limiting stops on the elevation quadrants to squeeze several more degrees out of them. Coupled with the broad base of fire from the way they were spread out around the fort's perimeter, they had elevation enough to form a cone much taller than would normally have been the case, and Janaki and chan Skrithik had thoughtfully provided something to help fill the gaps and thicken their total weight of fire. Every Faraika II which hadn't been emplaced in the hillside positions for the opening ambush had been clamped atop improvised post mounts, as well, and they had considerably more elevation than the pedestal guns did.

Now the men behind those guns watched over their sights as an incredible freight train of flying impossibilities dove straight towards them.

* * *

A black's lightning bolt would be far less effective than one of the reds' fireballs. Myr knew that. But after the losses he'd already taken, they needed every dragon. Even if that hadn't been true, Myr was a dragon pilot himself before he was anything else. No one else was going to lead the strike—not after what had happened to the 3012th.

He felt Razorwing's determination in the way the big dragon folded his wings and fell into a headlong, screaming dive. Despite the losses he'd already suffered, despite the possibility that he was going to suffer still more of them, Cerlohs Myr had never felt more alive, more confident . . . more powerful and focused.

That's not a machine gun! he thought abruptly. There wasn't time to try to puzzle out just what "that" was, but the weapon was bigger and bulkier. And the Sharonians were aiming it upward, as well.

Bigger probably means nastier, his racing mind decided, and he moved his aimpoint from the machine gun he'd already picked out to one of the unknown weapons. He barely had time to make the change before the crosshair stopped blinking as Razorwing's longer ranged breath weapon entered its effective range of the new target.

"*Kershai!*" Myr shouted, and the arm-thick column of lightning streaked downward.

* * *

Company-Captain Mesaion flinched as the solid shaft of lightning exploded across the sky. It was almost blindingly bright, even in the full daylight which had now settled over Fort Salby, and the thunderclap as it struck home was quite literally deafening.

It didn't appear to have that broad a threat zone—probably a circle no more than eight or ten yards across—but within that zone, it was lethal. It also appeared to be fiendishly accurate. It struck directly on top of one of his Yerthaks, and the gun crew didn't even have time to scream. They convulsed, smoke erupting from their clothing and hair, and then the ammunition in their weapon's magazine cooked off in an explosion that completely crippled the gun.

Mesaion saw it all, but only out of the corner of his eye, and there wasn't really time for it to register before his own people opened fire.

* * *

Myr saw the tracers streaking upward as Razorwing started to pull out of his screaming dive. The big dragon banked, twisting sideways, trading lift for evasion. It was a dangerous game to play this close to such mountainous terrain and at such low altitude after such a high-speed dive, but Razorwing was a skilled veteran, and the sheer adrenaline rush filled Myr with a wild sense of exultation. This—*this*—was what he'd been born for!

Then Razorwing bucked, bellowing a hoarse scream, as his low-altitude flightpath carried him straight in front of one of the pedestal guns. The rotating barrels flamed, the muzzle blast slammed at the faces and clothing of everyone near it, bronze cartridge cases flicked out of the opening breeches, bouncing and rolling, and Razorwing took two direct hits.

The high-explosive rounds slammed into belly scales which wouldn't have stopped even the far lighter rounds of the machine guns. They penetrated deep, and then exploded.

Cerlohs Myr and his dragon slammed into the neat houses of Salbyton at almost three hundred miles an hour.

* * *

Mesaion was never really able to sort it all out clearly later. It happened too quickly, too fast to be accurately recorded by the brains of the human beings caught in the chaos.

Machine guns and pedestal guns thundered and hammered insanely. The sky above Fort Salby was filled with stupendous creatures, and the gunners hurled their hate in copper-jacketed bolts and the sledgehammers of high-explosive.

The dragon pilots of Arcana had never experienced anything like it. For the first time, they encountered concentrated fire from a prepared, unshaken position, and the short range of their dragons' breath weapons left them no choice but to enter their enemies' reach.

Lightning bolts lanced downward. Only a handful of the shorter-ranged fireballs were successfully launched, and two of those went wide as defensive fire smashed into the firing reds. Sharonians screamed and died. The fireballs that landed inside the fort's confines exploded with tremendous force, and a tiny corner of Mesaion's mind thanked Prince Janaki fervently for insisting that his howitzer and mortar crews be kept under cover, out of their gun pits, until they were actually needed.

The overhead cover the prince had insisted with equal fanaticism upon providing for the riflemen spread out along the fort's fighting step proved its worth, as well. For all the heat and fury of the fireballs, they lacked the blast effect to penetrate those heaped sandbags.

What they did to Mesaion's exposed gunners, however, was something else entirely.

In less than two screaming minutes of savage action, fifty-three of Lorvam Mesaion's men were killed outright. Another eighteen were wounded so badly death would have been a mercy, and still another seventeen were put out of action. Four of his Yerthaks were destroyed or disabled. He lost five Faraikas, and two of his heavy mortars were thoroughly wrecked as all the ready ammunition in their—thankfully—unmanned pit went up in a thunderous chain of explosions.

But while all that was happening, his gunners brought down eight more dragons.

One mortally wounded beast crashed directly into the top of the northwestern tower like a forty-ton hammer of scales, blood, and bone, and the impact reduced the pedestal gun crew atop that tower to gruel. The parapet exploded outward in a meteor storm of broken adobe, stones, and dust, and the dragon came to rest, one shattered wing drooping down until its tip trailed on the ground beyond. Its pilot dangled from its broken neck, hanging limp and broken himself from the straps of his flight harness. Another dragon smashed into the southernmost stretch of the western wall. It just missed the corner tower where the wall turned to angle back to the east, and the plunging beast crushed the firing step's improvised overhead protection. At least another thirty men were killed as the dragon exploded through the parapet and slammed to earth between the wall and the nearest gun emplacement.

Smoke billowed up from the fort's interior. The top of the southern tower might have been missed by the plummeting dragon, but it was enveloped in a holocaust all its own where that dragon's fireball had struck yet another of the Yerthaks before it was killed itself. The fireball had ignited the destroyed gun's ready-use ammunition, and two dozen nearby infantry had been killed or wounded. But only four of the attacking dragons managed to pull out of their dives successfully, and two of them staggered off, obviously badly hurt.

CHAPTER TWENTY-EIGHT

MAYRKOS HARSHU'S FACE was completely expressionless as the imagery from Commander of Fifty Fahrlo's recon crystal played back before him. Klayrman Toralk wished *his* face could be equally disciplined, but that was more than he could manage.

Graholis! What the hells did Myr run into? *And what the* fuck *did he think he was doing with that second attack?!*

The imagery concluded with Deathclaw circling overhead while his two wounded wingmates came in for quick, clumsy landings. Toralk didn't have the Dragon-Healers' reports yet, but he'd be surprised if the more badly wounded of the two survived. And whether the beast lived or not, both of the injured dragons were going to be out of action for a long time.

Which means I have exactly three battle dragons left—all of them blacks, he thought grimly.

"Thank you," Harshu said almost absently to the Gifted technician. The man had done extraordinarily well to get the imagery transferred so quickly, but he didn't look very happy, despite the two thousand's well deserved thanks.

Probably because he isn't a total idiot, Toralk thought.

The technician departed, and Harshu and Toralk looked at one another across the map table.

"It would appear," Harshu said with a thin, humorless smile, "that it's fortunate I'd already decided to halt the offensive here in Traisum."

Toralk winced.

"Sir," he began, "I'd apologize for this . . . this debacle, if there were any way to excuse it. I—"

"That's enough, Klayrman," Harshu interrupted. The Air Force officer closed his mouth, and the Expeditionary Force's CO shook his head. "I saw your and Five Hundred Myr's attack plan. I was fully aware of the Intelligence appreciations upon which it was based, and I approved it. Whatever blame there may be, it belongs to me as much as it does to you."

Toralk started to disagree with his superior's assessment, then made himself stop and shook his own head.

"That's very understanding of you, Sir," he said instead. "But whoever's to blame, we've got a major problem here."

My, Klayrman, a corner of his brain mocked, *what a massive gift for understatement you* do *have*.

"For all practical purposes," he continued, "my battle dragon strength has just been wiped out. The blacks I have left are the least effective for this sort of attack. And, to be honest, despite all the smoke and explosions our pilots have reported, I doubt very much that they succeeded in neutralizing the fort's defensive fire."

"Probably not," Harshu agreed. The two thousand

gazed down at the map of the terrain around Fort Salby, rubbing his chin gently.

"All right," he said finally. "There's no point standing here beating ourselves up over our losses. What matters are our remaining resources for prosecuting the attack."

Toralk looked at him, then cleared his throat respectfully.

"Sir," he said diffidently, "as I understand our basic operational planning, the object was to secure a forward chokepoint we could hold against counterattack. That's what made this portal so attractive. But if we failed to secure that sort of chokepoint, our object became to conduct a mobile defensive withdrawal, slowing the enemy to the greatest possible extent while the Commandery found reinforcements for us."

"And you're thinking that if we take heavy losses—*additional* heavy losses—against Salby, we won't have anything left to conduct that mobile defense with." Harshu's voice sounded remarkably calm, and Toralk nodded.

"That's exactly what I'm thinking, Sir."

"Well, I'm not certain you're wrong," Harshu said frankly. "On the other hand, now that I've seen Fifty Fahrlo's recon images, I'm more convinced than ever that securing Fort Salby itself would be extremely valuable. The ground-level approach to the portal is even more constricted from the up-chain side than I'd thought it was, and thanks to the portal itself, there's no way—no practical way—they could flank us out of position. It would be a straight up fighting withdrawal to the portal, with our transport dragons giving us the ability to pull our men out at the very last minute."

"I can't disagree with that, Sir. But at the same time, the cliff face, alone, is going to be a major terrain obstacle for anyone without aerial capability. Frankly, if I were a Sharonian, I'd figure it was a pretty solid cork all by itself. We don't need to control the approaches, as well."

"I'm not as positive about that." Harshu shook his head. "I've been thinking about what they did to Hundred Thalmayr at the swamp portal. They used man and pack animal-portable weapons for that attack; for this one, they'd have their 'railroad' available to bring in really heavy weapons. And remember the sheer size of some of the machinery the overflight picked up. I've been trying to imagine what one of their artillery pieces might look like built on that scale and, to be honest, the thought scares the crap out of me.

"Whether they've got any *that* big or not, it's obvious that they have some which are at least a lot bigger and heavier than anything we've encountered so far. Obviously, we haven't seen those in action yet . . . which means I don't have any sort of measuring stick to evaluate how far through a portal *they* could shoot. I'd prefer to have some extra depth, enough room to at least get a good, solid feel for their capabilities, before we make a determined stand defending the cliffs. For that matter, simply deploying in well fortified defensive positions in this kind of terrain would force them to slow down, move cautiously. We wouldn't have that advantage anywhere else—or, at least, not to this extent—if they ever did get past the cliffs.

"Finally, as you yourself just pointed out, our whole object, when you come right down to it, is to buy time for the Commandery to get a real field army in here

Not only that, it's clear we're going to have to recall Carthos—or, at least, Hundred Helika's strike—to reinforce your surviving battle dragon strength, and we're going to have to buy time for that, as well. Well, if that's the case, then let's start buying it as far forward as we can."

"But, Sir—"

"It can be argued either way, Klayrman," Harshu said. "Unfortunately, we don't have time to debate it properly—not with their reinforcements as close as they probably are by now. That means I've got to make the decision right now, and, to be frank, with so much of our battle dragon combat strength written off, our ability to mount a mobile defense has just been pretty damned seriously compromised, even assuming we get Helika up here to reinforce you. Which leaves us with an interesting dilemma. Do we risk even more losses in a possibly unsuccessful attempt to secure a chokepoint we can hold without dragons, or do we avoid the losses but accept that slowing these people in the open field is going to be a lot harder without those same dragons?"

Toralk frowned as he realized he hadn't really considered that aspect of their suddenly unenviable strategic position. He'd been too focused on their disastrous losses and what it had done to their combat power right here, right now, to think that far ahead.

"We've still got the transports, Sir," he pointed out after a moment. "Some of them—some of the tactical transports, the transport-battle dragon crosses—have breath weapon capability. Not anything I'd like to take up against another dragon, you understand, but enough to make them effective against ground targets not covered by the kind of firepower they've got concentrated here. And whether or not we decided we could commit them as improvised stand-ins for the battle dragons, they'd still give us operational mobility that has to be enormously better than theirs."

"Agreed."

Harshu's eyes were hooded, his lips pursed in a thoughtful, silent whistle as he folded his hands behind him and stepped out of his tent into the morning sunlight.

Toralk followed him, gazing out across the dragonfield. If a man hadn't known about the nature of the losses the Expeditionary Force had just suffered, he might have been excused for wondering what all the doom and gloom were about. After all, their personnel losses amounted to only fifteen men out of a total force of over ten thousand. For that matter, they'd lost only fifteen—possibly sixteen—dragons out of a total dragon strength of well over two hundred. On the surface, their combat power should barely have been scratched.

"I agree with your point about the transports, Klayrman," Harshu reiterated after several moments. "But we still don't know exactly how powerful this reinforcement of theirs is going to be. Given what they just did to us, my estimate of what's likely to happen when *they're* allowed to attack *us* just got a lot more pessimistic. That leaves me even more strongly inclined to continue the attack."

"Sir—"

"I know what you're going to say, and you may be right," Harshu interrupted Toralk's nascent argument. "But we've still got a major force advantage, we haven't committed the gryphons or our cavalry, and these people still haven't seen our combat engineers at work. Under the circumstances, I'm inclined to risk additional casualties, considering the possible payoff if the attack succeeds. Be honest, Klayrman. We both know we've gotten off incredibly lightly to this point. I know we've just taken a truly heavy hit to your battle dragons, but I don't think we can justify simply turning around and retreating from a potential prize like this one when the rest of our force is still completely intact. We haven't been hauling all this cavalry and all this infantry around just so we could decide *not* to use it!"

Toralk nodded without speaking. After all, he couldn't argue with anything Harshu had just said.

"What I won't risk are the transports," the two thousand continued firmly. "You're right about the mobility advantage we'll retain as long we keep them intact. I'd prefer to keep the light cavalry intact, too. This is going to be a job for the dragoons and the heavy horse, I think."

And if you lose the heavy cav, you lose less of your tactical mobility down the road, Toralk added silently. *Of course, you lose* more *of your total* firepower, *but still . . .*

He considered the situation, his mind turning to the problem of how best to employ the aerial assets he could still muster. And, as he did, he discovered that he actually felt at least a flicker of optimism. The discovery astonished him, and he shook his head again, this time in rueful admiration.

Left to himself, he was almost certain, he would have called off the attack. Even now, he was far from convinced that *continuing* the attack was the proper decision. But there was really only one way to find out, and the two thousand had the intestinal fortitude to do just that.

He's right about the defensive advantages of this particular chokepoint, too . . . if we manage to pull it off after all, Toralk thought.

"All right, Sir," he said. "Let me go get with my staff for a few minutes and I'll be able to tell you what we've got to try again with."

* * *

"—then tell Master-Armsman chan Garath to get some more men on that fire," Regiment-Captain chan Skrithik said, pointing at the flames and thick, dense smoke pouring from the southeastern tower. The interior of the structure was burning now, although there wasn't actually that much in it that was flammable. He wasn't that concerned over the possibility that the fire might spread, but the gap all those roaring flames and dense smoke left in their defenses worried him quite a lot, considering that their limited infantry and field artillery strength was all concentrated *west* of the fort.

"Yes, Sir!" The runner saluted sharply and disappeared into the smoke and confusion. Chan Skrithik watched him go, then turned back to Janaki.

The crown prince had scarcely moved. Even during the aerial assault on the fort itself, he'd stood there, motionless, gray eyes unfocused on anything of the physical world about him. Not even the falcon on his shoulder had stirred, despite all the sound, fury and confusion swirling about them. The peregrine had been as still as a bird carved from stone, as if its human companion's total, focused concentration had reached out and enveloped it, as well.

Chan Skrithik felt awed by the realization that he was

seeing something very few people had ever witnessed: the legendary Talent of the Caliraths in action. Yet there was more than just awe inside the regiment-captain. There was desperate worry, concern for the safety of the young man who would one day wear the Winged Crown.

For all his years of service, all his hard-won experience and competence, Rof chan Skrithik's military service had been *peacetime* service, and he'd never seen anything like the last hour of chaos and destruction. In less than ten minutes, those diving monstrosities had killed more men than chan Skrithik had seen die in his entire previous military career, and they'd been *his* men. In the process, he'd discovered that it was something no man could truly prepare himself for ahead of time. The sense that he had somehow failed his men by not keeping them alive, that he would have lost fewer of them if only he'd been smarter, better, rolled around somewhere in the depths of his soul. His intellect knew better, knew no Sharonian had ever even imagined the possibility of facing this sort of attack, that no one could have prepared better. But this was a subject where intellect and emotions were scarcely even on speaking terms, and he knew it was going to take him a long, long time to resolve those feelings . . . assuming he ever *could* resolve them.

That, however, was something the future was going to have to take care of in its own good time. For the present, more pressing worries and responsibilities pushed that concern out of the forefront of his mind. And one of those worries was the way Crown Prince Janaki had insisted upon standing in this exposed position high atop the fortress wall.

He stepped towards the prince, reaching out one

hand to urge him to at least climb down from the gun platform to the parapet fighting step, but someone else's hand touched his own shoulder first.

The regiment-captain twitched in surprise. Then he turned his head, and Chief-Armsman Lorash chan Braikal shook his head with a small, sad smile.

"No, Sir," the Marine said softly. "Begging your pardon, but it wouldn't do any good."

"Chief," chan Skrithik told Janaki's senior noncom quietly, "I can't just leave him up here. Not after seeing all of this!" He jerked his head at the smoke, the fires, the corpsmen and their volunteer civilian assistants carrying broken and savagely burned bodies to Company-Captain Krilar's infirmary. "We've got to get him under cover."

"No, Sir." Chan Braikal's voice was respectful, but he shook his head again.

If he'd thought about it, chan Skrithik might have been surprised. No Ternathian officer with more brains than a rock ever doubted that while officers might *command*, it was the tough, experienced core of long-service noncoms who actually ran the Empire's military. Yet it was unusual, to say the very least, for one of those noncoms to argue with a full regiment-captain at a time like this . . . or about *something* like this.

As if any of us had ever experienced *"something" like this in the first place!*

The thought flickered somewhere down inside, and chan Skrithik cocked his head questioningly.

"That's not how Glimpses work, Sir." Chan Braikal's expression, chan Skrithik realized, was just as worried as his own, and the chief-armsman's voice was rough-edged. "I got a sort of crash course about his family's

Talent before he took over the platoon," the noncom continued. "What he's doing now—it's called 'fugue state,' Sir. And for it to work, he has to be at what they call the 'nexus.'"

"Nexus," chan Skrithik repeated carefully.

"Yes, Sir." Chan Braikal took off his helmet and tucked it under his left arm so that he could run the fingers of his right hand through his short, sweat-soaked hair in a gesture which shouted the depth of his worry more eloquently than any words. "The nexus is the place where whatever it is that makes his Talent work . . . flows together most strongly."

It seemed to the regiment-captain that chan Braikal was trying to find the exact words to express something that didn't really lend itself well to explanations.

"Sir," the chief-armsman said earnestly, "I never expected to see this. Gods! I never *wanted* to see it, because they told me that if I did, the shit would be neck-deep and rising fast, begging your pardon. But the thing is, for him to go into fugue state at all, he has to be in exactly the right place. No one else can tell where that 'right place' is. Triad—*he* couldn't've told you ahead of time, most likely. And that place could change, even in the middle of a Glimpse. But until it does, it's where he has to stay, and you won't be able to move him."

"I've never heard anything like that, Chief." It could have sounded accusatory, but it didn't. "According to all the legends—"

"Sir," chan Braikal grinned crookedly, "if you were a Calirath, would *you* want your enemies to know you'd be stuck in one place at a time like this?" Chan Skrithik shook his head, and the chief-armsman shrugged. "That's probably the main reason the stories never mention it. On the other hand, His Highness says that someone with a really strong Talent actually can move around in fugue state. Some of those with the very strongest Talents have actually been able to *fight* in fugue state, for that matter. He says *his* Talent isn't that strong, though. That's why he's just sort of . . . frozen like this."

Chan Skrithik heard the desperate unhappiness in the Marine's voice. Chan Braikal didn't want his crown prince—and a young man to whom he was obviously and deeply devoted—standing on this wall any more than Rof chan Skrithik did.

"I see, Chief." Chan Skrithik laid a hand on chan Braikal's shoulder. "I wish he'd explained that to *me* earlier."

"With all due respect, Sir, I think he probably figured that if he had, you'd've kicked us out before the bastards attacked."

"Maybe I would have," chan Skrithik admitted, and chan Braikal shrugged again.

"Maybe I wish you had, too, Sir. Gods know *I* wanted to argue with him about it. But he told me he *has* to be here, and somehow, when he says that, you just can't . . ."

Chan Braikal's voice trailed off and he shook his head in a helpless, bemused gesture chan Skrithik understood perfectly. He hadn't been prepared for the sheer force of Janaki's presence, either. Nor was he any more confident than chan Braikal of his ability to argue with the crown prince's decisions, and so he only smiled sadly and squeezed the chief-armsman's shoulder.

"Well, in that case, Chief, we'll just have to see to it that we keep him in one piece, won't we?"

* * *

"All right, Sir," Klayrman Toralk said. "Here's what we've got left."

He copied the files in his own crystal to Two Thousand Harshu's and waited while Harshu's quick, fierce eyes darted over the information. The two thousand digested it with his customary speed, then looked back up at Toralk.

"I remember your saying the gryphon-handlers were worried about their control spells."

"Yes, Sir. And they still are—worried, I mean. But they still don't have anything concrete to point to, either. I didn't want to use them before because, on the basis of our previous experience, neither Five Hundred Myr nor I thought we'd need them. Obviously, we were wrong."

"So was I," Harshu reminded him. The two thousand's tone was slightly absent as he looked back over Toralk's hastily recorded notes.

"Are you sure about bringing Urlan's transports in this close?" he asked after a moment.

"According to the maps, both of the designated LZs should be dead ground from their observed positions."

"Agreed. But don't forget that their artillery isn't like ours, Klayrman. They don't necessarily need direct lines of sight to their targets."

"Yes, Sir. I tried to allow for that by placing them far enough from their main position to be out of their range."

"I understand. Unfortunately, we've already encountered at least one weapon—those big, rotating things on the walls—that we'd never seen before. I'm not inclined to assume they don't have other, longer-ranged weapons we also haven't met up with before."

"Well," Toralk brought up his own copy of the information and paged through to a map generated from the Sharonian charts captured at Fort Ghartoun. "We could put them here or here, instead," he said, using his stylus to drop a pair of crosshairs onto the map. "Both spots are farther from the fort, so Urlan's cavalry would have farther to go, but there's a steep, solid mountain slope between both of them and the fort. From what we've seen tinkering around with those captured 'mortars' of theirs, I don't think even their weapons could drop something in that close on a reverse slope that steep."

"Um." Harshu frowned, contemplating the map. Then he nodded, although he still didn't look precisely enthralled.

"The other alternative, Sir, is to make it an infantry assault," Toralk pointed out. "If we throw the gryphons straight into their faces, and the tactical transports come in close behind them, we'd have the transports' breath weapons, such as they are, for support and the Sharonians would probably be too busy with the gryphons to knock many of them down."

"Tempting," Harshu acknowledged. "Very tempting, in some ways. But our men are going to need heavy weapons support if they're going to have a chance against Sharonian weapons at close range. And as you pointed out, we may need those transports' breath weapons later on, especially if this attack *doesn't* succeed. Besides, if we can take Salby, infantry is going to be more useful than cavalry afterward for defending the sort of terrain between the fort and the portal."

He gazed down at the map for several more minutes, rubbing his chin, then paused.

"You know," he said slowly, "if we timed it properly,

we might still be able to use the transports after all." Toralk's eyes narrowed, and his superior looked up at him with a smile. "If you were a Sharonian, Klayrman, and you'd never seen anything like a dragon or an augmented horse or a unicorn, which of the three would monopolize *your* attention if you saw all of them coming at you at once?"

CHAPTER TWENTY-NINE

"IMMORTAL ARUNCAS!" Tarnal Garsal, Windlord Garsal, muttered.

The second lord of horse stood in Sunlord Markan's command post, looking back at the smoke-streaming PAAF fort behind them, and he had ample reason to invoke the Uromathian god of war. Both cavalry officers, like Rof chan Skrithik, were veterans of long service. And, like chan Skrithik, neither of them had ever seen or imagined anything like this.

Actually, Garsal found the smoke and flames almost comforting in their normality. At least they were much less disconcerting than the enormous beast—the *dragon*, he told himself, using the Ternathian crown prince's terminology as he looked back at it—which had crashed to earth less than sixty yards from the CP. It loomed like a scaly mountain of broken bone and flesh where it had landed, crushing a dozen of Garsal's cavalry troopers in its death plunge.

"Aruncas, indeed," a voice said at Garsal's shoulder.

He turned his head and saw Sunlord Markan gazing out across the sandbags at the same sight. The first lord of horse was the second ranking officer of the Salby garrison, which had made him the proper choice to command the infantry and artillery positions outside the fort itself. He didn't exactly look shaken . . . but his expression came far closer to that than anything Garsal had ever seen from him before.

"I didn't really believe him, you know," Garsal said. Markan glanced at him and raised one eyebrow. "I suppose I didn't *want* to believe him," Garsal admitted, and this time Markan snorted.

"I imagine most of us would have preferred not to," the sunlord said after a moment. "It's like something out of a child's fairytale about monsters, ogres, and magic spells."

Garsal nodded, and Markan turned his eyes back to the monstrous, broken-winged carcass sprawled across the mangled bodies of his men.

There was another reason Garsal hadn't wanted to believe Prince Janaki, the sunlord thought. Another reason *he* hadn't wanted to, for that matter.

Markan had his own very private reservations about his emperor, but Chava Busar was still *his* emperor, and—up to this moment, at least—Markan had found himself forced to agree with Emperor Chava on at least one point: far too many people in Sharona were reacting with far too much panic to the reports from the frontiers.

Stories about "magic" simply didn't belong in the everyday world of hardheaded, practical men. Oh, no one had questioned the fact that the Arcanans were actually there, or that they had massacred the Chalgyn Consortium survey crew with frighteningly unknown weapons. But Hell's Gate was forty-eight thousand miles from Sharona, and hard on the news of the massacre had come the word that less than four hundred men had taken the swamp portal away from the enemy with ludicrous ease. Sharonian weapons had been clearly and obviously superior to anything they had yet faced, and nothing else the Arcanans had demonstrated since that short, brutal battle had been especially terrifying. Surely not enough to justify the almost hysterical response of certain of Sharona's political leaders!

Whatever happened out on the distant frontier, there was no real chance of an enemy successfully fighting his way through the portals and all of the wearisome miles between them to actually reach Sharona. Even assuming that all of those arguing in favor of some sort of worldwide—hells, *multiverse*-wide—empire were genuinely sincere in their motivations and not simply seeking to manipulate the political equation for their own advantage (which seemed unlikely, to say the least), it would have been foolish to allow oneself to be caught up in the hysteria.

Now, smelling the smoke from Fort Salby, looking at the huge, broken body of a genuine dragon while he awaited the second assault from a force which had advanced four thousand miles in less than two weeks, Jukan Darshu, Sunlord Markan, knew those "hysterical" leaders had been right all along. If the Arcanans had dragons that breathed fire and spat lightning, if they could cover eight percent of the total distance to Sharona in only two weeks, then the gods alone knew what *else* they might have or be able to do. It was entirely possible that they could fight their way clear to Sharona, after all . . . and that Zindel of Ternathia and Ronnel of Farnalia had been dead serious from the outset. That whatever Chava Busar might think, Zindel had *not* been manufacturing and manipulating the crisis which had impelled him to the throne of a united Sharona.

Firsoma help us all! he thought. *If the Crown Prince Saw this in a Glimpse, what has his* father *Seen?*

He didn't much care for that question, for a lot of reasons.

Of course you don't. You're a Uromathian, and Uromathians don't like *Ternathians, do they? But if the Arcanans have capabilities like* this, *then maybe the Conclave was right. Maybe we* can't *afford to be Uromathians or Ternathians any longer . . . even if it does mean putting another crown on Zindel chan Calirath's head.*

* * *

"They're coming back."

Regiment-Captain chan Skrithik twitched as Janaki spoke for the first time in at least half an hour.

"Your Highness?"

"They're coming back," Janaki repeated in that same otherworldly tone. "They're using their dragons to circle around the other aspect of the portal in Karys. Then they're going to use the western aspect in Traisum and swing wide, try to keep us from seeing them while they put cavalry on the ground."

"Cavalry? In the open against dug-in infantry and artillery?" Chan Skrithik couldn't believe what he was hearing.

"Yes," Janaki said. He turned those daunting eyes on the regiment-captain. "It's not going to be that easy. They can put them on the ground *east* of us and avoid most of our covering positions, and their cavalry is a lot faster than ours. And they've got something else. Something to cover them. I can't quite See it yet. And they're loading up other dragons with infantry. They'll be coming at us, too, and I think they're going to use those eagle-lions this time, as well."

Chan Skrithik's jaw tightened. He would have been totally confident of his entrenched infantry's ability to deal with any *Sharonian* cavalry attack. But as Janaki had just reminded him, he wasn't dealing with Sharonians . . . as their ability to *avoid* his entrenchments demonstrated.

"Can you See how they'll come at us, Your Highness?" he asked.

"Not yet," Janaki replied, and a hint of frustration shadowed his voice even through its detachment. "There are still too many possibilities. They're coming together . . . focusing. But they aren't there yet."

"Can you See where they'll land their cavalry?" Chan Skrithik asked, opening his map case.

"Here or here." Janaki's forefinger stabbed the map, and chan Skrithik looked up at Senior-Armsman Isia.

"Message for Company-Captain Mesaion. Give him these coordinates." Chan Skrithik read them off from the map grid. "Tell the Company-Captain I want chan Forcal to Watch both of them. And I want the howitzers ready to engage."

"Yes, Sir."

The Flicker had been writing quickly while the regiment-captain spoke. Now he read back his shorthand notations. Chan Skrithik nodded approval, and Isia Flicked the message canister to Mesaion's Flicker. The artillerist's acknowledgment appeared on the parapet beside chan Skrithik less than two minutes later.

* * *

Commander of Fifty Delthyr Fahrlo was still trying to come to grips with what had happened to the initial attack as he and Deathclaw led the line of transport dragons out of the portal's western aspect.

The maneuver wouldn't have been very practical without dragons. The nature of the portals between universes meant that any traveler from Karys found himself confronting the same sort of enormous cliffs no matter which way he passed through the portal, but the westernmost cliffs were quite a bit higher than those to the east. Wind erosion had softened and grooved the tops of those sheer walls until the pressures between the two sides of the portal had equalized, but the palisade of stone remained steeply and starkly unscalable.

Facing east into Traisum, from the opposite side of the portal, the cliffs were much shallower, and the wind screaming down the slopes beyond the cliffs' edges had carved deep ravines. The Sharonian construction engineers had taken advantage of that when they cut their road and "railroad" routes. As far as Fahrlo could see, they hadn't had very much choice about that, but the Expeditionary Force *did*, and Two Thousand Harshu and Thousand Toralk had decided to take advantage of that fact.

Too bad they didn't take advantage of it before, Fahrlo couldn't help thinking bitterly, even though he knew it was unfair. Nobody could have predicted what had happened to his fellow battle-dragon pilots and their mounts before they'd actually seen it. He knew that. But he also knew that somehow *he*, a mere commander of fifty, had become the senior battle-dragon pilot of the entire First Provisional Talon.

Of course, I'm a "commander of fifty" with only three dragons to command.

He grimaced behind his helmet visor at the thought, then shook his head. He had other things to be concentrating on at the moment.

* * *

"The dragons are landing at the second location, Sir," Chief-Armsman chan Forcal told Company-Captain Mesaion.

"Too bad," Mesaion grunted, then turned to his own Flicker. "Inform Regiment-Captain chan Skrithik that the enemy is landing at the second location and that we can't bring it under fire."

"Yes, Sir."

* * *

"Damn it," chan Skrithik muttered as Isia read him Mesaion's terse dispatch.

He'd been afraid of that when Janaki indicated the landing areas on the map. The one in question would have been out of range for the mortars, anyway, although the howitzers had the reach. He doubted these Arcanan bastards had any way of knowing that, but they'd lucked out and chosen a landing site in the dead ground beyond a steep, intervening ridgeline.

"Tell Company-Captain Mesaion I want chan Forcal to keep them under observation. Let me know the instant they begin to move out."

"Yes, Sir."

* * *

"Five Hundred Urlan's in position, Sir," the hummer-handler announced.

"Good." Harshu turned to Toralk. "I suppose that means it's time, Klayrman."

"Yes, Sir. It is." Toralk nodded, then looked at the hummer-handler. "Send Hundred Kormas the release order, Senior Sword."

"Yes, Sir!"

The hummer-handler opened the smaller cage in which he had set aside the hummer with the release order already recorded. Now he took the small, fiercely aggressive little creature in his hands, whispered something to it, and tossed it into the air. Its wings blurred into invisibility, and it turned like a questing hound, hovering in midair. Then, sudden as a snapping arbalest string, it flashed away.

Toralk watched it disappear and fought down an urge to inhale deeply and surreptitiously. He remained far from certain that continuing the attack was the right move, but that no longer really mattered. First, because it wasn't his decision; second, because everyone was committed now. Commander of One Hundred Surtel Kormas would release his gryphons five minutes after he received Toralk's dispatch, and the gryphons' onslaught would be the signal for the rest of the assault.

Graholis, I hope this works, the thousand thought fervently. Please *let this work!*

* * *

"Regiment-Captain!"

Rof chan Skrithik turned quickly back to Janaki. Something had changed in the prince's voice. The fort's commander couldn't quite identify what that change was, but whatever it was, it sent a fresher, deeper surge of anxiety through him.

"Yes, Your Highness?"

"It's starting." Janaki turned to look at him, and the distant focus in his eyes was deeper and darker than ever. "Listen to me," he said, and there was a stark edge of command in his voice. "I don't know how much time there'll be. It won't be enough, however much of it there is. So it's important. *Listen* to what I tell you."

"Of course, Your Highness." Chan Skrithik was puzzled. Of course anything Prince Janaki had to tell him was "important." Did Janaki think chan Skrithik would have allowed him to stand up here, Chief-Armsman chan Braikal or not, if it *wasn't* important?

"I can't tell yet," Janaki sounded far more frustrated. "I can't *tell* which is the real attack yet."

He wheeled back around, staring out across the parapet. Then his head tilted back. He looked up into the sky above the fort, his head swinging from side to side.

"Not yet," he told the bright, cloudless heavens in a strange tone which mingled command and entreaty in almost equal measure. "Not *yet*!"

For a moment, nothing else happened. Then his falcon launched from his shoulder with a high, fierce cry, and he sucked in a deep breath.

"They're coming!" His arm shot out and he pointed sharply to the northwest. *"There!"*

* * *

Fifty Fahrlo watched the strike gryphons go streaking past the transports and his escorting battle dragons. The gryphons were far smaller, tiny, compared to the dragons, but there were over a hundred of them, and he was delighted that they were at least a thousand feet higher than his own formation. Fahrlo had a lively respect for the men who worked as gryphon-handlers. He trusted their professionalism implicitly, yet he'd seen what gryphons could do, and he wanted no part of it. If the compulsion spells failed, or if those spells misidentified the gryphons' target, enough of them could swarm even a dragon out of the heavens.

This time, though, there was no mistake. The gryphons swept onward, driving towards the smoke-gouting fort like a plague of pony-sized locusts, and Fahrlo smiled thinly behind his visor.

Should've let them swarm the bastards in the first place, he thought, even though he knew precisely why it hadn't seemed necessary. *I bet they won't like* this *one little bit!*

* * *

"Sir, I think—yes!" The lookout floating on his levitation spell at the end of the long tether to his saddle shouted down to Commander of Five Hundred Gyras Urlan. "The gryphons are in position!"

"Good!" Urlan barked. "Now get your ass back down here!"

"Yes, Sir!"

"Bugler!"

"Yes, Sir?"

"Blow 'Walk'!"

"Yes, Sir!"

The bugle began to sound, and the big, heavily augmented horses of the Seventh Zydor Heavy Dragoons stirred into movement. They had a long way to go, and so they moved without haste. The time for that would come, but it wasn't here yet. Not yet. They were bigger—*much* bigger—than the light cavalry's unicorns, and despite their augmentation, that meant they were slower, with less endurance, as well. Their speed and strength had to be conserved for the final dash to their objective. But that was all right. The gryphons wouldn't attack immediately. The compulsion spells directing their strike had been carefully structured to give Urlan's cavalry time to get into position.

The heavy horses' larger size meant each of them could carry not one rider, but two, and two of Urlan's hundred-and-twenty-strong companies were configured as standard heavy dragoons. Each horse bore a two-man saddle, with the rear rider armed not with a saber or lance but with a cutdown version of an infantry-dragon. It was much shorter ranged than the infantry weapon, but longer ranged than any arbalest and far more deadly.

Each horse in Commander of One Hundred Orkal Kiliron's Charlie Company, on the other hand, carried only a standard saddle, instead of the two-man heavy dragoon version. In place of the normal second rider, a smaller version of the standard dragon cargo pod had been harnessed to each horse. Its comparatively diminutive size was small enough for an augmented horse to handle without too much trouble, but still big enough to carry a full twelve-man infantry squad. A quarter of those pods were occupied by Gifted engineering specialists; the others contained over a thousand picked infantry. And one basis for their selection was that at least half of them had at least some Gift.

Enough, at any rate, for them to be armed with daggerstones for the assault.

"Activate the glamour," Urlan said to the Gifted commander of fifty at his side.

"Yes, Sir."

* * *

"That's it."

Janaki's voice was suddenly calm, almost quiet, and chan Skrithik jerked his eyes away from the small dots, circling above Fort Salby with a hungry eagerness he could sense even from here. They seemed very close, those dots, but if they were the size the prince had described, then they were much higher than they looked.

"I beg your pardon, Your Highness?"

"I See now," Janaki said, and turned his back on the circling dots to face the regiment-captain with a strangely serene little smile. "I didn't think there was going to be enough time."

"Your Highness?" Something about Janaki's voice, the way his body language had somehow relaxed, worried chan Skrithik.

"Listen." Janaki put his hands on chan Skrithik's shoulders, pulling the older man so close to him their foreheads almost touched. "The eagle-lions are going to attack in just a few minutes. They'll come in from the west. When they do, we'll see the dragons coming in behind them."

The prince's words came quickly, with a sort of distant urgency. Chan Skrithik might have been fooled by their quietness, but he saw something behind the ghosts in those gray eyes. He saw ferocious purpose, determination, and his own eyes narrowed with the intensity of his concentration on what Janaki was saying.

"They'll have infantry on the dragons. Some of the dragons will be spitting fire or lightning. They'll have more infantry on lines, ready to drop over the parapet. They'll use the eagle-lions to try to suppress our fire. But the dragons aren't the real threat. They're a diversion, Regiment-Captain. They want us looking at *them* while the real attack comes in from behind us, from the east. Do you understand? The *dragons* and their infantry are the diversion, not the cavalry. Do you understand?"

Chan Skrithik nodded, and Janaki looked past him for a moment at Senior-Armsman Isia.

"Warn Company-Captain Mesaion. The cavalry have some sort of . . . spell. It's like a smokescreen, but different. It'll look more like a mirage—like heat shimmer. But the cavalry will be behind it. Most of the men won't be able to see through it, but chan Forcal can. He's got to get Mesaion's first rounds on target—on the ranks around their standard. It's a wind sock, like one of the Arpathian dragon-standards. That's where their commander is—where the spell will be coming from. Do you understand?"

Isia darted a look at chan Skrithik. The regiment-captain nodded, and the Flicker swallowed hard, then produced a jerky nod of his own.

"Yes. Yes, Your Highness!"

Janaki's head swiveled back to chan Skrithik while Isia's frenzied pencil started scribbling the message to Mesaion. The black dots overhead were beginning to widen their circle. Chan Skrithik was vaguely aware of them, sensed the way they were straining at some immaterial leash, but most of his attention was focused on Janaki chan Calirath and the prophetic fire burning in his eyes.

"They've got those fire-throwers on some of the horses. And some of the others are towing carriers—floating carriers, like hot-air balloons—with more infantry in them. They'll try to get the carriers in close enough to assault the parapet—use them like scaling ladders. And if they can't get *over* the wall, they'll go *through* it. They've got people with spells that can open breaches—like blasting charges, but different. They'll have to reach the wall to actually use them. They'll try for the dead spot at the southeast corner, where the fire will cover them and none of the machine guns or pedestal guns will bear. You have to get men with grenades over there now. Do you understand?"

Chan Skrithik felt himself nodding again as Janaki repeated the three-word question like some sort of mantra.

"See to it, Chief," he said to chan Braikal. The Marine stared at him for one instant, then turned almost agonized eyes to Janaki. He hesitated a heartbeat longer, but the crown prince gave him a smile and twitched his head, confirming chan Skrithik's order, and chan Braikal thundered off, shouting for the other members of his platoon.

"Some of the infantry have the same sort of smaller fire-throwers," Janaki went on, the machine-gun words coming with almost impossible clarity yet simultaneously seeming to trip and fall over one another. "If the ones with the blasting charges touch the wall, they'll blow through it. The fire-throwers have less range than a revolver, but they'll kill anyone they hit and each of them is good for several shots. And they've got other people with them—people with spells like a Lifter's, only better. They can actually Lift people up over the parapet without using ladders or the carriers if they can get close enough."

The circling dots were plunging downward now. Rifles began to crack. The surviving machine guns on the parapet began to fire, as well, but the gryphons were smaller, faster, and far more agile targets. The men Janaki had insisted on arming with the more rapidly firing Model 7s were going to be far more effective than riflemen, but the shotguns were also much shorter ranged. The men armed with them had to wait for the gryphons to come to them.

"Remember, Sir." Janaki's eyes burned into Roth chan Skrithik's soul, and his hands slid down from the regiment-captain's shoulders to grip the front of his uniform tunic. "Remember—the dragons are the diversion. They won't risk them in close. They've lost too many. It's the cavalry. You've *got* to stop the *cavalry*. If you stop it, they'll break off the attack. They won't take additional losses—not this far from home. But if the cavalry gets through, gets inside the walls, it's over. You can't—"

He broke off suddenly, and his eyes dropped abruptly back into focus. They were suddenly once again the clear, gray eyes of a young man, not the eyes of an avatar of legends.

"It's here."

His voice had changed, too. It was almost—almost—normal again.

"Good luck, Sir," he said, and his hands locked on chan Skrithik's tunic. The regiment-captain's eyes just had time to begin to widen, and then Janaki picked him bodily up and threw him off the gun platform. Chan Skrithik landed on the fighting step three feet below—landed so hard, so awkwardly, that he broke the bones in his left forearm into gravel.

He scarcely noticed the white-hot agony of those snapping, shattered bones. It was so small, so unimportant, in comparison.

Janaki chan Calirath never even turned his head. He was still looking at chan Skrithik when the gryphon he'd never seen with his physical eyes at all hit him from behind and killed him instantly.

CHAPTER THIRTY

THE GRYPHONS HIT Fort Salby like a tidal wave of ferocity wrapped up in feathers, talons, and fur.

The men on the fort's walls had never seen anything like them. But then, they'd never seen anything like quite a lot of what they were seeing this day. And if they'd never seen them before, at least they'd had them described to them by officers who had been briefed by Crown Prince Janaki. Those briefings defused much of the terror of the unknown. They didn't magically banish fear, didn't make dragons or gryphons any less monstrous, any less unnatural. But they set aside the paralyzing shock complete surprise might have achieved, and the men of Fort Salby were angry.

They knew about the negotiations. They knew the crown prince was right, that the Arcanans must have been carefully planning their offensive the entire time they'd been talking about negotiations and peaceful settlements. They'd drawn their own conclusions about what must have happened to the Voices down-chain from Traisum, and they knew *they'd* been supposed to be taken by surprise themselves and massacred in what they thought was peacetime.

They'd already smashed the first attack. The price might have been high, but they'd knocked those stupendous dragons out of the air, proven the Arcanans' magical creatures were indeed mortal, however wondrous they might appear. And so, as the gryphons swept down upon them, swinging wide to avoid overflying the infantry positions west of the fort, they were ready.

Rifle fire flamed across the parapet. The heavy machine guns which had wreaked such havoc against the dragons couldn't traverse quickly enough to engage the smaller, fleeter gryphons effectively, and even the rifles were less than completely effective. As good as the Model 10 was, it was still a bolt-action rifle engaging flying targets coming in at speeds of well over two hundred miles an hour.

Here and there, a gryphon's wings suddenly faltered, a beast fell out of the oncoming cloud of killers, but the rest kept coming.

The overhead cover which had been erected to protect the firing steps from fireballs proved at least partly effective against gryphons, as well. Some of the beasts flung themselves upon the sandbags, ripping at them, shredding them to get at the fragile human bodies beneath them. Others hurled themselves straight into the faces of the defenders, coming over the parapet, swarming into the gap between the overhead and the tops of the fort's walls. Still others swept past the parapets entirely, stooping on the unprotected men on the fort parade ground and in the gun pits.

Fourteen-inch bayonets turned rifles into short spears, thrusting frantically as two-foot beaks snapped like headsmen's axes. Here and there, wicked talons gripped rifles, snatching them aside, and everywhere men screamed in agony as bellies were opened, throats were ripped out, heads simply disappeared.

Revolvers cracked and shotguns began to bellow, thundering in rapid fire, spitting buckshot into tawny-hided killers, and gryphons shrieked in agony of their own. It was all one mad, swirling sea of chaos.

Rof chan Skrithik saw the gryphon which had killed his prince. The creature flung back its head, bloody beak gaping in a scream of triumph, and then a feathered thunderbolt struck from above. Janaki's falcon hurled itself into the monster's face with a hissing shriek of pure fury, and the guillotine beak snapped ferociously as its small tormentor ripped bleeding furrows across its face and blinded one eye.

Taleena distracted the gryphon just long enough for chan Skrithik to drag out his revolver. The regiment-captain was aware of his prince, bleeding under the gryphon's ferocious talons, and he bared his teeth in savage hatred as his thumb cocked the hammer and the heavy weapon roared.

The gryphon screamed in fresh pain as the heavy bullet smashed into it. It turned away from Taleena, back towards chan Skrithik, and the regiment-captain shot it again. And again!

It went down at last with the fourth shot, and chan Skrithik felt hands pulling him back to his feet.

It was Senior-Armsman Isia, bleeding from a deep cut in his right cheek, his eyes wild.

"Sir! Are you all right, Sir?"

Chan Skrithik stared at the Flicker for two or three eternal heartbeats. All right? How could he ever be "*all right*" again? He ripped his eyes away from Isia, and they burned with unshed tears as he looked down at the dead young man at his feet. But then he shook himself. His prince had died to give him his final orders, and his lips drew back.

"Message!" he barked at Isia.

"Yes, Sir!"

Isia dragged out his notepad, holding it to one side to avoid bleeding on it.

"I want Platoon-Captain chan Noth over at the southeastern tower—now! He's to do whatever it takes to hold that wall!"

"Yes, Sir!"

Isia's pencil slashed at the pad. He stuffed the hastily written order into a message canister and Flicked it on its way.

"Message to Sunlord Markan," chan Skrithik continued without a break. "Begin: Expect heavy cavalry attack from southeast. Expect fire-throwers. Imperative the enemy not reach the fort's walls with blasting spells."

He thought about adding specific instructions, but there was no need. Uromathian or not, Markan was smart and experienced. He'd know what to do.

Isia Flicked that message to its destination, as well, then took chan Skrithik's revolver and quickly replaced the expended rounds for the suddenly one-handed regiment-captain. Chan Skrithik thanked him absently and reholstered the weapon, then started down the steps from the parapet. He hated leaving that vantage point—and hated, almost as much, the feeling that he was somehow abandoning his prince—but with Janaki dead, he needed access to chan Forcal.

Movement jarred the shattered bones in his left forearm. A part of him almost welcomed the physical pain as a distraction from the anguish within, but he couldn't afford to be distracted by either of them. And so he pushed both of them aside, cradling his broken arm with his good one in an effort to at least minimize the hurt and trying not to think about what another fall might do to that arm while he ran down the steps faster than he really should have.

All about him he heard screams, rifle shots, shotguns, and pistols. Bodies and pieces of men's bodies fell from the walls. Sprays of blood and feathers seemed to be everywhere, and gryphons—most dead, some only wounded and even more dangerous for that—littered the parade ground.

Chan Skrithik let go of his left arm and drew his revolver once more as he and Isia headed out across that parade ground. Twice, wounded gryphons slashed at him with beaks or talons, and twice the heavy H&W revolver roared in his hand.

Then, ahead of him, he saw Company-Captain Mesaion. The New Farnalian company-captain had moved down to the ground level gun pits and he'd brought his Distance Viewer with him.

* * *

"I *understand* what His Highness said, Sir," Wesiar chan Forcal protested. "I'm trying. But they just gods-damned *disappeared* and I can't get them ba—"

The Distance Viewer broke off. For an instant, his eyes were distant, almost confused looking. And then, abruptly, they snapped back into focus.

"I've got them again," he said flat-voiced. "I See the standard, too. Gods, those are *big* fucking horses!"

"Screw their *size*!" Lorvam Mesaion snapped. "Give me a target!"

"Yes, Sir."

Chan Forcal closed his eyes once more, concentrating on his Talent. Distance Viewers were critical to accurate indirect artillery fire, but chan Forcal had a special Talent, and Mesaion had never been more glad that the chief-armsman had wound up assigned to Fort Salby. Men with his Talent were more often snapped up by the Navy, because chan Forcal was a *predictive* Distance Viewer. His particular Talent included just a touch of Precognition. The ability to project a moving target's position ever so briefly in advance.

"Six thousand yards," chan Forcal said suddenly, sharply. "One-seven-three degrees. Two minutes."

"Six thousand yards!" Mesaion bellowed. "One-seven-three degrees! *Move*, godsdamn you!"

* * *

"Bugler!"

"Sir?"

"Blow 'At the Trot'!"

"Yes, Sir!"

Five Hundred Urlan heard the urgent, golden notes flaring from the bell-mouthed bugle, and the Seventh Zydors sprang ponderously into a trot. Their horses might be slower than unicorns, but despite their size, the massive beasts were still faster than the finest unaugmented thoroughbred ever foaled. On the other hand, they still had over three miles to go.

"Bugler, blow 'Canter'!"

* * *

"*Now!*" chan Forcal shouted, and seven four-and-a-half-inch mortars coughed as one.

* * *

There was no warning.

One instant, the Seventh Zydor Heavy Dragoons were thundering forward, moving up from a trot to a hard canter in perfect order under the protection of their cloaking glamour. The next, thunderbolts came dropping out of the heavens without any warning at all.

Five Hundred Urlan swore savagely as the mortar bombs exploded. They clustered around his command standard with enough perverse accuracy to make a man actually believe in demons after all, and the sunbaked, stony earth was almost as hard as a paved street. The incoming mortar rounds scarcely dented it, and there was nothing to absorb the force of the explosions . . . or the deadly, whirling splinters those explosions threw out in all directions. Horses and men screamed as white-hot steel fragments drove into fragile flesh and bone. Half a dozen of the huge steeds went down, shrieking like tortured women as legs broke or whirling steel knives opened their bellies.

"Spread out! *Skirmish order!*" Urlan bellowed. Once again, the bugle's notes flared golden, and his men responded like the elite troopers they were. They opened their ranks, dispersing to deny their enemies a compact, concentrated target.

Urlan watched the evolution. The confines of the valley meant they couldn't open their ranks as widely as he would have preferred, but at least they were no longer riding knee-to-knee. He bared his teeth as more of those infernal explosions raked the Zydors, and then he swore again, hideously, as he realized the commander of fifty responsible for the glamour was down.

* * *

"There they are!" Lorash chan Braikal snapped.

He didn't know how the Arcanans had pulled it off. Still, if the bastards had dragons, why shouldn't they have cloaks of invisibility, as well?

The thought flickered through the back of his mind, but whatever it was and however it had worked, it obviously hadn't fooled Company-Captain Mesaion's Distance Viewer. The explosions sprouting amongst the oncoming cavalry looked like flame-cored toadstools, and he saw the huge horses going down, spilling their riders.

But not as many of them as I should *see*, something muttered in the back of his brain. *Vothan, those things must be tough!*

The howitzers were firing, as well, dropping their lighter shells in among the heavy mortar rounds, but they weren't going to stop that many pissed-off cavalrymen with less than a dozen tubes.

"Rifles!" he shouted as the range raced downward, and the platoon's Model 10s began to crack.

* * *

More of Urlan's men and horses went down as the Sharonian shoulder weapons—the "rifles"—opened fire from atop the wall. But at least the briefing from the recon crystal had been accurate. The tower that marked their objective was still on fire, and none of the machine guns and whatever-the-hells those other rapidfire weapons had been could bear on them from this angle. The rifle fire would be bad enough, but—

* * *

"Fire!"

Sunlord Markan heard the young commander of horse's shout as the company of dismounted cavalry

Markan had snatched away from the entrenched positions west of Fort Salby rounded the fort's flank.

Accuracy would have been too much to expect out of them after their hard run, and they'd lost at least ten or twelve men to stray, rampaging eagle-lions. But even unaimed fire from a hundred and twenty rifles had to get the other side's attention.

Of course, Markan thought distantly, *getting heavy cavalry's attention might not be the very best thing dispersed infantry could do when it's outnumbered three or four to one . . . in the open.*

* * *

"Mother Jambakol!"

Five Hundred Urlan spat the filthy curse as still more rifles began to fire, this time from ground level. His head whipped around, and his eyes narrowed as he saw the infantrymen. They were firing furiously, although with nowhere near the accuracy of the men on top of the wall.

For a moment, Urlan considered sending one of his dragoon companies to scatter them, but he quickly decided against it. They weren't hitting very many of his own men, and when the Zydors reached their objective, the fort itself would cover them against these new Sharonians' fire. They'd lose more men charging them than they would simply galloping straight into the waiting cover.

* * *

Chief-Armsman chan Braikal watched Arcanans dropping under his platoon's aimed fire. The mortar fire continued to rake their ranks, as well, but it wasn't going to be enough to keep them from reaching the wall, and they were going to run in under the mortars' effective arc of fire when they got a bit closer. His Marines weren't scoring as many hits as they should have been, either. Was that from excitement and too much adrenaline, he wondered? Or could it be that the bastards had some other spell protecting them? Not something that could make them *invisible*, perhaps, but something that made them harder to hit?

He didn't know, and it didn't matter. What *mattered* was that at least some of them were going to make it to the base of the wall after all, and Prince Janaki and Regiment-Captain chan Skrithik were counting on chan Braikal to keep them out of Fort Salby.

"Chan Yaran!"

"Yes, Chief?" Petty-Armsman Rokal chan Yaran, whose promotion had come through less than two weeks before, replied.

"Get your grenade party ready!"

"Yes, Chief!"

* * *

Windlord Garsal had suddenly become the senior officer in the infantry and artillery positions protecting the western approaches to Fort Salby. It was not, he discovered, a position he particularly wanted. Unfortunately, it was his.

Sunlord Markan's decision to personally lead the one company they'd retained as an immediate reserve struck Garsal as quixotic, at the very least. Nonetheless, he'd obeyed the sunlord's orders and his Flicker had sent out the orders that stripped an entire battalion out of its positions and sent them thudding across the barren, dusty earth in Markan's wake.

Which left Garsal to deal with the minor matter of

what looked like at least two or three hundred dragons headed straight for him.

And they're the diversion, *are they?*

The thought flashed through his brain, and for the first time in his life, he found himself devoutly hoping all the tall tales and legends about the Calirath Talent were actually accurate. Because, if they weren't . . .

He watched them coming on, and as he did, another thought occurred to him.

They may be supposed to be a diversion. In fact, I'll bet they are. They'd have followed closer behind those eagle-lions if this were a serious attack. But it looks like they may not have realized just how long ranged our artillery really is.

His smile was thin and feral as the huge dragons swooped and wove their intricate patterns. There was an awful lot of motion up there, but they weren't actually advancing all that quickly, and he looked at his Flicker once again.

"Message to the artillery. Prepare to load with shrapnel . . . but don't set the fuses until I give the order to fire."

* * *

Five Hundred Urlan's lead dragoons reached the foot of the fortress wall. The rear troopers leaned back, triggering their cutdown infantry-dragons, sending blasts of intolerable heat rolling up the outer face of the wall. A Sharonian who'd leaned out to fire down upon them shrieked horribly and plunged from the parapet, trailing fire like a human meteor. Others ducked back, cowering away from the searing fury.

But still others had been waiting.

Urlan saw the small objects plunging down from

above, and his stomach tightened. He didn't know what the godsdamned things were, but he was certain he was about to find out.

* * *

Chan Braikal heard the hand grenades exploding even through the thunder of the rest of the battle, and his eyes glittered with cold satisfaction as he listened to the screams from below. The bastards were too close to the wall for the artillery to drop on them any longer, but chan Yaran's grenades were obviously a different matter. Yet even as they exploded, the blasts of heat and fury continued to roar up from below, as well.

He looked out across the parapet, wondering if he had any eyebrows left, and swore with fresh inventiveness as he saw the floating . . . whatever-the-hells-they-were. He didn't know what to call them. They looked for all the world like some sort of airborne boats, towed by the massive horses to which they were tethered. But whatever they were, they floated even higher than Fort Salby's walls, and they were packed to the gunwales with Arcanans, some of whom obviously had fire-throwers of their own.

His men had the advantage of better cover, the fort's adobe had already proven itself virtually immune to the blast effect of the Arcanan fireballs, and the mortars could still reach the tow horses. Unfortunately, chan Braikal and the other defenders on the wall were also outnumbered by somewhere around ten-to-one, and when one of the fireballs *did* find a chink in the parapet, it killed or wounded four or five of his people at once.

Chan Yaran and his squad were still chucking hand grenades over the edge as quickly as they could pull the pins, and chan Braikal had another squad doing nothing but protecting the grenadiers. Which left him only three squads—less than thirty men, with the casualties he'd already taken—to hold off at least eight or nine hundred Arcanans in those floating boats.

It was not a winning proposition, even for Imperial Ternathian Marines.

* * *

Five Hundred Urlan grimaced in satisfaction as Charlie Company finally came up with the infantry assault force.

His two lead companies had taken at least thirty percent casualties, but they'd also managed to suppress a lot of the defensive fire. Now Kiliron's troopers had managed—not without taking serious losses of their own—to get close enough they were sheltered from the Sharonians' artillery fire by the wall itself, and *that* meant the infantry could damned well take over!

* * *

Chan Braikal felt someone pounding on his shoulder. He turned his head and found himself looking into Platoon-Captain Tarkel chan Noth's blue eyes.

"How bad, Chief?" chan Noth shouted in the Marine's ear, pointing downward to indicate the ground at the foot of the wall.

"I think we've got the first batch of bastards pinned—sort of, at least!" chan Braikal shouted back, then pointed out at the approaching "air boats." More and more fire was beginning to come from them, and chan Noth ducked as a fireball exploded just below the edge of the parapet directly in front of him.

"But if we don't stop *that*, Sir, we're fucked!" chan Braikal added . . . quite unnecessarily, he was certain.

"Then it's a good thing I brought this!"

Chan Braikal turned his head and saw a three-gun section of Faraika I machine guns setting up with frantic haste.

* * *

"Mother Jambakol!" Urlan snarled again as the distinctive, ripping-cloth sound of one of the Sharonians' accursed "machine guns" crackled above him. He whipped his head around in time to see splinters flying from two of the closer personnel pods as the Sharonians flayed them with fire. Then, suddenly, one of them plunged to shatter on the ground below as one of the Sharonian bullets either killed the Gifted engineer controlling the levitation spell or smashed the accumulator itself.

A second pod followed moments later, and the cavalry commander looked around quickly, then grunted as his eyes found what they'd been looking for.

"Fifty Rahndar!"

The dark-haired commander of fifty with the Engineers shoulder patch looked around sharply at the sound of his name.

"Yes, Sir!"

"I want a godsdamned hole, Fifty," Urlan snarled, jabbing a finger at the fort wall, "and I want it right fucking now!"

Rahndar darted a quick, anxious glance up the wall to where those infernal explosive devices were plunging down and swallowed hard. Apparently, however, the thought of being blown apart was less daunting than whatever he'd just seen in Urlan's eyes.

"Yes, Sir!"

Rahndar reined his horse around and started shouting for the rest of his engineering section.

* * *

Chan Braikal was just beginning to feel a certain cautious optimism when the world went crazy.

It wasn't really an *explosion*. It was too . . . quiet for that. There was no flash, no thunder, just the sudden concussive shattering of adobe and stone. It *should* have sounded like an explosion, but it actually sounded more like a frozen tree trunk snapping in an icy winter night.

But whatever it sounded like, the force of it shook Fort Salby to its bones. A section of wall at least eight feet across at the base simply disintegrated. It flew apart, spraying adobe, rock, and men as it opened a wedge-shaped gap which ran all the way to the parapet and measured better than forty feet across at the top.

Two of chan Noth's machine guns went with it . . . and so did Petty-Armsman chan Yaran and his grenadiers. Half of chan Braikal's platoon was simply gone, and the survivors were shocked, stunned by the sudden cataclysm.

Chan Noth's men had been hit less severely, but they'd also still been in the act of taking up their positions. Confusion swept through them, however briefly, and the defenders' fire faltered.

* * *

"*Now!*" Gyras Urlan bellowed as the fire from above slackened. "Now! Go—*go*, godsdamn it!"

Young Rahndar had done his job well. In fact, he'd done it too well for his own good. He and most of his section—and another twenty or so of Urlan's troopers—had been caught in the collapse his demolition spell had wreaked. That was unfortunate, but no one could control where the wreckage from a demo spell was going to fall, and at least they had a breach at last.

Half of Urlan's surviving men flung themselves off their horses. They took their swords, their infantry-dragons, and their daggerstones with them and charged forward, swarming up over the wreckage, into the clouds of billowing dust and smoke, with the high, howling cheer of the Seventh Zydors.

* * *

Lorash chan Braikal stared down into the gap which had suddenly appeared and shook himself. Despite its width, it was choked with rubble that rose to at least a third of the wall's original height. Unfortunately, enough of that rubble had spilled outward to provide a ramp, and he saw Arcanans in cavalry boots, breastplates, and helmets swarming up it. At least half of them seemed to be carrying the glittering tubes of their fire-throwers, and he snarled in fury.

He jerked the pin out of his final hand grenade and tossed it down into the gap, only to see it lodge in a hollow in the rubble before it exploded. The pocket into which it had fallen absorbed most of its power and only three or four men went down. The others kept coming, and a fireball roared past his ear.

Chan Braikal fired his rifle again and again, until the magazine was empty. He groped for another, but his hand came up empty. He cursed venomously, then kicked his feet over the edge of the gap and went slithering down into the dust and smoke, bayonet-first.

* * *

Five Hundred Urlan looked for his bugler, but the man was down with half his head blown away, and without the bugle, there was no way for him to communicate orders to Charlie Company. It should have already been here, and Urlan wanted to curse its commander as a coward. But that would have been unfair, and he knew it. Orkal Kiliron was no coward, but he was aware how valuable the Gifted engineers in his towed pods were. Although the fire from the wall directly in front of Urlan had been largely silenced, more and more rifle and light machine-gun fire was ripping out from the flanks. The smoke and dust hanging in the air was obviously affecting its accuracy, but at least two more pods had gone down, taking their infantry and engineers with them. If he'd been Kiliron, *he* probably would have assumed the defenders weren't being successfully suppressed and started falling back, too.

The five hundred reached out and grabbed the nearest trooper who was still mounted. The man's head whipped around.

"Sir?" His surprise was obvious, and Urlan shook him.

"Get your ass back there! Find Hundred Kiliron and tell him we need those pods up here right fucking *now*!"

* * *

Chan Braikal hit the bottom of the breach. His boots slipped and slithered in the ankle-deep rubble, and he found himself face-to-face with an Arcanan cavalry trooper.

The Arcanan reared back in obvious surprise, then swung his hand around. There was something in it. Chan Braikal didn't have a clue what it was, but given the things these people had already done, he didn't intend to sit there and find out the hard way. The other man was still trying to bring whatever-it-was to bear when a fourteen-inch, tempered steel bayonet slammed forward above his protective cuirass and opened his throat.

Chan Braikal drove a combat boot into the dead

man's breastplate, wrenched the blade free, and whirled to a second enemy.

* * *

More Sharonians hurled themselves forward. There was no unit organization to it. The breaching spell had buried at least sixty men inside the fort. Another forty or fifty had come down with the collapsing parapet. The platoons closest to it had taken the worst casualties, and some of those who weren't physically wounded were too stunned, too shaken, to respond coherently.

But others were like Lorash chan Braikal. They waited for no orders, didn't worry about where the rest of their platoon, or even the rest of their squad, might be. They drove forward to meet the charging Arcanans with rifles, pistols, shotguns, bayonets, rocks, or even their bare hands.

* * *

It was hand-to-hand in the breach.

Urlan could hardly believe the ferocity of the defense. The normal range advantage of the Sharonians' rifles was meaningless here. His troopers' infantry-dragons and daggerstones were far more lethal than firearms in such narrow confines . . . or would have been, if there'd been room to use them. But the Sharonians were charging straight into them, too close for them to use even daggerstones without killing themselves, as well as their enemies. Infantry-dragon gunners were being forced to discard their weapons and whip out sabers to defend themselves against lunatics with knives on the ends of their rifles. And unlike his men's daggerstones, the Sharonians with pistols didn't have to worry about back blast killing *them*.

They were actually pushing his men out of the breach

when a sudden rush of infantry surged past him. He looked around and realized Kiliron had given up on getting the pods in across the top of the wall. He'd grounded them, instead—or some of them, at least—and sent the infantry in at ground level.

"Yes!" Urlan bellowed as the fresh weight of men and weapons hammered the Sharonians back. "*Yes!*"

* * *

Chan Braikal staggered backward.

The cavalrymen had been falling back at last, but now men in infantry boots and equipment harnesses were charging forward. The ragged, disordered knots of Sharonians resisted stubbornly, but the Arcanan infantry were much better at this sort of game than their cavalry compatriots. They came forward with intact unit organization, and this time they were able to maintain enough separation to actually use their spell-powered weapons.

Blasts of flame and lightning swept the gap, maiming and incinerating, and chan Braikal flung himself down as an infantryman swung a daggerstone in his direction. His last-minute dodge saved him from a direct hit, but the very fringe of the bolt crashed over him. It slammed him into the rubble and broken adobe, and he slithered down it, alive but unconscious.

* * *

Five Hundred Urlan watched the infantry flowing unstoppably into the gap and groped in his saddlebag for the flare stone. He raised it and triggered the single green flare to announce his men's success.

* * *

Fifty Fahrlo saw the brilliant green flare arc up from the far side of the beleaguered fort.

He'd expected to see it sooner, but later was definitely better than never in this case. He looked over his shoulder to make certain the transport dragon who'd been told off to play messenger was already headed back towards the portal with the good news, then turned his attention back to the task at hand.

Now that Urlan was into the fort, it was more important than ever to keep as much as possible of the Sharonians' attention focused on the aerial demonstration. Aside from an occasional rifle shot, absolutely nothing had been fired in *his* direction this time around, and he felt no particular eagerness to change that. But if *he'd* been the Sharonians, he'd be looking for anyone he could possibly throw at the attacking infantry. So it was time to encourage the ones outside the fort to stay put.

* * *

Windlord Garsal watched through narrowed eyes as the intricately weaving dance of dragons flowed closer.

You really don't *know what our effective range is, do you?* he thought coldly. *Well, the* PAAF's *effective range, at any rate*, he amended, for his own horse artillery was shorter ranged and lighter than the heavier field guns from Fort Salby. Not that it mattered who the guns technically belonged to. At the moment, they were *his*, and he let the range fall to nine thousand yards, then nodded to his Flicker.

"Now," he said softly.

* * *

Only one thing saved them, Fahrlo realized later, and that was the fact that the Sharonians' supply of artillery was obviously limited.

The hammering the battle dragons had taken in

their direct attack upon the fort had imbued him with a healthy respect for the sheer destructiveness of Sharona's mechanical weapons. Nonetheless, he was unprepared for the puffs of smoke blossoming in midair. For an instant, he couldn't figure out what was happening—then he realized he'd just met another infernal Sharonian device.

Whatever they were firing at him were exploding into veritable clouds of smaller but still incredibly lethal projectiles. Each of those "puffs of smoke" spawned a cone-shaped pattern of death that carved its way into his formation.

Six transports went down in the first salvo, and three more were wounded. The other pilots reacted almost instantly in obedience to the orders they'd received before taking off for the operation. They wheeled, streaking back the way they'd come, and those innocuous looking puffballs of smoke followed them.

Five more transports crashed to the earth before they could get out of range, and Commander of Fifty Fahrlo swore with cold and bitter hatred as the Air Force found itself hammered yet again.

* * *

Five Hundred Urlan had no way to know what had just happened to the airborne diversion. Nor, to be completely honest, did he very much care as his assaulting column pushed forward.

He didn't want to think about the losses the Seventh Zydors had taken getting the infantry into position, but if it gave them the fort, it would be worth it. And it certainly looked as if—

The rifle bullet struck him behind the left ear and killed him instantly.

* * *

"Hit them!"

Had he stopped to think about it, Sunlord Markan might have felt just a bit ridiculous waving a sword in the middle of a modern battlefield to urge his men onward. Or perhaps not. There were swords in plenty on the other side of that "modern" battlefield, after all, as well as crossbows and daggers. Of course, there were also dragons, fireball-throwers, and the gods alone knew what else to go with them.

None of which mattered at the moment as he brought an entire dismounted battalion of elite Uromathian cavalry crunching in on the Arcanans' flank.

The Arcanans fought to turn and face the new threat, but the Uromathians had come out of the smoke and dust like ghosts, and the section of wall which had shielded the attackers from Markan's fire earlier had also hidden his own reinforcements' approach from them. No one had noticed him at all . . . until his troopers swept out and around the wall and opened fire. Now they sent disciplined, rapid, aimed volleys crashing into their enemies, and the battered Arcanan cavalry had had enough.

Those who were still mounted turned and galloped towards the rear, and most of those who *weren't* mounted took to their heels after them. The infantry force driving forward into the breached wall outnumbered the Uromathians by better than two-to-one, but it didn't *feel* that way when it found itself suddenly flanked by a thundering wall of Sharonian rifles.

The Arcanans recoiled, and even as they did, a counterattack came pounding back through the gap. No longer disorganized knots of men swarming instinctively towards the enemy, but an ordered, disciplined attack by two companies of Portal Authority infantry with rifles, shotguns, and grenades.

It was too much. Those who could, turned to flee. Those who couldn't, threw down their weapons and raised empty hands in token of surrender.

CHAPTER THIRTY-ONE

JUKAN DARSHU, SUNLORD MARKAN, climbed carefully down the loose, shifting slope of rubble which had spilled into Fort Salby from the breach in its eastern wall. It would have been easier to come in through the gate, but the gate was on the far side of the fort, and he was damned if he'd hike all the way back around just to use the front door.

He stepped off of the untidy ramp of wreckage and looked about him with a sense of disbelief. It didn't seem possible that so much carnage had been inflicted upon so many men—and so many . . . creatures—in so short a time.

The surrendered, unwounded Arcanans were still being shoved and pushed, none too gently in most cases, into a semblance of order, then searched while hard-eyed men with bayoneted shotguns watched them like hawks. Those searches were extraordinarily thorough, and no more pleasant than they had to be. It was plain the prisoners didn't care for the harshness of their treatment, but it was equally plain that they didn't have to be Empaths to sense the hatred radiating from their captors in waves and realize it was time to be very, very meek.

Markan felt his lips twitch in a slight, bitterly amused smile at the thought. It was the only thing remotely like amusement he'd felt in what seemed an eternity, and it vanished quickly as he picked his way around the sprawled, untidy carcasses of eagle-lions.

He wasn't the only man moving out there. At least a third of Fort Salby's garrison was down, and casualty parties were busy searching through the wreckage, concentrating on finding and collecting the wounded. There'd be time enough to collect the dead later.

An occasional pistol shot cracked as the search parties discovered an eagle-lion that wasn't quite dead yet, and Markan wondered what they were going to do with all the carcasses.

Hells, he thought with a snort, *why worry about* them? *What are we going to do with all the* dragon *carcasses?*

He reached the steps leading up to the gun platform where he'd left Crown Prince Janaki and Regiment-Captain chan Skrithik six hours and half a lifetime ago. The climb seemed much steeper, somehow, and he shook his head in weary bemusement as he started up them, rehearsing the apology he had to make when he got to the top. He hadn't attempted to hide his skepticism when Prince Janaki started describing his Glimpse, and now that he'd seen the reality, it was time—

Sunlord Markan's thoughts chopped off with brutal suddenness and he froze in mid-stride as he reached the head of the steps. He felt as if a sledgehammer had just hit him squarely in the pit of the stomach.

Crown Prince Janaki chan Calirath lay on the gun

platform where he had died. His body had been moved to a stretcher, but no one had been able to move him further, for painfully evident reasons. The two medical orderlies who'd brought the stretcher to the gun platform were backed up against the parapet, and the deeply bleeding gouges down the side of one orderly's face had obviously come from the talons and beak of the imperial peregrine falcon perched protectively on the dead prince's chest, wings half-spread and eyes blazing with battle fury. The bird's head snapped around as Markan stepped the rest of the way onto the gun platform, and its beak opened in a warning hiss of rage.

No one seemed to know what to do. *Markan* certainly didn't, and the stupefying shock of Janaki's death seemed to have shut his brain down entirely.

Then someone stepped past him, and his head turned to see Regiment-Captain chan Skrithik.

The Ternathian looked terrible. His left arm hung in an improvised sling which had been jury-rigged out of someone's pistol belt. His forearm was crudely splinted, and his filthy uniform tunic was torn in half a dozen places and covered with dust. An ugly, scabbed cut across the center of a livid bruise disfigured his left cheek, and dried bloodstains—most of them, obviously, from other people's blood—were spattered across both trouser legs.

But it was his face, his eyes, that truly struck Markan. The shock, deeper even than Markan's own. The loss. The *pain* . . . and the guilt.

Unlike Markan or the intimidated stretcher bearers, chan Skrithik didn't even flinch as Taleena hissed at him. He only walked straight across to her, slowly, holding out his good hand. That razor-sharp beak, fit to snap off fingers like a hatchet, opened as her head cocked threateningly, but then something seemed to flicker in the bird's golden-rimmed eyes. A memory, perhaps, Markan thought, recalling half-believed stories about the imperial falcons' fabled intelligence. Taleena's head swiveled toward the dead eagle-lion sprawled in ungainly death at the foot of the gun platform. Then she looked back at chan Skrithik and made a soft, almost entreating sound.

Markan was an experienced falconer, but he'd never heard anything like that cry of avian heartbreak out of another bird. Chan Skrithik seemed to flinch, but he only held out his hand patiently until, finally, the bird just brushed it with that sharp, wickedly curved beak.

"I'm sorry, My Lady." Chan Skrithik spoke then, so quietly Markan could barely hear him. "I tried. Gods know, we both tried."

Taleena looked at him for one another long moment, and then, without warning, her wings snapped once as she leapt from Janaki's chest to chan Skrithik's good shoulder. The regiment-captain's uniform lacked the nonregulation, reinforced leather patches Janaki's tunics had boasted, but the pistol belt-sling gave his shoulder some protection, and the falcon's powerful talons were careful, gentle. She stood on his shoulder and bent to press her beak into his hair, and chan Skrithik reached up to touch her folded wings with equally careful gentleness.

The litter bearers started to move away from the parapet towards the fallen prince, but the regiment-captain shook his head. They stopped again, and chan Skrithik went to his knees beside the stretcher. He knelt there, staring down at the face of a young man who would never grow old, and his own face was wrung with barely unshed tears.

Janaki's dead face was almost relaxed, Markan thought. The gray eyes were open, staring sightlessly into a void no Talent could See across. A trickle of blood had flowed from the corner of his mouth and dried, but there was no pain in that face . . . and no fear.

The Uromathian noble moved closer, and chan Skrithik laid his one working hand on Janaki's still chest and looked up at him.

"Sunlord," he said, and his voice was rusty and broken sounding.

"Regiment-Captain," Markan responded quietly.

"Thank you." Chan Skrithik had to stop, clear his throat. "Thank you," he repeated huskily. "Without your men—"

"My men would have been too late, if not for yours," Markan interrupted.

Chan Skrithik looked up at him for several seconds without speaking. Only his hand moved, the fingers stroking gently at the dead prince's tunic as if to somehow tidy it. Finally, the regiment-captain nodded, then looked down at his hand. He regarded it for a heartbeat or two as if it were a stranger's. Then he looked back up at Markan, and there was a strange, lost look in his eyes.

"My Crown Prince is dead."

Tears welled in those eyes at last, and his voice wavered. They were only five words, yet Markhan heard a universe of pain deep within them and felt his own eyes burn. Then the sunlord blinked once, hard, and looked away. Looked beyond the gun platform at the smoke, the bodies, the downed dragons and gryphons.

It was a scene of carnage such as no Sharonian had ever imagined, and yet in his mind's eye, Markan imagined another scene. One in which there were no dead dragons, no dead gryphons, no Arcanan prisoners marching sullenly into confinement . . . only a fort in flames and a garrison taken unawares and slaughtered.

He stared into that vision of what had never been. The vision, he realized, that Janaki chan Calirath had Seen in the Glimpses he'd tried to describe. The thought of his own cynical skepticism while Janaki had offered the warning which had saved them all filled him with shame, and he looked back down at chan Skrithik.

The tears had broken loose at last, cutting startlingly white tracks through the dust and grime and blood on the regiment-captain's face, and Markan went to his own knees beside Janaki's body across from him, with chan Skrithik's last words still ringing in his in ears.

"No, my friend," the Uromathian said quietly, and shook his head as he reached out to touch chan Skrithik's upper arm. "No. *Our* Crown Prince is dead."

* * *

"Still nothing?" Olvyr Banchu asked, as he climbed up the last few rungs of the ladder and stepped up onto the freight car roof beside Platoon-Captain Selan Vuras.

"Nothing." Vuras shook his head, gazing off to the north as if he thought he should somehow be able to see across the eight hundred miles between him and the Traisum portal.

"You don't think it could be some sort of normal glitch?" Banchu's question sounded a lot more like a statement, and Vuras shook his head again.

"The Regiment-Captain didn't set up his communications schedule just so he could ignore it, sir," he told the TTE's senior engineer. "If he hasn't said anything, then it's because Prince Janaki was right."

Banchu discovered that he had very seldom wished anything in his life as fervently as he wished that Vuras might be wrong. Unfortunately, he was certain the young Limathian wasn't. The question, of course, was whether chan Skrithik's silence resulted from an attack on Fort Salby or simply the cutting of the Voice relay between the railhead and the Traisum portal.

"Do you think they could have taken out the relay?" he asked, and Vuras snorted.

"I explained things very carefully to Voice Orma on our way through, sir. He understands, believe me. And unless the Arcanans have some sort of Voice Sniffer, they *aren't* going to find him. Even if they might somehow have known where he was before our train came through, we moved him over sixty miles and dropped him off at his own private waterhole with a camo net and tarp. We even found him some trees to hide under." The platoon-captain shook his head again. "Whatever's caused the communications break, it's not because the Arcanans found *him*, Master Banchu."

"Well." Banchu stood there, but unlike Vuras, his gaze was directed towards the worksite around them. He studied it for several minutes, then looked back at the PAAF officer.

"If you're right, I'm happy for Orma, Platoon-Captain, but it leaves us in a bit of a pickle, wouldn't you say?"

"Oh, I'd definitely say that, sir," Vuras agreed grimly.

"Then I suppose I'd better go see how our preparations are coming."

Banchu climbed down from the freight car and headed off in search of his assistants.

Platoon-Captain Vuras was the senior officer of the double platoon Regiment-Captain chan Skrithik had sent down to reinforce the railhead's security. Unfortunately, even after Vuras' arrival, that left Banchu with less than a company of regular troops to look after the better part of two thousand workers.

The good news was that at least a third of his labor force had at least some military experience. The Trans-Temporal Express had always given veterans preference when it came to hiring practices, and its personnel office vigorously recruited retired army engineers for its construction projects. And in this case, given all of the . . . uncertainties of the situation, Banchu had arrived with a freight car loaded with two thousand Model 10 rifles and a million rounds of ammunition. That was enough to issue virtually all of his workers—even those without actual previous military experience—a personal weapon, at least, and he'd put Foram chan Eris in charge of organizing them. Chan Eris was his senior assistant . . . and just happened to have retired from his first job as a company-captain in the Imperial Ternathian Army Corps of Engineers.

Unfortunately, neither Banchu, chan Eris, nor Vuras had very much in the way of heavy weapons to support those rifles, aside from the pair of Yerthak pedestal guns and single section of light machine guns Vuras had brought with him. There were no mortars, no field guns, no howitzers . . .

What they did have was ingenuity, lots of construction equipment, several hundred miles worth of stockpiled rails, and the mobile machine shops necessary to perform maintenance on millions of Ternathian marks worth of steam shovels, bulldozers, and tractors.

That thought carried Banchu over to the area where chan Eris and Platoon-Captain Harek chan Morak were overseeing the chief engineer's latest brainchild.

Sparks fountained from welding torches as sweating track layers and maintenance crews worked frantically on what had been standard freight cars up until a very few hours ago. Now the wooden sides of those freight cars were in the process of disappearing behind layers of steel rails. Banchu didn't know if a double layer of railroad iron would stand up to one of the "dragons" Petty-Captain chan Darma had described to Hersal Yoritam, Banchu's own assigned Voice. He doubted that anyone had any clear notion of exactly how powerful dragonfire or lightning might be. But his improvised armor ought to stand up to just about anything short of field artillery, and he'd been careful to leave enough loopholes to allow anyone inside the cars to bring at least a dozen Model 10s to bear in any direction.

"How's it coming, Foram?" he asked.

"Well as we could expect, I guess," chan Eris replied. "Mind you, I don't think we've got enough freight cars to put everyone into, even if we end up having time to stick rails on all of them."

"That's what I've always liked best about you, Foram—that sparkling Ternathian optimism of yours."

"What's to be optimistic about?" chan Eris responded sourly, although there was more than a hint of a gleam in his eyes.

"How about starting with the fact that we're all still alive, and we haven't seen any dragons diving on us?"

"Yet. We haven't seen any dragons diving on us *yet*," chan Eris said. "Of course, the day's still young, isn't it?"

"Yes, it is." Banchu thumped him on the shoulder, then cocked his head. "What about the locomotives?"

"I've got two of them just about ready. The cabs are protected at least as well as the freights, at any rate. And young chan Morak's working on another pair right now. We've done the best we could about protecting the boilers, too, but that's a lot tougher."

"As far as I can make out, these people don't have anything like rifles or machine guns," Banchu told him. "I don't know that they're going to be able to punch through the boilers with anything they've got."

"Maybe not. But all they really have to do to strand us is tear up the track, you know," chan Eris pointed out.

"They can tear up track if they want to," Banchu said more grimly. "Unless they're a lot more experienced with railroads than I think they are, though, they probably don't realize how quickly our people can put the track back together again."

"Assuming we've got enough firepower to keep the bastards off our people while they put it back."

Chan Eris might have sounded as if he were objecting to what Banchu had just said, but he wasn't, and he snorted when Banchu quirked an eyebrow at him.

"I don't know how many troops these people brought with them, Olvyr, but they'd better have a lot if they want to stop us and simultaneously take and hold Fort Salby—especially with Division-Captain chan Geraith as close as he is. I'm not too sure about these armored freight cars of yours. Mind you, I think they're a good idea—I just don't know *how* good an idea. But I do know that if the other side is stupid enough to spread its forces too thin, it's gonna get reamed."

"'Reamed,'" Banchu repeated. "Is that one of those

technical military terms a civilian like me wouldn't be familiar with?"

"Probably."

Chan Eris squinted up at the crew working on the current freight car, then looked back at Banchu.

"I've got this part of it pretty much under control, Olvyr. Why don't you go worry about something else? My 'Ternathian optimism' and I can handle this."

Banchu chuckled, shook his head, and headed off to see how much construction equipment they could load onto their available flat cars.

* * *

"What the—?"

Under-Armsman Verais lowered the field glasses for a moment, then shook his head and raised them once more.

"We've got three . . . horsemen coming down the valley, Armsman," he announced.

"What?" Junior-Armsman Paras chan Barsak seemed to materialize out of the dusty earth at Verais' elbow.

"There."

Verais passed over the field glasses and pointed at the roadway far below. Chan Barsak raised the binoculars to his own eyes, adjusting the focus, then grunted as the image sharpened.

Verais was right. Three men mounted on something horse-sized and vaguely horse-shaped were cantering along the roadway at a preposterous rate of speed. Afternoon sunlight glittered on what were apparently long, spiral horns sprouting from their "horses'" foreheads, and chan Barsak had never heard of a "horse" with what looked remarkably like a carnivore's tusks. Of course, the not-horses were just passing abreast of the shattered corpse of what was obviously a dragon, so he didn't suppose there was any reason they couldn't be equally preposterous.

His lips twitched at the thought, then his forehead creased in surprise.

"They're coming in under a parley banner," he said.

"Parley banner?" Verais hawked and spat over the edge of the drop-off. "How the fuck—pardon my Uromathian—would they know what a parley banner looks like? And if they did know, what makes them think we'd be stupid enough to trust anything they said?"

"I didn't say it was a proper parley banner," chan Barsak said rather more patiently than he felt. "But it's green, they're flying it, and there's just three of them. Whether we can trust 'em or not's really kind of beside the point, don't you think?"

Verais just scowled, and chan Barsak snorted, then shook his head and started calling for the Flicker assigned to his squad.

* * *

Rof chan Skrithik and Sunlord Markan stood side-by-side outside Markan's CP and watched the pair of Arcanan officers being escorted towards them. Both Arcanans were blindfolded, and their third companion had been held at the outer picket line where he could keep an eye on their peculiar horned horses . . . and couldn't see anything about the defenders' positions. Frankly, chan Skrithik was just as happy not to have those unnatural creatures any closer than they had to be.

Actually, he thought grimly, *I'd just as soon not*

have these Arcanan fuckers any closer than they have to be, either.

He thought about the dead prince lying in Company-Captain Krilar's infirmary and the palm of his pistol hand itched.

The Arcanans were marched into the command post. Chan Skrithik and Markan watched them go by, then followed them silently into the sandbagged bunker. It was obvious from the Arcanans' body language that they weren't as calm as they would have liked to appear, yet chan Skrithik found himself feeling an unwilling respect for their sheer nerve. Riding in to parley with someone against whom you'd just launched a sneak attack while in the midst of negotiations in time of peace was not a task for the faint hearted.

The Arcanans were turned to face him and the blindfolds were removed. They blinked as their eyes adjusted to the dim light inside the command post, then one of them looked at chan Skrithik and Markan. His eyes narrowed as he saw the three gold rifles of chan Skrithik's rank insignia and the splinted forearm suspended in the sling tied around the regiment-captain's neck.

"May I crystal back?" the Arcanan said in heavily accented Ternathian, gesturing at the petty-captain who'd escorted him and his companion to the CP.

"You want one of your crystals returned to you?" chan Skrithik responded, and the Arcanan nodded vigorously.

"Can talk better with," he said.

Chan Skrithik frowned for a moment, then glanced at the petty-captain.

"You took one of their rocks off of them?"

"Yes, Sir. We didn't find anything that looked like a

weapon—not even a knife—but after everything else, I figured, well . . ."

The youngster shrugged, and chan Skrithik nodded.

"You did exactly the right thing, son. On the other hand, I suppose if we actually want to hear what these . . . people have to say, we should give it back to them."

The regiment-captain held out his hand for the crystal in question, then turned back to the more talkative Arcanan with it on his palm.

"Understand," he said grimly, holding the other man's eyes with his own and letting him see the hate and barely leashed rage, "if we think you're going to do anything with this hunk of rock except talk, I'll shoot you dead where you stand."

"Understand," the Arcanan replied. Chan Skrithik wasn't at all certain that the other man's comprehension of Ternathian was genuinely up to understanding what he'd just said, but he suspected that he hadn't actually needed to say it in the first place.

He stared into the other man's eyes for another moment, then handed the crystal across. The Arcanan murmured something, and the piece of rock started to glow. Then he looked across it at chan Skrithik.

"I am Commander of Five Hundred Dayr Vaynair, Army of the Union of Arcana," he said crisply. Or, to be more precise, the crystal *translated* crisply. "This," he indicated the older man standing beside him, "is Commander of One Thousand Klayrman Toralk."

"I see."

Chan Skrithik gazed back at them, his eyes hard, but his brain was busy behind them. He knew nothing about how the Arcanans organized their military. For that matter, he didn't know whether the rank titles this

Vaynair had just rattled off had been literal or figurative interpretations of their actual ranks. Nonetheless, he didn't doubt for a moment that these were the two most senior Arcanan officers any official representative of Sharona had yet encountered.

Or, a mental voice amended coldly, *the most senior Arcanan officers any living,* uncaptured *official representative of Sharona has encountered.*

The Arcanans gazed back at him equally levelly, obviously waiting for him to introduce himself in response. For a moment, he toyed with the notion of refusing to do so, but he brushed the petty temptation aside.

"Regiment-Captain Rof chan Skrithik, Portal Authority Armed Forces," he said.

"Ah." Vaynair nodded. "May I assume I'm speaking to the senior Sharonian officer, in that case, Sir?" he inquired politely.

"At the moment," chan Skrithik replied curtly.

"Very good, Sir." Vaynair cleared his throat. "Thousand Toralk and I have been sent as envoys by Commander of Two Thousand Harshu."

"I see," chan Skrithik repeated. "So I suppose I should assume this 'Commander of Two Thousand Harshu' of yours is in command of this batch of cutthroats and murderers?"

Vaynair winced. His eyes tried to move sideways, towards his superior officer, but he stopped them. As for the superior officer in question, *his* expression didn't even flicker.

"I—" Vaynair began, then paused.

"You may assume that, Regiment-Captain," the commander of one thousand said into his junior's hesitation. He met chan Skrithik's eyes steadily. "Obviously,

I would prefer some other description of the men under my command. Under the circumstances, however, I can appreciate how you might fail to grasp the distinction."

Toralk's voice was firm, chan Skrithik noted.

"Nonetheless," the Arcanan continued, "Five Hundred Vaynair and I are here with a message. Two messages, in fact. Are you willing to listen to them?"

"The fact that you're here at all suggests to me that the last Sharonians who listened to what Arcanans had to say didn't make out very well," chan Skrithik replied coldly, and this time Toralk's eyes seemed to flinch ever so slightly.

"Regiment-Captain," he said after a moment, "I'm an officer in the Union Air Force. Policy decisions are made at a higher level than mine. I say that not in any effort to suggest that the anger you obviously feel is unreasonable, but because there's nothing I can do—or could have done—about the cause of that anger. I was sent here with a proposal based upon the situation in which we currently find ourselves. So, again, I ask you, are you willing to listen to my superior officer's messages?"

Chan Skrithik felt an unwilling flicker of sympathy for this Toralk even through the cold, bitter fury of Janaki's death. *He* wouldn't have cared to be sent on a mission like this one.

"Very well," he said finally, flatly. "Speak your piece."

"Five Hundred Vaynair," Toralk said quietly, looking at the other officer, and Vaynair cleared his throat again.

"Regiment-Captain chan Skrithik," he said, "I am Two Thousand Harshu's senior magistron—his senior medical officer. We realize that some Sharonians have what you refer to as the Healing Talent. What we've been able to discover about it so far, however, suggests that its primary functions are pain management and the enhancement of the natural healing process. A magistron like myself, however, has the healing Gift, which differs from your people's Talent. With proper training, that Gift can repair damages your own people's Talent can't. For example, a sufficiently powerful magistron can actually regenerate damaged nervous tissue."

Chan Skrithik managed to keep his eyes from widening and simply cocked his head, waiting, when Vaynair paused.

"The reason I, specifically, am here, Regiment-Captain," the commander of five hundred continued after a brief silence, "is to propose that my medical staff and I make our healing Gifts available to the wounded from both sides."

"Why?" chan Skrithik demanded.

"For several reasons, Sir. One of them, frankly, is to ensure the best possible treatment for the Arcanan prisoners currently in your hands, many of whom must have been wounded." Vaynair made the admission unflinchingly. "A second, which you may find more difficult to believe, is that magistrons swear an oath very similar to the one your Healers swear. The use of our Gift is supposed to be determined by our patients' needs, not by who those patients might happen to be or the uniform they might happen to wear. And a third is because we couldn't reasonably expect you to allow us access to our own wounded if we were to refuse to treat *your* wounded, as well."

"I see," chan Skrithik said for a third time. Somewhat to his own surprise, he was inclined to believe Vaynair was sincere about this magistron's oath. And whether the Arcanan was sincere about that or not, the other points he'd made were certainly reasonable enough.

And the least these whoresons can do is save *a few godsdamned lives for a change*, he thought bitterly.

It was hard, but he managed to keep his voice level. Straining the hate and fury out left it curiously flattened, but there wasn't much he could do about that.

"I'll certainly take your proposal under advisement," he said after several seconds. "Of course, before I could accept it, I would have to ask you to repeat it in the presence of a Sifter."

"That would be someone with your people's Talent for recognizing when someone is lying?"

"It would. Why?" Chan Skrithik's eyes narrowed. "Would you have some objection to that?"

"We would have no objection at all, Regiment-Captain," Toralk replied for the commander of five hundred, "so long as the questions we were required to answer were limited to the discussion of the proposals before us."

Chan Skrithik considered that, then shrugged.

"I suppose that wouldn't be unreasonable . . . assuming I feel inclined to consider those proposals in the first place. However, you said you have two messages."

"Yes," Toralk agreed. "At the moment, you have in your possession several hundred Arcanan prisoners. Two Thousand Harshu would like to propose an exchange—the prisoners you currently hold, for the free passage of your work crews in Karys back to Fort Salby."

"Our work crews?" chan Skrithik said. "Are you saying you've captured them? Or have you simply rounded up the survivors after massacring most of them?"

"We haven't 'massacred' any of them, Regiment-Captain. We bypassed them on our way to Fort Salby. However, they're now behind our lines, and it's necessary for us to do something about them." Toralk looked straight into chan Skrithik's eyes. "We can either go back and demand their surrender—and use force to compel them to surrender, if they refuse—or we can attempt to arrive at some other arrangement."

"Are you suggesting that you might hold them hostage for the return of your personnel?" chan Skrithik asked in a considerably icier voice.

"I suppose it might sound that way," Toralk conceded. "However, the point I'm trying to make is that at the moment there's been no contact between our forces and the *civilian* workers on your 'railroad.' What Two Thousand Harshu is offering you is an opportunity to protect them, in exchange for the return of his own personnel."

"What if I suggested that if he wants his people back he should return *all* of our people? Everyone you've captured from the moment you attacked us during the middle of the 'peace negotiations' *you* people proposed?"

Chan Skrithik watched the other man's expression narrowly and found himself wishing he'd had at least some experience in reading Arcanan body language. Not that he was certain it would have helped a great deal. Watching Toralk, he suspected that the Arcanan would have been a formidable opponent across the gaming table.

"Two Thousand Harshu thought you might make such a counter offer," Toralk said. "He instructed me to tell you that he doesn't have the authority to agree to such a broad exchange. He instructs me to point out to you that, as he's sure you'll appreciate, having transported at least some of the prisoners your people took when you attacked us beyond our reach, the prisoners in his hands represent an invaluable intelligence asset. He lacks the authority to surrender that asset until and unless both sides are in a position to discuss the return of *all* prisoners."

"Does he?"

There was something about Toralk's reply that bothered chan Skrithik. Something about the careful word selection. He couldn't put his finger on exactly what it was, yet it sent a chill through him, and he found himself hoping it was only because his bone-deep anger at Janaki's death had made him hyper-suspicious of anything an Arcanan said or did.

"Very well," he said, hoping his flicker of apprehension hadn't been obvious to Toralk and Vaynair, "suppose I make a different counter proposal. If he wants his soldiers back, I want not simply my civilians, but their construction equipment."

Toralk blinked. Clearly, chan Skrithik had managed to surprise him at least a little for the first time. The Arcanan frowned, cocking his head slightly while he considered what chan Skrithik had said, then shrugged.

"I can't say how Two Thousand Harshu would react to that suggestion," he admitted. "I would have to return and discuss it with him. Would that be acceptable?"

"Possibly." Chan Skrithik smiled thinly. "Your 'Two Thousand Harshu' is the fellow who first proposed the exchange. I hadn't even considered it. Obviously, I'll have to think about it, as well, won't I? However, at the moment, I'm . . . disinclined to settle for anything less. And I suppose I should point out to you that what we're talking about is a couple of thousand 'civilians' equipped with the same weapons which blew your first batch of butchers into dog shit at Fallen Timbers. You might find an effort to 'compel them' to surrender rather more expensive than you'd like."

Toralk's face tightened slightly at the words "first batch of butchers," but he had himself well under control. Instead of some angry response, he simply nodded.

"You might be right, Regiment-Captain. That doesn't mean either side would be happy about the expense involved, however."

"True enough," chan Skrithik agreed with a thin smile.

"I would like to add one more thing, Regiment-Captain," Vaynair said, and chan Skrithik swung his gaze back to the magistron.

"What?"

"The two proposals aren't necessarily linked, Sir. The offer of our medical personnel for the wounded of both sides is independent of any agreement on exchanging prisoners."

Chan Skrithik nodded.

"I understand. And, to be honest, we've got some men—on both sides—who probably aren't going to make it without the kind of Healing you seem to be describing."

"I thought that would probably be the case, Sir." Vaynair's expression was grim. "In fact, with your permission, I've already requested Two Thousand Harshu's permission to remain here and offer my own Gift for the immediate treatment of the most critically injured while you and he make up your minds about the other aspects of his proposals."

"And did 'Two Thousand Harshu' give you that permission?" chan Skrithik asked. "After all, you say you're his senior medical officer. Is he willing to effectively add you to our bag of prisoners if the negotiation of his 'proposals' falls through?"

"I'm sure he hopes that in that eventuality, you'll allow me to return to him," Vaynair said levelly. "In fact, he told me to ask you for assurances to that effect. However," Vaynair looked chan Skrithik straight in the eye, "he also authorized me to remain whether you gave that assurance or not."

Chan Skrithik's eyebrows rose.

"That was very generous of him," the Sharonian said. "Or else he's a lot more worried than he wants to admit about the care his wounded are likely to receive. In either case, I'm prepared to accept your offer—subject, of course, to that Sifter I mentioned. And," chan Skrithik added grudgingly, "if the Sifter passes you, I'm also prepared to guarantee your safe return whatever happens to the rest of our 'negotiations.' "

CHAPTER THIRTY-TWO

"—AND I DON'T give a good *godsdamn* what *you* think, Fifty! The next time you drag your sorry ass into *my* office and get into *my* face over this, I'll shove my boot so far up it you'll taste fucking leather for a godsdamned *week!* Now get the hells out of my sight!"

For the first time in his military career, Therman Ulthar failed to salute his commanding officer before he wheeled and marched furiously out of Hadrign Thalmayr's office. The wiry red-haired officer's blue eyes were cored with rage, his lips were white with compressed fury, and the care he took to shut the door very quietly behind him was a clearer statement of his seething anger and contempt than any violent slam could have been.

He stalked out of the office block at Fort Ghartoun literally trembling with combined fury, outrage, and humiliation, and Sword Keraik Nourm glanced up from where he'd been mending the buckle on his weapons harness.

"Guess the Hundred tied *his* balls in a knot," he remarked with a pronounced note of satisfaction. He shook his head and glanced at the other sword, sitting beside him on the barracks veranda and smoking a pipe. "Graholis, you'd think someone who'd been these fuckers' prisoner would get it, wouldn't you?"

Sword Evarl Harnak looked back at Nourm thoughtfully for several seconds. Then he took his pipe out of his mouth, tamped the tobacco down, and put the stem back between his teeth.

"Yeah, you would, wouldn't you?" he repeated in a very different tone, and Nourm's eyes narrowed.

"Don't tell me you *agree* with him!" the first noncom said incredulously.

"Fifty Ulthar's a right smart young fellow," Harnak replied indirectly, looking back out across the parade ground at the stables surrounded by infantry-dragons and alert sentries.

"He's only a *fifty*," Nourm pointed out. "You've been around as long as I have, Evarl. You've seen the dragon and smelled the smoke. You *know* most fifties still need swords like us to wipe their noses and change their diapers!"

"You think so?" Harnak looked back at him.

"Hells yes, I think so! I mean, take Fifty Sarma. He's a good kid, mostly. Still wet behind the ears and full of all that starry-eyed Academy crap, but a good kid. He just doesn't get it, though. Not where these bastards are concerned."

"Actually," Harnak said after a moment, his tone thoughtful, "it seems to me the real problem isn't snot-nosed kids fresh out of the Academy and too stupid to understand the real world, but some old sweats who're so stupid they aren't even bothering to try to 'get it.'"

Nourm stiffened and his face darkened.

"What d'you mean by *that* crack?" he demanded.

"I mean I'm getting tired of people who don't bother to listen to what's really going on out here, that's what I mean." Harnak's tone was harder, and his voice was lower pitched. "I mean I'm getting tired of people who eat up that asshole Neshok's so-called 'intelligence briefings' like they were handed down from the gods. And I mean I'm getting tired of idiots so locked up with the hate inside them that they can't even wake up and smell the fucking coffee!"

Nourm's eyes flared wide and he sat back in his cane-bottomed chair abruptly.

"What in the hells are you talking about?" Anger crackled in his own voice, but there was confusion, as well. "Godsdamn it, *you* were one of their prisoners! You know damned well they didn't even bother to give the Hundred a decent healer! And you were godsdamned there when they shot Magister Halathyn!"

"You poor, pathetic excuse for a sword," Harnak said almost pityingly. "My gods, you've been kicking around the Service for *this* long, and you don't recognize a pile of unicorn shit when they put it on your plate and call it scrambled eggs?"

Nourm's wide eyes narrowed at the slang phrase. It could be used to describe orders that were unusually stupid or confused or to describe someone's particularly blatant—and unconvincing—cover-his-ass excuses. But it was also used to describe "confirmed" intelligence that was just plain wrong . . . or a deliberate lie.

"What do you mean?" he demanded harshly.

"I mean I *was* there," Harnak grated, taking the pipe out of his mouth and stabbing the stem in Nourm's direction. "I was there at Fallen Timbers when it all fell into the shitter. Hells, Osmuna—the first man down—he was in *my* fucking platoon and I was the one who found him with a frigging hole blown all the way through his godsdamned chest! Don't you sit there and tell me what the fucking intelligence pukes have been feeding you! I was *there*, godsdamn it. I *saw* what the hells happened!"

The pipe in his hand quivered, and Nourm's expression changed suddenly as he recognized the barely leashed fury in that quiver.

"Then tell me," he said in a very different voice. "Tell me what happened."

Harnak looked at him for several heartbeats, as if weighing the risks, then inhaled deeply and shrugged ever so slightly.

"Hundred Olderhan was right all along," he said then, softly. "I don't know who shot first, Osmuna or their man. I don't think anyone ever *will* know. But I know who fucking shot first at Fallen Timbers, and it wasn't them. It wasn't the godsdamned civilian standing there with his hands *empty*, trying to fucking talk to us—just *talk* to us—when my own shitty excuse for a fifty shot him right in the throat against the hundred's direct orders!"

Nourm recognized the look in Harnak's eyes now, and the agonizing shame he saw there was more convincing than any anger might have been.

"Did you know Hundred Olderhan made the only two of them we didn't manage to kill his *shardonai*?" Harnak continued, glaring at the other sword. "You know whose son he is—you think he did that because we'd acted so fucking *honorably*? And I'll bet you didn't know the Hundred offered to cut Thalmayr down right there in front of everything that was left of my platoon when that asshole sitting in that office over there wanted to put manacles on the Hundred's *shardonai*. Well, *I* know. I was the sword Thalmayr ordered to do it . . . and the one the Hundred ordered to stand fast!

"And Magister Halathyn? They didn't kill him—*we* did." Anguish tightened Harnak's fierce, low voice. "It was an infantry-dragon, a godsdamned lightning-thrower—you seen any of them in *these* people's armory, Nourm? 'Cause *I* sure as fuck haven't seen any of 'em!"

Harnak jerked his head in the direction of the Fort Ghartoun armory building and his mouth twisted as if he wanted to spit.

"And all that crap about shooting prisoners, torturing them, denying medical care—dragon shit! *Dragon shit!* These people—the officers in that brig over there—saw to it that we were treated *well*. I never saw a single one of their guards as much as butt-stroke one of our guys with a rifle! You want to explain to me just how that compares with the way *we've* been treating *them*?

"And then there's that bastard Thalmayr and his lying shit about how they '*tortured* him.' " Harnak's tone dripped contempt. "Fifty Ulthar and I got left here because we were both wounded, too. I saw their healers at work—hells, they worked on *me*!—and I never saw one of them do less than the very best he could do. They aren't *like* our magistrons; they can't *do* the same things. Can't any of you get that through your godsdamned skulls? They did the best they fucking could, treated us every bit as well as they did their own people, without *once* asking whose uniform we were wearing, and *that's* who your precious Hundred Thalmayr's beating and stomping the shit out of every couple of days! It godsdamned makes me want to *puke*!"

Nourm stared at the other noncom in shock as he realized there were literally tears of fury—and shame—in Evarl Harnak's eyes.

"I—" he started, then broke off. It was too much for him to take in all at one sitting, stood too many preconceptions he'd spent too long cherishing on their heads. But in Evarl Harnak's rage and shame he recognized truth when he finally saw it.

"What?" Harnak half-snapped as Nourm hesitated.

"I guess, maybe, I should've spent a little more time listening to Fifty Sarma," Nourm replied finally, slowly. "Maybe then I wouldn't feel like as big a piece of shit as I do right now."

"Yeah?" Harnak growled. "Well, you aren't the only one who feels that way. Trust me."

"Maybe not."

Nourm sat staring out across the captured fort's parade ground, thinking about everything Harnak had just told him. Thinking about everything *he'd* said . . . and done.

"Maybe not," he repeated, "but what in Graholis' name do we do about it?"

"I don't know." Harnak put his pipe back into his mouth and turned away from the other man while he fished out an accumulator and used it to relight the tobacco, and his voice was even lower than before. "I know what I'd *like* to do, but I can't. And I wish the Fifty would remember the same advice he gave me," he added, turning to look in the direction in which Ulthar had disappeared. "If he keeps on with this, keeps getting in Thalmayr's way, I don't know what's going to happen."

Nourm's eyes followed Harnak's, and as they did, they deepened and darkened with fresh worry all their own.

I know exactly what's going to happen if Ulthar doesn't back off, he thought grimly. *And he's not the only officer it's going to happen to, either. So what the hells do I do about* my *Fifty? Because that "wet-behind-the-ears kid" I should've been listening to all along sure as* hells *isn't going to leave it alone either!*

Keraik Nourm looked into the future and didn't like what he saw there at all.

* * *

The miles-long train pulled into the Fort Salby station in a long, shuddering, clanking spasm of steam and hissing air brakes. It stretched as far back down the tracks as the eye could see, and Rof chan Skrithik's eyes narrowed in appreciation as he saw the machine guns and light pedestal guns which had been mounted on top of many of the freight cars.

The command and staff cars were at the head of the train, and chan Skrithik came to attention as the doors opened and an officer in the uniform and paired golden sunbursts of a Ternathian division-captain came down the short steps.

The division-captain was short, for a Ternathian, with dark hair beginning to be streaked with dramatic silver highlights. He was also wiry and fit, with a horseman's build and large, powerful hands which went well with his cavalry boots and the bone-handled grips of the H&W holstered at his side instead of the lighter Polshana many other officers preferred these days. But his brown eyes were dark, and the black mourning band on his right arm matched the identical mourning bands worn by every other person in sight.

"Division-Captain chan Geraith," chan Skrithik said quietly.

"Regiment-Captain," chan Geraith replied.

"I'm glad to see you, Sir. I only wish—"

"So do we all, Regiment-Captain," chan Geraith said as chan Skrithik broke off. The division-captain held out his hand and gripped chan Skrithik's firmly. "So do we all. But you did a fine job out here. A fine job."

"Thank you, Sir. We didn't do it all on our own, though, and, I'd like to intro—"

Chan Skrithik broke off again, but not this time because he couldn't find the words. This time, he was interrupted by the magnificent peregrine falcon which came slanting down across the station platform's roof and landed on his shoulder.

Chan Geraith's eyes widened. He hadn't actually noticed the leather pad on the regiment-captain's shoulder, he realized.

"I'm sorry, Sir," chan Skrithik began when he saw chan Geraith staring at the bird. "I know she's Prince Janaki's, and I'm sure there has to be some other arrangement, but since he was killed, she's . . ."

His voice trailed off helplessly. For a moment longer, chan Geraith just looked at him. Then the division-captain gave himself a visible shake.

"That's an Imperial Ternathian Peregrine, Regiment-Captain," he said. "No one tells them what to do in a case like this. On the thankfully rare occasions when they lose their human companions, *they* decide where to go and who, if anyone, to bond with. If she's chosen you, then that's *her* decision, not anyone else's."

"But, Sir, I don't know anything *about* falcons," chan Skrithik protested in a half-desperate voice. "If not for the Sunlord here, I wouldn't have had a clue what to do for her!"

"Then it would appear to me, Regiment-Captain," chan Geraith said, turning to extend his hand to the cavalry officer standing at chan Skrithik's shoulder with a matching mourning band on the right arm of his *Uromathian* uniform, "that we have two things to thank Sunlord Markan for. Believe me," he continued, speaking directly to the Uromathian, "I am as deeply and sincerely grateful to you and all of your men as Emperor Zindel himself will be, Sunlord."

"It was a cooperative effort, Division-Captain," Markan replied, gripping the offered hand firmly. "No one here at Fort Salby had a monopoly on courage . . . or sacrifice."

His dark, almond-shaped eyes dropped to the dark band around his own sleeve, matching the one on chan Geraith's, and the division-captain nodded soberly.

"Well said, Sunlord." He gave Markan's hand a final squeeze, then drew a deep breath.

"Gentlemen," he said, looking at both of them, "I suspect that my staff car is actually better equipped, at least until we can get your fort put back together again, for the briefings and discussions awaiting all of us. But before we start all of that, I would like to see my Prince."

* * *

Crown Prince Janaki chan Calirath, dressed in a clean uniform, lay on the bier in the Fort Salby chapel with his hands folded on the hilt of the dress sword on his chest. The presence lights of the Triad glowed above the altar where the three faces of Vothan the Protector, Mother Shalana, and Marinlay the Maiden gazed down upon him, and an honor guard composed of the seven surviving men of Janaki's platoon, under the command of Chief-Armsman chan Braikal, stood stiffly at attention around the bier. It was thankfully cool in the chapel, yet chan Geraith was surprised that there were no visible signs of corruption. He looked at chan Skrithik, and the regiment-captain shrugged.

"Maybe I shouldn't have done it, Sir, but the senior Arcanan Healer offered to put what he called a 'preservation spell' on the Prince's body."

"They've been informed he was killed?" chan Geraith asked sharply, with more than a hint of disapproval.

"He already knew when he approached me, Sir," chan Skrithik said levelly. "Apparently one of the wounded mentioned it where he and his . . . translating crystal could overhear. Since he already knew, I saw no reason not to accept his offer."

Chan Geraith grimaced, but chan Skrithik faced him squarely.

"Sir, every single one of your men is going to want to pay his respects to the Prince, just like every one of my men—and of the Sunlord's—did. They're going to need to see him, and there are going to be Voices among them. For that matter, I know you've got Voice correspondents with you. I didn't want his lady mother—*anyone*—to see him looking like—"

The regiment-captain stopped with another shrug, his eyes glittering under the presence lights, and chan Geraith felt his grimace smooth into something else.

"I hadn't thought about it that way," he admitted. "I'd rather they didn't know a thing about it, but if they already knew, then I think you probably made the right decision."

"Thank you, Sir," chan Skrithik said quietly. He shook his head slightly. "Actually, it seems to me—and Petty-Captain chan Darma, my Voice, agrees with me—that this Five Hundred Vaynair is a genuinely decent human being. I don't know what someone like him is doing in the Arcanan Army, but my Sifter agreed that he was sincere when he said he wanted to do this as a mark of his personal respect."

"Indeed?" Chan Geraith frowned thoughtfully.

He'd been surprised by the Arcanan commander's offer when chan Skrithik's Voice relayed its terms to him. In fact, he'd seriously contemplated ordering chan Skrithik to refuse. Like the regiment-captain, he was grimly suspicious of the real reasons this Harshu was mysteriously "not authorized" to release any other prisoners he might hold. And, as Harshu himself had pointed out through his mouthpieces, the Arcanan POWs constituted a potential intelligence treasure trove whose value was impossible to estimate.

But weighed against the release of fewer than three hundred military prisoners was the return of over two thousand civilians and most of their heavy equipment. Two Thousand Harshu had agreed to allow them to remove any and all equipment they could load in a twelve-hour window, starting when the exchange was agreed to. Since Olvyr Banchu had been loading cars with an eye to a retreat to Traisum for almost thirty-six hours at that point, the grace period actually amounted to almost two full days.

That, unfortunately, had still been a short enough time to preclude taking any of the really big excavators, since it would have been necessary to break them down into their component loads, and the lack of flatcars meant that almost a third of the other heavy equipment had been left behind, as well. Nonetheless, Banchu had returned to Fort Salby with millions of marks worth of construction machinery that was going to be worth considerably more than its weight in gold when it came time to resume the advance towards Hell's Gate. Indeed, chan Geraith had to wonder if Harshu had realized for a moment just how valuable that machinery was going to prove. If Sharona had lost all of it, it would have taken literally months to ship in replacements and the trained personnel to use it.

Chan Geraith had seen the endless lines of work cars, portable machine shops, flatcars loaded with bulldozers and scrapers, passenger cars, portable sawmills, auxiliary steam engines, loads of unused rails and ties, bolts, spikes, hammers, pickaxes. . . . The list seemed endless, and the cars and work locomotives filled the extensive sidings left behind when TTE finished construction of the Traisum Cut almost to capacity. He couldn't possibly have justified holding on to chan Skrithik's prisoners if they were the price of getting so many Sharonian civilians and so much priceless capability back.

He'd accepted the offer because he'd seen no choice, but he'd been more than a little surprised by how scrupulously the Arcanans had honored the terms of their agreement. According to chan Skrithik's post surgeon, for example, the regiment-captain would never have regained full use of his arm without the intervention of the Gifted Arcanan healers. At least fifteen of chan Skrithik's wounded—including Prince Janaki's chief-armsman—would almost certainly have died without that same intervention, and many more, like chan Skrithik, would have been crippled for life. Indeed, the Arcanans had ended up healing twice as many Uromathian and PAAF casualties as they had of their own men.

And then there was this, he thought, gazing down at the dead young man lying before him as if he were only sleeping.

"I suppose there have to be at least some decent men anywhere—even in Arcana," he said finally. "And I'm grateful. But I don't think this is going to soften public opinion back home an ounce when word gets back to Tajvana."

Chan Skrithik winced at the reminder that Janaki's parents still didn't know about his death.

"I wish, Sir—you don't know how badly I wish—that he hadn't been here," the regiment-captain said softly. "We'd never have held this post without him, but—*gods!*" He shook his head, eyes gleaming with remembered tears as he looked back down at the body. "To lose him like that, so young. So full of promise. I know we always think crown princes are 'full of promise,' but Triad above, he was. He really *was*!"

"I know." Chan Geraith reached out and squeezed chan Skrithik's left shoulder, careful to make no sudden movements near Taleena. "I know."

"He told me he had to be here," chan Skrithik continued. "I wanted to argue with him, but somehow I just couldn't. And gods know, I *needed* him. With all the civilians, the portal's strategic importance . . . I just couldn't tell him no. And to the very last moment of his life, he was totally focused on saving the rest of us. On doing his duty. On being certain *I* knew what he'd Glimpsed. Without that knowledge, that warning, we never would have held. Hells, without his warning we'd all have died in our beds! He saved us all, and at least I can honestly tell his parents that he died almost instantly. He never could have known what hit him."

"Oh, he knew, Regiment-Captain," chan Geraith said quietly. "He knew exactly. He Saw it coming—he *experienced* it—before the first Arcanan ever came into sight of your fort here."

"*Sir?*" The word came out half-strangled as chan Skrithik's head whipped back around. He stared into chan Geraith's eyes, and the division-captain nodded slowly.

"He was in fugue state," he said simply, "and his Talent was never as strong as his father's, or his sister's. For him to enter fugue state, it had to be a Death Glimpse. He *knew* he was going to die if he stayed here, Regiment-Captain chan Skrithik. He Saw it. He even sent me a message that *told* me he knew . . . and prevented me from ordering you to have him removed from Fort Salby, by force if necessary."

Chan Skrithik's face was twisted with a deeper, fresher anguish, and even though chan Geraith had no trace of Talent, he felt the other man's pain like his own. Part of him felt guilty for inflicting that fresh pain upon him, but it was important that chan Skrithik know, that *everyone* know, that Janaki chan Calirath had gone knowingly to his death, offering up his life to save thousands of others.

"It's the motto of his House, Regiment-Captain," Arlos chan Geraith said softly, quietly, into the silence, feeling Sunlord Markan at his elbow. "'I Stand Between.' I stand between evil and its victims, between darkness and light. I stand between right and wrong. I stand between my people and their enemies . . . and between the people I am sworn to protect and death. There's a reason men and women have followed Caliraths straight into the fire for thousands of years, Regiment-Captain, and we—you and I—have been honored to see precisely what that reason is."

CHAPTER THIRTY-THREE

"WHAT IS IT, Alazon?" Darcel Kinlafia's brown eyes looked into eyes of gray, and Alazon Yanamar didn't need the bond between them to recognize his deep concern. "What's worrying her so badly?"

He turned his head away once again, gazing down the palace corridor where Grand Princess Andrin had just disappeared. The young woman's spine was as straight, her carriage as graceful, as ever, but her eyes had been unquiet for days, cosmetics could not disguise the dark shadows under them, and she had walked past Alazon and Kinlafia without even noticing their presence.

"I can't tell you that, love."

Alazon reached up and touched his cheek gently, and his eyes narrowed. There were times when the closeness of a bond like theirs had its downside. He could tell that whatever was haunting Andrin was causing Alazon deep distress, as well. At the same time, he was a Voice himself. He understood the responsibilities, the privacy oaths of any Voice, far less the Emperor of Ternathia's Privy Voice.

"I'm sorry," he said contritely. "I shouldn't have asked you. It's just that . . . I hate seeing her this way."

"I know you do." Alazon stroked his cheek one more time, then tucked her arm through his and began walking him down the same corridor. "I think everyone does," she continued. "Triad knows I do, but then," she glanced up at him, "most of us have known her since she was a little girl."

"Point taken, My Lady," he said with a slightly lopsided smile.

<*If you don't want to tell me what's going on between the two of you, that's fine,*> she Said, deliberately using her Voice so there could be no question of her sincerity. <*But if it's something I can help with—help her or you—you know you only have to ask.*>

<*Of course I know,*> he Told her in reply. <*And it's certainly not that I don't want to tell you. It's just that I'm not really sure what's happening myself. And there are some . . . privacy issues of my own I have to work through.*>

<*I can understand that,*> she Said, and in the side traces of her Voice, he Heard her memory of the echoes she'd felt when his shared Glimpse with Zindel had hammered through him. She couldn't help feeling that memory, putting it together with a dozen other little clues, and realizing—in general terms, at least—what must have happened. Yet she made absolutely no effort to use the knowledge he knew she already possessed as some sort of opening wedge, and he sent a warm flood of love and gratitude over their bond.

<*You know she's already planning to organize our wedding for us, don't you?*> Alazon continued, her mental tone lighter as she deliberately changed the subject. <*From a few things she's said, I think she's planning on pulling out all the stops, too.*>

<Oh, wonderful!> Kinlafia's Voice was so tart Alazon chuckled out loud. *<You do realize that my parents—both of my parents—are good New Farnalian Social Republicans, don't you? They're going to have enough trouble with my marrying an emperor's privy voice without having said emperor's daughter organizing the ceremony!>*

<Oh, stop worrying!> she scolded. *<Every parent wants his or her child to do well in life. Just because your parents are Socialists doesn't change that! After you get elected to the new Imperial House of Talents, they'll be so proud of you they won't even notice who you're marrying. For that matter, you may find they've turned into staunch Imperialists once they see you wheeling and dealing in the very cockpit of power, as it were.>*

Kinlafia rolled his eyes.

<If simple confidence were enough to get elected, we wouldn't even have to count the ballots with you around,> he Said dryly. *<Unfortunately, I think it's a little more complicated than that.>*

<Not when Zindel chan Calirath puts his mind to it, it isn't,> she Told him serenely. *<And not when the candidate is as completely and totally right for the job as you are.>*

He squeezed her elbow against his side as the warmth and confidence flowed out of her into him, and yet her mention of the Emperor had brought him back his concern over Andrin. Zindel was older than Andrin, more experienced at dealing with—and concealing—the telltale symptoms of a Glimpse . . . despite which, it was obvious to Kinlafia that whatever was riding Andrin like some sort of unrelenting nightmare was also pursuing Zindel. And the ripples spreading from his and his daughter's anxiety were afflicting the empress and her younger daughters, as well, even if they had no idea what that anxiety's root cause might be.

<*Maybe the Ball will help,*> Alazon Said hopefully.

<*And maybe the Ball will send her right over the edge!*> Kinlafia shook his head. <*The mere thought of it is coming close to having that effect on* me, *at any rate!*>

<*Nonsense! You'll be the most handsome man there, not to mention the most famous. In fact, I'm planning to be intolerably jealous when all these court ladies come fluttering around you, asking to dance.*>

<*Oh, don't worry about* that!> Kinlafia chuckled. <*Did I forget to mention that I never learned to dance?*> His brown eyes danced wickedly. <*Trust me, as soon as I've crushed a few ladies' delicate toes, you won't have any trouble at all keeping me all to yourself!*>

"Voice Kinlafia?"

Alazon had been about to reply when the voice from behind cut them off. They stopped, looking over their shoulders, and saw an armsman in the green and gold of the Caliraths, who bowed to them both with grave courtesy.

"Your pardon, Voice Kinlafia, but His Majesty would be very grateful for a few moments of your time."

Kinlafia's mouth felt suddenly dry, and his pulse rate picked up.

"Of course," he said quickly. "Would now be a convenient time for him?"

"He hoped you could come promptly," the armsman agreed, and Kinlafia turned to peck a quick kiss on Alazon's cheek.

"I'll see you again as soon as I can, my dear," he told

her. "After all, we have that delightful appointment with the tailor this afternoon, don't we?"

Alazon smiled at him, then nodded and released his arm. He gave her an answering smile before he turned to the armsman and beckoned for the other man to lead the way. He followed the armsman down the passageway, and as he went, he felt Alazon's warm, loving touch on his mind and heart.

* * *

"Thank you for coming, Darcel."

Kinlafia's left eyebrow rose very slightly as Zindel chan Calirath turned from the view through his study windows to greet his guest. So far, the Emperor had always been careful to begin any interview or conversation with Kinlafia by greeting him formally, as "Voice Kinlafia." For a moment, Kinlafia wondered if today's change was some sort of deliberate tactic on Zindel's part, but then he felt that same mysterious something he'd felt at their very first meeting radiating from the Emperor. Using his given name hadn't been any sort of ploy; it was simply a measure of Zindel's concern that he'd forgotten the formal courtesy. And it was also, Kinlafia realized, a reflection of Zindel's awareness that whatever else might happen in this universe or any other, Darcel Kinlafia would face it at his daughter's side.

"Yes," Zindel said, almost as if he'd been the Voice, reading Kinlafia's surface thoughts, "it's about Andrin."

"Your Majesty, I'm sure there are other—" Kinlafia began, but then he stopped himself. There was no point in pretending, not when Zindel was as aware as he himself was of the bizarre fashion in which he had shared in the Emperor's Glimpse.

"I'm sorry, Your Majesty," he said instead. "It would be

pretty foolish, I suppose, to pretend I don't know what you're talking about. Of course," he managed a smile of sorts, "*understanding* it is something else again!"

"I'm sorry, too, Darcel," Zindel said with simple sincerity.

He walked over to the chair behind his desk and sank into it, then waved for Kinlafia to be seated in another chair at the end of the desk, close enough for comfortable conversation. Kinlafia was well aware that one was not supposed to sit in the Emperor's presence, yet it seemed the most natural thing in the world for him to accept the invitation. He sat, cocking his head to one side, and waited for Zindel to explain why he'd been summoned.

It took the Emperor several seconds of uncharacteristic hesitation, then he cleared his throat.

"I'm sure you've figured out by now that Janaki had more than one reason for suggesting you run for office," he said.

"Your Majesty, I realized that the first time he made the suggestion," Kinlafia replied. "I didn't ask him what those other reasons were, although perhaps I should have. But I knew they were there."

"And you accepted his suggestion anyway." The fleetingness of Zindel's smile seemed to shout his anxiety to the Voice. "It must have been that damned Calirath 'magnetism,'" the Emperor continued. "Janaki always has had more than his fair share of it."

"I think they issue it with your birth certificates, actually, Your Majesty." Kinlafia produced a small smile of his own, although he was beginning to suspect that what he'd just said came very close to being the literal truth.

"Well, at any rate," Zindel said, "after our little

shared experience at dinner, I strongly suspect—no, I don't *suspect*; I know—that you've figured out at least a part of what Janaki's other reasons were."

"Yes, I have, I think," Kinlafia admitted. "And if you'll pardon my saying so, Your Majesty, it scares the ever-living shit out of me. It's so far above anything I ever thought of as being my pay grade that I get a nosebleed just thinking about it."

"You'll get over it."

It could have been a simple conversational throw-away, and it could have been a condescension, but it was neither. It was a simple statement of fact, as if the Emperor had mentioned that the sun was likely to rise somewhere in the east tomorrow morning.

"I certainly hope you're right about that . . . even if it does seem a little unlikely at the moment."

Zindel chuckled, but then he shook his head and leaned slightly towards Kinlafia.

"Janaki's Talent isn't as strong as mine," he said, "and mine isn't as strong as Andrin's." His sea-gray eyes, so much like his son's and his elder daughter's, seemed to hold unquiet ghosts as his gaze met Kinlafia's. "In fact, I'm coming to the conclusion that Andrin has one of the truly legendary Talents. Her Glimpses are far stronger than mine *ever* were, much less than mine were at her age. I'm very much afraid that for her, like for many of her ancestors, her Talent's very strength is going to be the curse she bears. As an emperor, I'm delighted to see it, grateful it will be available to serve my people's need. As a father, I would sell my soul to protect her from it."

He fell silent, those gray eyes looking at something only they could see. He sat that way for several seconds before he inhaled again, deeply, and his eyes snapped back into focus.

"I suppose it's just as well for the Empire—and all of Sharona—that I can't protect her from her own Talent. But what Janaki Glimpsed fragments of, what I've Glimpsed in more detail, tells me she'll need you, Darcel. I don't pretend to know all of the reasons, all the ways in which you'll be there for her over the years. That isn't the way Glimpses work, especially for a member of the Glimpser's own family. But I know, beyond any question or doubt, that my daughter will come to love you as deeply as she's ever loved anyone in her life, and that you'll return that love just as deeply as if she had been the daughter of your own flesh. I *know* that, Darcel, but what I don't know is what the cost for *you* will be."

Kinlafia sat very quietly, looking into the eyes of the man who would become his Emperor in less than forty-eight hours. And as he did, he realized Zindel chan Calirath was already "his" Emperor.

"Your Majesty, I don't have any more idea about that than you do, and I won't say I don't *care* what the 'cost' will be. But I will say that, yes, I did share your Glimpse. And given what I Saw when I did, I'll pay that cost, whatever it is."

"Thank you," Zindel said with quiet, deep sincerity. "A father always wants—needs—to be there for his daughter. I hope to be there for many years to come for Andrin, as for Razial and Anbessa. But having Seen you and Andrin in my Glimpse, I know that if for some reason I can't be there, she will still have you, and that's one of the very few visions my Talent has ever given me which are unalloyed sources of relief and happiness.

"However, the reason I asked you to visit me this

morning," he continued more briskly, "is that I'm certain you've noticed that both Andrin and I have been more tense than usual over the past several days. And, as I'm almost equally certain you've deduced, that tension has been the result of a Glimpse we've shared.

"Given what you shared with me, you'll probably understand better than most non-Caliraths when I say it's been . . . difficult for us to nail down the exact significance of that Glimpse. However," his face turned grim and hard, "I've just received a dispatch from Division-Captain chan Geraith which has put a great deal of what I've Seen into perspective. A most disturbing perspective."

"Your Majesty?" Kinlafia stiffened in his chair.

"As you're better aware than most, any Voice message from the Division-Captain takes just over a week to reach us. This particular message relayed one from Janaki, at Fort Salby. It would appear, Darcel, that the Arcanans weren't negotiating in good faith with us, after all."

Kinlafia's eyes narrowed, and he felt something like sea ice sweeping through his veins.

"Janaki's message has put several things Andrin and I had Glimpsed earlier into perspective. I know, now, what we were Seeing, but Janaki's Glimpse is obviously far stronger, far more complete. At the time he sent his message to Division-Captain chan Geraith, he expected Fort Salby to be attacked within forty-eight hours by an Arcanan force which included dragons—literal, flying, fire-breathing dragons."

Kinlafia blinked in astonishment, and Zindel laughed. It was an ugly, harsh bark of sound, without any trace of humor.

"Believe me, I doubt very much that you could

be more surprised by that than I was, and I actually Glimpsed the things months ago! I simply didn't know what they were, didn't have enough other knowledge to put it into context or recognize what I was seeing. The very idea was so preposterous that my preconceptions got in the way until it was far too late."

"What do you mean, 'too late,' Your Majesty?" Kinlafia asked tautly.

"I mean Andrin and I have been Glimpsing Janaki in combat for the last eight days." Zindel's face suddenly looked years older. "I mean we can't tell from what we've Seen what happens to him. But what we have Glimpsed is terrifying, Darcel . . . and the message he sent to chan Geraith is even more frightening. Whatever Andrin and I may be Glimpsing, Janaki expects to die."

Kinlafia felt as if he'd just been shot through the chest, and his face went suddenly white under its deep tan. Memories of Janaki—of his laughter, his kindness and compassion, his zest for life, and his obviously deep and abiding dedication to the lifetime task to which an accident of birth had condemned him—rushed through the Voice, and his hands tightened like claws on the armrests of his chair.

"He may be wrong," Zindel said. "His Talent is weaker, as I've said. He may be misinterpreting something he's Seen, and I pray to the Triad that he is. But the very weakness of his Talent makes the clarity of his Glimpse more frightening. There are several reasons why it might have been clearer, sharper, than ours, but there's no point in pretending that the most likely reason isn't that he's interpreted it correctly."

"My gods, Your Majesty," Kinlafia whispered. "I don't know . . . I mean, what can I say? Do?"

"I don't know what you'll do if Janaki is right." Zindel's eyes were dark, glistening with the unshed tears of a strong man, an Emperor, who was also a father whose son had just prophesied his own death. "All I know is that if he is, Andrin will need you . . . and you *will* be there for her."

"Does she know? About Janaki's message, I mean?"

"No, she doesn't. Neither does her mother." Zindel looked away, gazing out the windows at the garden, and his voice had become distant, as if he were speaking to himself . . . or possibly to his son. "I don't know if I'm going to tell them. On the one hand, I should. They have a right to know. But, on the other hand, suppose Janaki's wrong, as I pray he is? Should I tell them, put that burden on them, now, of all times, when it may never come to pass at all? And even if Janaki is right, telling them now won't change what will happen. It will only let them worry, anticipate. It's bad enough knowing, myself; should I inflict that same pain, that same worry, on two of the five people I love most in all the multiverse?"

"I don't know what to say, Your Majesty," Kinlafia admitted softly. "I wish I did, but I don't."

"I know you don't, Darcel." The Emperor-elect of Sharona reached across and patted Darcel Kinlafia on the shoulder almost comfortingly. "I know you don't. But when Andrin needs you, you *will* know."

* * *

Andrin Calirath was not quite eighteen years old, and her mother had always had strict notions about proper etiquette and the degree of decorum expected out of a daughter of the aristocracy. Whereas many a young Ternathian noblewoman might have attended her first public ball by the time she was sixteen years old, or even as young as fifteen, Andrin's very first formal ball had been to celebrate the ratification and signing of the Act of Unification only twelve days earlier.

She'd expected to be giddy with excitement at the opportunity, and the truth was that she had enjoyed herself. But not as much as she'd expected to. Perhaps it was simply that pleasures anticipated always loomed greater than pleasures actually experienced. She suspected, however, that the answer was rather simpler than that.

Andrin was the eldest daughter of the man who would become the first emperor of a united Sharona tomorrow afternoon in the magnificent Temple of Saint Taiyr of Tajvana, the traditional site of Calirath coronations for almost two thousand years. Where other nobly born young ladies of her age could spend their formal "coming out" ball in a whirl of excitement and enjoyment, Her Grand Imperial Highness Andrin could not. Her entire evening had been rigorously regimented, planned out ahead of time with the precision of a professional military operation.

She hadn't really blamed anyone. She was who she was, and there was no point pretending it could have been any other way. But the fact that she understood why it had happened hadn't magically—she winced a little as that particular adverb occurred to her—restored some sort of spontaneity to the occasion.

Still, she'd enjoyed her first ball immeasurably more than she was enjoying her second.

One thing an imperial princess could count upon was that she would never find herself unattended. Not only was she accompanied everywhere—except on the dance floor itself, at any rate—by Lazima chan Zindico or one of her other bodyguards, but she was also the inevitable center of a veritable bison herd of young (and not so young) male aristocrats, all determined to impress her with their sparkle, their wit, their good looks, and—above all—their eligibility.

The only one of them who hadn't all too obviously been thinking of himself in terms of matrimonial prospects (and *her* in terms of breeding stock, she thought tartly) was Howan Fai Goutin. The Crown Prince of Eniath had partnered her for two dances, before he bowed to the dictates of etiquette and withdrew to allow others to seek her hand. Those two dances had been blessed interludes, in which she could enjoy the physicality of movement without being subjected to witty comments or bits of profound political—or literary, or philosophical, or even (gods help her) *religious*—insight. (Why, oh *why*, had the word that she was "bookish" had to get out amongst the "marry-me-because-I'm-so-impressive" crowd?) Unlike the others, Howan had simply *danced* with her, and most of her suitors had regarded him (while, no doubt, composing their own next witty sally) with a certain tolerant pity. For all its lengthy history, Eniath was a postage-stamp kingdom, and one which had already aligned its policy with the Caliraths. There was no need to buy Eniath's loyalty with an imperial marriage . . . and the entire kingdom was scarcely worth a Ternathian duchess' hand, far less that of an imperial grand princess who stood second in the line of succession to the throne of all of Sharona.

So they had allowed her two dances worth of freedom, waited while he'd bowed to her, kissed her hand, and withdrawn gracefully. And as soon as he had, they'd closed in once again to impress her with their own enormous suitability for her hand. It could even have been rather flattering, under the right circumstances . . . for all of, oh, fifteen seconds or so. By now, what she found herself hankering for most strongly was a good revolver and an extra box of ammunition.

Finena swiveled her head from her perch on the exquisitely stitched and gemmed leather gauntlet on Andrin's left wrist, looking up at her human friend with an eye Andrin was privately certain gleamed with approval. Her own lips twitched ever so slightly at the thought, yet not even that image, delectable though it might be, could break through the shell of . . . of what?

She couldn't answer that question, hard though she'd tried. She knew her terrifying Glimpses of Janaki were a huge part of it, of course. They were too strong, too persistent, for her to just brush them aside, however hard she tried. However frequently she reminded herself Glimpses often failed, or turned out to have been misunderstood or wrongly interpreted, especially when they concerned loved ones. She'd felt the bumblebees swarming under her skin again, felt the needles and pins of prophecy pricking in her bones, and she knew something—something dreadful—*was* going to happen to her brother.

Shalana the Merciful, please, she thought. *Please let* this *Glimpse be wrong. Protect Janaki.*

If only her father hadn't so obviously been Glimpsing something similar, it might have been easier for her to convince herself she was wrong. But she'd seen the same unspoken fears in his eyes, felt his Talent resonating against hers, and she knew what it was he hadn't told her mother.

Her haunted eyes tracked across the ballroom floor

to where Empress Varena swirled through the graceful measures of a Uromathian waltz with the Prince Regent of Limathia (who appeared to have finally forgiven her father for the famous "godsdamned fish" remark). The empress' head was tilted to one side as she smiled at her partner, moving with all the skilled grace which had seemed to elude Andrin, despite the best efforts of veritable troops of dancing masters, for so many years of her adolescence. Varena radiated vivacity, zest, confidence in the future, as she looked forward to her coronation as Empress of Sharona on the morrow.

But Andrin knew. She knew the burden of the Calirath Talent lay even heavier on the shoulders of imperial consorts who *lacked* that Talent than on any who possessed it. Her mother couldn't experience any Glimpse directly, yet she knew when her daughter and her husband were gripped by the cruel pincers of precognition. And she knew how desperately they sought to protect her from the often frustratingly murky visions of the future which haunted them. Despite her smiles, despite the confident, gracious image she projected, she knew they were protecting her now . . . and even someone far less intelligent than she would have had very little difficulty figuring out which of the people she loved was most probably in danger.

And yet, she did her duty. She shouldered the burden she had agreed to bear the day she accepted Zindel chan Calirath's hand in marriage, and the even greater one no one could have predicted, which would settle upon her tomorrow. She hid her fears, pretended she was unafraid. Pretended even to her husband and her daughter that she wasn't terrified by the future which they, unlike she, could at least Glimpse, however imperfectly.

As Andrin watched her dancing, smiling, she wanted to weep. Weep for her mother's courage, for the crushing weight of the duty she had accepted so many years before.

"Your Highness?"

Andrin blinked herself back into focus and turned her head.

"Yes, Voice Kinlafia?"

"I was hoping you might be kind enough to allow me to partner you for the next dance, Your Highness."

The tough-looking, brown-haired Voice looked out of place in the ballroom. Not because he wasn't perfectly attired, and one of the better-looking men present, but because he made the other, younger, far more nobly born males still orbiting Andrin look as callow and untried as they actually were. Many of them had the tanned, lean fitness of the sports field, but his bronzed, muscular hardness went far deeper than that, earned in a far harder school where the stakes had been infinitely higher than who won or lost some trophy. He was far too old for Andrin, of course—at least twice her age, and probably more—but for just a moment, as she looked into those warm, somehow compassionate brown eyes, she felt a deep envy of Alazon Yanamar.

"I promise I won't walk all over your slippers, Your Highness," Kinlafia told her with a twinkle. "Mind you, I wouldn't have promised any such thing for this waltz, but the next dance is from New Farnal, which means I actually know the steps."

He smiled so winningly she had to chuckle, despite her mood.

"I'd be delighted," she told him, and the crowd of disappointed aspirants parted like ice floes around the bows of a Farnalian icebreaker as he escorted her towards the head of the line forming for the next dance.

"You'll have to excuse me for a moment again, dearling," she told Finena, and the falcon launched from her gauntleted left wrist. Fortunately, the Caliraths' attachment to their falcons was sufficiently well known—not to say notorious—that no one seemed particularly astonished or upset when Finena went flashing overhead. The falcon settled on her perch, under the watchful eyes of Brahndys chan Gordahl and Ulthar chan Habikon, and Andrin offered her hand to Kinlafia.

"Thank you, Your Highness." He bent over it, pressed a kiss to its back, and then they took their places as the orchestra played the first few bars of a New Farnal country melody and the step-caller called out the circle dance's first movement.

The dance was far more lively than the stylized, refined waltz which had preceded it. Kinlafia was obviously familiar with the steps, although, despite his athleticism, he was not Howan Fai Goutin's equal as a dancer. Yet there was something profoundly soothing about him, and Andrin found herself actually laughing with delight as he twirled her through the dance's movements. And as she did, she realized it was precisely for that moment of escape that Kinlafia had asked her to dance.

It came to an end at last, and she tucked her hand into his elbow. He started to escort her back to where her abandoned suitors waited, but she looked up at him with a winsome smile.

"If you please, Voice Kinlafia," she said, "I think I'd prefer a glass of lemonade."

"Nothing could please me more, Your Highness."

From one of the nobly born butterflies who had been fluttering about her so assiduously all evening, it would have been a pleasant nothing. From Kinlafia, it was a completely sincere statement, and she squeezed his elbow gently. He glanced down at her with a small smile, and she realized there was no need to explain to him what that squeeze was for.

Lazima chan Zindico trailed watchfully along behind, his eyes searching constantly for any tiny flaw in the crowd, any possible sign of danger for his charge.

He didn't find one, of course, which didn't prevent him from settling into what Andrin privately thought of as his "brooding protector mode" as Kinlafia seated her at one of the small, candlelit tables placed to catch the pleasant evening breeze swirling in through the wall of opened double doors. Kinlafia glanced at chan Zindico with a much more measuring eye than most of the young sprouts who had pestered Andrin all night ever showed. Obviously, the Voice recognized chan Zindico for what—and who—he truly was, whereas most of the spoiled, pampered aristocrats saw him only as one more item of furniture. Andrin liked that.

Kinlafia disappeared for a moment or two, then returned with not one glass of punch, but four . . . and Prince Howan Fai Goutin and Alazon Yanamar. Andrin thanked the Voice for the glass and raised it to her lips a bit more quickly than she might otherwise have to hide her smile. She'd wondered when Alazon would turn up. She also wondered how long it would be before the reporters noticed that wherever "candidate Kinlafia" happened to be, the Emperor's Privy Voice was virtually certain to turn up, and vice versa. The thought tickled her fancy, and her eyes gleamed mischievously as she considered how she might twit the two of them. The two Voices were busy looking at one another, and Andrin's dancing eyes met Prince Howan's equally amused gaze for just a moment.

"Forgive me, Voice Kinlafia," she said then, lowering her glass, "but I've noticed that some of the papers and some of the Voice reports are commenting on how much time you seem to be spending here in the Palace. There's speculation that your presence here indicates you've decided to become one of 'Zindel's men.'"

She paused, and Kinlafia cocked his head slightly to one side.

"I've seen the reports, Your Highness," he said. "May I ask why you mention them?"

"I know from something Yanamar said that Father didn't want it to seem as if he was too openly supporting your candidacy. But I've also noticed he seems to be spending an extraordinary amount of time talking to you . . . especially for someone who hasn't even won election yet. I was just wondering if you and he had changed your minds about the possible implications of his openly supporting you. Or, at least, *appearing* to support you?"

She looked at him very steadily, and saw something like recognition flicker back in those brown eyes of his, but he didn't reply immediately. Instead, he sat there for several seconds, gazing at her thoughtfully—much as Shamir Taje might have. That thought danced through the back of Andrin's brain, and as it did, she realized that one of the things which most appealed to her about Kinlafia was that he and Taje were the only two men, apart from her father, who didn't seem to care about her youthfulness when she asked a question. They actually thought about those questions, about their responses to them, because they extended respect to the person asking them, not simply out of courtesy to the *title* of that person.

Then he tilted his head to one side, glancing at Prince Howan, and arched one eyebrow.

"King Junni has become one of Father's closer allies, Voice Kinlafia," Andrin told him. "I don't think we need to worry about the Prince's discretion, do we, Your Highness?"

"Most assuredly not, Your Grand Imperial Highness," Prince Howan responded with a slight smile. His Ternathian had improved enormously over the last couple of months, thanks in no small part to the services of a Voice language tutor, and the irony in his tone came through perfectly. Then his expression sobered. "Still, I will certainly understand if Voice Kinlafia would prefer to answer your question in privacy."

The Eniathian prince started to stand, but Kinlafia shook his head.

"If Her Highness trusts your discretion, Prince Howan, then certainly I do, as well," he said. The prince looked at him for a moment, then inclined his head in a small bow which mingled acknowledgment and appreciation of the implicit compliment. He sat back down, and Kinlafia turned to Andrin.

"Actually, Your Highness, I don't really think you were wondering about campaign strategies at all, were you?"

Andrin's eyes widened. Despite what she'd just been thinking, his directness—and perceptiveness—surprised her. No wonder Alazon was so attracted to him!

"You're right," she admitted. "I suppose I'm just not used to asking such questions directly."

"With all due respect, Your Highness," Alazon put in, "you should get used to it." Andrin looked at her, and the Privy Voice shrugged. "You happen to be Heir-Secondary, Your Highness. Yes, you're young. But don't let the natural deference of youth keep you from asking the questions you need to ask and demanding the answers to them."

Andrin glanced at Prince Howan, the only other person at the table remotely her own age. His expression gave away very little, but she thought she saw a trace of agreement in his almond eyes as he looked at the Privy Voice. And as Andrin considered the advice herself, she remembered that Alazon Yanamar was far more than simply her father's Privy Voice. She thought about it for several seconds, then nodded in acknowledgment and moved her eyes back to Kinlafia.

"Taking Alazon's advice, Voice Kinlafia, *am* I just imagining that Father—and First Councilor Taje—both seem to be treating you much more as if you'd been a family adviser for years than like someone who just got back from Hell's Gate less than two weeks ago?"

"I—" Kinlafia began, and paused. He looked very thoughtful for a moment or two, then he gave a little shrug of his own—very much like Alazon's had been—and nodded.

"I wouldn't say they regard me as any sort of *adviser*, Your Highness. And they certainly don't regard me as any sort of retainer, or as some sort of official member of your household or administration. But there have been certain . . . developments, since your brother sent that flatteringly inaccurate letter of recommendation to your father. I'd really rather not go into all of them at this point, but—" he looked into her eyes once more "—some of them, at least, concern you."

"Me?" Andrin's pulse fluttered ever so slightly as she remembered her own thoughts during the Unification Parade. "Is it something Father's Glimpsed?" she asked.

"To some extent, yes."

She could tell Kinlafia hadn't really wanted to admit that, yet she felt strangely certain he'd never been tempted to lie to her, however diplomatically. The front of her brain told her she should take her cue from him, let it rest where it was. She'd already learned more than she'd really expected to, after all.

"Can you tell me what he's Seen?" she asked, instead.

"No, Your Highness. Not without his permission, I'm afraid."

Andrin felt a quick, brief flicker of anger—a spike of almost-rage, made far stronger by the background of her endless days of anxiety and fear for Janaki—and Kinlafia was a Voice. She knew he'd felt her anger, but he only looked back at her steadily, and anger turned into respect.

"I can . . . appreciate your discretion, Voice Kinlafia," she told him after a moment. "That's not to say I don't wish you could be more forthcoming." She sipped from her lemonade glass once more, then lowered it. "I'm sure you're well aware that Father and I have been experiencing an entire cascade of Glimpses for the past several days. It's a very . . . uncomfortable sensation. It worries me. No, it *scares* me, and I suppose that makes me more anxious than usual for some kind of reassurance."

"I do know about the Glimpses, Your Highness."

He looked across the table at her, his eyes filled with a compassion which seemed somehow only warmer and deeper because of her awareness of what he himself had endured. He was like her father in some ways, she realized. From a different sequence of causes, perhaps, but with that same inner core of strength. Not so much of toughness, or hardness, but of purpose. Of determination to meet whatever challenges the Triad might see fit to throw before them.

Was he always like that, I wonder? Or did what happened to him at Fallen Timbers change him that deeply?

"I will tell you this, Your Highness," he continued. "Your father—as I'm sure you need no one in the multiverse to tell you—loves you very, very deeply. I haven't known you very long myself, but I can already understand why that is. I've told your father that if I win election to Parliament, my opinions will be my own, and that if I disagree with him, I'll say so. I meant that then, and I mean it now. But since then, I've been privileged to come to know him—and you—far better than I ever expected I would. And speaking as Darcel Kinlafia, not Voice Kinlafia, and not Parliamentary Representative Kinlafia, I would count it an honor if you would call upon me for anything you need."

Andrin's eyes widened once more in fresh surprise. People told her father—and her, to some extent—that sort of thing every day. Sometimes they even meant it. But coming from Kinlafia, it was . . . different, somehow. There was an echo almost of what she often sensed from chan Zindico and her other personal armsmen, and yet that wasn't quite correct, either. Chan Zindico and the others were her family's loyal retainers—her servants, when it came right down to it. Even though it would never have occurred to her to think of them as such, *they* were always aware of that relationship. It helped define not simply how they regarded her, but who they themselves *were*.

Darcel Kinlafia didn't see her that way. She'd never been "his" grand imperial princess, although she supposed that was technically going to change in about eighteen hours. There was no institutional, dynastic sense of loyalty in what he'd just said, and in a way Andrin doubted she would ever be able to explain, even to herself, that made the sincerity of what he'd just said indescribably precious. He meant it when he said he would be honored to help her, and there was no reason why he had to be. No basis for her to simply expect him to be.

"Voice Kinlafia, I—"

She paused, her eyes burning strangely, and he reached across the table and very gently took her hand. It could have been a presumption, an intrusion, but instead of drawing back, her wrist turned as if of its own volition, meeting his hand palm-to-palm, and as she felt him squeeze her fingers, something clicked almost audibly deep down inside her. The bumblebees buzzed louder under her skin, the sound almost deafening, and something seemed to literally flow from her fingers into his hand. She'd never experienced anything like it, never heard of anyone experiencing anything like it, and she inhaled sharply, her nostrils flared.

"Your Highness?" she heard chan Zindico say from behind her, his voice sharpening with the instinctive bristle of the deadly guard dog he truly was. "Are you all right, Your Highness?"

"I'm fine, Lazima."

She turned her head to smile reassuringly up at him, then looked back at Kinlafia. The Voice must have recognized chan Zindico's flare of suspicion, but his expression was calm, almost tranquil.

"Voice Kinlafia, I think—" she began, only to break off abruptly as Alazon Yanamar jerked upright in her chair.

The Privy Voice might have been carved from ice, so still she sat, as she Listened to whatever message had arrived with such abrupt, brutal unexpectedness. And then, her eyes filled suddenly with tears.

"*Alazon?*" Andrin said quickly, urgently. She took her hand from Kinlafia's, reaching out to the older woman as Alazon's pain reached out to her. "What is it? What's wrong?"

Alazon closed her eyes, her face wrung with an anguish so deep, so bitter, that Andrin literally flinched. She saw Kinlafia responding to his beloved's grief, as well. He reached out towards Alazon, and only later did Andrin realize that he'd reached out towards *her*, not Alazon, first.

Andrin leaned towards Alazon across the table, unable to imagine what had hurt the older woman so. And then, abruptly, she realized the music had stopped. That an ocean of utter silence was flowing out from the ballroom, sweeping over the entire palace. She turned her head, looking through the arched colonnade back into the ballroom, trying to understand the sudden stillness. And then, at last, Alazon spoke.

"Your Highness," the anguish, the grief, in Alazon's beautiful voice ripped at Andrin like a knife. "Your Highness," the Privy Voice said, "your father needs you."

CHAPTER THIRTY-FOUR

DARCEL KINLAFIA FOLLOWED Andrin and chan Zindico back into the ballroom. It was one of the hardest things he'd ever done, and his right arm tightened protectively around Alazon as the sledgehammers of shock, disbelief, grief, and fury hammered at their Voice's sensitivity.

Yet if it was terrible for them, it was still worse for Andrin, for she *knew* what her father was about to tell her.

He saw it in the way all color had drained out of her face, Felt it in the emotional aura trailing behind her like a fog of smoke and poison. Yet she crossed that ballroom floor tall, straight, and graceful.

"Yes, Papa?"

Her voice cut through the stillness, the silence, with an impossible clearness as she stopped before her parents. Her mother's face was as white as her own, but Empress Varena's eyes were filled with the dark terror of the unknown, not the even darker ghosts foreknowledge inflicted. Emperor Zindel's right arm was about his wife's shoulders, and his face was strained.

"Andrin." His deep, powerful voice sounded frayed about the edges, and his arm tightened around his wife. "We've just received word from Traisum. From Division-Captain chan Geraith. It's—"

His voice broke, and his left hand rose. It settled on the back of the empress' head, cradling it protectively, as he turned her and folded her against his massive chest. His own head bent as he bowed over her slenderness, and the tears of a strong man gleamed in his eyes.

"It's Janaki," Andrin said. Her father looked up, and she met his eyes levelly, steadily. "He's been killed."

The empress stiffened convulsively in her husband's arms. There was no word to describe the sound she made. It was far too soft to call a wail, yet too filled with pain to be called anything else. She shuddered, and the sound she'd made turned into something else—shattering sobs that filled the hollow silence.

"Yes," Andrin's father confirmed in a voice which had been pulverized and glued unskillfully back together once more.

Andrin swayed. Her regal head never drooped, yet Kinlafia could literally See the wave of agony that flowed through her. He stepped away from Alazon quickly, offering the princess his arm, and she took it blindly, without even looking at him.

Gods, he thought. *Dear sweet gods. If Janaki's dead, then* Andrin *is—*

"We have to go," her father told her across her sobbing mother's head.

"Of course, Papa." Andrin straightened her spine with a courage which made Kinlafia want to weep, and despite the tears which streaked her face and fogged her tone, her voice never wavered. "Razial and Anbessa will need us."

* * *

"How is she? How are *they*?"

Alazon looked up at the harsh, angry question, and shook her head.

"I don't know, love," she replied quietly. "The Empress and Razial are sedated. His Majesty is holding himself together—I don't know how. And I don't believe Anbessa really understands what's happened. Not yet."

"And Andrin?"

"She's just . . . sitting there," Alazon said sadly. "Sitting there in the nursery, beside Anbessa's bed. Razial's asleep in her arms—she cried herself out, poor little love, after the herbalist sedated her. Andrin—" Alazon's voice broke, and she raised gray eyes, soaked with tears, to Kinlafia's. "Andrin . . . sang them both to sleep," she managed to get out.

She began to weep once more, weep with deep, tearing shudders, and Kinlafia put his arms around her, hugging her tightly while his own eyes burned.

Again, he thought. *The bastards have done it* again.

His jaw clenched so tightly he thought his teeth would shatter as memories ripped through him, and white-hot rage boiled in their wake. The same Arcanan butchers who'd murdered Shaylar and all of his friends—his family—at Fallen Timbers. They'd done it *again*.

Despite his earlier conversation with the Emperor, or perhaps because of it, the pain of Janaki's death was like some huge, jagged splinter buried in his chest. And with that pain came the anger, the fury, that the Arcanans could wreak such carnage on the hearts and souls of those for whom he cared even here, even in the very heart of Sharona.

His eyes burned even hotter as he thought about

all the men he'd known, fought with. The men who'd avenged Shaylar's murder—Balkar chan Tesh, Grafin Halifu, Rokam Traygan, Delokahn Yar, Hulmok Arthag. . . . If the Arcanans had penetrated as deeply as Fort Salby, managed to kill Janaki, then all of those others—still more of Darcel Kinlafia's *friends*—must have been killed or captured first.

And now the treacherous murderers had killed the heir to the throne himself . . . and devastated his family.

"Is there anything *I* can do?" he whispered almost pleadingly into Alazon's hair. "Anything at all?"

"I—" she began.

"There *will* be something you can do, Voice Kinlafia," another, deeper voice interrupted Alazon's, and she and Kinlafia looked up quickly as Zindel chan Calirath strode into the room.

He looked in that moment, Kinlafia thought, like an Imperial Navy dreadnought with its main battery swinging out to bare its teeth as it forged into the teeth of a winter's gale. His face might have been hammered out of old iron, and his gray eyes were colder than chilled steel.

"Your Majesty?" Kinlafia said.

"There will be something," the Emperor repeated in a hard, flat voice. "I don't know what—not yet. But I know that much."

"Your Majesty, I—"

"You'll know what it is when the time comes, Darcel," Zindel said. "For now—" He drew a deep breath and raised both hands, scrubbing his face in his palms. "For now, all I know is that all the Arpathian hells together couldn't hold everything that's about to break loose right here in Tajvana."

His voice came out muffled by his hands, and Kinlafia looked at Alazon. Then both of them looked back at Zindel as the Emperor lowered his hands with a smile as bleak as northern sea-ice.

"Chava Busar is going to see his opportunity in this," the Emperor said. "Shamir Taje is out talking to the heads of the various delegations to the Conclave right now, and you can be damned certain Chava will soon have his . . . representatives doing exactly the same thing. They're going to use my son's death any way they can. As if what's happened to Janaki wasn't going to do damage enough all by itself."

"How bad is it, Your Majesty?" Alazon asked quietly.

"They've taken at least five universes," Zindel said flatly. "As far as we know, every soldier—and civilian—we had in those universes is either dead or prisoner. And somehow—" he met the two Voices' eyes "—they managed to keep a single Voice from getting the warning out, as well."

Kinlafia's belly muscles clenched, and he felt Alazon's sick awareness of what the Emperor was telling them.

"They've advanced over four thousand miles in less than *two weeks*," Zindel continued. "The sort of transport and logistics capability that suggests is going to be terrifying as soon as its implications sink in, and the existence of these . . . *dragons*, and these lion-eagle things of theirs, is going to be even worse. But, frankly, what's going to hit home the hardest, going to have the most catastrophic effect on public opinion, is that they launched this entire attack while they were *negotiating* with us."

Kinlafia's teeth grated together with fresh fury, and Zindel snorted with cold, bitter anger of his own.

"They've truly done it this time," he said harshly. "First, Shaylar's murder. Now this . . . this *treachery* and the murder of my son. The heir to the throne. The whole of Sharona is going to explode in fury. Any possible hope we ever had for stopping this insanity is gone forever. Whether we're ready for it or not, whether we want it or not, we're in a fight for our very survival, and my son—"

His voice broke savagely. It took him three tries to get it under control again.

"My son's death will *not* be in vain," he grated at last. "We're going to take every one of those portals back. We're going to drive those bastards back into the universe they came from. And I don't mean the universe on the other side of the portal you helped capture, Darcel—I mean their *home* universe. We're going to shove them back and bottle them up and blow them apart so hard it'll knock them back into the godsdamned *Stone Age*." He stared hard into Kinlafia's eyes. "And you, Parliamentary Representative Kinlafia, are going to help me do it."

"Yes, Sir." Kinlafia met that hard, bitter stare of steel across Alazon's head and nodded once, sharply. "Yes, Your Majesty," he agreed in the voice of a man swearing an oath. "No matter *what* it takes."

"Good."

Zindel's voice was different, too. It was the voice of an emperor accepting an oath of fealty. Then the grief, the anguish, in his eyes shifted. It turned into something else, equally hard, and yet somehow almost . . . desperate.

"And the other thing you're going to help me do, Darcel—" he added in a chilling tone "—you and Alazon both—is to find a way to keep that bastard Busar from forcing Andrin to marry one of his monstrous sons."

Kinlafia's heart lurched.

"*Oh, dear gods. . . .*" he half-whispered.

How could he have missed it? He'd already realized that Andrin had just become the Crown Princess of Sharona, or shortly would, and that meant—

"I will personally put a bullet through every last one of Chava Busar's sons before I let *any* of them marry your daughter, Your Majesty," he said, and felt Alazon shudder in his arms. Shudder with the thought of Andrin wed to any member of Chava's family . . . and with her Voice's knowledge that he meant every single word he'd just said.

"Good." Zindel chan Calirath's eyes could have frozen the heart of hell itself, but then he made himself inhale deeply.

"Good," he repeated. "But now let's try to figure out a way to stop it *without* throwing our world into a civil war at the same time we have to deal with these Arcanan butchers."

"Yes, Your Majesty."

Kinlafia nodded and the Emperor turned to Alazon.

"Shamir is canvassing our allies' delegations," he told her. It was a sign of his own grief and shock that, despite his outward self-control, he'd clearly forgotten that he'd already told them that. "I expect him back within the hour. Please contact the members of the Privy Council. This crisis won't wait; tell them we'll meet two hours from now, and I want Orem Limana present, as well. We'll need him to help us coordinate portal traffic."

"Yes, Your Majesty."

"Thank you. Thank you both," Zindel said.

Then he drew a deep breath, turned and walked back out the door through which he'd entered the room. Kinlafia heard the sound of weeping from beyond that door, and the Emperor moved like an exhausted swimmer in deep water as he returned to his grieving family.

The door closed behind him, and Alazon buried her face in Kinlafia's shoulder and spent one long, desperate moment weeping while he held her close. Then she tilted her face up and gave him a trembling smile full of courage, and he kissed her very gently.

"Let me know when you have a free moment," he said. "I'll feed you some dinner and rub your feet."

"*That's* an offer more precious than diamonds," she said, making herself smile once again even while her eyes swam with fresh tears. "Consider it a date."

She rose on her toes to kiss him once more, and then they both gathered themselves to face what must come next.

* * *

Chava Busar stood in his strategically chosen spot beside the buffet tables, watching the hysterics which were now fully underway in the Grand Ballroom, and worked hard to keep from smiling in delight.

The truth was still sinking in, he thought. Out on the dance floor, women sobbed into silk handkerchiefs and men wore murderous expressions. He heard curses and vows of dire vengeance in a score of languages, and the sound was sweet, sweet to his ears.

Janaki chan Calirath had gotten himself killed. Gotten his head nipped clean off like a chicken by some sort of huge bird or monster, if the rumors were to be believed.

It was absolutely delicious. In one fell swoop (his own choice of verb made him chuckle mentally behind his impassive expression, considering the nature of Janaki's executioner), the utter disaster which his political ambitions had suffered was reversed. All he had to do was grasp the opportunity swiftly and intelligently. By this time next week, that horse-shaped, gangling, hideous giant of a schoolgirl was going to find herself profoundly married. And not long after that . . .

He looked up as the Seneschal of Othmaliz waddled over to his corner of the ballroom. The seneschal contemplated the weepers and cursers, then looked Chava in the eye.

"What a pity," he said.

"Yes, isn't it?" Chava agreed, allowing one corner of his mouth to quirk upwards ever so slightly.

"I imagine tomorrow will be quite a busy day for us all," the seneschal continued. "There'll have to be another session of the Conclave to deal with this latest crisis. And, of course this is going to force a postponement of the Coronation. So sad." He sighed. "So very sad."

"True." Chava nodded, then cocked his head to one side. "One's heart goes out to the Emperor's family at such time, of course. Still, there are responsibilities which must be met, aren't there? And plans which must be adjusted. Or in some cases—" he looked deep into the seneschal's eyes "—accelerated. I do trust that the Comforters will be keeping the Emperor and his entire family in their thoughts."

"Oh, I think you need have no fear on those grounds, Your Majesty," the seneschal assured him.

* * *

Someone knocked on Darcel Kinlafia's door at three o'clock in the morning.

He jolted awake and jerked upright in bed, momentarily confused by the soft white moonlight falling through open windows where warm breeze stirred white draperies. He'd been dreaming of combat—a ghastly, nightmarish mishmash of his own memories, fighting at the swamp portal, the massacre of his survey crew, and the combat he'd seen through the Glimpse he'd shared with Zindel—and he wasn't certain, at first, what had awakened him.

Then the knock sounded again.

<*Darcel,*> a familiar Voice Called softly in the back of his brain, and he was out of bed in a heartbeat. He snatched up a night robe as he crossed the apartment, somehow managing, with the moonlight's aid, to avoid stubbing his toes as he dodged around the furniture of a living room to which he wasn't yet accustomed. Then he snatched the door open and found her standing in the hallway, trembling.

He didn't speak. He simply opened his arms, and she fell into them, weeping. He held her close, rocked her gently, then guided her into the living room. He drew her down beside him on the divan in a pool of moonlight, and she huddled against him while she sobbed.

He surrounded her with his arms, with his love, with the caress of his Voice and the bond between them. There were no words, for there was no need for words. There were only the two of them, clinging to one another in the midst of their grief, and that was enough.

"Reports are still coming in from Traisum," she whispered finally. "Chan Geraith's first report of the battle was relayed while he was still eleven hours out from Salbyton. He's sent three more since then. It's . . . horrible."

She relayed the images Kaliya chan Darma and Lisar chan Korthal had transmitted up the Voicenet. Images of Fort Salby, still smoking, with a huge, monstrous winged creature draped over one tower. Images of men burned into twisted charcoal, or lying like tattered scarecrows where lightning had left them. Bits and pieces of the bodies of Sharonian soldiers, and strewn among their mangled bodies the tumbled carcasses of the unnatural fusion of lion and eagle which had killed them. More bodies, breaches in a wall of adobe and stone, things which looked like horses, but obviously weren't, shattered platforms filled with the broken bodies of *Arcanan* soldiers, gun pits, row after row of bodies laid out in canvas shrouds . . .

They went on and on, a catalog of destruction and desecration, and Darcel Kinlafia fought the surge of acid trying to come up out of his belly. His arms tightened around Alazon, and he held her while she shared the horror with him.

The images ended at last, and he kissed her hair, murmuring wordlessly to her. He never knew how long they sat there, just being there for each other, clinging to their love like some last, unshakable rock of sanity in the midst of a multiverse gone mad.

"How are they holding up?" he asked finally.

"Andrin is sedated now, too," Alazon said. "She didn't want to take it, but His Majesty insisted. She wanted to stay with Razial and Anbessa, but she has to rest—really rest."

Kinlafia nodded, his jaw tightening once more.

"The Empress is in deep emotional shock," Alazon

continued. "She knew the danger was there, but somehow it seemed so remote, especially when Janaki was ordered home with the Arcanan prisoners. But I think . . . I think she'd guessed what's been worrying His Majesty and Andrin. She just didn't want to admit it to herself. He's her only son, Darcel, and—"

Her voice caught raggedly, and she shook herself.

"I already told you Razial had been sedated, but she's awake again. And Anbessa is finally realizing what's happened, I think. Both of them were clinging to their mother when I left the imperial apartments. And Zindel—"

Her voice broke off again.

"What about him?" Kinlafia pressed gently, and she inhaled deeply.

"I've never seen His Majesty like this. He can barely speak above a rasping whisper. It's more than just losing his only son. He feels responsible for the massacres, for failing to move quickly enough and get reinforcements forward soon enough."

"That's ridiculous!" Kinlafia snapped in hot defense. "I've worked that transit chain, Alazon. Nobody could have moved in troops or material any faster—*nobody*! He isn't a *god*, to wave one hand and magically transport a division!"

"I *know* all that, Darcel. And he knows that, too. But he's a Calirath. He feels responsible for the deaths, for the undermanned forts. And he's not the only one." Alazon shivered. "Orem Limana is nearly suicidal with remorse. He feels like he's betrayed them, all of them—soldiers and civilians—by trying to build new forts before he had troops in place to adequately man them. Before he had artillery in place to defend their walls."

"He's not a soldier," Kinlafia protested. "It's not his job to think like one. Besides, *no one* ever intended those portal forts to stand up to anything more dangerous than a few bands of brigands! There's never *been* anything more dangerous than a few bands of brigands—until now!"

"I know that, too." She nodded. "And the Emperor knows that. When Yaf Umani Spoke to me from Exploration Hall, he Said His Majesty's ordered two of the PA's Distance Viewers to watch the First Director twenty-four hours a day until this emotional shock passes. The Emperor has ordered Orem not to suicide."

That shocked Kinlafia. Orem Limana was one of the strongest men he'd ever known. If *he* was that shaken, then . . .

"What about the First Councilor's contacts with the other delegations?" he asked.

"It's going to be ugly," Alazon told him. "The Emperor was right about that, too. Isseth's requested an emergency meeting of the Conclave later this morning."

"*Isseth?*" Kinlafia repeated incredulously.

"Everyone knows perfectly well that Chava is really behind it," she said. "No one's going to admit it, though."

"And the Coronation?"

"That's been postponed," she said bitterly. "This 'spontaneous' request for a Conclave session supersedes it, under the circumstances."

"That's just wonderful."

"Actually," she said unwillingly, "it was inevitable. If Isseth hadn't requested it, we probably would have had to do it ourselves. Not that Isseth—or Chava—did it to do *us* any favors!"

Fresh anger swirled about deep inside Darcel Kinlafia,

but he made himself step back from it. He remembered what Janaki had told him about the deadliness of hatred, yet that wasn't what let him step away from the demons of his inner fury. No, it was the woman in his arms. The lifeline he clung to. And as he did, he felt her clinging to him, in turn. Their strength flowed together, melding, merging into something greater than the sum of its parts, and he turned her tear-soaked face up to his and kissed it gently.

"All right," he said softly. "His Majesty was right about Andrin needing to rest. Well, so do we. Come with me."

He stood, then scooped her up in his arms and carried her through the moonlight towards his bedroom door. She looked up at him, and he smiled crookedly.

<I said "rest," love,> he Told her, *<and I* meant *rest. There'll be time for other things later.>*

<I didn't realize you were so chivalrous,> her Voice murmured in the back of his mind. *<Refusing to take advantage of a maiden's grief.>*

He laughed softly, despite their grief, despite their loss, and kissed her once again.

<Chivalrous isn't exactly a word I'd apply to myself, love. Let's try . . . patient, instead.>

<I prefer chivalrous,> she Told him. *<And in this case, I think I may just know you better than you know yourself.>*

<Maybe. But either way, woman,> he turned back the light spread at one side of the enormous bed and tucked her under it, *<you need* rest. *And so do I. So—>* he bent over to kiss her once again, very gently *<—go to sleep.>*

CHAPTER THIRTY-FIVE

THE TENSION IN the Emperor Garim Chancellery could have been used to chip flint as Darcel Kinlafia settled into the place in the gallery to which his candidacy for the House of Talents entitled him.

The sunlight streaming in through the windows framed in the black-and-white banners of mourning revealed a very different set of faces from the ones he'd seen there just the day before. The vast majority of naysayers and fence-sitters had disappeared. Today's faces were shaken, sick . . . and enraged.

Zindel chan Calirath, who should have been at the Temple of Saint Taiy, preparing for his coronation, sat like a statue of Ternathian granite. The black mourning band around his right arm was matched by the bands around the arms of every other man and woman in that enormous chamber, and the flags of every nation of Sharona flew at half-mast. The death of the heir to any imperial throne was always a world-shaking event; the death of this particular heir had shaken an entire universe to its foundation.

Andrin Calirath sat beside her father, her own face

pale and drawn with grief. The preparation of her Glimpse had done nothing to lessen her sorrow or the profound, brutal shock of her loss, and nothing could have prepared her to deal with her younger sisters' grief. She'd argued against her father's decision the night before, but she knew now that he'd been correct. She *had* needed rest . . . and she was profoundly grateful that her mother and sisters had no official reason to be here this morning. Indeed, she wished desperately that *she* hadn't had to be here, either. But there was absolutely no choice about that, despite her youth.

With Janaki's death, Andrin Calirath, at seventeen, had become not Heir-Secondary to the Winged Crown of Ternathia, but Heir Apparent to the Throne of Sharona, and all the crushing weight of the multiverse seemed to be bearing down upon her shoulders.

I should still be with my tutors, a small voice wailed in the back of her mind. *I'm not* ready *for this—it wasn't supposed to be* my *job!*

Yet even as that little voice cried out in protest, she knew it *was* her job. That it had always been here, waiting for her, if anything happened to Janaki.

Shamir Taje, unlike Andrin, was not in his place at his Emperor's elbow. Since the formal ratification of the Act of Unification, Taje, as the effective First Councilor of the worldwide empire to be, had replaced Orem Limana as the presiding officer of the Conclave. Under the terms of the Unification, the Conclave was to continue to function as the effective caretaker government of the new empire until after the formal parliamentary elections scheduled for two months after the official Coronation. Now, that Conclave's members sat almost as still as Zindel as Taje stepped up to the podium Orem Limana had occupied when it first assembled.

"This Conclave is now in session," Taje announced. "All rise for the invocation."

That morning, the invocation was short and to the point: *Guard us, heavenly protectors, and help us choose wisely in this battle to save ourselves.*

Then Taje took the podium once again.

"As all of us, I'm sure, have already been informed," he said, his voice harsh and rusty with fatigue, "Crown Prince Janaki chan Calirath has fallen in battle against the enemies of Sharona. Regiment-Captain chan Skrithik and Division-Captain chan Geraith both agree that it was only the Prince's Glimpses which allowed Fort Salby to hold. And—" he looked up, forced to clear his throat hard, despite all his years of political experience "—the Division-Captain has confirmed that Prince Janaki knew it was a Death Glimpse before he chose to remain as part of the garrison defending Fort Salby and Salbyton's civilian population."

There was a moment of profound silence, and then Taje straightened his shoulders.

"Rather than rehearse the truly harrowing details, which have been summarized in reports that are being bound for distribution as we speak, I will turn the podium over to His Imperial Majesty, the Emperor-Elect of Sharona. But first, I ask that all please rise and bow heads for a moment of silence to honor the Crown Prince and the thousands of others that we estimate have been murdered in this Arcanan assault."

Kinlafia heard Temple bells tolling in the distance as the word raced out through Tajvana and the rest of Sharona, signaling Voices across the world to sound the bells in honor of their dead, royal and common, military and civilian. He shivered as he listened to those deep, rolling tones of grief and respect. He'd never heard so many Temple bells at one time. The sound reverberated through the city, through his bones. They rang out their dirge for five full minutes, calling to the thousands of Sharonian souls trying to find their way to the heavens of home.

In the end, the last shivery tone died into silence, and Zindel chan Calirath took the podium.

It was obvious he hadn't slept. Kinlafia's seat was close enough for him to see the bloodshot eyes, haggard with dark circles. The Emperor gripped the sides of the podium for long, silent moments, simply standing there in the heartlessly plain black and white mourning tunic and trousers instead of the jeweled coronation robes he ought to have been wearing.

Then he began to speak.

"Over the past several weeks," he rasped, his deep voice rough-edged with fatigure and grief, "we have wondered and debated over Arcana's possible intentions. Those intentions are now brutally clear. We neither asked for nor provoked this war. We attempted to deal fairly and openly with the enemy—only to be met with treachery and escalating violence.

"I have been closeted with the Chiefs of Staff, the elected Speakers of this Conclave, and the first Director of the Portal Authority for most of the night. We've discussed threats and options for meeting them, and we have reached the following decisions.

"We are instituting an immediate recall to active duty of every soldier, sailor, and marine under the age of forty. We realize the terrible hardship this will place on families and businesses, but we have no choice. Our standing army is far too small to fight a war of this magnitude. If circumstances force our hand, we will recall all former military personnel under the age of *fifty*, placing those with health and eyesight difficulties in administrative slots that must also be filled in order to make this war effort succeed.

"We are also asking for emergency volunteers from the Talents to fill critical positions in communications, intelligence gathering, medical care, and many other areas. If we cannot fill those needed positions through volunteerism, we will have no choice but to institute conscription."

Shock detonated through every Talented delegate to the Conclave. Even Darcel was stunned by the suggestion. Of all the major Sharonan nations, only Uromathia practiced conscription. Ternathia, Farnalia, Harkala, and New Ternath and New Farnal all relied upon a tradition of voluntary military service. So did virtually all of the smaller Sharonian nations, and even in Uromathia, the Talents were automatically exempt from conscription because they were so relatively scarce, as necessary to the civilian infrastructure as to the military. What Zindel had just suggested—or threatened—was unprecedented, hadn't happened in over four hundred years, and a roar of protest rose. It hammered at the Chancellery's banner-hung walls and—

"You will be silent!"

Zindel chan Calirath's bull-throated bellow stunned the entire vast chamber into silence.

"By our best estimate, judging from when we initially lost contact with our forces in Hell's Gate," he said into the ringing stillness, biting off each rough-edged, husky word like a sliver of bone, "the Arcanans advanced over four thousand miles in approximately *twelve days*. They are now little more than forty-four thousand miles from Sharona. If they launch a second—and successful—assault on Fort Salby and continue to advance at the same pace, they could cover the remaining distance to this very city in barely three months. Do not presume to protest *anything* the Throne demands in a war of survival. We don't have time for it, and I will *not* let any of you jeopardize all of us. *Is that clear?*"

No one said a word, and Zindel chan Calirath's nostrils flared with satisfaction.

"Good," he said much more quietly. "Then understand this, as well—all of you. We did not start this war, but we *will* finish it. We will take back the portals they've taken from us in their treacherous attack. We will punish the atrocities they have committed against our people. And we will insure that this 'Union of Arcana' will never again pose a threat to us, to our children, or to our *grand*children."

A roar of approval went up, louder by far than the previous protest. Kinlafia found himself on his feet with the rest, applauding madly, yet even as he did, he looked down from the gallery at Chava Busar's face and saw the cold, calculating eyes that watched Zindel with carefully veiled contempt.

When the tumult finally died, Zindel continued his implacable, methodical outline of his preparations. Troops to be raised and trained, railroads to be extended, shipyards to be built, munitions factories to be expanded, fortifications to be planned and built, weapons to be improved, developed, and deployed . . . the list went on and on, marshaling the resources of every universe

Sharona had ever explored and hammering them into a weapon of war.

"What I require from you," he finished finally, "is the immediate passage of sufficient taxation to pay for these utterly critical measures. We do not have time to wait for formal parliamentary elections. The Arcanans have taken that luxury out of our hands. When those elections are held, I will seek approval of our present emergency revenue measures from that Parliament, but they must be passed *now*, and they will not be a negligible burden for anyone. This will be an expensive war. Never doubt that. Every Sharonian will feel the bite of higher taxes, and that bite will be deep. Many will protest when they realize just *how* deep. But when they do, ask them this question. Which do you prefer—higher taxes and higher prices, or Arcanan dragons in your skies, burning down your homes and loved ones? *That* is their choice. We did not ask for this war, but we will, by the Triad, fight it with everything we have—with every ounce of strength we possess!"

Another ovation met that statement, although it was more subdued than the last one. Talk of things like higher taxes and conscripted labor forces had that effect.

"That concludes my prepared remarks," Zindel said when silence had fallen once again. "Does anyone have questions? Not debate—questions?"

No one spoke for several seconds, but then the Emperor of Uromathia stood in the heart of his own delegation.

"Your Majesty," he began, bowing in Zindel's direction, "and esteemed colleagues, Uromathia shares the profound grief which the heroic death of Crown Prince Janaki has brought to all of Sharona and applauds the

Emperor of Ternathia's determination to deal with this crisis."

Something flared deep inside Kinlafia as Chava said the word "Ternathia."

"However," Chava continued, "while no one could deny the necessity of the measures which he has outlined, Uromathia must question whether or not he possesses the authority to demand them." A stir of protest began, but he continued speaking, clearly and strongly. "It is unfortunately true that Crown Prince Janaki's death has reordered both the Ternathian imperial succession and the proposed succession of the Empire of Sharona. And it is also unfortunately true that as of this moment, there *is* no 'Emperor of Sharona,' nor an Empire for him to rule. There has been no Coronation, and the conditions specified by the Act of Unification for the Empire he is to rule have not been—and cannot, as written, be—satisfied."

"What are you suggesting?" Ronnel of Farnalia demanded furiously.

"I am simply suggesting," Chava replied, "that this is a time of enormous uncertainty, and that under those circumstances, it is particularly important that all these matters be handled in strict accordance with the provisions under which the nations represented at this Conclave agreed to surrender their sovereignty. Yes, we are at war. Yes, it may be a war for our very survival. But if we are to face our enemies as a single, cohesive whole, we *must* be truly united, and there must be no question of the legality and legitimacy of the government under which we will fight."

"Come to the point—quickly," Zindel chan Calirath said icily.

"Very well, Your Majesty." Chava bowed once more. "My point is this. The death of your son has invalidated Section Three of Article Two of the Act of Unification. Unless the provisions of that article and section are satisfied, the Act is not binding upon Uromathia or any other signatory power. If there is to be a true Empire of Sharona, then I must respectfully request that the succession be secured as contemplated by Article Two in light of the changed circumstances resulting from your son's lamentable death. Is Crown Princess Andrin ready to marry the son I designate as her groom?"

A savage roar of outrage erupted. Half the members of the Conclave were on their feet, shouting and demanding Chava's ejection from the Chancellery, and Zindel's hands tightened on the podium with such force that Kinlafia expected the wood to crack. Then the gavel crashed down again and again, hammering for order, and all the while, Chava stood in the tumult, eyes defiantly insolent and wearing a smug little half-smile of satisfaction.

The furor died down at last, trickling slowly away into silence. When the entire Chancellery was still once more, the Emperor turned his attention back to Chava Busar.

The Uromathian's smile faltered as Zindel chan Calirath's icy gray eyes bored into him with scalpel-sharp contempt.

"The son *you* designate?" the Emperor said, and Chava actually blanched at the menace in his deadly soft voice. "Haven't you overstepped your authority by presuming to name which of your lecherous, ill-bred mongrels will have the right to rape my daughter?"

Chava Busar's face went sickly white with shock, then purple with rage.

"How *dare* you—?!" he began.

"*Do not presume to dictate terms to me!*" Zindel thundered.

"I—" Chava began again, but a third voice interrupted him. It was a youthful voice, a soprano, which had never been raised in that Chancellery before.

"Do not discuss me as if I were not here!" that voice said with icy precision, and every eye turned to the Ternathian delegation.

Andrin Calirath stood there, and the golden strands in her midnight hair seemed thicker, brighter than ever, gleaming as she faced the combined leaders and rulers of her entire planet. She stood in her black mourning gown, with its bodice of stark, pitilessly unadorned white, like a votive candle burning before the Triad's altar in its holder of polished ebony, and her eyes were Calirath eyes—haunted by portents of a future dark as the mourning band about her sleeve, yet hard with the lightning flash of purpose. In some indefinable fashion she looked like both the teenaged girl she was and the avatar of Sharona's future—tall, strong, fearless, and wounded.

Emperor Zindel stared at his daughter, and his eyes were no longer those of an emperor. They were the eyes of a father, stark with fear for a daughter he loved more than life itself. They were the eyes of a man who had been asked for one sacrifice too many, of a man who could not—*would* not—give his family's juggernaut destiny his daughter, as well as his son. And they were the eyes, Darcel Kinlafia realized, of someone who recognized in this instant one fragment of the Glimpse he and Kinlafia had shared.

That man opened his mouth, his face hard with bitter

determination, but the daughter looked up at her father and shook her head.

"Chanaka s'hari, Halian. Sho warak," Crown Princess Andrin Calirath said softly, and her father's face twisted as if the words had been bullets.

Yaf Umani was one of Sharona's foremost linguisticians. He'd never held a position in any university's Department of Ancient Languages—his career as the Portal Authority's Chief Voice had precluded that—but he had a true Voice's love for languages . . . and he was one of the very few people in that enormous chamber who recognized the language in which she'd spoken. He was also a man of impeccable integrity, but the shocks had come too hard and fast over the past fourteen hours; his recognition of what Andrin had said leaked out to every Voice in the Chancellery.

"I am your daughter, Halian. I remember."

Silence hovered, and then, slowly—so slowly—Zindel chan Calirath bowed his head.

Andrin smiled at him almost gently. But then she turned to look across the Chancellery, with its endless tiers of men and women, and there was no gentleness in the tempered steel of the eyes which fixed themselves upon the Emperor of Uromathia.

"I beg leave to inform Emperor Chava that his concerns are premature," she said clearly and distinctly. "The Act of Unification has been neither nullified nor invalidated by my brother's death, nor will the House of Calirath seek to evade its obligations under that Act. There is still an heir to the throne of Ternathia, and that heir is prepared to accept *her* obligations under the subsection Emperor Chava has just cited.

"But I am the Imperial Crown Princess of Ternathia,

Heir to the Winged Crown of Celaryon, daughter of the House of Calirath, descendent of Halian and Erthain the Great!" Her eyes flashed gray lightning, and her voice rang out like a soprano sword. It was no longer the voice of a teenaged girl. The voice of the most ancient lineage in human history had taken its place in that Conclave. It stood before them in a gown of mourning, crowned in hair of golden-stranded black silk, and all the weight of that lineage crackled in its pride and defiance . . . and anger. "My ancestors were emperors of half the world while yours were still picking lice, raiding their neighbors' sheep, and stealing their neighbors' wives. You will *not* dictate to me the man I will marry, Chava Busar!"

Busar's face darkened in fresh rage, but Andrin's eyes were deadly, and she continued speaking with that cold, lethal precision.

"Subsection Three of Article Two requires the Heir to Ternathia to wed a Uromathian royal prince within three months of the ratification of the Act of Unification, and that Act was ratified two weeks ago. Very well. You will submit to me no later than noon tomorrow a list of those you wish to nominate as my husband. You may list every unmarried male of your lineage, if such is your desire. But I, Chava Busar—*I*, and no one else—will make *my* choice from all the eligible nominees. I will marry as the Act requires, within the next ten weeks, but do not *ever* make the mistake of attempting to dictate to a member of *my* House again!"

EPILOGUE

THE SUN HAD SET hours ago.

The slider car raced up what should have been the valley of the Razinta River almost silently, but for the rush of wind. It was a cloudy, moonless night, cold and still . . . and very, very empty.

The Arcanans called the Razinta the "Kosal," and they'd traveled almost eighteen hundred miles across the face of the universe they called Lamia to reach it, racing steadily southwest towards the next portal in their endless journey. From the maps Jasak had shown them, that portal lay some miles south of Usarlah, the capital of the province of Delkrath back in Sharona, almost in the center of the Narhathan Peninsula. But *this* Usarlah lay almost a hundred thousand miles from the Usarlah Shaylar had visited as a young university student so long ago.

I've come almost half the distance to the moon from home, she thought, staring out into the darkness, *and that's as a bird—or a dragon—might have flown it. Halfway to the moon.* She shook her head, trying to wrap her mind around the sheer distance involved. *And we still have almost forty thousand* more *miles to go.*

"You seem . . . pensive tonight, Shaylar," Gadrial said, and Shaylar turned back from the window.

The Ransaran magister sat across the small table from her, shuffling the sixty-card deck with slender, adroit fingers. She'd been teaching Shaylar and Jathmar an Arcanan card game called Old Basilisk. The rules weren't all that complex—certainly not any more complicated than several Sharonian card games Shaylar could think of—but the deck had five twelve-card suits instead of the three eighteen-card suits she was accustomed to, which made keeping track of exactly what had been played challenging. Or would have, if Voices hadn't had photographic memories, at any rate.

"I *feel* pensive," Shaylar admitted. "We're such a long way away from everything I've ever known. And it's so . . . empty out there."

"Appearances can be deceiving," Gadrial told her, looking out the window herself. "Back home, all of this is part of the Duchy of Forkasa, one of the oldest and wealthiest independent territories of Shaloma. Of course, the factors that made Forkasa so wealthy back in Arcana don't necessarily apply in the out-universes. And we're still a long way from Arcana or New Andara. But the last time I checked the census figures, Lamia had a population of somewhere around three million, I think."

"Three million," Shaylar repeated. She had to remind herself that Arcana had been expanding into the multiverse for two centuries, almost three times as long as Sharona. Still, the thought that they had *three million* people living in a universe forty thousand miles from their home universe was sobering, to say the least.

"Well, Lamia's attracted more colonization than a lot of other universes," Gadrial said as she offered the deck for Shaylar to cut. "The distance between portals is shorter than in some, and it's all overland, which helps. And the natural tendency is to spread out to either side of the slider right-of-way, which just happens to run across some of Shaloma's best real estate. Not to mention the fact that some of the most beautiful beaches of the Western Hesmiryan are less than a hundred miles from where we are right now."

She began to deal, and Shaylar nodded in understanding. The Hesmiryan Sea was what the Arcanans called the Mbisi Sea, and Gadrial was certainly right about the Narhathan beaches. Tourism was one of Teramandor Province's most lucrative industries back home in Sharona, and Teramandor beach resorts were famous throughout the multiverse.

"Anyway," Gadrial continued, "I think every universe looks emptier when you see it in the dark. It always makes *me* feel like there's nothing really quite real out there."

"I've felt that way a lot, lately," Shaylar said in a low voice, and Gadrial's hands paused. She looked across the table at the other woman, and her almond-shaped eyes were dark with sympathy.

"I know you have. And I wish none of this had happened to you and Jathmar."

"We know that, Gadrial." Shaylar managed a smile. "Go ahead and deal, silly!"

Gadrial smiled back and resumed dealing cards. Shaylar watched them fall, listening to the quiet, snapping sounds the cardboard rectangles made as they landed on the table top. She would never have been able to hear that sound aboard a Sharonian train moving at this speed. Indeed, the quiet, vibrationless slider cars continued to amaze her, although she and Jathmar had noticed several weaknesses, compared to old-fashioned, noisy, vibrating railroads.

It had taken them a while to realize just how big a disadvantage the absence of engines was. There was no doubt that the fact that each slider was self-propelled made the slider cars far more flexible, but the price for that flexibility was high. Each slider required its own spell accumulator, and for all their luxury, they were much more lightly built than Sharonian rolling stock . . . for reasons which had become obvious as they'd watched the Gifted technicians recharge the accumulators at the stations where they'd stopped. The spells which propelled the sliders were obviously complicated, and it took quite a while to recharge each slider's accumulator. And as Gadrial had explained, when they'd finally asked her about it, there was a reason the cars were so light. The sliders relied upon a variant of the levitation spells used by the cargo pods dragon transports often towed, and those really weren't very efficient on a tonnage basis. From what she'd said, Jathmar (who knew far more about railroads and steam engines than Shaylar did) had calculated that the Arcanans would be lucky if one of their slider cars could transport a quarter of the tonnage one of the TTE's freight cars routinely carted across the multiverse.

It's nice to think we have at least some advantages, she thought moodily as she gathered up her cards and began sorting her hand.

She glanced across the compartment to where Chief Sword Threbuch and Jathmar were engaged in a game the Arcanans called battle squares. It was a complicated, highly stylized wargame using eighteen carved pieces on each side, played across a gameboard that was nine squares wide and nine squares deep. Jathmar had turned out to be surprisingly good at it, and he was pushing Threbuch hard while Jugthar Sendahli kibitzed. She could feel his concentration—and enjoyment—through their marriage bond, and it was obvious that Sendahli was amused by Threbuch's predicament.

Shaylar was glad Jathmar was enjoying himself, but even that was flawed for her tonight. She could feel his concentration and enjoyment, yes, but not as clearly as she should have been able to. Their wedding bond was definitely weaker, and when they'd stopped for the last accumulator charge, Jathmar had tested his Mapping Talent.

It was weaker, too.

In a way, Shaylar was almost relieved. Even in Sharona, marriages and relationships sometimes proved less enduring than the people involved in them might have wished, especially in the face of unexpected stress or anxiety. Very few people could ever have been under more stress than the two of them, and she'd seen more than one marriage bond simply wither and die as the partners drifted apart. The thought of that happening to her and Jathmar was more than she could have borne, and she was almost desperately glad that there was some other reason for what was happening. But even so, the implications of their weakening bond and Jathmar's weakening Talent were nearly as frightening as the thought of losing Jathmar might have been.

They had no idea what was causing it, and Shaylar looked up from her cards. Gadrial's head was bent as she sorted her own hand, and she failed to notice the intense, almost plaintive quality of the look Shaylar gave her. The Voice wished with all her heart that she and Jathmar could discuss what was happening to them with *someone*, and the most reasonable someone would have been Gadrial. But Jathmar was right. They couldn't mention this to anyone—not when it was possible that the effect could be deliberately induced, even used against other Talents, by a sorceress who figured out what was happening.

Gadrial looked up, and Shaylar quickly banished her worries from her expression, if not from her emotions.

"Ready to bid?" Gadrial asked.

"Sure," Shaylar said, with a cheerfulness she was far from feeling. "Fifteen."

* * *

Afternoon sunlight slanted in through the narrow, barred windows as the outside door slammed open. Two Arcanan guards came through it, dragging a limp, semi-conscious body between them, and a third guard followed behind them, with one of their repeating crossbows cocked and loaded in his hands. The armed guard stood back, weapon ready, while one of the other two unlocked the cell door so that his companion could toss their burden through it.

Namir Velvelig moved quickly, catching Company-Captain Silkash before the all but unconscious Healer could hit the cell floor. Silkash cried out in pain as the regiment-captain caught him, and Velvelig's eyes could have frozen the heart of any Arpathian hell as he glared up at the guards.

One of them sneered at him, obviously amused by his glare, and made a taunting gesture with one hand. His mocking expression and obvious satisfaction at Silkash's broken, bloodied condition was almost enough. Almost.

Yet Velvelig's iron expression never even twitched. Only those frozen eyes spoke of the fury blazing within him. The time would come. He already knew that much. The time would come when he would finally make his try and die.

But not today. Not until the moment was right and he could count on taking at least one of them with him before the bastard with the crossbow shot him down.

The guard who'd mocked him snorted with contempt, spat on the floor, then slammed the cell shut and locked it. He said something to his companion, and all three of the guards sauntered out.

Velvelig eased Silkash down on the pallet he and the other officers in their cell had put together, and the Healer twitched, hissing in anguish as Velvelig's gently testing fingers found fresh breaks in his ribs.

The regiment-captain had cuts and bruises in plenty of his own. The last two times they'd come for Silkash, Velvelig had stood in front of the Healer. He hadn't launched a single blow, hadn't threatened the guards in any way, but they'd had to club him out of the way before they could get at the Healer.

Not that it had done any good in the end.

"Sir?"

He looked down at the faint, thready voice. Silkash's left eye was open; his right was swollen shut. He'd lost several teeth along the way, as well, and his speech wasn't very clear.

"I'm here, Silky," Velvelig said quietly. "You don't look too good."

"Well, I don't *feel* so good, either," Silkash got out, and Velvelig's eyes burned at the Healer's feeble attempt at humor.

"Tobis?" Velvelig asked after a moment, and Silkash shook his head.

"Don't know, Sir." The bruised, bloodied face twisted. "That son-of-a-bitch was still working on him when they dragged me out."

"*Whoreson!*" somebody snarled behind Velvelig, but the regiment-captain only patted Silkash gently on the shoulder.

"All right, Silky. Take it easy. We'll take care of you."

"I know, Sir," Silkash whispered, and his eye slid shut.

Velvelig held up one hand, and one of the other prisoners handed him the scrap of blanket they'd soaked in their water bucket. The regiment-captain began cleaning his Healer's face, and his touch was as gentle as any woman's, while black murder seethed in his heart.

Hadrign Thalmayr's sadism had a certain brutal cunning. There was no doubt in Velvelig's mind that he was going to kill Silkash and Makree in the end, but he was in no hurry to end his entertainment. Perhaps it had begun as some sort of punishment, vengeance for the "torment" he believed the Healers had deliberately inflicted upon him. If that was how it had started, though, it had gone far beyond that by now. Vengeance might have offered him the pretext, but the truth was that he *enjoyed* what he was doing.

He was pacing himself, rationing himself . . . giving his victims time to recover between sessions. Yet Silkash and—especially—Makree were growing steadily weaker, and no one seemed to care. Certainly no one was offering them the magical healing which had saved Velvelig's own life. However spectacular their healing powers might be, the Arcanan healers were obviously content to watch their Sharonian counterparts being slowly and brutally beaten to death without raising a finger to repair the damage.

"I don't think Tobis can take much more, Sir." Silkash's voice was a little stronger, which only made the despair in it that much clearer. "It's worse for him. It blasts his Talent open. Makes him *Feel* how much the son-of-a-bitch enjoys what he's doing to him."

"I know, Silky. I—"

Velvelig broke off, and his belly muscles tightened in anticipation as the outside door opened once more. But it wasn't the guards dragging Tobis Makree back into the brig, after all.

Velvelig straightened, and the fury in his heart redoubled as he recognized the wiry redhead. Thalmayr was bad enough, yet at least he appeared to genuinely believe his captors had deliberately tortured him when he was in their power. The Arcanan standing outside their cell now, looking in at them, had no such excuse, and Velvelig knew that if he would only come within arm's reach of the bars . . .

He wasn't that stupid, unfortunately. He only stood there, glaring at the prisoners, his face tight with hatred as he drank up the extent of Silkash's injuries. Then he turned around, as wordlessly as he'd come, and stalked back out.

Namir Velvelig watched him go, then knelt slowly back down beside his Healer and started wiping blood off his face once more.

* * *

Therman Ulthar closed the door very carefully behind him, then stood on the walkway outside the brig. His left hand dropped to the hilt of the short sword sheathed at his hip, and his knuckles whitened with the force of his grip.

He refused to let himself look at the administration block. He couldn't, because he knew what was happening in there right this moment. He didn't have to hear the blows, listen to the gasping screams, to know what Hadrign Thalmayr was doing, and if he let himself think about it, let himself *feel*, then—

He closed his eyes and inhaled deeply.

You're an officer in the Union Army, godsdamn it, he told himself despairingly. *You can't just* stand *here, whatever Iftar said! If you don't take a stand for* something, *then what the fuck use* are *you?*

There was a sickness spreading through the garrison of the captured Sharonian fort, radiating from the man who'd been placed in command, and Ulthar was afraid. Afraid of where it would end, who might find himself added to the list of Hadrign Thalmayr's "enemies." Someone had to *do* something, yet Ulthar was only one man, and a man Thalmayr obviously distrusted as much as he loathed him.

You don't even have a platoon anymore, Therman, he thought, and it was true. He had exactly five men, the other Andaran Scout wounded POWs who'd been left behind here with him and Thalmayr, under his "command." Thalmayr had been careful not to assign him to anything which might have required more men, and Ulthar knew exactly why that was.

He also knew all five of them would have followed him into any open confrontation with Thalmayr . . . for all the good it would have done.

I can't take them with me, he told himself yet again. *I don't have that right. But, gods, I've got to do* something!

At least the Healers Five Hundred Vaynair had left behind were refusing to go along with Thalmayr. No doubt the other prisoners didn't understand, but if Thalmayr had had *his* way, the Healers would have repaired the damages he inflicted on a daily basis . . . so that he could inflict *fresh* damages on a daily basis. But they'd refused. They couldn't stop him from torturing his prisoners, but they could refuse to become his accomplices by helping him do it.

Ulthar snarled in frustration. How pathetic was it when the best he could find to say was that the Healers *wouldn't* heal someone?

Something snapped down inside him at that thought. The iron self-control he'd forced himself to exert slipped, and he spun on his heel and started stalking across the parade ground towards the office block, unsnapping the retaining strap across his short sword as he went.

"Fifty Ulthar?"

The voice reached him even through the red haze of his fury, and he paused, looking over his shoulder. He didn't really know the man who'd called out to him. He'd seen him around the fort, but he wasn't an Andaran Scout, and Ulthar had been too focused on what Thalmayr was up to to pay him much attention.

"Yes?" Ulthar's one-word response came out sounding strangled and strange, even to his own ears, and the other man grimaced.

"I think we need to talk, Fifty Ulthar," Commander of Fifty Jaralt Sarma said.

* * *

Commander of Two Thousand Mayrkos Harshu sat in his tent at the foot of the precipitous cliffs and pushed the last few bites of his supper around the bowl with a spoon. A glass of wine sat largely untasted at his elbow, and his expression was unusually grim.

The sentry outside the tent called out a challenge to someone, and Harshu raised his head, looking towards the entrance. A moment later, the sentry lifted the flap and looked in at him.

"Thousand Toralk is here, Sir. He says you're expecting him."

"I am, Sword. Send him in, please."

"Sir!"

The noncom snapped a salute and disappeared. A moment later, the flap rose again, and Klayrman Toralk came through it.

"You wanted to see me, Sir?"

"Yes, please. Have a seat."

Harshu gestured at the camp chair floating on the far side of the table, and Toralk settled himself onto it. The thousand never looked away from Harshu as he sat, and Harshu smiled sourly.

"I've just received some . . . interesting dispatches, Klayrman."

"Sir?" Toralk's eyebrows rose as Harshu paused.

"One set is from Carthos," the two thousand said. "That's the good news, such as it is. He's detached Hundred Helika's strike. We should see Helika in about three more days. The only bad news from *him* is that I'd asked him how much transport he needed to move his prisoners to the rear. If I were the Sharonians and I had the capability, I'd try pushing down the secondary chain before I tried to fight my way down these cliffs. I don't think they *do* have the capability, but if it turns out they do, there's no way we can reinforce Carthos enough to hold against a serious attack. The best we can do is to keep the approaches picketed and make sure they don't manage to get past him and sneak up on us undetected from the rear. So I thought to myself we should send his POWs back to Five Hundred Klian so he could move quickly, without any encumbrances. Fortunately, we don't have to worry about that."

"What do you mean, Sir?" Toralk asked, his expression unhappy, when Harshu paused once more.

"I mean he doesn't *have* any prisoners. Not one. Apparently—" Harshu met Toralk's eyes levelly across the table "—every single Sharonian died fighting rather than surrender."

Klayrman Toralk's belly muscles tightened. It wasn't really a surprise, of course. And a part of him couldn't help feeling a sudden surge of fury directed not at the distant Thousand Carthos but at Two Thousand Harshu. It was just a bit late for Harshu to be feeling upset with anyone over violations of the Kerellian Accords after he'd sown the seeds for everything Carthos had done by what he'd allowed Neshok to do!

Something of the thousand's emotions must have shown in his face, because Harshu's jaw tightened. But then the two thousand inhaled deeply and made himself nod.

"You're right, Klayrman. It *is* my fault. And if I'd listened to you in the beginning, it wouldn't have happened. But it has, and it's going to be a hell of a lot harder to stop it than it would have been simply to never let it start."

He shook his head, then leaned back in his chair with a smile that was even more sour than before.

"Of course, there's always that second set of dispatches to help distract me from the Carthos situation."

"Second set, Sir?" Toralk asked cautiously.

"Oh, yes. The set from Two Thousand mul Gurthak."

"From Two Thousand mul Gurthak?"

Surprise startled the repetition out of Toralk. Mul Gurthak had been oddly silent ever since the Arcanan Expeditionary Force began its advance. In fact, as far as Toralk was aware, he hadn't sent Harshu a single message in all that time.

"Indeed," Harshu told him. "It would appear that Two Thousand mul Gurthak is most distressed over the way in which I have misinterpreted his desires and grossly exceeded his intentions."

Toralk's eyes went wide. He couldn't help it. He'd read most of the official instructions and memoranda mul Gurthak had sent forward to Mahritha before Harshu launched his attack.

"But, Sir, that's rid—" he began.

"Don't say it," Harshu interrupted. Toralk closed his mouth with a click, and Harshu grimaced. "Given a couple of things he said in his dispatches, Klayrman," he said very quietly, "I think he probably has his own eyes and ears out here, keeping him informed. It might not be very wise to . . . express your opinion overly freely in front of anyone besides myself, if you take my meaning."

It was Toralk's turn to sit back, and his jaw muscles tensed as the implications began to percolate through his brain.

"That's better," Harshu told him. The two thousand picked up his almost forgotten wineglass and sipped from it, then set it back down again.

"According to Two Thousand mul Gurthak, it was never his intention for us to advance beyond Hell's Gate. And, in fact, *he* always regarded the use of force to retake even Hell's Gate as an action of *last* resort."

"Sir," Toralk said, despite Harshu's warning, "I don't see how any reasonable individual could have interpreted his instructions to mean anything of the sort. Certainly not in light of the verbal briefings he gave both of us before he deployed us forward!"

"Klayrman," Harshu said in a chiding way, shaking a finger at him, "you're letting your opinions run away with you again."

Toralk clamped his mouth shut, and Harshu snorted harshly.

"The interesting thing is that if you read his written instructions *without* those verbal briefings of his, they can actually be interpreted exactly the way he's interpreting them at the moment. While I would never wish to impute duplicity to a superior officer, I find that I can't quite shake the suspicion that the discrepancy between his current very clearly expressed views and what you and I understood his instructions to be isn't . . . accidental, shall we say?"

"Sir, I don't like what you seem to be saying."

"I'm not overjoyed with it myself. In fact, the thing that bothers me most right now is that I can't decide whether mul Gurthak is simply trying to cover his own ass now that the shit's hit the fan, or if he deliberately set us up—well, set *me* up, at least—from the start. Did he simply shape his written instructions this way so he'd be covered if something went wrong, or did he want us to do exactly what I went ahead and did, but clearly—for the record, at least—without his authorization?"

Toralk started to open his mouth again, but Harshu's raised finger stopped him. Not, the Air Force officer reflected a second later, that it was really necessary for him to say what he was thinking.

But why? Why would mul Gurthak want *us to start a shooting war out here "without his authorization"? He's still the senior officer in command, even if he did delegate the field command to Harshu. Ultimately, surely the Commandery is going to hold him responsible for what happens in his command area. So why go to such elaborate lengths?*

The thoughts flashed through his brain. He had no answers for any of the questions, but he was sinkingly certain that if he'd had those answers, he wouldn't have liked them.

"Of course," Harshu continued in a lighter tone which fooled neither of them, "Two Thousand mul Gurthak is not yet aware that we've managed to kill the heir to the Ternathian Crown, is he? That's going to be just a bit unexpected, I imagine. As is the way the Sharonians are going to respond to it."

He showed his teeth in a smile which contained no humor at all, and Toralk winced. Unlike Harshu, he'd actually met the senior Sharonian officers at Fort Salby. There wasn't much question in his mind about how the Ternathian Empire, at least, was going to respond.

He looked across the table at Mayrkos Harshu and wondered if he looked as sick as he felt.

* * *

Rof chan Skrithik stood stiffly to attention as the haunting bugle notes of "Sunset," the call the Ternathian Empire's military had used to close the day for almost three thousand years, floated out under the smoldering embers of a spectacular sunset.

It was a beautiful bugle call, with a sweet, clear purity that no soldier ever forgot. And it was also, by a tradition so ancient no one even knew when it had begun, the call used at military funerals.

The last sweet notes flared out, and chan Skrithik inhaled deeply, gazing out across the neat rows of graves. At least a third of them were marked with the triangular memorial symbol of the Triad. Others showed the horsetails of Arpathia, or the many-spired star of Aruncas of the Sword.

And out there, in the midst of the men who had died to hold Fort Salby, was the young man who had died to *save* Fort Salby.

Chan Skrithik reached up, gently stroking the falcon on his right shoulder. For millennia, since the death of Emperor Halian, the House of Calirath's tradition had been that when one of its own died in battle, he was buried where he fell. Buried with the battle companions who had fallen at his side, and with his enemies. Chan Skrithik would have preferred to send Janaki home to his mother. To let him sleep where he had earned the right to sleep, beside Erthain the Great. But like Halian himself, Janaki chan Calirath would rest where he had fallen, farther away from Estafel and Tajvana than any other Calirath.

And where he slept would be Ternathian soil forever.

"It doesn't seem right, Sir."

Chan Skrithik turned. Chief-Armsman chan Braikal stood beside him, looking out across the same cemetery.

"What doesn't seem right, Chief?"

"It doesn't seem right that he's not here, Sir." Grief clouded the chief-armsman's voice. "None of us would be here without *him*, and—"

Chan Braikal broke off, and chan Skrithik reached out and touched him lightly on the shoulder.

"It was his choice, Chief. Remember that. He *chose* to die for the rest of us. Never let anyone forget that."

"No, Sir. I won't." Chan Braikal's wounded voice hardened. "And none of us will be forgetting *how* he died, either."

Chan Skrithik only nodded.

Division-Captain chan Geraith's entire First Brigade had marched past Janaki's body. Every surviving man of the fort's PAAF garrison had done the same, and Sunlord Markan had personally led his surviving Uromathian cavalry troopers past the bier in total silence, helmets removed, weapons reversed, while the mounted drummers kept slow, mournful time.

Janaki chan Calirath's death had done more than save Fort Salby. Rof chan Skrithik already understood that. Janaki had been added to the legend of the Caliraths, and the fighting men of Sharona would never forget that the attack which had killed him had been launched in time of peace by the very nation which had asked for the negotiations in the first place.

He wasn't the only victim of their treachery. In fact, chan Skrithik never doubted that Janaki would have been dismayed—even angry—if anyone had suggested anything of the sort. Yet it was inevitable that the young man who would one day have been emperor of all Sharona should be the focal point for all the grief, all the rage—all the *hate*—Arcana had fanned into a roaring furnace.

"I Stand Between," chan Skrithik thought. *Well, you did, Janaki. You stood between all of us and Arcana. And you stood between* me *and the gryphon that killed you. It's a hard thing, knowing a legend died for you. But that's what Caliraths do, isn't it? They make legends.*

They become *legends, and, gods, the price they pay for it!*

Taleena made a soft sound on his shoulder, and he reached up and stroked her wings once again.

"I know, My Lady," he said gently. "I know. I miss him, too."

Taleena touched the back of his hand very gently with her razor-sharp beak, and chan Skrithik looked across at chan Braikal once more.

"His horses and his sword are going home, Chief," he said. "And you and his platoon are taking them."

"Yes, Sir." Chan Braikal's voice was husky again.

"Tell them for us, Chief." Chan Skrithik looked into the Marine's eyes. "Tell them all. This fort, the cemetery, it's *ours*. He bought it for us, and no one and *nothing* will ever take it away from us."

* * *

"I can't believe she did that." Alazon Yanamar shook her head. "What was she *thinking*?"

"You know exactly what she was thinking, love," Kinlafia chided her sadly.

The two of them stood in Alazon's office in Calirath Palace, surrounded by her collection of horses as they gazed out the windows. The lamps were turned low, the sun had set hours ago, and a silver moon drifted over the palace gardens. It was a serene and beautiful sight, utterly at odds with the chaos and confusion which had enveloped the people who lived and worked in the palace.

"You just don't want to admit that she was right," Kinlafia continued.

"Right?" Alazon stared at him in stark disbelief. "Gods, Darcel! She's *seventeen*! And she's a Ternathian!

The youngest of that bastard's sons is twenty-nine, and they're all just as bad as he is! Can you imagine what will happen to her when she marries one of *them*? Especially after humiliating his father the way she did this morning? Why not just invite him to rape her on the floor of the Conclave and be done with it?!"

"Yes." The word came out harshly, but Kinlafia met her angry eyes levelly. "I can imagine exactly what will happen. Vothan! Do you think I *like* the thought? But that doesn't change the fact that she's right. That we've got to unify, and that we don't have time to give Chava the opportunity to reopen the entire unification debate."

"Yes we do!" Alazon protested. "And if Chava's going to open the door then I say we should use the opportunity *he's* given us to delete that entire subsection from the Act!"

"You know better than that." Kinlafia regarded her sternly. "In fact, I *know* you know better than that—you've been the one teaching *me* to think in strategic political terms for the last two weeks! Do you really think Chava would have opened this entire subject if he wasn't prepared to announce that Uromathia would use the pretext of Janaki's death and the 'invalidation' of the Act to justify refusing to accept unification after all unless it's revised once again? This time to give him more power, more room to spin his webs? And do you think he waited until *after* the Emperor detailed his requirements by *accident*? He wanted every member of the Conclave to accept, gut-deep, just how serious the threat is. And *then* he issued his demand.

"He wanted them to know how big a pistol he was prepared to hold to all of their heads. If he claims the

Act is nullified, if he refuses to acknowledge Zindel's rightful coronation, then what happens to all of the preparations we need to make? Do you think for an instant that once that sack of snakes was untied, there wouldn't be enormous pressure from other members of the Conclave to give him more of what he wanted in the first place if that was the only way to get him to sign back up quickly now that the Arcanans have proven they're a genuine, *immediate* threat?

"He might as well have handed us a written memo about his new strategy, Alazon! The way he saw it, he won either way. Either he got to name Andrin's husband under the terms of the Act, or else Zindel told him to go straight to the Arpathian hells before he gave one of Chava's sons *his* daughter. And if that happened, if Zindel refused to honor the Act's terms, then Chava could declare that *Zindel's* decision to invalidate the Act absolved him of his agreement to surrender the sovereignty of Uromathia *to* Zindel . . . and that would have given him all the leverage in the world, unless we chose to fight that very civil war the Emperor told me last night he wanted to avoid!

"It's obvious from the Voice reports and print articles you've had me Watching and reading ever since I got back that Chava never really regarded the original Arcanan massacre as a genuine threat. He was doing his best to game the situation then, and he's doing exactly the same thing now. He's just changing technique, using the threat everyone else sees as genuine to frighten them into conceding the points they refused to give him before. If he can simultaneously frighten the other members of the Conclave badly enough and appear sufficiently intransigent, he'll get at least some of his demands—maybe even *most* of them. And he won't give a good godsdamn how long he delays unification, how much damage he does to our ability to deal with the Arcanans, as long as there's a chance of improving *his* position."

"But—"

"'But' nothing, love," Kinlafia said softly, sadly. "You know that's what would happen. And so does her father. My gods, Alazon, you know how much he loves her, and you saw as well as I did what he was prepared to do out there today! Yes, it was her decision, and I know as well as you do that she never even warned him she was going to do it. That she *deliberately* didn't give him time to think about ways to stop her, or for the father in him to find some justification—*any* justification—for keeping her from doing this. But if he hadn't realized in the end that she was right, he would never have let her get away with it. Never."

"But there *has* to be another way." Alazon was no longer protesting or denying. She was almost pleading. "We can't just let her do this, Darcel. We *can't*!"

Tears glittered in the Privy Voice's eyes, and Darcel put his arm around her and hugged her tightly.

"I don't see how we can stop her," he said, and in the back of his brain he saw once again the image of Andrin weeping. "I'm finally beginning to understand—*really* understand—what sort of price being born a Calirath can exact. She's going to do this. The only person who could stop her is her father, and he won't—he can't. He'll do everything he can to protect her, but this is the one thing he can't stop her from doing."

"It will kill her," Alazon said softly. "Maybe not physically—not quickly. But it *will* kill her." She looked up at Kinlafia, and a single tear broke free and trickled down her cheek. "I never really knew her until this entire impossible crisis just exploded in our faces. But now that's changed. And if she marries someone like one of Chava Busar's sons, it will just *destroy* her inside."

Kinlafia nodded, hearing the pain in her beautiful voice. That pain, he knew, was the reason someone with Alazon's sharp intelligence and grasp of politics could insist that Andrin had to be stopped. And gods knew she was right. If there'd been *any* way to avoid this . . .

"We're just going to have to hope she's stronger than that," he said. "I've read the entire Act since you gave me a copy. If I could see any way for her to—"

He paused suddenly, and Alazon stiffened in the circle of his arm as she Felt a sudden, incredible cascade of thoughts and emotions tumbling through him. Then he inhaled sharply and looked into her eyes.

"Gods!" he half-whispered. "That's *it*."

"What?" Alazon demanded.

"I've just had an idea," he told her. "My gods, it's what Janaki Glimpsed!"

"*What's* what Janaki Glimpsed?!"

"We've got to go find Andrin," Kinlafia told her. "And be sure you bring your copy of the Act!"

* * *

Andrin Calirath sat on her bedroom window seat, staring out into the moon-soaked gardens of Calirath Palace, and wept.

Her tears were nearly silent, and she sat very still, watching the moonlight waver through them. She wept for the brother she would never see again. She wept for her parents, who would never again see their son. She wept for all the other mothers, fathers, sisters, brothers, and daughters who would never see their loved ones again.

And she wept for herself.

In the cold, still hours of the night, it was hard. She was only seventeen, and knowing that what she must do would save thousands, possibly even millions of lives—even *agreeing* that it was what she must do—was cold and bitter compensation for the destruction of her own life. She was frightened, and despite her youth, she had few illusions about what sort of marriage Chava Busar and his sons had in mind for her. She knew her strengths, knew the strength of her parents' love, how fiercely they would strive to protect her. Yet in the end, no one *could* protect her from the cold, merciless demands of the Calirath destiny. At best, it would be a marriage without love, without tenderness. And at worst—

She folded her arms, trying to wrap them around herself, not because she was physically cold, but because of the chill deep inside.

She was going to spend her life married to the son of her father's worst enemy. Her children would be the grandchildren of her family's most deadly foe. She could already feel the ice closing in, already sense the way the years to come would wound and maim her spirit, and she wished—wished with all her heart—that there could be some escape. That Shalana could somehow find that single, small scrap of mercy for her. Could let her somehow evade this last, bitter measure of duty and responsibility.

But Shalana wouldn't. She couldn't. "I Stand Between." How many Caliraths had given themselves to that simple, three-word promise over the millennia? Janaki had given his life to that promise, and Andrin could do no less than sacrifice her life to it, as well.

"*Sho warak*, Janaki," she whispered. "*Sho warak*. Sleep, Janaki. Sleep until we all wake once more. I love you."

She put her head down on the back of the padded window seat and let her tears soak into the upholstery.

She never knew how long she wept into the window seat's satin, but somehow, despite her determination not to, she must have made some sound. She had to have, because her bedroom door opened abruptly, with absolutely no warning, spilling lamplight into the darkened room. She jerked upright, spinning towards the brightness, but her angry rebuke for whoever had dared to intrude upon her died unspoken.

Lady Merissa Vankhal stood in the doorway, silhouetted against the light. There was a chair just outside the door behind her, one which hadn't been there when Andrin went to bed, with a blanket tossed untidily across it, and Lady Merissa herself was clad in a silken sleep robe over her night dress, devoid of the least trace of make-up, her hair all awry. Andrin had never seen—never imagined—her fussy, propriety-obsessed chief lady-in-waiting in such disarray, and she wondered what fresh cosmic disaster could have driven Lady Merissa to her bedroom in such a state.

Yet before she could even start to frame the question, Lady Merissa crossed the bedroom to her and, to her utter astonishment, Andrin found herself enfolded in a tight embrace.

"Oh, my love," Merissa whispered in her ear. "Oh, my poor love. I didn't *hear* you—I didn't know."

Andrin felt herself beginning to crumble in that

totally unexpected, immensely comforting embrace. Lady Merissa sat down on the window seat beside her, and a corner of Andrin's brain wondered just how ridiculous they looked. She was a foot taller than Lady Merissa, yet Merissa cradled her as if she were a child, and Andrin abandoned herself to the comfort of that touch.

"There, love," Merissa murmured, stroking her back while she sobbed. "There, love."

Andrin clung to her, as if the fussy, fluffy, irritating lady-in-waiting were the last solid rock in her universe, for that was precisely what Lady Merissa had become.

And then someone knocked gently on the bedroom door.

Andrin stiffened, and Lady Merissa's spine straightened with an almost audible snap.

"*Really!*" she huffed. "Is this a grand imperial princess' bedroom, or is it the waiting room down at the local train station?!"

She set Andrin aside gently, then came to her feet, straightening her robe, and stalked across the enormous bedroom towards the door, muttering as she went.

"Can't leave the poor girl in peace," Andrin heard floating malevolently back from her remorselessly advancing lady-in-waiting. "Middle of the night, for goodness sake! Coming bursting in on her, keeping her awake at all hours! I'll give *you* a piece of my mind, just wait and see if I—!"

Lady Merissa reached the door and yanked it open. A palace maid stood there, hands folded anxiously, and the poor young woman ought by rights to have burst spontaneously into flame under Lady Merissa's fiery glare.

"*Well?*" Merissa snapped at her luckless victim.

"Beg pardon, Lady Merissa!" the maid said quickly. "I wouldn't ever have disturbed Her Grand Imperial Highness, not ever! But they insisted."

"*Who* insisted, girl?" Lady Merissa demanded. "And what could possibly be so important that it couldn't wait until morning?!"

"I'm sure I don't know what's important, My Lady!" the maid said. "But it's Privy Voice Yanamar and Voice Kinlafia. They say they have to talk to Her Grand Imperial Highness right away!"

GLOSSARY

Aeravas—a Sharonian city in Harkala; located in approximately the same place as Shiraz, Iran.

Alathia—one of the provinces of the Ternathian Empire, it is the trans-temporal analogue of Italy.

Andara—the Arcanan equivalent of the continent of North America. Andara is the home of the warrior kingdoms of the Andarans and provides the backbone of the Union of Arcana's military.

Arau Mountains—the Sharonian equivalent of the Yoblonovy Khrebet mountain range east of Lake Baikal.

Arcana—the home universe and Earth of the Union of Arcana. Its physics are based on "magic."

Arpathia—the Sharonian equivalent of the area stretching from the Caspian Sea through the Siberian tundra north of Mongolia to the Pacific Ocean. While there is no united government for this region, it is often referred to as the Septentrion, which is a trade union developed by the septs (see Septs and Septentrion, below).

Aruncas of the Sword—the Uromathian god of war.

Baranal—literally, "protector" in old Andaran. A baranal is the individual responsible for protecting a shardon (see below).

Barkesh—a city in Sharona located at the approximate trans-temporal site of Barcelona, Spain.

Bergahl—the dominant deity of the Order of Bergahl. Bergahl is a god of both war and justice. His order is a militant one, which has traditionally provided the judges and law enforcement mechanism in the Kingdom of Othmaliz.

Bergahl's Comforters—an ironic nickname for Berghal's Dagger (see below).

Bergahl's Dagger—a highly militant cult within the Order of Bergahl. The Dagger was officially disbanded over a hundred years ago.

Bernith Island—the Sharonian analogue of the island of Great Britain.

Bernith Channel—the Sharonian analogue of the English Channel.

Bernithian Highlands—the Sharonian analogue of Scotland.

Bison—the steam-powered tractor portion of the Ternathian Army's experimental mechanized transport.

Blade of Ibral—the Sharonian analogue of the Gallipoli Peninsula.

blood debt—an ancient Ransaran concept of justice based on the principle of "an eye for an eye and a tooth for a tooth." It also has personal connotations of vengeance, but has been renounced by modern Ransarans as a barbaric and horrific basis for true justice. The term is sometimes still used as a slang phrase to describe a highly personal form of redress for wrongful actions.

blood vendetta—Shurkhali blood vendetta is triggered when a massive miscarriage of justice leads to someone's death. Shaylar Nargra-Kolmayr's apparent murder by Arcanans triggers a blood vendetta reaction in every Shurkhali alive.

Bolakin, Queens of—the queens who collectively rule the ten Bolakini city-states which control the southern shore of the Mbisi Sea.

Bolakini Strait—the Sharonian analogue of the Strait of Gibraltar.

Book of the Double-Three—the holy book of the Church of the Double Triads, the imperial religion of Ternathia.

Book of Secrets—one of the two seminal holy books of the Mythalan *shakira* caste.

Book of the Shakira—one of the two seminal holy books of the Mythalan *shakira* caste.

Calirath—the imperial dynasty of Ternathia. The Caliraths have ruled Ternathia for more than four millennia.

Celaryon II—King of Ancient Ternathia who negotiated the treaty which bound Ternathia and Farnalia as allies in the year 203 of the Ternathian calendar.

Central Bank of Mythal—the largest, wealthiest, and most powerful of the Mythalan banks. The CBM, unlike the private Mythalan banks, is directly subject to government supervision, and a full third of the seats on its Board of Directors are held by government appointees.

Cerakondian Mountains—the Sharonian equivalent of the Altai Mountains.

Cetacean Institute/Shurkahli Aquatic Realms Embassy—the Sharonian research institute and embassy founded and operated by Shaylar's mother, Thalassar Kolmayr-Brintal, who is a cetacean translator. Similar embassies serve the sentient great apes and higher primates of Ricathia (Africa), Uromathia (Asia), and New Farnal (South America, with its New World monkeys).

Chairifon—the Sharonian equivalent of the Eurasian supercontinent.

Chalar—an Arcanan maritime empire, based on the island of Chalar (Cuba) and dominating the Chalaran Sea (Caribbean Sea) and Gulf of Hilmar (Gulf of Mexico). Chalar is the dominant naval power of Arcana.

Chalgyn Consortium—survey company that employs Jathmar Nargra and Shaylar Nargra-Kolmayr. The Chalgyn Consortium is an independent survey company based in Shurkhal.

chan—"veteran" in Ternathian. This is an honorific indicating someone who is currently or has been a member of the Ternathian military.

Chinthai—a Sharonian breed of horses very similar to Percherons.

Commandery—the Arcanan equivalent of the Joint Chiefs of Staff.

Conclave—The formal multi-nation crisis-management organization established when the first portal opened in Sharona. Its members are the heads of state of every sovereign nation in Sharona and, on paper, Sharona's new, independent colony universes.

Cratak Mountains—the Arcanan equivalent of the Sierra Nevada Mountains.

Crown of fire—the Sharonian term for our own volcanically active "ring of fire" in the Pacific.

Daggerstone—a sarkolis crystal used to store short-range combat spells. Maximum range is no more than twenty feet, and they are impossible to conceal from any Gifted person, but they can store anti-personnel spells of great power.

Dalazan River—the Sharonian analogue of the Amazon River.

Daykassian—the premier Arpathian breed of cavalry horse. Very similar to the Turkoman.

Delkrath Mountains—a mountain range in Delkrathia Province; the Sharonian equivalent of the Santa de Guararrma Mountains of Spain.

Delkrathia Province—a province of the Ternathian Empire north of Narhath and east of Teramandor; it consists of the equivalent of central Spain, from just south of Madrid to the Bay of Biscay.

Dosaru—the Uromathian god of justice. Also known as "Dosaru of the Watching Eyes" and "Dosaru of the Scales."

Ekros—an Arcanian demon; the equivalent of our own Demon Murphy.

Elath—an Andaran kingdom whose territory covers roughly the area of the United States as far west as Kansas and Nebraska and extends as far north as Newfoundland.

Emergency Voice Network—a planet-wide network of Voices capable of linking all Sharonian heads of state in a real-time conference.

Emergency Transportation System—a Sharona-wide teleportation system capable of transporting very small groups of passengers. The ETS is designed for the emergency use of heads of state and diplomats in time-critical crises.

Emperor Edvar Mountains—the Sharonian equivalent of the Pyrenees Mountains.

Empress Wailyana II—Wailyana Calirath, Empress of Ternathia, 4172–4207. Generally referred to as Wailyana the Great.

Eniath—a technically Uromathian Kingdom in the eastern region of the equivalent of Mongolia. A land renowned for its falcons, its people are as much Arpathian as Uromathian and not particularly fond of the Empire of Uromathia.

Eraythas Mountains—the Sharonian analogue of the Cantabrian Mountains along the Biscay Coast of Spain.

Ermandia—a province of the Ternathian Empire, corresponding to Austria.

Erthain the Great—semi-legendary founder of the House of Calirath and the Ternathian Empire.

Esferia—the Sharonian analogue of Cuba.

Estafel—the capital city of the Ternathian Empire.

Evanos Ocean—the Arcanan name for the Pacific Ocean.

Faltharia—a republic in New Ternath, located in the general vicinity of the Great Lakes. The homeland of Jathmar Nargra.

Farnalia—the Sharonian equivalent of the Scandinavian peninsula.

Farnalian Sea—the Sharonian equivalent of the Baltic Sea.

Farnalian Empire—a Sharonian empire stretching from its home Farnalia across the northern periphery of the Sharonian equivalent of Europe to the equivalent of the Sea of Japan.

Farshal—a Hilmaran Kingdom in Arcana whose territory includes the equivalent of Guyana, Surinam, and French Guiana.

Finger Sea—the Sharonian analogue of the Red Sea.

Firsoma—Uromathian goddess of wisdom and fate. Also known as "Firsoma of the Shears" and "The Cutter."

Fist of Bolakin—the Sharonian analogue of the Rock of Gibraltar.

Flicker—a Talented Sharonian capable of teleporting, or "Flicking," relatively small objects over long distances with considerable precision.

Flight—an Arcanan Air Force formation consisting of four combat dragons, organized into two pairs of wingmen.

Fort Brithik—Sharonian portal fort in the universe of Thermyn, covering the outbound portal to New Uromath. Located roughly on the trans-temporal site of Lincoln, Nebraska.

Fort Ghartoun—formerly Fort Raylthar, Sharonian portal fort in the universe of Thermyn, covering the inbound portal from Failcham. Located roughly on the trans-temporal site of Carson City, Nevada.

Fort Losaltha—the Sharonian portal fortress protecting the entry portal of the Salym Universe. Located approximately at the trans-temporal site of Barcelona, Spain.

Fort Mosanik—Sharnonian portal fort in the universe of Karys, covering the outbound portal to Failcham. Located roughly on the trans-temporal site of Astana, Kazakhstan.

Fort Rycharn—the Arcanan coastal enclave in the universe of Gharys, serving the swamp portal to Hell's Gate. Located roughly on the trans-temporal site of Belém. Brazil.

Fort Salby—Sharonian portal fort in the universe of Traisum, covering the outbound portal to Karys. Located roughly on the trans-temporal site of the Sharonian city of Narshalla, or our own Medina, Saudi Arabia.

Fort Shaylar—Company Captain Halifu's portal fort in New Uromath.

Fort Talon—Arcanan fortress in Erthos located roughly on the transtemporal site of Ust Ilimsk, Siberia.

Fort Tharkoma—Sharonian portal fort in the universe of Salym covering the outbound portal to Traisum. Located roughly on the trans-temporal site of Sofia, Bulgaria.

Fort Wyvern—the Arcanan fortress and base in the universe of Gharys at the entry portal from the universe of Erthos. Located roughly on the trans-temporal site of Manzanilla, Cuba.

Gariyan VI—the Ternathian emperor who began the phased withdrawal from the easternmost provinces of the Ternathian Empire.

Gariyan VII—the son of Gariyan VI; the last Ternathian emperor to rule from Tajvana.

Garmoy, Sunhold of—a Sharonian dukedom in southeastern Uromathia. Roughly equivalent to the country of Laos.

Garouoma—a Sharonian city located on the Narhathan Peninsula; roughly equivalent to Cordoba, Spain.

Garsulthan—a Manisthuan word which translates roughly as "real politics." Its practitioners believe that all international relations ultimately rest upon the balance of military power and that morality and ethics must take second place to that reality when formulating foreign policy.

Gartasa Mountains—the Sharonian analogue of the Iberian Mountains in Spain, separating Teramandor from Delkrathia.

Garth Showma Institute—the Academy established by Magister Halathyn vos Dulainah at the site of Showma Falls in New Arcana. It is the second largest magical academy anywhere and its prestige is rapidly overtaking that of the Mythal Falls Academy.

Garth Showma—a large and powerful duchy and city in the universe of New Arcana. Located at the Arcanan equivalent of Niagara Falls and the headquarters site of the Arcanan Army.

Garthan—the non-magic users of the Mythalan culture. They make up at least eighty percent of the Mythalan population but possess only extremely circumscribed legal rights.

Gerynth—a city in the southern portion of the Andaran Kingdom of Yanko roughly analogous to Durango, Mexico.

Gorhadyn Protocol—a Mythalan assassination technique.

Grand Ternathian Canal—the Sharonian equivalent of the Suez Canal.

Grocyra—the Sharonian equivalent of Siberia.

Grocyran Plain—the Sharonian equivalent of the West Siberian Plain.

Gulf of Shurkhal—the Sharonian equivalent of the Gulf of Aden.

Hammerfell Lake—the Arcanan equivalent of Lake Huron.

Harkala—the Sharonian equivalent of India. The ancient Harkalian Empire extended from India through Afghanistan and into Iran.

Hell's Gate—the Sharonian name assigned to the universe where their survey personnel first encountered the Arcanans. Later adopted by Arcana, as well.

Hesmiryan Sea—the Arcanan analogue of the Mediterranean.

High Commandery—the high command of the Union of Arcanan's Army. Essentially, the equivalent of the Pentagon and the Chiefs of Staff, rolled into one. Traditionally, the High Commandery is heavily dominated by a senior Andaran officers.

Hilmar—the Arcanan equivalent of South America.

Hinorean Empire—the smaller of the two empires which dominate Uromath. The Hinorean Empire includes the Sharonian equivalent of western India and Bangladesh, Burma, Thailand, the Philippines, and Malaysia.

Hook of Ricathia—the Sharonian equivalent of the southern side of the Strait of Gibraltar; the trans-temporal equivalent of Morocco and Ceuta, Spain.

Horn of Ricathia—the Sharonian analogue of the Horn of Africa between the Gulf of Aden and the Indian Ocean.

Hummer—a magically enhanced bird developed from normal hummingbirds by Arcanan sorcerers as high-speed, highly aggressive "carrier pigeons."

Hurkaym—a small town/communications post located at the trans-temporal site of Palermo, Sicily, in the Salym Universe expressly as a Voice link between Fort Tharkoma and Fort Losaltha.

Hurlbane—a Ricathian deity associated with the Queens of Bolakin. She is a warrior goddess who protects the Bolakini (see Bolakin, Queens of), and her clergy have always been very influential in the Bolakini city-states. Hurlbane's High Priestess, for example, advised the Queens of Bolakin to ally with Ternathia thousands of years ago.

Ibral Strait—the Sharonian equivalent of the Dardanelles.

Ibral's Blade—the Sharonian equivalent of the Gallipoli Peninsula.

Indelbu—Ternathian port city; the trans-temporal analogue of Belfast.

Inkara—the Arcanan equivalent of the island of Great Britain.

Isseth—a kingdom situated between Harkala and Arpathia in the Sharonian equivalent of Kashmir, Tajikistan, and northeastern Pakistan.

Isseth-Liada—a portal exploration company owned/ sponsored by the Kingdom of Isseth.

Ithal Mountains—the Sharonian analogue of the Hejaz Mountains.

Janu River—the Sharonian analogue of the Rhine River.

Jerekhas—the Sharonian analogue of the island of Sicily.

Journeyman—a formal rank for Arcanan practitioners of sorcery who have completed their formal education but have not contributed a new application of sorcery. The majority of sorcerers do not progress beyond this rank. (See also "novice," "magister," and "magistron."

Judaih—a city in Sharona located on the site of Ghat, Libya.

Juhali—a volcanic island on Sharona; the Sharonian analogue of Krakatoa.

Kanaiya—a duchy in central Lokan, consisting of much of the central portion of the equivalent of Manitoba. Its capital, also called Kanaiya is located on the eastern shore of Lake Kanaiya.

Karmalia—the Sharonian analogue of Hungary.

Kerellian Accords—the Andaran military accords drafted centuries ago by the Andaran Commander of Armies Housip Kerellia and adopted by the Union of Arcana as the official standard for treatment of POWs and as the code of conduct to be followed by Arcanan personnel who become POWs.

Kershai—the ancient Mythalan word for "lightning"; the release code for a black dragon's breath weapon.

Kingdom of Shartha—a Ricathian kingdom in Sharona; it occupies roughly the area of Somalia, eastern Ethiopia, and most of Kenya. (See also "Lubnasi.")

Kosal River—the Arcanan analogue of Spain's Ebro River.

Kythia—a region of Arcana roughly equivalent to Gujarat, India.

Lake Arau—the Sharonian equivalent of Lake Baikal.

Lake Kanaiyar—the Arcanan equivalent of Lake Winnipeg.

Lake Wind Daughter—the Arcanan equivalent of Lake Michigan.

Larakesh—the site of the first Sharonian trans-temporal portal on the Ylani Sea. The Sharonian analogue of Varna, Bulgaria.

Larkima—the ancient Mythalan word for "strangle"; the release code for a yellow dragon's breath weapon.

Lifter—a Sharonian telekinetic Talent. Most Lifters can handle only very small objects; a very small percentage of exceptionally powerful Lifters can manipulate objects weighing as much as thirty or forty pounds.

Limathia—a kingdom in New Farnal, located between the Sharonian equivalent of Chile and Argentina. One of the Directors of the Portal Authority is from Limathia.

Lissia—the Sharonian equivalent of Australia; the main landmass of the Lissian Republic, which also includes New Zealand, the islands of Oceania, and a fair percentage of the South Pacific Islands of Polynesia. Shaylar Nargra-Kolmayr's mother is Lissian.

Lokan—an Andaran kingdom whose territory covers the equivalent of most of Canada and Alaska, but sweeps down to include Oregon and most of California, as well.

Losaltha—the Sharonian city located at the entry portal of the Salym universe. Located roughly at the trans-temporal location of Barcelona, Spain.

Lubnasi—an ancient independent city-state located within the boundaries of the Kingdom of Shartha (see above) in Sharona. Like the Bolakini city-states (see "Bolakin, Queens of"), Lubnasi was an ancient treaty partner of Ternathia, which is the historic guarantor of its independence.

Lugathia—a province of the Ternathian Empire, equivalent to France.

Magister—a formal title earned by Arcanan practitioners of sorcery. It requires the completion of an arduous formal education and the creation of at least one new, previously unknown application of sorcery. There are additional ranks within the broader title of magister. (See also "novice," "journeyman," and "magistron.")

Magistron—a formal title, equivalent to "magister," but reserved for those whose Gift and training are specialized for working with living things. There are additional ranks within the broader title of magistron. (See also "novice," "journeyman," and "magister.")

Mahritha—the Arcanan-explored universe connecting to Hell's Gate. Named by Magister Halathyn in his wife's honor.

Manisthu, Kingdom of—the dominant political unit of the Manisthu Islands.

Manisthu Islands—the Arcanan analogue of Japan.

Marnilay—a Sharonian goddess, "Sweet Marnilay the Maiden" is one of the Ternathian Double Triads, which are the foundation of the religion for at least half of Sharona, as Ternathia once controlled and/or colonized so much of that world.

Mbisi Sea—the Sharonian equivalent of the Mediterranean Sea.

Melwain the Great—the Andaran equivalent of King Arthur. Melwain lived well over a thousand years ago and is revered as the perfect example of Andaran honor.

Mind Healer—a Sharonian with a complex of Talents which permits him to treat mental disorders.

Mithanan—the Mythalan god of cosmic destruction.

Monarch Lake—the Arcanan equivalent of Lake Superior.

Mother Jambakol—an Arcanan evil goddess or demoness, both worshiped and feared in Hilmar. She is the personification of destruction, vengeance, and hatred.

Mother Marthea—a Sharonian deity. In the Shurkhali pantheon, she is revered as the water-bringer and life-bringer. She is called the Mother of Rivers, the Mother of Springs, and the Mother of the Sea. Revered as Mother of the Sea, she brings wealth in the form of pearls and coral, and watches over Shurkhali ships. She is viewed as a mother of abundance, whether from the sea, agricultural crops, or herds and flocks.

Mount Karek—a mountain peak west of Fort Salby in the Ithal Mountains.

mul—"warrior" in ancient Mythalan. As a part of a Mythalan's name, it indicates that he springs from one of the family lines of the *multhari* warrior caste. If the individual is also *shakira*, the higher caste indicator vos is used for most purposes instead of mul, but the proper formal usage is "vos and mul," so a *shakira* officer named Sythak of the Yuran line would properly be "Sythak vos and mul Yuran," but would normally be referred to as "Sythak vos Yuran."

Mulgethia—a Ternathian province, equivalent to Germany/Switzerland.

Multhari—the second most important caste group of Mythalan society. The *multhari* are the military caste. Some members of *multhari* are also *shakira*. These normally tend to dominate the upper ranks of the Mythalan military.

Mythal Falls Academy—the oldest and most prestigious magical research and teaching Academy in Arcana.

Mythal River—the Arcanan equivalent of the Nile River.

Mythal—the Arcanan equivalent of Africa. Mythal is dominated by a caste-based society which enshrines the total superiority of the *shakira* magic-using caste to the *garthan* caste of non-magic users.

Mythal Falls—the Arcanan equivalent of Victoria Falls.

Mythalan Hegemony—the supranational Mythalan political body representing all Mythalan states. Effectively, the governing body of the Mythalan Empire, although there is no *official* Empire of Mythal.

Narhath—an affluent province of the Ternathian Empire, consisting of the equivalent of southern Spain and Portugal.

Narhathan Peninsula—the Sharonian equivalent of the Iberian peninsula.

Narshalla—a Sharonian city located approximately on the site of Medina, Saudi Arabia.

Nessia—eastern-most modern Ternathian province, equivalent to Greece.

New Ramath—the port city built specifically to serve the rail line to Fort Tharkoma in Salym. Located on the trans-temporal equivalent of Durrës, Albania.

New Sharona—the first additional universe surveyed from Sharona.

New Ternath—the Sharonian equivalent of North America.

New Farnal—the Sharonian equivalent of South America.

Norgamar Works—one of the great locomotive foundries of Sharona. A prime supplier to the Trans-Temporal Express.

Nosikor—a Sharonian city located at the southwestern end of Lake Arau.

Novice—the title awarded to a Gifted student in Arcana. A student remains a novice, regardless of age, until his or her graduation from formal training. (See also "journeyman," "magister," and "magistron.")

Order of Bergahl—the religious order of the war god Bergahl (see above). Because of its special position in the Kingdom of Othmaliz, the Kingdom's Seneschal must, by tradition, be selected from the Order's priesthood.

Osmaria—the Sharonian analogue of Italy.

Othmaliz—the kingdom which dominates the eastern end of the Mbisi Sea and the outlet from the Ylani Sea. It is roughly equivalent to the western half of Turkey and the southern third of Bulgaria. Its capital is Tajvana, the ancient Imperial capital of the Ternathian Empire.

PAAF—the Portal Authority Armed Forces. The military units of various Sharonian nations placed under the Portal Authority's command for frontier security operations.

Paerystia—a region of Arcana roughly equivalent to Oman.

Pairhys Island—the Sharonian equivalent of the Isle of Man. The premier training camp of the Imperial Ternathian Marines is located there.

Plotter—a Sharonian with the "Plotting" Talent. Plotting is a specialized sub-variant of the Mapping Talent which is particularly useful in military service. Plotters, unlike Mappers, detect the presence and location of living creatures, like human beings.

Portal Hound—a Sharonian psionic sensitive to trans-temporal portals.

Porter—a Sharonian Talent with the telekinetic ability to teleport (or "Port") passengers or limited freight via the Emergency Transportation System.

Projective—a Sharonian psionic with the ability to project detailed and accurate mental images for non-telepaths. All Projectives are also Voices, but less than .01% of all Voices are Projectives.

Queen Kalthra's Lake—the Arcanan equivalent of Lake Ontario.

Queriz—a city in Arpathia, located at the equivalent position of Astana, Kazakhstan.

Queriz Depression—the Sharonian equivalent of the Caspian Depression.

Rahil—the Great Prophetess, the founder of and patron saint of mercy and healing in the Fellowship of Rahil, one of the dominant religions of Ransar.

Rahilian—an adherent of the Fellowship of Rahil.

Rankadi—Mythalan ritual suicide.

Ransar—the Arcanan equivalent of Asia. Ransar is home to a highly humanistic, democratic, and innovative culture which places an extremely high value on the worth of the individual. This makes Ransar an uncomfortable fit with the Andaran warrior aristocracy at times, but an even more uncomfortable fit with Mythal's caste-based society. Ransarans enjoy the most comfortable life styles of any Arcanan social group.

Razinta Basin—the depression between the Gartasa Mountains, Teramandor Mountains, and Emperor Edvar Mountains of the Narhathan Penninsula; drained by the Razinta River.

Razinta River—the Sharonian analogue of Spain's Ebro River.

Recon crystal—also called "RC"; a sarkolis-based reconnaissance device capable of recording and storing visual imagery and sounds within specified radii of the crystal. It is a *storage* device, and has no ability to transmit reconnaissance data across any distance.

Ricathia—the Sharonian equivalent of Africa.

Ricathian Desert—the Sharonian equivalent of the Libyan Desert.

Rindor Ocean—the Sharonian equivalent of the Indian Ocean.

Rokhana—a nation of New Ternath on Sharona which occupies the western coast from what would be our own Oregon to just about the line of the Mexican border.

Saint Taiyr—also called Taiyr of Estafal, the patron saint of the House of Calirath.

Saramash—the Shurkhali devil.

Sarkolis crystal—the extremely strong, quartz-like "stone" (actually an artificially manufactured crystal) used as the matrices and storage components for Arcanan spell-based technology.

Sarlayn River—the Sharonian analogue of the Nile River.

Sarthan Desert—the Sharonian analogue of the Sahara Desert.

Scurlis Sea—the Sharonian equivalent of the Sea of Japan.

Sea of Ibral—the Sharonian equivalent of the Sea of Marmara.

Septs—Arpathian clan-based social units, most of which are nomadic herders. Arpathian septs breed some of the finest horses in Sharona. Septs are mistrustful of outsiders, due to unscrupulous traders who sought to take advantage of "nomadic barbarians" and due to the tendency of other cultures to view them as primitive and make them the butt of unpleasant humor.

Septentrion—Most septs of Arpathia do not have a formal government outside the ruler of each tribe/clan-based sept. Their territories are somewhat fluid, particularly in the region of the Siberian plains. The septs banded together in the matter of trade, however, creating the Septentrion as a trade union that protects the financial interests of all the septs. The representatives of the septs who serve in the Septentrion deal with outside merchants and bargain the best prices for Arpathian goods, including the legendary work of Arpathian goldsmiths. The Septentrion established regional trade centers along the borders with Arpathia's neighbors. The Septentrion also sends a delegate to serve as a director of the Portal Authority and assists septmen who want to join the PAAF as soldiers or to apply to the Portal Authority for training to explore the multiverse as members of a civilian survey crew.

Serikai—"City of Snow," a lakeside city in Sharona, which is the equivalent of Buffalo, New York. Serikai is the capital city of the Republic of Faltharia.

Sethdona—the capital of the Sharonian Kingdom of Shurkhal. Located at the trans-temporal equivalent of Jiddah on the Arabian peninsula's Red Sea shore.

Shakira—the magic-using caste which totally dominates and controls the culture of Mythal. These are the researchers, theoreticians, etc., and control virtually all of Mythal's "white collar" occupations.

Shalana—"Mother Shalana" is one of the Ternathian Double Triads and one of the most-revered and powerful deities of that Double Triad. Blue is her sacred color, which is why her Temple in Tajvana is covered with lapis lazuli and sapphires. She is also known as Shalana the Merciful. Her priestess-hood is one of the wealthiest in Sharona.

Shaloma—The Arcanan equivalent of Western Europe.

Shardon—a technical term, from the Old Andaran. It translates literally as "shieldling," and indicates an individual under the protection of an Andaran warrior and his family. (See *baranal*, above.)

Sharona—the home universe and Earth of the Ternathian Empire. Its physics are similar, but not identical, to our own, and its society is largely based upon highly developed psionic Talents.

Shartahk—the main Andaran religion's devil.

Shartha Highlands—high, rugged mountains in northwestern Shartha; the Sharonian analogue of Ethiopia's Eastern Highlands.

Shartha—a kingdom in eastern Ricathia (see "Kingdom of Shartha," above).

Sherkaya—the ancient Mythalan word for "fire;" the release code which triggers a red dragon's breath weapon.

Shikowr—a breed of riding/cavalry horse developed in Ternathia over the space of several thousand years. The Shikowr resembles the Morgan horse in conformation and stance, but stands between sixteen and seventeen hands in height. The name is taken from a type of Shurkhali cavalry saber which was adopted by the Ternathian cavalry.

Showma Falls—the Arcanan equivalent (in New Arcana) of Niagara Falls. Site of the Garth Showma Institute of Magic.

Shurkhal—a Sharonian kingdom, roughly equivalent to Saudi Arabia, Jordan, and the Sinai Peninsula. The Kingdom of Shurkhal is the largest of several "Shurkhalian" kingdoms, closely related culturally to Harkala, but clearly a distinct subculture, which dominates the area of Syria, Iraq, and most of Iran.

Sifter—a Sharonian psionic whose Talent allows him to determine whether or not any statement is the truth or a lie.

Sky Blood Mountains—the Sharonian name for the Sierra Nevada Mountains.

Sky Blood Lode—the Sharonian name for the Comstock Lode.

Slide rail—also "slider." The Arcanan equivalent of a railroad.

Sniffer—another term for a "Tracer." (See "Tracer," below.)

Snow Sapphire Lake—the Sharonian name for Lake Tahoe, Nevada.

Strait of Tears—the Sharonian equivalent of the Bab el-Mandeb Strait connecting the Red Sea with the Gulf of Aden.

Strait of Bolakin—the Sharonian equivalent of the Strait of Gibraltar.

Strike—an Arcanan Air Force formation consisting of three "flights," for a total of twelve dragons.

Sunhold—the Uromathian feudal territory held by a "sunlord" (see below); roughly equivalent to a duchy or grand duchy.

Sunlord—a Uromathian aristocratic title roughly equivalent to that of duke.

SUNN—Sharona's Universal News Network, the largest news organization in Sharona's multiple-universe civilization, with both print and telepathic broadcast divisions.

Tajvana—the capital of the First Ternathian Empire at its height; the Sharonian equivalent of Constantinople or Istanbul.

Talon—an Arcanan Air Force formation consisting of three "strikes," for a total of thirty-six dragons.

Temple of Saint Taiyr of Tajvana—a temple in Tajvana, comemorating Saint Taiyr of Estafel, built by Empress Wailyana I in 3016. Traditional site of Calirath coronations for almost two thousand years.

Teramandor—a province of the Empire of Ternathia located in northwest Narhath; roughly analogous to Catalonia and western Aragon, Spain.

Teramandor Mountains—the Sharonian analogue of the Cataluna Mountains of Spain.

Ternath Island—the ancient homeland of the Emperors of Ternathia; the Arcanan equivalent of Ireland.

Ternathian Empire—the most ancient human polity known in any of the explored universes. The Ternathians established an effective world-state during the Copper and early Iron Age eras of Sharona, largely through the recognition, development and use of psionic talents. Originally located on Ternath Island (Ireland), it is the largest, oldest, most prestigious empire on Sharona. Its major component states include, besides Ternath Island:

> **Alathia:** Italy; **Jerekhas**: Sicily; **Bernith Island:** Britain (Scotland, England, Wales); **Delkrathia**: part of Spain; **Ermandia:** Austria; **Karmalia:** Hungary; **Lugathia:** France; **Mulgethia:** Germany/ Switzerland; **Narhath:** part of Spain; **Nessia:** Greece; **Pairhys Island:** Isle of Man; **Teramandor:** part of Spain.

Tharkan—a grand Duchy in Shaloma, an imperial territory of the Kingdom of Elath located in the Arcanan equivalent of Poland where the first Arcanan trans-temporal portal was discovered.

Time of Conquest—the period of ancient Ternathia's most sustained, militant expansion. Generally dated by Sharonian historians as extending from approximately 2025 to 3650.

Torkash—the chief deity of the ancient Manisthu pantheon in Arcana.

Tosaria—an ancient Ransaran kingdom on Arcana. Its capital was located in the same approximate geographical spot as Shanghai. Tosaria had attained a high and sophisticated level of civilization while most of the rest of present day Ransara was still in a state of primitivism.

Tracer—a Sharonian with the Tracer Talent. One who is sensitive to the current location, or at least direction to, another individual or object. They are also called "Sniffers."

Trans-Temporal Express—a privately-held corporation responsible for building and maintaining the primary rail and shipping connections linking the Sharonian home universe to the expanding frontier. Although it is the single largest, wealthiest privately-held corporation in Sharonian history, the TTE is subject to close regulation and oversight by the Portal Authority, which has granted—and retains the legal right to revoke—the TTE's multi-universal right-of-way.

Tukoria—the largest and most powerful of the Hilmaran kingdoms, consisting of the equivalent of most of Argentina and Chile. Tukoria was the only Hilmaran state which maintained its independence against Andaran conquest and colonization.

Union of Arcana—the world government of the home universe of Arcana.

Union City—a city at the entry portal into New Sharona, located about fifty miles east of Bloemfontein, South Africa.

Union Trans-Temporal Transit Authority—the agency of the Union of Arcana's government charged with overseeing trans-temporal travel and commerce, including regulation of sliderails and maritime transport infrastructure.

Union Arbitration Commission (UAC)—a quasi-diplomatic commission which answers to the Union Senate's committee on inter-universal disputes.

Uromathia—a general term applied to the Sharonian equivalent of Asia south of Mongolia and west of India. This area is divided into many smaller kingdoms and two empires, all of which share many common cultural traits.

Uromathian Empire—the larger of the two empires found in Uromathia. It occupies the Sharonian equivalent of China and includes the equivalent of Vietnam and Cambodia.

Usarlah—a Sharonian city located in the Delkrath Mountains (just north of Madrid) in the Ternathian province of Delkrathia.

UTTTA—see Union Trans-Temporal Transit Authority, above.

Vandor Ocean—the Sharonian equivalent of the Atlantic Ocean.

vos—"of the line of" in ancient Mythalan. The use in a Mythalan's name indicates that the individual is of high *shakira* caste. (See also "mul," above.)

Vothan—the Ternathian deity called "Father Vothan," who serves as Ternathia's war god, is one of the Ternathian Double Triads. "Father Vothan" protects the Empire in military combat and is therefore also called Protector Vothan or "The Protector" by the people of Ternathia and those regions colonized by Ternathia.

Vothan's chariot—the armored chariot of the Ternathian Double Triad deity who serves as Ternathia's Protector, or god of war.

Vyrlair—an Arpathian region of Sharona roughly equivalent to our own Turkmenistan.

Western Ocean—the Sharonian name for the Pacific Ocean.

Whiffer—a Sharonian with the Whiffer Talent. One who is sensitive to residual psychic impressions.

White Mist Lake—the Arcanan equivalent of Lake Erie.

Windhold—the feudal territory held by a Uromathian "windlord" (see below); roughly equivalent to an earldom.

Windlord—a Uromathian aristocratic title, roughly equivalent to that of earl.

Winged Crown—the imperial crown of Ternathia. This ancient crown (still used in coronations) was made by Farnalian goldsmiths almost 5,000 years ago as a surety for the treaty negotiated between the Kingdom of Ternathia and Farnalia by Celaryon II of Ternathia (see above).

Yamali Mountains—the Sharonian analogue of the Himalaya Mountains, they lie north of Harkala, stretching from Isseth in the west into the Uromathian Empire in the east.

Yanko—the third major Andaran kingdom, which includes the equivalent of most of central North America, from the Canadian border south, and virtually all of Mexico.

Yarahk—an Arcanan city located at the equivalent of Aswan, Egypt.

Yirshan River—the Sharonian equivalent of the Columbia River.

Ylani Strait—the Sharonian equivalent of the Bosporus.

Ylani Sea—the Sharonian equivalent of the Black Sea.

Yurha—the soul as conceptualized by Mythalan religion. The *yurha* is the basis of Mythalan reincarnation beliefs, which enshrine the concept of "spiritual evolution" to a higher state of being.

Zaithag—an Arpathian city in Vyrlair, located at approximately the same spot as Ashgabat, Turkmenistan.

CAST OF CHARACTERS

[HG] = appears in *Hell's Gate.*

[HHNF] = appears in *Hell Hath No Fury.*

Ambor, Shield Layrak, Union of Arcana Army— [HG] assistant surgeon, Charlie Company, First Battalion, First Regiment, Second Andaran Temporal Scouts.

Anzeti, Djoser—[HG] a director of the Sharonian Portal Authority board, representing the Arpathian Septentrion.

Arthag, Petty-Captain Hulmok, Portal Authority Armed Forces—[HG, HHNF] acting platoon-captain, CO, Second Platoon, Argent Company, Ninety-Second Independent Cavalry Battalion. Formally promoted to platoon-captain in HHNF.

Balithar, Sathee—[HG] Princess Andrin's personal maid from childhood.

Banchu, Olvyr—[HG, HHNF] the Trans-Temporal Express's chief construction engineer.

Bantha, Petty-Armsman Grethar, Portal Authority Armed Forces—[HG] Company-Captain Halifu's senior Flicker.

Baskay, Charazan—[HG] Platoon-Captain chan Baskay's sixteen-year-old sister.

Baulwan, Petty-Captain Shansair, Portal Authority Armed Forces—[HHNF] a Voice assigned to Company-Captain Halifu at Fort Shaylar.

Berhala, Commander of Twenty-Five Tahlos, Union of Arcana Air Force—[HHNF] a pilot attached to the 3012th Strike; pilot of red battle dragon Skyfire.

Bolsh, Tarlin—[HG] international news division chief, Sharonian Universal News Network.

Borkaz, Trooper Emiyet, Union of Arcana Army—[HG] First Squad, Charlie Company, First Battalion, First Regiment, Second Andaran Temporal Scouts.

Breasal, Ordras—[HG] a director of the Sharonian Portal Authority Board, representing the Kingdom of Isseth.

Bright Wind—[HG, HHNF] Hulmok Arthag's prized Palomino stallion.

Busar, Emperor Chava IX—[HG, HHNF] Emperor of Uromathia.

Calirath, Her Imperial Grand Highness Anbessa—[HG, HHNF] the youngest of Zindel chan Calirath's daughters.

Calirath, Her Imperial Grand Highness Andrin—[HG, HHNF] the eldest of Zindel chan Calirath's three daughters, next in the imperial line of succession after her brother, Crown Prince Janaki.

Calirath, Her Imperial Grand Highness Razial— [HG, HHNF] the second eldest of Zindel chan Calirath's daughters.

Calirath, Her Imperial Majesty Varena—[HG, HHNF] Empress Consort of Ternathia; Zindel chan Calirath's wife.

Carthos, Commander of One Thousand Tayrgal, Union of Arcana Army—[HHNF] Two Thousand Harshu's senior ground commander.

Chan Barsak, Junior-Armsman Paras, Portal Authority Armed Forces—[HHNF] a noncommissioned officer assigned to Fort Salby.

Chan Baskay, Platoon-Captain Dorzon, Portal Authority Armed Forces—[HG, HHNF] Viscount Simrath; a Ternathian cavalry officer assigned to Balkar chan Tesh.

Chan Braikal, Chief-Armsman Lorash, Portal Authority Armed Forces—[HG, HHNF] Prince Janaki's senior noncom, Third Platoon, Copper Company, Second Battalion, 117th Imperial Ternathian Marines, assigned to duty with the PAAF.

Chan Calirath, Platoon-Captain Crown Prince Janaki, Portal Authority Armed Forces— [HG, HHNF] the eldest child and heir of Emperor Zindel chan Calirath of Ternathia. CO, Third Platoon, Copper Company, Second Battalion, 117th Imperial Ternathian Marines, assigned to duty with the PAAF.

Chan Calirath, His Imperial Majesty Zindel—[HG, HHNF] Zindel XXIV, Duke of Ternathia, Grand Duke of Farnalia, Warlord of the West, Protector of the Peace, Wing-Crowned, and, by the gods' grace, Emperor of Ternathia.

Chan Darma, Petty-Captain Kaliya, Portal Authority Armed Forces—[HHNF] the Voice assigned to Fort Salby.

Chan Dersal, Platoon-Captain Parai, Portal Authority Armed Forces—[HG, HHNF] the senior of the two Ternathian Imperial Marine platoon COs assigned to Balkar chan Tesh.

Chan Eris, Foram—[HHNF] a retired Ternathian Army officer serving as Olvyr Banchu's second-in-command in Karys.

Chan Forcal, Chief-Armsman Wesiar, Portal Authority Armed Forces—[HHNF] a Distance Viewer assigned to Fort Salby.

Chan Garath, Master-Armsman Tesan, Portal Authority Armed Forces—[HHNF] senior noncommissioned officer, Fort Salby.

Chan Geraith, Division-Captain Arlos, Imperial Ternathian Army—[HG, HHNF] CO, Third Dragoon Division, Fifth Corps.

Chan Gordahl, Brahndys—[HG, HHNF] one of Princess Andrin's personal guardsmen.

Chan Gristhane, Captain-of-the-Army Thalyar, Imperial Ternathian Army—[HG] senior uniformed officer of the Ternathian Army and Ternathian Defense Councilor.

Chan Habikon, Ulthar—[HG, HHNF] one of Princess Andrin's personal guardsmen.

Chan Hagrahyl, Ghartoun—[HG] crew chief for the Chalgyn Consortium crew which first contacts the Arcanans.

Chan Harthu, Platoon-Captain Gerail, Portal Authority Armed Forces—[HG] the junior of the two Ternathian Imperial Marine platoon COs assigned to Balkar chan Tesh.

Chan Hathas, Chief-Armsman Rayl, Portal Authority Armed Forces—[HG, HHNF] Hulmok Arthag's senior noncommissioned officer.

Chan Himidi, Fanthi—[HG] a Ternathian military veteran assigned to the Chalgyn Consortium crew which first contacts the Arcanans.

Chan Isail, Regiment-Captain Merkan, Imperial Ternathian Army—[HHNF] Division-Captain chan Geraith's chief of staff.

Chan Jassian, Division-Captain Ustace, Imperial Ternathian Army—[HG] CO Twenty-First Infantry Division, Fifth Corps.

Chan Kormai, Master-Armsman Frai, Portal Authority Armed Forces—[HG, HHNF] Balkar chan Tesh's senior noncommissioned officer.

Chan Korthal, Company-Captain Lisar, Imperial Ternathian Army—[HHNF] Division-Captain chan Geraith's staff Voice.

Chan Lyrosk, Petty-Captain Waird, Portal Authority Armed Forces—[HHNF] a Voice assigned to Fort Brithik.

Chan Manthau, Division-Captain Yarkowan, Imperial Ternathian Army—[HG] CO, Ninth Infantry Division, Fifth Corps.

Chan Milhenai, Under-Armsman Sirda, Portal Authority Armed Forces—[HHNF] a Ternathian soldier assigned to Fort Shaylar.

Chan Morak, Platoon-Captain Harek, Portal Authority Armed Forces—[HHNF] Company-Captain Nalkhar's assistant engineer at Fort Salby.

Chan Morthain, Master-Captain Farsal, Imperial Ternathian Navy—[HG] the CO of Emperor Zindel's escorting cruisers for the voyage to Tajvana.

Chan Noth, Platoon-Captain Tarkel, Portal Authority Armed Forces—[HHNF] a platoon commander assigned to Fort Salby.

Chan Quay, Brigade-Captain Renyl, Imperial Ternathian Army—[HHNF] CO, First Brigade, Third Dragoon Division, Imperial Ternathian Army.

Chan Rakail, Josam, Portal Authority Armed Forces—[HG] the Voice assigned to Fort Tharkoma in the universe of Salym.

Chan Robarik, Company-Captain Feryal, Portal Authority Armed Forces—[HHNF] CO, Fort Brithik.

Chan Rodair, Petty-Captain Esalk, Portal Authority Armed Forces—[HG] the senior Talented Healer at Fort Brithik.

Chan Rowlan, Corps-Captain Fairlain, Imperial Ternathian Army—[HG] CO, Fifth Corps.

Chan Sairath, Senior-Armsman Quelovak, Portal Authority Armed Forces—[HG] Platoon-Captain chan Talmarha's senior noncom.

Chan Salgmun, Falsan—[HG] a member of the Chalgyn Consortium crew which first contacts the Arcanans.

Chan Skrithik, Regiment-Captain Rof, Portal Authority Armed Forces—[HG, HHNF] CO, Fort Salby, in the universe of Traisum.

Chan Synarch, Junior-Armsman Tairsal, Portal Authority Armed Forces—[HG, HHNF] Balkar chan Tesh's senior Flicker.

Chan Talmarha, Platoon-Captain Morek, Portal Authority Armed Forces—[HG, HHNF] CO of the mortar company assigned to Balkar chan Tesh.

Chan Tergis, Senior-Armsman Folsar, Portal Authority Armed Forces—[HHNF] the Voice assigned to Fort Ghartoun.

Chan Tesh, Company-Captain Balkar, Portal Authority Armed Forces—[HG, HHNF] CO Copper Company, First Battalion, Ninth Cavalry Regiment.

Chan Therson, Chief-Armsman Dunyar, Portal Authority Armed Forces—[HG] Company-Captain Halifu's senior noncommissioned officer.

Chan Treskin, Chief-Armsman Virak, Portal Authority Armed Forces—[HHNF] the Flicker assigned to Dorzon chan Baskay's negotiating team.

Chan Turkan, Under-Armsman Lyntail, Portal Authority Armed Forces—[HHNF] a soldier assigned to the Fort Ghartoun garrison.

Chan Yaran, Under-Armsman Rokal, Portal Authority Armed Forces—[HG, HHNF] Third

Platoon, Copper Company, Second Battalion, 117th Imperial Ternathian Marines. Promoted to petty-armsman in HHNF.

Chan Zindico, Lazima—[HG, HHNF] Princess Andrin's senior personal guardsman.

Charaeil—[HG] Emperor Zindel's peregrine falcon.

Chusal, Train Master Yakhan—[HG] the senior train master of the Trans-Temporal Express.

Cloudtiger—[HHNF] a red battle dragon; pilot, Commander of Twenty-Five Lairys Urkora.

Company-Captain Golvar Silkash, Portal Authority Armed Forces—[HG, HHNF] senior surgeon, Fort Ghartoun.

Crown Prince Danith Fyysel—[HG] heir to the throne of Shurkhal.

Darshu, Lord of Horse Jukan, Uromathian Imperial Cavalry—[HG, HHNF] Sunlord Markan, senior officer of the Uromathian cavalry detachment sent to reinforce Fort Salby.

Dastiri, Uthik—[HG, HHNF] a member of the Union Arbitration Commission; Rithmar Skirvon's subordinate.

Desmar, Commander of One Hundred Sahlis, Union of Arcana Air Force—[HHNF] CO, 2029th Strike; pilot of black battle dragon Thunderclap.

Dulan, Brithum—[HG] Ternathian Internal Affairs Councilor.

Elivath, Darl—[HG] the Sharonian Universal News Network's senior Voice correspondent at the Sharonian Portal Authority's headquarters.

Erkol, Divis—[HG] Ghartoun chan Hagrahyl's Ricathian clerk, assigned to the Chalgyn Consortium crew which first contacts the Arcanans.

Eswayr, Commander of Five Hundred Pahkrys, Union of Arcana Army—[HHNF] senior battalion commander assigned to Thousand Carthos' detached command.

Fahrlo, Commander of Fifty Delthyr, Union of Arcana Air Force—[HHNF] a pilot attached to the First Provisional Talon; pilot of black battle dragon Deathclaw.

Fai Yujin, His Majesty Junni—[HG] the King of Eniath (see also King Junni).

Fai Goutin, Prince Howan—[HG, HHNF] Crown Prince of Eniath (see also Prince Howan).

Farl, Lance Yirman, Union of Arcana Army—[HHNF] a soldier assigned to Fifty Halesak's First Platoon, Able Company, Second Andaran Temporal Scouts.

Finena—[HG, HHNF] Princess Andrin's peregrine falcon.

Firefang—[HHNF] a red battle dragon; pilot, Commander of One Hundred Faryx Helika.

Fornath, Lord Mancy—[HG] fifty-first Baron Fornath and forty-fifth Earl of Ilforth, the Speaker of the Ternathian House of Lords.

Futhai, Braiheri—[HG] a Ternathian noble and naturalist assigned to the Chalgyn Consortium crew which first contacts the Arcanans.

Garlath, Commander of Fifty Shevan, Union of Arcana Army—[HG] CO, First Platoon, Charlie Company, First Battalion, First Regiment, Second Andaran Temporal Scouts.

Garsal, Second Lord of Horse Tarnal, Uromathian Imperial Cavalry—[HG, HHNF] Windlord Garsal, Sunlord Markan's senior subordinate officer and XO.

Geraith, Misanya—[HHNF] Division-Captain chan Geraith's wife.

Geyrsof, Commander of One Hundred Horban, Union of Arcana Air Force—[HHNF] CO, 3012th Strike; pilot of yellow battle dragon Graycloud.

Gitel, Elevu—[HG] a geologist assigned to the Chalgyn Consortium crew which first contacts the Arcanans.

Grantyl, Commander of Five Hundred Waysal, Union of Arcana Army—[HG] CO, Fort Wyvern, universe of Mahritha.

Graycloud—[HHNF] a yellow battle dragon; pilot, Commander of One Hundred Horban Geyrsof.

Grigthir, Trooper Mikal, Portal Authority Armed Forces—[HG] a Scout assigned to Hulmok Arthag's cavalry platoon.

Haimas, Chathee—[HG] Orem Limana's assistant.

Halesak, Commander of Fifty Iftar, Union of Arcana Army—[HHNF] CO, First Platoon, Able Company, Second Andaran Temporal Scouts. Commander of Fifty Ulthar's brother-in-law.

Halifu, Company-Captain Grafin, Portal Authority Armed Forces—[HG, HHNF] CO of the newly established portal fort in the universe of New Uromath.

Hansara, Rayjhari—[HG] an ancient Ransaran magistron who devised the technique of genetic manipulation which produced Arcana's dragons and other magically enhanced creatures.

Hardoran, Petty-Armsman Joral, Portal Authority Armed Forces—[HHNF] a Farnalian noncom assigned to Fort Shaylar.

Harklan, Shield Gaythar, Union of Arcana Army—[HG] squad shield, Second Squad, First Platoon, Charlie Company, First Battalion, First Regiment, Second Andaran Temporal Scouts.

Harnak, Sword Evarl, Union of Arcana Army—[HG, HHNF] senior noncom, First Platoon, Charlie Company, Second Andaran Temporal Scouts.

Harshu, Commander of Two Thousand Mayrkos, Union of Arcana Army—[HG, HHNF] CO, Arcanan Expeditionary Force.

Harwal, Falgayn—[HG] an extremely powerful and Talented Sharonian Projective Voice.

Helika, Commander of One Hundred Faryx, Union of Arcana Air Force—[HHNF] CO, 5001st Strike; pilot of red battle dragon Fire-fang.

Hilovar, Junior-Armsman Soral, Portal Authority Armed Forces—[HG] a Ricathian Tracer temporarily attached to Hulmok Arthag's cavalry platoon.

Hordan, Chenrys—[HG] the Voice assigned to Hurkaym as the link between Fort Tharkoma and Fort Losaltha.

Ilthyr, Lamir—[HHNF] a civilian Voice assigned to the Portal Authority Voicenet in the universe of Traisum.

Isia, Senior-Armsman Orek, Portal Authority Armed Forces—[HHNF] Regiment-Captain chan Skrithik's Flicker at Fort Salby.

Israin, Commander of Five Hundred Chalbos, Union of Arcana Army—[HHNF] one of Two Thousand Harshu's senior infantry battalion commanders.

Jaboth, Lance Inkar, Union of Arcana Army—[HG] cook, Charlie Company, First Battalion, First Regiment, Second Andaran Temporal Scouts.

Jalkanthi, Master Engineer Hardar—[HG] a senior engineer of the Trans-Temporal Express.

Jalkanthi-Ishar, Jesmanar—[HG] Hardar Jalkanthi's Shurkhali wife.

Jastyr, Ulantha—[HHNF] Alazon Yanamar's assistant Voice and protégée.

Kalcyr, Senior Sword Barcan, Union of Arcana Army—[HHNF] senior noncom, Company Bravo, 901st Light Cavalry.

Karone, His Imperial Majesty Ronnel XVI—[HG, HHNF] Emperor of Farnalia.

Karuk, Master-Armsman Hordal, Portal Authority Armed Forces—[HHNF] the senior noncom assigned to Fort Ghartoun.

Karym, Lady Jagtha—[HG] a director of the Sharonian Portal Authority Board representing the Kingdom of Limathia.

Kasell, Barris—[HG] an Arpathian ex-soldier assigned to the Chalgyn Consortium crew which first contacts the Arcanans.

Kavilkan, Jali—[HG] executive manager, Sharonian Universal News Network.

Kelbryan, Magister Gadrial—[HG, HHNF] former student of Magister Halathyn vos Dulainah; Department Chairwoman, Theoretical Magic, Garth Showma Institute of Magic.

Kiliron, Commander of One Hundred Orkal, Union of Arcana Army—[HHNF] CO, Charlie Company, Seventh Zydor Heavy Dragoons.

Kindare, Relatha—[HG] a serving girl from Hawkwing Palace and Ternathia who replaces Sathee Balithar as Princess Andrin's personal maid after Balithar's injury.

King Junni—[HG, HHNF] Junni Fai Yujin, King of Eniath (see also Fai Yujin, His Majesty Junni)

King Fyysel—[HG] the monarch of Shurkhal.

Kinlafia, Darcel—[HG, HHNF] the second Voice assigned to the Chalgyn Consortium crew which first contacts the Arcanans.

Kinshe, Halidar—[HG] a director of the Sharonian Portal Authority and a Parliamentary Representative in the Kingdom of Shurkhal.

Kinshe-Falis, Lady Alimar—[HG] Halidar Kinshe's wife; a Talented Healer.

Klian, Commander of Five Hundred Sarr, Union of Arcana Army—[HG] CO, Fort Rycharn, universe of Mahritha.

Kolmayr, Thaminar—[HG] the father of Shaylar Nargra-Kolmayr and husband of Shalassar Kolmayr-Brintal.

Kolmayr-Brintal, Shalassar—[HG] a Talented ambassador to the cetaceans for the Kingdom of Shurkhal. Shaylar Nargra-Kolmayr's mother.

Kormas, Commander of One Hundred Surtel, Union of Arcana Air Force—[HHNF] Thousand Toralk's senior gryphon-handler.

Krankark, Javelin Sherlan—[HG] Third Squad, First Platoon, Charlie Company, First Battalion, First Regiment, Second Andaran Temporal Scouts.

Krilar, Company-Captain Gairion, Portal Authority Armed Forces—[HHNF] senior medical officer, Fort Salby.

Kuralk, Senior-Armsman Yairkan, Portal Authority Armed Forces—[HHNF] an Arpathian noncom assigned to Fort Shaylar.

Kurthal, Trooper Branak—[HG] Second Squad, Charlie Company, First Battalion, First Regiment, Second Andaran Temporal Scouts.

Laresk, Sword Seltym, Union of Arcana Army—[HHNF] Fifty Tharian Narshu's SpecOps' senior noncom.

Larshal, Commander of Fifty Jolika, Union of Arcana Air Force—[HHNF] Thousand Toralk's command dragon pilot.

Limana, Director Orem—[HG, HHNF] First Director, Sharonian Portal Authority.

Loumas, Petty-Armsman Harth, Portal Authority Armed Forces—[HG, HHNF] a Plotter assigned to Hulmok Arthag's command.

Mahrkrai, Commander of Five Hundred Herak, Union of Arcana Army—[HHNF] Two Thousand Harshu's chief of staff.

Makree, Platoon-Captain Tobis, Portal Authority Armed Forces—[HG, HHNF] Company-Captain

Silkash's assistant surgeon. He is also a very Talented Healer.

Mala, Commander of Five Hundred Karth, Union of Arcana Air Force—[HHNF] senior Air Force officer assigned to Thousand Carthos' detached command.

Malthayr, Gayrzal—[HG] Princess Razial's art instructor.

Mankahr, Commander Twenty-Five Sherlahk, Union of Arcana Air Force—[HHNF] a pilot assigned to the 3012th Strike; pilot of yellow battle dragon Skykill.

Mesaion, Company-Captain Lorvam, Portal Authority Armed Forces—[HHNF] senior artillery officer, Fort Salby.

Morikan, Sword Naf, Union of Arcana Army—[HG] Gifted healer, Charlie Company, First Battalion, First Regiment, Second Andaran Temporal Scouts.

Myr, Commander of Five Hundred Cerlohs, Union of Arcana Air Force—[HHNF] CO, First Provisional Talon, pilot of black battle dragon Razorwing.

Naldar, Yorlahn—[HG] the cook assigned to the Chalgyn Consortium crew which first contacts the Arcanans.

Nalkhar, Company-Captain Meris, Portal Authority Armed Forces—[HHNF] senior engineering officer, Fort Salby.

Nargra, Jathmar—[HG, HHNF] a Mapper assigned to the Chalgyn Consortium crew which first encounters the Arcanans. The husband of Shaylar Nargra-Kolmayr.

Nargra-Kolmayr, Shaylar—[HG, HHNF] a powerfully Talented Voice, assigned to the Chalgyn Consortium crew which first encounters the Arcanans. The wife of Jathmar Nargra.

Narmayla, Haliyar—[HG] the Voice assigned to New Ramath in the universe of Salym.

Narshu, Commander of Fifty Tharian, Union of Arcana Army—[HG, HHNF] a Special Operations officer assigned to command Rithmar Skirvon's escort at the Fallen Timbers negotiations.

Neshok, Commander of Five Hundred (acting) Alivar, Union of Arcana Army—[HG, HHNF] Two Thousand Harshu's senior Intelligence officer.

Nourm, Sword Keraik, Union of Arcana Army—[HHNF] senior noncom, Second Platoon, Able Company, Fifth Battalion, 306th Regiment.

Olderhan, Commander of One Hundred Sir Jasak, Union of Arcana Army—[HG, HHNF] CO, Charlie Company, First Battalion, First Regiment, Second Andaran Temporal Scouts.

Olderhan, Sir Thankhar—[HG] Duke of Garth Showma, planetary governor of New Arcana, father of Sir Jasak Olderhan.

Olderhan, Sathmin—[HG] Duchess of Garth Showma, wife of Sir Thankhar Olderhan, mother of Sir Jasak Olderhan.

Orma, Jaerika—[HHNF] a civilian Portal Authority Voice assigned to the Voicenet in Karys.

Osmuna, Trooper Yurak, Union of Arcana Army—[HG] Second Squad, First Platoon, Charlie

Company, First Battalion, First Regiment, Second Andaran Temporal Scouts.

Palben, Irthan—[HG] a director of the Sharonian Portal Authority Board, representing the Empire of Farnalia.

Parcanthi, Petty-Armsman Nolis, Portal Authority Armed Forces—[HG] a Whiffer temporarily attached to Hulmok Arthag's platoon.

Partha, Junior-Armsman Farzak, Portal Authority Armed Forces—[HHNF] Company-Captain Halifu's orderly at Fort Shaylar.

Perthis, Davir—[HG] Chief Voice, Sharonian Universal News Network.

Porath, Javelin Lisaro, Union Of Arcana Army—[HHNF] a noncom assigned to Five Hundred Neshok's Intelligence section.

Prince Howan—[HG, HHNF] Prince Howan Fai Goutin, Crown Prince of Eniath (see also Fai Goutin, Prince Howan.)

Rahndar, Commander of Fifty Imal, Union of Arcana Army—[HHNF] a Gifted combat engineer attached to the Seventh Zydor Heavy Dragoons.

Ranlak, Lance Yurain, Union of Arcana Army—[HHNF] cavalry trooper, Company Bravo, 901st Light Cavalry.

Raynarg, Fairlain—[HHNF] birth-name of His Crowned Eminence, the Seneschal of Othmaliz.

Raynor, Division-Captain Thersahl, Portal Authority Armed Forces—[HG] the senior uniformed officer of the PAAF at the time of first contact with Andara.

Razorwing—[HHNF] a black battle dragon; pilot, Commander of Five Hundred Cerlohs Myr.

Rilthan, Lerok—[HG] the gunsmith assigned to the Chalgyn Consortium crew which first contacts the Arcanans.

Rothag, Under-Captain Trekar, Portal Authority Armed Forces—[HG, HHNF] a Sifter assigned as Dorzon chan Baskay's "aide" for his negotiations with Rithmar Skirvon.

Salmeer, Squire Muthok, Union of Arcana Air Force—[HG] pilot of transport dragon Windclaw.

Sandrick, Gortho—[HG] a retired portal survey crewman used for local color and expert coverage of trans-temporal affairs by the Sharonian Universal News Network.

Sarma, Commander of Fifty Jaralt, Union of Arcana Army—[HHNF] CO, Second Platoon, Alpha Company, Fifth Battalion, 306th Regiment; assigned to Two Thousand Harshu's Arcanan Expeditionary Force.

Scleppis, Tymo—[HG] the Talented Healer attached to the Chalgyn Consortium crew which first contacts the Arcanans.

Sendahli, Trooper Jugthar, Union of Arcana Army—[HG, HHNF] Third Squad, First Platoon, Charlie Company, First Battalion, First Regiment, Second Andaran Temporal Scouts. Sendahli is a *garthan* who has fled Mythal and enlisted in the Union Army.

Sheltim, Train Master Hayrdar—[HG] a protégé of Yakhan Chusal, assigned as the train master for the Trans-Temporal Express transporting the Third Dragoons, Imperial Ternathian Army.

Shilvass, Ekthar—[HG] Imperial Ternathian Treasury Councilor.

Shulthan, Javelin Iggar, Union of Arcana Army— [HG] senior hummer-handler, Charlie Company, First Battalion, First Regiment, Second Andaran Temporal Scouts.

Silbeth, Nanthee—[HG] Imperial Ternathian Education Councilor.

Silkash, Company-Captain Golvar, Portal Authority Armed Forces—[HG, HHNF] Regiment-Captain Velvelig's senior physician; a brilliant surgeon, but not a Talented Healer.

Skirvon, Rithmar—[HG, HHNF] a representative of the Union Arbitration Commission, an internal, quasi-diplomatic organ of the Union of Arcana. He is the senior diplomat available for negotiations with the Sharonians.

Skrithik, Chalendra—[HHNF] Regiment-Captain Rof chan Skrithik's wife.

Skyfire—[HHNF] a red battle dragon; pilot, Commander of Twenty-Five Tahlos Berhala.

Skykill—[HHNF] a yellow battle dragon; pilot, Commander of Twenty-Five Sherlahk Mankahr.

Taje, First Councilor Shamir—[HG, HHNF] head of the Ternathian Imperial Privy Council; effectively, Zindel chan Calirath's prime minister.

Taleena—[HG, HHNF] Crown Prince Janaki's peregrine falcon.

Targal, Raysith—[HHNF] "Kersai" Targal's wife.

Targal, Syrail—[HHNF] an emerging Voice; the thirteen-year old son of "Kersai" and Raysith Targal.

Targal, Syrail ("Kersai")—[HHNF] a Fairnos Consortium's geologist assigned to the universe of Thermyn.

Tarka, Irnay—[HHNF] a Trans-Temporal Express employee assigned to the construction crews in the universe of Karys.

Tarku, Charak—[HG] Hardar Jalkanthi's Arpathian fireman.

Taymish, Director Gahlreen—[HG] First Director of the Sharonian Trans-Temporal Express.

Thalmayr, Commander of One Hundred Hadrign, Union of Arcana Army—[HG, HHNF] CO, Charlie Company, Second Andaran Temporal Scouts.

Tharsayl, Dalisar—[HG] the head of the staff assigned to Shalassar Kolmayr-Brintal and Thaminar Kolmayr by King Fyysel of Shurkhal.

Threbuch, Chief Sword Otwal, Union of Arcana Army—[HG, HHNF] Battalion Chief Sword, Charlie Company, First Battalion, First Regiment, Second Andaran Temporal Scouts.

Thunderclap—[HHNF] a black battle dragon; pilot, Commander of One Hundred Sahlis Desmar.

Tiris, Lance Rewelyn, Union of Arcana Army—[HG, HHNF] a trooper assigned to Charlie Company, Second Andaran Temporal Scouts.

Toralk, Commander of One Thousand Klayrman, Union of Arcana Air Force—[HG, HHNF] Two Thousand Harshu's senior Air Force officer;

senior Air Force officer, Arcanan Expeditionary Force.

Traith, Sword Garmak, Union of Arcana Army—[HG] surgeon, Charlie Company, First Battalion, First Regiment, Second Andaran Temporal Scouts.

Traygan, Petty-Captain Rokam, Portal Authority Armed Forces—[HG, HHNF] the Voice designated for permanent assignment to Company-Captain Halifu's fort but ultimately assigned to the Fallen Timbers negotiations.

Ula, Captain Chairmok—[HG] CO of the passenger liner IMS *Windtreader*.

Ulthar, Commander of Fifty Therman, Union of Arcana Army—[HG, HHNF] CO, Third Platoon, Charlie Company, Second Andaran Temporal Scouts. Commander of Fifty Halesak's brother-in-law.

Ulthar, Arylis—[HHNF] Commander of Fifty Therman Ulthar's wife.

Umani, Yaf—[HG, HHNF] Head Voice of the Sharonian Portal Authority.

Urkora, Commander of Twenty-Five Lairys, Union of Arcana Air Force—[HHNF] a pilot attached to the 3012th Strike; pilot of red battle dragon Cloudtiger.

Urlan, Commander of Five Hundred Gyras, Union of Arcana Army—[HHNF] CO, Seventh Zydor Heavy Dragoons.

Vankhal, Lady Merissa—[HG, HHNF] Princess Andrin's chief lady-in-waiting and protocol instructor.

Vardan, Erthek—[HHNF] a civilian Voice assigned to the Portal Authority Voicenet chain in the universe of Thermyn.

Vargan, Company-Captain Orkam, Portal Authority Armed Forces—[HHNF] Regiment-Captain chan Skrithik's executive officer at Fort Salby.

Varkal, Commander of Fifty Daris, Union of Arcana Air Force—[HG] pilot of transport dragon Skyfang, Union of Arcana Air Force.

Varla, Petty-Armsman Erkam, Portal Authority Armed Forces—[HHNF] a noncom assigned to Fort Ghartoun.

Vaynair, Commander of Five Hundred Dayr, Union of Arcana Army—[HHNF] the senior Gifted healer assigned to Two Thousand Harshu's Arcanan Expeditionary Force.

Velvelig, Regiment-Captain Namir, Portal Authority Armed Forces—[HG, HHNF] CO of Fort Ghartoun.

Verais, Under-Armsman Kardan, Portal Authority Armed Forces—[HHNF] a soldier assigned to Fort Salby.

Vormak, Sword Chul, Union of Arcana Army—[HG] surgeon, Charlie Company, First Battalion, First Regiment, Second Andaran Temporal Scouts.

Vos and mul Gurthak, Commander of Two Thousand Nith, Union of Arcana Army—[HG, HHNF] CO, Fort Talon, universe of Erthos, senior officer for a nine-universe command area running from Esthiya through Mahritha. He is both *shakira* and *multhari*.

Vos Dulainah, Magister Halathyn—[HG] *shakira* theoretical magister. Ex-instructor and department head, Mythalan Falls Academy; currently founder and chancellor of the Garth Showma Institute of Magic.

Vos Hoven, Lance Bok, Union of Arcana Army—[HG] a Gifted *shakira* combat engineer assigned to Charlie Company, First Battalion, First Regiment, Second Andaran Temporal Scouts.

Vuras, Platoon-Captain Selan, Portal Authority Armed Forces—[HHNF] an infantry platoon commander assigned to Fort Salby.

Wilkon, Samari—[HG] a Voice assigned by Yaf Umani to accompany Halidar Kinshe to Shurkhal.

Wiltash, Linar—[HG] Jali Kavilkan's private secretary.

Wilthy, Lance Erdar, Union of Arcana Army—[HG] senior baggage handler, First Platoon, Charlie Company, First Battalion, First Regiment, Second Andaran Temporal Scouts.

Windclaw—[HG] a tactical transport dragon piloted by Squire Muthok Salmeer.

Windslasher—[HHNF] a yellow battle dragon; pilot, Commander of Fifty Nairdag Yorhan.

Worka, Commander of One Hundred Sylair, Union of Arcana Army—[HHNF] CO, Company Bravo, 901st Light Cavalry.

Yanamar, Alazon—[HG, HHNF] Zindel chan Calirath's Privy Voice.

Yar, Petty-Captain Delokahn, Portal Authority Armed Forces—[HG, HHNF] the Talented Healer assigned to Balkar chan Tesh.

Yorhan, Commander of Fifty Nairdag, Union of Arcana Air Force—[HHNF] a pilot assigned to the 3012th Strike; pilot of yellow battle dragon Windslasher.

Yoritam, Hersal—[HHNF] a civilian Portal Authority Voice assigned to Olvyr Banchu's work crews in Karys.

Flag in Exile 0-7434-3575-3 • $7.99

"Packs enough punch to smash a starship to smithereens."—*Publishers Weekly*

Honor Among Enemies 0-671-87723-2 • $21.00
0-671-87783-6 • $7.99

"Star Wars as it might have been written by C.S. Forester...fast-paced entertainment."—*Booklist*

In Enemy Hands 0-671-87793-3 • $22.00
0-671-57770-0 • $7.99

After being ambushed, Honor finds herself aboard an enemy cruiser, bound for her scheduled execution. But one lesson Honor has never learned is how to give up!

Echoes of Honor 0-671-87892-1 • $24.00
0-671-57833-2 • $7.99

"Brilliant! Brilliant! Brilliant!"—Anne McCaffrey

Ashes of Victory 0-671-57854-5 • $25.00
0-671-31977-9 • $7.99

Honor has escaped from the prison planet called Hell and returned to the Manticoran Alliance, to the heart of a furnace of new weapons, new strategies, new tactics, spies, diplomacy, and assassination.

War of Honor 0-7434-3545-1 • $26.00
0-7434-7167-9 • $7.99

No one wanted another war. Neither the Republic of Haven, nor Manticore—and certainly not Honor Harrington. Unfortunately, what they wanted didn't matter.

At All Costs 1-4165-0911-9 • $26.00

The war with the Republic of Haven has resumed...disastrously for the Star Kingdom of Manticore. The alternative to victory is total defeat, yet this time the cost of victory will be agonizingly high.

THE BAHZELL SAGA:

Oath of Swords 0-671-87642-2 • $7.99

The War God's Own hc • 0-671-87873-5 • $22.00
pb • 0-671-57792-1 • $7.99

Wind Rider's Oath hc • 0-7434-8821-0 • $26.00
pb • 1-4165-0895-3 • $7.99

Bahzell Bahnakson of the hradani is no knight in shining armor and doesn't want to deal with anybody else's problems, let alone the War God's. The War God thinks otherwise.

BOLO VOLUMES:

Bolo! hc • 0-7434-9872-0 • $25.00
pb • 1-4165-2062-7 • $7.99

Keith Laumer's popular saga of the Bolos continues.

Old Soldiers hc • 1-4165-0898-8 • $26.00
pb • 1-4165-2104-6 • $7.99

A new Bolo novel.

OTHER NOVELS:

The Excalibur Alternative hc • 0-671-31860-8 • $21.00
pb • 0-7434-3584-2 • $7.99

An English knight and an alien dragon join forces to overthrow the alien slavers who captured them. Set in the world of David Drake's *Ranks of Bronze*.

In Fury Born pb • 1-4165-2131-3 • $7.99

A greatly expanded new version of *Path of the Fury*, with almost twice the original wordage.

BAEN

PRAISE FOR STEVE WHITE

"Exciting extraterrestrial battle scenes served up with a measure of thought and science."—*Kliatt*

"White offers fast action and historically informed world-building."—*Publishers Weekly*

"White perfectly blends background information, technical and historical details, vivid battle scenes and well-written characters. . . . a great package."—*Starlog*

BLOOD OF THE HEROES

1-4165-0924-0 • $24.00 • HC

Jason Thanoi of the Temporal Regulatory Authority was nurse-maiding an academic mission to ancient Greece to view one of the biggest volcanoes at the dawn of human history. He and his charges were about to find that there was more to those old legends of gods and heroes than anyone had imagined. . .

DEMON'S GATE

0-7434-7176-8 • $24.00 • HC

1-4165-0922-4 • $7.99 • PB

Long ago, demons ruled the world, until they were exiled to the nether realm. Now, someone is trying to reopen the gate to that realm. Unless Prince Valdar can stop them, darkness will rule the world forever.

FORGE OF THE TITANS

0-7434-3611-3 • $22.00 • HC

0-7434-9895-X •* $7.99 • PB

The old gods—actually extra-dimensional aliens with awesome powers—have returned, requesting human help against the evil Titans. But, judging from mythology, how much can you actually trust a god?

THE PROMETHEUS PROJECT

0-7434-9891-7 • $24.00 • HC

Only a gigantic hoax kept Earth from being taken over by aliens, and the secret was about to be leaked by a traitor in the project—unless one man could stop it.

EAGLE AGAINST THE STARS

0-671-57846-4 • $6.99 • PB

One burned-out secret agent against the new alien masters of Earth.

PRINCE OF SUNSET

0-671-87869-7 • $6.99 • PB

EMPEROR OF DAWN

0-671-57797-2 • $6.99 • PB

A grand two-book saga of love and war. Basil, Sonja and Torval, recent graduates of the Imperial Deep Space Fleet Academy, were looking forward to their future. But with a dying Empire and a rebellion threatening to engulf the galaxy in war, only they and powerful dragon-like beings held the key to stave off utter destruction.

And don't miss White's bestselling collaborations with David Weber:

THE STARS AT WAR

0-7434-8841-5 • $25.00 • HC

Crusade and *In Death Ground* in one large volume.

THE STARS AT WAR II

0-7434-9912-3 • $27.00 • HC

The Shiva Option and *Insurrection* (revised version) in one large mega-volume.

Available in bookstores everywhere.
Or order online at our secure, easy to use website:
www.baen.com